THE YEAR'S BEST DARK FANTASY & HORROR

2014 Edition

THE YEAR'S BEST DARK FANTASY & HORROR

2014 Edition

EDITED BY PAULA GURAN

○
PRIME BOOKS

Contents

For You, the Reader—
Thank you.

"In the tale, in the telling, we are all one blood. Take the tale in your teeth, then, and bite till the blood runs, hoping it's not poison; and we will all come to the end together, and even to the beginning: living, as we do, in the middle."

—Ursula K. Le Guin

Dancing at the Edge of the World: Thoughts on Words, Women, Places

INTRODUCTION

Paula Guran

This is the fifth time I've had the honor of assembling a volume for this series. Each year I write an introduction that contains about the same information explaining the intent of the Year's Best Dark Fantasy and Horror. I am sure it is tedious to those of you who have read a few of them, but—because we are dealing with an anthology that takes a different approach to dark fiction than others of its kind—I always feel some information needs to be more-or-less restated each time.

I do have a few *new* things to say this time though, so let's start there. Then you "veterans" can skip the rest . . . or read on and see if I slipped anything new in. (I did.)

First, I read more fiction this year than ever before. A great deal of it was quite good and made decisions even more difficult. This doesn't mean I'm seeing *all* that I should, but I am seeing more. Perhaps I've gotten a little better at seeking it out, but I also suspect it is because more folks now know this series exists and clue me in.

There's also a chance there's simply there is more dark fiction being published—often rather obscurely or in publications that don't consider what they publish as horror or dark fantasy. This year's selections were taken from many diverse sources—check them out in the "Acknowledgements" section— and there are many more I read and could have chosen stories from. In fact, one outstanding British periodical this year—*Black Static*—had such a stellar year for fiction, I feel I should single it out for special mention. Although a story from its sister publication, *Interzone*, made the final content, *Black Static* wound up not only being under-represented here, but not represented at all. These things happen—but in this case it probably shouldn't have.

As for not seeing as much fiction as I should—there are many ways to publish these days and I begin to wonder if new online magazines, small speciality presses, and crowd-funded anthology editors realize that I (and others) need to be made aware of what is being published. This is particularly true of non-genre sources.

So, spread the word. The most recent call for submissions can be found on my website: paulaguran.com. The URL is lengthy, so use this abbreviated URL: http://tinyurl.com/kkuxc97—or just go to paulaguran.com and search for "submissions"—you'll find it right away.

Also, I edited two anthologies myself this year containing outstanding original stories. I think a couple of them have been honored elsewhere, but I chose not to select any stories for this anthology from either *Halloween: Magic, Mystery, & the Macabre* or *Once Upon a Time: New Fairy Tales*. It would have been almost like trying to pick one's favorite child to settle on one or two of them to include here. Not all the stories are dark, but I do hope you seek them out, read them, and gain your own appreciation for the talented authors who contributed to both.

And now for some of the usual stuff. And, yes, I'm self-plagiarizing portions of this. Forgive me—I have my reasons, most of which have to do with deadlines and a rather nasty virus—but I still feel I need to touch on a few points, even if I must recycle a bit this time around.

The scope, intent, and theme of The Year's Best Dark Fantasy and Horror series is unique. There are two other established year's "best" horror series and several year's "best" science and fantasy series. This year, there's a new entry in the field featuring the best of the "weird." Our content can, naturally, overlap at times. But no other series considers *dark fantasy* and *horror*.

Of course the words *dark fantasy* and *horror* are highly debatable and constantly changing literary terms. There's no single definition. "Dark fantasy" isn't universally defined—the definition depends on the context in which the phrase is used or who is elucidating it. It has, from time to time, even been considered as nothing more than a marketing term for various types of fiction.

A dark fantasy story might be only a bit unsettling or perhaps somewhat eerie. It might be revelatory or baffling. It can be simply a small glimpse of life seen "through a glass, darkly." Or, in highly inclusive literary terms, it might be any number of things—as long as the darkness is there: weird fiction (new or old) or supernatural fiction or magical realism or surrealism or the *fantastique* or the ever-ambiguous horror fiction.

As for defining horror . . . The easiest definition is that horror is "scary" or inspires fright. But that's a little too simplistic.

Since horror is something we feel—it's an emotion, an affect—what each of us experiences, responds or reacts to differs.

What you feel may not be what I feel. Maybe you can't stand the thought of, oh . . . spiders. Understandably, one doesn't want to encounter one of the poisonous types, but *I* think of spiders, for the most part, as helpful arachnids that eat harmful insects. You, however, might shiver at the very thought of eight spindly legs creeping down your wall.

Once upon a time I felt the term "horror" could be broadened, accepted by the public, and generally regarded as a fiction [to quote Douglas E. Winter who wrote in *Revelations* (1997)] that was "evolving, ever-changing—because it is about our relentless need to confront the unknown, the unknowable, and the emotion we experience while in its thrall."

For me, horror is about finding, even seeking, that which we do not know. When we encounter the unknowable we react with emotion. And the unknowable, the unthinkable need not be supernatural. We constantly confront it in real life

One reason Winter was reminding us of his definition of horror in the introduction to his anthology was because the word "horror" had already been devalued. His opinion was (and is) as good as anyone's about what horror literature is, but the word itself had previously been slapped on a generic marketing category that had, by then, pretty much disappeared from major trade publishing. Even then—seventeen years ago—the word had become a pejorative.

The appellation has now been hijacked even more completely. I feel the word "horror" is associated in the public hive mind—an amorphous organism far more frequently influenced by the seductive images, motion, sounds, and effects that appear on a screen of any size than by written words (even when they are on a screen)—with entertainments that depend on shock for any value they may (or may not) possess rather than eliciting the more subtle emotion of fear.

And while fine and highly diverse horror literature—some of the best ever created—continues to be written in forms short and long, the masses for the most part have identified "horror" as either a certain kind of cinema or a generic type of fiction (of which they have certain expectations or ignore entirely because it delivers only a specific formula for which they evidently do not care.)

The term has been expropriated, and I doubt we'll ever be able to convince the world it means what we alleged horror mavens might want it to mean.

For this anthology series, I might have used only "dark fantasy" in the title, but I wanted to include stories with nothing supernatural in them at all. I mean, fantasy of any type must have a supernatural element . . .

Doesn't it?

Maybe not.

Fantasy, I think, takes us out of our usual mundane world of consensual reality and gives us a glimpse or a larger revelation of the possibilities of the "impossible." Far from being mere escapism or dealing only with "good" versus "evil," it confronts us with new ways to view complexities we may never have considered.

Fantasy is sometimes, but far from always, rooted in myth and legend. (But then myths were once believed to be part of accepted reality. If one believes in the supernatural or the magical, is it still fantasy?) It also creates new mythologies for modern culture. This can affect us profoundly, even become a part of who and what we are.

And, as with horror, the word "fantasy" alone—no matter its "shade"— conjures various notions in the mass mind, not to mention differing opinions among those who read it, study it, write about it, and seem to love to argue about it.

See why I'm not offering definitions?

Elements of "the dark" and horror and the fantastic are increasingly found in modern stories that do not conform to established tropes. What was once mainstream or "literary" fiction frequently treads paths that once were reserved for "genre."

Even other genres stride into the dark without hesitation. Stories of mystery and detection mixed with the supernatural may also be amusing and adventurous or have upbeat endings, but that doesn't mean such stories have not also taken the reader into stygian abysses along the why.

Crime fiction may have no supernatural element, but it is frequently extremely effective horror.

Horror is also interwoven—essentially—into many science fiction themes. Bleak fictional futures abound these days. Ultimately, the reader may come away with a hopeful attitude, but not until after having to confront some very scary scenarios and face some very basic fears.

Darkness seeps naturally into weird and surreal fiction too. The strange may be mixed with whimsy, but the fanciful does not negate the shadows.

So, if I don't offer definitions, I do offer a selection of outstanding stories— all published within the calendar year 2013—that seemed to fit my personal concept of outstanding fiction that more or less fits the ideas I've touched on.

As in the years before, the stories selected often take twists and turns into the unexpected. There are monsters, yes, but they aren't always monstrous. And, of course, we are often the monsters ourselves (or we know them). Sometimes we find ourselves doing the darkest of deeds for the best reasons. The darkly humorous can be both delightful and deadly.

There are tales to remind us that discovering disquietude, disintegration, and loss are evocative for most of us. Human relationships can be more terrifying than anything supernatural, or so strong they call the unnatural into being.

These stories take us back to the past, be it historical, altered, or completely imagined; into a few futures; keep us in the present; and sometimes take us outside of time altogether. They guide us into utterly different worlds than our own; keep us perhaps a little too close to home; journey into the strange terrains of the soul and the mind; sidestep into settings not unfamiliar, but never quite comfortable either.

Most of all, they take us into many shades and variations of the dark.

Paula Guran
11 April 2014

Long angular shadows carved into the wheat lifted out of their places,
turning over then flapping, rising into the turbulent air where they
became knife rips in the fabric of the sky . . .

WHEATFIELD WITH CROWS

Steve Rasnic Tem

Sometimes when he sketched out what he remembered of that place, new revelations appeared in the shading, or displayed between the layering of a series of lines, or implied in a shape suggested in some darker spot in the drawing. The back of her head, or some bit of her face, dead or merely sleeping he could never quite tell. He was no Van Gogh, but Dan's art still told him things about how he felt and what he saw, and he'd always sensed that if he could just find her eyes among those lines or perhaps even in an accidental smear, he might better understand what happened to her.

In this eastern part of the state the air was still, clear and empty. An overabundance of sky spilled out in all directions with nothing to stop it, the wheat fields stirring impatiently below. Driving up from Denver, seeing these fields again, Dan thought the wheat nothing special. He made himself think of bread, and the golden energy that fed thousands of years of human evolution, but the actual presence of the grain was drab, if overwhelming. When he'd been here as a child, he'd thought these merely fields of weeds, but so tall— they had been pretty much all he could see, wild and uncontrolled. But when he was a child everything was like that—so limitless, so hard to understand.

In the decade and a half since his sister's disappearance, Dan had been back to this tiny no-place by the highway only once, when at fifteen he'd stolen a car to get here. He'd never done anything like that before, and he wasn't sure the trip had accomplished much. He'd just felt the need to be here, to try to understand why he no longer had a sister. And although the wheat had moved, and shuddered, and acted as if it might lift off the ground to reveal its secrets, it did not, and Dan had returned home.

Certainly this trip—driving the hour from Denver (legally this time), with his mother in the passenger seat staring catatonically out the window—was unlikely to change anything in their lives. She'd barely said two words since he picked her up at her apartment. He had to give her some credit, though— she had a job now, and no terrible boyfriends in her life as far as he knew. But it was hard to be generous.

Roggen, Colorado, near Interstate 76 and Colorado Road 73, lay at the heart of the state's grain crop. 'Main Street' was a dirt road that ran alongside a railroad track. A few empty store fronts leaned attentively but appeared to have nothing to say. The same abandoned house he remembered puffed out its gray-streaked cheeks as it continued its slow-motion collapse. The derelict Prairie Lodge Motel sat near the middle of the town, its doors wide open, various pieces of worn, overstuffed furniture dragged out for absent observers to sit on and watch.

Every few months when Dan did an Internet search, it came up as a "ghost town." He wondered how the people who still lived here—and there were a few of them, tucked away on distant farms or hiding in houses behind closed blinds—felt about that.

"There, there's where it happened," his mother whispered, tapping the glass gently as if hesitant to disturb him. "There's where my baby disappeared."

Dan pulled the car over slowly at this ragged edge of town, easing carefully off the dirt road as he watched for ditches, holes, anything that might trap them here longer than necessary. They'd started much later than he'd planned. First his mother had been unsure what to wear, trying on various outfits, worrying over what might be too casual, what might be "too much." Dan wanted to say it wasn't as if they were going to Caroline's funeral, but did not. His mother had put on too much makeup, but when she'd asked how she looked he was reluctant to tell her. The encroaching grief of the day only made her face look worse.

Then she'd decided to make sandwiches in case they got hungry, in case there was no place to stop, and of course out here there wouldn't be. Dan had struggled for patience, knowing that if they started to argue it would never end. It had been mid-afternoon by the time they left Denver, meaning this visit would have to be a short one, but it just couldn't be helped.

As soon as he stopped the car his mother was out and pacing in front of the rows of wheat that lapped the edge of the road. He got out quickly, not wanting her to get too far ahead of him. The clouds were lower, heavier, leaking darkness toward the ground in long narrow plumes. He could see the wind coming from a distance, the fields farther off beginning to move like water rolling on the ocean, all so restless, aimless, and, by the time the disturbance arrived at the field where they stood, the wind brought the sound with it, a constant and persistent crackle and fuzz, shifting randomly in volume and tone.

It occurred to him there was no one in charge here to watch this field, to witness its presence in the world, to wonder at its peace or fury. No doubt the owners and the field hands lived some distance away. This was the way of things with modern farming, vast acreages irrigated and cultivated by machinery, and nobody watched what might be going on in the fields. It had been much the same when Caroline vanished. It had seemed almost as if the fields had no owners, but were powers unto themselves, somehow managing on their own, like some ancient place.

Dan took continuous visual notes. He itched to rough these into his typical awkward sketches, but although he always kept sketching supplies in the glove compartment he couldn't bring himself to do so in front of his mother. He never showed his stuff to anyone, but his untrained expressions were all he had to quell his sometimes runaway anxiety.

So, like Van Gogh's "Wheatfield With Crows," Dan saw long angular shadows carved into the wheat beginning to lift out of their places, turning over then flapping, rising into the turbulent air where they became knife rips in the fabric of the sky.

"She was right here, right here." His mother's voice was like old screen shredding to rust. She was standing near the edge of the field, her head down, eyes intent on the plants as if waiting for something to come out of the rows. "My baby was *right here.*"

The wheat was less than three feet tall, even shorter when whipped back and forth like this, a tortured texture of shiny and dull golds. At six, his sister had been much taller. Had she crouched so that her head didn't show? Had she been brave enough to crawl into the field? Or had she been taken like his mother always thought, and dragged, her abductor's back hunched as he'd pulled her into the rows of vibrating wheat?

Out in the field the wheat opened and closed, swirling, now and then revealing pockets of shade, moments of dark opportunity. The long flexible stalks twisted themselves into sheaves and limbs, humanoid forms and moving rivers of grainy muscle, backs and heads made and unmade in the changing shadows teased open by the wind. Overhead the crows screeched their unpleasant proclamations. Dan could not see them but they sounded tormented, ripped apart.

His mother knelt, wept eerily like a child. He had to convince himself it wasn't Caroline. He stepped up behind his mother and laid his hand on her shoulder, confirming that she was shaking, crying. She reached up and laid her hand over his, mistaking his reality check for concern.

A red glow had crept beneath the dark clouds along the horizon, and that along with the increasingly frayed black plumes clawing the ground made him think of forest fires, but there were no forests in that direction to burn— just sky, and wheat, and wind blowing away anything too insubstantial to hold on.

Suddenly a brilliant blaze silvered the front surface of wheat and his mother sprang up, her hands raised in alarm. Dan looked around and, seeing that the pole lamp behind them had come on automatically at dusk, he turned her face gently in that direction and pointed. It seemed a strange place for a street lamp, but he supposed even the smallest towns had at least one for safety.

That light might have been on at the time of his sister's disappearance. He'd been only five, but in his memory there had been a light that had washed all their faces in silver, or had it been more of a bluish cast? There had been Caroline, himself, their mother, and Mom's boyfriend at the time. Ted had been his name, and he'd been the reason they were all out there. Ted said he used to work in the wheat fields, and Dan's mother said it had been a long time since she'd seen a wheat field. They'd both been drinking, and impulsively they took Caroline and Dan on that frightening ride out into the middle of nowhere.

Ted had interacted very little with Dan, so all Dan remembered about him was that he had this big black moustache and that he was quite muscular— he walked around without his shirt on most of the time. Little Danny had thought Ted was a cartoon character, and how it was kind of nice that they had a cartoon character living with them, but like most cartoon characters Ted was a little too loud and a little too scary.

"I never should have dated that Ted. We were all pretty happy until Ted came along," his mother muttered beside him now. She hadn't had a drink in several years as far as he knew, but like many long time drinkers she still sounded slightly drunk much of the time—drink appeared to have altered how she moved her mouth.

This was all old stuff, and Dan tuned it out. His mother had always blamed ex-husbands and ex-boyfriends for her mistakes, as if she'd been helpless to choose, to do what needed to be done. Just once Dan wished she would do what needed to be done.

When Dan had come here at age fifteen it had been the middle of the day, so this oh-so-brilliant light had not been on. He hadn't wanted to be here in the dark. He didn't want to be here in the dark now.

But the night his sister Caroline disappeared had also been bathed in this selective brilliance. That high light had been on that night as well. No doubt a different type of bulb back in those days. Sodium perhaps, or an arc light. Dan just remembered being five years old and sitting in the back of that smelly old car with his sister. The adults stank of liquor, and they'd gotten out of the car and gone off somewhere to do something, and they'd told Danny and Caroline to stay there. "Don't get off that seat, kids," his mother had ordered. "Do you hear me? No matter what. It's not *safe*. Who knows what might be out there in that field?"

Danny had cried a little—he couldn't even see over the back of the seat and there were noises outside, buzzes and crackles and the sound of the wind over everything, like an angry giant's breath. Caroline kept saying she needed to go to the bathroom, and she was going to open the car door just a little bit, run out and use the bathroom and come right back. Dan kept telling her no, don't do that, but Caroline was a little bit older and never did anything he said.

The only good thing, really, had been the light. Danny told himself the bright light was there because an angel was watching over them, and as long as an angel was watching nothing too terrible could happen. He decided that no matter how confusing everything was, what he believed about the angel was true.

Caroline had climbed out of the car and gone toward the wheat field to use the bathroom. She'd left the car door part way open and that was scary for Danny, looking out the door and seeing the wheat field moving around like that, so he had used every bit of strength he had to pull the car door shut behind her. But what if she couldn't open the door? What if she couldn't get back in? That was the last time he saw his sister.

"I left you two in the car, Dan. I told you two to stay. Why did she get out?"

Dan stared at his mother as she stood with one foot on the edge of the road, the other not quite touching, but almost, the first few stalks of wheat. Behind her the rows dissolved and reformed, shadows moving frenetically, the spaces inside the spaces in constant transformation. He'd answered her questions hundreds of times over the years, so although he wanted to say *because she had to go to the bathroom, you idiot*, he said nothing. He just watched her feet, waiting for something to happen. Overhead was the deafening sound of crows shredding.

There used to be a telephone mounted below the light pole, he remembered. He and his mother and Ted had waited there all those years ago until a highway patrolman came. Ted and his mother had searched the wheat field for over an hour before they made the call. At least that's what his mother had always told him. Danny had stayed in the car with the doors shut, afraid to move.

He guessed they had looked hard for his sister, he guessed that part was true. But they obviously did a bad job because they never found her. They also told the officer they had been standing just a few feet away at the time, gazing up at the stars. What else had they lied about?

The brilliant high light carved a confusing array of shadows out of the wheat, Dan's car, and his mother. His own shadow, too, was part of the mix, but he had some difficulty identifying it. As his mother paced back and forth in front of the field, her shadow self appeared to multiply, times two, times three, more. As the wind increased the wheat parted in strips like hair, the stalks writhing as if in religious fervor, bowing almost horizontal at times, the wind threatening to tear out the plants completely and expose what lay beneath. Pockets of shadow were sent running, some isolated and left standing by themselves closer to the road. Dan could hear wings flapping over him, the sound descending as if the crows might be seeking shelter on the ground.

"She might still be out there, you know," his mother said. "I was so confused that night, I just don't think we covered enough of the field. We could have done a better job."

"The officers searched most of the night." Dan raised his voice to be heard above the wind. "They had spotlights, and dogs. And volunteers were out here the rest of the week looking, and for some time after. I've read all the newspaper articles, Mom, every single one. And even when they harvested the wheat that year, they did this section *manually*, remember? They didn't want to damage—they wanted to be careful not to—" He was trying to be careful, calm and logical, but he wasn't sure he even believed what he was saying himself.

"They didn't want to damage her *remains*. That's what you were trying to say, right? Well, I've always thought that was a terrible word. She was a sweet little *girl*."

"I'm just trying to say that after the wheat was gone there was nothing here. Caroline wasn't here."

"You don't know for sure."

"What? You think she got plowed under? That she's down under the furrows somewhere? Mom, it's been *years*. Something would have turned up."

"Then she might be alive. We just have to go find her. I've read about this kind of thing. It happens all the time. They find the child years later. She's too scared to tell all these years, and then she does. There's a reunion. It's awkward and it's hard, but she becomes their daughter again. It happens like that sometimes, Danny."

He noticed how she called him by his childhood name. Danny this and Danny that. It was also the only name Caroline had ever had for him. But more than that, he was taken by her story. To argue with his mother about such a fairy tale seemed too cruel, even for her.

He barely noticed the small shadow that had fallen into place not more than a foot or two away from her, a dark hollow shaking with the wind, perhaps thrown out of the body of wheat, vibrating as if barely whole or contained, its edges ragged, discontinuous. At first he thought it was one of the large crows that had finally landed to escape the fierce winds above, ready to take its chances with the winds blowing along the ground, but its feathers so damaged, so torn, Dan couldn't see how it could ever fly again.

Until it opened its indistinct eyes, and looked at him, and he knew himself incapable of understanding exactly what he was seeing. If he were Van Gogh he might take these urgent, multi-directional slashes and whorls and assemble them into the recognizable face of his sister Caroline, whose eyes had now gone cold, and no more sympathetic or understandable than the other mysteries that traveled through the natural and unnatural world.

His mother wept so softly now, but he was close enough to hear her above the wind, the hollowed-out change in her voice as this shadow gathered her in and took her deep into the field.

And because he had no right to object, he knew that this time there would be no phone call, there would be no search.

Steve Rasnic Tem is a past winner of the Bram Stoker, World Fantasy, and British Fantasy awards. His two books from 2012 were the novel *Deadfall Hotel* and the noir collection *Ugly Behavior* (New Pulp Press). Three Tem collections: *Onion Songs* (Chomu), *Celestial Inventories* (ChiZine), and *Twember* (NewCon Press) were released in 2013. Southern gothic *Blood Kin* (Solaris) is his latest novel.

In the movies, monsters are always defeated by something ordinary and obvious, usually discovered by accident—seawater, dog whistles, paprika, Slim Whitman music . . . this is no movie . . .

BLUE AMBER

David J. Schow

When Senior Patrol Agent Rixson first spotted the shed human skin draped over the barbed-wire fence, she thought it was an item of discarded clothing. Then she saw it had empty arms, legs, fingers, an empty mouth-hole stretched oval in a silent scream, and vacant Hallowe'en-mask eye sockets. Carrion birds had already picked it over. Presently it was covered with ants. It stank.

If you had asked her, before, what her single worst experience working for the Border Patrol had been, Carrie Rixson might have related the story of how she and her partner Cash Dunhill had happened upon a hijacked U-Haul box trailer full of dead Mexicans eighteen feet shy of the Sonora side of Buster Lippert's pony ranch. Something had gone wrong, and the coyotes—the wetback enablers, not the scavengers—had left their clients locked in the box, abandoned, under one hundred and one-degree heat for over three days. The Cochise County Coroner concluded that the occupants had died at least two days prior to that. The smell was enough to make even the vultures doubtful. The victims had deliquesced into a undifferentiated mass of meat that had broiled in convection heat that topped four hundred degrees, about the same as you'd use to bake a frozen pizza.

That had been bad, but the flyblown husk on the fence seemed somehow worse.

"Should I call it in?" said Dunhill, sweating in the pilot seat of their Bronco. He was a deputy and answerable to Carrie, but neither of them were high enough in the grade chain to warrant collar insignia.

"As what?" Carrie shouted back, from the fence. She was already snapping digital photographs.

Dunhill unsaddled and ambled over for a look-see. No need to hurry, not in this heat. "I think this falls out of the purview of 'accidental death,'" he said.

"Unless this ole boy was running away so fast he jumped the bobwire and it shucked off his hide."

"That happened once," said his partner. "Dude in New Jersey. Hefty guy, running away from the cops, tried to jump an iron railing and got his chin caught on the metal spike up top. Tore his head clean off. It was still stuck on the end of the spike. I saw it on the internet."

Cash and Carrie had been the target of department punsters ever since their first pair-up assignment. She was older, thirty-seven to his twenty-nine years. They had never been romantically inclined, although they teased each other a lot. Cash's high school sweetie had divorced him in a legal battle only slightly less acrimonious than the firebombing of Dresden, and Carrie had been about to marry her ten-year live-in life partner—Thomas "Truck" Fitzgerald, a former Pima County sheriff turned Jeep customizer—when he up and died of cancer that took him away in six weeks flat. Neither Cash nor Carrie was in the market for loving just now, although they both suffered the pangs in their own different ways.

"Oh, don't *touch* it, for christsake," Cash told her.

"I'm thinking cartel guys," she said as her hand stopped short of making actual fleshy contact. "This is the sort of shit they do. Skin your enemies. Cut off their heads, stuff their balls into their mouths, dismember them and leave the pieces in a public place with the name of the *cliqua* written in blood."

"You see that on the internet, too?" Cash dug out a toothpick. He was battling mightily to stop smoking.

"Nahh," she said. "I usually only look at lesbian porn. Girl-on-girl, slurpy-burpy." The way Cash usually rose to the bait when she egged him on was reliably amusing, under normal circumstances.

She used a dried stick of ironwood to lift one of the flaps. "Definitely not a scuba suit or a mannequin. There used to be a person wearing this, and not so long ago." The shadow side of the castoff skin was dotted with oily moisture, as though it was still perspiring.

"Whose property is this?" Cash was looking around for landmarks.

"This is outside Puzzi Ranch. I guess it might be Thayer McMillan's fence."

Cash and Carrie's daily grind was to patrol the strip of International Highway (both a description of the actual road and its real name) between Douglas, Arizona and Naco Highway. Naco—the town—straddled the

US-Mexico border and had always been a sizzling hot spot for violations of all sorts.

In the dead-ass stretches of high desert separating the two towns, there was just too goddamned much open space for something not to go wrong.

"Secure Fence Act, my ass," said Cash, for about the zillionth time. His views on a wetback-proof fence were abundantly known. "I'll call base; see if we can get a number for McMillan." He popped an energy drink from the Bronco's cooler and blew down half the can in one gulp.

"Gross," said Carrie. "That candy-flavored salt water is bad for you."

The logo on the can shrieked *Kamikaze!* " 'Divine wind.' 'Empty wind' is more like it."

Then Cash would say . . .

"May the wind at your back never be your own."

They were okay, as partners. When the meatwagon arrived over an hour later, Billy Szwakop, the coroner's assistant, scowled at them at though he was the butt of yet another in an endless series of corpse gags. It wasn't even really a dead body, he said. It was just the skin part. For all they knew, no murder had been committed. "Yeah, he's probably still walking around, all wound up in duct tape to keep from leaking," Cash said. Billy's gentle disentanglement of the . . . item . . . had revealed it to be male.

It had also revealed a broad split from sternum to crotch, not an incision.

After it was bagged, Billy added, "I don't think this was a Mex, either."

Carrie got interested. "What makes you say that?"

"Most Mexicans are Catholic, and most Catholic males are circumcised."

"Ugh," said Carrie. "Too much information."

From the concealment of a broad, shaded thicket of skunkbush and screwbean mesquite, bulbous indigo eyes watched them, then died.

The zigzag access road to the McMillan compound was dead on the eastern property edge, about half a mile back from where Carrie Rixson had spotted the thing on the fence. It paralleled several secure horse corrals before it widened into a gated archway featuring a wrought iron double M (itself a zigzag) up top. The building cluster was organized around a broad donut of paved road—big barn, smaller barn, main house, guesthouse, and a generator-driven industrial icehouse side-by-side with a smaller smokehouse. Further north, in the rear, would be a long, narrow greenhouse with solar panels. Thayer McMillan had made part of his pile breeding quarter horses and Appaloosas. In residence were several trainers and wranglers, in addition to a cook, a housekeeper, and an on-call executive personal assistant. Two of the eight McMillan children still lived at home—Lester, the heir apparent to King Daddy's throne, and his younger sister Desiree, a recent divorcee with two children of her own, both under ten years old. Thayer, the patriarch, was on his fourth wife, a brassy Houston fireball named Celandine, twenty-five years his junior, or about Desiree's age. Call it fortyish.

There was also, it was rumored, security staff.

It was further rumored that McMillan was pouring concrete to the north of the greenhouse for a private helicopter landing pad.

There were many other rumors about the McMillans, mostly of the sort slathered about by jealous inferiors, but the one about the chopper pad piqued Cash Dunhill's interest. That close to the border? Cash had always wanted an excuse to investigate further.

The light green Bronco kicked up a tailwind of grit as it barreled along the access road. Half a mile in, there was a red pickup truck parked on the shoulder.

One of those show-offy, urban cowboy rigs with a mega-cab, a Hemi V-8 and double rear tires. Nobody inside or close by. The clearcoat was covered in dust.

Cash checked it out. "The keys are inside," he said. It was as though someone had pulled over for a piss and just sank into the earth before he or she could zip up.

"Nobody on the home line," said Carrie, snapping her cellphone shut. "Just voice mail."

"No horses, either," said Cash. He could see the corrals from where they'd stopped. "Not a single one."

"It's midday; maybe they're cooling off in the barn." No doubt the barn was air conditioned.

"Guess we guessed wrong about the security, too," he said, a bit distantly, the way he did when he was trying to puzzle out evidence. "Nobody on us yet, nobody at the gate."

"Maybe they upgraded," said Carrie. "Cameras and lasers instead of people."

"Maybe." You could score useful points by agreeing with your partner on things that did not matter. They rumbled over the cowcatcher rails at the gate, within sight of the Cliff May architectural masterpiece that was the main house—a classic of the modernist California Ranch style that blended hacienda elements with the Western aesthetic of building "out" instead of "up." There was a lot of woodgrain and natural stone. The bold, elongated A-frame of the roof line allowed sunlight to heat the huge pool.

"How many bedrooms, you figure?" said Cash.

"Five," said Carrie. "No, six, and probably at least one bathroom for each. Japanese soaking tubs, I bet. I love those."

A large blob of brown was piled near the gate to the northernmost corral.

"What the hell is that?"

"Horsehide."

"No, it isn't," said Cash, stopping the vehicle again. "Horse."

Hollow, split and empty, just like the thing they had found on the barbed-wire fence.

Carrie already had her weapon out. "There's a dog over there. But a whole dog, not just skin." She moved closer to verify. There were spent shotgun cartridges strewn around a dead Rottweiler near the front walkway. "We'd better —"

"Call this in, now!" Partners often completed each other's sentences.

Cash was advised that available law enforcement, this far out, was on a triage basis and they would be required to wait at the scene.

"Cash, look at this."

Carrie indicated a smear of blackish fragments in the dirt, like ash or charcoal. "I stepped on it. But look, here's another one."

It was a dried-up bug. There were several of them in the yard. "Looks like a cicada," said Cash. "Or one of them cockroaches; you know they get three inches long around here."

"But it isn't. Look."

She stabbed it with a Bic pen and held it aloft for inspection. It sounded crispy, desiccated. What resembled an opaque, thornlike stinger protruded from one end, its razor-sharp edge contoured to flare and avoid contact with the body.

"This isn't right," she said. "It can't be. This is mutated or something. Or a hybrid. No bilateral symmetry."

"I don't understand a thing you just said."

"Bilateral," Carrie said. "Identical on both sides. We're all base two—two eyes, two arms, two legs. Ants have six legs. Spiders have eight, and eight eyes. One side of the body is a mirror of the other. But not this. Nothing I know of is based on three."

Cash, prepared to blow her off, grew more interested. "Maybe it's missing a leg."

"From where?" She turned the thing over in the waning sunlight.

"There's no obvious wound."

"Maybe that stinger thing is really a leg? Or a tail?"

"Yeah, and maybe it's a dick," she said, disliking patronization.

"Leave it for the plastic bag boys," said Cash. "Just don't touch the sharp thing, okay?"

"No way."

"You suppose maybe a swarm of these locusty things flew in and ate everybody from the inside out?"

"Then why aren't there dead ones inside the . . . " Carrie sputtered out, groping for the right word. "Carcasses? That much fine dining, there should be a couple thousand of them around."

Cash knocked loudly and rang the bell while Carrie thumbed the latch on a door handle that probably cost three weeks of her pay. "It's open," she said.

"Probable cause?"

"You've gotta be shitting me, Cash."

Then Cash would say . . .

"I wouldn't shit you, darlin, you're my favorite turd."

But he, too, had his weapon limbered up, a Ruger GP100 double-action revolver in .357 Mag. Carrie packed a full-sized Smith & Wesson M&P-40 that held sixteen rounds with one in the pipe—cartridges that Cash knew to be semiwadcutters.

Feeling increasingly absurd, they both called into the acoustically vacant recesses of the house. The coolers were on full-blast.

"Jesus," she said. "It must be below fifty degrees in here."

"Like the frozen food aisle at the supermarket." They covered each other excellently. Goosebumps speckled their sun-licked flesh.

Cash shook his head. Think of the utility bill.

"Well, room by room, I guess," he said, uncertainly.

The showplace central room was large and vaulted, with a grape-stake ceiling and a fireplace large enough to roast a Smart Car. Very open. All other rooms were peripheral.

The deeper they ventured, the more tenantless the house seemed. Neither one of them called out any more—that was just instinctive, the old telepathy of partners sharing a silent warning.

Carrie checked the behemoth Sub-Zero Pro fridge for sealed bottled water, just for hydration's sake. Do it when you can. Several more of the bugs, chilled and lifeless, were on the top shelf near an open half gallon of milk.

Keeping her voice low, Carrie said, "I'm thinking disease, Cash; what are you thinking?"

Cash nodded. "Something insect-borne, something special. That means government spooks and security. But not here; the goddamned door was open."

He gratefully plugged water down his throat. It was so cold it gave him a migraine spike.

"Either that or a really pissed-off butcher with some kind of vendetta. But I don't see any blood anywhere. How about we just back off?"

"Crime scene," said Cash. "We've got to stay."

"What's the crime?"

"We really oughta leave this for larger minds," he said, full up with doubt.

"Don't you chicken out on me, Cash Dunhill. It's not seemly."

"Something is going on; we're just not smart enough to figure it ou —"

She held up her free hand to cut him off. "Hold."

A noise; they both heard it. A soft noise. A soft, shuffling, sliding noise.

Something was moving toward them in the hallway.

"Mommy," said the thing.

It appeared at a fast glance to be a little girl in blue jeans and a bright yellow Taylor Swift T-shirt (logoed *You Are the Best Thing That's Ever Been Mine*), lurching along as though drugged, in a pair of blocky K-Swiss Tubes. Her bronze-colored hair was lank and damp.

"Holy shit," whispered Carrie.

The voice was all wrong. That "Mommy" had come out as a froggy, guttural croak. The front of the T-shirt was soaked, as though she had vomited. She looked past the two officers, not at them. Half her face seemed to be melting off. The whole left side was slack and drooping, elongating her eye and hanging her jaw crookedly down.

"Mommy make samwich peen butter gahh."

Thick yellow mucus was cascading out of her nose.

Carrie moved to kneel, arms out. "Honey . . . ?"

"Don't touch her, for godsake!"

"Found it," the girl said, voice hitching with phlegm.

"Found what, sweetie?" Carrie was keeping her distance.

"Pretty," said the girl. She opened her hand. One of the bugs was there.

Crouching at the abrupt light, tripod legs tensing. It was alive.

"Oh my god," Carrie said as the bug sprang across the three feet between them like a grasshopper, hit her in the face, and sank its wicked-looking barb into her cheek. In the light, Cash swore he could see fluid drain from the translucent stinger.

Cash shouted and charged, kicking sidelong to lay out the kid, swatting with his hand to dispose of the attacking bug. It hit the floor with its legs up, dead already, like the ones they'd found in the yard.

"Stupid, stupid!" Carrie had landed on her ass.

"Lemme see that. Quick, now."

"Squeeze it. Cut it if you have to!" Her cheek was swelling and darkening already. Her right eye was going crimson.

Cash put his thumbs together to try to evacuate the poison—if that's what it was—from the entry wound, but no dice. A tiny dot of bluish wetness welled up at the puncture, but nothing was coming out. He almost tried to suck it, using snakebite protocol.

"Don't put your *mouth* on it, Cash, for fuck's sake!" Carrie was sweeping her arms around, preparatory to trying to stand again, but her movements went thick and wide.

"Astringent," Cash said. "Disinfectant." There had to be something in the kitchen or a nearby bathroom. In a glass-doored liquor cabinet he found some 120-proof Stolichnaya vodka. Stashed behind it was a crumpled soft pack of Camel Lights with two bent cigarettes inside, which he stashed in his uniform blouse's flap pocket. Two wouldn't kill him.

He dashed vodka over Carrie's wound. "I can't even feel it," she said. "It should burn."

The kid was standing back up.

"Bike," she said. Her eyes were looking two different directions. The skin on one arm seemed skewed, as though her hand was mounted backward on the bone. With the other hand, the girl pawed at her face and caught hold of her slack, hanging lower lip. She pulled it downward and it began to peel away. The buttery flesh on her neck split and began to slough. Her yellow shirt absorbed more discharge, from within.

For that single second, Cash and Carrie were transfixed in mute witness.

The little girl's face flopped around her neck like a rubber cowl. In its place was a knob of pale meat resembling a clenched fist, with two bulging button eyes, shiny, featureless orbs that were not black, but a very deep indigo.

Together, Cash and Carrie opened fire.

Their slugs hoisted and dumped the thing, which had begun to walk toward them again. It fell back into the corridor in a broken jackstraw sprawl.

"It was starting to tear off the skin," Carrie said, distantly. Its raised arm lingered, clenching a handful of wadded-up neck. Then it toppled over and hit the marble floor tiles with a juicy slaughterhouse *smack*.

Whatever was leaking out of the bullet holes looked like plain water. Faintly bluish.

"Come on," urged Cash. "To hell with this. We've got to get you out of here, pronto."

"Good idea," said Carrie. Her voice was going furry and opiate, as from a severe allergic reaction. Congestion, histamine levels redlining.

He lifted her bodily, not thinking of all the times he'd wanted to brush her boobs, her butt, just playfully.

Then Cash would say . . .

"Hang on, darlin, you and me are traveling." Warily he observed the pewter light in the windows. Twilight had already fallen. Sundown came fast in the desert.

Just get to the vehicle, he thought. *Just burn ass outta here.*

But the Bronco, sitting in the front turnaround, had already been dumped on its side, partially spiderwebbing the windshield.

And two more things of full-grown human size were waiting for them, with their bulging, dark, ratlike eyes.

They had shucked their human envelopes and stood on either side of the upended Bronco. Like UFO "grays," but lumpier and mottled. Two arms with pincer hands. Two legs. Bilateral symmetry. No facial features except the convex eyes, deep blue, no pupils or irises. They looked spindly. But they had turned the Bronco over.

Cash had to place Carrie on the ground in order to execute a speed reload. If he shot them center mass, they only flinched. Headshots put them down more definitively.

"Shotgun," said Carrie from the ground. "Truck. Keys. Run."

Then Cash would say . . .

"I'm not leaving you!"

"Don't be an idiot," she said. She managed to prop herself on one elbow to dump the Smith's clip and refresh. "Get the shotgun. Run as fast as you can to the truck and bring it back. I'm not going anywhagh . . . "

She coughed viscously.

"You sure?" Weapon up, Cash was scanning the perimeter nervously. *Go. Stay. Go. Stay.*

"Go," Carrie said. "I'm a big girl."

Cash wasted several more seconds trying to upright the Bronco by himself. No go. The adrenalin surge of legendary vehicular rescues had failed him. He retrieved the Mossberg pump from the cabin mount (he never locked it unless he was handing over the vehicle; in his worldview, speedy readiness outranked rules). The veins in his head were livid and throbbing. Thirty yards distant was the structure that shaded the big freezer unit and the smokehouse.

The freezer. The cold house. Sunset. These monsters did not like the light or the heat. They coffined up in the daytime. Now it was nighttime.

The bugs stung you, injected you. These things grew inside you, then peeled you off like a chrysalis. When they did, there wasn't any you left. You had become nutrient and a medium for gestation.

Their purpose or motive could be hashed out later by others, people with degrees and ordnance and expensive backup. Right now, Carrie was stung and waning. Who knew what her timetable was, or whether the effect could be neutralized? In the movies, monsters who upset the status quo were always defeated by something ordinary and obvious, usually discovered by accident—seawater, dog whistles, paprika, Slim Whitman music. In movies, the salvational curative was always set up in the first act as a throwaway, sure to encore later with deeper meaning.

In movies, you found a cure, gave the victim a pill or an injection, and they were instantly okay. A miracle, wrap it up, the end, roll credits.

Cash ran faster, his boot heels thudding on the roadway, the sound reminding him of a shopping cart with a bum wheel, the kind he always seemed to draw at the market. How did the wheels get those bumps, anyway?

With proper warmup and training, track sprinters could do eight hundred meters in three minutes. That was without a gunbelt and equipment, without cowboy boots or Cash's lamentable diet. Without panic or terror. What a laugh, if he ran himself right into a heart attack.

Then they'd find his body and use him as an incubator.

Then Carrie would say . . .

Man up. Don't be afraid. Solve the problem. Work fast and sure.

But he was afraid. Normally fear got shoved behind revulsion or duty. Fear was tamped down and tucked away. Cash did not want to go back. He wanted to show this place his ass and taillights, never to return.

Carrie would have come for him, so he forced himself to stay on track. To do the manly thing, the brave-and-true thing. He did not wish to look bad in her eyes.

Gunshots echoed behind him. Five, six, seven rounds.

"Dammit to hell!" He spit the toothpick from his already arid mouth.

The red Ram pickup was twenty yards away, chrome bumpers glinting.

Cash roared the truck through the archway, cutting hard left to skid clear of where he had left Carrie. The dual rear wheels churned a broad curtain of dust.

Carrie was not to be seen in the yard or near the porch. Two more of the bipedal things were spread-eagled in the dirt, missing most of their heads, forming big, wet puddles around themselves. Carrie's .40 was there on the ground, too. The action was not locked back; it still had rounds in it.

Cash was sure that if he wanted trouble, he'd find it in the big freezer. The creatures he had seen were pallid, like cadavers; featurelessly smooth, like a reptile's clammy underbelly; undoubtedly alien or aberrant, which suggested a moist toxicity as incomprehensible as a biowar germ. The smart thing to do was leave.

The right thing to do was rescue Carrie, if she could still be saved.

Reverse out the strangeness—that's what Cash's thinking mind told him to do. Put yourself in their place. Somehow, some way, they come to consciousness on McMillan's ranch. Maybe they had no idea where they were. Perhaps they lacked the facility to process sounds or smells. Maybe their vision was into the infrared spectrum, like a rattler's. Anyway, they hit the ground (or came up out of the ground, if they didn't fall from outer space or burst out of radioactive pods) and commence reproducing, to strengthen their numbers or gain some kind of immediate survival foothold. They discover that for the most part, they cannot walk around in the daytime because it's too hot, too bright. They wander around and maybe incur a few casualties in their experiential curve. They're like men on the moon, seeking a shelter with oxygen and environment. Perhaps they were transitional beings in the process of adaptation, evolving to live in new circumstances.

Illegal aliens, Cash thought with a sting of irony.

Edging up in the icehouse door was one of the hardest things Cash had ever done. There might not be any ceiling to this madness, but there might be a floor, and that bedrock had to be composed of Cash's own resolve. This could not be about anything, right now, except retrieving his partner. All the rest, the theories, the what-ifs and mad speculation, had to be left for later. And yes, the fear, too. All Cash needed to know was that bullets seemed to put the creatures down just dandy.

The icehouse door was latched by a large silver handle. It made a complicated clockwork sound when Cash cranked it, as though he was breaching an immense safe. Cold air and condensation ghosted out around the insulating gaskets.

Nobody home.

He could not find a light switch and so brought up his baton flashlight. There *was* something in here, but it wasn't a cadre of shufflers waiting to eat his face or a line of frozen beef sides to mock his fear.

The object looked like a big, broken section of latticework, laced with frost, propped against the stainless steel wall. About five-by-five, it was obviously a segment of something larger, something elsewhere, or perhaps the sole piece worth salvage. When Cash tilted his head to one side he saw that it resembled a big honeycomb, with rows of orderly, stop-sign-shaped pockets. Each octagonal chamber held one of the bugs, suspended like prehistoric scorpions in amber, although this medium was a pliable, transparent blue gel the consistency of modeling clay. It gave when Cash pressed it with the tip of his ballpoint pen, then sprang back.

Twenty or thirty of the little compartments were empty.

Peek: There were—head count—sixteen creatures outside now, cutting him off from the truck. They had hidden themselves, and waited for him to enter the freezer. The empty area between Cash and his opponents hinted that they had gotten the idea to keep their distance.

They were learning.

Best tally, he could clear twelve with the shotgun and the Ruger before he had to reload, if he did not miss once. He still had little idea of how fast they could move when motivated. He could hang tight and wait for dawn, a fat ten or eleven hours . . . but not in the freezer. They might not even disperse at dawn. They might wait until noon, when it got hotter.

Beyond fear was exhaustion. How long could Cash keep his eyes open and guard up?

Longer, he realized, than he could go without taking a dump. His last visit to the throne had been over twenty hours ago, and his bowels were threatening to burst like a sausage casing in a centrifuge. Great.

He could surrender. But not yet.

He could spy on them and pick a moment. They might dither around trying to form a plan of attack, or an ambush, or a diversion. Not yet.

He checked the door again. They hadn't moved. He tried to squeeze his ass cheeks to interrupt the inevitable. *Go or no go?* He did not laugh at his own folly, because if he started, he might not be able to stop, and when authorities locked him in a padded cell, he'd still be laughing.

Utterly humiliated, he moved to the back corner of the freezer, dropped his pants and tried to move his bowels as fast as possible. The tang of his own refrigerated shit brought him about as low as he'd ever felt, and rendered him infantile.

The pack with the two cigarettes rustled in his pocket, beckoning his attention. He craved a smoke, just to purchase a smoke's worth of time.

Brilliantly, he lacked the means to light up.

"Emerge. Cash emerge now."

It was a voice from outside. It sounded like a very bad imitation of Carrie's voice, clotted and syrupy.

Cash hurried his pants on and buckled up so he could refill his hands with guns.

All right, full disclosure: Cash had always wanted to see Carrie's breasts. But not this way.

She was naked, striding through the group, her flesh disorganized and baggy. Her face was melting right off her skull. Cash saw her breasts. They hung offsides due to the V-neck rip in the center of her chest. The skin that had drooped along her arms accordioned at the wrists the same way as a paper wrapper mashed down from a drinking straw. She reached up with elephantine hands to grab at the tear in her chest. The tissue rended apart, gone fishy and rotten, as the mouthless being stepped out of the incubation envelope that used to be Cash's partner. Its knot of throat bulged as it mimicked speech via some unguessable mechanism.

"Cash. Emerge."

It had been less than an hour since Carrie had been stung.

When Cash came out, shotgun-first, the entire group moved forward several emboldened steps. He shot one, then another, and they dropped. In the nightmare slow-motion of a fever dream, he saw the one that had issued from Carrie pick up her Smith from the ground. One tendril of the clawlike pincer wrapped the butt while the other sought the trigger. It leveled the pistol at Cash and fired.

The slug went high and wide.

It's not her, not any more . . .

That hesitation almost killed him. As he brought the Mossberg to bear, a second shot flew in true and punched him in the upper left chest, spoiling his aim. A hot rivet of pain fried his nerves. He grimaced, corrected his muzzle, and cut loose. The thing that had peeled off Carrie's body lost half of its knoblike head and spun down in a shower of gluey mulch, dropping the pistol, slide open.

While the rest rushed him.

Cash side-stepped to the smokehouse, dealing out the remaining rounds from the shotgun and getting one more hit, one miss, and one wing-strike that blew away a pincer at the elbow.

It was at least ninety degrees inside the smokehouse. The air was ripe with cured pork. There was an interior crank handle that could be barricaded if he could find something to wedge under it.

Carrie had favored light loads for diminished recoil. As a result, the semiwadcutter had lodged in Cash's breast and failed to exit. Dense blood, not completely oxygenated, was already blotting his shirt. Heart blood.

The creature had picked up Carrie's gun, fired once, corrected, and hit him on the second shot. They were learning. Now they would know the purpose of any other firearms loitering around, say, inside the house, if . . .

Cash remembered the spent shotgun shells in the yard. Someone else had tried earlier, and failed. Someone had shot their own dog, the Rottie, to keep it from changing, too.

Cash hoped they would not come into the smokehouse due to the heat.

They might waste time deciding what to do, but wouldn't breeze on in. Not yet. He should have just bolted. Run for the hills and made it someone else's problem. Now he was cornered, low on ammo, and in need of medical attention. But if he ran, he still had no idea of how fast they could pursue him.

Or maybe Cash could wait until they adapted more, or learned enough to come in after him, at which time he still had the option of putting a slug into his own head.

But not yet.

Thudding and thumping, next door. They were inside the icehouse.

They could imprint off horses, dogs, people, anything. Until Cash was all that was left to use.

Outside there came a sputtering noise, like a motor missing cylinder strokes. The generator for the icehouse had been chugging away for the better part of a day or two without being refueled. It was running out of gas. Cash knew the sound. The icehouse would thaw and the stored bugs would melt free. Would the smokehouse cool off as the freezer warmed up?

Buttoning up for hours was no longer an option. Cash had scant cognizance of the passage of time. He did not wear a wristwatch. Almost nobody did, any more; everybody had mobile devices. Cash's own cell was still in the door pocket of the Bronco.

Not yet.

Cash used his fist to hammer a pork shank under the door handle, because the creatures outside had come to test it. Right outside the smokehouse door, they were less than a foot away from his face.

Shooting through the door would get Cash nothing except ricochets and a less secure door. Maybe, if he could get to the roof . . .

The smokehouse was a wood frame veneered in sheet metal. There was a white oak curing barrel that could be flipped to provide a step-up. Every time Cash tried to correct his balance to bulldog his way through the ceiling, his wounded shoulder blew new spikes of pain all the way down to his feet and the bullet hole began to pump fresh. His life was dribbling out.

Obscured from view was a tiny skylight, probably for ventilation. It was difficult to see since the ceiling had browned to a uniform pattern. Too small for his body, but there. He had to bang the corroded hasp back with the grip of his Ruger.

Yeah, don't attract any attention to yourself with the noise.

The hinges squeaked as he pushed against the hatch with the heel of his good hand. His entire right side was going numb and his vision was getting spotty. Shock was setting in. He could just get his head through the hole if he was willing to sacrifice an ear. Outstanding; his last tetanus shot had been years ago. Amoebic infections from tainted meat were the worst.

Soon he would not be able to trust the evidence of his own senses. He would hallucinate, grow dopey, pass out.

Cash had to clamber down to find a plastic crate for more elevation, then repeat his unsteady ascent. He could just get his head through the hatch. The ceiling was as solid as a carpenter's warranty, no rusty nails to auger loose, firm framing or your money back.

Cash could see the pickup truck. There were no creatures in sight except the ones he'd terminated. They were knocked down in their own mud, near the hideous skin-pile that used to be Senior Patrol Agent Carrie Rixson.

To the left, clear; to the right, ditto. The view to the rear was harder since Cash had to peer through the interstice between the hatch and the roof, but it looked okay behind him, too.

This calm could not hold. They had retreated to regroup, find weapons, or make more. Cash could belay his fear and move now, or try to clench and await what came next, as he grew more helpless by the second. The tension was far worse than trying not to shit. You couldn't win. Your own biology would doom you.

He nearly fell on his face getting down from the clumsy barrel-and-crate arrangement. He nearly started weeping when the chunk of pork stuck under the door handle refused to wiggle loose. But in three more heartbeats, the door was open and he was moving as fast as he could manage for the truck, hoping his adversaries had not become savvy enough to take the keys.

They were gone from the yard.

"I'm sorry," he said to Carrie's remains. She deserved better. "God, am I sorry."

That did not slow him down, though. The pickup's cab door was still open. The keys were still in the ignition. And Cash was alone in the turnaround.

"You fuckers!" he shouted hoarsely. "I'm coming back! I'm coming back for all of you! I'm gonna kill every single one of you!"

No response. Locked into the cab, windows up, Cash unbuckled his gunbelt to get at his trouser belt, which he unthreaded to bind his own wadded up T-shirt tight against the oozing bullet ditch in his shoulder. The Ram truck fired up positively on the first try. Not like in the movies, where the vehicle won't start while the monsters close in. The seatbelt alarm pinged annoyingly.

Cash laid the pedal down and thundered over the cow-catcher at the archway, highbeams up to max. The fuel stood at half a tank. He did not allow himself to breathe until he rocketed back onto the International Highway. Now it was safe to crack the windows and blow the AC on high.

He remembered the cigarettes in his pocket, dug one out, and lipped it. A little nicotine would be better than nothing at all. But the truck did not have a dashboard lighter. Few of them did, anymore.

The black tarp in the pickup bed, unsecured, blew free just in time for Cash to glimpse the big section of blue amber honeycomb, his cargo, before his dulled eyesight focused on the bug that had been left for him inside the cab. It tensed to spring, just out of swatting reach. That's what the monsters had been up to in the icehouse—setting a trap and backing off, to let Cash ambush himself.

The big Ram truck swerved off the road and stopped. It would sit for a while, metal pinging as it cooled, the AC still blasting. Then, eventually, it would resume its journey into the city.

David J. Schow is a multimedia writer whose work includes the script for the dark cult classic, *The Crow*, and episodes for television series *Masters of Horror*. The author of nine novels, his acclaimed short stories are featured in dozens of anthologies and collected in seven volumes. He is also the author of an award-winning book of essays on modern media, *Wild Hairs* and *The Outer Limits Companion* (on the classic TV series). Schow recently updated the latter with a new fiftieth anniversary source for all things *Outer Limits*: *The Outer Limits at 50*. He lives in Los Angeles, California.

*What happened to the Scouts in Troop 13? Why did they not come back
from that last patrol, when we patted their little green hats
and kissed them goodbye so happily?*

THE LEGEND OF TROOP 13

Kit Reed

The Lost Troop

In the mountains tonight, in the jagged hills below the observatory, the Girl
Scouts' voices ring—just not where you can hear, for the missing girls of
Troop 13 are as wary as they are spirited.

"Beautiful," Louie says. He paints the observatory dome, top to bottom on
his revolving scaffold, so he's in a position to know. He says, "It's a little bit
like angels singing."

It would lift your heart to hear them, tourists claim, because tourists
believe everything they hear, whether or not they actually heard it.

Although they've been missing for years, some people think the legendary
lost Girl Scouts of Troop 13 are still out there on Palamountain, camping
in the shadow of the great white dome. We don't know how it happened
or where our girls went when they went missing, but tourists come to the
mountain in hopes, and business is booming.

They claim they came to see the cosmos through the world's largest
telescope, but the men's wet mouths tell you different.

As for our girls, there have been signs, e.g.: surprise raids on picnic tables,
although it could be bears. Outsiders swear the Last Incline is booby-trapped
with broken glass and sharp objects, but they can't prove it. They have to lug
their ruined tires downhill to Elbow and by the time the wrecker brings these
tourists back uphill with their new tires, the road is clear—no Scouts, no sign
of Scouts, but their cars have been rifled.

So there's a chance our girls are running through the woods in their green hats at this very minute, with their badge sashes thrown over items missing from our clotheslines. It's like a party every night, twelve Girl Scouts on their Sit-Upons around the campfire—feasting on candy and s'mores, judging from supplies stolen in midnight break-ins at Piney's Store. Our sheriff and the State Police looked for months; the FBI came, but the cold trail just got colder. It's been so long that even their mothers have stopped looking.

Now, you may come to Palamountain expecting to find dead campfires, skeletal teepees, abandoned Sit-Upons; you may think you spotted little green hats bobbing up there on the West Slope, but don't expect to catch up with them. You won't find our lost girls, no matter how hungry you are for love or adventure, so forget about easing whatever itch you thought you'd scratch here. They haven't been seen or heard from since the day Tracie Marsters threw the gaudy Troop Leader Scarf around her throat and led them up the mountain.

What happened to the Scouts in Troop 13, really? Why did they not come back from that last patrol, when we patted their little green hats and kissed them goodbye so happily? Did they not love us, or are there things on Palamountain that we don't know about? Were they wiped out in a rockfall or kidnapped by Persons Unknown, or are they just plain lost in the woods, and still trying to find their way back to us? Our Scouts couldn't be carried off against their will, that's unthinkable. Their motto is "Be Prepared," and they'd know what to do. We would have found markers: bits of crumpled paper on the trail, blazes on the trees, to signify which way they were taken.

We're afraid they went looking for someplace better than the settlement at Elbow, halfway up the East Grade on Palamountain, or our boring home town in the foothills. Prepared or not, we don't want to think about them running around in some big city. Unless they were running away from home and us personally, which is even worse.

Better to think of them as still up there, somewhere on Palamountain.

Listen, there have been sightings!

A tourist staggers into Mike's bar in the Elbow and he is all, *I alone am left to tell the tale, I alone am left to tell . . .* At this point words desert him; it was that intense. No, he can't tell you where, or what, exactly, and that's the least of it.

We need to shush him, so we shush him. That kind of talk is bad for business.

If they're still up there, they're too happy to hurt you. They're probably fine, running along to: "Ash Grove" or "Daisy, Daisy, we honor your memory true," that's the Girl Scout version, "We are Girl Scouts, all because of you . . . "—wonderful songs. You won't hear them singing as they bound along, because Scouts are trained to be careful, they'd be trilling.

It's a pretty sound but it chills your blood, according to Louie, who has heard it. He says, "If you hear them coming, *run.*"

No, we think. Not our girls. How could those sweet things be dangerous?

Edwin Ebersole III

Five a.m., and we've been on this bus for so long that the babies are panicking, not all at once, but more or less sequentially. Yow, one cries. Wawww, goes the next; uuuck and aaah aaah aaaa; and the big ones erupt in counterpoint, *Are we there yet*, wawww, *are we there yet*, aaaah aaaah aaaa, *Are we there yet?* Bwaaaaaa, *Are we . . .* it's like a class project on chain reaction. The racket is exponential and we're all too anxious and depressed to make it stop and the only thing that keeps me going on this excursion is the glittering secret in my pocket and the chance that I can get what I want out of this trip, up there at the top. It's taking too long!

Fifty movers and shakers with wives and kids, riding into the experience of a lifetime in a stinking, overloaded repurposed Grayhound bus, and why? Evanescent Tours sold us on the trip of a lifetime. It was the card. Triple cream stock. Engraved. Gold ink.

EVANESCENT TOURS PRESENTS:
THE TOP OF THE WORLD, VIA LUXURY COACH.
PALAMOUNTAIN OBSERVATORY EXCLUSIVE

And the kicker?

by invitation only

Who wouldn't bite? No riffraff, just us, the business elite, and, better? Every man on this tour is like me, tough, successful, rich. No ordinary guys on this bus. They can't afford it, and for us, top of the world, with more TK. See, these pretty little Girl Scouts vanished up there when they were small, nobody knows how. The lost little girls must be big girls by now. Every man on this bus has stated reasons for riding up the mountain, but at bottom, there are babes in those woods and they need us.

We're going up the mountain to hunt. Like we can get back something we lost before we even knew it was missing.

The hell of it is, Serena's on to me. I plugged this trip as our second honeymoon, that I'd booked especially for her, but she knows. Nowhere is it written, but she knows we've never been happy. She jumped up in the middle of the night and dragged our girl Maggie off to sit in the back, and for what? All I did was move on my wife in the dark because she is after all my wife, and we've been traveling for so long that my want ran ahead of me.

Dammit, the bus was dark. They were all asleep.

I thought, 2 a.m., okay, let's make the time go by a little faster—you know. Serena slapped my hand away. "Back off, you horny fuck!" and I went, "I was just . . . " which devolved into the usual.

Serena: You always . . .

Me: I never, and besides, you . . .

Her: I always, and you say you love me but you never . . .

This happens to couples in enclosed situations: the vacation house, the Carnival Cruise. This bus.

Thousands I spent to get us here, high-end launch party at a luxury hotel on the coast, with us done up like kings: for me, Gucci shoes, the Hugo Boss tux with the Armani vest. I even bought Serena a Valentino gown. Champagne smashed across the prow of our private vehicle, full access to the Observatory, satisfaction guaranteed, I bought front row seats for the spectacle of the century, and where are we?

Nowhere.

We've been rolling for days, all the toilets are stopped up and the video player is kaput. We're running out of food, probably because the driver got us lost back there. Worse yet, he isn't speaking to us.

We don't know if he's sworn to secrecy by Evanescent Tours, or if he's pissed at us for bitching, or just plain out of control.

I personally think the captain is mad. This Clyde Pritchard is one hostile hick. He drives without stopping except for gas, at which point, given the sticker price on this extravaganza, he should let us get out, relieve ourselves at the Roaming Mountains Dine and Dance that we whizzed past an hour ago instead of in one of his rolling cesspools, he should let us visit our luggage for necessaries and eat hot food for a change, instead of the freeze-dried dinners Evanescent Tours Incorporated vacuum-packed for the days or is it weeks we'll be in this rat trap.

—Later

Last night the judgmental knuckle-dragger threw packs of beef jerky and rattler paté at us, one each, and warned us to limit fluids because, well, you don't want to know. Today it was oyster crackers, one miserable packet each, stamped with the name of some crap diner in the flatlands. Are we low on food? What if he runs off the road out here where I can't get a signal? What if we have to kill and eat each other, in hopes somebody will see the vultures circling and rescue whoever's left?

I parleyed with the guys. "Does he know who we *are*? Nobody treats us like trailer trash. We're *rich*." A bunch of us got together and went up there to stick it to the slack-jawed hick. At least he could tell us which route he is taking, the East Slope Road, or the West Slope Incline, which is, like, our polite way of saying, Jerkoff, *do you know what you're doing?*

He won't answer. He snaps his head around, glaring, and when we don't back off, he pulls a sidearm out of his belt. "Back to your seats or I fire," he says, and he's not kidding.

I pass a note to Serena, and watch it going hand over hand to the bench seat in the back, where she is braiding fishermen's lures into our daughter's hair. Without bothering to open my heartfelt apology, she tears it to shreds and braids paper butterflies in with all the other junk in Maggie's hair.

My son Eugene the felon drags his paw across my arm. "Dad."

"Shut up, Eugene."

Kid goes, "I saw a sign!"

A sign. Like we're pilgrims, looking for the golden calf or something. Oh wait. It says . . . but this pissed-off fool is whipping around curves so fast that I catch it out of the corner of my eye. *Mount Palamountain.* "Guys!"

Our heads snap back on our necks so fast that nobody hears. We take a sharp turn and start the climb. Our hearts rise up.

We are going to the mountain! The mountain, where I get mine.

Clyde Pritchard

I thought you'd be excited, but you don't give a crap. I stop at the Overlook to let you look up at Palamountain and around at territory surrounding, it's a perfect 360 but you don't care, you just circle like bears fixing to take a dump right here on Overlook Point and the next thing I know, you're wandering across the road sniffing for something in the woods, this Ebersole guy in the lead. Look at you, with candy wrappers stuck to your camp shorts and pork rinds ground into your big, white Jell-O thighs, drooling red because of the gummy rattlesnakes I threw you after lunch. Cover those legs, they're disgusting! If I left you off right here I'd be doing you a favor, you wouldn't be smarter by the time you made it back downhill to the highway exit ramp, but by God you'd be thinner.

I show you the nth wonder of the world, the full 360, and . . .

Okay, Clyde, try. "Friends, look up! From here, you can see the monster telescope move! At this height, critters you've never seen before streak by so fast that you don't even know they're stalking you, these woods bristle with undergrowth that you don't see anywhere, winding suckers around petrified trees, and . . . " *Oh shit.* "Wait a minute. Where are you going?" *Uncouth fuckers.* "Come back!"

But you run for the woods with your pants on fire, like you'll find those girls hiding behind the next tree, so I do what I have to, it's company regulations. I yell.

"Okay then, watch out! There's rattlesnakes in those ferns and the last thing you want is for one of those mean suckers to bite you, they can strike up to six feet high," *but nobody stops.*

"Okay, dammit. Go ahead and get bit." *I'd be glad, but I have to read off the warning card: Evanescent policy.*

"When it happens, do not make a cross and try to suck the venom out. You have to raise the part that got bit higher than your head and hightail it for the observatory gift shop. Agatha can help you . . . if you get back on the goddam bus. Do you hear me? There's antivenin in the gift shop and Agatha can call 911 for you on the landline, that is, if we get there before closing time . . .

"I warned you."

Like you care. You crunch after Ebersole, loaded for bear. Agatha's visiting her great-granddaughter in Scottsdale at the moment, and she might not get back until Thursday, but I did what I could, and you brought it on yourselves.

"Okay, assholes. Be careful out there."

The Lost Girls

Oh yay hurray, another great day, running along in our badge sashes and deerskin shoes for we are, first of all, Girl Scouts, and so very proud! Melody Harkness is our leader now, and she's the best! Moira's put Girl Scout trefoils on the moccasins she made for us, for with the needles Stephanie carved from bones cut out of the last deer we brought down, and beads sewn on with hair pulled out of Delia, who has plenty to spare because it grew until it was long enough to sit on, Moira can make anything. For wild girls we're pretty well dressed, considering. Scouting makes you resourceful. Steal a bed-sheet or two from the line behind the P.O. when Miss Archibald's out delivering the mail and, man, Nancy will whip up a sweet outfit, and if anything rips, Ella will patch it, that's her job.

There's tons of food for girls who know how to find it, you can kill it in the woods or dig it out of the dirt, plus, there's food in gangs of places you wouldn't think to look, like, there's food in the day trippers' cars and summer cabins and down at Piney's store in Elbow; there's food on picnic blankets and food on windowsills just asking for it so don't you moms worry about us.

In spite of what you think happened, your Scouts that used to be so little and cute are fat and sassy now, and we're doing fine, fine, fine. We run along singing, just not so anybody but us can hear, we are that fine, and our songs are wonderful! We move fast and keep it low, so you can't hunt us down and catch us, and the fun will never end. If it did, that would be the end of us so if you were thinking of catching us, forget it or it will be the end of you. Nobody sneaks up on Troop 13, our motto is *Be Prepared*, don't even try.

We get what we want and we keep what we have which is fun, fun, fun, Troop 13 is forever, so beware.

Ida Mae Howells

19—

I'm so lucky! I'm a happy, lucky girl, running free with my sister Scouts, and all because I chased a kitty in the woods when I was little, and got lost for good which was lucky, *lucky* because it was so awful at home.

It was the day our grade came up Palamountain to see the stars.

I got so lost!

I wouldn't of, if everybody wasn't so mean to me, so I guess that was lucky too. We were up to stars in first grade so Mrs. Greevey brought us all the way up in the school bus to see stars through the giant telescope. Ahead of time I was very excited to come, but it was awful on the bus. Betty Ann and them said eeeww, dirty underpants, when I fell down getting on the bus. They wouldn't sit with me, which, it's not my fault Uncle Martha's always gone and never did the wash, so I had to ride all the way up the mountain in my dirty underpants all by myself. Also it was loud and ugly in the bus, because of all those boys yelling at you and rubbing stuff in your hair and them all fighting in the aisles. Mrs. Greevey yelled that she would buy us all ice cream sandwiches at Piney's Store when we got to the Elbow if we would only shut up, she yelled and yelled but it only got worse.

Mrs. Greevey made the driver stop at Piney's anyway, either it was them ganging up on her or she forgot. Kids jumped down and ran into Piney's so fast that Mrs. Greevey fell down and hurt herself, I think she even cried. She was too upset to count when we went into the store and I guess she wasn't counting when they all came back after, except not me.

They left without me, and you know what? I was glad!

See, Gerald pushed me down the back steps and my ice cream all squoze out of the sandwich and got mooshed into the dirt. They all laughed, so I had to get down and play like I had a rock in my shoe until they got bored of waiting for me to get up and forgot. Then Jane threw a rock at Billy Carson and Gerald and them piled on her, which pretty much served her right. I ran into the woods while nobody was looking so I wouldn't have to mess, I went way, way up there on the hill where it was quiet, so I never even saw them get back on the bus.

The cutest little kitty came up to me!

I tried to pet it, but it ran away so I ran after it, it looked so cuddly and soft. By the time I gave up, I was lost and it was getting dark. Well, I could of screamed and hollered until somebody down at Piney's Store would of heard me and they came up and found me, but then I would of had to go sit in the store and wait for the bus to come back down and I'd have to go home to Uncle Martha and them. I'm not never going back, I'd rather die. So I just set there doing nothing and waiting for the kitty to come back, and my bones would still be sitting there waiting except there were noises in the woods like kids trying not to laugh and the next minute, they came.

It was this wonderful lady Miss Tracie, with a special scarf around her hair. I found out later that meant she was the troop leader, and those cute things on the girls were badge sashes and Girl Scout pins with three gold leaves, so just when I could of starved to death or died of loneliness, Troop 13 found me and I went home with them.

They didn't ask who was I or was I lost or what was I doing up there. They just brought me back to their camp and fed me on pigs in the blanket and s'mores until I couldn't eat any more so when I felt better, I explained. Miss Tracie said be glad that kitty was too fast for me because there are no kitties in these woods, just mountain lions, and if the mother had found me I would be dead by now.

She said I should thank my stars, but I was already thanking my stars because by the time the fire went out and everybody sang "Day is done . . ." Miss Tracie decided I could stay. She called Council and they voted me in. This girl Myrna whispered that it was either that *or*, but she never told me the *or*. I was way happy because nobody voted to send me downhill to Piney's, so I would never, ever have to go back to Uncle Martha and the bike gang, they said Piney would of sent me home and they might torture me until I told on Troop 13.

Now this is my home! Wherever we set down our Sit-Upons and build a fire and put up our tents. Camp is so, so much nicer than Uncle Martha's big old shed on the freeway down at the tippy bottom of the hills, where they were so mean to me, plus I had to do all their dirty dishes and they made me sleep in the loft.

The first week Miss Tracie taught me the Girl Scout Promise and a bunch of other Girl Scout things, she asked did I want to be one. Yes! So by Saturday I was a brand new member of Troop 13 although I was only in first grade. See, Miss Tracie was a great, great troop leader, and they don't have Brownies here. Plus something happened to this other girl in the troop and they needed one more.

That was so wonderful, they *needed* me!

That night we all stood around the fire saying the Girl Scout Promise, "On my honor I will try . . . " where we promise to follow the Girl Scout Law. Miss Tracie and them and me, we all put our hands over our hearts and swore to "make the world better and be a sister to every Girl Scout," and that is what we do.

Clyde Pritchard

"Here we are, people. It's a short walk to the top from this point, but you have to stay in line and follow me. It's steep."

So what if the bus broke down on the West Grade and we're here after closing time? I left voicemail so Gavin and Lionel will hang in long enough to give you the tour.

This is all your fault and I want you off my back. Eli had to truck new parts uphill from Elbow because you fat fucks overloaded my bus and it blew a Thing and now you're bitching because we got here late, when it was you that ditched the wives and kids at the Overlook, two hours wasted sitting on our thumbs. Like your lost girls would be in there rubbing up against trees, all hot and ready to give you what you want. Believe me, you don't want to tangle with them.

Two hours, and you come back empty-handed, red in the face and pissed off at me, and Ebersole reams me out for making you late.

Shut up, asshole. We're here.

Look at you looking back, like you'll spot them flitting through the woods at the bottom of Observatory Hill. One of your women goes to look over the edge before I can head her off. She jams her fists in her mouth, all, eek *and I have to grab her elbow and help her pull herself together before the others freak, but you don't care. You don't even see. The air is so thick with your desire that it's hard to corral you and aim you toward the stone steps to the top.*

Time to grab the walkie and start the spiel. I bang on the mouthpiece. "A-hem."
I heard that dirty laugh.

"Welcome to the Palamountain observatory, crown jewel of the western range.
We usually walk up from the parking lot, but I parked on the Last Incline because
we're late. Excited much?"

*Parking on the ledge is risky, given that we're nosed into an eight thousand-
foot drop, but so is shoving you up the long, windy path from the parking lot at
this hour, when tourists are more likely to stray and get lost or snakebit or worse.*

*I funnel you into the straight and narrow, a hundred stairsteps to the brass
double doors as daylight thins out and starts to go. I think up mountain gods so
I can pray that Gavin and Lionel are still on deck when we hit the top.* "Light's
going, so watch your step."

You're all mutter grumble, mutter mutter, " . . . food in this place,"
". . . restaurant," "bloody starving," ". . . restaurant," *Ebersole, belching,* ". . . food!"

The sun is in a nosedive and you're thinking food? "There's plenty to see once we
get into the rotunda, plus the amazing Palamountain gift shop has snacks." *Yeah,
I hear you snarling,* "snacks!" *Okay, Clyde, think fast.* "Fountain pens and snow
globes with the Palamountain dome. Observatory patches, spyglass mini-scopes.
Sky's the limit, you can get meteorite fragments, powerful pills for what ails you,
moon rocks! Baseball caps and warmup jackets with the Palamountain emblem,
show the people where you've been!"

Like that works. " . . . Starving, get it?"

"Food."

The nth wonder of the universe and you're all, food. "There are marvels in the
rotunda, and you can get food and drink in the gift shop on the exit side. Beef
jerky, volcanic stew, moon pies." *I invent, to keep you quiet.* "Whiskey singles,
Palamountain wines . . . "

("Restaurant!")

*About the restaurant. There is no restaurant, which is not my problem. And
there's more, and this is what I'm dreading, laying out the* more.

*I could tell you outright, but you don't want to hear. You bang on your chests
like uncaged gorillas in the fading light, yelling* "Top of the world," *and* "Bring it
on," *like our lost girls will hear what big men you are and swarm out of the woods
all warmed up* down there *and waiting for you to come out when the tour is done.
Well, I can tell you about that. Your women are over you, and our girls . . . You
don't want to know. You don't need to know that there have been Incidents, not
to mention the lawsuit, so whatever you thought you heard about Troop 13, you're
wrong.*

There is no Troop 13, trust me, there are no wild girls out there, get it? But if you see them coming, run! Shit, who am I to tell you rich, ravenous pigs what to look out for when you can't even be bothered to field strip your cigarettes? You and your hidden desires can rot in hell. I waste my life hauling you up here by the busload, with your fat wallets and I-can-buy-and-sell-you squints and I am done with you.

Ebersole straight-arms me. "I want in!"

I want him dead. "And on this level, the Waiting Room."

This is bad. The observatory's dark, just the one light over the keyhole to the double doors to the Waiting Room. I check my phone: no texts, no missed calls. Usually I unlock the doors and give a little speech in the Waiting Room while you file in, saying this is the air lock, the last chamber between you and the wonders of space, which is Gavin's cue to come out and give his speech and unlock the rotunda, but the observatory is dark and Gavin isn't here.

Where is everybody?

So I stall. "Before we go in, you need to take the circular staircase up to the observation deck and get your vanity shots. Snap the wife and kids in front of the Palamountain dome." *Good thing you're easily distracted. Every one of you tenses up, like, where to pose them and who's first. Like the family matters. You're all about getting off your crap screen shots so the homefolks can start feeling bad right now because you're here, and they can't afford it. I pretend to consult my watch.* "And be back here in um. Oh, fifteen."

By that time, Gavin had better be here. There's the Evanescent regulation for late arrivals like us, and I want you toured and gift shopped before I break the news.

As soon as you guys tramp up the steps to the observation deck, I pull out my phone, but even Lionel isn't picking up.

Where is everybody anyway?

"Problem?" *Ebersole is back, all suspicious and mean.*

"No problem." *I lock my face up tight and throw away the key.* "Better hurry or you'll lose the light."

Randy slutgrubbers, you're back in five, agitating to get inside the rotunda and get your tour because you can't wait to get out. You expect to ditch me and the family when you're done and go have your way in the woods. Well, good luck with that. I hear it in your ugly laughter and your muttered asides, all rank and gross. I can smell it on you. I want to yell into the microphone, but, company regulations: I'm not allowed to say shut up, shut up. Whether or not Gavin shows I need you inside, where I can keep track, so I say, "Welcome to the world-famous

Palamountain Observatory, the largest and finest in the world." I unlock the doors and herd you into the Waiting Room with a tired "Ta-DA."

You damn near trample me, getting in. Good thing you don't hear the clang as the doors behind you shut. I switch on the lights and the women relax a little bit but you guys bang on the doors to the rotunda like you bought and paid for it, "Open up!"

"Sorry for the delay, folks. The keys . . . "

"Let's get this over with." You turn into a monster with twenty heads, teeth bared in angry growls and your flabby bodies bunched like that's all muscle: big men. Used to getting what you want.

Sooner or later, I have to break the news.

Nobody gets into the rotunda unless Gavin shows up with the keys and nobody leaves until Lionel fires up the telescope after which the docents talk, after which there's the light show so when I explain that we're stuck here until morning, at least you got your money's worth. See, after the tour I let you into the gift shop so you can load up on junk food before I lock you into the Waiting Room. If you're eating when I tell you what happens next, it will soften the blow. Except Agatha's in New Mexico and we're waiting for Gavin, and Gavin isn't anywhere.

I've looked.

The Lost Girls

—Now

My my, where did the time go?

Day is done, gone the sun and we're still rollicking, laughing and frolicking in our special place, eating the catch of the day while Marcia toasts a yummy batch of s'mores over our sweet little fire. We're down to our last mini-marshies but nobody really cares, nobody worries because that cute Claude from the valley brought another busload up the mountain today. They stopped at the Overlook, and, Melody saw. You can see practically everything from there!

Melody's the oldest, but she wears the tattered badge sash with pride, over a sweet pink dimity something she snatched from a clothesline back in the day. Melody sees everything, and Melody knows. That girl runs these woods.

"Freeze dried eggs and fresh orange juice on that bus," she says, "Lots of good things!"

"And Clyde'll leave them off when he goes."

He will, he's never seen us but he must love us, he always puts leftovers on the rock at the Overlook when the bus goes back downhill.

Patsy giggles. "Plus whatever they're carrying, if . . . "

"If . . . " It's catching, like music. "Whatever they're carrying if . . . " If we happen to *want*.

Day is done, yay for fun!

It's not Ida Mae's fault how she talks, she didn't get much education; she goes, "And whoever they brung."

Stephanie is all, "Girls, let's hold back on this one," but nobody listens, because she's only been in this troop since her folks' car broke down and she replaced Sallie Traub that was in the bear trap accident, even Melody couldn't save her.

Marcia is like, "Stephanie, shut up," and Steph goes, "No, you shut up," which is not to say that Girl Scouts fight among themselves, because that would be a violation of the Girl Scout code, so Melody goes, "Girls, shhhh!"

Melody is in charge and for a minute, we do.

But Stephanie's all this and Marcia's all that, and people are taking sides because when we finished the BBQ tonight, enough wasn't, well, quite enough. Melody's extra worried because there'll be tourists at the observatory tonight, and it's after hours. If anything happens, she has to say who and what we take and if we take somebody, what we do with them, which is a lot, so she sings:

"Day is done . . . "

And we all sing, "Gone the sun," and by the time we finish we're pretty much chill, because that's what Melody really means when she starts singing, she means, "Chill."

We all lay back with our heads on our Sit-Upons and Melody's all happy to see us settled in the firelight so she starts our most favorite, favorite story to keep us settled. It's "The Bloody Finger of Ghostine Deck," about something awful that happens on a boat. She strings it along and *strings* it along until the moon is high and everyone but Ida Mae Howells is snuggled down in the canebrake and sound asleep because Melody put Ida Mae on guard. She has to wake us all up if one of them strays down here, it's so exciting!

She kind of whispers, just like this, it's so low and so *sharp* that we know it even in our sleep:

"They're here."

Clyde Pritchard

Back off, assholes. It's hard to breathe without you all up in my face. Rich fat pricks closing in, all puffed up and pushy with your needs, you're overflowing the space.

"Sorry for the delay, folks. In the old days the telescope was hand operated, staff here around the clock. These days it's all computerized, and our research

assistant . . . " I don't know where Lionel is, but I can tell you what Lionel is. Lionel is late. " . . . will be with you after he does a couple more things."

I fill some time with a little spiel about the Bleeding Heart restaurant on down in the Elbow, at which point you all perk up because you've been agitating about the no-restaurant ever since we arrived. You finished your last pork rinds and candy bars on the Overlook and I can hear you gulping drool. I hit the high spots on the Bleeding Heart menu, from Mountain Ash Venison all the way down to Palamountain Passion, Mag's sensational dessert, to distract you until Gavin comes, which should be any minute now except it isn't and yeah, I know where your minds are wandering, it's stuffy in here and it's getting late.

Too late. Okay then. Break the news. Tour or no tour, you will not be leaving the observatory tonight. Whatever you think you heard about Troop 13 and those wild girls, *for your safety and mine, you're socked in here until it gets light. I pull out the card and read the Evanescent Night-time Regulation:* Late arrivals must remain on the premises until 8 a.m. *It's my job to lug thirty bedrolls out of the lockers when the tour's done and we're back in the Waiting Room, show you the toilets and vending machines and lock you in for the night.*

Break it gently.

"Okay folks, you'll eat well at the Bleeding Heart, but it won't be tonight. Trust me, you'll get your tour tomorrow morning as soon as Gavin, comes in. We'll be back in Elbow by noon, but right now . . . For your comfort and safety, we're bunking here." *The women groan but you . . .*

"The fuck we are."

"Where it's warm and safe."

Ebersole. "We're not paying for safe."

I know what you want. You stink of it. "Bathrooms and vending machines down the hall to your left, soft drinks, Slim Jims and Pocky Sticks so you won't starve. Gavin's always here by eight. You'll get your your private tour."

The noise you make is ugly, ugly.

" . . . out of here."

Oh hell, I go, "I know you're sick of waiting, but trust me, it's worth waiting for."

Your minds go running along ahead to the dirty place. There are things I could tell you about Troop 13, but you don't like me any more than I like you, so why should I? As the Evanescent tour driver, I am forced to add, "People, it's not safe out there!"

But you're all stampeding, threatening legal action or worse.

Okay, in situations like this, the foyer is the safest place to sleep, but no way

am I bedding down with you ignorant, flatulent, loud-mouthed fools. You want
out? Okay, you asked for it.

You'll bitch when I fill your pockets with food from the machines and frog-
march you down the steep staircase to the ledge, but the bus is almost as safe as the
Waiting Room, so get used to it. See, I don't mind your women or the kids but I
can't stand another minute of you, and don't go thinking I don't have the power.
You backed off when I pulled my gun? Now the Evanescent taser shows its teeth.
You'll let me shovel you back onto the bus and lock you in for the night, which I am
obligated to do, because even though you signed off on the liability clause before you
came on this tour and I don't like you, I am responsible, so sleep safe and fuck you.

By the time you look for me I'll be laying out my bedroll back here in the
Waiting Room, drunk on the silence, happy as a rat in a barrel of rum.

Edwin Ebersole III

One more sleepless night on that toilet of a tour bus, one more dinner of crap
freeze-dried packets supplied by Evanescent Tours, no way am I walking back
into that.

Why are we still here? I'll tell you why. The technician never showed
up. Docents never showed up. We jammed that retard driver's face into the
surveillcam and an old lady came. It took forever and she was mad as a cow
in heat, but she unlocked the gift shop so this Clyde could herd us out past
astronaut T-shirts and bogus moon rocks, shoving us through like a bunch
of mountain mice. Six figures blown on this excursion and not one shot of us
looking through the giant telescope or any other damn thing and Serena is
even more pissed at me because I can't call a taxi and I damn well won't fake
a heart attack so Life Star will come and lift us out of here.

As if this dumb hick marching us down a hundred steps in the dark could
get Life Star to do anything but take a piss on him and besides, how's Life Star
landing on this Godforsaken crag which I don't mind, because . . .

I am damn well not leaving until I get what I came for. Just watch me
boogie, all fake-walking down the steps with you, marking time while
everybody follows this Clyde like lemmings to the slaughter. Well, fuck you
Clyde, while you herd my family *down* the steps I'm fake-walking backward,
up the steps, and I'll hide at the top until you've loaded them on and locked
everybody in. No way am I piling into that rolling garbage can they call a
luxury coach. I'll luxury you, Evanescent Tours Incorporated, I'll sue your
brains out as soon as I get what I came for and bring her back at which point
you might as well know, Serena, you and I are done.

I came up the mountain to get me a sweet, sexy, grown-up Girl Scout. I know she's out there, like, you think a babe like her wants to stay up here all funky in the woods when she can have me, and everything that comes with? E.g., the little diamond something-something that I brought to lure her out of the hills. It's in the security pocket in my cargo pants, and in case you were worried about me hunting sweet pussy all alone out here in the dark, I came prepared. Cavalry boots laced up to the knees under the leg extensions I zipped on while you were all flopping around the Overlook, so if there are snakes out there, no worries, this beekeeper's hat with a see-through veil thing will keep me safe.

I rolled it down like a theater curtain as soon as the hick led us out into the dark. Winners get what they pay for and I'm here to get mine, so don't think you can stiff me. The minute you slam the door on that death trap and run for the waiting room I hum a few bars to let her know that I am here and I love her already, and everything good will happen, all she has to do is show herself.

Do you hear me, sweetheart?

This is me not-singing, not-crooning this love song that I wrote inside my head on those long, terrible nights in the luxury coach, I'm rolling it out right now, for you.

"Are you lonely, do you miss it, do you want it, do you hate running wild and sleeping in the dirt, would you like something pretty, see I brought it, just for you . . . " going into a sort of ooo oooo ooooo . . . as I come down the steps and I let it get a little bit louder after I pass that stinking sardine can full of losers and head downhill into the parking lot by the woods where I happen to know you're hiding out. I get a little bit louder because I love you already and I want to hear, how old are you now, sweetheart, twenty? Eighteen?

Babe, listen to me singing, see me crouching low like a tiger romancing his mate, come to me, sweet baby, let me show you diamonds, and if you like them, I'll buy you a diamond collar and lead you out of these filthy woods on a diamond leash, and the first thing we'll do when we get off this stupid mountain is get you into a nice hot shower and scrub you down until your nipples lift and all your skin turns pink and then, you and I can . . . and then . . .

Ida May Howells
—Now

I'm a Scout and I have sisters now, and Uncle, Martha, and them can go to hell. It's sad what happened to Miss Tracie, but they gave me her Girl Scout pin after it happened because she didn't need it any more, and then we sang "Day is done" and gave her a really nice funeral before we put her in next to Ellie DeVere and some girl named Sallie inside the lime cave under the ledge on the Last Incline.

I love my troop and, you know what? After Uncle Martha and all, I love that there's only us *sisters* around. We live together and we play together and we belong together and when one of us gets too big for what we were wearing, Melody sees to it, and Martha makes alterations and if there's nothing on hand Stephanie goes out with the raiding party and they bring back such cute things! Melody's the oldest, and Melody knows what we need and who gets what when we're one short, and she knows if a girl is lost in the woods and she knows if that lost girl needs us, and after we find her or if she finds us, Melody decides whether or not this girl belongs, and if not, Melody knows what to do about it, and if something worse happens, she knows what to do and how, and Melody decides when.

Melody decided and now it's my turn to be up on the hill all by myself, she gave me the Midnight Watch. This is so cool! Me, hiding on the slope by the parking lot keeping watch, so my sister Scouts can sleep safe.

She trusts me to stay awake and be vigilant, so they can't sneak up on us while we sleep.

Like, these guys come crunching into the woods in the dead of night acting all heroic, like they're here to be nice, but we know they all want to Do Things to girls in the woods up here where nobody sees it and nobody can hear. Twice we caught men hunting us for the reward, like they could drag us back down the mountain in their teeth, back to our boring, stupid old lives. Well, we took care of them.

Sleep safe, girls. Nobody gets past me. I'm watching them people in the bus away up the Last Incline, no problem. Clyde marched them down and locked them all in the bus. They're asleep, so I can relax.

Wait! What's that? Did I dream it? Did I accidentally fall asleep? Who's out there anyway?

Ooooh nooooo!

And why am I all weird right now, thinking about all those outsiders, this close. We all hung back today when the bus left the Overlook, and when Clyde drove past, up the Last Incline, we were glad. See, in the parking lot, they get out and bop around and sometimes one gets lost. Then Stephanie warns us so low that only we can hear, "Run!" So we pick up and run.

We can't let them find us. If they find us, it will be bad.

Except this time it isn't them, it's only me.

And he's singing. Somebody is out here singing, I can hear him, it's for me!

Are you lonely, do you miss it, do you want it, it's so weird, and then, in the bushes something sparkles just above my head and the sneaky, nice-nasty sound comes with, too low for anybody but Ida Mae to hear, *it's so pretty, would you like it,* and the sparkle hangs closer, *do you want it, see I brought it just for you* and all of a sudden I don't want to move, I don't jump, I don't sound the alarm because I want to listen, I have to see, *if you want it you can have it . . .* and I should hoot to warn my sister Scouts but instead I just let the song happen until I see him through the leaves, he's singing and singing, he's close!

He looks huge in *all that stuff,* and, oh! Miss Tracie, I talked to him, I did! I kept it low, so as not to reach the others, I whispered, "Oh, you can take off the hat, our rattlers are all curled up sleeping in their holes," which is a lie, but I had to see what he looked like in the face behind the veil.

"Oh," he said, "are you in there? Let me see you, come out and look at me, and let me look at you." If he Tried Something I would have bopped him but he didn't move, he just waited in what was left of the moonlight, dangling this sparkly thing and singing his long, sweet song thing that made me squirm Down There, *if you want it you can have it, I brought diamonds just for you . . .*

And they're so shiny and he's so close that I almost, almost betrayed the spirit of Miss Tracie and Melody and Stephanie and all my other sister Scouts sleeping under my watch. I'm weak! I think: *It's okay, I don't even have to warn.*

I tell myself: *I just want to see him. Then I'll decide.*

I tell myself: *be careful, careful, Ida Mae, there are gangs of big city folks asleep on the ledge up there, right there, in the bus,* but his song is so sweet, so soft and so all about me and my chain of diamonds that I squirm forward on my elbows like a rattler in heat and at the last second I rear up so he sees me and like he promised, he takes off the veil hat and I'm all, "Oh, crap."

"You," he says, in a different voice, he's so *ugly,* and this is awful. He says it like: *ewwwww.* "You aren't . . ."

And I think: *fine!* so I say, too low to wake up my sister Scouts, "Well neither are you. Go away!" but I keep coming at him because I want the sparkly. I'll just grab it and let him go.

But he snaps off a branch and starts swinging at me like I'm a monster that he has to kill but it's *okay,* I have my rock.

I really think I can just bop him and roll him off the edge before my sisters come but he yells "Get away from me" mean enough to scare the whole mountain and I vomit one last warning, "Shut up, shut *up*!"

But he howls in my face, "Get away, you ugly dirtbag." Then he shouts out the worst thing ever. "You're too damn old!"

So I smash him with the rock. Then I bash his head and bash it and bash it, I have to wipe that disgusting, hurtful word off his disgusting face. By the time my sister Scouts are wide awake and charging uphill to join, there's not much left to bash but, oh boy, he screamed so loud that up there on the ledge, lights pop on all over Clyde's bus and we hear them hammering to get out. Usually we're such good Scouts that we come and go without anybody knowing, but this time it got loud, and it's all my fault.

"Ohhhh, Melody, I'm so sorry."

Her voice goes hard. "Don't worry, I heard."

"Old." This is awful, it comes out in a sob. I'm so *embarrassed*. Everybody is. "Old!"

Stephanie looks down at what's left of the man, like he's a rattler we had to squash. "We all heard."

"*Okay* girls, Scout council." Melody points and we squat in a circle around what's left of what we just did, wondering what to do.

Sisters, worrying. "Tomorrow they'll find out."

"They don't have to." Melody is the one who decides *whether*.

This is so *hard*. I say, "They can't find out."

We shudder. "Nobody can."

"They might." Even Stephanie is scared.

Melody comes down on that like a hammer, "They won't find out," and we all feel better because Melody also decides *when*.

Day and night, summer, winter, year after year for a really long time, we have protected our sweet life on the mountainside. Nothing gets between Troop 13 and our freedom, and nothing will.

"*Okay*," Melody says, "Council," Melody says, and we squat in a circle and begin. After Council, she will say *how*.

Either we do what we usually do, break camp and fade away to the East Grade and do like it says the Girl Scout prayer, "Help us to see where we may serve / In some new place in some new way," praying that nobody looks out the window when the sun comes up and Clyde backs that bus around and comes downhill and that Louie doesn't care what the vultures are eating when he cranks himself up the dome . . .

Or we go up to the ledge and do something else about it tonight.

Clyde never unlocks the bus until the sun comes up. There are enough of us to get it rolling, all it takes is one little push.

Kit Reed's most recent collection *The Story Until Now* (The Wesleyan University Press), was published in 2013; Severn House published her latest novel, *Son of Destruction,* in the UK in 2012 and US in 2013. Her 2011 collection, *What Wolves Know,* was nominated for the Shirley Jackson Award. Her many other novels include *Enclave, The Baby Merchant,* and *Thinner Than Thou,* a winner of the ALA. Alex Award. A Guggenheim fellow, Reed is the first American recipient of an international literary grant from the Abraham Woursell Foundation. Her stories appear in venues including *The Yale Review, Asimov's, The Magazine of Fantasy & Science Fiction, Omni, The Norton Anthology of Contemporary Literature,* and *The Kenyon Review.* Her books *Weird Women, Wired Women* and *Little Sisters of the Apocalypse* were finalists for the Tiptree Prize. A member of the board of the Authors League Fund, she serves as Resident Writer at Wesleyan University.

"I don't understand anything anymore," she said.
"Everything is strange."

THE GOOD HUSBAND

Nathan Ballingrud

The water makes her nightgown diaphanous, like the ghost of something, and she is naked underneath. Her breasts are full, her nipples large and pale, and her soft stomach, where he once loved to rest his head as he ran his hand through the soft tangle of hair between her legs, is stretched with the marks of age. He sits on the lid of the toilet, feeling a removed horror as his cock stirs beneath his robe. Her eyes are flat and shiny as dimes and she doesn't blink as the water splashes over her face. Wispy clouds of blood drift through the water, obscuring his view of her. An empty prescription bottle lies beside the tub, a few bright pills scattered like candy on the floor.

He was not meant to see this, and he feels a minor spasm of guilt, as though he has caught her at something shameful and private. This woman with whom he had once shared all the shabby secrets of his life. The slice in her forearm is an open curtain, blood flowing out in billowing dark banners.

"You're going to be okay, Katie," he says. He has not called her Katie in ten years. He makes no move to save her.

Sean shifted his legs out of bed and pressed his bare feet onto the hardwood floor; it was cold, and his nerves jumped. A spike of life. A sign of movement in the blood. He sat there for a moment, his eyes closed, and concentrated on that. He slid his feet into his slippers and willed himself into a standing position.

He walked naked across the bedroom and fetched his robe from the closet. He threw it around himself and tied it closed. He walked by the vanity, with its alchemies of perfumes and eyeshadows, ignoring the mirror, and left the bedroom. Down the hallway, past the closed bathroom door with light still bleeding from underneath, descending the stairs to the sunlit order of his home.

He was alert to each contraction of muscle, to each creak of bone and ligament. To the pressure of the floor against the soles of his feet, to the slide of the bannister's polished wood against the soft white flesh of his hand.

His mind skated across the frozen surface of each moment. He pushed it along, he pushed it along.

They'd been married twenty-one years, and Katie had tried to kill herself four times in that span. Three times in the last year and a half. Last night, she'd finally gotten it right.

The night had started out wonderfully. They dressed up, went out for dinner, had fun for the first time in recent memory. He bought her flowers, and they walked downtown after dinner and admired the lights and the easy flow of life. He took her to a chocolate shop. Her face was radiant, and a picture of her that final night was locked into his memory: the silver in her hair shining in the reflected light of an overhead lamp, her cheeks rounded into a smile, the soft weight of life turning her body beautiful and inviting, like a blanket, or a hearth. She looked like the girl she used to be. He'd started to believe that with patience and fortitude they could keep at bay the despair that had been seeping into her from some unknown, subterranean hell, flowing around the barricades of antidepressants and anxiety pills, filling her brain with cold water.

When they got home they opened up another bottle and took it to the bedroom. And somehow, they started talking about Heather, who had gone away to college and had recently informed them that she did not want to come home for spring break. It wasn't that she wanted to go anywhere special; she wanted to stay at the dorm, which would be nearly emptied of people, and read, or work, or fuck her new boyfriend if she had one, or whatever it was college girls wanted to do when they didn't want to come home to their parents.

It worked away at Kate like a worm, burrowing tunnels in her gut. She viewed Sean's acceptance of Heather's decision as a callous indifference. When the subject came up again that night, he knew the mood was destroyed.

He resented her for it. For spoiling, once again and with what seemed a frivolous cause, the peace and happiness he was trying so hard to give her. If only she would take it. If only she would believe in it. Like she used to do, before her brain turned against her, and against them all.

They drank the bottle even as the despair settled over her. They ended the night sitting on the edge of the bed, she wearing her sexy nightgown, her breasts mostly exposed and moon-pale in the light, weeping soundlessly, a little furrow between her eyebrows but otherwise without affect, and the light sheen of tears which flowed and flowed, as though a foundation had cracked; and he in the red robe she'd bought him for Christmas, his arm around her, trying once again to reason her away from a precipice which reason did not know. Eventually he laid back and put his arm over his eyes, frustrated and angry. And then he fell asleep.

He awoke sometime later to the sound of splashing water. It should have been too small a sound to reach him, but it did anyway, worming its way into the black and pulling him to the surface. When he discovered that he was alone in the bedroom, and sensed the deepness of the hour, he walked to the bathroom, where the noise came from, without urgency and with a full knowledge of what he would find.

She spasmed every few seconds, as though something in the body, separate from the mind, fought against this.

He sat down on the toilet, watching her. Later he would examine this moment and try to gauge what he had been feeling. It would seem important to take some measure of himself, to find out what kind of man he really was.

He would come to the conclusion that he'd felt tired. It was as though his blood had turned to lead. He knew the procedure he was meant to follow here; he'd done it before. Already his muscles tightened to abide by the routine, signals blew across his nerves like a brushfire: rush to the tub, waste a crucial moment in simple denial brushing the hair from her face and cradling her head in his warm hands. Hook his arms underneath her body and lift her heavily from the water. Carry her streaming blood and water to the bed. Call 911. Wait. Wait. Wait. Ride with her, and sit unmoving in the waiting room as they pump her stomach and fill her with a stranger's blood. Answer questions. Does she take drugs. Do you. Were you fighting. Sir, a social worker will be by to talk to you. Sir, you have to fill out these forms. Sir, your wife is broken, and you are, too.

And then wait some more as she convalesces in the psych ward. Visit her, try not to cry in front of her as you see her haunting that corridor with the rest of the damned, dwelling like a fading thought in her assigned room.

Bring this pale thing home. This husk, this hollowed vessel. Nurse her to a false health. Listen to her apologize, and accept her apologies. Profess your reinvigorated love. Fuck her with the urgency of pity and mortality and fear, which you both have come to know and to rely on the way you once relied on love and physical desire.

If they could save her.

And if, having saved her, they decided to let her come home at all.

She will never be happy.

The thought came to him with the force of a revelation. It was as though god spoke a judgment, and he recognized its truth as though it had been with them all along, the buzzard companion of their late marriage. Some people, he thought, are just incapable of happiness. Maybe it was because of some ancient trauma, or maybe it was just a bad equation in the brain. Kate's reasons were mysterious to him, a fact which appalled him after so many years of intimacy. If he pulled her from the water now, he would just be welcoming her back to hell.

With a flutter of some obscure emotion—some solution of terror and relief—he closed the door on her. He went back to bed and, after a few sleeping pills of his own, he fell into a black sleep. He dreamed of silence.

In the kitchen, light streamed in through the bay window. It was a big kitchen, with a stand-alone chopping table, wide crumb-flecked counters, ranks of silver knives agleam in the morning sun. Dirty dishes were stacked in the sink and on the counter beside it. The trash hadn't been taken out on time, and its odor was a dull oppression. The kitchen had once been the pride of their home. It seemed to have decayed without his noticing.

A small breakfast nook accommodated a kitchen table in a narrow passage joining the kitchen to the dining room. It still bore the scars and markings of the younger Heather's attentions: divots in the wood where she once tested the effectiveness of a butter knife, a spray of red paint left there during one of her innumerable art projects, and the word "kichen" gouged into the side of the table with a ballpoint pen, years ago, when she thought everything should carry its name. It had become an inadvertent shrine to her childhood, and since she'd left Kate had shifted their morning coffee to the larger and less welcoming dining room table in the adjoining room. The little breakfast nook had been surrendered to the natural entropy of a household, becoming little more than a receptacle for car keys and unopened mail.

Sean filled the French press with coffee grounds and put the water on to boil.

For a few crucial minutes he had nothing to do, and a ferocious panic began to chew at the border of his thoughts. He felt a weight descending from the floor above him. An unseen face. He thought for a moment that he could hear her footsteps. He thought for a moment that nothing had changed.

He was looking through the bay window to the garden out front, which had ceded vital ground to weeds and ivy. Across the street he watched his neighbor's grandkids tear around the corner of their house like crazed orangutans: ill-built yet strangely graceful, spurred by an unknowable animal purpose. It was Saturday; though winter still lingered at night, spring was warming the daylight hours.

Apparently it was a beautiful day.

The kettle began to hiss and he returned to his rote tasks. Pour the water into the press. Stir the contents. Fit the lid into place and wait for the contents to steep. He fetched a single mug from the cabinet and waited at the counter.

He heard something move behind him, the soft pad of a foot on the linoleum, the staccato tap of dripping water. He turned and saw his wife standing at the kitchen's threshold, the nightgown still soaked through and clinging intimately to her body, streams of water running from the gown and from her hair which hung in a thick black sheet, and pooling brightly around her.

A sound escaped him, a syllable shot like a hard pellet, high-pitched and meaningless.

His body jerked as though yanked by some invisible cord and the coffee mug launched from his hand and shattered on the floor between them. Kate sat down in the nook; the first time she'd sat there in almost a year. She did not look at him, or react to the smashed mug. Water pit-patted from her hair and her clothes, onto the table. "Where's mine?" she said.

"Kate? What?"

"Where's my coffee? I want coffee. I'm cold. You forgot mine."

He worked his jaw, trying to coax some sound. Finally he said, "All right." His voice was weak and undirected. "All right," he said again. He opened the cabinet and fetched two mugs.

She'd had a bad dream. It was the only thing that made sense. She was cold and wet and something in her brain tried to make sense of it. She remembered seeing Sean's face through a veil of water. Watching it recede from her. She felt a buckle of nausea at the memory. She took a drink from the coffee and felt the heat course through her body. It only made her feel worse.

She rubbed her hands at her temples.

"Why am I all wet?" she said. "I don't feel right. Something's wrong with me. Something's really wrong."

• • •

Sean guided her upstairs. She reacted to his gentle guidance, but did not seem to be acting under any will of her own; except when he tried to steer her into the bathroom. She resisted then, turning to stone in the hallway. "No," she said. Her eyes were hard and bright with fear. She turned her head away from the door. He took her wrist to pull her but she resisted. His fingers inadvertently slid over the incision there, and he jerked his hand away.

"Honey. We need to fix you up."

"No."

He relented, taking her to the bedroom instead, where he removed her wet nightgown. It struck him that he had not seen her like this, standing naked in the plain light of day, for a long time. They had been married for over twenty years and they'd lost interest in each other's bodies long ago. When she was naked in front of him now he barely noticed. Her body was part of the furniture of their marriage, utilized but ignored, with occasional benign observations from them both about its declining condition.

In a sudden resurgence of his feelings of the previous night, he became achingly aware of her physicality. She was so pale: the marble white of statues, or of sunbleached bones. Her flesh hung loosely on her body, the extra weight suddenly obvious, as though she had no muscle tone remaining at all. Her breasts, her stomach, her unshaven hair: the human frailty of her, the beauty of a lived-in body, which he knew was reflected in his own body, called up a surge of tenderness and sympathy.

"Let's put some clothes on," he said, turning away from her.

He helped her step into her underwear, found a bra and hooked her into it. He found some comfortable, loose-fitting clothes for her, things he knew she liked to wear when she had nowhere special to go. It was not until he was fitting her old college reunion T-shirt over her head that he allowed himself to look at her wrist for the first time, and the sight of it made him step back and clasp a hand over his mouth.

Her left arm bore a long incision from wrist to elbow. The flesh puckered like lips, and as she bent her arm into the shirt he was afforded a glimpse at the awful depth of the wound. It was easily deep enough to affect its purpose, and as bloodless as the belly of a gutted fish.

"Katie," he said, and brought her wrist to his lips. "What's happening to you?" He pressed her fingers to her cheek; they were cool, and limp. "Are you okay?" It was the stupidest question of his life. But he didn't know what else to ask. "Katie?"

She turned her face to him, and after a few moments he could see her eyes begin to focus on him, as though she had to travel a terrible span to find him there. "I don't know," she said.

"Something doesn't feel right."

"Do you want to lie down?"

"I guess."

He eased her toward her side of the bed, which was smooth and untroubled: she had slept underwater last night; not here. He laid her there like folded laundry.

He sat beside her as she drifted off. Her eyes remained open but she seemed gone; she seemed truly dead. Maybe, this time, she was.

Does she remember? he thought. Does she remember that I left her? He stretched himself out beside her and ran his hand through her hair, repetitively, a kind of prayer.

Oh my god, he thought, what have I done. What is happening to me.

Eventually she wanted to go outside. Not at first, because she was scared, and the world did not make any sense to her. The air tasted strange on her tongue, and her body felt heavy and foreign—she felt very much like a thought wrapped in meat. She spent a few days drifting through the house in a lethargic haze, trying to shed the feeling of unease which she had woken with the morning after her bath, and which had stayed rooted in her throat and in her gut the whole time since. Sean came and went to work. He was solicitous and kind; he was always extra attentive after she tried to kill herself, though; and although she welcomed the attention she had learned to distrust it. She knew it would fade, once the nearness of death receded.

She watched the world through the window. It was like a moving picture in a frame; the details did not change, but the wind blew through the grass and the trees and the neighbors came and went in their cars, giving the scene the illusion of reality. Once, in the late afternoon before Sean came home, she was seen. The older man who lived across the street, whose cat she fed when he went out of town and who was a friend to them both, caught sight of her as he stepped out of his car and waved. She only stared back. After a moment, the man turned from her and disappeared into his own house.

The outside world was a dream of another place. She found herself wondering if she would fit better there.

On the evening of the third day, while they were sitting at dinner— something wretched and cooling that Sean had picked up on his way home— she told him. "I want to go outside."

Sean kept eating as though he didn't hear her.

This was not new. He'd been behaving with an almost manic enthusiasm around her, as though he could convince her that their lives were unskewed and smooth through sheer force of will. But he would not look at her face; when he looked at her at all he would focus on her cheek, or her shoulder, or her hairline. He would almost look at her. But not quite.

"I don't know if that's a good idea," he said at last. He ate ferociously, forking more into his mouth before he was finished with the last bite.

"Why not?"

He paused, his eyes lifting briefly to the salt and pepper shakers in the middle of the table. "You still don't seem . . . I don't know. Yourself."

"And what would that be like?" She had not touched her food, except to prod it the way a child pokes a stick at roadkill. It cooled on the plate in front of her, congealing cheese and oils. It made her sick.

His mood swung abruptly into something more withdrawn and depressed; she could watch his face and see it happen. This made her feel better. This was more like the man she had known for the past several years of their marriage.

"Am I a prisoner here?"

He finally looked at her, shocked and hurt. "What? How could you even say that?"

She said nothing. She just held his gaze.

He looked terrified. "I'm just worried about you, babe. You don't—you're not—"

"You mean this?" She raised her left arm and slipped her finger into the open wound. It was as clean and bloodless as rubber.

Sean lowered his face. "Don't do that."

"If you're really worried about me, why don't you take me to the hospital? Why didn't you call an ambulance? I've been sleeping so much the past few days. But you just go on to work like everything's fine."

"Everything *is* fine."

"I don't think so."

He was looking out the window now. The sun was going down and the light was thick and golden. Their garden was flowering, and a light dusting of pollen coated the left side of their car in the driveway. Sean's eyes were unblinking and reflective as water. He stared at it all.

"There's nothing wrong with you," he said.

Silence filled the space between them as they each sat still in their own thoughts. The refrigerator hummed to life. Katie finally pushed herself away from the table and headed toward the door, scooping up the car keys on her way.

"I'm going out," she said.

"Where?" His voice was thick with resignation.

"Maybe to the store. Maybe no where. I'll be back soon."

He moved to stand. "I'll come with."

"No thanks," she said, and he slumped back into his chair.

Once, she would have felt guilty for that. She would have chastised herself for failing to take into account his wishes or his fears, for failing to protect his fragile ego. He was a delicate man, though he did not know it, and she had long considered it part of her obligation to the marriage to accommodate that frailty of spirit.

But she felt a separation from that now. And from him too, though she remembered loving him once. If anything inspired guilt, it was that she could not seem to find that love anymore. He was a good man, and deserved to be loved. She wondered if the ghost of a feeling could substitute for the feeling itself.

But worse than all of that was the separation she felt from herself. She'd felt like a passenger in her own body the last three days, the pilot of some arcane machine. She watched from a remove as the flesh of her hand tightened around the doorknob and rotated it clockwise, setting into motion the mechanical process which would free the door from its jamb and allow it to swing open, freeing her avenue of escape. The flesh was a mechanism too, a contracting of muscle and ligament, an exertion of pull.

There's nothing wrong with you, he'd said.

She opened the door.

The light was like ground glass in her eyes. It was the most astonishing pain she had ever experienced. She screamed, dropped to the floor, and curled into herself. Very distantly she heard something heavy fall over, followed by crashing footsteps which thrummed the floor beneath her head, and then the door slammed shut. Her husband's hands fell on her and she twisted away from them. The light was a paste on her eyes; she couldn't seem to claw it off of them. It bled into her skull and filled it like a poisonous radiation. She lurched to her feet, shouldering Sean aside, and ran away from the door and into the living room, where she tripped over the carpet and landed hard on her side. Her husband's hysterical voice followed her, a blast of panic. She pushed her body forward with her feet, wedged her face into the space beneath the couch, the cool darkness there, and tried to claw away the astounding misery of the light.

• • •

That night she would not come to bed. They'd been sleeping beside each other since the suicide, though he was careful to keep space between them, and had taken to wearing pajamas to bed. She slept fitfully at night, seeming to rest better in the daylight, and this troubled his own sleep, too. She would be as still as stone and then struggle elaborately with the sheets for a few moments before settling into stillness again, like a drowning woman. He turned his head toward the wall when this happened. And then he would remember that he'd turned away from her that night, too. And he would stay awake into the small hours, feeling her struggle, knowing that he'd missed his chance to help her.

The incident at the door had galvanized him, though. Her pain was terrifying in its intensity, and it was his fault. He would not let his guilt or his shame prevent him from doing whatever was necessary to keep her safe, and comfortable from now on. Love still lived in him, like some hibernating serpent, and it stirred now, it tasted the air with its tongue.

It took her some time to calm down. He fixed her a martini and brought it to her, watched her sip it disinterestedly as she sat on the couch and stared at the floor, her voice breaking every once in a while in small hiccups of distress. Long nail marks scored her skin; her right eye seemed jostled in its orbit, angled fractionally lower than the other. He had drawn the curtains and pulled the blinds, though by now the sun had sunk and the world outside was blue and cool.

He turned off all but a few lights in the house, filling it with shadows. Whether it was this, or the vodka, or something else that did it, she finally settled into a fraught silence.

He eased himself onto the couch beside her, and he took her chin in his fingers and turned her face toward him. An echo of his thought from the night of the suicide passed through his mind: *She will never get better.*

He felt his throat constrict, and heat gathered in his eyes.

"Katie?" He put his hand on her knee. "Talk to me, babe."

She was motionless. He didn't even know if she could hear him.

"Are you all right? Are you in any pain?"

After a long moment, she said, "It was in my head."

"What was?"

"The light. I couldn't get it out."

He nodded, trying to figure out what this meant. "Well. It's dark now."

"Thank you," she said.

This small gratitude caused an absurd swelling in his heart, and he cupped her cheek in his hand. "Oh baby," he said. "I was so scared. I don't know what's going on. I don't know what to do for you."

She put her own hand over his, and pressed her cheek into his palm. Her eyes remained unfocused though, one askew, almost as if this was a learned reaction. A muscle memory. Nothing more.

"I don't understand anything anymore," she said. "Everything is strange."

"I know."

She seemed to consider something for a moment. "I should go somewhere else," she said.

"No," Sean said. A violence moved inside him, the idea of her leaving calling forth an animal fury, aimless and electric. "No, Katie. You don't understand. They'll take you away from me. If I take you somewhere, if I take you to see someone, they will not let you come back. You just stay here. You're safe here. We'll keep things dark, like you like it. We'll do whatever it takes. Okay?"

She looked at him. The lamplight from the other room reflected from her irises, giving them a creamy whiteness that looked warm and soft, incongruous in her torn face, like saucers of milk left out after the end of the world. "Why?"

The question shamed him.

"Because I love you, Katie. Jesus Christ. You're my wife. I love you."

"I love you too," she said, and like pressing her cheek into his hand, this response seemed an automatic action. A programmed response. He ignored this, though, and chose to accept what she said as truth—perhaps because this was the first time she'd said it to him since the suicide, when her body had stopped behaving in the way it was meant to and conformed to a new logic, a biology he did not recognize and could not understand and which made a mystery of her again. It had been so long since she'd been a mystery to him. He knew every detail of her life, every dull complaint and every stillborn dream, and she knew his; but now he knew nothing. Every nerve ending in his body was turned in her direction, like flowers bending to the sun.

Or perhaps he only accepted it because the light was soft, and it exalted her.

His free hand found her breast. She did not react in any way. He squeezed it gently in his hand, his thumb rolling over her nipple, still soft under her shirt. She allowed all of this, but her face was empty. He pulled away from her. "Let's go upstairs," he said.

He rose and, taking her hand, moved to help her to her feet. She resisted.

"Katie, come on. Let's go to bed."

"I don't want to."

"But don't you . . . " He took her hand and pressed it against his cock, stiff under in his pants. "Can you feel that? Can you feel what you do to me?"

"I don't want to go upstairs. The light will come in in the morning. I want to sleep in the cellar."

He released her hand, and it dropped to her side. He thought for a minute. The cellar was used for storage, and was in a chaotic state. But there was room for a mattress down there, and tomorrow he could move things around, make some arrangements, and make it livable. It did not occur to him to argue with her. This was part of the mystery, and it excited him. He was like a high school boy with a mad new crush, prepared to go to any length.

"Okay," he said. "Give me a few minutes. I'll make it nice for you."

He left her sitting in the dark, his heart pounding, red and strong.

He fucked her with the ardor one brings to a new lover, sliding into the surprising coolness of her, tangling his fingers into her hair and biting her neck, her chin, her ears. He wanted to devour her, to breathe her like oxygen. He hadn't been so hard in years; his body moved like a piston and he felt he could go on for hours. He slid his arms beneath her and held her shoulders from behind as he powered into her, the mattress silent beneath them, the darkness of the cellar as gentle and welcoming as a mother's heart. At first she wrapped her legs around his back, put her arms over his shoulders, but by the time he finished she had abandoned the pretense and simply lay still beneath him, one eye focused on the underbeams of the ceiling, one eye peering into the black.

Afterwards he lay beside her, staring up at the underside of his house. The cellar was cold and stank of mildew. The piled clutter of a long and settled life loomed around them in mounted stacks, tall black shadows which gazed down upon them like some alien congress. The mattress beneath them came from their own bed; he'd resolved to sleep down here with her, if this was where she wanted to be. Three candles were gathered in a little group by their heads, not because he thought it would be romantic—though he felt that it was—but because he had no idea where the outlets were down here to set up a lamp, and he didn't want to risk upsetting her by turning on the bare bulb in the ceiling. The candlelight didn't seem to bother her at all, though; maybe it was just the sun.

He turned his head on the pillow to look at her, and ran his hand along the length of her body. It was cool to the touch, cool inside and out.

"This other light doesn't bother you, does it, babe?"

She turned her head too, slowly, and looked at him. Her wounds cast garish shadows across her face in the candlelight. "Hm?"

"The light?"

" . . . Oh, I know you," she said, something like relief in her voice. "You're the man who left me in the water."

Something cold flowed through his body. "What?"

She settled back against the mattress, closing her eyes and pulling the sheet up to her chin. She seemed very content. "I couldn't remember you for a minute, but then I did."

"Do you remember that night?"

"What night?"

" . . . You said I'm the man who left you in the water."

"I looked up and I saw you. I was scared of something. I thought you were going to help, but then you went away. What was I scared of? Do you know?"

He shook his head, but her eyes were closed and she couldn't see him. "No," he said at last.

"I wish I could remember."

She climbed off the mattress, leaving the man to sleep. He snored loudly, and this made her think of machines again. His was a clumsy one, loud and rattling, and its inefficiency irritated her. It was corpulent and heavy, uncared for, and breaking down. She decided at that moment that she would not let it touch her again.

She slipped her nightgown on over her head and walked upstairs. Cautiously, she opened the door at the top and peered into the ground floor of the house. It was welcomingly dark. Crossing the living room floor and parting the curtains, she saw that night had fallen.

Within moments she was outside, walking briskly along the sidewalk, crackling with an energy she hadn't felt in as long as she could remember. The houses on either side of the street were high-shouldered monsters, their windows as black and silent as the sky above her. The yawn of space opened just beneath the surface of her thoughts with a gorgeous silence. She wanted to sink into it, but she couldn't figure out how. Each darkened building held the promise of tombs, and she had to remind herself that she could not go inside them because people lived there, those churning, squirting biologies, and that the quietude she sought would not be there.

She remembered a place she could go, though. She quickened her pace, her nightgown—the one she had worn that night, when the man had left her in the water, now clean and white—almost ephemeral in the chilly air and trailing behind her like a ghostly film. The narrow suburban road crested a hill a few hundred feet ahead, and beyond it breached a low dome of light. The city, burning light against the darkness.

Something lay on the sidewalk in front of her, and she slowed as she approached. It was a robin, its middle torn open, its guts eaten away. A curtain of ants flowed inside it, and lead away from it in a meandering trail into the grass. She picked it up and cradled it close to her face. The ants seethed, spreading through its feathers, over her hand, down her arm. She ignored them.

The bird's eyes were glassy and black, like tiny onyx stones. Its beak was open and in it she could see the soft red muscle of its tongue. Something moved and glistened in the back of its throat.

She continued on, holding the robin at her side. She didn't feel the ants crawling up her arm, onto her neck, into her hair. The bird was a miracle of beauty.

The suburbs stopped at the highway, like an island against the sea. She turned east, the city lights brighter now at her right, and continued walking. The sidewalk roughened as she continued along, broken in places, seasoned with stones and broken glass. She was oblivious to it all. Traffic was light but not incidental, and the rush of cars blowing by lifted her hair and flattened the nightgown against her body. Someone leaned on the horn as he drove past, whooping through an open window.

The clamor of the highway, the stink of oil and gasoline, the buffeting rush of traffic, all served to deepen her sense of displacement. The world was a bewildering, foreign place, the light a low-grade burn and a stain on the air, the rushing cars on the highway a row of gnashing teeth.

But ahead, finally, opening in long, silent acres to her left, was the cemetery.

It was gated and locked, but finding a tree to get over the wall was no difficulty. She scraped her skin on the bark and then on the stone, and she tore her nightgown, but that was of no consequence. She tumbled gracelessly to the ground, like a dropped sack, and felt a sharp snap in her right ankle. When she tried to walk, the ankle rolled beneath her and she fell.

Meat, getting in the way.

Disgusted by this, she used the wall to pull herself to a standing position. She found that if she let the foot just roll to the side and walked on the ankle itself, she could make a clumsy progress.

Clouds obscured the sky, and the cemetery stretched over a rolling landscape, bristling with headstones and plaques, monuments and crypts, like a scattering of teeth. It was old; many generations were buried here. The sound of the highway, muffled by the wall, faded entirely from her awareness. She stood amidst the graves and let their silence fill her.

The flutter of unease that she'd felt since waking after the suicide abated. The sense of disconnection was gone. Her heart was a still lake. Nothing in her moved. She wanted to cry from relief.

Still holding the dead robin in her hand, she lurched more deeply into the cemetery.

She found a hollow between the stones, a trough between the stilled waves of earth, where no burial was marked. She eased herself to the ground and curled up in the grass. The clouds were heavy and thick, the air was cold. She closed her eyes and felt the cooling of her brain.

Sounds rose from the earth. New sounds: cobwebs of exhalations, pauses of the heart, the monastic work of the worms translating flesh to soil, the slow crawl of rock. There was another kind of industry, somewhere beneath her. Another kind of machine.

It was new knowledge, and she felt the root of a purpose. She set the robin aside and tore grass away, dug her nails into the dark soil, pushed through. She scooped aside handfuls of dirt.

At some point in her labors she became aware of something awaiting her beneath the earth.

Moving silences, the cloudy breaths of the moon, magnificent shapes unrecognizable to her novice intelligence, like strange old galleons of the sea.

And then, something awful.

A rough bark, a perverse intrusion into this quiet celebration, a rape of the silence. Her husband's voice.

She was alone again, and she felt his rough hands upon her.

It had been nothing more than instinct which guided him to her, finally. He panicked when he awoke to her missing, careened through the house, shouted like a fool in his front yard until lights began to pop on in the neighbors' houses. Afraid that they would offer to help, or call the police for him, he got into the car and started driving. He crisscrossed the neighborhood to no avail, until finally it occurred to him that she might go to the cemetery. That she might, in some fit of delirium, decide that she belonged there.

The thought tore at him. The guilt over leaving her to die in the bathtub threatened to crack his ribs. It was too big to contain.

He scaled the cemetery wall and called until he found her, a small white form in a sea of graves and dark grass, huddled and scared, clawing desperately in the dirt. Her ankle was broken and hung at a sickening angle.

He pulled her up by her shoulders and wrapped his arms around her, hugged her tightly against him.

"Oh Katie, oh baby," he said. "It's okay. It's okay. I've got you. You scared me so bad. You're going to be okay."

An ant emerged from her hairline and idled on her forehead. Another crawled out of her nose. He brushed them furiously away.

She returned to the cellar. He spent a few days getting it into some kind of order, moving precarious stacks into smaller and sturdier piles, and giving her some room to move around in.

While she slept in the daytime he brought down the television set and its stand, a lamp, and a small box where he kept the books she had once liked to read. He left the mattress on the floor but changed the sheets regularly. When he was not at work he spent all his time down there with her, though he had taken to sleeping upstairs so that he could lock her in when she was most likely to try to wander.

"I can't risk you getting lost again," he told her. "It would kill me." Then he closed the door and turned the lock. She heard his steps tread the floor above her. She had taken the dead robin and nailed it to one of the support beams beside the mattress. It was the only beautiful thing in the room, and it calmed her to look at it. Her foot was more trouble than it was worth so she wrenched it off and tossed it into the corner.

"That was Heather," Sean said, closing the cellar door and tromping down the stairs. He sat beside her on the mattress and put his arm around her shoulders. She did not lean into him the way she used to do, so he gave her a little pull until it seemed like she was.

When he'd noticed her missing foot the other night he'd quietly gone back upstairs and dry heaved over the sink. Then he came back down, searched until he located it in a corner, and took it outside to bury it. The crucified bird had not bothered him initially, but over the days it had gathered company: two mice, three cockroaches, a wasp, some moths. Their dry little bodies were arrayed like art. She had even pulled the bones from one of the mice, fixing them with wood glue onto the post in some arcane hieroglyph.

He was frightened by its alienness. He was frightened because it meant something to her and it was indecipherable to him.

She was watching something on TV with the sound off: men in suits talking to each other across a table. They seemed very earnest.

"She wants to come home for the weekend," he said. "I said it would be okay."

She pulled her gaze from the screen and looked at him. The light from the television made small blue squares in her eyes, which had begun to film over in a creamy haze. It was getting hard to tell that one eye was askew, which made him feel better when he talked to her.

"Heather," she said. "I like Heather."

He put his fingers in her hair, hooked a dark lock behind her ear. "Of course you do, baby. You remember her, don't you."

She stared for a moment, then her brow furrowed. "She used to live here."

"That's right. She went to college, and she lives there now. She's our daughter. We love her."

"I forgot."

"And you love me, too."

"Okay."

She looked back at the television. One of the men was standing now, and laughing so hard his face was red. His mouth was wide open. He was going to swallow the world. "Can you say it?"

"Say what?"

"That you love me. Can you say that to me? Please?"

"I love you."

"Oh baby," he said, and leaned his head against hers, his arm still around her. "Thank you. Thank you. I love you too." They sat there and watched the silent images. His mind crept ahead to Heather's visit. He wondered what the hell he was going to tell her. She was going to have a hard time with this.

What is the story of our marriage?

He went back to that night again and again. He remembered standing over her, watching her body struggle against the pull of a death she had called upon herself. It is the nature of the body to want to live, and once her mind had shut down her muscles spasmed in the water, splashing blood onto the floor as it fought to save itself.

But her mind, apparently, had not completely shut down after all. She remembered him standing over her. She looked up as the water lapped over her face and saw him staring down at her. She saw him turn and close the door.

What did she see behind his face? Did she believe it was impassive? Did she believe it was unmoved by love? How could he explain that he had done it because he could not bear to watch her suffer anymore?

On the rare occasions that he remembered the other thoughts—the weariness, the dread of the medical routine, and especially the flaring anger he'd felt earlier that same night, when the depression took her and he knew he'd have to steer her through it *yet again*—he buried them.

That is not the story of our marriage, he thought. The story is that I love her, and that's what guided my actions. As it always has.

He was losing her, though. The change which kindled his interest also pulled her farther and farther away, and he feared that his love for her, and hers for him, would not be enough to tether her to this world.

So he called Heather and told her to come home for spring break. Not for the whole week, he knew that she was an adult now, she had friends, that was fine. But she had family obligations and her mother was lonely for her, and she should come home for at least the weekend.

Is she sick? Heather asked.

No. She just misses her girl.

Dad, you told me it was okay if I stayed here spring break. You told me you would talk to Mom about it.

I did talk, Heather. She won. Come on home, just for the weekend. Please.

Heather agreed, finally. Her reluctance was palpable, but she would come.

That was step one.

Step two would be coaxing Katie out of the cellar for her arrival. He'd thought that being locked down there at night, and whenever he was out, would have made coming upstairs something to look forward to. He'd been wrong; she showed no signs of wanting to leave the cellar at all, possibly ever again. She had regressed even further, not getting up to walk at all since losing her foot, and forsaking clothing altogether; she crawled palely naked across the floor when she wanted to move anywhere—a want which rarely troubled her mind anymore. She allowed him to wash her when he approached her with soap and warm water, but only because she was passive in this as she had become in all things.

Unless he wanted to touch her with another purpose.

Then she would turn on him with an anger that terrified him. Her eyes were pale as moon rocks. Her breath was cold. And when she turned on him with that fury he would imagine her breathing that chill into his lungs, stuffing it down into his heart. It terrified him. He would not approach her for sex anymore, though the rejection hurt him more than he would have dreamed.

He decided to woo her. He searched the roads at night, crawling at under twenty miles an hour, looking for roadkill. The first time he found some, a gut-crushed possum, he brought the carcass into the house and dropped it onto the floor in front of the cellar door, hoping the smell would lure her out. It did not; but he did not sulk, nor did he deprive her of her gift. He opened the door and rolled the animal wreckage down the stairs.

On the night he told her about Heather, he was propelled by romantic impulse to greater heights. He poisoned the cat that lived across the street, the one she watched over when its owner left town, and brought it to her on a pillow; he'd curled it into a semblance of sleep, and laid it at the foot of her mattress. She fixed her flat, pale eyes on it, not acknowledging his presence at all. Slowly she scooped it into her arms, and she held it close to her body. Satisfied, he sat beside her on the bed. He smiled as she got to work.

The floor was packed dirt. It seemed as hard as concrete, but ultimately it was just earth. It could be opened. She bent herself to this task. She found a corner behind some boxes of old china, where her work would not be obvious to the man when he came down to visit, and picked at the ground with a garden spade. It took a long time, but finally she began to make serious progress, upturning the packed ground until she got to the dark soil beneath it, bringing pale earthworms and slick, black insects to their first, shocked exposure to the upside world. When she got deep enough she abandoned the small spade and used her hands. Her fingernails snapped off like little plastic tabs, and she examined her fingers with a mild curiosity.

Staring at the ruined flesh reminded her of how the man's face would sometimes leak fluid when he came down here, and of his occasional wet cough. It was all so disgusting.

She took one of the cat's bones from its place on the wall and snapped it in half. The end was sharp and she scraped the flesh from her fingers until hard bone gleamed. Then she went to work again, and was pleased with the difference.

"Hey, Dad." Heather stood in the doorway, her overnight bag slung over her shoulder. Considering how little she wanted to be here, Sean thought she was doing a good job of putting up a positive front.

"Hey, kiddo." He looked over her shoulder and saw that she had parked directly behind his car again, like she always used to do, and like he had asked her not to do a million times. He actually felt a happy nostalgia at the sight of it. He kissed her cheek and took the bag from her shoulder. "Come on in."

She followed him in, rubbing her arms and shuddering. "Jeez, Dad, crank up the AC why don't you."

"Heh, sorry. Your mother likes it cold."

"*Mom?* Since when?"

"Since recently I guess. Listen, why don't you go on up to your room and get changed or whatever. I'll get dinner started."

"Sentimental as always, Dad. I've been in the car all day and I *really* need a shower. Just call me when you're ready." She brushed past him on her way to the stairs.

"Hey," he said.

She stopped.

He held an arm out. "I'm sorry. Come here." She did, and he folded his arm around her, drawing her close. He kissed her forehead. "It means a lot that you came."

"I know."

"I'm serious. It matters. Thank you."

"Okay. You're welcome." She returned his hug and he soaked it in. "So where is she?"

"Downstairs. She'll be up."

She pulled back. "In the cellar? Okay, weird."

"She'll be up. Go on now. Get yourself ready."

She shook her head with the muted exasperation of a child long-accustomed to her parents' eccentricities, and mounted the stairs. Sean turned his attention to the kitchen. He'd made some pot roast in the crockpot, and he tilted the lid to give it a look. The warm, heavy smell of it washed over his face and he took it into his lungs with gratitude. He hadn't prepared anything real to eat in a month, it seemed, living instead off of frozen pizzas and TV dinners. The thought of real food made him lightheaded.

He walked over to the basement door and slid open the lock. He paused briefly, resting his head against the doorjamb. He breathed deeply. Then he cracked it open and poked his head in. A thick, loamy odor rode over him on cool air. There was no light downstairs at all.

"Katie?"

Silence.

"Katie, Heather's here. You remember, we talked about Heather."

His voice did not seem to carry at all on the heavy air. It was like speaking into a cloth.

"She's our daughter." His voice grew small. "You love her, remember?" He thought he heard something shift down there, a sliding of something. Good, he thought. She remembers.

Heather came downstairs a little later. He waited for her, ladling the pot roast into two bowls. The little breakfast nook was set up for them both. Seeing her, he was struck, as he was so often, by how much like a younger version of Katie she looked. The same roundness in her face, the same way she tended to angle her shoulders when she stood still, even the same bob to her hair. It was as though a young Katie had slipped sideways through a hole in the world and come here to see him again, to see what kind of man he had become. What manner of man she had married.

He lowered his eyes.

I'm a good man, he thought.

"Dad?"

He looked up, blinking his eyes rapidly. "Hey you."

"Why isn't there a mattress on your bed? And why is there a sleeping bag on the floor?"

He shook his head. "What were you doing in our bedroom?"

"The door was wide open. It's kind of hard to miss."

He wasn't expecting this. "It's . . . I've been sleeping on the floor." She just stared at him. He could see the pain in her face, the old familiar fear. "What's been going on here, Dad? What's she done this time?"

"She uh . . . she's not doing very well, Heather."

He watched tears gather in her eyes. Then her face darkened and she rubbed them roughly away. "You told me she was fine," she said quietly.

"I didn't want to upset you. I wanted you to come home."

"You didn't want to *upset me*?" Her voice rose into a shout. Her hand clenched at her side and he watched her wrestle down the anger. It took her a minute.

"I'm sorry, Heather."

She shook her head. She wouldn't look at him. "Whatever. Did she try to kill herself again? She's not even here at all, is she Is she in the psych ward?"

"No, she's here. And yes, she did."

She turned her back to him and walked into the living room, where she dropped onto the couch and slouched back, her arms crossed over her chest like a child. Sean followed her, pried loose one of her hands and held onto it as he sat beside her.

"She needs us, kiddo."

"I would *never* have come back!" she said, her rage cresting like a sun. "God damn it!"

"Hey! Now listen to me. She needs us."

"She needs to be committed!"

"Stop it. Stop that. I know this is hard."

"Oh do you?" She glared at him, her face red. He had never seen her like this; anger made her face into something ugly and unrecognizable. "*How* do you know, Dad? When did you ever have to deal with it? It was always me! I was the one at home with her. I was the one who had to call the hospital that one time I found her in her own blood and then call you so you could come! I was the one who—" She gave in then, abruptly and catastrophically, like a battlement falling; sobs broke up whatever else she was going to say. She pulled in a shuddering breath and said, "I can't believe you *tricked* me!"

"Every night!" Sean hissed, his own large hands wrapped into fists, cudgels on his lap. He saw them there and caught himself. He felt something slide down over his mind. The emotions pulled away, the guilt and the horror and the shame, until he was only looking at someone having a fit. People, it seemed, were always having some kind of breakdown or another. Somebody had to keep it together. Somebody always had to keep it together.

"It was not just you. Every night I came home to it. Will she be okay tonight? Will she be normal? Or will she talk about walking in front of a bus? Will she be crying because of something I said, or she thinks I said, last fucking week? Every night. Do you think it all just went away when you went to sleep? Come out of your narcissistic little bubble and realize that the world is bigger than you."

She looked at him, shocked and hurt. Her lower lip was trembling, and the tears came back in force.

"But I always stood by her side. Always." He took her lightly by the arm stood with her.

"Your mother needs us. And we're going to go see her. Right now."

He led her toward the basement door.

What is the story of our family?

He led her down the stairs, into the cool, earthy musk of the basement, the smell of upturned soil a dank bloom in the air. His grip on her arm was firm as he descended one step ahead of her. The light from the kitchen behind them was an ax blade in the darkness, cutting a narrow wedge. It illuminated the corner of the mattress, powdered with a layer of dirt. Beside it, the bottom two feet of the support beam she had nailed the bird to; something new was screwed into place there, but he could intuit from the glistening mass only gristle and hair, a sheet of dried blood beneath it.

"What's going on here? Oh my god, Dad, what's going on?"

"Your mom's in trouble. She needs us."

Heather made a noise and he clamped down harder on her arm. "Katie?" he said. "Heather's here." His voice did not carry, the words dropping like stones at his feet.

Our family has weathered great upheaval. Our family is bound together by love.

They heard something shift, in the darkness beyond the reach of the light. "Mom?"

"Katie? Where are you, honey?"

"Dad, what happened to her?"

"Just tell me where you are, sweetheart. We'll come to you."

They reached the bottom of the steps and as he moved out of the path of the kitchen light it shone more fully on the thing fixed to the post: a gory mass of scrambled flesh, a ragged web of graying black hair. Something moved in the shadows beyond it, small and hunched and pale, its back buckling with each grunted effort, like something caught in the act of love.

Our family will not abandon itself.

Heather stepped backward; her heel caught on the lowest step and she fell onto the stairs.

Sean approached his wife. She labored weakly in the bottom of a small declivity, grave-shaped, worm-spangled, her dull white bones poking through the parchment skin of her back, her spine bending as she burrowed into the earth. Her denuded skull still bore the tatters of its face, like the flag of a ruined army.

"Daddy, come on." Sean turned to see his daughter crawling up the stairs. She reached the top and crawled through the doorway, pulling her legs in after her. In the light, he could see the tears on her face, the twist of anguish. "Daddy, please. Come on. Come on."

Sean put his hand on Katie's back. "Don't you remember me? I'm your husband. Don't you remember?"

She continued to work, slowly, her arms like pistons powered by a fading battery.

He lifted her from her place in the earth, dirt sifting from her body like a snowfall, and clutched her tightly to his chest. He rested his head against the blood-greased curve of her skull, cradled her forehead in his hand. "Stay with me."

Heather, one more time, from somewhere above him: "Daddy, oh no, please come up. Please."

"Get down here," Sean said. "Goddamn you, get down here." The door shut, cutting off the wedge of light. He held his wife in his arms, rocking her back and forth, cooing into the ear that still remained.

He pulled her away, but she barely knew it. Everything was quiet now. Silence blew from the hole she had dug like smoke. She could feel what lay just beyond. The new countryside. The unspeaking multitude. Steeples and arches of bone; temples of silence. She felt the great shapes that moved there, majestic and unfurled, utterly silent, utterly dark.

He held her, breathing air onto the last cinder in her skull. Her fingers scraped at empty air, the remains of her body engaged in this one final enterprise, working with a machine's unguided industry, divorced at last from its practical function. Working only because that was its purpose; its rote, inelegant chore.

Nathan Ballingrud is the author of *North American Lake Monsters*, from Small Beer Press. Several of his stories have been reprinted in "year's best" anthologies, and his story "The Monsters of Heaven" won a Shirley Jackson Award. He's worked as a bartender in New Orleans, a cook on oil rigs in the Gulf of Mexico, and a waiter in a fancy restaurant. Currently he lives in Asheville, NC, with his daughter, where he's at work on his first novel. You can find him online at nathanballingrud.wordpress.com.

Chimeric with secrets, she was amazed the whole house did not lurch into motion, pulling up its deep roots and walls to run somewhere that wasn't bathed in madness and the footsteps of the dead . . .

THE SOUL IN THE BELL JAR

KJ Kabza

Ten lonely miles from the shores of the Gneiss Sea, where the low town of Hume rots beneath the mist, runs a half-wild road without a name. Flanked by brambles and the black, it turns through wolf-thick hollows, watched by yellow eyes that glitter with hunger and the moon. The wolves, of course, are nothing, and no cutthroat highwayman ever waited beneath the shadows of those oaks. There are far worse things that shamble in the dark. This is the road that skirts Long Hill.

So the coachman declared, and so Lindsome Glass already knew. She also knew whose fault the shambling things were, and where their nursery lay: in the great, moaning house at Long Hill's apex.

She knew anxiety and sorrow, for having to approach it.

"Can't imagine what business a nice young miss like you has with the Stitchman," said the coachman.

Lindsome knew he was fishing for gossip. She did not reply.

"A pretty young miss like you?" pressed the coachman. Their vehicle was a simple horse trap, and there was nowhere to sit that was away from his dirty trousers and wine-stained smile. "You can't be, what, more than eleven? Twelve? Only them scienticians go up there. Unless you's a new Help, is that it? The ol' Stitchman could use a new pair of hands, says me. That big ol' house, rottin' up in the weeds with hardly nobody to tend to it none." He laughed. "Course, it's no wonder. You couldn't get Help up there for all the gold in Yorken." He eyed her sideways. "So what's he have on *you?*"

The road wound upward, the branches overhead thinned, and the stones beneath the wheels took on the dreary glow of an overcast sky. November in Tattenlane meant sunshine, but Lindsome was not in Tattenlane anymore.

"Eh?" the coachman pressed.

Lindsome turned her pale face away. She fought against the quiver in her jaw. "Mama and Papa have gone on a trip around the world. They didn't say for how long, but I'm to stay here until they return. The Stitchman is my great-uncle."

Startled into silence, the coachman looked away.

The nameless road flattened, and the mad, untamed lawn of Apsis House sprawled into view. It clawed to the horizons, large as night, lonely as the world.

When Lindsome alighted with her single hatbox and carpetbag, there was only one sour-mouthed, middle-aged man to meet her. He was tall and stooped, with shoulders too square and a neck too short, giving him an altogether looming air of menace. "Took your time, didn't you?"

Behind Lindsome, the coachman was already retreating down Long Hill. "I—I'm sorry. The roads were—"

"Where are you manners?" the sour-mouthed man demanded. "Introduce yourself."

Lindsome bit her lip. The quiver in her jaw threatened to return. *I must not cry*, she told herself. *I am a young lady.* Lindsome gripped the hem of her white dress and dropped into a graceful curtsey. "I . . . beg your pardon, sir. My name is Lindsome Glass. How do you do? Our meeting is well."

"S'well," the man replied shortly. "That's better. Now take your things and come inside. Ghost knows where that lack-about Thomlin is. Doctor Dandridge is on the cusp of a singular work, one of the greatest in his career, and he and I have far more valuable things to do with our time than coddle you in welcome."

Lindsome nearly had to run to keep up with the man's long, loping strides. "The house has three main floors, one attic, and two basements," he said, leading her past a half-collapsed carriage house. "Attic is dangerous and off-limits. Third floor is Help's quarters and off-limits. Basements are the laboratories, so they are *definitely* off limits, especially to careless little children."

The man pushed through a back door that cried on rust-thick hinges. Lindsome followed. The interior had a damp, close smell of things forgotten in the rain, and the air was clammy and chill. A small, useless fire guttered in a distant grate. Pots and pans, dingy with age and wear, hung from beams like gutted animals. Lindsome set down her hatbox and touched a bunch of drying sage. It crumbled like a desiccated spiderweb.

The man grabbed her wrist. "And don't. Touch. Anything."

Lindsome fearfully withdrew her hand. "Yes, sir."

A middle-aged woman, generous in girth but mousy in the face, hobbled out from a pantry, wiping her hands on her flour-smeared apron. "Good afternoon, Mister Chaswick, sir." She turned to Lindsome. Her smile was kind. "Is this the young miss? Oh, so pale, with such lovely dark hair. You'll be a heartbreaker someday, won't you? What's your name?"

"This is Lindsome Glass," said Chaswick. "Mind you watch her."

"Yes, Mister Chaswick."

"Don't trouble to see her up. I'll do it."

"Thank you, Mister Chaswick."

"Don't thank me. With your knees it takes you a century to get up the bloody staircase."

Chaswick led Lindsome deeper into the house, under moldering lintels, through crooked doorways, past water-damaged wainscoting and rooms hung with peeling wallpaper. The carcasses of upturned insects lay in corners, legs folded neatly in rictus. Paintings lined the soot-blackened walls, and Lindsome thought that perhaps they had portrayed beautiful scenes, once, but now most were so caked with filth that it was hard to divine their subjects. Here, a lake? There, a table of hunting bounty? Many were portraits with tarnished nameplates. Any names still legible meant nothing. Who was Marilda Dandridge, anyway?

"Are you paying attention?" Chaswick demanded. "Breakfast's at seven, supper's at noon, and dinner's at seven. We don't have tea or any of that Tatterlane nonsense here. Bath day is Sunday, wash day is Monday, and if you'd like to occupy yourself, I suggest the library on the second floor, as it contains a number of volumes that will ensure the moral betterment of a young person such as yourself."

"Do you have any picture books?" Lindsome asked.

Chaswick frowned. "I suppose you could borrow one of your great-uncle's illustrated medical atlases. Perhaps Porphyry's *Intestinal Arrangements of the Dispeptic* or Gharison's *Common Melancholia in the Spleen of the Breeding Female.*"

Lindsome looked down at her shoes. "Never mind."

"You may also explore the grounds," Chaswick continued. "But don't cross paths with the gardener. Understand? If you ever hear the gardener working, turn around and go back at once.

"And mind the vivifieds. Doctor Dandridge is a brilliant, highly prolific man, and you'll see a great many examples of his work roaming throughout the area, many of which do not have souls consanguineous to their bodies. However, none of the vivifieds that Doctor Dandridge and I have created for practical purposes is chimeric, so you may safely pat the house cats and the horses in the stables. If you'd like to go for a ride . . . "

Something colorful moved at the edge of Lindsome's vision. Surprised at something so bright in so dreary a place, she stopped and backtracked. She peered around a corner, down a short hall sandwiched between a pair of much grander rooms.

The door at the end of the hall stood ajar. A hand's-breadth of room beckoned, sunny-yellow and smelling of lavender. A bookcase stood partially in view, crammed with spinning tops, painted wooden blocks, tin soldiers, stuffed animals, rattles, little blankets, papers cleverly folded into birds . . .

Lindsome stepped forward.

A woman exited the room. Her movements were quick, though she was old and excessively thin, with dark circles about her despairing eyes. She grasped the doorknob with bloodless talons, pulling it shut and locking it with a tiny iron key.

She turned and saw Lindsome.

Her transformation into rage was instantaneous. "What are you doing?" the woman bellowed, baring her long, gray teeth. "Get out of this hall! Get away from here!"

Lindsome fled to Chaswick.

"What's this?" said Chaswick, turning. "What! Have you not been following me?"

"There was a woman!" Lindsome said, dropping her things. "A thin woman!"

Chaswick grabbed Lindsome's wrist again. He bent over and pulled her close—lifted her, even, until she was nearly on her tiptoes and squirming with discomfort and alarm.

"That's Emlee, the housekeeper. Mind her too." Chaswick narrowed his eyes. "And that little hallway between the study and the card room? Definitely, *absolutely* off limits."

Chaswick deposited Lindsome in front of a room on the second floor. As soon as he had withdrawn down the grand staircase, Lindsome set her things inside and made a survey of the rest of the level. The aforementioned library was spacious and well stocked but poorly kept, with uneven layers of dust and bookbindings faded by sun. Many volumes had been reshelved unevenly, incorrectly, or even upside-down, if at all.

Most of the other rooms were unused, their furniture wholly absent or in deep slumber beneath moth-eaten sheets. Two of the rooms were locked, or perhaps even rusted shut, including one next to what she assumed were her great-uncle's personal quarters, since they were the largest and, she could only surmise, at one time, the grandest. Now, like all else in Apsis House, their colors and details had darkened with soot and neglect, and Lindsome wondered how, if Dr. Dandridge were so brilliant, he could fail to control such misery and decay.

While exploring the first floor more thoroughly, she came across a squat, surly man in overalls who was pasting paper over a broken window in the Piano Room. He introduced himself as Thomlin, the Housemaster. Lindsome politely asked how did he do. Thomlin said he did fine, as long as he took his medicine, and as an illustration produced a silver flask, from which he took a hearty pull.

"May I ask you something, Mister Thomlin? What's at the end of the little hallway? In the yellow room?"

The house'm scowled as he lifted his paste brush from the bucket and slapped it desultorily over the glass. "Nothin'," he said. "Nothin' that a good girl should stick 'er nose in. How a man wants to grieve, that's his business. No, no, I've said too much already." Juggling flask and brush, he took another medicinal dose. "I know everything that happens and ever did happen in these walls, you understand, inside and out. Wish I didn't, but I do. Housemaster, that's me. All these poor bastards—oops, pardon my language, young miss—I mean all these poor folks walk around in a fog a' their own problems, but a Housemaster sees everything as The Ghost sees it: absolute and clear as finest crystal, as not a soul else can ever understand. But good men tell no tales anyway. An' a gooder man you won't find either side of this whole blasphemous Long Hill heap. Why don't you go play outside? But don't never interrupt the gardener. Hear?"

Lindsome did not want to explore the grounds, but she told herself, *I must be brave, because I am a young lady*, and went outside with her head held high. Nonetheless, she did not get far. The weeds and brambles of the neglected lawn had long since matured into an impenetrable thicket, and Lindsome could barely see the rooftops of the nearby outbuildings above the wild creepers, dying leaves, needle-thin thorns, and drab, stenchful flowers. The late autumnal blossoms stank of carrion and sulfur, mingled with the ghastly sickly-sweetness of mothballs. Lindsome pulled one sleeve over her hand and held it to her wrinkled nose as she picked her way along a downward-sloping animal trail that ran near the main house, the closest navigational relief in this unrelenting jungle, but she could get no corresponding relief from the smell.

She rounded a barberry bush. A little scream squeezed from behind her hand.

The stench wasn't the flowers. It was vivifieds.

In her path, blocking it completely, stood a white billy goat. He did not breathe or move. His peculiar, tipped-over eyes were motionless, his sideways pupils like twin cracks to the Abyss.

His belly had burst, and flies looped around his gaping bowels in humming droves.

Heart pounding, Lindsome backed away. The goat did nothing. Its gaze remained fixed at some point beyond her shoulder. As she watched, bits of its flesh grew misty, then re-solidified. *It's all right*, Lindsome told herself. *It's just an old vivified, rotten enough for the soul to start coming loose. It's so old it doesn't know what it is or how to act. See? It's staying right there.*

Push past it. It will never notice.

Lindsome shuddered. But she was a young lady, and young ladies were always calm and regal and never afraid.

So Lindsome lifted the hem of her dress, as if preparing to step through a mud puddle, and inched her way toward and around the burst-open creature.

Its foul-smelling fur, tacky with ichor, brushed the whiteness of her garment. Lindsome closed her eyes and bit her lip, enough to bring pain, and a fly buzzed greedily in her ear. *I am not afraid. I am not afraid.*

She passed the goat.

At the first possible moment, she dropped her hem and sprinted down the path. The thicket thinned out into a place where the trail wasn't as clear, but she kept going, crashing through brittle twigs and dead undergrowth, prompting vivified birds to take wing. The corpses were poor fliers, dropping as swiftly as they'd risen. One splatted onto a boulder at the edge of the path, hard enough for the stitched-on soul to be shaken loose entirely in a shimmer of mist; the physical shell, without anything to vivify it, shrank in volume like a dried-up fruit.

The faint trail turned abruptly into a long, empty clearing that stretched back toward the house. The vista had been created with brisk violence: every stubborn plant, whether still verdant or dormant for the season, had been uprooted and lay in careless, half-dried piles, revealing tough, rocky soil. A second path connecting to this space had been widened and its vegetation thoroughly trampled. Lindsome silently blessed the unseen gardener's vigorous but futile work ethic and, slowing to a breathless, nervous walk, crossed the clearing. Despite the portending stink, there were no vivifieds in sight.

But as the path resumed, the stench grew stronger yet. Rot and cloying sweetness clogged Lindsome's nose so badly that her eyes watered and she breathed through her mouth. Young ladies remained calm and regal, Lindsome supposed, but they were also not stupid. Perhaps it was time to turn back.

The path ended at a set of heavy double doors.

To be truthful, a number of paths ended at these doors, with at least four distinct trails converging at the edges of the small, filth-caked patio. Lindsome imagined that her great-uncle, along with the unpleasant Chaswick, exited from these doors when making expeditions into the haunted thicket for the few live specimens that must remain. *Do they only catch the old and injured,* she wondered, *or do they murder creatures in their prime, only to sew their souls right back on again?*

Lindsome tried the doors. They opened with ease.

The revealed space was not some dingy mudroom or rear hall, as Lindsome had expected, but a room so wide, it could have served as a stable were it not for its low ceiling and unfinished back. Instead of meeting a rear wall, the flagstone floor disintegrated into irregular fragments and piled up onto a slope of earth.

Three long tables ran down the center of the room to Lindsome's right, the final one disappearing into the total blackness of the room's far end. The tables were stone, their surfaces carved with deep grooves that terminated at the edges, above stained and waiting buckets.

Melted candles spattered the tables' surfaces. There were no windows.

The stench of the place flowed outward like an icy draft. Lindsome left a door open behind her, held her nose, and took a step inside. Even when breathing through her mouth, the vivified odor was a soup of putrification that clotted at the back of her throat, thick enough to drip into her belly. The sensation was unendurable. Surely that was a stone staircase leading up over the unfinished back wall, into less offensive parts of the house?

Three steps toward the staircase, Lindsome made the mistake of glancing behind her.

The entire front wall, lined floor to ceiling with cages and bars, bore an unliving library of vivifieds, every creature too large for its pen. Stoats stood shoulder-to-shoulder with badgers and owls, and serpents had no room to uncurl in their tiny cubes. Rabbit fur commingled with hawk feathers. Paws tapped and noses twitched, and bodies lurched gently from side to side, but that great wall of shifting corpses, scales and hide and stripes, made no sound. Each rotting throat was silent.

Three hundred pairs of eyes watched Lindsome, flashing yellow and green, white and red. She fell into a table, hitting her shoulder against the stone.

Get up. Run away. She daren't breathe. *You silly fool. The ground was sloping outside. Remember? This is a basement.*

You cannot be here.

A door squealed open. A trickle of light dribbled down the steps.

Lindsome dove away from the table and behind the staircase's concealing bulk.

The door at the top opened fully. Candlelight flowed down the steps now, making hundreds of vivified eyes sparkle. "The sea lion, I think," said a voice. It was papery and thin, like a flake of ash that would crumble at the barest touch. "At the far end."

"Really, Albion," said Chaswick, stepping down onto the flagstones. He held high a five-branched candelabrum, his shadow stretching behind him. "We're overpreparing, don't you think?"

"Oh no, not hardly." An old, old man shuffled in Chaswick's wake. His head, wreathed in a wispy halo of white and framed by sizeable ears, seemed bowed under the weight of constant thought across many decades. His knobby fingers would not stop undulating, like twin spiders in a restless sleep. "One last test, before Thursday. I'm certain that a Kell Stitch at the brain stem, instead of a Raymund, will surprise us."

Chaswick's back heaved in a sigh. "I maintain that the original protocol would have sufficed. The first time around—"

"I was lucky," interrupted the man. "Very, very lucky. That ghastly knot was nothing but shaking hands and fortunate bungling. And besides—" He sighed, too, but instead of deflating, the exhalation appeared to lift him up. "Think of the advances, Chaswick. The discoveries I've made since then. How all these newer elements might work in concert—well. We cannot be too careful. I don't have to tell you what's at stake."

The two men moved into the blackness of the room's far end. The candelabrum revealed that the distant third of the wall was hidden behind a heavy black curtain.

"Of course, Doctor Dandridge," said Chaswick.

"The sea lion," Dr. Dandridge repeated.

Chaswick passed the candelabrum to his superior. When he turned to grip the curtain, Lindsome noticed what he was wearing.

Waders?

The curtain hissed partway aside upon its track. The candlelight fell upon tanks, tanks and tanks and tanks, each filled with an evil, yellowing liquid. Each held a shrunken animal corpse, embalmed. The lowest third of the wall was but a single tank, stretching back behind the half-closed curtain.

A great, bloated shadow rolled within.

Chaswick knelt by a tank on the second shelf, obscuring the monstrosity below. He fitted a length of rubber hose to a stopcock at the bottom of the tank, then ran the hose along the floor and out the open door. "Door's blown loose again. That useless Thomlin—I've asked him to fix the latch thrice this week. I swear to Ghost, I'd stick him in one of the tanks myself if he weren't a man and would leave behind anything more useful than ghostgrease."

Chaswick returned and opened the stopcock. The end of the hose, limp over the edge of the patio, dribbled its foul load into the weeds. The large corpse within the tank settled to the bottom as it drained, a limp, matted mess. Chaswick did something to the glass to make it open outward, like the door to an oven.

He gathered the dead thing to his chest and stood. Ichor ran in rivulets down his waders. "I don't mean to rush you, but—"

"Of course." Candelabrum in tow, Dr. Dandridge shuffled back to the stairs. "I'll do my best to hurry."

They ascended the steps, pulling the light with them and the squealing door shut.

Lindsome fled outside. After that chamber of horrors, the sticking burdock, Raven's Kiss, and cruel thorns of the sunlit world were the hallmarks of Paradise.

At seven o'clock, some unseen, stentorian timepiece tolled the hour. Lindsome, who had elected to spend the rest of the afternoon in the library in a fort constructed from the oldest, fattest, dullest (and surely therefore safest) books she could find, reluctantly emerged to search for the dining room.

The murmur of voices and clink of silverware guided her steps into a room on the first floor nearly large enough to be a proper banquet hall. Only the far end of the long table, near the wall abutting the kitchen, was occupied. A fire on the wall's hearth cast the head of the table in shadow while illuminating Chaswick's disdain.

"You are late," Chaswick said. "Don't you know what they say about first impressions?"

Lindsome slunk across the floor. "I'm sorry, Mister Chaswick."

From the shadows of a wingback chair, the master of the house leaned forward. "No matter," said Dr. Dandridge. "Good evening. I am Professor Albion Edgarton Dandridge. Our meeting is well. Please pardon me for not arising; I'm an old man, and my bones grow reluctant, even at the welcome sight of a face so fresh and kind as yours."

Lindsome had not expected this. "I . . . thank you, sir."

"Uncle Albion will do. Come, sit, sit."

Opposite Chaswick, Lindsome pulled out her own massive chair with some difficulty, working it over the threadbare carpet in small scoots. "Thank you, sir. Our meeting is well."

Chaswick snorted. "Mind her, Doctor. She's got a streak in her."

"Oh, I don't doubt it. Comes from my side." The old man smiled at her. His teeth were surprisingly intact. "Are you making yourself at home, my dear?"

Lindsome served herself a ladle-full of shapeless brown stew. "Yes, sir."

"Don't mumble," said Chaswick, picking debris from his teeth with his fingernails. "It's uncouth."

"I am delighted that you're staying with us," continued Dr. Dandridge. Outside of the nightmarish basement, he looked ordinary and gentle. His halo of hair, Lindsome now saw, wandered off his head into a pair of bedraggled dundrearies, and the fine wrinkles around his eyes made him look kind. His clothes were dusty and ill-fitting, tailored for a more robust man at least thirty years his junior. She could not imagine a less threatening person.

"Thank you, sir."

"Uncle. I am dear old Uncle—" Dr. Dandridge coughed, a dry, wheezing sound, and put an embroidered handkerchief to his mouth. Chaswick nudged the old man's water glass closer. "Albion," he managed, taking a sip from the glass. "Thank you, Chaswick."

"Yes, Uncle."

"And how is your papa?"

Lindsome did not want to think of him, arm in arm with Mama, strolling up the pier to the great boat and laughing, his long legs wavering under a film of tears. "He is very well, thank you."

"Excellent, excellent. And your mama?"

"Also well."

"Good, good." The doctor nibbled at his stew, apparently unfazed by its utter lack of flavor. "I trust that the staff have been kind, and have answered all of your questions."

"Well . . . " Lindsome started, but Chaswick shot her a dangerous look. Lindsome fell silent.

"Yes?" asked Dr. Dandridge, focused on teasing apart a gravy-smothered nodule.

"I was wondering . . . " dared Lindsome, but Chaswick's face sharpened into a scowl. " . . . about your work."

"Oh!" said Dr. Dandridge. His efforts on the nodule of stew redoubled. "My work. My great work! You are right to ask, young lady. It is always pleasing to hear that the youth of today have an interest in science. Young people are our future, you know."

"I—"

"The work, of course, builds on the fundamentals of Wittard and Blacke from the thirties, going beyond the Skin Stitch and into the essential vital nodes. But unlike Havarttgartt and his school (and here's the key, now), we don't hold that the heart, brain, and genitals, aka the Life Triad, are the necessary fulcrums. We hold—that is, I hold—that is, Chaswick agrees, and he's a very smart lad—*we* hold that a diversified architecture of fulcrums is key to extending the ambulatory period of a vivified, and we have extensive data to back this hypothesis, to the extent where we've produced a curve—a Dandridge curve, I call it, if I may be so modest, ha-ha—that illustrates the correlation between the number of fulcrums and hours of ambulatory function, and clearly demonstrates that while *quality* of fulcrums does indeed play a role, it is not nearly so prominent as the role of *quantity*. Or, in layman's terms, if you stitch a soul silly to a corpse at every major mechanical joint—ankles, knees, hips, shoulders, elbows, wrists—you'll still get a far better outcome than you would had you used a Butterfly Stitch to the heart itself! Can you imagine?"

Lost, Lindsome stared at her plate. She could feel Chaswick's smug gaze upon her, the awful look that grown-ups use when they want to say, *Not so smart now, are you?*

"And furthermore," Dr. Dandridge went on gaily, setting down his fork and withdrawing a different utensil from his pocket with which to attack his clump of stew, "we have discovered a hitherto unknown role of the Life Triad in host plasticity. Did Chaswick explain to you about our chimeras? The dogs with souls of finches, and the blackbirds with the souls of chipmunks, and in one exceptional case, the little red fox with the soul of a prize-winning hog? Goodness, was I proud of that one!" The old man laughed.

Lindsome smiled weakly.

"It is upon the brain, you see, not the heart," Dr. Dandridge went on, "that the configuration, amount, and type of stitches are key, because—and this is already well known in the higher animals—a great deal of soul is enfleshed in the brain. You may think of the brain as a tiny little seed that floats in the center of every skull, but not so! When an animal is alive, the brain takes up the *entire* skull cavity. Can you imagine? Of course, the higher the animal, the more the overall corpse shrinks at the moment of death, aka soul separation, due to the soul composing a greater percentage of the creature. This is why Humankind (with its large and complex souls) leaves no deathhusk, or corpse, at all—nothing but a film of ghostgrease. Which, incidentally, popular doggerel will tell you is absent from the deathbeds of holy people, being that they are so *very* above their animal natures and are one hundred percent ethereal, but goodness, don't get me started about all *that* ugsome rot."

Dr. Dandridge stopped. He frowned at his plate. "Good grief. What am I doing?"

"A Clatham Stitch, looks like," said Chaswick gently. "On your beef stew."

"Heavens!" Dr. Dandridge put down his utensil, which Lindsome could now see was an aetherhook. He removed what looked like a monocle made of cobalt glass from a breast pocket, then peered through it at his plate. "There weren't any souls passing by just now, were there? The leycurrents are strong here in the early winter, dear Lindsome, and sometimes the departed souls of lesser creatures will blow into the house if we have the windows open. And when *that* happens—"

The lump of beef quivered. Lindsome dropped her fork and clapped a hand to her mouth.

From beneath the stew crawled a beetle, looking very put out.

Dr. Dandridge and Chaswick burst into guffaws. "A beetle!" cried the old man. "A beetle in the stew! Oh, that is precious, too precious for words! Oh, how funny!"

Chaswick, laughing, looked to Lindsome, her eyes saucer-wide. "Oh, come now," he said. "Surely you see the humor."

Dr. Dandridge wiped his eyes. The beetle, tracking tiny spots of stew, crawled off across the tablecloth at speed. "A beetle! Oh, mercy. Mercy me. Excuse us—that's not a joke for a young lady at all. Forgive me, child—we've grown uncivilized out here, isolated as we are. A Clatham Stitch upon my stew, as if to vivify it! And then came a beetle—"

Lindsome couldn't take it anymore. She stood. "May I be excused?"

"Already?" said Chaswick, still chuckling. "No more questions for your great-uncle, demonstrating your *very* thorough interest in and understanding of his work?"

Lindsome colored beneath the increasing heat of her discomfort. This remark, on top of all else, was too much. "Oh, I understand a great deal. I understand that you can stitch a soul to an embalmed deathhusk instead of an unpreserved one—"

Chaswick stopped laughing immediately.

"—even though *everybody knows* that's impossible," said Lindsome.

Chaswick's eyes tightened in suspicion. Dr. Dandridge, unaware of the ferocity between their interlocked stares, sat as erect as his ancient bones would permit. "Why, that's right! That's absolutely right! You must have understood the implications of Bainbridge's supplemental index in her report last spring!"

"Yes," said Chaswick coldly. "She must have."

Lindsome colored further and looked away. She focused on her great-uncle, who, in his excitement, had picked up the aetherhook once again and was attempting to cut a bit of potato with it. "Your mama was right to send you here. I never imagined—a blossoming, fine young scientific mind in the family! Why, the conversations we can have, you and I! Great Apocrypha, I'm doing it again, aren't I?" The old man put the aetherhook, with no further comment or explanation, tip-down in his water glass. "We shall have a chat in my study after dinner. Truth be told, you arrived at the perfect time. Chaswick and I are at the cusp of an astounding attempt, a true milestone in—"

Chaswick arose sharply from his chair. "A moment, Doctor! I need a word with your niece first." He rounded the table and grabbed Lindsome's arm before anyone could protest. "She'll await you in your study. Excuse us."

Chaswick dragged her toward the small, forbidden hallway, but rather than entering the door at the end into the mysterious yellow room, he dragged Lindsome into one of the rooms that flanked the corridor. Lindsome did not have an opportunity to observe the interior, for Chaswick slammed the door behind them.

"What have you seen?"

A match flared to life with a pop and Lindsome shielded her eyes. Chaswick lit a single candle, tossed the match aside, and lifted the candle to chest-level. Its flicker turned his expression eerie and demonic. "I said, what have you seen?"

"Nothing!" Lindsome kept her free hand over her eyes, pretending the shock of the light hurt worse than it did, so that Chaswick could not see the lie upon her face.

"Listen to me, you little brat," Chaswick hissed. "You might think you can breeze in here and destroy everything I've built with a bit of flattery and deception, but I have news for you. You and the rest of your shallow, showy, flighty, backstabbing kindred? You abandoned this brilliant man long ago, thinking his work would come to nothing, and that these beautiful grounds and marvels of creation weren't worth the rocks the building crew dug from the soil, but with The Ghost as my witness, I swear that I am not allowing your pampered, money-grubbing hands to trick me out of my inheritance. Do you understand me? I love this man. I love his work. I love what he stands for. Apsis House will remain willed to *me*. And if I so much as see you bat your wicked little eyes in the doctor's direction, I will *ensure* that you are not in my way.

"Do I make myself clear?"

Lindsome lowered her hand. It was trembling. Every part of her was. "You think I'm—are you saying—?"

The vise of Chaswick's hand, honed over long hours of tension around a Stitchman's instruments, crushed her wrist in its grip. "Do I make myself clear?"

Lindsome squirmed, now in genuine pain. "Let me go! I don't even want your ruined old house!"

"What did you see?"

"Stop it!"

"Tell me what you've seen!"

"Yes," announced Dr. Dandridge, and in half a second, Chaswick had released Lindsome and stepped back, and the old man entered the room, a blazing candelabrum in hand. "Yes, stitching a soul to an embalmed, or even mummified, deathhusk would be a tremendous feat. Just imagine how long something like that could last. Ages, maybe. And ages more . . . " His expression turned distant and calculating. "Just imagine. A soul you never wanted to lose? Why, you could keep it here forever . . . "

Chaswick straightened. He smiled at Lindsome, a poisonous thing that Dr. Dandridge, lost in daydreams, did not see. "Good night, Doctor. And good night, Lindsome. Mind whose house you're in."

• • •

Surviving the fervid conversation of her great-uncle was one thing, but after just five days, Lindsome wasn't sure how long she could survive the mysteries of his house. Chimeric with secrets, every joint and blackened picture was near bursting with the souls of untold stories. Lindsome was amazed that the whole great edifice did not lurch into motion, pulling up its deep roots and walls to run somewhere that wasn't bathed in madness and the footsteps of the dead. She searched the place over for answers, but the chambers yielded no clues, and any living thing who might supply them remained stitched to secrets of their own.

The only person she hadn't spoken with yet was the gardener.

Lindsome finally set off one evening to find him, under a gash of orange-red that hung over the bare trees to the west. She left the loop trail around the house. Bowers of bramble, vines of Heart-Be-Still, and immature Honeylocusts rife with spines surrounded her. A chorus of splintering twigs whispered beyond as unseen vivifieds moved on ill-fitted instinct.

"Hello? Mister Gardener?"

Only the twigs, whispering.

Lindsome slipped her right hand into her pocket, grasping what lay within. A grade-2 aetherblade, capped tight. She'd found it on the desk in Uncle Albion's study one afternoon. Lindsome couldn't say why she'd taken it. An aetherblade was only useful, after all, if one wanted to cut spirit-stitches and knew where those stitches lay, and Lindsome had neither expertise nor aetherglass to make solid the invisible threads. It would have done her just as much good to pocket one of Cook's paring knives, which is to say, not much good at all.

"Hello?"

Beneath the constant stink of corpses came something sweet. At first, Lindsome thought it was a freshly vivified, exuding the cloyingly sweet fragrance of the finishing chemicals. But it was too gentle and mild.

A dark thing, soft as a moth, fluttered onto her cheek.

A rose petal.

"Mister Gardener? Are you growing—"

A savagely cleared vista opened before her, twisting back toward the house, now a looming shadow against the dimming sky. The murdered plants waited in neat piles, rootballs wet and dark. Lindsome squeezed her stolen aetherblade tighter in relief. The things were newly pulled. He'd be resting at the end of this trail, close to the house, preparing to come in for the evening.

But he wasn't.

At the end of the vista, Lindsome halted in surprise. In front of her lay another clearing, but this one was old and well maintained. Its floor held a fine carpet of grass, dormant and littered with leaves. The grass stretched up to the house itself and terminated at the edge of a patio. The double doors leading out were twin mosaics of diamond-shaped panes. Through them, Lindsome could see sheer curtains drawn back on the other side. Within the room, a gaslamp burned.

Its light flickered over yellow walls.

Lindsome's breath stuck in her throat like a lump of ice. She could see the shelves now, the stacks of toys, the painted blocks and tops and bright pictures of animals hung above the chair-rail molding. A tiny, overlooked chair at the patio's edge. An overlooked iron crib within.

Nobody had said the room was forbidden to approach from the outside.

Lindsome drifted across the grass. As she drew closer, she noticed something new. In the center of the room, between her and the iron crib, stood a three-legged table. Upon the table sat a bell jar. Perfectly clean, its translucence had rendered it invisible, until Lindsome saw the gaslight glance from its surface at the proper angle.

Within the bell jar, something moved.

Lindsome drew even closer. The bell jar was large, the size of a birdcage, but not so large as to dwarf the blur within. The blur's presence, too, had been obscured from behind by the stark pattern of the crib's bars, but it was not so translucent as the bell jar itself. The thing inside the glass was wispy. Shimmering.

Lindsome stepped onto the patio. The icy lump in her throat froze it shut.

Within the bell jar, a tiny, tiny fist pressed its knuckles against the glass.

Lindsome's scream woke Long Hill's last surviving raven, which took wing into the night, cawing.

Thorns tore Lindsome's dress to tatters as she ran. "Chaswick!"

She fled toward the squares of gaslight, jumping over a fallen tree and flying up the main steps into the house. She called again, running from room to empty room, scattering dust and mice, the lamplight painting black ghosts behind crooked settees and broken chairs. "Someone help! Chaswick!"

Lindsome reached the kitchen. Cook was kneeling by the hearth, roasting a pan of cabbage-wrapped beef rolls atop the glowing coals. "Cook! Help! The yellow room! There's a baby!"

Cook maintained her watchful crouch, not even turning. "Sst!" She put a plump finger to her lips. "Hush, child!"

"The yellow room," cried Lindsome, gripping Cook's elbow. "I saw it. I was outside and followed a path the gardener made. There's a bell jar inside. It's got a soul in it. A human soul. He's keeping a—"

Cook planted her sooty hand over Lindsome's mouth. She leaned toward her, beady eyes pinching. "I said hush, child," Cook whispered. "Hush. That was nothing you saw. That fancy gaslight the doctor likes, it plays tricks on your eyes."

Lindsome shook her head, but Cook pressed harder. "It plays tricks." Her expression pleaded. "Be a good girl, now. Stop telling tales. Lock your door at night. And don't you bring the gardener into this—don't you dare. That's a good girl?" Her eyes pinched further. "Yes?"

Lindsome wrenched herself away and ran.

"Chaswick!" She ran to the second floor, so upset that she grew disoriented. Had she already searched this corridor? This cloister of rooms? She could smell it. Fresh vivified. No—something milder. Right behind this locked door . . .

A hand touched Lindsome's shoulder. She squealed.

"Saint Ransome's Blood, child!" Chaswick said, spinning her about. A pair of spectacles perched on his nose, gleaming in the hall's gaslight. His other, dangling hand held a half-open book, as though it were a carcass to be trussed. "What's all this howling?"

Lindsome threw her arms about him. "Chaswick!"

He stiffened. "Goodness. Control yourself. Come now, stop that. Did you see a mouse?"

"No," said Lindsome, pressing her face into Chaswick's chest. "It was—"

"How many times must I tell you not to mumble?" Chaswick asked. "Now listen. I was in the midst of a very important—"

"A BABY!" Lindsome shouted.

Chaswick grew very still.

"It was—"

Chaswick drew back, gripped Lindsome's shoulder, and without another word marched her down the hall and through a door that had always been locked.

Lindsome glanced about. The place appeared to be Chaswick's quarters. The room was in surprisingly good repair, clean and recently painted, but all carpets, tapestries, cushions, and wallpaper had been removed. The only furniture was a desk, chair, and narrow bed, the only thing of any comfort a mean, straw mattress. The fire in the grate helped soften the room's hard lines, and Lindsome's fear of this stern and jealous man melted further under her larger one. "I'm sorry, Mister Chaswick, but I was walking outside, and there was a path that took me past the yellow room, and inside I saw a bell jar. And in it was an infant's soul. It put its fist against the glass. I swear I'm not fibbing, Mister Chaswick. I swear by Mama's virtue, I'm not."

Chaswick sighed. He placed his book upon his desk. "I know you're not."

"You *know*?"

Chaswick shook his head, the flames highlighting the firm lines around his mouth. "I have said. The doctor is a brilliant man."

"But he—but you *can't* just—" Lindsome sputtered. "You can't stop a soul from going to Heaven! It's wrong! You'll—The Ghost will—you'll freeze in the Abyss! Forever and ever! The Second Ghostscroll says—"

"Don't quote scripture at me, girl, it's tiresome." Chaswick withdrew a small leather case from a pocket in his trousers, removed his spectacles, and slid them inside. "The Ghost is nothing but a fairy tale for adults who never grow up. Humankind is alone in the universe, and there are no rules save for those which we agree upon ourselves. If Doctor Dandridge has the knowledge, the means, the willingness, and the bravery to experiment upon a human soul—well, then, what of it?"

Lindsome shrank back. "He's going to—what?"

Chaswick set his mouth, the firelight carving his sternness deeper. "It's not my place to stop him."

Lindsome took a full step backward, barely able to speak. "You can't mean that. He can't. He wouldn't."

"In fact, I rather encourage it," said Chaswick. "Fortune favors the bold."

"But it's illegal," Lindsome stammered. "It's sick! They'd think he's gone mad! They'd put him away, and then they'd—"

She stopped. She stared at Chaswick.

They'd take away all of Uncle's property.

And they'd look in Uncle's will and give it to . . .

"You," Lindsome whispered. "It's you. You put this idea into his head."

Chaswick sneered. "Marilda died in childbirth, and the doctor chose his method of grieving, well before I ever set foot on Long Hill. Not that you'd know, considering how very little your ilk cared to associate with him, after the tragedy. Ask your precious mama. She doesn't approve of the yellow room, either." Chaswick's laugh was nasty. "Not that she thinks it's anything more than an empty shrine."

Lindsome backed toward the door. Chaswick advanced, matching her step for step. *You monster. You brute. What has my poor uncle done? What awful things has he already done?*

And what else is he going to do?

The door was nearly at her back. Chaswick loomed above her. "Go to bed, little girl," he warned. "Nobody is going to listen to your foolish histrionics. Not in this house."

Lindsome turned and fled.

She ran down the hall and into her own bedroom, where the bed sagged, the mold billowed across the ceiling like thunderheads, and the vivified mice ran back and forth, back and forth against the baseboards, without thinking, all night long.

Lindsome locked the door. *Cook would be proud.*

Then she lay on her bed and wept.

The night stretched like a cat, smothering future and past alike with its inky paws. Lindsome tossed in broken sleep. She dreamed of light glinting off of curved glass, and something lancing through her heart. Chaswick above her, flames of gaslight for eyes, probing her beating flesh with an aetherhook. "What's all this howling?"

Under everything, roses.

An hour before dawn, Lindsome dressed and left the house. The sky was too dark and the clouds too swollen, but she couldn't stand this wretched place another moment. Even the stables, which held nothing but vivifieds, would be an improvement. *The matted fur of dead horses is just as well for sponging away tears.*

In the stables, Lindsome buried her face against the cold nose of a gelding. Did he have the same soul he'd had in life, she wondered, or did some other horse now command this body? What did it feel like, to be stitched imperfectly to a body that was not yours? She remembered the grade-2 aetherblade in the pocket of her coat. She recalled the few comprehensible bits of her great-uncle's post-dinner lectures. Lindsome drew away from the horse, wiped her face on her sleeve, and produced the aetherblade.

The horse watched her, exhibiting no sign of feeling.

Lindsome plunged the tool behind the horse's knee, between the physical stitches of a deep, telltale cut that could never heal. She circled the creature, straining to see in the poor light, plunging the aetherblade into every such cut she could find.

The horse's legs buckled. It collapsed to the floor.

Its neck still functioned. The horse looked up at her, expressionless.

Lindsome searched through its mane, shuddering, trying to find the final knot of stitching that would—

Set it free.

Lindsome stopped.

The horse did not react.

"Wait for me," Lindsome said, setting down the aetherblade on the floor. "There's something I have to do. I'll be right back."

The horse, unable to do anything else, waited.

But she didn't come back.

Something was wrong with the sky, Lindsome thought, as she trotted toward the house. It was too gray and too warm, after last night's chill. There shouldn't be thunderheads gathering now. Not so late in autumn.

And something was wrong with the vivifieds. Instead of rustling in the depths of the thicket, they lurched up and down the irregular paths in a sluggish remembrance of flight. A snake with a crushed spine lolled in a hollow. A pack of coyotes, moving in rolling prowls like house cats, moved single file in a line from the stables to the well, not even swiveling an ear as Lindsome squeezed past.

Near the main steps of the house, the burst-open billy goat had gotten ensnared in a tangle of creepers, its blackened entrails commingling with blackened vines.

Lindsome resolutely ran past it.

A dead sparrow fell from the sky and pelted her shoulder, and a frog corpse crunched beneath her foot. A hundred awful things could smear her with their putrescence—but oh, let them, because she was a lady. And ladies always did what needed doing.

There.

The gardener's path to the yellow room.

She was at the final vista, now. Then the private patio. The sheer curtains were closed, but one of the patio doors was open, swinging to and fro on the fretful breeze.

In the center of the room, the three-legged table waited, but the bell jar was gone.

Lindsome slumped in gratitude. Uncle Albion had finally come to his senses. Or Chaswick had felt guilty about their talk last night, or careless Thomlin had knocked it over and broken it, even.

But then Lindsome remembered.

Today is Thursday.

Her throat made an awful squeak. She turned back and ran, up the vista and through wilderness to the ring path.

To the basement. Where ranks of monsters rotted as they stood, and the flesh of nightmares yet to be born floated in tanks, dreaming inscrutable dreams.

One of the doors to the basement stood open, too, swinging in the mounting wind. Lindsome ran inside. By now, she was panting, her back moist with sweat, her heart fighting to escape the hot prison of her chest. The foul air choked her. She bent double and gagged, falling to her knees on the icy stones.

Scores of waiting eyes watched her.

The wall of bodies began to moan, hundreds of bastard vocalizations from bastardized throats that had long ago forgotten how to speak. Pulpy flesh surged forward against bars and railings, jaws unhinging, the sound rising like the discordant sirens of an army from the Abyss.

Beneath them, Lindsome began a keening of her own, tiny and devoid of reason.

She did not know how she stepped to that far corner, where the future nightmares waited, but step she did, into a forest of burning candles. Some had toppled over onto the floor, frozen in sprays of wax. Some had melted into puddles, now aflame. The plentiful light showed all the tanks and that long, black curtain pulled fully back.

The giant tank on the bottom, as long as two men laid end to end, was drained, empty, and open.

The moaning grew. Lindsome's keening grew into a wail, though she could not hear it, only watch as her feet pointed her around and sent her across the basement and up the stone steps.

The door at the top was already open.

Lindsome's wail squeezed down into words, screamed loud enough to tear her throat as thorns will tear a dress. "Uncle Albion!"

Someone emitted a distant, ringing scream.

Lindsome couldn't breathe. She stumbled through the first floor, gasping, her uncle's name a mere whisper on her wide-open lips.

She found a door that Chaswick had forbidden, the door to the other basement-cum-laboratory. Or rather, she found the space where the door should have been. Both door and molding had been torn away.

The steps led down into pure blackness.

"Uncle," Lindsome gasped. Outside, lightning flickered, and Lindsome saw four steps down. Dark smears daubed the floorboards. Further within, the glitter of metal and broken glass.

A bloody handprint on the wall.

The scream came again, an animalistic screech of distilled and mortal terror. Lindsome backed away from the stairs. Her legs quaked too much to run now.

She walked to the grand staircase. A painful flash of lightning illuminated the entire house—the puddles of ichor through which Lindsome trod, the monstrous gouges in the wood and wallpaper on either side of her, the gaslamps torn from their mounts.

The mental image of a tiny fist, its knuckles bumping the inside of a tank as long as two men laid end to end.

Lindsome found Chaswick on the staircase. He had ended up like the billy goat outside, his stomach torn open, his entrails tangled in the shattered spindles of the banister.

"Linds . . . " One of his hands, slimy and bright, pawed at the banister.

She stared at him.

"Up . . . " Chaswick whispered. "Up . . . " His head twitched in the direction of the second floor. "If you . . . love . . . then up . . . "

Lindsome's head nodded. "Yes, Mister Chaswick," her mouth said.

His gaze clouded. The room flickered, as if under a second touch of lightning, and the pools of blood below him flashed into a sizzle.

Lindsome blinked, and Chaswick was gone. In his place, a pile of clothing lay tossed against the spindles, commingled with heavy black ghostgrease.

Somehow, Lindsome was running.

Sprinting, even. Up the stairs. "Uncle Albion!" she cried, and realized that she could speak again, too. Yet again, Lindsome heard that scream, that inhuman terror.

"Albion!" someone else called. Emlee, the gaunt old housekeeper. Third floor. The devastation continued up the staircase.

"Get out!" Her uncle. Alive. "Go!"

"No—not when—" A crash.

"Run, damn your miserable old hide! If ever you loved me as I loved you, Albion, then *run!*"

And that scream. That Ghost-forsaken scream.

Lindsome ran, up and up and out, tripping over shredded carpet, torn-down paintings, shattered vases and urns. From around a corner came a ghastly crunch, then booms and bangs, the sound of something mighty hurtling down a staircase.

"No, Marilda!"

Lindsome rounded the corner. The servants' staircase lay before her, walls half-ripped asunder, ichor on the steps.

Lindsome took them one flight down. At the bottom lay the housekeeper's clothes, black with ghostgrease.

"Uncle!" Lindsome wailed. "Uncle, where are you? We have to hide!"

His bedroom. Outside in the hall. Uncle Albion's door was open.

So was the door next to his, the one that had looked rusted shut.

The stench inside was unspeakable. Lindsome fell to the carpet and vomited, despite her empty stomach, hard enough for bile to dribble over her lips. Vivified. An ark of freshly vivified. They had to be stacked to the ceiling, packed like earth in a grave.

But when she looked up, all she saw were briars.

Roses. Thousands upon thousands of roses. Fresh, dried, rotting, trampled, entire bushes of them, as though a giant had uprooted them and brought them in here.

They were woven into a gigantic nest.

In the center sat Thomlin. His eyes were rolled up, showing nothing but white. He grasped his knees to his chest and rocked, like all those windblown, yawning doors, moaning like that wall of rotting flesh. A frothy river of drool dribbled down his chin.

Lindsome did not speak to him. It was clear that Thomlin would never speak again.

The siren song of that inhuman scream rang out, and Lindsome ran out into the hall. She called her uncle's name, shouted it, even, but received no answer.

She ran into his room, searching. The knobs of a rope ladder lay bolted into his windowsill.

"Uncle!" Lindsome peered over the sill. The ladder still wobbled from a recent descent, trailing down into a tight copse of saplings. Lindsome scrambled down. "Uncle Albion! Wait!"

Lightning cut her shadow from the air. The boom that answered split the sky, a rolling bang that made Lindsome squeal and cover her ears. In seconds, its echoes vanished under static, the sound of a million gallons pouring down. Lindsome was immediately soaked. The tatters of her dress slapped at her legs as she ran, and so heavy was the downpour, Lindsome couldn't see.

The path became slick. Lindsome slipped and went sprawling, face-first, and a fallen branch tore a gash in her arm. Lindsome screamed and rolled aside, curling around her wound, blinded by rain and tears.

Get up.

The thing will get you. Get up!

Weeping, squeezing her arm, Lindsome struggled to her feet. She stumbled along a trough of mud. She ripped off a strip of her soaked dress and tried to tie it around her wound to protect it.

A vivified hunting dog lumbered past, Cook's sodden apron hanging from its jaws.

The sky lit up again, illuminating a great gash in the thicket. Uprooted plants, unearthed rocks, and crushed branches paved the way. How dare anyone keep working in the shadow of such horrors? Lindsome yelled for her uncle, for the gardener, for someone and anyone as she stumbled down that fresh avenue, arm throbbing and poorly tied scrap of dress soaking through with red.

No creature hindered her. The fleeing vivifieds had disappeared.

Instead came roses. Thicker and thicker still, the tangled walls burst with roses, like puddles of gore on a battlefield. She moved in a forest of them, boughs bending to enclose the path overhead, their stink so strong not even the downpour could erase it. It was black beneath the boughs, black and dripping. Torn-off petals dribbled down between the branches, sticking to her hair, her hands, her face.

The tunnel turned and opened.

Not even the looming branches of this deadly forest could cover a space so large. The clearing was a pit of trampled thorns and bowed-in walls, canes of briars thrashing in the gusts, petals smeared everywhere like a violent snowfall. It stank of roses and death, water and undeath, and though naked sky arced above this grove of wreckage, the light was not strong enough for Lindsome to understand the pair of shapes that waited at the far end.

But then the lightning came.

Its brilliance bore down, and Lindsome understood even less, though what she saw burned itself into her vision with the force of a dying sun. One was large, impossibly large. A mountain of fur and rot, waiting on trunk-thick limbs, bearing eyes that knew—even if the throat could not speak, even if those ghastly hands could not move with the mastery and grace that memory still begged for.

And one was small. The size of two men, laid end to end.

Lindsome did not know that she kept screaming. There was only feeling, a single feeling of eclipsing terror so hot she felt her own soul struggling to tear free. The pain in her arm disappeared. She felt neither cold nor wet. Only this searing moment, as the small one rolled in its nest of thorns and flailed, as though its soul had never learned to walk.

The mountain of rot took a step forward, until it towered protectively over the wriggling thing below.

It reached out a hand toward Lindsome.

The eclipse reached totality. Lindsome went down, her heartbeat a ringing roar.

"Miss?"

Something struck the front of her thighs with brisk force. Lindsome grunted.

"Miss?"

"Leave her. She's a woodcutter's child, innit? Girl a' the woods?"

"In woods like these? Not on yer hat. An' look at her bleedin' arm, ye piece-wit. That's no small hurt. Miss?"

Lindsome opened her eyes. She was lying on her side in the sodden leaves, at the edge of a nameless road. The earth smelled good, of dirt and wind and water, and the branches of the bare trees overhead swayed and knocked in the bleak sunshine.

Two men stood over her, one holding the reins of a pair of horses. The other held a staff, with which he rapped Lindsome's thighs again.

Lindsome's eyes went to the horses. They were the horses of poor men, witless, subpar animals bought for cheap with zero cost of upkeep: vivifieds.

Lindsome began to cry.

One of the men mounted, and the other placed Lindsome at his comrade's back. She clung to his coat and sobbed as they rode out of the deserted wood.

They asked her questions, but Lindsome did not answer. They rode to the low town of Hume and deposited her on the steps of the orphanage, where kinder, cleaner, better-dressed men and women asked her the same things, but Lindsome only wept. She did not protest when they steered her inside, bathed her, tended her arm, dressed her in worn but clean things, and gave her a bowl of oatmeal and honey. She hardly ate half before falling dead asleep at the table, and barely noticed when a pair of strong, gentle arms lifted her up and placed her upon a cot.

The streets of Hume were buried in the snow of the new year before Lindsome spoke a single word.

· · ·

She had to tell them something. So Lindsome, in the course of explaining who she was and that she did in fact have living parents who might someday appear to fetch her, decided to say that the household of her Great-Uncle Albion had succumbed to a foolish but gruesome accident. He had planned to perform a stitching experiment on a pack of wolves that were not yet dead, Lindsome claimed, and the rest of the household, making heated bets on whether this holy grail of vivology was in fact possible to obtain, had gathered in the laboratory to watch. Lindsome had been spared from the ensuing tragedy because she did not care about the bet and had been playing outside, alone. The constable's men, who went to Apsis House to investigate as soon as the spring thaw came, found evidence to corroborate her story. The interior of Apsis House was torn apart, as if indeed by a pack of infuriated wolves, and not a trace of anyone living could be found.

The spring after that, Lindsome's parents returned, refreshed from travel but baffled and scornful of the personal and legal complications that had evolved in their absence. At the conclusion of the affair, the judge gave them the property deed to Apsis House. They wanted to know what on Earth they were supposed do with such a terribly located, wolf-infested wreck, and told Lindsome that she would have it, when she came of age.

The day she did, Lindsome attempted to sell it, but nobody could be persuaded to buy. She couldn't even give it away. The deed finally sat unused in a drawer in her dressing table, in a far-away city in her far-away grown-up life, next to the tin of cosmetic power she used to cover up a long, ugly scar upon her arm. Her husband, to whom she never told the entire truth, agreed that the property was probably worthless, and never suggested that they visit Long Hill or take any action regarding Apsis House's restoration. Nor did their three daughters, once they were grown enough to be told the family legends about mad Uncle Albion, and old enough to understand that some things are best left where they fall.

And besides—now that Lindsome knew what it was to have and love a child, she couldn't bear to interrupt what might still move up there, within that blooming forest of thorns. If they were both intact, still, the least Lindsome could do was give them their peace; and if they were not, Lindsome could not bear the thought of finding one of them alone, endlessly screaming that desperate, lonely scream, until however long it took for Albion's sturdy handiwork to unravel.

As Chaswick had said, Uncle Albion was a brilliant man.

It could take a very long time.

KJ Kabza has sold over fifty stories to venues such as *The Magazine of Fantasy & Science Fiction, Nature, Daily Science Fiction, Beneath Ceaseless Skies, AE: The Canadian Science Fiction Review, Buzzy Mag, Flash Fiction Online,* and many more. He's been anthologized in *The Best Horror of the Year, The Best of Every Day Fiction,* and *The Best of Beneath Ceaseless Skies.* For updates on and free fiction, follow him on Twitter @KJKabza and peruse www.kjkabza.com.

It was only once he left the Lagoon that he realized how good he'd had it there . . . the murky bottom where he'd nested among the drifting fronds of plants . . . the hidden channel that led to his underground lair . . .

THE CREATURE RECANTS

Dale Bailey

During breaks in shooting, the Creature from the Black Lagoon usually rests in a pond on the studio back lot and dreams of home. The pond isn't much even as ponds go. It's maybe four feet deep at its deepest point and a hundred yards or so around, an abandoned set carved out of the scorched southern California earth for some forgotten film or other: cattails and reeds and occasionally a little arrow of ripples when a dry breeze skates across the surface. Not even a fish if he's feeling peckish. Which he often is. The catering is suspect at the best of times, and it's even more so when you're accustomed to a diet of raw fish and turtle flesh prized living from the shell.

This is Hollywood.

"Don't expect too much," Karloff had advised him over sushi not long after he'd arrived, full of ambition and optimism, and Lugosi, strung out on morphine and methadone by the time the Creature made the scene, had been even more blunt. "They vill fuck you every time," he'd said in that thick Hungarian accent. The both of them typecast by their most famous roles. The Creature had assumed he could beat the odds, but on those blazing afternoons in the pond, now and again scooping up handfuls of water to moisten his gills, he'd begun to reconsider. The water was unkind, perpetually casting his reflection back at him: the bald, barnacle-encrusted skull, the eyes sunk beneath shelves of armored bone, the frills of tissue encasing the gills around his neck. Not what you would call leading-man material.

To think, he'd once been the king of his little world—the vast, dark Lagoon, overhung with the boughs of enormous trees, and the mighty

Amazon itself, where anacondas slithered through the algae-clotted water, caiman slid into the flood without a splash, their tails lashing, and catfish the size of Chevrolets trolled the mossy bottom. Not to mention the jungle, humid, rank, and festering, clamorous with the chitinous roar of millions of insects. And here he was in southern California instead, spending his days in waist-deep water and sleeping his nights in an oversized bathtub in a crummy apartment.

Such are the Creature's thoughts when a member of the crew—it's Bill, a gopher who's trying to break into the biz as a lighting tech—walks down to the pond to tell him that Jack's finished setting up the next shot. It's time for the Creature to come back up to the set and stagger around the deck of the *Rita*—not even a real boat, just a cheap mock-up in one of the soundstages on the Universal lot—and menace Julie Adams for another hour or so. She's a real scream queen, Julie, the genuine article, but she's nice enough in real life; she even walks down to the pond to chat once in a while between set-ups. They're all nice enough. Even Jack's okay, though he's always badgering the Creature to focus on his motivation when the Creature has enough trouble just hitting his marks. To tell the truth, the Creature's heart isn't in it anymore, but he's signed a deal with Universal, and his agent—who rarely returns his calls anyway—tells him there's no way to break the contract.

So the Creature hauls himself out of the pond, and tramps back up to the soundstage, trying not to think about the fact that he could decapitate Bill with a single stroke of his taloned hand. Trying not to think that at some level he wants to.

It wasn't supposed to turn out this way.

You never know happiness until it's gone, that's the way the Creature figures it. The present always seems like a mess. It was only once he left the Lagoon that he realized how good he'd had it there. In Hollywood, he recalls its dark waters with longing. Sometimes at night, his head pillowed on the bottom of his brimming bathtub and his webbed feet slung over either side to brush the peeling vinyl floor, he even dreams of it. How perfect it seems now, the murky bottom where he'd nested for hours among the drifting fronds of plants he cannot name and the hidden channel that led to his rocky underground lair. Armored with scales and impervious to jaguar and piranha alike, the Creature had hunted both the overgrown shores and the black fathoms, snatching spider monkeys screaming from their roosts and feasting on the great fish that slipped through the Lagoon's sulfurous depths. He recalls even his isolation with melancholy regret. What had seemed like loneliness—he'd never known another of his kind—now seemed like autonomy, and when the boat that spelled his expulsion from paradise had first steamed into the lagoon he had approached it with a curiosity that now seemed like folly.

He hadn't planned to leave the Black Lagoon, but life always takes the unexpected turn: caiman poachers in this case, though he hadn't known that then. It had been the boat, anchored in a sun-dappled inlet, that fascinated him. He'd taken it for some kind of novel creature, and because no denizen of the Amazon posed a threat to him—because he pined for novelty in those days—he hadn't given a second thought to approaching the thing. He'd been backstroking along, his face turned to the sun, when it came chugging into the Lagoon, stinking of gasoline. When he saw it, the Creature dove into the sun-spangled water, surfaced in the shadow of the boat, and dragged a talon along its rusting keel. He hadn't seen the net until it was too late. He found himself entangled. Panicked, he began to claw at it. He'd have freed himself had the poachers not reacted so quickly, winching him out of the water even as his talons tore long rents in the ropy mesh.

"My God," one of the poachers screamed, staggering back.

"Jesus, what the hell is that thing?" his companion cried, reaching for a spear gun. (The Creature reconstructed this dialogue only later.) The Creature was thinking the same thing. What could these soft, distorted reflections of his scaly self be, he wondered—

Then the harpoon punctured his shoulder and he stumbled flailing into the water. He'd never felt such agony. By the time he bobbed to the surface, he was unconscious. When he woke he found himself imprisoned behind steel bars.

The poachers weren't dumb—grimy, stubbled, and foul-mouthed—but not dumb. Three times a day, they tossed a fish, still flopping, between the bars of his cage. When they saw him pour his bucket of drinking water over his head, they realized that he needed to moisten his gills regularly. Using a spare gaff, they poked fresh buckets into his pen on the hour. The rest of the time he spent curled in a corner, whimpering. His terror of the boat at first overwhelmed him: the roar of the engine, the stench of his own waste, the curious faces (if you could call such doughy parodies of his own batrachian features faces) staring at him jaws agape from outside his cage. But you can get used to anything. By the time they anchored in the headwaters of Peru, his terror had dwindled to a dull simmer of anxiety.

What next?

He had no concept of the worst possibilities—not then, anyway. He could have been sold to a marine biology institute, where sooner or later scientists would have gotten around to dissecting him to see what made him tick (the Creature's rudimentary knowledge of scientists derives mostly from horror movies; scientists were all mad, as far as he is concerned). He could have been sold to a zoo, and spent the rest of his life paddling around in a wading pool, while small children gawped at him and tossed half-eaten ice cream cones through the bars. These would no doubt have been more profitable avenues. But the caiman poachers weren't anxious to disclose their reasons for cruising the Amazon. So he was sold instead to a carny scout combing the region for freak-show specimens, shipped north, and sold yet again, this time to Southeby & Sons Traveling Carnival, a fly-by-night operation that worked the south-western circuit through the spring and fall, wintering in Gibsonton, Florida, along with most of the other carnies in North America.

And here was happiness again—sort of, anyway—though he didn't recognize it at the time. By then, he'd pretty well been tamed. After he'd raked the shoulder of one of the poachers with his claws, a cattle prod had been brought into play, and three or four applications of *that* had been sufficient to cool his heels. So when he came to Southeby & Sons he'd been pliable enough. Besides, he fit right in with the freaks. They too were unique: the Living Skeleton, the Fat Lady (fat hardly did her justice), Daisy and Violet, the Siamese Twins, and half a dozen others, midgets and bearded ladies and the Monkey Boy: a community of sorts, a family that assuaged the loneliness that had been his lot back home in the Black Lagoon.

What's more, he had a vertical glass aquarium he could call his own, smaller than he might have wished, true, but brimful of water. Southeby billed him as the Gill Man and his sideshow performances were no hardship. He could bob in the green water, or kick to the surface for a breath of rank air (the Monkey Boy wasn't particular in matters of personal hygiene), or even doze if so inclined. Something of a romance—unconsummated, for the Creature's sexual organs, if he had any, were incompatible with those of human beings—blossomed between him and Daisy, much to Violet's dismay, who for unknown reasons took an immediate and abiding dislike of him. It was Daisy who taught him to talk, though his vocal cords, unfit for human speech, rendered his voice guttural and unintelligible to the untutored ear. And there was a kind of freedom during the winters in Gibsonton, this perhaps most precious of all. A simple walk of a mile or so brought him to the beach, and he sometimes lazed for hours in the warm, briny waters of the Gulf.

So he might have passed his life, or at least a longer portion of it, for who could say how long he might yet exist? The Creature had no memory of his birth and growth. He was then as he always had been and might always be. But restlessness possessed him. Violet's inescapable abhorrence was a constant blight on the affection he shared with Daisy, his tank grew cramped, and even his sojourns in the waters of the Gulf too brief, restricted by nine months on the road, burning the lot in one town to set up the next day in another. The midway—the flashing lights of the rides, the alluring chants of the barkers, the sugary reek of cotton candy and funnel cake—grew oppressive.

So when the chance to escape presented itself, in the person of a low-rent Hollywood agent who paused before his tank, the Creature was quick to take it. The agent took the time to decipher his rasping tones, sensed his discontent, and persuaded him to give the silver screen a try. L.A. was close to the beach year round, after all, and the Creature was already in show biz. If stardom didn't suit him, he could always return to the carny circuit. So it was the Creature signed up to be a contract player for Universal. He didn't count on being typecast as, well, the Creature, forever flapping about on his great rubbery feet after one nubile beauty or another, his scaly green arms outstretched. Didn't count on being mistaken for a stunt man in a rubber suit. Didn't count on the bathtub or the crummy apartment.

Most of all he didn't count on Julie Adams.

This is Hollywood.

As Bela Lugosi put it, "They vill fuck you every time."

The Creature has begun to believe that he might be in love with Julie Adams.

"Are you lonely?" she asks him one day down by the pond.

He floats on his back in a stand of cattails, keeping an eye on her through a screen of gently bending stalks. He understands all too well what it's like to be stared at. Every time he strolls outside his apartment, people stare. He's learned to ignore the occasional cries of "Hey, fish man," and no longer stops to explain that he's not a fish, but an amphibian. Yet the mockery has had its effect. The Creature has begun to wonder if there's something cannibalistic about him every time he chomps into a fish taco or spears a sushi roll on a single curved claw—with his webbed fingers, chopsticks and silverware are out of the question. The truth is, that's another reason the Creature has given up on the set's catering: he senses that people would just as soon not see him eat. He's never quite overcome the gastronomic habits of the jungle. He wolfs down his meals, smacks his oversized red lips, chews with his mouth open, gets unsightly gobs of food caught in his fangs. The whole thing is unsightly. The studio has ignored his requests to stock the pond with bluegills and catfish so that he can eat in privacy, and rather than protest—the negligent agent again—the Creature elects to spend his days hungry. He figures it sharpens his hostile motivations in the film; he's become a student of Stanislavsky.

The Creature has, in short, begun to accept the norms of Hollywood. He no longer sees any beauty in his fellow denizens of the freak show (the mere thought of Daisy now repulses him)—but he has very much come to see the beauty in Julie Adams, a tall busty brunette who spends most of her days in their scenes together wearing a white one-piece bathing suit that accentuates her considerable curves. He's not sure that what he feels is love—love is a relatively new concept to him—but he knows that he eagerly anticipates her occasional visits to the pond, that the sound of her voice sets his heart racing, that sometimes he has trouble sleeping nights, and not merely because the bathtub provides no comfortable accommodation for his dorsal ridge. No, he has trouble sleeping because he can't stop thinking of Julie Adams.

Is he lonely? In a word, yes.

But the question begs closer examination. He glides out of the bed of cattails and gives Julie his full attention. Perhaps she's come to suspect his amorous intentions, for she has taken to wrapping herself in a thick white bathrobe before she walks down to the pond. Perhaps she's merely cold. It's hard to know.

"Lonely?" he says, hating his inhuman rasp. He cannot help comparing it to the rich, clear timbre of Richard Carlson, the (let's face it) star of the movie, despite the Creature's eponymous billing. With a languid kick he turns to face Julie. She sits at the edge of the shore, with her knees drawn up and her hands clasped around her legs. The Creature can't help staring at her bare ankles. Lonely? He muses on the question.

"That's right."

"I suppose I haven't really thought about it."

"Well, there are no other Creatures, are there?"

"None that I know of," he says, recalling the splendid isolation of the Lagoon.

"It must be very lonely, then. I wouldn't like to be all alone."

"I'm not alone anymore."

Implying that he has become a companion to the human race in general, and perhaps, hopefully, to Julie in particular.

She doesn't take his meaning. "Sometimes I think we're all alone, every one of us. Do you ever think that?"

The Creature composes his largely immobile features into an expression of tragic acceptance. "I suppose we are," he says. "But if you can find someone to love—"

She interrupts him. "I guess that's true. But it must be especially difficult for you. You're not human, but you're not . . . not human, either, if you see what I mean." She sighs, resting her chin on her knees. "Dick says you're the Missing Link." She seems to be blind to the cruelty of this statement, but the Creature has become as accustomed to this appellation as he is to "Fish Man." If he really thinks about it, he supposes he does stand somewhere between the modern human and his piscine ancestry, but he doesn't much like what this implies about his place on the evolutionary spectrum.

Annoyed, he backstrokes off in a snit, arcs his body gracefully backward, and dives, dragging his armored belly on the muddy bottom of the shallow pond (oh, how he longs for the fathomless depths of the Black Lagoon!) He surfaces to face Julie across the stretch of sun-shot water—only to find her striding back to the soundstage. Bill is waving him in from the water's edge. It must be time to resume shooting. Sighing, the Creature breaststrokes toward shore. Once the scourge of the Amazon, he has been reduced to a bit player in his own story.

For it *is* his story. Or was supposed to be.

History will record it differently—attributing the film's origins to Maurice Zimm, but Zimm did little more than transcribe the Creature's narrative during a series of interviews conducted while the Creature lounged in producer William Alland's swimming pool. That's how the Creature remembers it anyway. He would have pounded out the screenplay himself if he could have. That task fell instead to two inveterate Hollywood journeymen, Harry Essex and Arthur Ross. When the final draft fell into the Creature's hands, he recoiled in disbelief. The caiman poachers had been transformed into intrepid paleontologists, the Black Lagoon into an arena of horrors, the Creature himself—an innocent victim!—into a vicious monster. About the only thing the trio of scribes had managed to do right was add a love interest—otherwise, the Creature thinks, he might never have met Julie Adams.

"I won't do it," the Creature protested. "I'll go back to the carnival. Hell, I'll go back to the Amazon!"

His agent—a balding, mousy little man named Henry Duvall—shook his head dolefully. "You've signed a contract."

"I didn't sign anything," the Creature growled. "I can't even hold a pen."

"I signed *for* you in the presence of two witnesses and a notary public," Duvall replied. "Same difference."

Cue Bela Lugosi.

So the Creature reported to the set as ordered, climbed aboard the *Rita* to terrorize Julie as required, shrank before the virile posturings of Richard Carlson (as required)—and fell in love.

"Love," he tells Karloff, pacing the actor's capacious study. By this time, Karloff has long since settled into stardom. He lives comfortably in L.A. and has steady work, though he's still typecast as a horror icon. Smaller than the Creature expected—the Creature towers a good two feet above him—Karloff in his late sixties remains handsome and slim, his dark hair silvering. Five times married, he is perhaps not the best person to approach for romantic advice, but the Creature's options are limited. His film, the first of a projected trilogy, is not yet completed, much less released, and he is beginning to see that he has been played for a fool. If Boris Karloff can't escape his defining role—if this charming, gentle man still clumps around in the American zeitgeist wearing elevator boots and bolts in his neck—then what hope has the Creature, who cannot even shuck his costume? There are no Oscars in his future, just endless sequels to this initial pack of lies. *Revenge of the Creature. The Creature Walks Among Us.* Even *Abbot and Costello Meet the Creature,* if things go badly enough (or well enough, from Universal's perspective).

"Love?" Karloff says. He leans back in his armchair and steeples his fingers. "Love is always a delicate matter."

"Tell me about it," says the Creature.

"If your love is unrequited"—Karloff retains a trace of his native British accent, a genteel formality—"then there is little you can do."

This is not the advice the Creature sought. This is not advice at all. This is a statement of fact. The Creature has come to suspect that Julie's visits to his pond are little more than kindnesses. After all, he sees the way she looks at Richard Carlson, the way she moistens her lips and gazes up at him in adoration. Carlson is nice enough to him, but nice won't do. While the Creature occasionally daydreams of raking Bill's head off in annoyance, his fantasies of violence toward Carlson burn icy and pure. He would like to kill him slowly, to spear each eyeball upon a talon and pop them into his mouth like jellybeans, to unseam his belly and feed upon the steaming offal, to wrench off his limbs one by one. For a start. The Creature does what he can to repress these unsavory flights of imagination, but they retain a vividness he cannot deny. He may work in a black-and-white 3D horror flick, but his fantasies are projected in widescreen Technicolor. Perhaps this is his true nature, savage and immutable, antediluvian and, yes, appropriate to the Missing Link. You can take the Creature out of the jungle, but you can't take the jungle out of the Creature.

He senses that this is not the way to Julie's heart.

Karloff clears his throat. "You face many obstacles, of course. You are not handsome. You are not human. You have, insofar as you have been able to detect, no potential for procreation. Yet there might be a way."

A way? The Creature pauses. He takes a seat across from Karloff. He'd like to lean back, but his goddamn dorsal ridge is, as always, in the way. Another reminder of his inhumanity. Yet there might be a way past even that.

He is all attention.

"Beauty comes in many forms," Karloff says. "It is, as the expression goes, in the eye of the beholder. But that eye is often best attuned when its object is set against its natural environment."

"What are you saying?"

Now Karloff leans forward. He smiles. "Underwater, my friend. Water is your natural milieu."

True enough. In his pond on the Universal lot, submerged to the waist and ladling up clear freshets with one spade-like hand, the Creature looks ridiculous. In the Black Lagoon, however, he glides through the water with a grace and beauty no man can hope to match. Human beings are no more suited to thrive underwater than he is suited to a purely land-bound existence. Clumsy and ill equipped for a submarine life, they don wet suits that are but sad reflections of his own glistening hide. They have rubber flippers where he has feet, heavy oxygen tanks and re-breathers where he has gills. If he shambles gasping across the Universal lot, his adversary in love will shamble—or anyway flail—beneath the surface. In the water, Carlson's beauty will be but a paltry thing. And while a return to the Black Lagoon is cost-prohibitive, the underwater scenes are scheduled to be filmed in Wakulla Springs, Florida, a return to his beloved Gulf and (yes, he has researched the location shoots) the largest freshwater cave system in the world—if not his beloved Lagoon, the next best thing. Flush with renewed optimism, the Creature thanks Karloff and takes his leave.

The same optimism carries him across the continent, canted awkwardly in his seat—his dorsal ridge; again—and staring out at the blur of the propellers. Halfway through the flight, Julie walks down the aisle to take the seat beside him. She leans past him to look out the window, so close that he can smell the faint lavender scent of her perfume. "Isn't it beautiful?" she says, gazing down at the green hills unscrolling below the streaming scud. "It makes me think of the film."

"How?" says the Creature, who can see no clear connection.

"Well, it seems so deep, you know, so . . . dimensional . . . looking down from up here like this. I imagine the way the audience will experience it when they see us swimming out of the screen like that."

Ah. 3D. If he's been told once he's been told a thousand times. Alland's ambitions for the film hinge upon two factors: the realistic creature effects (which certainly *should* look realistic, the Creature ruminates) and the use of 3D, only the second Universal film to be released in the innovative format. But then he realizes that Julie has dozed off against his shoulder, and he wonders if he too can have a three-dimensioned life.

Wakulla Springs is everything the Creature had hoped it would be. There are shortcomings, to be sure. He could have wished for a more tropical setting—strangler figs, lianas, and buttress-rooted trees—but there is much to be thankful for as well. The alligators slipping into the murky water recall the caiman of the Black Lagoon; the bulky manatees the nine-foot piracuru and catfish that call his native waters home; the boom of insects the constant roar of the jungle. And the springs themselves are fathoms deep and riddled with caverns. Against his better judgment—Julie will think him hardly human at all, he fears—the Creature dispenses with the pretense of his trailer and abandons the on-set catering altogether. Halfway abandons the film, in fact. More often than not, when Jack dispatches Bill to summon the Creature to the set, he's off touring the depths. He explores the cave system in search of a rocky grotto like the one he had in the Amazon. He dozes in deep, cold currents where no human being can follow. He gluts himself on the abundance of prey, devouring fish raw in clouds of ichthyic blood. Life is good, or better anyway, but he is not happy (or if he is, he does not recognize it). Thoughts of Julie torture him like an inflamed scale under a ridge of his armored breast.

Finally, Jack calls him in for a meeting. Like Karloff, Jack is a kind man. Anger is not his natural métier, yet the Creature is forced to stand dripping on the carpet in the director's trailer, listening to his gentle rebuke. Somehow that makes it worse, Jack's generosity of spirit. "I have no choice, you see," the director admonishes him. "We're on a tight schedule. We're not making *Gone With the Wind*, you know."

"It's going to be a good picture," the Creature says.

"I didn't say it wasn't going to be a good picture. I said that we have to make our release date or both our careers are on the line."

"Your career," the Creature rasps. "What kind of career am I likely to have, Jack?"

"You're unique. After people see this picture, offers are going to come rolling in."

"Don't patronize me, Jack. We both know there's only one role I can play."

Jack sighs. "I guess you're right. But still, this is going to be a good film. You'll get to play *this* role again."

The Creature laughs humorlessly, snared in a dilemma even his human colleagues must share, forever trapped in the prisonhouse of self. That's the appeal of acting, he supposes: the chance to be someone else, if only for a little while. And isn't that what he's doing here, playing at being something he's not? He's not a monster. He never has been. If his range of roles is limited—if he is doomed to be the Creature from the Black Lagoon--well that's Hollywood. He thinks of Karloff and Lugosi. Who does he want to become? Does he wish to accept his fate with grace or does he wish to rail perpetually against it, strung out on drugs and bitterness? Is being the Creature any different than being a carnival freak? Yet still he longs for his lost home. How he hates the poachers who have done this to him. He'd like to poke *their* eyeballs out, too. And eat them.

So maybe he's a monster, after all.

"I need you on the set on time," Jack is saying while these thoughts run through the Creature's head. "It's expensive to shoot underwater, especially with the 3D rig. Every time you don't show up when you're supposed to, you cost us money."

"I'm sorry, Jack," the Creature says.

"Look, I know this is hard for you. Nobody ever said acting was easy. Look at Brando. Channel your anger into the role. I need you to be the Creature I know you can be."

The Creature doesn't know quite what Jack means by this. He doesn't even know who—or what—he is anymore. Yet he vows to himself that he will try for something more complex than a B-movie monster—to draw not only upon his fury and resentment, but upon his passion for Julie. He vows to do better.

He does, too.

The Creature shows up promptly as requested. He lingers between shots. He tries to make small talk with the crew. But what is there to say, really? He's an eight-foot amphibian, finned and armored in plates of bone. He could eviscerate any one of them with the twitch of a talon. Monster or not, he is a monster to them.

Not Julie, though, or so he tells himself. Perhaps Karloff is right: set against his natural environment, she seems to recognize his natural grace. Indeed she seems to share it. Unburdened by the clunky scuba tanks the men's roles demand, she glides through the water. And between shots she dispenses with the bathrobe she'd taken to draping herself in on the Universal lot, as if swimming together has drawn them closer. Of all the actors on the set, she alone seems entirely at ease with him. They spend more and more time talking. As he lolls in the shallows, she tells him about her recent divorce and about growing up in Arkansas; she tells him about her first days in Hollywood, working as a secretary and taking voice lessons on the side. Yet she is still capable of blind cruelty.

"You're lucky," she says. "You never had to fight for your dreams."

The Creature hardly knows how to respond. So what if Universal picked him up the minute William Alland laid eyes on him? Unlike Julie, he'll never play another role in his life; all the elocution lessons in the world won't change his inhuman growl. He's not even sure what he aspires to anymore. Stardom? Freedom? A return to the Black Lagoon? In his dreams, he sweeps Julie into his embrace, carries her off to the Amazon, unveils to her the wonders of his vanished life: the splendid isolation of the Lagoon, the sluggish currents of the great river, the mystery of the crepuscular forest.

Maybe this newfound intimacy accounts for the otherworldly beauty of the Wakulla scenes. In the dailies, Julie cuts the surface, her white bathing suit shining down through the gloom like god light. The Creature stalks her from below, half-hidden among drifting fronds of thalassic flora, rapt by her ethereal beauty. His webbed hands cleave the water. Bubbles erupt skyward with his every kick. As she swims, he glides toward her from below, up, up, up, until he is swimming on his back beneath her and closing fast: a dozen feet, half a dozen, less, his immovable face frozen in an expression of impossible longing. He reaches out a tentative hand to brush her ankle as she treads water—and pulls it away at the last moment, as terrified of her rejection on celluloid as he is terrified of her rejection in life. What one does not risk, one cannot lose; worse yet, he thinks, what one does not risk, one cannot gain. A sense of inconsolable despair seizes him. In the images projected on the screen, he sees now how little their worlds can connect. She is a creature of the daylit skin of the planet, he of the shadowy submarine depths.

Jack praises the silent yearning in the Creature's performance.

Yet the whole thing drives the director crazy nonetheless. Frustrated by the task of stitching the haunting underwater scenes together with the mundane L.A footage, he asks the studio for reshoots and is denied. For the first time—

the only time—the Creature sees Jack angry, his face a mask of fury. "This could be so much more than another goddamn monster flick," he says in the dim projection trailer, flinging away the 3D glasses perched on his nose. Even this angry gesture drives home the Creature's inhumanity. Alone in the back row, he must pinch his glasses between two delicate claws. His flattened nose provides no bridge to support them. He has no external ears to hook them over. Everything about him is streamlined for his underwater existence.

The Creature grinds his cardboard glasses under one webbed foot. He slams out of the trailer, the door crumpling with a screech of tortured metal as he hurtles into the moonlit night. He is halfway to the water when Julie catches up with him. "Wait," she says, "Wait—"

Her voice hitches in the place where his name ought to be—for of course he has no name, does he? He is the Creature, the Gill Man, nothing more. There has been no one to name him—even the freaks did not name him— and he has never thought to name himself. He would not know how to begin. Fred? John? Earl? Such human names fall leaden on the tongue, inadequate to describe a . . . a creature, a fiend, an inhuman monster. How will they credit him in the film? *The Creature as the Creature*?

"Wait," Julie says again. "Creature, wa—"

The Creature whirls to face her, one massive hand drawn back to strike.

"Don't," she whispers, and the Creature checks the blow. For an instant, everything hangs balanced on a breath. Then the Creature lowers his hand, turns away, and shambles toward the water, his great feet flapping. Something feels broken inside him. Jack's words—

—*another goddamn monster flick*—

—echo inside his head. That's all he is, isn't he? A monster. A monster who in a moment of fury, would have with a single swipe of his claws torn from her shoulders the head of the woman he loved. A monster who would in the grip of his rage, feed upon her blood. The Creature would cry, but even that simple human solace is denied him. The dark waters beckon.

"Wait," Julie says. "Please."

Almost against his will, the Creature turns to face her. She stands maybe a dozen feet away. In the moonlight, tears glint upon her cheeks. Beyond her, the men—Jack and Dick and Richard Denning, the third lead—stand silhouetted against the beacon of golden light pouring through the trailer's shattered door.

"Why?" the Creature says, knowing the doom that will come upon him if he stays.

"Because," Julie says, "because I love you."

So Karloff was right. For a heartbeat, happiness—a great and abiding contentment that no mere human being can plumb—settles over the Creature like a benediction. But what is the depth of love, he wonders, its strange currents and dimensions? What is its price, and is he willing to pay it? And a line from another monster movie comes to him, one that Jack showed him in pre-production: *It was beauty killed the beast.*

This is Hollywood.

It vill fuck you every time.

"I love you, too," he says in his inhuman rasp, and in the same instant, in his heart, he recants that love, refuses and renounces it. For Julie. For himself. He will not be the monster that loves. He will not be the monster that dies. He will not be their freak, their creature. He will not haunt their dreams. They can finish their fucking film with a man in a rubber suit.

The Creature puts his back to Julie and wades into the water, glimmering with moonlight. It welcomes him home, rising to his shins and thighs before the bottom drops away beneath him, and he dives. He has studied the locations, he has explored the Springs' network of caverns: from here the Wakulla River to the Saint. Marks and Apalachee Bay, and thence to the Gulf. The Black Lagoon calls out to him across the endless miles, and so the Creature strikes off for home, knowing now how fleeting are the heart's desires, knowing that Julie too would ebb into memory, this perfect moment lost, this happiness receding forever into the past.

Dale Bailey lives in North Carolina with his family, and has published three novels, *The Fallen, House of Bones,* and *Sleeping Policemen* (with Jack Slay, Jr.), as well as a collection of short fiction, *The Resurrection Man's Legacy and Other Stories.* He has been a four-time finalist for the International Horror Guild Award, a two-time finalist for the Nebula Award, and a finalist for the Bram Stoker and the Shirley Jackson awards. His fiction has appeared in *Alchemy, Amazing Stories, Asimov's, Clarkesworld, The Magazine of Fantasy & Science Fiction, Lightspeed, Nightmare, SciFiction, and Tor.com,* among other places. "Death and Suffrage," his award-winning novelette, was adapted by director Joe Dante as part of the television series, *Masters of Horror.* He has two books due out in 2015, *The End of the End of Everything: Stories* and *Acheron: A City in Seven Stories.*

What is in you is ancient as the black tar between stars.
A void that howls in hunger and mindless antipathy
against the heat of the living.

TERMINATION DUST

❯❯➤

Laird Barron

Let be be finale of seem.
—Wallace Stevens

Hunting in Alaska, especially as one who enjoys the intimacy of knives, bludgeons, and cords, is fraught with peril. Politically speaking, the difference between a conservative and a liberal in the forty-ninth state is the caliber of handgun one carries. Le sigh. Despite a couple of close calls, you've not been shot. Never been shot, never been caught, knock on wood.

That's what you used to say, in any event.

People look at you every day. People look at you every day, but they don't see you. People will ask why and you will reply, Why not?

Tyson Langtree's last words: "I tell you, man. Andy Kaufman is alive, man. He's alive, bigger than shit, and cuttin' throats. He's Elvis, man. He's the king of death." This was overheard at the packed Caribou Creek Tavern on a Friday night about thirty seconds before bartender Lonnie DeForrest tossed his sorry ass out onto a snowbank. Eighteen below zero Fahrenheit and a two and a half mile walk home. Dead drunk, wearing coveralls and a Miners Do It Deeper *ball cap.*

Nobody's seen the old boy since. Deputy Newcastle found a lot of blood in Langtree's bed, though. Splattered on the walls and ceiling of his shack on Midnight Road. Hell of a lot of blood. That much blood and no corpse, well, you got to wonder, right? Got to wonder why Langtree didn't just keep his mouth shut.

Everybody knows Andy Kaufman is crazy as a motherfucker. He been whacking motormouth fools since '84.

You were in the bar that night and you followed Langtree back to his humble abode. Man, he was surprised to see you step from the shadows.

For the record, his last words were actually, "Please don't kill me, E!"

Jessica Mace lies in darkness, slightly drunk, wholly frustrated. Heavy bass thuds through the ceiling from Snodgrass' party. She'd left early and in a huff after locking horns with Julie Vellum, her honorable enemy since the hazy days of high school. Is hate too strong an emotion to describe how she feels about Julie? Nope, hatred seems quite perfect, although she's long since forgotten why they are at eternal war. Vellum—what kind of name is that, anyhow? It describes either ancient paper or a sheepskin condom. The bitch is ridiculous. Mobile home trash, bottom drawer sorority sister, tits sliding toward earth with a vengeful quickness. Easiest lay of the Last Frontier. A whore in name and deed.

JV called *her* a whore and splashed a glass of beer on her dress. Cliché, bitch, so very cliché. Obviously JV hadn't gotten the memo that Jessica and Nate were through as of an hour prior to the party. The evil slut had carried a torch for him since he cruised into town with his James Dean too-cool-for school shtick and set all the girlies' hearts aflutter a few weeks before the Twin Towers crumbled a continent away.

Snodgrass, Wannamaker, and Ophelia, the beehive-hairdo lady from 510, jumped between them before the fur could fly. Snodgrass was an old hand at breaking up fist fights. Lucky for Julie, too. Jessica made up her mind to fix that girl's wagon once and for all, had broken a champagne glass for an impromptu weapon when Snodgrass locked her in a bear hug. Meanwhile, Deputy Newcastle stood near the wet bar, grimly shaking his huge blond head. Or it might've been the deputy's evil twin, Elam. Hard to tell through the crush of the crowd, the smoke, and the din. If she'd seen him with his pants down, she'd have known with certainty.

Here she is after the fracas, sulking while the rest of town let down its hair and would continue to do so deep into the night. Gusts from the blizzard shake the building. Power comes from an emergency generator in the basement. However, cable is on the fritz. She would have another go at Nate, but Nate isn't around, he is gone-Johnson after she'd told him to hit the bricks and never come back no more, no more. Hasty words uttered in fury, a carbon copy of her own sweet ma who'd run through half the contractors and fishermen in the southeast during a thirty year career of bar fights and flights from the law. Elizabeth Taylor of the Tundra, Ma. Nate, an even poorer man's Richard Burton. Her father, she thought of nevermore.

Why hadn't Nate been at the party? He *always* made an appearance. Could it be she's really and truly broken his icy heart? Good!

She fumbles in the bedside drawer, pushing aside the cell charger, Jack's photograph, the revolver her brother Elwood gave her before he got shredded by a claymore mine in Afghanistan, and locates the "personal massager" she ordered from Fredericks of Hollywood and has a go with that instead. Stalwart comrade, loyal stand-in when she's between boyfriends and lovers, Buzz hasn't let her down yet.

Jessica opens her eyes as the mattress sags. A shadow enters her blurry vision. She smells cologne or perfume or hairspray, very subtle and totally androgynous. Almost familiar. Breathless from the climax it takes her a moment to collect her wits.

She says, "Jack, is that you?" Which was a strange conclusion, since Jack presumably drifts along deep sea currents, his rugged redneck frame reduced to bones and sweet melancholy memories. All hands of the *Prince Valiant* lost to Davey Jones's Locker, wasn't it? That makes three out of the four main men of her life dead. Only Nate is still kicking. Does he count now that she's banished him to a purgatory absent her affection?

Fingers clamp her mouth and ram her head into the pillow hard enough that stars shoot everywhere. Her mind flashes to a vivid image: Gothic oil paintings of demons perched atop the bosoms of swooning women. So morbidly beautiful, those antique pictures. She thinks of the pistol in the dresser that she might've grabbed instead of the vibrator. Too late baby, too late now.

A knife glints as it arcs downward. Her attacker is dressed in black so the weapon appears to levitate under its own motive force. The figure slashes her throat with vicious inelegance. An untutored butcher. It is cold and she tastes the metal. But it doesn't hurt.

Problem is, constant reader, you can't believe a damned word of this story. The killer could be anyone. Cops recovered some bodies reduced to charcoal briquettes. Two of those charred corpses were never properly identified, and what with all the folks who went missing prior to the Christmas party . . .

My life flashed before my eyes as I died of a slashed throat and a dozen other terrible injuries. My life, the life of countless others who were in proximity.

Wasn't pretty, wasn't neat or orderly, or linear. I experienced the fugue as an exploding kaleidoscope of imagery. Those images replay at different velocities, over and over in a film spliced together out of sequence. My hell is to watch a bad horror movie until the stars burn out.

I get the gist of the plot, but the nuances escape into the vacuum. The upshot being that I know hella lot about my friends and neighbors; just not everything. Many of the juiciest details elude me as I wander Purgatory, reliving a life of sin. Semi-omniscience is a drag.

In recent years, some pundits have theorized I was the Eagle Talon Ripper. Others have raised the possibility it was Jackson Bane, that he'd been spotted in San Francisco months after the *Prince Valiant* went down, that he'd been overheard plotting bloody revenge against me, Jessica, a dozen others. Laughable, isn't it? The majority of retired FBI profilers agree.

Nah, I'm the hot pick these days. Experts say the trauma I underwent in Moose Valley twisted my mind. Getting shot in the head did something to my brain. Gave me a lobotomy of sorts. Except instead of going passive, I turned into a monster, waited twenty-plus years, and went on a killing spree.

It's a sexy theory what with the destroyed and missing bodies, mine included. The killer could've been a man or woman, but the authorities bet on a man. Simple probability and the fact some of the murders required a great deal of physical strength and a working knowledge of knots and knives. I fit the bill on all counts. There's also the matter of my journal. Fragments of it were pieced together by a forensics team and the shit in there could be misconstrued. What nobody knows is that after the earlier event in Moose Valley, I read a few psychology textbooks. The journal was just therapy, not some veiled admission of guilt. Unfortunately, I was also self-medicating with booze and that muddied the waters even more.

Oh, well. What the hell am I going to do about it now?

If you ask me, Final Girl herownself massacred all those people. What's my proof? Nothing except instinct. Call me a cynic—it doesn't seem plausible a person can survive a gashed throat and still possess the presence to retrieve a pistol, in the dark, no less, and plug the alleged killer to save the day. How convenient that she couldn't testify to the killer's identity on account of the poor lighting. Even more convenient how that fire erased all the evidence. In the end, it's her word, her version of events.

Yeah, it's a regular cluster. Take the wrong peg from this creaky narrative and the whole log pile falls on you. Nonetheless, you know. You know.

What if . . . What if they were in it together?

• • •

Nights grow long in the tooth. A light veil of snow descends the peaks. Termination dust, the sourdoughs call it. You wait and watch for signs. Geese fly backwards in honking droves, south. Sunsets flare crimson, then fade to black as fog rolls over the beach. People leave the village and do not return. A few others never left but are gone just the same. They won't be returning either.

The last of the cruise ships migrated from Eagle Talon on Saturday. The Princess Wing blared klaxons and horns and sloshed up the channel in a shower of streamers and confetti, its running lights blazing holes through the mist. A few hardy passengers in red and yellow slickers braved the drizzle to perch along the rails. Some waved to the dockworkers. Others cheered over the rumble of the diesels. Seagulls bobbed aloft, dark scraps and tatters against the low clouds that always curtain this place.

You mingled with the people on the dock and smiled at the birds, enjoying their faint screams. Only animals seem to recognize what you are. You hate them too. That's why you smile, really. Hate keeps you warm come the freeze.

Ice will soon clog the harbor. Jagged mountains encircle the village on three sides in a slack-jawed Ouroboros. The other route out of town is a two-mile tunnel that opens onto the Seward Highway. This tunnel is known as the Throat. Anchorage lies eighty miles north, as the gull flies. Might as well be the moon when winter storms come crashing in on you. Long-range forecasts call for heavy snow and lots of wind. There will come a day when all roads and ways shall be impassable.

You've watched. You've waited. Salivated.

You'll retreat into the Estate with the sheep. It's a dirty white concrete superstructure plonked in the shadow of a glacier. Bailey Frazier & Sons built the Frazier Estate Apartments in 1952 along with the Frazier Tower that same year. History books claim these were the largest buildings in Alaska for nearly three decades, and outside of the post office, cop shop, library, little red schoolhouse, the Caribou Tavern, and a few warehouses, that's it for the village proper. Both were heavily damaged by the '64 quake and subsequent tsunami. Thirteen villagers were swept away on the wave. Four more got crushed in falling debris. The Tower stands empty and ruined to this day, but the Estate is mostly functional; a secure, if decrepit, bulwark against the wilderness.

You are an earthquake, a tidal wave, a mountain of collapsing stone, waiting to happen. You are the implacable wilderness personified. What is in you is ancient as the black tar between stars. A void that howls in hunger and mindless antipathy against the heat of the living.

Meanwhile, this winter will be business as usual. Snowbirds flee south to California and Florida while the hardcore few hunker in dim apartments like animals in burrows and play cribbage or video games, or gnaw yourselves bloody with regret. You'll read, and drink, and fuck. Emmitt Snodgrass will throw his annual winter gala. More drinking and even more fucking, but with the sanction of costume and that soul-warping hash Bobby Aickman passes around. By spring, the survivors will emerge, pale as moles, voracious for light as you are for the dark.

With the official close of tourist season, Eagle Talon population stands at one hundred and eighty-nine full-time residents. Three may be subtracted from that number, subtracted from the face of the earth, in fact, although nobody besides the unlucky trio and you know anything about that.

Dolly Sammerdyke. Regis and Thora Lugar. And the Lugars' cat, Frenchy. The cat died hardest of them all. Nearly took out your eye. Maybe that will come back to haunt you. The devil's in the . . .

Elam Newcastle is interviewed by the FBI at Providence Hospital. He has survived the Frazier Estate inferno with second degree burns and frostbite of his left hand. Two fingers may have to be amputated and the flesh of his neck and back possess the texture of melted wax. In total, a small price to pay considering the hell-on-Earth-scenario he's escaped. His New Year's vow is to find a better trade than digging ditches.

He tells the suit what he knows as the King of Pop hovers in the background, partially hidden by curtains and shadows. This phantom, or figment, has shown up regularly since the evening of the massacre at the Estate. Elam is not a fan and doesn't understand why he's having this hallucination of the singer grinning and gesticulating with that infamous rhinestone-studded glove. It is rather disturbing. Doubly disturbing since it's impossible to attribute it to the codeine.

The investigator blandly reveals how the local authorities have recently found Elam's twin brother deceased in the Frazier Tower. It was, according to the account, a gruesome spectacle, even by police standards. The investigator describes the scene in brief, albeit vivid, detail.

Elam takes in this information, one eye on the moonwalking apparition behind the FBI agent. Finally, he says, "Whaddaya mean they stole his hat?"

Scenes from an apocalypse:

Viewed from the harbor, Eagle Talon is an inkblot with a steadily brightening dot of flame at its heart. The Frazier Estate Apartments have been set ablaze. Meanwhile, the worst blizzard to hit Alaska since 1947 rages on. Flames leap from the upper stories, whipped by the wind. Window glass shatters. Fire, smoke, and driving snow boil off into outer darkness. That faint keening is either the shrieks of the damned as they roast in the penthouse, or metal dissolving like Styrofoam as the inferno licks it to ash. Or both.

Men and women in capes and masks, gossamer wings and top hats, mill in the icy courtyard. Their shadows caper in the bloody glare. They are the congregants of a frigid circle of Hell, summoned to the Wendigo's altar. They join hands and begin to waltz. Flakes of snow and ash cover them, bury them.

The angry fire is snapping yellow. Pull farther out into the cold and the dark and fire becomes red through the filter of the blizzard, then shivers to black. Keep pulling back until there are no stars, no fire, no light of any kind. Only the snow sifting upward from the void to fill the world with silence and sleep.

We make love with the lights off. The last time, I figure. She calls me Jack when she comes and probably has no idea. Jackson Bane died on the Bering Sea two winters gone. His ghost makes itself known. He knocks stuff over to demonstrate he's unhappy, like when I'm fucking his former girlfriend. Not hard to imagine him raving impotently behind the wall of sleep, working himself toward a splendorous vengeance. Perhaps that makes him more of a revenant.

My name is Nathan Custer. I fear the sea. Summertime sees me guiding tours on the glacier for Emmitt Snodgrass. Winter, I lie low and collect unemployment. Cash most of those checks down at the Caribou. Laphroaig is my scotch of choice and it's a choice I make every livelong day, and twice a day once snow flies. Hell of an existence. I fought with Jack at Emmitt Snodgrass' annual winter party in '07. Blacked his eye and demolished a coffee table. Don't even recall what precipitated the brawl. I only recall Jessica in a white tee and cotton shorts standing there with a bottle of Lowenbrau in her hand. Snodgrass forgave me the mess. We never patched it up, Jack and I.

Too late, now. Baby, it's too late.

While Jessica showers, I prowl her apartment naked, peering into cupboards and out the window at snowflakes reflected in a shaft of illumination pitched by the twin lamps over the lobby foyer. Ten feet beyond the Estate wall lies a slate of nothingness. Depending on the direction, it's either sea ice and, eventually, open black water, or mountains. This is five-oh-something in the p.m., December. Sun has been down for half an hour.

"What are you doing?" Jessica, head wrapped in a towel, strikes a Venus pose in the bathroom doorway. The backlighting lends her a halo. She's probably concerned about the butcher knife I pulled from the cutlery block. Wasn't quick enough to hide it behind my leg. Naked guy with a knife presents an environmental hazard even if you don't suspect him of being a homicidal maniac, which she might.

"Getting ready for the party," I say, disingenuous as ever.

"Yeah, you look ready." She folds her arms. She thinks I've been using again; it's in her posture. "What the hell, Nate?"

Unfortunately for everyone, I'm not an outwardly articulate man. I'm my father's son. Mom didn't hate his guts because he slapped her at the '88 Alaska State Fair; she hated him because he refused to argue. When the going got shouty, Dad was a walker-awayer. I realize, here in my incipient middle age, that his tendency to clam up under stress wasn't from disrespect. He simply lost his ability to address the women in his life coherently.

"Uh," is what I come up with. Instead of, *Baby, I heard a noise. Somebody was trying the door. Swear to God, I saw the knob jiggle.* I don't have the facility to ask her, *If I was jacked up, wouldn't you have noticed it while we were in bed?* More than anything, I want to tell her of my suspicions. Something is terribly wrong in our enclave. People are missing. Strange shadows are on the move and I have a feeling the end is near for some of us.

"Jesus. Cal's right. He's right. The bastard is right. My god."

"Cal's right? He's not right. What did he say?" Add Building Superintendent Calvin Wannamaker to my little black book of hate. I grip the knife harder, am conscious of my oversized knuckles and their immediate ache. Arthritis, that harbinger of old age and death, nips at me.

"Hit the road, Jack." She points the Finger of Doom, illustrating where I should go. Presumably Hell lies in that general direction.

Maybe I can bulldoze through this scene. "That makes twice you called me Jack today. We have to get ready for the party. Where the hell are my pants?" I look everywhere but directly into the sun that is her gaze.

"You've lost your damned mind," she says in a tone of wonderment, as if waking from a long, violent dream and seeing everything for how it really is. "You need to leave."

"The party. My pants."

"Find another pair. Goodbye. And put that back. It was a present. From Jack!" She's hollering now.

"Wait a second . . . Are you and Cal—"

"Shut your mouth and go."

I put the cleaver in the block, mightily struggling to conjure the magic words to reverse the course of this shipwreck. This isn't love, but it's the best thing I've had in recent memory. No dice. Naked guy hurled from the nest by his naked girlfriend. This is trailer park drama. Julie Vellum will cream over the details once the gossip train gets chugging. Maybe, just maybe, I'll throw a fuck into her. Ah, sweet revenge, hey? The prospect doesn't thrill me, for some reason. I walk into the hall and lurk there a while, completely at a loss. I press the buzzer twice. Give up when there's no answer, and start the long, shameful trudge to my apartment.

The corridors of the Estate are gloomy. Tan paneled walls and muddy recessed lights spaced far enough apart it feels like you're walking along the bottom of a lake. The effect is heightened due to the tears in my eyes. By the time I get to the elevator, I'm freezing. The super keeps this joint about three degrees above an ice-locker.

"Nate!" The whisper is muted and sexless. A shadow materializes from behind the wooden statue of McKinley Frazier that haunts this end of the fifth floor. It's particularly murky here because the overhead has been busted. A splinter of glass stabs my bare foot. I'm hopping around, trying to cover my balls and also act naturally.

"Nate, hold still, pal." Still whispering. Whoever it is, they're in all black and they've got a hammer.

Oh, wait, I recognize this person. I'm convinced it's impossible that this could be happening to me for the second time in twenty years. This isn't even connected to that infamous Moose Valley slaughter. It's like winning top prize in a sweepstakes twice in one's lifetime. Why me, oh gods above and below? I'm such a likeable guy. Kurt Russell wishes he was as handsome as I am. So much to live for. Living looks to be all done for me.

The hammer catches the faint light. It gleams and levitates.

"What are you going to do with that?" I say. It's a rhetorical question.

Jessica Mace can't actually speak when the feds interview her. She's still eating through tubes. The wound at her neck missed severing the carotid by a millimeter. She scribbles curt responses to their interrogation on a portable whiteboard. Her rage is palpable, scarcely blunted by exhaustion and painkillers.

Ma'am, after this individual assaulted you in bed, what happened?

Came to. Choking on blood. Alive. Grabbed gun. Heard noises from living room. The killer had someone in a chair and was torturing them.

Who was in the chair?

Nate Custer.

Nathan Custer?

I think so. Yes.

Did you see the suspect's face?

No.

Approximately how tall was the suspect?

I don't know. Was dark. Was bleeding out. Confused.

Right. But you saw something. And you discharged your firearm.

Yes. It was him. I'm sure.

Him?

Him, her. The killer. My vision was blurry. They were a big, fuzzy shadow.

Are you admitting that you fired your weapon multiple times at . . . at a shadow?

No. I shot a goddamned psycho five times and killed him dead. You're welcome.

How can you be certain, Ms. Mace?

Maybe I can't. Killer could've been anyone. Could *be* anyone. The doctor. The nurse. Maybe it was you. YOU look fucking suspicious.

Calvin Wannamaker and his major domo Hendricks are bellied up to the bar at the Caribou Tavern for their weekly confab. They've already downed several rounds.

DeForrest is polishing glasses and watching the new waitress's skirt cling in exactly the right places as she leans over table No. 9 to flirt with big Luke Tucker. Tucker is a longshoreman married to a cute young stay-at-home mom named Gladys. Morphine is playing "Thursday" on the jukebox while the village's resident Hell's Angel, Vince Diamond, shoots pool against himself. VD got paroled from Goose Bay Correctional Facility last month. He has spent nineteen of his forty-eight years in various prisons. His is the face of an axe murderer. His left cheek is marred by a savage gash, freshly scabbed. Claims he got the wound in a fight with his newest old lady. Deputy Newcastle has been over to their apartment three times to make peace.

The bar is otherwise unoccupied.

"Found a dead cat in the bin." Wannamaker lights a cigarette. A Winston. It's the brand that he thinks best suits his Alaska image. He prefers Kools, alas. "Neck was broke, eyes buggin' out. Gruesome." The super loves cats. He keeps three Persians in his suite on the first floor. He's short and thin and wears a round bushy beard and plaid sweaters, or if it's a special occasion, black turtlenecks. Hendricks started calling him "Cat Piss Man" behind his back and the name kind of stuck. Neither man was born in Alaska. Wannamaker comes from New York, Hendricks from Illinois. They've never adjusted to life on the frontier. They behave like uneasy foreigners in their own land.

"Oh, yeah?" Hendricks says with a patent couldn't-give-a-shit-less tone. No cat lover, Hendricks. *Don't like cats, love pussy,* he's been quoted time and again. He's taller than Wannamaker, and broad-shouldered. Legend says he worked for the Chicago Outfit before he got exiled to Alaska. Everyone considers him a goon and that's a fairly accurate assessment.

"Floyd found it, I guess is what I mean," Wannamaker says.

Floyd is the chief custodian and handyman for the Estate. He was also a train-hopping hobo for three decades prior to landing the Estate gig.

"The hell was Floyd doing in the bin?"

"Makin' a nest. Divin' for pearls. I dunno. He found a dead cat is all I know. Thinks it belonged to the Lugars. They split ten days ago. Must a been in a rush, cause they locked their doors and dropped the keys in my box without so much as a by your leave. Earlier and earlier every year, you know that? I don't get why they even make the trip anymore. I get three or four calls a day, people looking for an apartment. At least."

Hendricks sips his beer. He doesn't say anything. He too is checking out the posterior of Tammy, the new girl.

"Yeah, exactly." Wannamaker nods wisely in response to some ghost of a comment. "I hate snowbirds. Hate. Too cheap to pack their old cat and ship him to Florida. What's Lugar do? Snaps the poor critter's neck and dumps him in the garbage. Bah. Tell you what I'm gonna do, I'm gonna file a report with Newcastle. Sic the ever lovin' law on that sick jerk. Shouldn't have a cat. If he didn't own his apartment I'd yank his lease faster than you can spit."

Hendricks pushes his bottle aside. "That's a weird story."

"Lugar's a weird dude. He sells inflatable dolls and whatcha call 'em, body pillows."

"Is that what he does?"

"Oh, yeah, man. He flies to Japan every so often and wines and dines a bunch of CEOs in Tokyo. They're nuts for that stuff over there."

"Huh. I figured he'd be retired. Guy's gotta be pushing seventy."

"I guess when you love what you do it ain't work."

Words to live by.

• • •

Last words of Mark Ferro, aged thirty-three as he is executed by lethal injection for a homicide unrelated to the Frazier Estate Massacre: "It was meeeeeee!"

You've exercised a certain amount of restraint prior to the blizzard. That's over. Now, matters will escalate. While everybody else has gathered upstairs for Snodgrass' annual bash, you sneak away to share a special moment with Nathan Custer.

Does it hurt when I do this? *It's a rhetorical question.*

You don't expect Custer can hear you after you popped his eardrums with a slot screwdriver. Can't see you either. Blood pumps from the crack in his skull. Smack from a ball peen hammer took the starch right out of our hero. He coughs bubbles. Don't need tongue or teeth to blow bubbles, though it helps.

It may not even be Custer under that mask of gore. Could be Deputy Newcastle or Hendricks. Shit, could be that arrogant little prick Wannamaker at this rate. True story, you've fantasized about killing each of them so often that the lines might well be erased.

Except, haven't you wanted to end your existence? Sure you have. You'd love nothing more than to take your own miserable head off with a cleaver, string your own guts over the tree the way those cheap Victorian saps strung popcorn before Christmas went electric.

This is where it gets very, very confusing.

For a lunatic moment you're convinced it's you, slumped there, mewling like a kitten, soul floating free and formless while an angel of vengeance goes to work on your body with hammer and tongs. Yeah, maybe it's you in the chair and Custer, or Newcastle, or Wannamaker, has been the killer all along. It ain't pretty, having one's mind blown like this.

You were certain it was Custer when you put him in the chair, but that was a long time ago. So much has changed since then. The continents have drifted closer together, the geography of his features has altered for the worse. It's gotten dark. There's the storm and your sabotage of the reserve generator to thank. You've gathered wool and lost the plot. Can't even remember why you'd reserve special tortures for this one.

Why are your hands so fascinating all of the sudden?

Oh, Jesus, what if Snodgrass spiked the punch? He'd once threatened to dose his party-goers with LSD. Nobody took him seriously. But, what if? That would explain why the darkness itself has begun to shine, why your nipples are hard as nail-heads, why you've suddenly developed spidey-sense. Oh, Emmitt Snodgrass, that silly bastard; his guts are going to get extracted through his nose, and soon.

You detect the creak of a loose board and turn in time to see a snub-nosed revolver extending from a crouched silhouette. A lady's gun, so sleek and petite. Here's a flash of fire from the barrel that reveals the bruised face of the final girl. Don't she know you're invulnerable to lead? Didn't she read the rules inside the box top? Problem is, it's another sign that your version of reality is shaky, because you are sure as hell that you killed her already. Sliced her throat, ear to lovely ear. Yet, here she is, blasting you into Kingdom Come with her itty-bitty toy pistol. What the fuck is up with that?

Double tap. Triple, dipple, quadruple tap. Bitch ain't taking any chances, is she? You're down, sprawled next to your beloved victim, whoever he is. Your last. The final girl done seen to that, hasn't she?

Custer, is that you? you ask the body in the chair. He don't give anything away, only grins at you through the blood. Luckily you're made of sterner stuff. Four bullets isn't the end. You manage to get your knees and elbows underneath you for a lethal spring in the penultimate frame of the flick of your life, the lunge where you take the girl into your arms and squeeze until her bones crack and her tongue protrudes. When you're done, you'll crawl away to lick your wounds and plot the sequel. Four shots ain't enough to kill the very beating heart of evil.

Turns out, funny thing, the final girl has one more bullet. She hobbles over and puts it in your head.

Well, shit—

"Christ on a pony, what are you *dooo-ing*?" This plaintive utterance issues from Eliza Overstreet's ripe mouth. She's dressed as a cabaret dancer or Liza Minnelli, or some such bullshit. White, white makeup and sequins and tights. A tight, tight wig cropped as a Coptic monk's skullcap. All *sparkly*.

Emmitt Snodgrass cackles and pops another tab of acid. The rest of the batch he crushes into the rich red clot of punch in a crystal bowl shaped as a furious eagle. The furious eagle punch bowl is courtesy of Luke Tucker, collector of guns, motorcycles, and fine crystal. The suite is prepared—big Christmas tree, wall-to-wall tinsel, stockings and disco balls hung with care. Yeah, Snodgrass is ready for action, Jackson.

Eliza gives him a look. "Everybody is going to drink that!"

He grabs her ass and gives it a comforting squeeze. "Hey, hey, baby. Don't worry. This shit is perfectly safe to fry."

"But it's all we've got, you crazy sonofabitch!"

The doorbell goes ding-dong and the first guests come piling in from the hallway. It will be Bob Aickman, bare-assed and goggle-eyed on acid, who will eventually trip over the wires that cause the electrical short that starts the tragic fire that consumes the top three floors of the Estate.

Deputy Newcastle operates two official vehicles: an eleven-year-old police cruiser with spider web cracks in the windshield and a bashed in passenger side door, and an Alpine snowmobile that, by his best estimate, was likely manufactured during the 1980s. Currently, he's parked in the cruiser on Main Street across from the condemned hulk that is the Frazier Tower. The sun won't set for another forty-five minutes, give or take, but already the shadows are thick as his wife's blueberry cobbler. It's snowing and blowing. Gusts rock the car. He listens to the weather forecast. Going to be cold as hell, as usual. Twenty-seven degrees Fahrenheit and sinking fast. He unscrews the thermos and has a sip of cocoa Hannah packed in his lunchbox. Cocoa, macaroni salad and a tuna sandwich on white bread. He loathes macaroni and tuna, loves cocoa, and adores dear Hannah, so it's a wash.

His beat is usually quiet. The geographic jurisdiction extends from the village of Eagle Talon to a fourteen-mile stretch north and south along the Seward Highway. Normally, he deals with drunks and domestic arguments, tourists with flat tires and the occasional car accident.

Then along came this business with Langtree and the slaughterhouse scene at his shack on Midnight Road. A forensics team flew in from Anchorage and did their thing, and left again. Deputy Newcastle still hasn't heard anything from headquarters. Nobody's taking it seriously. Langtree was a nut. Loons like him are a dime a dozen in Alaska. Violence is part of the warp and woof of everyday existence here. Takes a hell of a lot to raise eyebrows among the locals. The deputy is worried, and with good reason. The angel on his shoulder keeps whispering in his ear. The angel warns him a blood moon is on the rise.

Despite the fact his shift ended at two o'clock, Deputy Newcastle has spent the better part of an hour staring at the entrance of the abandoned Frazier Tower. Should have gotten leveled long ago, replaced by a hotel or a community center, or any old thing. Lord knows the village could use some recreational facilities. Instead, the building festers like a rotten tooth. It's a nest for vermin—animals and otherwise—and a magnet for thrill-seeking kids and ne'er-do-wells on the lam.

Custodian Floyd is supposed to keep the front door covered in plywood. The plywood is torn loose and lying in the bushes. A hole leads into gloom. This actually happens frequently. The aforementioned kids and ne'er-do-wells habitually break into the tower to seek their fun. Deputy Newcastle's cop intuition tells him the usual suspects aren't to blame.

"I'm going in," he says.

"You better not," says MJ. The King of Pop inhabits the back seat, his scrawny form crosshatched by the grilled partition between them. His pale features are obscured in the shade of a slouch hat. He is the metaphorical shoulder-sitting angel.

"Got to. It's my job."

"You're a swell guy, deputy. Don't do it."

"Who then?"

"You're gonna die if you go in there alone."

"I can call someone. Hendricks will back my play."

"Can't trust him."

"Elam."

"Your brother is a psychopath."

"Hmm. Fair enough. I could ring Custer or Pearson. Heck, I could deputize both of them for the day."

"Look, you can't trust anyone."

"I don't." Newcastle stows the thermos and slides on his wool gloves. He unclips the twelve-gauge pump action from its rack and shoulders his way out of the cruiser. The road is slick beneath the tread of his boots, the breeze searing cold against his cheek. Snowflakes stick to his eyelashes. He takes a deep breath and trudges toward the entrance of the Frazier Tower. The dark gap recedes and blurs like a mirage.

True Romance isn't Deputy Newcastle's favorite movie. Too much blood and thunder for his taste. Nonetheless, he identifies with the protagonist, Clarence. In times of doubt Elvis Presley manifests and advises Clarence as a ghostly mentor.

The deputy adores the incomparable E, so he's doubly disconcerted regarding his own hallucinations. Why in the heck does he receive visions of MJ, a pop icon who fills him with dread and loathing?

MJ visited him for the first time the previous spring and has appeared with increasing frequency. The deputy wonders if he's gestating a brain tumor or if he's slowly going mad like his grandfather allegedly did after Korea. He wonders if he's got extra sensory powers or powers from God, although he hasn't been exposed to toxic waste or radiation, nor is he particularly devout. Church for Christmas and Easter potluck basically does it for him. Normally a brave man, he's too chicken to take himself into Anchorage for a CAT scan to settle the issue. He's also afraid to mention his invisible friend to anyone for fear of enforced medical leave and/or reassignment to a desk in the city.

In the beginning, Deputy Newcastle protested to his phantom partner: "You aren't real!" and "Leave me alone! You're a figment!" and so on. MJ had smiled ghoulishly and said, "I wanna be your friend, Deputy. I've come to lend you a hand. Hee-hee!"

Deputy Newcastle steps through the doorway into a decrepit foyer. Icicle stalactites descend in glistening clusters. The carpet has eroded to bare concrete. Cracks run through the concrete to the subflooring. It is a wasteland of fallen ceiling tiles, squirrel nests, and collapsed wiring. He creeps through the debris, shotgun clutched to his waist.

What does he find? An escaped convict, dirty and hypothermic, like in the fall of 2006? Kids smoking dope and spraying slogans of rebellion on the walls? A salmon-fattened black bear hibernating beneath a berm of dirt and leaves? No, he does not find a derelict, or children, or a snoozing ursine.

The Killer awaits him, as the King of Pop predicted.

Deputy Newcastle sees shadow bloom within shadow, yet barely feels the blade that opens him from stem to stern. It is happening to someone else. The razor-sharp tip punches through layers of insulating fabric, enters his navel, and rips upward. The sound of his undoing resonates in the small bones of his ears. He experiences an inexplicable rush of euphoria that is frightening in its intensity, then he is on his knees, bowed as if in prayer. His mind has become so disoriented he is beyond awareness of confusion. His parka is heavy, dragged low by the sheer volume of blood pouring from him. He laughs and groans as steam fills his throat.

The Killer takes the trooper hat from where it has rolled across the ground, dusts away snow and dirt, and puts it on as a souvenir. The Killer smiles in the fuzzy gloom, watching the deputy bleed and bleed.

Deputy Newcastle has dropped the shotgun somewhere along the way. Not that it matters—he has no recollection of the service pistol in his belt, much less the knowledge of how to work such a complicated mechanism. The most he can manage at this point is a dumb, meaningless smile that doesn't even reflect upon the presence of his murderer.

His final thought isn't of Hannah, or of the King of Pop standing at his side and mouthing the words to "Smooth Criminal," eyes shining golden. No, the deputy's final thought isn't a thought, it is inchoate awe at the leading edge of darkness rushing toward him like the crown of a tidal wave.

• • •

A storm rolls in off the sea on the morning of the big Estate Christmas party. Nobody stirs anywhere outdoors except for Duke Pearson's two-ton snowplow with its twinkling amber beacon, and a police cruiser as the deputy makes his rounds. Both vehicles have been swallowed by swirls of white.

Tammy Ferro's fourteen-year-old son Mark is perched at the table like a raven. Clad in a black trench coat and exceptionally tall for his tender age, he's picking at a bowl of cereal and doing homework he shirked the previous evening. His mother is reading a back issue of the *Journal of the American Medical Association*. The cover illustration is of a mechanical heart cross-sectioned by a scalpel.

Tammy divorced her husband and moved into the village in September, having inherited apartment 202 from her Aunt Millicent. Tammy is thirty-three but can pass for twenty-five. Lonnie DeForrest's appreciation of her ass aided her in snagging a job at the Caribou Tavern waiting tables. She earned a degree in psychology from the University of Washington, fat lot of good that's done her. Pole dancing in her youth continues to pay infinitely greater dividends than the college education it financed.

She and Mark haven't spoken much since they came to Eagle Talon. She tells herself it's a natural byproduct of teenage reticence, adapting to a radically new environment, and less to do with resentment over the big blowup of his parents' marriage. They are not exactly in hiding. It is also safe to say her former husband, Matt, doesn't know anything about Aunt Millicent or the apartment in Alaska.

Out of the blue, Mark says, "I found out something really cool about Nate Custer."

Tammy has seen Custer around. Impossible not to when everyone occupies the village's only residence. Nice looking guy in his late forties. Devilish smile, carefree. Heavy drinker, not that that is so unusual in the Land of the Midnight Sun, but he wears it well. Definitely a Trouble with a capital T sort. He goes with that marine biologist Jessica Mace who lives on the fifth. Mace is kind of a cold fish, which seems apropos, considering her profession.

She says, "The glacier tour guide. Sure." She affects casualness by not glancing up from her magazine. She dislikes the fascination in her son's tone. Dislikes it on an instinctual level. It's the kind of tone a kid uses when he's going to show you a nasty wound, or some gross thing he's discovered in the woods.

"He survived the Moose Valley Slaughter. Got shot in the head, but he made it. Isn't that crazy? Man, I never met anybody that got shot before."

"That sounds dire." Guns and gun violence frighten Tammy. She doesn't know if she'll ever acclimate to Alaska gun culture. However, she is quite certain that she prefers grown men leave her impressionable teen son out of such morbid conversations, much less parade their scars for his delectation. Barbarians aren't at the gate; they are running the village.

"It happened twenty years ago. Moose Valley's a small town, even smaller than Eagle Talon. Only thirty people live there. It's in the interior . . . You got to fly supplies in or take a river barge." Mark isn't looking at her directly, either. He studies his black nails, idly flicking the chipped polish.

"Gee, that's definitely remote. What do people do there?" Besides shoot each other, obviously.

"Yeah, lame. They had Pong, maybe, and that's it. Nate says everybody was into gold mining and junk."

"Nate says?"

Mark blushes. "He was a little older than me when it all went down. This ex-Army guy moved in from the Lower Forty-Eight to look for gold, or whatever. Everybody thought he was okay. Turns out he was a psycho. He snapped and went around shooting everybody in town one night. Him and Nate were playing dominoes and the dude pulled a gun out of his pocket. Shot Nate right in the head and left him on the floor of his cabin. Nate didn't die. Heh. The psycho murdered eleven people before the state troopers bagged him as he was floating downriver on a raft."

"Honey!"

"Sorry, sorry. The cops *apprehended* him. With a sniper rifle."

"Did Nate tell you this?"

"I heard it around. It's common knowledge, Mom. I was helping Tucker and Hendricks get an acetylene bottle into the back of his rig."

She hasn't heard this tale of massacre. Of course, she hasn't made many friends in town. At least Mark is coming out of his shell. Despite the black duds and surly demeanor, he enjoys company, especially that of adults. Good thing since there are only half a dozen kids his age in the area. She's noticed him mooning after a girl named Lilly. It seems pretty certain the pair are carrying on a rich, extracurricular social life via Skype and text . . .

"Working on English?" She sets aside her magazine and nods at his pile of textbooks and papers. "Need any help?"

He shrugs.

"C'mon. Watch ya got?"

"An essay," he says. "Mrs. Chandler asked us to write five hundred words on what historical figure we'd invite to dinner."

"Who'd you pick? Me, I'd go with Cervantes, or Freud. Or Vivien Leigh. She was dreamy."

"Jack the Ripper."

"Oh . . . That's nice."

A young, famous journalist drives to a rural home in Upstate New York. The house rests alone near the end of a lane. A simple rambler painted red with white trim. Hills and woods begin at the backyard. This is late autumn and the sun is red and gold as it comes through the trees. Just cool enough that folks have begun to put the occasional log into the fireplace, so the crisp air smells of applewood and maple.

He and the woman who is the subject of his latest literary endeavor sip lemonade and regard the sky and exchange pleasantries. An enormous pit bull suns itself on the porch a few feet from where the interview occurs. Allegedly, the dog is attack-trained. It yawns and farts.

The journalist finds it difficult not to stare at the old lady's throat where a scar cuts, so vivid and white, through the dewlapped flesh. He is aware that in days gone by his subject used to camouflage the wound with gypsy scarves and collared shirts. Hundreds of photographs and she's always covered up.

Mrs. Jessica Mace Goldwood knows the score. She drags on her Camel No. 9 and winks at him, says once her tits started hitting her in the knees she gave up vanity as a bad business. Her voice is harsh, only partially restored after a series of operations. According to the data, she recently retired from training security dogs. Her husband, Gerry Goldwood, passed away the previous year. There are no children or surviving relatives on record.

"Been a while since anybody bothered to track me down," she says. "Why the sudden interest? You writing a book?"

"Yeah," the journalist says. "I'm writing a book."

"Huh. I kinda thought there might be a movie about what happened at the Estate. A producer called me every now and again, kept saying the studio was 'this close' to green-lighting the project. I was gonna make a boatload of cash, and blah, blah, blah. That was, Jesus, twenty years ago." She exhales a stream of smoke and studies him with a shrewd glint in her eyes. "Maybe I shoulda written a book."

"Maybe so," says the journalist. He notices, at last, a pistol nestled under a pillow on the porch swing. It is within easy reach of her left hand. His research indicates she is a competent shot. The presence of the gun doesn't make him nervous—he has, in his decade of international correspondence, sat among war chiefs in Northern Pakistan, and ridden alongside Taliban fighters in ancient half-tracks seized from Russian armored cavalry divisions. He has visited Palestine and Georgia and seen the streets burn. He thinks this woman would be right at home with the hardest of the hard-bitten warriors he's interviewed.

"Life is one freaky coincidence, ain't it though?" She stares into the woods. Her expression is mysterious. "Julie Vellum died last week. Ticker finally crapped out."

"Julie Vellum . . . " He scans his notes. "Right. She cashed in big time. Author of how many bestselling New Age tracts? Friend of yours?"

"Nah, I despised the bitch. She's the last, that's all. Well, there's that guy who did psychedelic music for a while. He's in prison for aggravated homicide. Got involved with a cult and did in some college kids over in Greece. Can't really count him, huh? I'm getting sentimental in my dotage. Lonely."

"Lavender McGee. He's not in prison. They transferred him to an institution for the criminally insane. He gets day passes if you can believe it."

"The fuck is this world coming to? What is it you wanna ask me?"

"I have one question for you."

"Just one?" Her smile is amused, but sharp. It has been honed by a grief that has persisted for more than the latter half of her long life.

"Just one." He takes a small recorder from his shirt pocket, clicks a button, and sets it on the table between them. "More than one, of course. But this one is the biggie. Are you ready?"

"Sure, yeah. I'm ready."

"Mrs. Goldwood, why are you alive?"

Wind moves the trees behind the house. A flurry of red and brown leaves funnel across the yard, smack against the cute skirting. A black cloud covers the sun and hangs there. The temperature plummets. Gravel crunches in the lane.

The dog growls, and is on its feet, head low, mouth open to bare many, many teeth. The fur on its back is standing in a ridge. It is Cerberus's very own pup.

"Oh, motherfucker," says Jessica Mace Goldwood. She's got the revolver in her hand, hammer cocked. Her eyes blaze with a gunfighter's fire as she half crouches, elbows in tight, knees wide. "It's never over with these sonsofbitches."

"What's happening?" The journalist has ducked for cover, hands upraised in the universal sign of surrender. "Jesus H., lady! Don't shoot me!" He glances over his shoulder and sees a man in the uniform of a popular parcel delivery service slamming the door of a van and roaring away in a cloud of smoking rubber.

"Aw, don't fret. Me and Atticus just don't appreciate those delivery guys comin' around," she says. The pit bull snarls and throws himself down at her feet. She uncocks the revolver and tucks it into the waistband of her track pants. "So, young man. Where were we?"

He wipes his face and composes himself. In a hoarse voice he says, "I guess what happened in Alaska doesn't let go."

"Huh? Don't be silly—I smoked that psycho. Nah, I hate visitors. You're kinda cute, so I made an exception. Besides, you're gonna pay me for this story, kiddo."

He tries for a sip of lemonade and ice rattles in the empty glass. His hand trembles. She pats his arm and takes the glass inside for a refill. Atticus follows on her heel. The journalist draws a breath to steady himself. He switches off the recorder. A ray of sun burns through the clouds and spotlights him while the rest of the world blurs into an impressionistic watercolor. A snowflake drifts down from outer space and freezes to his cheek.

She returns with a fresh glass of lemonade to find the journalist slumped in the lawn chair. Someone has placed an ancient state trooper's hat on his head and tilted it so that the man's face is partially covered. The crown of the hat is matted with dried gore that has, with the passing decades, indelibly stained the fabric. A smooth, vertical slice begins at the hollow of his throat and continues to belt level. His intestines are piled beneath his trendy hiking shoes. His ears lie upon the table. Steam rises from the corpse.

Atticus growls at the odors of shit and blood.

Jessica gazes at him in amazement. "Goddamnit, dog. *Now* you growl. Thanks a heap." She notices a wet crimson thumbprint on the recorder. She sighs and lights another cigarette and presses PLAY. Comes the static-inflected sound of wind rushing across ice, of snow shushing against tin, of arctic darkness and slow, sliding fog. Fire crackles in the background. These sounds have crept across the span of forty years.

A voice, garbled and muted by interference, whispers, "Jessica, we need to know. Why are you alive?" Snow and wind fill a long gap. Then, "Did you cut your own throat? Did you? Are you dead, Jessica? Are you dead, or are you playing? How much longer do you think you have?" Nothing but static after that, and the tape ends.

Intuition tells her that the journalist didn't file a plan with his network, that he rolled into the boondocks alone, that when he doesn't arrive at the office on Monday morning it will be a fulfillment of the same pattern he's followed countless times previously. The universe won't skip a beat. A man such as he has enemies waiting in the woodwork, ready to wrap him in a carpet and take him far away. It will be a minor unsolved mystery that his colleagues have awaited since his first jaunt into a war-torn region in the Middle East.

She can't decide whether to call the cops or hide the body, roll the rental car into a ditch somewhere and torch it. *Why, yes, Officer, the young fellow was here for a while the other day. Missing? Oh, dear, that's terrible . . .*

"Jack?" she says to the hissing leaves. Her hand is at her neck, caressing the scar that defines her existence. "Nate? Are you out there?"

The sun sets and night is with her again.

Three years, six months, and fifteen days before Dolly Sammerdyke is eviscerated and dropped down a mineshaft, where her bones rest to this very day, she tells her brother Tom she's moving from Fairbanks to Eagle Talon. She's got an in with a woman who keeps the books at a shipping company and there's an opening for an on-site clerk. Tom doesn't like it. He lived in the village during a stretch in the 1980s when his luck was running bad.

"Listen, kid. It's a bum deal."

"Not as if I have a better option," she says.

"Bad place, sis."

"Yeah? What's bad about it? The people?"

"Bad people, sure. Bad neighborhood, bad history. Only one place to live in Eagle Talon. Six-floor apartment building. Ginormus old tenement. Dark, drafty, creepy as shit. It's a culture thing. People there are weird and clannish. You'll hate it."

"I'll call you every week."

Dolly calls Tom every week until her death. He doesn't miss her calls at first because he's landed a gig as a luthier in Nashville and his new girlfriend, an aspiring country and western musician, commands all of his attention these days.

Did the Final Girl do it? Was it this person or that? You can only laugh at the preposterousness of such conceits. You can only weep. As the omniscient narrator of some antique fairy tale once declaimed: Fool! Rub your eyes and look again!

You will never die—nothing does.

From the journal of Nathan E. Custer as transcribed from the original text by the Federal Bureau of Investigation, Anchorage:

I've never told anyone the whole truth about Moose Valley, or this recurring dream I've suffered in the following years. Probably not a dream; more of a vision. Nonetheless, for clarity's sake, we'll go with it being a dream. The dream has two parts. The first part is true to life, a memory of events with the tedious details edited from the narrative.

In the true-to-life part of the dream, Michael Allen and I are playing dominoes in the dim kitchen of my old place in Moose Valley. I'd seen him standing in the yard, a ghostly shape in the darkness, and had invited him to come out of the weather without thinking to ask why he was lurking.

It is fall of '93, around four in the morning. He's winning, he always wins at these games—pool, checkers, cards, dominoes— although everybody likes him anyway.

Allen has only been in town for a few months. An ex-Army guy, so he's capable, with an easy smile and a wry wit. Long hair, but kempt. Keeps to himself for the most part in a one-room cottage by the river. He's passionate about Golden Age comic books and the poetry of James Dickey. I was in the cottage for maybe five minutes once. Dude kept it to a minimum and neat as you please. Gun oil scent, although no guns in view. Yeah.

He pockets my last eleven dollars with a shrug and an apologetic grin. Says, Thanks for the game, and pulls on his orange sock cap and stands. I turn away to grab a beer from the icebox, hair of the dog that bit me, and the bullet passes through my skull above my ear and I'm on the floor, facedown. He squeezes the trigger again and I hear the hammer snap, a dud in the chamber. Or he hadn't reloaded from slaughtering the Haden family across the street. We'll never know. Anyway, I'm unblinking, unresponsive, paralyzed, so he leaves me for dead. The front door slams and sunlight creeps across the tiles and makes the spreading blood shiny.

The second part of the dream is a fantasy cobbled and spliced from real events. I have a disembodied view of everything that happens next.

Allen slips down to the launch and steals a rubber raft. He lets the flow carry him downstream. He's packed sandwiches and beer, and has a small picnic. God, it's a beautiful day. The mountain peaks are white with fresh snow, but the lower elevations are yet green and gold. The air is brisk, only hinting at the bitter chill to come. A beaver circles the raft, occasionally slapping the water with its tail. The crack is like a gunshot. Allen chuckles and scans the eggshell-blue sky from behind a pair of tinted aviator glasses.

The current gradually picks up as it approaches a stretch of falls and rapids. A black dot detaches from the sun and drops toward the earth. Allen unlimbers the 30.06 bolt-action rifle he's stowed under a blanket. His balance is uncertain and the first round pings harmlessly through the fuselage of the police chopper. He ejects the empty and sights again, cool as the ice on the mountains, and this will be a kill shot. The SWAT sniper is a hair quicker and Allen is knocked from the raft. He plunges into the water and sinks instantly. The raft zips over the falls and is demolished.

A sad, tragic case closes.

The fact is, Allen survives for a few minutes. He is a tough, passionless piece of work, a few cells short of Homo sapiens status, and that helps him experience a brutal and agonizing last few moments on the mortal plane. He is sucked into a vortex and wedged under and between some rocks where he eventually suffocates and drowns. This is a remote and dangerous area. The cops never recover the body.

Small fish nibble away his fingers, then his face, then the rest of it.

Laird Barron was born and raised in Alaska, did time in the wilderness, and raced in several Iditarods. Later, he migrated to Washington State where he devoted himself to American Combato and reading authors like Robert B. Parker, James Ellroy, and Cormac McCarthy. At night he wrote tales that combined noir, crime, and horror. He was a 2007 and 2010 Shirley Jackson Award winner for his collections *The Imago Sequence and Other Stories* and *Occultation and Other Stories* and a 2009 nominee for his novelette "Catch Hell." Other award nominations include the Crawford Award, Sturgeon Award, International Horror Guild Award, World Fantasy Award, Bram Stoker Award, and the Locus Award. His first novel, *The Croning*, was published in 2012; his latest collection, *The Beautiful Thing That Awaits Us All*, was published last year. Barron currently resides in Upstate New York and is writing a novel about the evil that men do.

"You know what it's like—they've got me on a clock back at the office. Can we get back to this Banshee you mentioned?"

POSTCARDS FROM ABROAD

⊸⊷

Peter Atkins

The house was nothing special, just another Liverpool semi-detached, one of those blink-and-there'll-be-ten-more-of-the-fuckers types of places. If *you* don't have a Granny who lives in one, you've got a mate who does, know what I mean?

There were a lot of them strung along the half-mile drag of Woolton Road as it fled Wavertree for pastures snootier, most of them dating from the dull and deco-free end of the nineteen-thirties. This one hadn't even kept the stained glass fanlights that were one of the few things that gave them any character at all, but at least it didn't have a name—you know, *Dunroamin* or something equally witty—so there was that.

I rang the bell and waited and, eventually, the front door swung open. The look that the little old lady in the hall gave me once she'd blinked away the glare of the sunlight was neither suspicious nor welcoming, just mildly surprised as if she thought her life had long ago run out of visitors.

"Mornin', luv," I said. "I'm from the Council." Which is lower middle class for *Open Sesame*.

"Oh," she said, as if already worried she'd done something wrong. "You'd better come in."

She stepped back, ushering me past her into the hall. It was narrow, of course, and made narrower halfway down its length by the stairs that led up to the bedrooms. I stopped before reaching any of the doors to the downstairs rooms and turned back to her, figuring I needed to do me bit for civic responsibility. "You know," I said. "You really should ask to see some identification before you let someone in your house."

"Why?" she said. "Are you a murderer?" Very deadpan. Not even a twinkle in the eyes. I liked her.

"No," I said. "I'm not a murderer."

"And you've not come to read the meter, have you?"

"I've not, luv. No."

"Then you must have come about the Banshee," she said. "Kettle's boiling. Go and sit down."

I hadn't reckoned to be out in the field when the day'd started. Morning had found me down by the Pier Head getting slapped around by a nasty wind off the Mersey as I made my way to the Liver Buildings.

Like a lot of government jobs these days, mine didn't really *need* me to show up at the office—even the paperwork can be done via telecommute and, given the nature of the department, anything that didn't draw attention to our existence was considered a score—but I'd been told to come in for a face-to-face with a visiting Higher Grade up from London.

We're on the seventh floor of the Liver Buildings and, while there's no specific *rule* about not using the big flashy main entrance that fronts the river, the standing policy is keep your fucking heads down whenever possible and so we're encouraged to enter through one of the various smaller side entrances, all of which have the benefit of relative anonymity. I like the one opposite the India Buildings because there's a lift right the other side of it that doesn't get as stop and starty as those in the main bank in the front lobby.

If it's still start-of-the-working-day sort of time, the lift can be packed with a bunch of the Internal Revenue birds from the fourth floor but it was already gone half nine when I got in it so my only fellow passenger was Toni from our mob, on her way back up from Records in the basement. She'd fetched a folder that must've been down there since before Victoria died—yellowed, damp-stained, all-but-cobwebbed—and was holding it face in as per policy. Surprising how a glimpse of file-names like *Necromancy/Mossley Hill/1897* can start rumors among the civilians.

Toni, who I'm not sure was even twenty yet, wore her hair like Barbara Stanwyck in *Ball of Fire* and dressed like it had never stopped being 1942. In Manhattan. But have a conversation with her and there's no mistaking where she's from. I'd once made the mistake of asking if her name was short for Antoinette.

"Antoinette?" she'd said. "What are you, fucking stupid? Me mum likes Toni Braxton." Winsome and delicate, these Liverpool girls. It's why we love 'em.

"Mornin', Tone," I said now.

She tutted at me. "Could've worn a tie," she said. "Top Brass coming in special to see you. What're you like?"

"I don't think I own a tie," I said. "Tell you what; give his mobile a jingle. Ask him to pick me one up on his way in."

"He's already here," Toni said, and I resented the hushed and impressed tone in her voice. I'd met James Arcadia before and I was a lot less fond of him than he was.

The parlor—that's what the old lady called the front room, like me Nan used to—was clean and tidy but it had a bit of a musty smell like it had kept its windows closed on the world a little too long.

Her mantelpiece ornaments—probably only Woolworth's to begin with but chosen with taste and now improved with the accidental gravitas of age—sat below a big oval mirror in a genuinely impressive gilded frame. Between the ornaments and the mirror, tacked across the wall in a ribboning sprawl, were dozens of postcards.

"Our Carol," she said, when she saw me looking at them. "She's in the diplomatic service. All over the world, she's been."

"Very nice," I said. "She ever anywhere long enough for her Mum to visit?"

"Ooh, yes, luv," she said, and I could hear the pride and wonder in her voice at what her daughter's life had allowed for her—world travel hadn't been for the likes of her when she herself was young. "I've been to America, you know. And Sardinia. Very nice. Most recently the Caribbean. That was probably me last trip though. Can't take those long flights anymore, I were running a fever all the way back on this last one. Ooh, and Berlin. Had a lovely time there, I did. Almost forgave 'em for the Blitz. I don't know if—"

"I don't mean to cut you off," I said. "But you know what it's like—they've got me on a clock back at the office. Can we get back to this Banshee you mentioned?"

"Well, I thought you'd know all about them," she said. "You're here to take care of it, aren't you?"

"Well, possibly, luv, possibly," I said. "Look, I'll be honest with you." I lowered my voice a bit like I was letting her in on government secrets. "We *have* had a few . . . well, I don't want to say complaints . . . let's say expressions of concern. From the neighbors. About the noises. But I don't think anybody said *Banshee*, specifically."

"Well, perhaps they're not as well read as me," she said. "To be honest, I'm not sure some of them *can* read. That Mrs. Bennett in number forty-seven, she—"

"Again," I said, as gently as I could. "If we could stay on—"

"Isn't it Banshees that howl?"

"Aye, I think so."

"Well, *something's* howling," she said, as if that was that. "So what do you do?"

"Eh?"

"With a Banshee. What do you do? What's the procedure?"

She didn't come over as pushy, just interested. And she seemed much more alive than when she had opened the front door. Like most civilians, she found this shit fascinating as long as it stayed on the other side of scary.

"Well," I said. "It'd be your garden that'd be the issue. If it was a Banshee, I mean. And I'd . . . well, I'd spray it. The bushes. The hedgerows."

"Spray it?" she said, all disappointed, like her date had shown up with a tandem instead of a Bentley. "No bell, book, and candle and all that stuff?"

"Well, it—"

"*Spray.* Tch. What sort of spray?" she asked. "Is it like poison? Like rat poison?"

"No," I said. "It's—"

"'Cause if there's something dead there in the morning, *I* won't be the one shifting it."

"There wouldn't be anything dead," I said. "It's not poison. It's more like a warning."

"Oh," she said. "*Keep off the grass* sort of thing?"

I smiled at her. "A little more aggressive," I said. "*Get out of Town* sort of thing."

"How does it work?"

"Can I be indelicate?"

"I was a nurse, luv. Seen it all, heard it all."

"Fair enough. It's like piss-marking territory. Spraying the area to tell a smaller predator that it's had its fun. That it can sling its hook now, because something bigger and nastier is claiming the manor."

She gave me a pointed up and down. "You don't *look* big and nasty," she said.

"Day's not over," I said, and winked.

When the lift opened on the seventh floor, Arcadia had been standing there. Three-piece suit. Pocket watch. Trademark gray leather gloves. That handsome forty-ish face, and those ancient eyes within it.

"Antoinette," he said, as if just the sight of Toni had saved him from suicide. "As radiant as ever."

Not a word of objection from not-Antoinette. Just a smile that was almost a simper and a little wiggle that was almost a fucking curtsey. He took her hand, raising it to his lips as he glided her elegantly out of the lift and gestured her down the corridor.

"Go and further brighten the lives of your lucky colleagues," he said, "while I take our young friend here topside."

He stepped into the lift with me and we rode to the top floor, or to what I'd always believed to be the top floor until—via an obscure door that looked like it should lead only to a closet and the spiral staircase that actually lay behind it—we came to a small circular room that I guessed was inside one of the towers that, from the street twenty flights below, appeared to be purely ornamental.

"One of my favorite rooms in the place," he said.

"You've been to Liverpool before, then?" I said. Which was really stupid. He'd obviously been to Liverpool before; he apparently knew Toni well enough to get away with shit that would have had some poor local bastard up on sexual harassment charges.

"Oh, many times," he said. "I was actually based here for nearly a year." He paused for a half-smile. "During the War."

I nearly bit. I'd heard what he'd said—*the War*, not *the Falklands War*, not *the recent unpleasantness in Iraq*, just *the War*—but I was buggered if I was going to play his let's-flirt-with-my-legend game this early in the day.

Apart from a couple of chairs, the room contained only a large circular white table set below a brass and mahogany contraption that disappeared into the ceiling.

"It's a *Camera Obscura*," Arcadia said. "A shadow cabinet. Do you know what that is?"

"Of course I know what that is," I said. Bit of a spin on the tone, I admit. I hadn't liked the way he'd used a foreign accent for the Latin phrase. Bad enough when people do that with French or Spanish, but at least we know what they sound like. Nobody knows what *Latin* sounded like so, you know, fuckoff. It annoyed me that he could well have been simply making the accent up, confident that no one up here in the barbarous north would challenge him on it, him being such a toff and all. But it annoyed me more that he might *not* have been making it up, that he might very well have heard it spoken and spoken it himself.

"A device to capture images via light," he said, like he wasn't going to let the inconvenience of any pre-existing knowledge on my part slow his gallop. Arcadia's one of those blokes who regards a conversation as a good lecture spoiled. "The name came from Kepler, of course, but the Chinese and the Greeks knew the principle long before."

"Shame they had to wait two thousand years for someone to invent celluloid," I said.

"That *was* inconvenient," Arcadia said, and I could tell from the delight in his voice that I'd just played straight man to his coming punchline. "Of course, not everyone was as patient as they should have been. Chap who made *this* one, for example." He patted the curved housing of the device with the kind of proprietorial affection a well-heeled Victorian roué might have shown a chorus girl's bottom. "It's from the early Seventeenth century," he said. "There've been whispers it was once owned by John Dee, but we can't be sure."

His eyes lost focus for a second or two, and I knew he was remembering the old days when, if the fancy took him, he could have popped off for a minute or two to find John Dee and just fucking ask him. But Mr. Sweets was dead and, though Arcadia still had plenty of tricks up his impeccably tailored sleeve, Time was as closed to him now as it was to the rest of us.

"So it's a *magic* Camera Obscura," I said. "It takes pictures. Well, no offense, but these days so does me fucking cell phone."

"No, it doesn't take pictures," Arcadia said. "Not as we understand it. But, still, it's unique."

"So what *does* it do?"

"It remembers," he said, and my eyes snapped back instantly to the machine.

"Ah," said Arcadia. "There it is." He was looking at me rather than the machine, and he sounded genuinely pleased. And not just with himself for once.

"There what is?" I asked.

"The first of my three Cs," he said. "Curiosity."

"Oh," I said. "Cars? Cancer?"

"I'm sorry?"

"Are we not playing *Things that Killed the Cat*, then?"

"No, we're playing things that make us good at our job. Not, you understand, things we need to *do* the job. Lots of people can *do* the job. The three Cs are what I consider vital to doing it *well*."

"Oh, aye?" I said. "So what are the other two?"

"Well, the second is Competence. You've already demonstrated that. I read the report on that mass clearing you did in Wavertree Playground a couple of weeks ago."

"The Mystery," I said, and then, off his questioning look, "nobody local calls it Wavertree Playground. It's The Mystery."

"Oh," he said, like he'd just had a hit of something good. "How . . . apt."

"Aye," I said. "What's the third C?"

"The most important one of all."

"Which is . . . ?

He gave me his half-smile again. "That would be telling," he said.

"So these noises," I said. "This *howling*. Is it constant?"

She pursed her lips, thinking about it. "No," she said. "No, not constant."

"Is it daytime, nighttime? Both?"

"I'm not sure. I hear it sometimes, but not others."

"Are you hearing it now?"

"Eh? Don't be daft. Are *you* hearing it now?"

"I'm asking if *you* are," I said, and glanced around the room as if only now appreciating its architectural splendors. "From the thirties, isn't it, the house?"

"Aye," she said. "Just like me."

"But you weren't *born* here or anything," I said. "Weren't here as a little girl?"

"Oh, no. No. Me husband bought it just after the war—he were a bit older than me, been gone near enough twenty years now—and just moved me in once he'd made an honest woman of me. Our *Carol* was born here. Well, I mean, she was born in the hospital, but we were living here when—"

"But the house is as it was?" I said. I didn't like to keep interrupting her but, you know, meant to be working here.

"How d'you mean, *as it was*?" she said, ready to be insulted, like I was saying she hadn't once redecorated or something.

"No, I just mean, you know, original features and fittings and things."

"What, like banisters and windows and stuff?"

"Like the coal cellar," I said.

"Coal cellar?"

"Yeah. Is there still a coal cellar down there? Hasn't been bricked up or anything?"

"*Coal*," she said, like I was an idiot. "It hasn't had coal in it for forty years."

"Then what *has* it got in it?"

"Eh?"

I stood up. The racket was getting fucking unbearable. "What is it in the coal cellar," I said, "that's making all that noise?"

Arcadia hadn't had a lot more to say. Pulled a few further details out of me about the job in The Mystery, congratulated me on it again, handed me the file on the Woolton Road semi, and that was it.

"Off you pop then," he said. "Got everything you might need?" He raised an eyebrow and mimed an example, his left hand sketching in the air in a way that no passer-by would have put down to anything more than an unusually elegant Tourette's spasm but which I recognized as an Assyrian scattering spell known as much for its difficulty as for its usefulness. I suppose he wasn't *just* showing off, but it's so fucking hard to tell with him.

"Well, I've got me charm and me good looks," I said. "See how far they get me, eh?"

"Quite," Arcadia said, and smiled like he was comfortable with a certain degree of humor from among the enlisted men. I was just turning to go when he spoke again.

"Actually," he said. "There's something else I think you should take." He reached into a desk drawer and handed me something from it.

I weighed it in my hand and gave him a look. "Hardly standard issue," I said.

He shrugged. "I just have a hunch about this one," he said.

The roars from below only increased in intensity and ferocity as I approached the little three-quarter door at the top of the steps that led down to the coal cellar. But the second I slammed back the top and bottom bolts that had been holding the door shut, the sounds stopped dead. Something knew I was up there and had no wish to discourage my descent.

Banshee, my arse.

I suppose the old lady had been technically right to have called them howls, but howls always suggest an element of the plaintive to me, dizzy young romantic that I am, and these things hadn't had a trace of melancholy in them. They were feral, angry, and—not a comfortable concept as I made my crouched way down the cramped wooden stairs—hungry.

The cellar was long but low—its ceiling not even high enough to let me stand upright—and if there'd ever been a light down there, it was long gone. There was a little residual spill coming down from the house, but whatever it was that was in the cellar had moved way back into the shadows at the rear. Its silence and its retreat didn't mean that it was hiding, though. They meant that it was trying to draw me in.

Fuck. I froze for a moment, trying to get my breathing under control and pondering my choice of career, and then I stepped in. One yard. Two. A third, and suddenly the thing lurched out of the shadows and came at me.

It was the old lady from upstairs. Or used to be.

The rot of the dead flesh had left one hand entirely skeletal and half the chin was naked jawbone. From what I'd heard, these things didn't breathe but I'd swear those gray desiccated nostrils twitched as if catching a whiff of the warm meat I was wearing on my bones.

It raced towards me. Not graceful, but fucking fast. Much faster than the manual says. I thought about writing the editors a stern letter, but I didn't think about it for long.

Fuck knows, if I'd come here with just the standard issue kit, this undead thing would have had half my face off while I was still trying to weave a circle round it thrice and say something in Phoenician. But Arcadia'd had a hunch. I was pissed off that I owed him one, but I can't deny the tingle of gratitude and admiration I felt as I lifted the ancient service Webley and aimed for the head.

She was sitting on the couch looking up at her postcards from abroad when I came back into the parlor.

"Everything all right?" she said.

"It will be," I said, and sat down next to her. I took her hand and closed mine around it gently. Still stuns me how solid they can feel.

"Ooh," she said. "Getting a bit familiar, aren't we? It's not grab-a-granny night down at the Grafton Rooms, you know."

"The Grafton Rooms?" I said, smiling. "Before my time. Been closed for nigh on thirty years now."

"Christ," she said. "That long? It all goes so fast."

I gave her hand a gentle pat. It was a little more yielding now, like water within a thin membrane trying to maintain a half-remembered shape.

"Are you starting to get a handle on what's going on, luv?" I asked her.

She sighed. "I think I knew as soon as I bolted the cellar door on it," she said. "I just didn't want to admit it to meself."

She looked up above the mantelpiece to the postcards from her daughter again and was silent for a while. I kept stroking her hand, less substantial by the minute.

"Downstairs," she said, suddenly. "Will someone tidy—"

"They'll send a team," I said.

"When?"

"Once I call them."

"You should call them," she said. "You're on the clock."

"Bugger the clock," I said, still holding where her hand used to be. "I'm right here. You just relax, luv. Take as long as you need."

She didn't need long. And I had nowhere better to be.

Peter Atkins is the author of the novels *Morningstar, Big Thunder,* and *Moontown* and the screenplays *Hellraiser II, Hellraiser III, Hellraiser IV,* and *Wishmaster.* His short fiction has appeared in such anthologies as *The Museum of Horrors, Dark Delicacies II, Hellbound Hearts, Gutshot,* and *The Alchemy Press Book of Pulp Heroes.* His most recent book, *Rumours of the Marvellous,* was a finalist for the British Fantasy Award. "Postcards from Abroad," set in the author's native Liverpool, was written for the 2013 performances of *The Rolling Darkness Revue,* an annual folly he commits with Glen Hirshberg. He blogs at peteratkins.blogspot.com.

In the seven years leading up to 1888, the women had struck three times.
They were unsuccessful, to be sure, but practice makes perfect.

PHOSPHOROUS

Veronica Schanoes

A man can strike a Lucifer on anything—the wall, the bottom of a shoe, a barstool. Sometimes the white head of the match flares up from the friction of being packed at the factory, and an entire box bursts into flames, releasing the rough poison of white phosphorus into the air, and the box goes on burning until the girl who was packing them stamps it out, and then the Bryant and May Match Company fines her.

London in the nineteenth century is marked, inside and out, by the black, burnt trails left whenever a Lucifer is struck. A series of black marks, scoring the city's face, like scars.

The Lucifer allows an easy way to kindle fires, to provide light and heat and smoke without the unreliable and frustrating business of flint or the danger of Congreves, matches prone to exploding into burning pieces upon being struck, and so banned in France and Germany. And Lucifers are cheap, much cheaper than matches made from red phosphorus, which can be struck only on the side of the box, anyway. Lucifers are so cheap that, in the words of William Morris, "the public buy twice as much as they want, and waste half."

Herbert Spencer calls the Lucifer "the greatest boon and blessing to come to mankind in the nineteenth century."

The pathways the Bryant and May matchwomen take home from the factory every night are marked by piles of phosphorescent vomit.

It begins with a toothache. And those are not uncommon, not where you live, not when you live. Not uncommon at all. But you know what it means, and you know what comes next, no matter how hard you try to put it out of your mind. For now, the important thing is to keep it from the foreman. And for a while, you can. You can swallow the clawing pain in your mouth just as you swallow the blood from your tender gums, along with your bread during the lunch break. If you have bread, that day. A mist of droplets floats through the room, making the air hazy, hard to see through. They settle on your bread.

Your teeth hurt, but you can keep that from the foreman. You can eat your bit of bread and keep that secret.

But then your face begins to swell.

Property is theft, wrote Karl Marx, and for almost thirty-five years, Karl Marx lived in London. Private property, he said, is the theft from the people of resources hitherto held in common. And then that property can be turned to capital, which can be used to extort labor from workingmen and women for far less than its value. Another theft. Theft of communal resources, theft of labor, and for these women and girls, the matchmakers of the Bryant and May match factory at Bow, it could also become theft of bone, theft of flesh, and, finally, theft of life.

Not that they don't put up a good fight. Fighting is something they're good at. Fighting, dancing, and drinking, those wild Irish girls of London's East End. That's what reformers and journalists say, anyway.

Your old Nan came over with her husband back in 1848, during the famine forty years ago, long before you were born, but you and your siblings and cousins, you still have the map of Eire stamped into your souls.

Your Nan has the sight, or so she says. When you were naught but a small girl, not working yet, but only a nuisance underfoot, hungry all the time, she would distract you by telling you all the lovely things she could see in your future a husband handsome and brave, fine strapping sons and lively daughters, and a home back in Ireland, with cows lowing on the hills, and ceilis with the neighbors every weekend, and all the cheese and bread you could eat.

You couldn't quite picture the countryside she described—the closest you could come was a blurred memory of Hampstead Heath, where your family had once gone on a bank-holiday outing, and being a London girl, you weren't quite sure that you wanted to live there, but you liked the sound of the cheese and the ceilis and the husband that your Nan promised you. And you believed her implicitly, because your Nan had the sight, didn't everyone on the street know that?

But perhaps she'd been mistaken because now your teeth hurt like hellfire and your face has started to swell. You can think of only one way for this to end, and it doesn't involve any ceilis.

When you were little, the youngest of your family, the first thing you remember is your mum telling you to be quiet while she counted out the matchboxes she made at home. Your mum would put you into the arms of your sister, Janey, four years older, and shoo the two of you and your brother, and any cousins who happened to be around, outside to play, and there'd you be until late at night, when the matchboxes were dry and could be stacked in a corner out of the way, and you kids could unroll mats and blankets and sleep fitfully on the floor.

When you were old enough to be a bit more useful, soon after your mum died birthing one baby too many, you would sit with your Nan, cutting the rotten bits out of the potatoes so that she could cook them more easily, back in the days before she lost her vision, the vision of this world, anyway. Once you'd lost your temper and complained about how many rotten spots there were, and your Nan shook her head and told you that the half or third of good flesh you got out of one of these potatoes was a bounty compared to the famine years. "All rot and nothing else," she said, "and you could hear the keening throughout the countryside, until you couldn't, and that was all the worse, the despair and silence of those left behind." She looked at the potato in your hand, took it from you, and dropped it in the pot. "And every crop melting into slime, and the English shipping out fat cows and calves and anything else they could get their hands on."

Sometimes your Nan would lapse into Irish, the language she and your granddad had spoken before emigrating. You don't speak; your mum spoke a bit, and so did your dad. Janey and some of your older cousins speak some, but after that, there were just too many kiddies to make sure of what they were saying. When your Nan uses Irish, you don't know what her words mean, but it's easy to make out the general tone.

In Irish, the potato famine of 1845-52 is called *an Gorta Mór*, the Great Hunger, or *an Drochshaol*, the Bad Times. During those seven years, around one million Irish died, most likely more, and at least another one million emigrated, reducing the country's population by one-quarter.

England exported crops and livestock, off-limits to the impoverished Irish, to its own shores throughout the disaster. The food was exported under armed guard from ports in the areas of Ireland most affected by the potato blight.

The sultan of the Ottoman Empire attempted to send ten thousand pounds in aid to the people of Ireland; Queen Victoria requested that he reduce his charity to the sum of one thousand, as she herself had sent only two thousand. The sultan agreed, but nonetheless sent three ships of food to Ireland as well. The English courts attempted, unsuccessfully, to block the ships.

In America, the Choctaws had endured the death march known as the Trail of Tears sixteen years prior and apparently saw something familiar in a people being starved to death and forced off their land. They sent $710 for the relief of the Irish.

Sir Charles Trevelyan, the government official responsible for England's relief efforts, considered that "the judgment of God sent this calamity [the potato blight] to teach the Irish a lesson."

Your Nan lost her first two babbies, a little girl of two years who starved to death before she and your granddad left his farm, and another one that had yet to be born on the way over to England. Now she looks forward to holding both her babes once more when she meets them in paradise, which she describes as sounding much like county Cork in happier times.

When she used to tell you of your future life in Ireland, an Ireland under home rule, perhaps, an Ireland of Parnell's making, and blessed O'Connell's memory, she put herself there, too, back in county Cork in her old age, sitting by your fire.

When you were a little girl, you promised that you would bring her back to Ireland with you, and that when she died, you'd see her buried in the graveyard of the church where she'd been baptized and married.

Where will she see you buried, you now wonder.

There are no outside agitators in the factory at the end of June, and the only socialists are the same socialists who are there every day, dipping and cutting and packing for five shillings a week.

The only new thing is a bit of newspaper being passed around furtively, read out in whispers by the girls who can read to those who cannot: an article from *The Link* entitled "White Slavery in London," telling the middle-class folk of London about work at the Bryant and May factories.

You read with interest the details of your own life, and you make haste to hide the paper when the foremen come in.

A letter at your workstation states that the article is a lie, and that you are happy, well paid, and well treated in your work.

You rub the place at the bottom of your swollen cheek where the sores first opened up.

Instead of signing the preprinted letter to *The Times*, which has become the mouthpiece for middle-class outrage at Bryant and May, you spit on it.

Not one of the women in the entire factory signs the letter.

In the entire factory, the only letter with a mark at the bottom is the one with your spittle on it, shining faintly in the dark.

Fourteen-year-old Lizzie collects the unsigned letters and hands them to the foreman, staring him straight in the eye, and in that moment you know that it was Lizzie who'd gone to *The Link* with the story. And so does the foreman, perhaps, because he smacks her across the face with the sheaf of papers. Lizzie spits between the foreman's feet.

Lizzie is sacked the following Monday. When she's told to leave, she considers for a moment, then breaks the foreman's jaw with a single punch.

As she turns to leave, all of you, you and your friends and rivals, put on your hats and follow her out.

The strike flares up like a Lucifer. When you look back at the long line of women behind you, you have to blink to be sure that there aren't white trails of phosphorus smoke floating off all of you, disappearing into the sky.

They said it was Annie Besant's doing, that Mrs. Besant had been the ringleader, an outside Fabian socialist agitator. And perhaps there is some truth to it, as she did write and publish "White Slavery in London," the article that so shamed Mr. Bryant that he tried to get his workers to repudiate it.

But Mrs. Besant called for a respectable middle-class boycott, not for working-class girls and women to take matters into their own hands. The strikers did not contact her until some days after the initial walkout.

The East End of London did not need middle-class Fabians to explain socialism.

In the seven years leading up to 1888, the women of Bryant and May had struck three times. They were unsuccessful, to be sure, but practice makes perfect.

You're getting ready to go out marching, collecting for the strike fund, when you hear your Nan calling for you. You hold off on wrapping up your suppurating face and turn to find her, bent almost double with her dowager's hump, staring up at you with her milky, sightless eyes.

"Yeh've got the phoss, a cushla," she says. "Had it for a while, I reckon. When were yeh plannin' to tell me?"

You shrug, saying nothing, then remember that your Nan can't see you. You open your mouth to talk when she turns and shuffles back to the chair she had been sitting in.

You find your tongue. "You can smell it, eh, Nan?"

She swats at the air. "Can't smell a damn thing. Haven't been able to since before you were born. Makes all the mush I eat taste the same. Not that I figure what I eat tastes of anything worth eating anyways." She shakes her head. "Nah. I just know. Known for a while."

You wait to see what, if anything, she'll say next. Her eyelids droop, and before you know what you're doing, you burst out angrily, "And what about my children and husband and cows and ceilis every weekend? When will I get them, Nan?"

Her eyelids snap up again. She makes a sort of feeble fluttering gesture with her hands, which still look surprisingly youthful. "Never, a cushla, my darling. Never for you."

Your eyes widen in shock, and for the first time you realize that part of you had been hoping that your wise, witchy Nan would pull an ould Irish trick from up her sleeve, send the phoss packing, and send you away to Ireland, away from Bryant and May.

"I lied to you, my love," she says. "All those times, for all those years, I lied. I never saw nothing for you. Just a greenish glow where your long life should have been."

"Why?" you ask, glacial with the loss of hope.

"Ah, darling. Don't you know yeh've always been my favorite?"

You turn abruptly and resume tucking your scarf around your decaying jaw.

After a few seconds, your Nan speaks again, softly. "Darling, don't be so wretched, the phoss in your jaw is a horror, it's true, but it'll soon be over, it won't be long now."

You picture yourself coughing up blood, your jaw twisted, black, and falling to pieces, and you take little comfort in the image.

"Worse off by far," says your Nan, "are those who get the phoss in their souls. "They'll never see paradise at all."

> *We'll hang Old Bryant on the sour apple tree,*
> *We'll hang Old Bryant on the sour apple tree,*
> *We'll hang Old Bryant on the sour apple tree,*

As we go marching on.

Glory, glory hallelujah . . .

> —Matchgirl strikers' marching song, 1888, sung to the
> tune of "John Brown's Body," a song popular among
> Union soldiers and abolitionists during the US Civil War

A few days after the walkout, you and Annie Ryan from next door make your way to the Mile End Waste. You don't say much on the walk. Moving your jaw has become too painful, every slight flex of your facial muscles redoubling the bone-grinding ache, the soreness stretching poisoned tentacles out from your slowly decaying jaw to grip your skull and bore into your brain.

You've taken to eating the same soft, gray pap your Nan lives on. It saves you chewing and leaves more hard bread for your brothers and sisters and their kiddies. And since you're constantly queasy if not worse, you don't even miss it.

Some days you don't want the gray mush either, but your Nan won't eat unless you do. And some days you've half a mind to let the ould bitch starve, serve her right for lying to you all these years.

But after all, she is your Nan.

You leave your scarf on inside, even at home, so as not to scare the kiddies, but they avoid you anyway. It's the smell.

When you were a wee lass yourself, you and the others used to play on the corpses of horses, worked to death and left to putrefy in the street.

Nothing still walking around should smell like that.

So you walk in silence toward the rally, even as the men and girls around you break into song. And in a crowd of thousands, your patch of silence isn't likely to be noticed.

Annie draws your arm through hers. "You've a marvelous singing voice, Lucy," she says, pulling you near, near enough that you can see her nostrils flare as she works to give no sign that she's noticed the smell. "Don't you remember when we were only small, and you made up that skipping rhyme about Mrs. Rattagan's warts? You sounded like an angel, counting off her warts as you skipped."

You nod, and even that hurts.

"They've got to hear us, Lucy. All the way to Mayfair and Parliament. Maybe all the way back to Ireland. That'd make old Parnell proud, wouldn't it?"

Annie leans in even closer. "You know nobody'd ever put you out, Lucy, don't you? And even if they did, well, you'd just trot down the block and come stop with me and mine. Take care of you right to the end, we would."

You nod slightly and she squeezes your hand. "Make the end come a bit sooner, too, if need be."

She draws away again, and after a moment you find your voice.

You can barely hear your own singing above the noise of your headache, but you see that Annie and the other girls can, and that, you suppose, is what counts.

When you return home, you finally relax and remove your hat and scarf. Something small, like a pebble, falls to the floor.

It's a piece of your jaw.

In 1889, Annie Besant exchanged socialism for theosophy. Despite its esoteric reputation, theosophy reflected conventional Victorian values in at least one way.

According to the teachings of Madame Blavatsky, theosophy's founding mother, each and every person has exactly what he or she deserves in this life. Theosophists believed that sickness, suffering, deformity, and poverty were punishments for sins committed in a past life. "This belief can be dressed as God's will, or as social Darwinism, but it comes to the same thing.

It is a reassuring thought to those whose lives are not thoroughly saturated with such suffering. Sometimes it can be a comfort even as one is led to the guillotine or faces the firing squad.

When Besant traded in socialism for theosophy, she bought spiritual certainty at the price of her compassion.

Though Annie Besant was by no means a strike leader—indeed, she had written on more than one occasion about the futility of trying to organize unskilled labourers—she'd had enough sympathy with the strikers and care for her good journalistic name to counter management's claims of innocence by publicizing the working conditions, wages, and abuse that Bryant and May expected the striking matchwomen to accept.

And she had a word with her good friend Charles Bradlaugh, MP.

As you and the other girls make your way to parliament, heads turn at the sight of so many tattered dresses, the sound of so many rough accents outside the East End, and not in any uniform, either.

"What're you lookin' at?" Lizzie shouts at a group of young ladies who, having forgotten the manners drilled into them by their governesses, stare and gape as you walk past.

The young ladies drop their eyes and turn away quickly. After a few seconds, you hear a shriek of laughter.

By the time you reached Westminster, traffic in the streets has slowed to a crawl as cabs and buses come to a full stop so their drivers and passengers can take a good, long look at the poor women walking en masse toward parliament, just as if they have a right to.

Perhaps if you weren't in so much pain, you tell yourself, you could be as brave as Jenny, old Jenny Rotlegh, forty if she's a day, and bald as an egg from years of carrying wooden pallets on her head. Jenny sweeps off her bonnet right then and there, in front of the three MPs who had received your delegation.

"Look," she says. "Look what they done to me! Ain't that worth more 'n four shillings a week, less fines?"

You listen to the gasps from the fine gentlemen and wonder if you should undo your scarf and expose what remains of your blackened jaw, and the line of sores reaching now up to your temples. You come as near as raising your hand to the scarf around your throat and taking one of the ends in your fingers. You untuck it and pause, thinking of the gentlemen staring at your melting face.

Jenny is an object of pity, an exemplar of abused and mistreated femininity.

But you have become a monster.

There is a difference between shocked pity and horrified disgust. It is human nature to turn away from the latter. You tighten the scarf and retie the knot, more tightly than before.

Annie Besant wasn't the only established activist late to the party. There was also the London Trades Council, the last leading bastion of craft unionism, which had previously turned up its nose at unskilled laborers. The council met with a delegation of matchwomen. Perhaps out of the desire to retain its preeminent place as the voice of the urban worker, perhaps out of a paternalistic sense of noblesse oblige, perhaps even out of a genuine sense of fellow feeling and solidarity, the LTC offered to send a delegation of workmen to negotiate a settlement agreeable to both parties.

The firm received the overture genteelly, which must have made it all the more humiliating when that deputation returned empty-handed. The men reported only that Bryant and May were willing to allow most of the strikers to resume their old places, if they returned immediately, while reserving the right to refuse reemployment to the women they termed "the ringleaders."

The strikers didn't bother to send a reply.

• • •

The evening after the meeting with the MPs, your Nan asks you to lay your head on her lap. When you do, she rests her hand on your hair.

"You're angry with me, a cushla," she says.

You say nothing. You watch your words more carefully than your sisters watch their farthings now that you slough off flesh with every motion of your mouth.

"Well, you've a right," she continues. When you remain silent, she sighs and is quiet herself for a while. After some minutes drift by, she draws breath to begin again.

"The strike will end," she says conversationally. "I seen it." This time she doesn't bother to pause for responses you will not give. "But you won't see it. You'll die first. I seen that, too."

Sooner's better than later, you think dully, and wonder if she'll tell you how long the strike will last, and if any of you will have jobs by the time it is over. You'd like to know that Annie won't starve, at least. If your Nan really does have any sight at all, if she hasn't been lying about everything, all this time. If she isn't just some crazy ould biddy.

"You won't see the end of this strike," she repeats. "Not unless I help you out. And I figure, I figure, I owe you at least that much." You gently take her hand from your head and sit up, moving slowly, the way you have been for a while now. You hold her rough hand between two of yours, and you know for sure now, her mind is broken and gone, and she'll never see Ireland again.

She pulls her hand away from you irritably, as though she can hear your thoughts, and swats at you.

"Not a crazy ould one," she says. "Not like my own gran, there was madness for you, if that's what you're thinking. A life, it's like a flame, y'see, a candle flame. An' if I put that flame into a real flame, a real candle, well, you'll keep right on living as long as that candle keeps burning.

"And a candle held in the left hand of a hanged man, that candle, it can't go out. You can't put that out with wind nor water nor snuff it with yer fingers. Only good white milk can put out a Hand o' Glory.

"I can do that fer you," she says. "I can do it, if yeh can bring me what I need. It won't exactly be living, more sort of not dyin'. But I don't know that what yeh're doing now is living, so much, either."

You say nothing once more, but this time more out of shock than deliberately.

"I'll give you a list," she says.

"Hand of a dead man?" you manage to slur.

"Hanged," she corrects you. "Left hand of a hanged man. Or woman'll do as well, o' course. Dunno how we'll get that one. We're neither of us well enough for grave robbing. But we'll manage."

After a doubtful pause, she repeats, "We'll manage.

"And those pieces of your jawbone that keep fallin' off. Start saving 'em."

Here are some of the reasons given by Bryant and May for fines taken g from their workers' pay packets:
—dirty feet (3d.)
—ground under bench left untidy (3d.)
—putting burnt-out matches on the bench (ls.)
—talking (amount not specified)
—lateness, for which the worker was then shut out for half the day (5d.)

Here are deductions regularly taken from the matchwomen's pay packets:
—6d. for brushes to clean the machines (every six months)
—3d. to pay for children to fetch packing paper (weekly)
—2d. to pay the packer who books the number of packages (weekly)
—6d. to pay for stamps, to stamp the packages (weekly
—ld. to pay for children to fetch and carry for the box-fillers (weekly)

Bryant and May employed no children to fetch and carry for the box-fillers. The box-fillers fetched and carried for themselves.

Nan says that you don't have the time to make a tallow dip. You wonder how much time you do have, as you collect what she told you to, and if it's worth living as you do now until the strike is over and broken.

Perhaps it would be better to go now, while the girls are still going strong, fuelled by high hopes.

But love is a hard habit to break, so you do as she tells you, scavenging strips of paper, a wide-mouth jar, and a length of wire from the trash heaps, and stopping at the butcher's for what lumps of pork fat he'll give you for your pennies. You've found that shopkeepers give you better prices these days. Perhaps they feel sorry for you.

Perhaps they just want you out of the shop as quickly as possible, so you don't scare off custom.

Either way is fine by you, as long as you can walk away with all the pork fat you need, which isn't much. You bring your parcels home to your Nan and lay them at her feet, like offerings.

What you do next isn't hard; you've made paper wicks before, rendered pork fat before, and it stinks, but it doesn't stink as badly as you do. While you do these things, your Nan takes the pieces of your jawbone that you've saved and grinds them into a fine powder, using a mortar and pestle. They crumble so easily.

Dust to dust.

While you stir the melted fat, your Nan leans over from her chair by the fire and tips the dust of your bones into the small pot. Then she slices across the veins of your forearm with an old knife. Straining against her arthritic knuckles, she squeezes and massages your arm to get as much of your blood into the mix as she can.

After you give the pot a few more stirs, the tallow looks no different from any other bit of tallow you've ever seen, grubby and nasty, and smells no different either, rank and putrid. You pour it into the glass jar, watching it pool and pile up around the paper wick held stiff by the scavenged wire.

While you scrub out the pot, your Nan mutters some Irish over the makeshift candle and sets it aside to harden.

"It's a good thing we neither of us eat much," she says to you. "With neither of us bringing anything in."

You nod. After a minute, you ask her the same thing you did the previous evening.

"Hand of a hanged man?" you force out.

She seems troubled, but she pats your hand. "Leave that to me," she says, and then again, more slowly, "leave that to me."

Before you sleep that night, she whispers in your ear, "I'm goin' out tonight. You be in the cemetery. The unconsecrated ground, an hour before dawn. Bring the small axe and the candle. And a few matches, o' course."

Your sleep has been unquiet for a long time now, with the effect that you find it harder and harder to rouse yourself. This is probably because you are dying.

Whatever the reason, by the time you force yourself fully awake, it's long past when you should have left for Bow Cemetery. On your way, you wonder anxiously if you'll be there in time. However it is that your Nan plans to find you a hanged man, you want the cover of darkness.

You don't know the way as well as you do to the churchyard at Saints

Michael and Mary on Commercial Road, the Catholic church not yet built when your Nan came over. You've been there plenty, standing by the gravesides of the very young, the very old, and all between.

But your Nan wouldn't dig up a good Catholic.

Surely she didn't have the strength to dig up anybody else, either, come to that. And she didn't tell you to bring a shovel.

It's summer, and small pink flowers dot the ground of the graveyard.

They remind you of the morning that an anonymous benefactor sent a cartload of pink roses down to all the girls on the picket, to wear as badges. That morning, the fragrance of roses had blotted out even the stench you did your best to trap in the folds of your scarf. For that one morning, the scent of roses surrounded you, and you let yourself pretend that you weren't rotting away, like the corpses interred in the ground beneath your feet.

The unconsecrated ground is a newer part of the graveyard, and it holds unbaptized babies, suicides, and those of strange and foreign faiths, or perhaps even no faith at all.

But they all rot in the same way, you figure, 'cause the worms probably don't know the difference.

Or maybe they do. Maybe they feel a tingle of the divine wind round them as they cross from unconsecrated to holy soil, and the whisper of loss and chilly despair as they pass back the other way.

You spot your Nan's figure swaying by an oak tree. That's to be expected, of course, the swaying, but she seems somehow to be taller than you think of her being, and she's not holding her stick.

When you draw nearer, you see your Nan's stick lying on the ground where she dropped it, next to the lidded milk pail and near the kicked-over step stool, all of which she must have dragged out to the cemetery last night. Nan herself sways and twists gently, her feet a foot and a half off the ground, one end of a stout rope around her neck, the other tied to a branch over your head, a branch high enough to keep her feet from the ground, but low enough that she could reach it from the step stool.

She rocks back and forth, and you watch her, waiting for the tears to come. They don't, though, perhaps because there's nothing left inside you at all.

"Oh, Nan," you whisper, and you don't even feel the pain as what remains of your jaw and tongue move clumsily.

You sit just near her swaying feet and begin to feel a certain leaden weight in your limbs, beginning at your hands and feet, and creeping upward. It is death come for you, you know. As you decide to sit calmly and wait for the leaden feeling to spread, a gust of wind sets your Nan's corpse to swinging violently. You look up at her contorted face.

It is less repellent than you imagine your own to be.

You get to your feet, straighten the stool, and pick up the axe, so your Nan, who had loved you enough to lie to you, enough to relinquish her place in paradise and her chance to see her lost babbies again, shouldn't have done so for nothing at all.

For isn't suicide a mortal sin?

Using the axe, you cut her down and lay the body on the ground, her left arm stretched to the side. And as the sun rises, you bring the axe down on her left wrist.

You move mechanically, so as not to waste a moment, and in any case, the cool, rough skin of your Nan's hand is less horrifying than the dead flesh of your face and neck. You close her fingers around the candle, and they grip it tightly, as if your Nan is still there, holding on to what remains of your life for all she is worth.

You take a match from your pocket and strike it against the handle of the axe. It flares up, and for a moment the familiar smell of white phosphorus hovers in the air.

You hide the axe in the bushes on the grounds of the cemetery and walk home carrying the corpse, the burning candle protected by her good left hand hidden in the lidded milk pail dangling from your arm.

The old lady is heavy, so much heavier than she had seemed when she was alive. She'd become small and frail, but the body that lies in your arms is heavy as sin.

Even in the East End, people do not usually stroll out just after dawn carrying a corpse. Heads turn as you go, and your neighbors recognize you, recognize your Nan. Nobody speaks.

You lay your Nan's body down in the room you shared with her and your sister, her husband, and their kiddies, and then you rouse the rest of the family.

You say little when they ask what happened. But then, you say very little these days anyway. They assume that your Nan's hand was missing when you found her.

At least, you think they do. You do catch Janey looking at you intently, her brow wrinkled, her head tilted to one side, a bit suspicious-like, and for a minute she looks so much like your late mother, with her constant expression of worry, that it takes your breath away.

Or it would.

You realize that you are no longer breathing. You bring your fingers to your throat, pushing through the layers of your scarf, and feel for a pulse.

You find none.

Later, in private, you peer into the milk pail, and the candle your Nan made and holds is still burning.

Early in the afternoon, you go back for the axe.

Bryant and May gave in, just over two weeks after the walkout. They gave in so quickly and so completely that with the benefit of historical hindsight, one wonders if the matchwomen should have demanded more. On July 18, 1888, Bryant and May acceded to every one of the strikers' terms.

> —The firm agreed to recognize the newly formed Union of Women Matchmakers, the largest union of women and girls in England.
> —The firm agreed to abolish all fines.
> —The firm agreed to abolish all deductions.
> —Matchworkers could take any and all problems directly to the managing director of the firm rather than having to go through the foremen.
> —The firm agreed to provide a room for eating lunch separate and apart from the working rooms.

This last item was so that the matchwomen could eat without white phosphorous settling onto their food and from there making its way into their teeth.

It starts with a toothache, after all.

On August 14, 1889, just over a year after the matchwomen's victory, a group of London dockworkers walked off the job. These workers were mainly Irishmen: the husbands, sons, brothers, and sweethearts of the matchwomen of the East End. Within two days, twenty-five hundred men had turned out, demanding a wage of 6d. an hour, a penny more than they had been earning. Solidarity with the dockworkers spread across London. Black workers, usually brought in as cheap replacement labor, refused to scab. Jewish tailors went out. Hyde Park played host to a rally of one hundred thousand people, serenaded by bands playing "The Marseillaise."

By the end of August, over one hundred thirty thousand workers were out on strike, and the families that were making do without their men's wages were withholding rent.

The strike lasted a month, and the dockworkers won nearly all they asked for. Years later, historians refer to the Great Dock Strike of 1889 as the beginning of the militant New Unionism: the organization of unskilled and industrial labor that swept Britain and replaced the old craft union model. By the end of 1890, almost two million of Britain's workers held a union card.

John Burns, one of the dockworkers' great leaders, spoke out at rallies, urging solidarity in the face of the starvation that threatened strikers and their families.

"Stand shoulder to shoulder," he thundered. "Stand shoulder to shoulder and remember the matchgirls, who won their fight and formed a union!"

On 18 July 1890, the new terms are settled and accepted by the newly born union and by Bryant and May, still in shock (but also pleased that they'd not had to cede more). That afternoon and evening, there is jubilation in the East End.

Streets and homes fill with happy, loud women in the bright, loud clothing the matchgirls are known to favor. Women talk, laugh, dance, and drink. There might even be a few fights, to tell the truth, but if so, they are all in good fun.

Even journalists are right, some of the time.

You switch out your regular scarf for one in bright blue and your everyday hat for your best one, all over red roses and feathers. You wear your best clothing and spend the evening with Annie at the Eagle in the City Road, even dancing on the crystal platform, just as you did before, when your heart beat and your jaw was whole.

When your Nan was alive.

Your Nan, your poor Nan, not laid in the rich soil of county Cork, not now in a better place clutching once more her babbies to her breast, but lost to heaven completely, for had she not been a witch, and a suicide to boot? Sure, she was laid to rest in the consecrated ground of the Catholic churchyard, but only because when Father Keene had interviewed your sisters and brothers, they had all sworn that she had been out of her head with grief for some time, ever since her favorite granddaughter had started showing the signs of phossy jaw. Sure to God, she'd never have done a thing like this while in her right mind, never.

And Father Keene had looked over at you, you sitting in the corner with your face hidden in shadows, and had felt in his heart that what they said was the truth, and he had thought, wouldn't it be a shame to bring scandal and more suffering to this family?

But your Nan hadn't been out of her head at all. All you had to do to see that was to look into the covered pail where her candle still burned, or to search in vain for the heartbeat that used to pulse under your left breast. Your Nan hadn't hanged herself because she was out of her mind with grief.

Your Nan had hanged herself for this: so that this night you could dance a breakdown on The Eagle's crystal platform, so that you could put your arm through Annie's and watch the sun come up, knowing that she and the others were going to be all right, maybe. That when she'd told her man, Mick O'Dell, lived over a few streets and worked on the docks, that she was expecting, he'd told her to set the date just as soon she could.

But you aren't going to hang around for the wedding. Nothing less lucky than a corpse at a wedding, even one that can dance.

You and Annie watch the sun rise from the churchyard at Saints Michael and Mary. You have one arm through hers, and in the other, you hold the pail with the candle inside, still burning, and a small bottle of milk.

Just a bit, you figure, to dowse the candle, and then the rest for Annie to drink, for the coming babby, and you'll do it yourself. No need to make a murderer out of Annie, no matter her offer, and then you'll follow your Nan to perdition, so she won't be without family to help her in her trials.

You and Annie turn and walk slowly and a bit unsteadily (the worse for drink, both of you) through the churchyard, toward the freshly filled-in grave of your Nan. There's a small headstone, just her name, Bridget O'Hea, and the years, 1827-1888. You'd been there yesterday to lay flowers. Other than the pink and yellow wildflowers you'd picked on Hampstead Heath, already wilting and going brown by the time you placed them on the grave, there had been nothing.

But now the flowers you laid yesterday are not wilted at all. They've taken root and are blooming. You give them a gentle tug to make sure they're real, not a trick.

You and Annie clutch at each other's waists as you watch an honest-to-God oak tree sprout from the grave, from sapling to full grown in an instant, with a rich canopy of leaves, wreathed in mistletoe. You step forward and run your hand across the rough bark. A large snake coils around the trunk of the oak, several times, and the thing must be yards long.

You stare for a moment before turning to look at Annie, to see if she's seeing what you are, or if what is left of your brain is playing tricks on you.

She steps forward and plucks a leaf from the oak and holds it to her lips in wonder.

The snake turns its head to look at you, and you find yourself looking into your Nan's eyes.

You blink and the snake, the oak, and the mistletoe are gone, but the flowers you brought are still growing from the grave soil. After a moment's pause, you meet Annie's eyes and step carefully onto your Nan's grave.

You settle yourself against the headstone, and Annie sits next to you. You take the candle, still held in your Nan's left hand and set it on the ground and pass the bottle of milk to Annie. She begins to pry the cork loose, but you still her hand.

Instead, you slide the fingers of your Nan's hand back, and they uncurl as smoothly and gracefully as barley bending in the wind. The candle slips free.

It begins to burn in earnest then, guttering and smoking like the cheap tallow that it is, but burning more quickly than any candle should have a right to, as if making up for lost time. You have ten, maybe fifteen minutes, at the rate it is going.

Annie takes your hand, and together you watch the candle burn down.

Near the end, her grip on your hand tightens, and you close your eyes.

We have remaining to us two photographs, and only two photographs, of the striking Bryant and May matchworkers. The second photograph is more formal. It is of the official strike committee, and the women in it have done their hair and put on their Sunday best. They are arrayed across a stage, carefully posed in chairs. They seem confident, proud, intent.

But the first photograph is the more interesting one. It is of seven women standing in front of the Bryant and May factory. Their faces are gaunt, taut, and serious. More than one look a bit dazed, as if unsure of what they have done and what future it will bring them.

This photograph is famous now. More than that, it has become a symbol of working-class courage and resolve, displayed in the windows of London union offices.

Two of the seven women have almost certainly been identified by recent scholarship.

At the leftmost edge of the photo stands a woman half cut out of the picture. We see her left arm, the left half of her body, and most of her head, which she must have turned toward the camera. She is wearing a velvet hat, like some of the other women, and has a fringe of straight hair reaching almost down to where her eyes should be. Her face is nearly impossible to make out. It is a blur. Perhaps she moved as the photograph was being taken, though nothing else is blurred, not her hat, not her hand, not the scarf knotted around her neck, not a hair of her fringe.

The original print, now lost, belonged to John Burns, the leader of the dockworkers' strike, who urged his men to remember the matchgirls, who had won their fight and formed a union.

But her face is gone

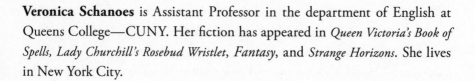

Veronica Schanoes is Assistant Professor in the department of English at Queens College—CUNY. Her fiction has appeared in *Queen Victoria's Book of Spells, Lady Churchill's Rosebud Wristlet, Fantasy,* and *Strange Horizons.* She lives in New York City.

They talk about the labyrinth of Minos, but that was nothing by comparison to
this. Just some tunnels with a hornheaded fellow wandering
lonely and scared and hungry

A LUNAR LABYRINTH

Neil Gaiman

We were walking up a gentle hill on a summer's evening. It was gone eight-thirty, but it still felt like midafternoon. The sky was blue. The sun was low on the horizon, and it splashed the clouds with gold and salmon and purple-gray.

"So how did it end?" I asked my guide.

"It never ends," he said.

"But you said it's gone," I said. "It isn't there any longer. What happened to it?"

I had found the lunar labyrinth mentioned online, a small footnote on a website that told you what was interesting and noteworthy wherever you were in the world. Unusual local attractions: the tackier and more handmade the better. I do not know why I am drawn to them: stoneless henges made of cars or of yellow school buses, polystyrene models of enormous blocks of cheese, unconvincing dinosaurs made of crusted powdery concrete and all the rest.

I need them, and they give me an excuse to stop driving, wherever I am, and to talk to people. I have been invited into people's houses and into their lives because I wholeheartedly appreciated the zoos they made from engine parts, the houses they had built from tin cans and stone blocks then covered with aluminum foil, the historical pageants made from shop-window dummies, the paint on their faces always flaking off. And those people, the ones who made the roadside attractions, they would accept me for what I am.

"We burned it down," said my guide. He was elderly, and he walked with a stick. I had met him sitting on a bench in front of the town's hardware store, and he had agreed to show me the site that the lunar labyrinth had once been built upon. Our progress across the meadow was not fast. "The end of the lunar labyrinth. It was easy. The rosemary hedges caught fire and they crackled and flared. The smoke was thick and drifted down the hill and made us all think of roast lamb."

"Why was it called a lunar labyrinth?" I asked. "Was it just the alliteration?"

He thought about this. "I wouldn't rightly know," he said. "Not one way or the other. We called it a labyrinth, but I guess it's just a maze . . . "

"Just amazed," I repeated.

"There were traditions," he said. "We would only start to walk it the day *after* the full moon. Begin at the entrance. Make your way to the center, then turn around and trace your way back. Like I say, we'd only start walking the day the moon began to wane. It would still be bright enough to walk. We'd walk it any night the moon was bright enough to see by. Come out here. Walk. Mostly in couples. We'd walk until the dark of the moon."

"Nobody walked it in the dark?"

"Oh, some of them did. But they weren't like us. They were kids, and they brought flashlights, when the moon went dark. They walked it, the bad kids, the bad seeds, the ones who wanted to scare each other. For those kids it was Hallowe'en every month. They loved to be scared. Some of them said they saw a torturer."

"What kind of a torturer?" The word had surprised me. You did not hear it often, not in conversation.

"Just someone who tortured people, I guess. I never saw him." A breeze came down toward us from the hilltop. I sniffed the air but smelled no burning herbs, no ash, nothing that seemed unusual on a summer evening. Somewhere there were gardenias.

"It was only kids when the moon was dark. When the crescent moon appeared, then the children got younger, and parents would come up to the hill and walk with them. Parents and children. They'd walk the maze together to its center and the adults would point up to the new moon, how it looks like a smile in the sky, a huge yellow smile and little Romulus and Remus, or whatever the kids were called, they'd smile and laugh, and wave their hands as if they were trying to pull the moon out of the sky and put it on their little faces.

"Then, as the moon waxed, the couples would come. Young couples would come up here, courting, and elderly couples, comfortable in each other's company, the ones whose courting days were long forgotten." He leaned heavily on his stick. "Not forgotten," he said. "You never forget. It must be somewhere inside you. Even if the brain has forgotten, perhaps the teeth remember. Or the fingers."

"Did they have flashlights?"

"Some nights they did. Some nights they didn't. The popular nights were always the nights where no clouds covered the moon, and you could just walk the labyrinth. And sooner or later, everybody did. As the moonlight increased, day by day—night by night, I should say. That world was so beautiful.

"They parked their cars down there, back where you parked yours, at the edge of the property, and they'd come up the hill on foot. Always on foot, except for the ones in wheelchairs, or the ones whose parents carried them. Then, at the top of the hill, some of them'd stop to canoodle. They'd walk the labyrinth, too. There were benches, places to stop as you walked it. And they'd stop and canoodle some more. You'd think it was just the young ones, canoodling, but the older folk did it, too. Flesh to flesh. You would hear them sometimes, on the other side of the hedge, making noises like animals, and that always was your cue to slow down, or maybe explore another branch of the path for a little while. Doesn't come by too often, but when it does I think I appreciate it more now than I did then. Lips touching skin. Under the moonlight."

"How many years exactly was the lunar labyrinth here before it was burned down? Did it come before or after the house was built?"

My guide made a dismissive noise. "After, before . . . these things all go back. They talk about the labyrinth of Minos, but that was nothing by comparison to this. Just some tunnels with a hornheaded fellow wandering lonely and scared and hungry. He wasn't really a bull-head. You know that?"

"How do you know?"

"Teeth. Bulls and cows are ruminants. They don't eat flesh. The minotaur did."

"I hadn't thought of that."

"People don't." The hill was getting steeper now.

I thought, *there are no torturers, not any longer.* And I was not a real torturer. But all I said was, "How high were the bushes that made up the maze? Were they real hedges?"

"They were real. They were high as they needed to be."

"I don't know how high rosemary grows in these parts." I didn't. I was far from home.

"We have gentle winters. Rosemary flourishes here."

"So why exactly did the people burn it all down?"

He paused. "You'll get a better idea of how things lie when we get to the top of the hill."

"How do they lie?"

"At the top of the hill."

The hill was getting steeper and steeper. My left knee had been injured the previous winter, in a fall on the ice, which meant I could no longer run fast, and these days I found hills and steps extremely taxing. With each step my knee would twinge, reminding me, angrily, of its existence.

Many people, on learning that the local oddity they wished to visit had burned down some years before, would simply have gotten back into their cars and driven on toward their final destination. I am not so easily deterred. The finest things I have seen are dead places: a shuttered amusement park I entered by bribing a night watchman with the price of a drink; an abandoned barn in which, the farmer said, half a dozen bigfoots had been living the previous summer. He said they howled at night, and that they stank, but that they had moved on almost a year ago. There was a rank animal smell that lingered in that place, but it might have been coyotes.

"When the moon waned, they walked the lunar labyrinth with love," said my guide. "As it waxed, they walked with desire, not with love. Do I have to explain the difference to you? The sheep and the goats?"

"I don't think so."

"The sick came, too, sometimes. The damaged and the disabled came, and some of them needed to be wheeled through the labyrinth, or carried. But even they had to choose the path they traveled, not the people carrying them or wheeling them. Nobody chose their paths but them. When I was a boy people called them cripples. I'm glad we don't call them cripples any longer. The lovelorn came, too. The alone. The lunatics—they were brought here, sometimes. Got their name from the moon, it was only fair the moon had a chance to fix things."

We were approaching the top of the hill. It was dusk. The sky was the color of wine, now, and the clouds in the west glowed with the light of the setting sun, although from where we were standing it had already dropped below the horizon.

"You'll see, when we get up there. It's perfectly flat, the top of the hill."

I wanted to contribute something, so I said, "Where I come from, five hundred years ago the local lord was visiting the king. And the king showed off his enormous table, his candles, his beautiful painted ceiling, and as each one was displayed, instead of praising it, the lord simply said, 'I have a finer, and bigger, and better one.' The king wanted to call his bluff, so he told him that the following month he would come and eat at this table, bigger and finer than the king's, lit by candles in candleholders bigger and finer than the king's, under a ceiling painting bigger and better than the king's."

My guide said, "Did he lay out a tablecloth on the flatness of the hill, and have twenty brave men holding candles, and did they dine beneath God's own stars? They tell a story like that in these parts, too."

"That's the story," I admitted, slightly miffed that my contribution had been so casually dismissed. "And the king acknowledged that the lord was right."

"Didn't the boss have him imprisoned, and tortured?" asked my guide. "That's what happened in the version of the story they tell hereabouts. They say that the man never even made it as far as the Cordon Bleu dessert his chef had whipped up. They found him on the following day with his hands cut off, his severed tongue placed neatly in his breast pocket and a final bullet hole in his forehead."

"Here? In the house back there?"

"Good Lord, no. They left his body in his nightclub. Over in the city."

I was surprised how quickly dusk had ended. There was still a glow in the west, but the rest of the sky' had become night, plum-purple in its majesty.

"The days before the full of the moon, in the labyrinth," he said, "They were set aside for the infirm, and those in need. My sister had a women's condition. They told her it would be fatal if she didn't have her insides all scraped out, and then it might be fatal anyway."

Her stomach had swollen up as if she was carrying a baby, not a tumor, although she must have been pushing fifty. She came up here when the moon was a day from full and she walked the labyrinth. Walked it from the outside in, in the moon's light, and she walked it from the center back to the outside, with no false steps or mistakes."

"What happened to her?"

"She lived," he said, shortly.

We crested the hill, but I could not see what I was looking at. It was too dark.

"They delivered her of the thing inside her. It lived as well, for a while." He paused. Then he tapped my arm. "Look over there." I turned and looked. The size of the moon astonished me. I know it's an optical illusion, that the moon grows no smaller as it rises, but this moon seemed to take up so much of the horizon as it rose that I found myself thinking of the old Frank Frazetta paperback covers, in which men with their swords raised would be silhouetted in front of huge moons, and I remembered paintings of wolves howling on hilltops, black cutouts against the circle of snow-white moon that framed them. The enormous moon that was rising was the creamy yellow of freshly churned butter.

"Is the moon full?" I asked.

"That's a full moon, all right." He sounded satisfied. "And there's the labyrinth."

We walked toward it. I had expected to see ash on the ground, or nothing. Instead, in the buttery moonlight, I saw a maze, complex and elegant, made of circles and whorls arranged inside a huge square. I could not judge distances properly in that light, but I thought that each side of the square must be two hundred feet or more.

The plants that outlined the maze were low to the ground, though.

None of them was more than a foot tall. I bent down, picked a needle-like leaf, black in the moonlight, and crushed it between finger and thumb. I inhaled, and thought of raw lamb, carefully dismembered and prepared, and placed in an oven on a bed of branch-like leaves that smelled just like this.

"I thought you people burned all this to the ground," I said.

"We did. They aren't hedges, not any longer. But things grow again, in their season. There's no killing some things. Rosemary's tough."

"Where's the entrance?"

"You're standing in it," he said He was an old man who walked with a stick and talked to strangers, I thought. Nobody would ever miss him.

"So what happened up here when the moon was full?"

"Locals didn't walk the labyrinth then. That was the one night that paid for all."

I took a step into the maze. There was nothing difficult about it, not with the little rosemary hedges that marked it no higher than my shins, no higher than a kitchen garden. If I got lost, I could simply step over the bushes, walk back out. But for now I followed the path into the labyrinth. It was easy to make out the way in the light of the full moon. I could hear my guide, as he continued to talk.

"Some folk thought even that price was too high. That was why we came up here, why we burned the lunar labyrinth. We came up that hill when the moon was dark, and we carried burning torches, like in the old black-and-white movies. We all did. Even me. But you can't kill everything. It don't work like that."

"Why rosemary?" I asked.

"Rosemary's for remembering," his voice explained. The butter-yellow moon was rising faster than I imagined or expected. Now it was a pale ghost-face in the sky, calm and compassionate, and white, bone-white.

The man said, "There's always a chance that you could get out safely. Even on the night of the full moon. First you have to get to the center of the labyrinth. There's a fountain there. You'll see. You can't mistake it. Then you have to make it back from the center. No missteps, no dead ends, no mistakes on the way in or on the way out. It's probably easier now than it was when the bushes were high. It's a chance. Otherwise, the labyrinth gets to cure you of all that ails you. Of course, you'll have to run."

I looked back. I could not see my guide. Not any longer. There was something in front of me, beyond the bush-path-pattern, a black shadow padding silently along the perimeter of the square. It was the size of a large dog, but it did not move like a dog.

It threw back its head and howled to the moon, with amusement and with merriment. The huge flat table at the top of the hill echoed with joyous howls, and, my left knee aching from the long hill climb, I stumbled forward.

The maze had a pattern; I could trace it. Above me, the moon shone, bright as day. She had always accepted my gifts in the past. She would not play me false at the end.

"Run," said a voice that was almost a growl.

I ran like a lamb to his laughter.

Neil Gaiman is a *New York Times* bestselling author of more than twenty books for adults and children, including the novels *Neverwhere*, *Stardust*, *American Gods*, *Anansi Boys*, *Coraline*, and *The Graveyard Book*; the Sandman series of graphic novels; and *Make Good Art*, the text of a commencement speech he delivered at Philadelphia's University of the Arts. *The Ocean at the End of the Lane* is his most recent novel for adults and, for younger readers, *Fortunately, the Milk*. He is the recipient of numerous literary honors, including the Locus and Hugo Awards and the Newbery and Carnegie Medals. Born and raised in England, Neil Gaiman now lives in Cambridge, Massachusetts.

The old theatre is a temple, holy in its way, and you've come to worship,
to find epiphany in truths captured by a camera's lens

THE PRAYER OF NINETY CATS

Caitlín R. Kiernan

In this darkened theatre, the screen shines like the moon. More like the moon than this simile might imply, as the moon makes no light of her own, but instead adamantly casts off whatever the sun sends her way. The silver screen reflects the light pouring from the projector booth. And this particular screen truly *is* a silver screen, the real deal, not some careless metonym lazily recalling more glamorous Hollywood movie-palace days. There's silver dust embedded in its tightly-woven silk matte, an apotropaic which might console any Slovak grandmothers in attendance, given the evening's bill of fare. But, then again, is it not also said that the silvered-glass of mirrors offends these hungry phantoms? And isn't the screen itself a mirror, not so very unlike the moon? The moon flashes back the sun, the screen flashes back the dazzling glow from the projector's Xenon arc lamp. Here, then, is an irony, of sorts, as it is sometimes claimed the *moroaică, strigoi mort, vampir,* and *vrykolakas,* are incapable of casting reflections— apparently consuming light much as the gravity well of a black hole does. In these flickering, moving pictures, there must surely be some incongruity or paradox, beginning with Murnau's Orlok, Browning's titular Dracula, and Carl Theodor Dreyer's sinister Marguerite Chopin.

Of course, pretend demons need no potent, tried-and-true charm to ward them off, no matter how much we may wish to fear them. Still, we go through the motions. We need to fear, and when summoning forth these simulacra, to convince ourselves of their authenticity, we must also have a means of dispelling them. We sit in darkness and watch the monsters, and smugly remind ourselves these are merely actors playing unsavory parts, reciting dialogue written to shock, scandalize, and unnerve. All shadows are carefully planned. That face is clever makeup, and a man becoming a bat no more than a bit of trick photography accomplished with flash powder, splicing, and a lump of felt and rabbit fur dangled from piano wire. We sit in the darkness, safely reenacting and mocking and laughing at the silly, delicious fears of our ignorant forbearers. If all else fails, we leave our seats and escape to the lobby. We turn on the light. No need to invoke crucified messiahs and the Queen of Heaven, not when we have Saint Thomas Edison on our side. Though, still another irony arises (we are gathering a veritable platoon of ironies, certainly), as these same monsters were brought to you courtesy of Mr. Edison's tinkerings and profiteering. Any truly wily sorcerer, any witch worth her weight in mandrake and foxglove, knows how very little value there is in conjuring a fearful thing if it may not then be banished at will.

The theatre air is musty and has a sickly sweet sourness to it. It swims with the rancid ghosts of popcorn butter, spilled sodas, discarded chewing gum, and half a hundred varieties of candy lost beneath velvet seats and between the carpeted aisles. Let's say these are the top notes of our perfume. Beneath them lurk the much fainter heart notes of sweat, piss, vomit, cum, soiled diapers—all the pungent gases and fluids a human body may casually expel. Also, though smoking has been forbidden here for decades, the reek of stale cigarettes and cigars persists. Finally, now, the base notes, not to be recognized right away, but registering after half an hour or more has passed, settling in to bestow solidity and depth to this complex *Eau de Parfum*. In the main, it strikes the nostrils as dust, though more perceptive noses may discern dry rot, mold, and aging mortar. Considered thusly, the atmosphere of this theatre might, appropriately, echo that of a sepulcher, shut away and ripe from generations of use.

Crossing the street, you might have noticed a title and the names of the players splashed across the gaudy marquee. After purchasing your ticket from the young man with a death's head tattooed on the back of his left hand (he has a story, if you care to hear), you might have paused to view the relevant lobby cards or posters on display. You might have considered the concessions. These are the rituals before the rite. You might have wished you'd brought along an umbrella, because it's beginning to look like there might be rain later. You may even go to the payphone near the restrooms, but, these days, that happens less and less, and there's talk of having it removed.

Your ticket is torn in half, and you find a place to sit. The lights do not go down, because they were never up. You wait, gazing nowhere in particular, thinking no especial thoughts, until that immense moth-gnawed curtain the color of pomegranates opens wide to reveal the silver screen.

And so we come back to where we began.

With no fanfare or overture, the darkness is split apart as the antique projector sputters reluctantly to life. The auditorium is filled with the noisy, familiar cadence of wheels and sprockets, the pressure roller and the take-up reel, as the film speeds along at twenty-four frames per second and the shutter tricks the eyes and brain into perceiving continuous motion instead of a blurred procession of still photographs. By design, it is all a lie, start to finish. It is all an illusion.

There are no trailers for coming attractions. There might have been in the past, as there might have been cartoons featuring Bugs Bunny and Daffy Duck, or newsreels extolling the evils of Communism and the virtues of soldiers who go away to die in foreign countries. Tonight, there's only the feature presentation, and it begins with jarring abruptness, without so much as a title sequence or the name of the director. Possibly, a few feet of the opening reel were destroyed by the projectionist at the last theatre that screen the film, a disagreeable, ham-fisted man who drinks on the job and has been known to nod off in the booth. We can blame him, if we like. But it may also be there never were such niceties, and that *this* 35mm strip of acetate, celluloid, and polyester was always meant to begin *just so.*

Likewise, the film's score—which has been compared favorably to Wojciech Kilar's score for Campion's *Portrait of a Lady*—seems to begin not at any proper beginning. As cellos and violins compete with kettledrums in a whirl of syncopated rhythms, there is the distinct impression of having stumbled upon a thing already in progress. This may well be the director's desired effect.

EXT. ČACHTICE CASTLE HILL, LITTLE CARPATHIANS. SUNSET.
WOMAN'S VOICE (fearfully):
Katarína, is that you?
(pause)
Katarína? If it is you, say so.

The camera lingers on this bleak spire of evergreens, brush, and sandstone, gray-white rock tinted pink as the sun sinks below the horizon and night claims the wild Hungarian countryside. There are sheer ravines, talus slopes, and wide ledges carpeted with mountain ash, fenugreek, tatra blush, orchids, and thick stands of feather reed grass. The music grows quieter now, drums diminishing, strings receding to a steady vibrato undercurrent as the score hushes itself, permitting the night to be heard. The soundtrack fills with the calls of nocturnal birds, chiefly tawny and long-eared owls, but also nightingales, swifts, and nightjars. From streams and hidden pools, there comes the chorus of frog song. Foxes cry out to one another. The scene is at once breathtaking and forbidding, and you lean forward in your seat, arrested by this austere beauty.

WOMAN'S VOICE (angry):
It is a poor jest, Katarína. It is a poor, poor jest, indeed, and I've no patience for your games tonight.

GIRL'S VOICE (soft, not unkind):
I'm not Katarína. Have you forgotten my name already?

The camera's eye doesn't waver, even at the risk of this shot becoming monotonous. And we see that atop the rocky prominence stands the tumble-down ruins of Čachtice Castle, *Csejte vára* in the mother tongue. Here it has stood since the 1200s, when Kazimir of Hunt-Poznan found himself in need of a sentry post on the troubled road to Moravia. And later, it was claimed by the Hungarian oligarch Máté Csák of Trencsén, the heroic Count Matthew. Then it went to Rudolf II, Holy Roman Emperor, who spent much of his life in alchemical study, searching for the Philosopher's Stone. And, finally, in 1575, the castle was presented as a wedding gift from Lord Chief Justice Ferenc Nádasdy to his fifteen-year-old bride, Báthory Erzsébet, or Alžbeta, the Countess Elizabeth Báthory. The name (one or another of the lot) will doubtless ring a bell, though infamy has seen she's better known to many as the Blood Countess.

The cinematographer works more sleight of hand, and the jagged lineament of the ruins is restored to that of Csejte as it would have stood when the Countess was alive. A grand patchwork of Romanesque and Gothic architecture, its formidable walls and towers loom high above the drowsy village of Vrbové. The castle rises—no, it sprouts—the castle sprouts from the bluff in such a way as to seem almost a natural, integral part of the local geography, something *in situ*, carved by wind and rain rather than by the labors of man.

The film jump cuts to an owl perched on a pine branch. The bird blinks— once, twice—spreads its wings, and takes to the air. The camera lets it go and doesn't follow, preferring to remain with the now-vacant branch. Several seconds pass before the high-pitched scream of a rabbit reveals the reason for the owl's departure.

GIRL'S VOICE:
Ever is it the small things that suffer. That's what they say, you know?
The Tigress of Csejte, she will have them all, because there is
no end to her hunger.

Another jump cut brings us to the castle gates, and the camera pans slowly across the masonry of curtain walls, parapets, and up the steep sides of a horseshoe-shaped watchtower. Jump cut again, and we are shown a room illuminated by the flickering light of candles. There is a noblewoman seated in an enormous and somewhat fanciful chair, upholstered with fine brocade, its oaken legs and arms ending with the paws of a lion, or a dragon.

Or possibly a tigress.

So, a woman seated in an enormous, bestial chair. She wears the "Spanish Farthingale" and stiffened undergarments fashionable during this century. Her dress is made of the finest Florentine silk. Her waist is tightly cinched, her ample breasts flattened by the stays. Were she standing, her dress might remind us of an hourglass. Her head is framed with a wide ruff of starched lace, and her arms held properly within trumpet sleeves, more lace at the cuffs to ring her delicate hands. There is a wolf pelt across her lap, and another covers her bare feet. The candlelight is gracious, and she might pass for a woman of forty, though she's more than a decade older. Her hair, which is the color of cracked acorn shells, has been meticulously braided and pulled back from her round face and high forehead. Her eyes seem dark as rubies.

INT. COUNTESS BÁTHORY'S CHAMBER. NIGHT.
COUNTESS (tersely):
Why are you awake at this hour, child? You should be sleeping.
Haven't I given you a splendid bed?

GIRL (seen dimly, in silhouette):
I don't like being in that room alone. I don't like the shadows in that room.
I try not to see them—

COUNTESS (close up, her eyes fixed on the child):
Oh, don't be silly. A shadow has not yet harmed anyone.

GIRL (almost whispering):
Begging your pardon, My Lady, but these shadows mean to do me mischief.
I hear them whisper, and they do. They are shadows cast by wicked spirits.
They do not speak to you?

COUNTESS (sighs, frowning):
I don't speak with shadows.

GIRL (coyly):
That isn't what they say in the village.
(pause)
Do you truly know the Prayer of Ninety Cats?

By now, it is likely that the theatre, which only a short time ago so filled your thoughts, has receded, fading almost entirely from your conscious mind. This is usually the way of theatres, if the films they offer have any merit at all. The building is the spectacle which precedes the spectacle it has been built to contain, not so different from the relationship of colorful wrapping paper and elaborately tied bows to the gifts hidden within. You're greeted by a mock-grand façade and the blazing electric marquee, and are then admitted into the catchpenny splendor of the lobby. All these things make an impression, and set a mood, but all will fall by the wayside. Exiting the theatre after a film, you'll hardly note a single detail. Your mind will be elsewhere, processing, reflecting, critiquing, amazed, or disappointed.

Onscreen, the Countess' candlelit bedchamber has been replaced by the haggard faces of peasant women, mothers and grandmothers, gazing up at the terrible edifice of Csejte. Over the years, so many among them have sent their daughters away to the castle, hearing that servants are cared for and well compensated. Over the years, none have returned. There are rumors of black magic and butchery, and, from time to time, girls have simply vanished from Vrbové, and also from the nearby town of Čachtice, from whence the fortress took its name. The women cross themselves and look away.

Dissolve to scenes of the daughters of landed aristocracy and the lesser gentry preparing their beautiful daughters for the *gynaeceum* of ecsedi Báthory Erzsébet, where they will be schooled in all the social graces, that they might make more desirable brides and find the best marriages possible. Carriages rattle along the narrow, precipitous road leading up to the castle, wheels and hooves trailing wakes of dust. Oblivious lambs driven to the slaughter, freely delivered by ambitious and unwitting mothers.

Another dissolve, to winter in a soundstage forest, and the Countess walks between artificial sycamore maples, ash, linden, beech, and elderberry. The studio "greens men" have worked wonders, meticulously crafting this forest from plaster, burlap, epoxy, wire, Styrofoam, from lumber armatures and the limbs and leaves of actual trees. The snow is as phony as the trees, but no less convincing, a combination of SnowCel, SnowEx foam, and Powderfrost, dry-foam plastic snow spewed from machines; biodegradable, nontoxic polymers to simulate a gentle snowfall after a January blizzard. But the mockery is perfection. The Countess stalks through drifts so convincing that they may as well be real. Her furs drag behind her, and her boots leave deep tracks. Two huge wolves follow close behind, and when she stops, they come to her and she scratches their shaggy heads and pats their lean flanks and plants kisses behind their ears. A trained crow perches on a limb overhead, cawing, cawing, cawing, but neither the woman nor the wolves pay it any heed. The Countess speaks, and her breath fogs.

COUNTESS (to wolves):
You are my true children. Not Ursula or Pál or Miklós. And you are also my true inamoratos, my most beloved, not Ferenc, who was only ever a husband.

If tabloid gossip and backlot hearsay is to be trusted, this scene has been considerably shortened and toned down from the original script. We do not see the Countess' sexual congress with the wolves. It is only implied by her affections, her words, and by the lewd canticle of a voyeur crow. The scene is both stark and magnificent. It is a final still point before the coming tempest, before the horrors, a moment imbued with grace and menacing tranquility. The camera cuts to Herr Kramer in its counterfeit tree, and you're watching its golden eyes watching the Countess and her wolves, and anything more is implied.

INT. ČACHTICE CASTLE/DRESSING ROOM. MORNING.
The Countess is seated before a looking glass held inside a carved wooden frame, motif of dryads and satyrs. We see the Countess as a reflection, and behind her, a servant girl. The servant is combing the Countess' brown hair with an ivory comb. The Countess is no longer a young woman. There are lines at the edges of her mouth and beneath her eyes.

COUNTESS (furrowing her brows):
You're pulling my hair again. How many times must I tell
you to be careful. You're not deaf, are you?

SERVANT (almost whispering):
No, My Lady.

COUNTESS (icily):
Then when I speak to you, you hear me perfectly well.

SERVANT:
Yes, My Lady.

*The ivory comb snags in the Countess' hair, and she stands, spinning about to face
the terrified servant girl. She snatches the comb from the girl's hand. Strands of
Elizabeth's hair are caught between the teeth.*

COUNTESS (tone of disbelief):
You wretched little beast. Look what you've done.

*The Countess slaps the servant with enough force to split her lip. Blood spatters the
Countess' hand as the servant falls to the floor. The Countess is entranced by the
crimson beads speckling her pale skin.*

COUNTESS (whisper)
You . . . filthy . . . wretch . . .

FADE TO BLACK
FADE IN:
INT. DREAM MIRROR.
*The Countess stands in a dim pool of light, before a towering mirror, a grotesque
nightmare version of the one on her dressing table. The nymphs, satyrs, and dryads
are life-size, and move, engaged in various and sundry acts of sexual abandon.
This dark place is filled with sounds of desire, orgasm, drunken debauchery. In
the mirror is a far younger Elizabeth Báthory. But, as we watch, as the Countess
watches, this young woman rapidly ages, rushing through her twenties, thirties,
her forties. The Countess screams, commanding the mirror cease these awful
visions. The writhing creatures that form the frame laugh and mock her screams.*

FLASH CUT TO:
EXT. SNOW-COVERED FIELD. DAYLIGHT.
*The Countess stands naked in the falling snow, her feet buried up to the ankles.
The snowflakes turn red. The red snow becomes a red rain, and she's drenched.
The air is a red mist.*

FLASH CUT TO:
INT. DREAM MIRROR.
*Nude and drenched in blood, the Countess gazes at her reflection, her face and
body growing young before her eyes. The looking glass shatters.*

FADE TO BLACK

   The Hungary of the film has more in common with the landscape of Hans
Christian Andersen and the Brothers Grimm than with any Hungary that
exists now or ever has existed. It is an archetypal vista, as much a myth as
Stoker's Transylvania and Sheridan Le Fanu's Styria. A real place that has,
inconveniently, never existed. Little or nothing is said of the political and
religious turmoil of Elizabeth's time, or of the war with the Ottoman Turks,
aside from the death of the Countess' husband at the hands of General Giorgio
Basta. If you're a stickler for accuracy, these omissions are unforgivable. But
most of the men and women who sit in the theatre, entranced by the light
flashed back from the screen, will never notice. People do not generally come
to the movies hoping for recitations of dry history. Few will care that pivotal
events in the film never occurred, because they are happening *now*, unfolding
before the eyes of all who have paid the price of admission.

INT. COUNTESS' BEDCHAMBER. NIGHT.
GIRL:
If you have been taught the prayer, say the words aloud.

COUNTESS:
How would you ever know such things, child?

GIRL (turning away)
We have had some of the same tutors, you and I.

The second reel begins with the arrival at Csejte of a woman named Anna Darvulia. In hushed tones, a servant (who dies an especially messy death farther along) refers to her as "the Witch of the Forest." She becomes Elizabeth's lover and teaches her sorcery and the Prayer of Ninety Cats to protect her from all harm. As Darvulia is depicted here, she may as well have inhabited a gingerbread cottage before she came to the Countess, a house of sugary confections where she regularly feasted on lost children. Indeed, shortly after her arrival, and following an admittedly gratuitous sex scene, the subject of cannibalism is introduced. A peasant girl named Júlia, stolen from her home, is brought to the Countess by two of her handmaids and partners in crime, Dorottya and Ilona. The girl is stripped naked and forced to kneel before Elizabeth while the handmaids burn the bare flesh of her back and shoulders with coins and needles that have been placed over an open flame. Darvulia watches on approvingly from the shadows.

INT. KITCHEN. NIGHT.

COUNTESS (smiling):

You shouldn't fret so about your dear mother and father. I know they're poor, but I will see to it they're compensated for the loss of their only daughter.

JÚLIA (sobbing):

There is never enough wood in winter, and never enough food. We have no shoes and wear rags.

COUNTESS:

And haven't I liberated you from those rags?

JÚLIA:

They need me. Please, My Lady, send me home to them.

The Countess glances over her shoulder to Darvulia, as if seeking approval/ instruction. Darvulia nods once, then the Countess turns back to the sobbing girl.

COUNTESS:

Very well. I'll make you a promise, Júlia. And I keep my promises. In the morning, I will send your mother and your father warm clothing and good shoes and enough firewood to see them through the snows. And, what's more, I will send you back to them, as well.

JÚLIA:
You would do that?

COUNTESS:
Certainly, I will. I'll not have any use for you after this evening,
and I detest wastefulness.

This scene has been cut from most prints. If you have any familiarity with
the trials and tribulations of the film's production, and with the censorship
that followed, you'll be surprised, and possibly pleased, to find it has not been
excised from this copy. It may also strike you as relatively tame, compared to
many less controversial, but far more graphic, portions of the film.

COUNTESS:
When we are finished here . . .
(pause)
When we're finished, and my hunger is satisfied, I will speak with my
butcher—a skilled man with a knife and cleaver—and he will see to it
that your corpse is dressed in such a way that it can never be mistaken for
anything but that of a sow. I'll have the meat salted and smoked, then
sent to them, as evidence of my generosity. They will have their daughter
back, and, in the bargain, will not go hungry. Are they fond of sausage.
Júlia? I'd think you would make a marvelous *debreceni*.

Critics and movie buffs who lament the severe treatment the film has
suffered at the hands of nervous studio executives, skittish distributors, and
the MPAA often point to Júlia's screams, following these lines, as an example
of how great cinema may be lost to censorship. Sound editors and Foley artists
are said to have crafted the unsettling and completely inhuman effect by
mixing the cries of several species of birds, the squeal of a pig, and the steam
whistle of a locomotive. The scream continues as this scene dissolves to a
delirious montage of torture and murder. The Countess' notorious iron maiden
makes an appearance. A servant is dragged out into a snowy courtyard, and
once her dress and underclothes have been savagely ripped away, the woman
is bound to a wooden stake. Elizabeth Báthory pours buckets of cold water
over the servant's body until she freezes to death and her body glistens like an
ice sculpture.

The theatre is so quiet that you begin to suspect everyone else has had enough and left before The End. But you don't dare look away long enough to see whether this is in fact the case.

The Countess sits in her enormous lion- (or dragon- or tigress-) footed chair, in that bedchamber lit only by candlelight. She strokes the wolf pelt on her lap as lovingly as she stroked the fur of those living wolves.

"We've had some of the same tutors, you and I," the strange brown girl says, the gypsy child who claims to be afraid of the shadows in the small room that has been provided for her.

"Anna's never mentioned you."

"*She* and I have had some of the same tutors," the child whispers. "Now, My Lady, please speak the words aloud and drive away the evil spirits."

"I have heard of no such prayer," the Countess tells the girl, but the actress' air and intonation make it's obvious she's lying. "I've received no such catechism."

"Then shall I teach it to you? For when they are done with me, the shadows might come looking after you, and if you don't know the prayer, how will you hope to defend yourself, My Lady?"

The Countess frowns and mutters, half to herself, half to the child, "I need no defense against shadows. Rather, let the shadows blanch and wilt at the thought of me."

"That same arrogance will be your undoing," the child replies. Then all the candles gutter and are extinguished, and the only light remaining is cold moonlight, getting in through the parted draperies. The child is gone. The Countess sits in her clawed chair and squeezes her eyes tightly shut. You may once have done very much the same thing, hearing some bump in the night. Fearing an open closet or the space beneath your bed, a window or a hallway. In this moment, Elizabeth Bathory von Ecsed, Alžbeta Bátoriová, the Bloody Lady of Čachtice, she seems no more fearsome for all her fearsome reputation than the child you once were. The boyish girl she herself was, forty-seven, forty-six, forty-eight years before this night. The girl given to tantrums and seizures and dressing up in boy's clothes. She cringes in this dark, moon-washed room, eyelids drawn against the night, and begins, haltingly, to recite the prayer Anna Darvulia has taught her.

"I am in peril, O cloud. Send, O send, you most powerful of Clouds, send ninety cats, for thou are the supreme Lord of Cats. I command you, King of the Cats, I pray you. May you gather them together, even if you are in the mountains, or on the waters, or on the roofs, or on the other side of the ocean . . . tell them to come to me."

Fade to black.

Fade up.

The bedchamber is filled with the feeble colors of a January morning. With the wan luminance of the winter sun in these mountains. The balcony doors have blown open in the night, and a drift of snow has crept into the room. Pressed into the snow there are the barefoot tracks of a child. The Countess opens her eyes. She looks her age, and then some.

Fade to black.

Fade up.

The Countess in her finest farthingale and ruff stands before the altar of Csejte's austere chapel. She gazes upwards at a stained-glass narrative set into the frames of three very tall and very narrow lancet windows. Her expression is distant, detached, unreadable. Following an establishing shot, and then a brief close up of the Countess' face, the trio of stained-glass windows dominates the screen. The production designer had them manufactured in Prague, by an artisan who was provided detailed sketches mimicking the style of windows fashioned by Harry Clarke and the Irish cooperative *An Túr Gloine*. As with so many aspects of the film, this window has inspired heated debate, chiefly regarding its subject matter. The most popular interpretation favors one of the hagiographies from the *Legenda sanctorum*, the tale of Saint. George and the dragon of Silene.

The stillness of the chapel is shattered by squealing hinges and quick footsteps, as Anna Darvulia rushes in from the bailey. She approaches the Countess, who has turned to meet her.

DARVULIA (angry):
What you seek, Elizabeth, you'll not find it here.

COUNTESS (feigning dismay):
I only wanted an hour's solitude. It's quiet here.

DARVULIA (sneering):
Liar. You came seeking after a solace that shall forever be denied you,
as it has always been denied me. We have no place here, Elizabeth.
Let us leave together.

COUNTESS
She came to me again last night. How can your prayer protect me
from her, when she also knows it?

Anna Darvulia whispers something in the Countess' ear, then kisses her cheek and leads her from the chapel.

DISSOLVE TO:
Two guards or soldiers thread heavy iron chain through the handles of the chapel doors, then slide the shackle of a large padlock through the links of chain and clamp the lock firmly shut.

Somewhere towards the back of the theatre, a man coughs loudly, and a woman laughs. The man coughs a second time, then mutters (presumably to the woman), and she laughs again. You're tempted to turn about in your seat and ask them to please hold it down, that there are people who came to see the movie. But you don't. You don't take your eyes off the screen, and, besides, you've never been much for confrontation. You also consider going out to the lobby and complaining to the management, but you won't do that, either. It sounds like the man is telling a dirty joke, and you do your best to ignore him.

The film has returned to the snowy soundstage forest. Only now there are many more trees, spaced more closely together. Their trunks and branches are as dark as charcoal, as dark as the snow is light. Together these two elements—trees and snow, snow and trees—form a proper joyance for any chiaroscurist. In the foreground of this *mise-en-scène*, an assortment of taxidermied wildlife (two does, a rabbit, a badger, etc.) watches on with blind acrylic eyes as Anna Darvulia follows a path through the wood. She wears an enormous crimson cloak, the hood all but concealing her face. Her cloak completes the palette of the scene: the black trees, the white of the snow, this red slash of wool. There is a small falcon, a merlin, perched on the woman's left shoulder, and gripped in her left hand (she isn't wearing gloves) is a leather leash. As the music swells—strings, woodwinds, piano, the thunderous kettledrum—the camera pans slowly to the right, tracing the leash from Darvulia's hand to the heavy collar clasped about the Countess' pale throat. Elizabeth is entirely naked, scrambling through the snow on all fours. Her hair is a matted tangle of twigs and dead leaves. Briars have left bloody welts on her arms, legs, and buttocks. There are wolves following close behind her, famished wolves starving in the dead of this endless Carpathian winter. The pack is growing bold, and one of the animals rushes in close, pushing its muzzle between her exposed thighs, thrusting about with its wet nose, lapping obscenely at the Countess' ass and genitals. Elizabeth bares her sharp teeth and, wheeling around, straining against the leash, she snaps viciously at this churlish rake of a wolf. She growls as convincingly as any lunatic or lycanthrope might hope to growl.

All wolves are churlish. All wolves are rakes, especially in fairy tales, and especially this far from spring.

"Have you forgotten the prayer so soon?" Darvulia calls back, her voice cruel and mocking. Elizabeth doesn't answer, but the wolves yelp and retreat.

And as the witch and her pupil pick their way deeper into the forest, we see that the gypsy girl, dressed in a cloak almost identical to Darvulia's—wool died that same vivid red—stands among the wolves as they whine and mill about her legs.

Elizabeth awakens in her bed, screaming.

In a series of jump cuts, her screams echo through the empty corridors of Csejte.

(This scene is present in all prints, having somehow escaped the same fate as the unfilmed climax of the Countess' earlier trek through the forest—a testament to the fickle inconsistency of censors. In an interview she gave to the Croatian periodical *Hrvatski filmski ljetopis* [Autumn 2003], the actress who played Elizabeth reports that she actually did suffer a spate of terrible nightmares after making the film, and that most of them revolved around this particular scene. She says, "I have only been able to watch it [the scene] twice. Even now, it's hard to imagine myself having been on the set that day. I've always been afraid of dogs, and those were *real* wolves.")

In the fourth reel, you find you're slightly irritated when film briefly loses its otherwise superbly claustrophobic focus, during a Viennese interlude surely meant, instead, to build tension. The Countess' depravity is finally, inevitably brought to the attention of the Hungarian Parliament and King Matthias. The plaintiff is a woman named Imre Megyery, the Steward of Sávár, who became the guardian of the Countess' son, Pál Nádasdy, after the death of her husband. It doesn't help that the actor who plays György Thurzó, Matthias' palatine, is an Australian who seems almost incapable of getting the Hungarian accent right. Perhaps he needed a better dialect coach. Perhaps he was lazy. Possibly, he isn't a very good actor.

INT. COUNTESS' BEDCHAMBER. NIGHT.
Elizabeth and Darvulia in the Countess' bed, after a vigorous bout of lovemaking. Lovemaking, sex, fucking, whatever. Both women are nude. The corpse of a third woman lies between them. There's no blood, so how she died is unclear.

DARVULIA:

Megyery the Red, she plots against you. She has gone to the King, and very, very soon Thurzó's notaries will arrive to poke and pry and be the King's eyes and ears.

COUNTESS:

But you will keep me safe, Anna. And there is the prayer . . .

DARVULIA (gravely):

These are men, with all the power of the King and the Church at their backs. You must take this matter seriously, Elizabeth. The dark gods will concern themselves only so far, and after that we are on our own. Again, I beg you to at least consider abandoning Csejte.

COUNTESS:

No. No, and don't ask again. It is my home. Let Thurzó's men come. I will show them nothing. I will let them see nothing.

DARVULIA:

It isn't so simple, my sweet Erzsébet. Ferenc is gone, and without a husband to protect you . . . you must consider the greed of relatives who covet your estates, and consider, also, debts owed to you by a king who has no intention of ever settling them. Many have much to gain from your fall.

COUNTESS (stubbornly):

There will be no fall.

You sit up straight in your reclining theatre seat. You've needed to urinate for the last half hour, but you're not about to miss however much of the film you'd miss during a quick trip to the restroom. You try not to think about it; you concentrate on the screen and not your aching bladder.

INT. COUNTESS' BEDCHAMBER. NIGHT.

The Countess sits in her lion-footed chair, facing the open balcony doors. There are no candles burning, but we can see the silhouette of the gypsy girl outlined in the winter moonlight pouring into the room. She is all but naked. The wind blows loudly, howling about the walls of the castle.

COUNTESS (distressed):

No, you're not mine. I can't recall ever having seen you before. You are nothing of mine. You are some demon sent by the moon to harry me.

GIRL (calmly):

It is true I serve the moon, Mother, as do you. She is mistress to us both. We have both run naked while she watched on. We have both enjoyed her favors. We are each the moon's bitch.

COUNTESS (turning away):

Lies. Every word you say is a wicked lie. And I'll not hear any more of it. Begone, *strigoi*. Go back to whatever stinking hole was dug to cradle your filthy gypsy bones.

GIRL (suddenly near tears)

Please do no not say such things, Mother.

COUNTESS (through clenched teeth)

You are not my daughter! This is the price of my sins, to be visited by phantoms, to be haunted.

GIRL:

I only want to be held, Mother. I only want to be held, as any daughter would. I want to be kissed.

Slowly, the Countess looks back at the girl. Snow blows in through the draperies, swirling about the child. The girl's eyes flash red-gold. She takes a step nearer the Countess.

GIRL (cont'd.):

I can protect you, Mother.

COUNTESS:

From what? From whom?

GIRL:

You know from what, and you know from whom. You would know, even if Anna hadn't told you. You are not a stupid woman.

COUNTESS:
You do not come to protect me, but to damn me.

GIRL (kind):
I only want to be held, and sung to sleep.

COUNTESS (shuddering):
My damnation.

GIRL (smiling sadly):
No, Mother. You've tended well-enough to that on your own. You've no
need of anyone to hurry you along to the pit.

CLOSE UP — THE COUNTESS
*The Countess' face is filled with a mixture of dread and defeat, exhaustion and
horror. She shuts her eyes a moment, muttering silently, then opens them again.*

COUNTESS (resigned):
Come, child.

MEDIUM SHOT — THE COUNTESS
*The Countess sits in her chair, head bowed now, seemingly too exhausted to
continue arguing with the girl. From the foreground, the gypsy girl approaches
her. Strange shadows seem to loom behind the Countess' chair. The child begins to
sing in a sweet, sad, lilting voice, a song that might be a hymn or a dirge.*

FADE TO BLACK.

This scene will stay with you. You will find yourself thinking, *That's where
it should have ended. That would have made a better ending.* The child's song—
only two lines of which are intelligible—will remain with you long after many
of the grimmer, more graphic details are forgotten. Two eerie, poignant lines:
Stay with me and together we will live forever. / Death is the road to awe. Later,
you'll come across an article in *American Cinematographer* (April 2006), and
discover that the screenwriter originally intended this to be the final scene,
but was overruled by the director, who insisted it was too anticlimactic.

Which isn't to imply that the remaining twenty minutes are without merit, but only that they steer the film in a different and less subtle, less dreamlike direction. Like so many of the films you most admire—Bergman's *Det sjunde inseglet*, Charlie Kaufman's *Synecdoche, New York*, Herzog's *Herz aus Glas*, David Lynch's *Lost Highway*—this one is speaking to you in the language of dreams, and after the child's song, you have the distinct sense that the film has awakened, jolted from the subconscious to the conscious, the self aware. It's ironic, therefore, that the next scene is a dream sequence. And it is a dream sequence that has left critics divided over the movie's conclusion and what the director intended to convey. There is a disjointed, tumbling series of images, and it is usually assumed that this is simply a nightmare delivered to the Countess by the child. However, one critic, writing for *Slovenska Kinoteka* (June 2005), has proposed it represents a literal divergence of two timelines, dividing the historical Báthory's fate from that of the fictional Báthory portrayed in the film. She notes the obvious, that the dream closely parallels the events of December 29, 1610, the day of the Countess' arrest. A few have argued the series of scenes was never meant to be perceived as a dream (neither the director nor the screenwriter have revealed their intent). The sequence may be ordered as follows:

The Arrival: A retinue on horseback—Thurzó, Imre Megyery, the Countess' sons-in-law, Counts Drugeth de Homonnay and Zrínyi, together with an armed escort. The party reaches the Csejte, and the iron gates swing open to admit them.

The Descent: The Palatine's men following a narrow, spiraling stairwell into the depth of the castle. They cover their mouths and noses against some horrible stench.

The Discovery: A dungeon cell strewn with corpses, in various stages of dismemberment and decay. Two women, still living, though clearly mad, their bodies naked and beaten and streaked with filth, are manacled to the stone walls. They scream at the sight of the men.

The Trial: Theodosious Syrmiensis de Szulo of the Royal Supreme Court pronounces a sentence of *perpetuis carceribus*, sparing the Countess from execution, but condemning her to lifelong confinement at Csejte.

The Execution/Pardon of the Accomplices: Three women and one man. Two of the women, Jó Ilona and Dorottya Szentes, are found guilty, publicly tortured, and burned alive. The man, Ujváry János (portrayed as a deformed dwarf), is beheaded before being thrown onto the bonfire with Jó and Dorottya. The third woman, Katarína Beniezky, is spared (this is not explained, and none of the four are named in the film).

The Imprisonment: The Countess sits on her bed as stonemasons brick up the chamber's windows and the door leading out onto the balcony. Then the door is sealed. Close ups of trowels, mortar, callused hands, Elizabeth's eyes, a Bible in her lap. Last shot from Elizabeth's POV, her head turned away from the camera, as the final few bricks are set in place. She is alone. Fade to black.

Anna Darvulia, "the Witch of the Forest," appears nowhere in this sequence.

FADE IN:
EXT. CSETJE STABLES. DAY.
The Countess watches as Anna Darvulia climbs onto the back of a horse. Once in the saddle, her feet in the stirrups, she stares sorrowfully down at the Countess.

DARVULIA:
I beg you, Erzsébet. Come with me. We'll be safe in the forest. There are places where no man knows to look.

COUNTESS:
This is my home. Please, don't ask me again. I won't run from them. I won't.

DARVULIA (speaking French and Croatian):
Ma petite bête douce. Volim te, Erzsébet.
(pause)
Ne m'oublie pas.

COUNTESS (slapping the horse's rump)
Go! Go now, love, before I lose my will.

CUT TO:
EXT. ČACHTICE CASTLE HILL. WINTER. DAY.
Anna Darvulia racing away from the snowbound castle, while the Countess watches from her tower.

COUNTESS (off):
I command you, O King of the Cats, I pray you.
May you gather them together,
Give them thy orders and tell them,
Wherever they may be, to assemble together,
To come from the mountains,

From the waters, from the rivers,

From the rainwater on the roofs, and from the oceans.

Tell them to come to me.

FADE TO BLACK.

FADE IN:

INT. COUNTESS' BEDCHAMBER. NIGHT.

The Countess in her enormous chair. The gypsy girl stands before her. As before, she is almost naked. There is candlelight and moonlight. Snow blows in from the open balcony doors.

GIRL:

She left you all alone.

COUNTESS:

No, child. I sent her away.

GIRL:

Back to the wood?

COUNTESS:

Back to the wood.

You sit in your seat and breathe the musty theatre smells, the smells which may as well be ghosts as they are surely remnants of long ago moments come and gone. Your full bladder has been all but forgotten. Likewise, the muttering, laughing man and woman seated somewhere behind you. There is room for nothing now but the illusion of moving pictures splashed across the screen. Your eyes and your ears translate the interplay of light and sound into story. The old theatre is a temple, holy in its way, and you've come to worship, to find epiphany in truths captured by a camera's lens. There's no need of plaster saints and liturgies. No need of the intermediary services of a priest. Your god— and the analogy has occurred to you on many occasions—is speaking to you directly, calling down from that wide silk-and-silver window and from Dolby speakers mounted high on the walls. Your god speaks in many voices, and its angels are an orchestra, and every frame is a page of scripture. This mass is rapidly winding down towards benediction.

GIRL:
May I sit at your feet, Mother?

COUNTESS:
Wouldn't you rather have my lap?

GIRL (smiling)
Yes, Mother. I would much rather have your lap.

The gypsy girl climbs into the Countess' lap, her small brown body nestling in the voluminous folds of Elizabeth's dress. The Countess puts her arms around the child, and holds her close. The girl rests her head on the Countess' breast.

GIRL (whisper):
They will come, you know? The men. The soldiers.

COUNTESS:
I know. But let's not think of that, not now. Let's not think on anything much at all.

GIRL:
But you recall the prayer, yes?

COUNTESS:
Yes, child. I recall the prayer. Anna taught me the prayer, just as you taught it to her.

GIRL:
You are so clever, Mother.

CLOSE UP.
The Countess' hand reaching into a fold of her dress, withdrawing a small silver dagger. The handle is black and polished wood, maybe jet or mahogany. There are occult symbols etched deeply into the metal, all down the length of the blade.

GIRL:
Will you say the prayer for me? No one ever prays for me.

COUNTESS:

I would rather hear you sing, dear. Please, sing for me.

The gypsy girl smiles and begins her song.

GIRL:

Stay with me, and together we will live forever.
Death is the road to awe—

The Countess clamps a hand over the girl's mouth, and plunges the silver dagger into her throat. The girl's eyes go very wide, as blood spurts from the wound. She falls backwards to the floor, and writhes there for a moment. The Countess gets to her feet, triumph in her eyes.

COUNTESS:

You think I didn't know you? You think I did not see?

The girl's eyes flash red-gold, and she hisses loudly, then begins to crawl across the floor towards the balcony. She pulls the knife from her throat and flings it away. It clatters loudly against the floor. The girl's teeth are stained with blood.

GIRL (hoarsely)

You deny me. You dare deny me.

COUNTESS:

You are none of mine.

GIRL:

You send me to face the cold alone? To face the moon alone?

The Countess doesn't reply, but begins to recite the Prayer of Ninety Cats. As she does, the girl stands, almost as if she hasn't been wounded. She backs away, stepping through the balcony doors, out into snow and brilliant moonlight. The child climbs onto the balustrade, and it seems for a moment she might grow wings and fly away into the Carpathian night.

COUNTESS:

May these ninety cats appear to tear and destroy

The hearts of kings and princes,
And in the same way the hearts of teachers and judges,
And all who mean me harm,
That they shall harm me not.
(pause)
Holy Trinity, protect me.
And guard Erzsébet from all evil.

The girl turns her back on the Countess, gazing down at the snowy courtyard below.

GIRL:
I'm the one who guarded you, Mother. I'm the one who has kept you safe.

COUNTESS (raising her voice):
Tell them to come to me.
And to hasten them to bite the heart.
Let them rip to pieces and bite again and again . . .

GIRL:
There's no love in you anywhere. There never was.

COUNTESS:
Do not say that! Don't you dare say that! I have loved—

GIRL (sadly):
You have lusted and called it love. You tangle appetite and desire. Let me
fall, and be done with you.

COUNTESS (suddenly confused)
No. No, child. Come back. No one falls this night.

INT./EXT. NIGHT.
*As the Countess moves towards the balcony, the gypsy girl steps off the balustrade
and tumbles to the courtyard below. The Countess cries out in horror and rushes
out onto the balcony.*

EXT. NIGHT.

The broken body of the girl on the snow-covered flagstones of the courtyard. Blood still oozes from the wound in her throat, but also from her open mouth and her nostrils. Her eyes are open. Her blood steams in the cold air. A large crow lands near her body. The camera pans upwards, and we see the Countess gazing down in horror at the broken body of the dead girl. In the distance, wolves begin to howl.

EXT. BALCONY. NIGHT.
The Countess is sitting now, her back pressed to the stone columns of the balustrade. She's sobbing, her hands tearing at her hair. She is the very portrait here of loss and madness.

COUNTESS (weeping):
I didn't know. God help me, I did not know.

FADE UP TO WHITE.
EXT. CSEJTE. MORNING.
A small cemetery near the castle's chapel. Heavy snow covers everything. The dwarf Ujváry János has managed to hack a shallow grave into the frozen earth. The Countess watches as the gypsy girl's small body, wrapped in a makeshift burial shroud, is lowered into the hole. The Countess turns and hurries away across the bailey, and János begins filling the grave in again. Shovelful after shovelful of dirt and frost and snow falls on the body, and slowly it disappears from view. Perched on a nearby headstone, an owl watches. It blinks, and rotates its head and neck 180 degrees, so it appears to be watching the burial upside down.

In a week, you'll write your review of the film, the review you're being paid to write, and you'll note that the genus and species of owl watching János as he buries the dead girl is *Bubo virginianus*, the Great Horned Owl. You'll also note the bird is native to North America, and not naturally found in Europe, but that to fret over these sorts of inaccuracies is, at best, pedantic. At worst, you'll write, it means that one has entirely missed the point and would have been better off staying at home and not wasting the price of a movie ticket.

This is not the life of Erzsébet Báthory.

No one has ever lived this exact life.

Beyond the establishing shot of the ruins at the beginning of the film, the castle is not Csejte. Likewise, the forest that surrounds it is the forest that this story requires it to be, and whether or not it's an accurate depiction of the forests of the Piešťany region of Slovakia is irrelevant.

The Countess may or may not have been Anna Darvulia's lover. Erzsébet Báthory may have been a lesbian. Or she may not. Anna Darvulia may or may not have existed.

There is no evidence whatsoever that Erzsébet was repeatedly visited in the dead of night by a strange gypsy child.

Or that the Countess' fixation with blood began when she struck a servant who'd accidentally pulled her hair.

Or that Erzsébet was ever led naked through those inaccurate forests while lustful wolves sniffed at her sex.

Pedantry and nitpicking is fatal to all fairy tales. You will write that there are people who would argue a wolf lacks the lung capacity to blow down a house of straw and that any beanstalk tall enough to reach the clouds would collapse under its own weight. They are, you'll say, the same lot who'd dismiss Shakespeare for mixing Greek and Celtic mythology, or on the grounds that there was never a prince of Verona named Escalus. "The facts are neither here nor there," you will write. "We have entered a realm where facts may not even exist." You'll be paid a pittance for the review, which virtually no one will read.

There will be one letter to the editor, complaining that your review was "too defensive" and that you are "an apologist for shoddy, prurient filmmaking." You'll remember this letter (though not the name of its author), many years after the paltry check has been spent.

The facts are neither here nor there.

Sitting in your theatre seat, these words have not yet happened, the words you'll write. At best, they're thoughts at the outermost edges of conception. Sitting here, there is nothing but the film, another's fever dreams you have been permitted to share. And you are keenly aware how little remains of the fifth reel, that the fever will break very soon.

EXT. FOREST. NIGHT.
MEDIUM SHOT.
Anna Darvulia sits before a small campfire, her horse's reins tied to a tree behind her. A hare is roasting on a spit above the fire. There's a sudden gust of wind, and, briefly, the flames burn a ghostly blue. She narrows her eyes, trying to see something beyond the firelight.

DARVULIA:
You think I don't see you? You think I can't smell you?
(pause)

You've no right claim left on me. I've passed my debt to the Báthory woman. I've prepared her for you. Now, leave me be, spirit. Do not trouble me this night or any other.

The fire flares blue again, and Darvulia lowers her head, no longer gazing into the darkness.

DISSOLVE TO:
EXT. ČACHTICE CASTLE HILL. NIGHT.
The full moon shines down on Csejte. The castle is dark. There's no light in any of its windows.

CUT TO:
The gypsy girl's unmarked grave. But much of the earth that filled the hole now lies heaped about the edges, as if someone has hastily exhumed the corpse. Or as if the dead girl might have dug her way out. The ground is white with snow and frost, and sparkles beneath the moon.

CUT TO:
EXT. BALCONY OUTSIDE COUNTESS' BEDCHAMBER. NIGHT.
The owl that watched Ujváry János bury the girl is perched on the stone balustrade. The doors to the balcony have been left standing open. Draperies billow in the freezing wind.

CLOSE UP:
Owl's round face. It blinks several times, and the bird's eyes flash an iridescent red-gold.

The Countess sits in her bedchamber, in that enormous chair with its six savage feet. A wolf pelt lies draped across her lap, emptied of its wolf. Like a dragon, the Countess breathes steam. She holds a wooden cross in her shaking hands.

"Tell the cats to come to me," she says, uttering the prayer hardly above a whisper. There is no need to raise her voice; all gods and angels must surely have good ears. "And hasten them," she continues, "to bite the hearts of my enemies and all who would do me harm. Let them rip to pieces and bite again and again the heart of my foes. And guard Erzsébet from all evil. *O Quam Misericors est Deus, Pius et Justus.*"

Elizabeth was raised a Calvinist, and her devout mother, Anna, saw that she attended a fine Protestant school in Erdöd. She was taught mathematics and learned to write and speak Greek, German, Slovak, and Latin. She learned Latin prayers against the demons and the night.

"O Quam Misericors est Deus. Justus et Paciens," she whispers, though she's shivering so badly that her teeth have begun to chatter and the words no longer come easily. They fall from her lips like stones. Or rotten fruit. Or lies. She cringes in her chair, and gazes intently towards the billowing, diaphanous drapes and the night and balcony beyond them. A shadow slips into the room, moving across the floor like spilled oil. The drapes part as if they have a will all their own (they were pulled to the sides with hooks and nylon fishing line, you've read), and the gypsy girl steps into the room. She is entirely nude, and her tawny body and black hair are caked with the earth of her abandoned grave. There are feathers caught in her hair, and a few drift from her shoulders to lie on the floor at her feet. She is bathed in moonlight, as cliché as that may sound. She has the iridescent eyes of an owl. The girl's face is the very picture of sorrow.

"Why did you bury me, Mother?"

"You were dead . . . "

The girl takes a step nearer the Countess. "I was so cold down there. You cannot ever imagine anything even half so cold as the deadlands."

The Countess clutches her wood cross. She is shaking, near tears. "You cannot be here. I said the prayers Anna taught me."

The girl has moved very near the chair now. She is close enough that she could reach out and stroke Elizabeth's pale cheek, if she wished to do so.

"The cats aren't coming, Mother. Her prayer was no more than any other prayer. Just pretty words against that which has never had cause to fear pretty words."

"The cats aren't coming," the Countess whispers, and the cross slips from her fingers.

The gypsy child reaches out and strokes Elizabeth's pale cheek. The girl's short nails are broken and caked with dirt. "It doesn't matter, Mother, because I'm here. What need have you of cats, when your daughter has come to keep you safe?"

The Countess looks up at the girl, who seems to have grown four or five inches taller since entering the room. "You are my daughter?" Elizabeth asks, the question a mouthful of fog.

"I am," the girl replies, kneeling to gently kiss the Countess' right cheek. "I have many mothers, as I have many daughters of my own. I watch over them all. I hold them to me and keep them safe."

"I've lost my mind," the Countess whispers. "long, long ago, I lost my mind." She hesitantly raises her left hand, brushing back the girl's filthy, matted hair, dislodging another feather. The Countess looks like an old woman. All traces of the youth she clung to with such ferocity have left her face, and her eyes have grown cloudy. "I am a madwoman."

"It makes no difference," the gypsy girl replies.

"Anna lied to me."

"Let that go, Mother. Let it all go. There are things I would show you. Wondrous things."

"I thought she loved me."

"She is a sorceress, Mother, and an inconstant lover. But I am true. And you'll need no other's love but mine."

The movie's score has dwindled to a slow smattering of piano notes, a bow drawn slowly, nimbly across the string of a cello. A hint of flute.

The Countess whispers, "I called to the King of Cats."

The girl answers, "Cats rarely ever come when called. And certainly not ninety all at once."

And the brown girl leans forward, her lips pressed to the pale Countess' right ear. Whatever she says, it's nothing you can make out from your seat, from your side of the silver mirror. The gypsy girl kisses the Countess on the forehead.

"I'm so very tired."

"Shhhhh, Mother. I know. It's okay. You can rest now."

The Countess asks, "Who are you?"

"I am the peace at the end of all things."

EXT. COURTYARD BELOW COUNTESS' BALCONY. MORNING.
The body of Elizabeth Báthory lies shattered on the flagstones, her face and clothes a mask of frozen blood. Fresh snow is falling on her corpse. A number of noisy crows surround the body. No music now, only the wind and the birds.

FADE TO BLACK:
ROLL CREDITS.
THE END.

As always, you don't leave your seat until the credits are finished and the curtain has swept shut again, hiding the screen from view. As always, you've made no notes, preferring to rely on your memories.

You follow the aisle to the auditorium doors and step out into the almost deserted lobby. The lights seem painfully bright. You hurry to the restroom. When you're finished, you wash your hands, dry them, then spend almost an entire minute staring at your face in the mirror above the sink.

Outside, it's started to rain, and you wish you'd brought an umbrella.

The *New York Times* recently hailed **Caitlín R. Kiernan** as "one of our essential writers of dark fiction." Her novels include *The Red Tree* (nominated for the Shirley Jackson and World Fantasy awards) and *The Drowning Girl: A Memoir* (winner of the James Tiptree, Jr. Award and the Bram Stoker Award, nominated for the Nebula, Locus, Shirley Jackson, World Fantasy, British Fantasy, and Mythopoeic awards). To date, her short fiction has been collected in thirteen volumes, most recently *Confessions of a Five-Chambered Heart, Two Worlds and In Between: The Best of Caitlín R. Kiernan (Volume One)*, and *The Ape's Wife and Other Stories*. Currently, she's writing the graphic novel series Alabaster for Dark Horse Comics and working on her next novel, *Cherry Bomb*.

She knew to look the Forests straight on. She knew the surveyors were wrong.
There was a predator out there. The Forest itself was one . . .

SHADOWS FOR SILENCE
IN THE FORESTS OF HELL

Brandon Sanderson

"The one you have to watch for is the White Fox," Daggon said, sipping his beer. "They say he shook hands with the Evil itself, that he visited the Fallen World and came back with strange powers. He can kindle fire on even the deepest of nights, and no shade will dare come for his soul. Yes, the White Fox. Meanest bastard in these parts for sure. Pray he doesn't set his eyes on you, friend. If he does, you're dead."

Daggon's drinking companion had a neck like a slender wine bottle and a head like a potato stuck sideways on the top. He squeaked as he spoke, a Lastport accent, voice echoing in the eaves of the waystop's common room. "Why . . . why would he set his eyes on me?"

"That depends, friend," Daggon said, looking about as a few overdressed merchants sauntered in. They wore black coats, ruffled lace poking out the front, and the tall-topped, wide-brimmed hats of fortfolk. They wouldn't last two weeks out here, in the Forests.

"It depends?" Daggon's dining companion prompted. "It depends on what?"

"On a lot of things, friend. The White Fox is a bounty hunter, you know. What crimes have you committed? What have you done?"

"Nothing." That squeak was like a rusty wheel.

"Nothing? Men don't come out into the Forests to do 'nothing,' friend."

His companion glanced from side to side. He'd given his name as Earnest. But, then, Daggon had given his name as Amity. Names didn't mean a whole lot in the Forests. Or maybe they meant everything. The right ones, that was.

Earnest leaned back, scrunching down that fishing-pole neck of his, as if trying to disappear into his beer. He'd bite. People liked hearing about the White Fox, and Daggon considered himself an expert. At least, he was an expert at telling stories to get ratty men like Earnest to pay for his drinks.

I'll give him some time to stew, Daggon thought, smiling to himself. *Let him worry.* Earnest would pry him for more information in a bit.

While he waited, Daggon leaned back, surveying the room. The merchants were making a nuisance of themselves, calling for food, saying they meant to be on their way in an hour. That *proved* them to be fools. Traveling at night in the Forests? Good homesteader stock would do it. Men like these, though . . . they'd probably take less than an hour to violate one of the Simple Rules and bring the shades upon them. Daggon put the idiots out of his mind.

That fellow in the corner, though . . . dressed all in brown, still wearing his hat despite being indoors. That fellow looked truly dangerous. I wonder if it's him, Daggon thought. So far as he knew, nobody had ever seen the White Fox and lived. Ten years, over a hundred bounties turned in. Surely someone knew his name. The authorities in the forts paid him the bounties, after all.

The waystop's owner, Madam Silence, passed by the table and deposited Daggon's meal with an unceremonious thump. Scowling, she topped off his beer, spilling a sudsy dribble onto his hand, before limping off. She was a stout woman. Tough. Everyone in the Forests was tough. The ones that survived, at least.

He'd learned that a scowl from Silence was just her way of saying hello. She'd given him an extra helping of venison; she often did that. He liked to think that she had a fondness for him. Maybe someday . . .

Don't be a fool, he thought to himself, as he dug into the heavily gravied food. Better to marry a stone than Silence Montane. A stone showed more affection. Likely, she gave him the extra slice because she recognized the value of a repeat customer. Fewer and fewer people came this way lately. Too many shades. And then, there was Chesterton. Nasty business, that.

"So . . . he's a bounty hunter, this Fox?" The man who called himself Earnest seemed to be sweating.

Daggon smiled. Hooked right good, this one was. "He's not just a bounty hunter. He's *the* bounty hunter. Though, the White Fox doesn't go for the small timers—and no offense, friend, but you seem pretty small time."

His friend grew more nervous. What *had* he done? "But," the man stammered, "he wouldn't come for me—er, pretending I'd done something, of course— anyway, he wouldn't come in here, would he? I mean, Madam Silence's waystop, it's protected. Everyone knows that. Shade of her dead husband lurks here. I had a cousin who saw it, I did."

"The White Fox doesn't fear shades," Daggon said, leaning in. "Now, mind you, I don't *think* he'd risk coming in here—but not because of some shade. Everyone knows this is neutral ground. You've got to have some safe places, even in the Forests. But . . . "

Daggon smiled at Silence as she passed him by on the way to the kitchens again. This time she didn't scowl at him. He was getting through to her for certain.

"But?" Earnest squeaked.

"Well . . . " Daggon said. "I could tell you a few things about how the White Fox takes men, but you see, my beer is nearly empty. A shame. I think you'd be very interested in how the White Fox caught Makepeace Hapshire. Great story, that."

Earnest squeaked for Silence to bring another beer, though she bustled into the kitchen and didn't hear. Daggon frowned, but Earnest put a coin on the side of the table, indicating he'd like a refill when Silence or her daughter returned. That would do. Daggon smiled to himself and launched into the story.

Silence Montane closed the door to the common room, then turned and pressed her back against it. She tried to still her racing heart by breathing in and out. Had she made any obvious signs? Did they know she'd recognized them?

William Ann passed by, wiping her hands on a cloth. "Mother?" the young woman asked, pausing. "Mother, are you—"

"Fetch the book. Quickly, child!"

William Ann's face went pale, then she hurried into the back pantry. Silence clutched her apron to still her nerves, then joined William Ann as the girl came out of the pantry with a thick, leather satchel. White flour dusted its cover and spine from the hiding place.

Silence took the satchel and opened it on the high kitchen counter, revealing a collection of loose-leaf papers. Most had faces drawn on them. As Silence rifled through the pages, William Ann moved to look through the peephole back into the common room.

For a few moments, the only sound to accompany Silence's thumping heart was that of hastily turned pages.

"It's the man with the long neck, isn't it?" William Ann asked. "I remember his face from one of the bounties."

"That's just Lamentation Winebare, a petty horse thief. He's barely worth two measures of silver."

"Who, then? The man in the back, with the hat?"

Silence shook her head, finding a sequence of pages at the bottom of her pile. She inspected the drawings. *God Beyond*, she thought. *I can't decide if I want it to be them, or not.* At least her hands had stopped shaking.

William Ann scurried back and craned her neck over Silence's shoulder. At fourteen, the girl was already taller than her mother. A fine thing to suffer, a child taller than you. Though William Ann grumbled about being awkward and lanky, her slender build foreshadowed a beauty to come. She took after her father.

"Oh, God *Beyond*," William Ann said, raising a hand to her mouth. "You mean—"

"Chesterton Divide," Silence said. The shape of the chin, the look in the eyes . . . they were the same. "He walked right into our hands, with four of his men." The bounty on those five would be enough to pay her supply needs for a year. Maybe two.

Her eyes flickered to the words below the pictures, printed in harsh, bold letters. Extremely dangerous. Wanted for murder, rape, extortion. And, of course, there was the big one at the end: And assassination.

Silence had always wondered if Chesterton and his men had intended to kill the governor of the most powerful city on this continent, or if it had it been an accident. A simple robbery gone wrong. Either way, Chesterton understood what he'd done. Before the incident, he had been a common—if accomplished—highway bandit.

Now he was something greater, something far more dangerous. Chesterton knew that if he were captured, there would be no mercy, no quarter. Lastport had painted Chesterton as an anarchist, a menace, and a psychopath.

Chesterton had no reason to hold back. So he didn't.

Oh, God Beyond, Silence thought, looking at the continuing list of his crimes on the next page.

Beside her, William Ann whispered the words to herself. "He's out there?" she asked. "But where?"

"The merchants," Silence said.

"What?" William Ann rushed back to the peephole. The wood there— indeed, all around the kitchen—had been scrubbed so hard that it had been bleached white. Sebruki had been cleaning again.

"I can't see it," William Ann said.

"Look closer." Silence hadn't seen it at first either, even though she spent each night with the book, memorizing its faces.

A few moments later, William Ann gasped, raising her hand to her mouth. "That seems so *foolish* of him. Why is he going about perfectly visible like this? Even in disguise."

"Everyone will remember just another band of fool merchants from the fort who thought they could brave the Forests. It's a clever disguise. When they vanish from the paths in a few days, it will be assumed—if anyone cares to wonder—that the shades got them. Besides, this way Chesterton can travel quickly and in the open, visiting waystops and listening for information."

Was this how Chesterton discovered good targets to hit? Had they come through her waystop before? The thought made her stomach turn. She had fed criminals many times; some were regulars. Every man was probably a criminal out in the Forests, if only for ignoring taxes imposed by the fortfolk.

Chesterton and his men were different. She didn't need the list of crimes to know what they were capable of doing.

"Where's Sebruki?" Silence said.

William Ann shook herself, as if coming out of a stupor. "She's feeding the pigs. Shadows! You don't think they'd recognize her, do you?"

"No," Silence said. "I'm worried she'll recognize them." Sebruki might only be eight, but she could be shockingly—disturbingly—observant.

Silence closed the book of bounties. She rested her fingers on its leather.

"We're going to kill them, aren't we?" William Ann asked.

"Yes."

"How much are they worth?"

"Sometimes, child, it's not about what a man is worth." Silence heard the faint lie in her voice. Times were increasingly tight, with the price of silver from both Bastion Hill and Lastport on the rise.

Sometimes it wasn't about what a man was worth. But this wasn't one of those times.

"I'll get the poison." William Ann left the peephole and crossed the room.

"Something light, child," Silence cautioned. "These are dangerous men. They'll notice if things are out of the ordinary."

"I'm not a fool, Mother," William Ann said dryly. "I'll use fenweed. They won't taste it in the beer."

"Half dose. I don't want them collapsing at the table."

William Ann nodded, entering the old storage room, where she closed the door and began prying up floorboards to get to the poisons. Fenweed would leave the men cloudy-headed and dizzy, but wouldn't kill them.

Silence didn't dare risk something more deadly. If suspicion ever came back to her waystop, her career—and likely her life—would end. She needed to remain, in the minds of travelers, the crotchety but fair innkeeper who didn't ask too many questions. Her waystop was a place of perceived safety, even for the roughest of criminals. She bedded down each night with a heart full of fear that someone would realize a suspicious number of the White Fox's bounties stayed at Silence's waystop in the days preceding their demise.

She went into the pantry to put away the bounty book. Here, too, the walls had been scrubbed clean, the shelves freshly sanded and dusted. That child. Who had heard of a child who would rather clean than play? Of course, given what Sebruki had been through . . .

Silence could not help reaching onto the top shelf and feeling the crossbow she kept there. Silver boltheads. She kept it for shades, and hadn't yet turned it against a man. Drawing blood was too dangerous in the Forests. It still comforted her to know that in a true emergency, she had the weapon at hand.

Bounty book stowed, she went to check on Sebruki. The child was indeed caring for the pigs. Silence liked to keep a healthy stock, though of course not for eating. Pigs were said to ward away shades. She used any tool she could to make the waystop seem more safe.

Sebruki knelt inside the pig shack. The short girl had dark skin and long, black hair. Nobody would have taken her for Silence's daughter, even if they hadn't heard of Sebruki's unfortunate history. The child hummed to herself, scrubbing at the wall of the enclosure.

"Child?" Silence asked.

Sebruki turned to her and smiled. What a difference one year could make. Once, Silence would have sworn that this child would never smile again. Sebruki had spent her first three months at the waystop staring at walls. No matter where Silence had put her, the child had moved to the nearest wall, sat down, and stared at it all day. Never speaking a word. Eyes dead as those of a shade . . .

"Aunt Silence?" Sebruki asked. "Are you well?"

"I'm fine, child. Just plagued by memories. You're . . . cleaning the *pig shack* now?"

"The walls need a good scrubbing," Sebruki said. "The pigs do so like it to be clean. Well, Jarom and Ezekiel prefer it that way. The others don't seem to care."

"You don't need to clean so hard, child."

"I like doing it," Sebruki said. "It feels good. It's something I can do. To help."

Well, it was better to clean the walls than stare blankly at them all day. Today, Silence was happy for anything that kept the child busy. Anything, so long as she didn't enter the common room.

"I think the pigs will like it," Silence said. "Why don't you keep at it in here for a while?"

Sebruki eyed her. "What's wrong?"

Shadows. She was so observant. "There are some men with rough tongues in the common room," Silence said. "I won't have you picking up their cussing."

"I'm not a child, Aunt Silence."

"Yes you are," Silence said firmly. "And you'll obey. Don't think I won't take a switch to your backside."

Sebruki rolled her eyes, but went back to work and began humming to herself. Silence let a little of her grandmother's ways out when she spoke with Sebruki. The child responded well to sternness. She seemed to crave it, perhaps as a symbol that someone was in control.

Silence wished she actually were in control. But she was a Forescout—the surname taken by her grandparents and the others who had left Homeland first and explored this continent. Yes, she was a Forescout, and she'd be damned before she'd let anyone know how absolutely powerless she felt much of the time.

Silence crossed the backyard of the large inn, noting William Ann inside the kitchen mixing a paste to dissolve in the beer. Silence passed her by and looked in on the stable. Unsurprisingly, Chesterton had said they'd be leaving after their meal. While a lot of folk sought the relative safety of a waystop at night, Chesterton and his men would be accustomed to sleeping in the Forests. Even with the shades about, they would feel more comfortable in a camp of their own devising than they would in a waystop bed.

Inside the stable, Dob—the old stable hand—had just finished brushing down the horses. He wouldn't have watered them. Silence had a standing order to not do that until last.

"This is well done, Dob," Silence said. "Why don't you take your break now?"

He nodded to her with a mumbled, "Thank'ya mam." He'd find the front porch and his pipe, as always. Dob hadn't two wits to rub together, and he hadn't a clue about what she really did at the waystop, but he'd been with her since before William's death. He was as loyal a man as she'd ever found.

Silence shut the door after him, then fetched some pouches from the locked cabinet at the back of the stable. She checked each one in the dim light, then set them on the grooming table and heaved the first saddle back onto its owner's back.

She was near finished with the saddling when the door eased open. She froze, immediately thinking of the pouches on the table. Why hadn't she stuffed them in her apron? Sloppy!

"Silence Forescout," a smooth voice said from the doorway.

Silence stifled a groan and turned to confront her visitor. "Theopolis," she said. "It's not polite to sneak about on a woman's property. I should have you thrown out for trespassing."

"Now, now. That would be rather like . . . the horse kicking at the man who feeds him, hmmm?" Theopolis leaned his gangly frame against the doorway, folding his arms. He wore simple clothing, no markings of his station. A fort tax collector often didn't want random passers to know of his profession. Clean-shaven, his face always had that same patronizing smile on it. His clothing was too clean, too new, to be that of one who lived out in the Forests. Not that he was a dandy, nor was he a fool. Theopolis was dangerous, just a different kind of dangerous from most.

"Why are you here, Theopolis?" she said, hefting the last saddle onto the back of a snorting roan gelding.

"Why do I always come to you, Silence? It's not because of your cheerful countenance, hmmm?"

"I'm paid up on taxes."

"That's because you're mostly exempt from taxes," Theopolis said. "But you haven't paid me for last month's shipment of silver."

"Things have been a little dry lately. It's coming."

"And the bolts for your crossbow?" Theopolis asked. "One wonders if you're trying to forget about the price of those silver boltheads, hmmm? And the shipment of replacement sections for your protection rings?"

His whining accent made her wince as she buckled the saddle on. Theopolis. Shadows, what a day!

"Oh my," Theopolis said, walking over to the grooming tale. He picked up one of the pouches. "What are these, now? That looks like wetleek sap. I've heard that it glows at night if you shine the right kind of light upon it. Is this one of the White Fox's mysterious secrets?"

She snatched the pouch away. "Don't say that name," she hissed.

He grinned. "You have a bounty! Delightful. I have always wondered how you tracked them. Poke a pinhole in that, attach it to the underside of the saddle, then follow the dripping trail it leaves? Hmmm? You could probably track them a long way, kill them far from here. Keep suspicion off the little waystop?"

Yes, Theopolis was dangerous, but she needed *someone* to turn in her bounties for her. Theopolis was a rat, and like all rats, he knew the best holes, troughs, and crannies. He had connections in Lastport, and had managed to get her the money in the name of the White Fox without revealing her.

"I've been tempted to turn you in lately, you know," Theopolis said. "Many a group keeps a betting pool on the identity of the infamous fox. I could be a rich man with this knowledge, hmmm?"

"You're already a rich man," she snapped. "And, though you're many things, you are not an idiot. This has worked just fine for a decade. Don't tell me you'd trade wealth for a little notoriety?"

He smiled, but did not contradict her. He kept half of what she earned from each bounty. It was a fine arrangement for Theopolis. No danger to him, which was how she knew he liked it. He was a civil servant, not a bounty hunter. The only time she'd seen him kill, the man he'd murdered couldn't fight back.

"You know me too well, Silence," Theopolis said with a laugh. "Too well indeed. My, my. A bounty! I wonder who it is. I'll have to go look in the common room."

"You'll do nothing of the sort. Shadows! You think the face of a tax collector won't spook them? Don't you go walking in and spoiling things."

"Peace, Silence," he said, still grinning. "I obey your rules. I am careful not to show myself around here often, and I don't bring suspicion to you. I couldn't stay today anyway; I merely came to give you an offer. Only now you probably won't need it! Ah, such a pity. After all the trouble I went to in your name, hmmm?"

She felt cold. "What help could you possibly give me?"

He took a sheet of paper from his satchel, then carefully unfolded it with too-long fingers. He moved to hold it up, but she snatched it from him.

"What is this?"

"A way to relieve you of your debt, Silence! A way to prevent you from ever having to worry again."

The paper was a writ of seizure, an authorization for Silence's creditors— Theopolis—to claim her property as payment. The forts claimed jurisdiction over the roadways and the land to either side of them. They did send soldiers out to patrol them. Occasionally.

"I take it back, Theopolis," she spat. "You most certainly *are* a fool. You'd give up everything we have for a greedy land snatch?"

"Of course not, Silence. This wouldn't be giving up anything at all! Why, I *do* so feel bad seeing you constantly in my debt. Wouldn't it be more efficient if I took over the finances of the waystop? You would remain working here, and hunting bounties, as you always have. Only, you would no longer have to worry about your debts, hmmm?"

She crumpled the paper in her hand. "You'd turn me and mine into slaves, Theopolis."

"Oh, don't be so dramatic. Those in Lastport have begun to worry that such an important waypoint as this is owned by an unknown element. You are drawing attention, Silence. I should think that is the last thing you want."

Silence crumpled the paper further in her hand, fist tight. Horses shuffled in their stalls. Theopolis grinned.

"Well," he said. "Perhaps it won't be needed. Perhaps this bounty of yours is a big one, hmmm? Any clues to give me, so I don't sit wondering all day?"

"Get out," she whispered.

"Dear Silence," he said. "Forescout blood, stubborn to the last breath. They say your grandparents were the first of the first. The first people to come scout this continent, the first to homestead the Forests . . . first to stake a claim on hell itself."

"Don't call the Forests that. This is my home."

"But it is how men saw this land, before the Evil. Doesn't that make you curious? Hell, land of the damned, where the shadows of the dead made their home. I keep wondering. Is there really a shade of your departed husband guarding this place, or is it just another story you tell people? To make them feel safe, hmmm? You spend a fortune in silver. That offers the real protection, and I never *have* been able to find record of your marriage. Of course, if there wasn't one, that would make dear William Ann a—"

"*Go.*"

He grinned, but tipped his hat to her and stepped out. She heard him climb into the saddle, then ride off. Night would come before too long; it was probably too much to hope that the shades would take Theopolis. She'd long suspected that he had a hiding hole somewhere near, probably a cavern he kept lined with silver.

She breathed in and out, trying to calm herself. Theopolis was frustrating, but he didn't know everything. She forced her attention back to the horses and got out a bucket of water. She dumped the contents of the pouches into it, then gave a hearty dose to the horses, who each drank thirstily.

Pouches that dripped sap in the way Theopolis indicated would be too easy to spot. What would happen when her bounties removed their saddles at night and found the sap packets? They'd know someone was coming for them. No, she needed something less obvious.

"How am I going to manage this?" she whispered as a horse drank from her bucket. "Shadows. They're reaching for me on all sides."

Kill Theopolis. That was probably what Grandmother would have done. She considered it.

No, she thought. *I won't become that. I won't become her.* Theopolis was a thug and a scoundrel, but he had not broken any laws, nor had he done anyone direct harm that she knew. There had to be rules, even out here. There had to be lines. Perhaps in that respect, she wasn't so different from the fortfolk.

She'd find another way. Theopolis only had a writ of debt; he had been required to show it to her. That meant she had a day or two to come up with his money. All neat and orderly. In the Fortress Towns, they claimed to have civilization. Those rules gave her a chance.

She left the stable. A glance through the window into the common room showed her William Ann delivering drinks to the "merchants" of Chesterton's gang. Silence stopped to watch.

Behind her, the Forests shivered in the wind.

Silence listened, then turned to face them. You could tell fortfolk by the way they refused to face the Forests. They averted their eyes, never looking into the depths. Those solemn trees covered almost every inch of this continent, those leaves shading the ground. Still. Silent. Animals lived out there, but fort surveyors declared that there were no predators. The shades had gotten those long ago, drawn by the shedding of blood.

Staring into the Forests seemed to make them . . . retreat. The darkness of their depths withdrew, the stillness give way to the sound of rodents picking through fallen leaves. A Forescout knew to look the Forests straight on. A Forescout knew that the surveyors were wrong. There *was* a predator out there. The Forest itself was one.

Silence turned and walked to the door into the kitchen. Keeping the waystop had to be her first goal, so she was committed to collecting Chesterton's bounty now. If she couldn't pay Theopolis, she had little faith that everything would stay the same. He'd have a hand around her throat, as she couldn't leave the waystop. She had no fort citizenship, and times were too tight for the local homesteaders to take her in. No, she'd *have* to stay and work the waystop for Theopolis, and he would squeeze her dry, taking larger and larger percentages of the bounties.

She pushed open the door to the kitchen. It—

Sebruki sat at the kitchen table holding the crossbow in her lap.

"God Beyond!" Silence gasped, pulling the door closed as she stepped inside. "Child, what are you—"

Sebruki looked up at her. Those haunted eyes were back, eyes void of life and emotion. Eyes like a shade.

"We have visitors, Aunt Silence," Sebruki said in a cold, monotone voice. The crossbow's winding crank sat next to her. She had managed to load the thing and cock it, all on her own. "I coated the bolt's tip with black blood. I did that right, didn't I? That way, the poison will kill him for sure."

"Child . . . " Silence stepped forward.

Sebruki turned the crossbow in her lap, holding it at an angle to support it, one small hand holding the trigger. The point turned toward Silence.

Sebruki stared ahead, eyes blank.

"This won't work, Sebruki," Silence said, stern. "Even if you were able to lift that thing into the common room, you wouldn't hit him—and even if you did, his men would kill us all in retribution!"

"I wouldn't mind," Sebruki said softly. "So long as I got to kill him. So long as I pulled the trigger."

"You care nothing for us?" Silence snapped. "I take you in, give you a home, and this is your payment? You steal a weapon? You *threaten* me?"

Sebruki blinked.

"What is wrong with you?" Silence said. "You'd shed blood in this place of sanctuary? Bring the shades down upon us, beating at our protections? If they got through, they'd kill everyone under my roof! People I've promised safety. How *dare* you!"

Sebruki shook, as if coming awake. Her mask broke, and she dropped the crossbow. Silence heard a snap, and the catch released. She felt the bolt pass within an inch of her cheek, then break the window behind.

Shadows! Had the bolt grazed Silence? Had Sebruki *drawn blood*? Silence reached up with a shaking hand, but blessedly felt no blood. The bolt hadn't hit her.

A moment later, Sebruki was in her arms, sobbing. Silence knelt down, holding the child close. "Hush, dear one. It's all right. It's all right."

"I heard it all," Sebruki whispered. "Mother never cried out. She knew I was there. She was strong, Aunt Silence. That was why I could be strong, even when the blood came down. Soaking my hair. I heard it. *I heard it all.*"

Silence closed her eyes, holding Sebruki tight. She herself had been the only one willing to investigate the smoking homestead. Sebruki's father had stayed at the waystop on occasion. A good man. As good a man as was left after the Evil took Homeland, that was.

In the smoldering remains of the homestead, Silence had found the corpses of a dozen people. Each family member had been slaughtered by Chesterton and his men, right down to the children. The only one left had been Sebruki, the youngest, who had been shoved into the crawl space under the floorboards in the bedroom.

She'd lain there, soaked in her mother's blood, soundless even as Silence found her. She'd only found the girl because Chesterton had been careful, lining the room with silver dust to protect against shades as he prepared to kill. Silence had tried to recover some of the dust that had trickled between the floorboards, and had run across eyes staring up at her through the slits.

Chesterton had burned thirteen different homesteads over the last year. Over fifty people murdered. Sebruki was the only one who had escaped him.

The girl trembled as she heaved with sobs. "Why . . . Why?"

"There is no reason. I'm sorry." What else could she do? Offer some foolish platitude or comfort about the God Beyond? These were the Forests. You didn't survive on platitudes.

Silence did hold the girl until her crying began to subside. William Ann entered, then stilled beside the kitchen table, holding a tray of empty mugs. Her eyes flickered toward the fallen crossbow, then at the broken window.

"You'll kill him?" Sebruki whispered. "You'll bring him to justice?"

"Justice died in Homeland," Silence said. "But yes, I'll kill him. I promise it to you, child."

Stepping timidly, William Ann picked up the crossbow, then turned it, displaying its now-broken bow. Silence breathed out. She should never have left the thing where Sebruki could get to it.

"Care for the patrons, William Ann," Silence said. "I'll take Sebruki upstairs."

William Ann nodded, glancing at the broken window.

"No blood was shed," Silence said. "We will be fine. Though if you get a moment, see if you can find the bolt. The head is silver . . . " This was hardly a time when they could afford to waste money.

William Ann stowed the crossbow in the pantry as Silence carefully set Sebruki on a kitchen stool. The girl clung to her, refusing to let go, so Silence relented and held her for a time longer.

William Ann took a few deep breaths, as if to calm herself, then pushed back out into the common room to distribute drinks.

Eventually, Sebruki let go long enough for Silence to mix a draught. She carried the girl up the stairs to the loft above the common room, where the three of them made their beds. Dob slept in the stable and the guests in the nicer rooms on the second floor.

"You're going to make me sleep," Sebruki said, regarding the cup with reddened eyes.

"The world will seem a brighter place in the morning," Silence said. *And I can't risk you sneaking out after me tonight.*

The girl reluctantly took the draught, then drank it down. "I'm sorry. About the crossbow."

"We will find a way for you to work off the cost of fixing it."

That seemed to comfort Sebruki. She was a homesteader, Forests born. "You used to sing to me at night," Sebruki said softly, closing her eyes, laying back. "When you first brought me here. After . . . after . . . " She swallowed.

"I wasn't certain you noticed." Silence hadn't been certain Sebruki noticed anything, during those times.

"I did."

Silence sat down on the stool beside Sebruki's cot. She didn't feel like singing, so she began humming. It was the lullaby she'd sung to William Ann during the hard times right after her birth.

Before long, the words came out, unbidden.

"Hush now, my dear one . . . be not afraid. Night comes upon us, but sunlight will break. Sleep now, my dear one . . . let your tears fade. Darkness surrounds us, but someday we'll wake . . . "

She held Sebruki's hand until the child fell asleep. The window by the bed overlooked the courtyard, so Silence could see as Dob brought out Chesterton's horses. The five men in their fancy merchant clothing stomped down off the porch and climbed into their saddles.

They rode in a file out onto the roadway; then the Forests enveloped them.

One hour after nightfall, Silence packed her rucksack by the light of the hearth.

Her grandmother had kindled that hearth's flame, and it had been burning ever since. She'd nearly lost her life lighting the fire, but she hadn't been willing to pay any of the fire merchants for a start. Silence shook her head. Grandmother always had bucked convention. But, then, was Silence any better?

Don't kindle flame, don't shed the blood of another, don't run at night. These things draw shades. The Simple Rules, by which every homesteader lived.

She'd broken all three on more than on occasion. It was a wonder she hadn't been withered away into a shade by now.

The fire's warmth seemed a distant thing as she prepared to kill. Silence glanced at the old shrine, really just a closet, she kept locked. The flames reminded her of her grandmother. At times, she thought of the fire *as* her grandmother. Defiant of both the shades and the forts, right until the end. She'd purged the waystop of other reminders of Grandmother, all save the shrine to the God Beyond. That was set behind a locked door beside the pantry, and next to the door had once hung her grandmother's silver dagger, symbol of the old religion.

That dagger was etched with the symbols of divinity as a warding. Silence carried it, not for its wardings, but because it was silver. One could never have too much silver, in the Forests.

She packed the sack carefully, first putting in her medicine kit and then a good-sized pouch of silver dust to heal withering. She followed that with ten empty sacks of thick burlap, tarred on the inside to prevent their contents from leaking. Finally, she added an oil lamp. She wouldn't want to use it, as she didn't trust fire. Fire could draw shades. However, she'd found it useful to have on prior outings, so she brought it. She'd only light it if she ran across someone who already had a fire start.

Once done, she hesitated, then went to the old storage room. She removed the floorboards and took out the small, dry-packed keg that lay beside the poisons.

Gunpowder.

"Mother?" William Ann asked, causing her to jump. She hadn't heard the girl enter the kitchen.

Silence nearly dropped the keg in her startlement, and that nearly stopped her heart. She cursed herself for a fool, tucking the keg under her arm. It couldn't explode without fire. She knew that much.

"Mother!" William Ann said, looking at the keg.

"I probably won't need it."

"But—"

"I know. Hush." She walked over and placed the keg into her sack. Attached to the side of the keg, with cloth stuffed between the metal arms, was her grandmother's firestarter. Igniting gunpowder counted as kindling flames, at least in the eyes of the shades. It drew them almost as quickly as blood did, day or night. The early refugees from Homeland had discovered that in short order.

In some ways, blood was easier to avoid. A simple nosebleed or issue of blood wouldn't draw the shades; they wouldn't even notice. It had to be the blood of another, shed by your hands—and they would go for the one who shed the blood first. Of course, after that person was dead, they often didn't care who they killed next. Once enraged, shades were dangerous to all nearby.

Only after Silence had the gunpowder packed did she notice that William Ann was dressed for traveling in trousers and boots. She carried a sack like Silence's.

"What do you think you're about, William Ann?" Silence asked.

"You intend to kill five men who had only half a dose of fenweed by yourself, Mother?"

"I've done similar before. I've learned to work on my own."

"Only because you didn't have anyone else to help." William Ann slung her sack onto her shoulder. "That's no longer the case."

"You're too young. Go back to bed; watch the waystop until I return."

William Ann remained firm.

"Child, I told you—"

"Mother," William Ann said, taking her arm firmly, "you aren't a *youth* anymore! You think I don't see your limp getting worse? You can't do everything by yourself! You're going to have to start letting me help you sometime, dammit!"

Silence regarded her daughter. Where had that fierceness come from? It was hard to remember that William Ann, too, was Forescout stock. Grandmother would have been disgusted by her, and that made Silence proud. William Ann had actually had a childhood. She wasn't weak, she was just . . . normal. A woman could be strong without having the emotions of a brick.

"Don't you cuss at your mother," Silence finally told the girl.

William Ann raised an eyebrow.

"You may come," Silence said, prying her arm out of her daughter's grip. "But you *will* do as you are told."

William Ann let out a deep breath, then nodded eagerly. "I'll warn Dob we're going." She walked out, adopting the natural slow step of a Homesteader as she entered the darkness. Even though she was within the protection of the waystop's silver rings, she knew to follow the Simple Rules. Ignoring them when you were safe led to lapses when you weren't.

Silence got out two bowls, then mixed two different types of glowpaste. When finished, she poured them into separate jars, which she packed into her sack.

She stepped outside into the night. The air was crisp, chill. The Forests had gone silent.

The shades were out, of course.

A few of them moved across the grassy ground, visible by their own soft glow. Ethereal, translucent, the ones nearby right now were old shades—they barely had the forms of men any longer. The heads rippled, faces shifting like smoke rings. They trailed waves of whiteness about an arm's length behind them. Silence had always imagined that as tattered remains of their clothing.

No woman, not even a Forescout, looked upon shades without feeling a coldness inside of her. The shades were about during the day, of course, you just couldn't see them. Kindle fire, draw blood, and they'd come for you even then. At night, though, they were different. Quicker to respond to infractions. At night they also responded to quick motions, which they never did during the day.

Silence took out one of the glowpaste jars, bathing the area around her in a pale green light. The light was dim, but was even and steady, unlike torchlight. Torches were unreliable, since you couldn't relight them if they went out.

William Ann waited at the front with the lantern poles. "We will need to move quietly," Silence told her while affixing the jars to the poles. "You may speak, but do so in a whisper. I said you will obey me. You will, in all things, immediately. These men we're after . . . they will kill you, or worse, without giving the deed a passing thought."

William Ann nodded.

"You're not scared enough," Silence said, slipping a black covering around the jar with the brighter glowpaste. That plunged them into darkness, but the Starbelt was high in the sky today. Some of that light would filter down through the leaves, particularly if they stayed near the road.

"I—" William Ann began.

"You remember when Harold's hound went mad last spring?" Silence asked. "Do you remember that look in the hound's eyes? No recognition? Eyes that lusted for the kill? Well, that's what these men are, William Ann. Rabid. They need to be put down, same as that hound. They won't see you as a person. They'll see you as meat. Do you understand?"

William Ann nodded. Silence could see that she was still more excited than afraid, but there was no helping that. Silence handed William Ann the pole with the darker glowpaste. It had a faintly blue light to it, but didn't illuminate much. Silence put the other pole to her shoulder, sack over the other, then nodded toward the roadway.

Nearby, a shade drifted toward the boundary of the waystop. When it touched the thin barrier of silver on the ground, it crackled like sparks and drove the thing backward with a sudden jerk. The shade floated the other way.

Each touch like that cost Silence money. The touch of a shade ruined silver. That was what her patrons paid for: a waystop whose boundary had not been broke for over a hundred years, with a longstanding tradition that no unwanted shades were trapped within. Peace, of a sort. The best the Forests offered.

William Ann stepped across the boundary, which was marked by the curve of the large silver hoops jutting from the ground. They were anchored below by concrete so you couldn't just pull one up. Replacing an overlapping section from one of the rings—she had three concentric ones surrounding her waystop—required digging down and unchaining the section. It was a lot of work, which Silence knew intimately. A week didn't pass that they didn't rotate or replace one section or another.

The shade nearby drifted away. It didn't acknowledge them. Silence didn't know if regular people were invisible to them unless the rules were broken, or if the people just weren't worthy of attention until then.

She and William Ann moved out onto the dark roadway, which was somewhat overgrown. No road in the Forests was well maintained. Perhaps if the forts ever made good on their promises, that would change. Still, there was travel. Homesteaders traveling to one fort or another to trade food. The grains grown out in Forest clearings were richer, tastier, than what could be produced up in the mountains. Rabbits and turkeys caught in snares or raised in hutches could be sold for good silver.

Not hogs. Only someone in one of the Forts would be so crass as to eat a pig.

Anyway, there *was* trade, and that kept the roadway worn, even if the trees around did have a tendency to reach down their boughs—like grasping arms—to try to cover up the pathway. Reclaim it. The Forests did not like that men had infested them.

The two women walked carefully and deliberately. No quick motions. Walking so, it seemed an eternity before something appeared on the road in front of them.

"There!" William Ann whispered.

Silence released her tension in a breath. Something glowing blue marked the roadway in the light of the glowpaste. Theopolis's guess at how she tracked her quarries had been a good one, but incomplete. Yes, the light of the paste known as Abraham's Fire did make drops of wetleek sap glow. By coincidence, wetleek sap *also* caused a horse's bladder to loosen.

Silence inspected the line of glowing sap and urine on the ground. She'd been worried that Chesterton and his men would cut into the Forests soon after leaving the waystop. That hadn't been likely, but still, she'd worried.

Now she was sure she had the trail. If Chesterton cut into the Forests, he'd do it a few hours after leaving the waystop, to be more certain their cover was safe. She closed her eyes and breathed a sigh of relief, then found herself offering a prayer of thanks by rote. She hesitated. Where had that come from? It had been a long time.

She shook her head, rising and continuing down the road. By drugging all five horses, she got a steady sequence of markings to follow.

The Forests felt . . . dark this night. The light of the Starbelt above didn't seem to filter through the branches as well as it should. And there seemed to be more shades than normal, prowling between the trunks of trees, glowing just faintly.

William Ann clung to her lantern pole. The child had been out in the night before, of course. No Homesteader looked forward to doing so, but none shied away from it either. You couldn't spend your life trapped inside, frozen by fear of the darkness. Live like that, and . . . well, you were no better off than the people in the forts. Life in the Forests was hard, often deadly. But it was also free.

"Mother," William Ann whispered as they walked. "Why don't you believe in God anymore?"

"Is this really the time, girl?"

William Ann looked down as they passed another line of urine, glowing blue on the roadway. "You always say something like that."

"And I'm usually trying to avoid the question when you ask it," Silence said. "But I'm also not usually walking the Forests at night."

"It just seems important to me now. You're wrong about me not being afraid enough. I can hardly breathe, but I do know how much trouble the waystop is in. You're always so angry after Master Theopolis visits. You don't change our border silver as often as you used to. One out of two days, you don't eat anything but bread."

"And you think this has to do with God, why?"

William Ann kept looking down.

Oh, shadows, Silence thought. *She thinks we're being punished.* Fool girl. Foolish as her father.

They passed the Old Bridge, walking its rickety wooden planks. When the light was better, you could still pick out timbers from the New Bridge down in the chasm below, representing the promises of the forts and their gifts, which always looked pretty but frayed before long. Sebruki's father had been one of those who had come put the Old Bridge back up.

"I believe in the God Beyond," Silence said, after they reached the other side.

"But—"

"I don't worship," Silence said, "but that doesn't mean I don't believe. The old books, they called this land the home of the damned. I doubt that worshiping does any good, if you're already damned. That's all."

William Ann didn't reply.

They walked another good two hours. Silence considered taking a shortcut thorough the woods, but the risk of losing the trail and having to double back felt too dangerous. Besides. Those markings, glowing a soft blue-white in the unseen light of the glowpaste . . . those were something *real*. A lifeline of light in the shadows all around. Those lines represented safety for her and her children.

With both of them counting the moments between urine markings, they didn't miss the turnoff by much. A few minutes walking without seeing a mark, and they turned back without a word, searching the sides of the path. Silence had worried this would be the most difficult part of the hunt, but they easily found where the men had turned into the Forests. A glowing hoofprint formed the sign; one of the horses had stepped in another's urine on the roadway, then tracked it into the Forests.

Silence set down her pack and opened it to retrieve her garrote, then held a finger to her lips and motioned for William Ann to wait by the road. The girl nodded. Silence couldn't make out much of her features in the darkness, but she did hear the girl's breathing grow more rapid. Being a Homesteader and accustomed to going out at night was one thing. Being alone in the Forests . . .

Silence took the blue glowpaste jar and covered it with her handkerchief. Then she took off her shoes and stockings and crept out into the night. Each time she did this, she felt like a child again, going into the Forests with her grandfather. Toes in the dirt, testing for crackling leaves or twigs that would snap and give her away.

She could almost hear his voice, giving instructions, telling her how to judge the wind and use the sound of rustling leaves to mask her as she crossed noisy patches. He'd loved the Forests until the day they'd claimed him. *Never call this land hell*, he had said. *Respect the land as you would a dangerous beast, but do not hate it.*

Shades slid through the trees nearby, almost invisible with nothing to illuminate them. She kept her distance, but even so, she occasionally turned to see one of the things drifting past her. Stumbling into a shade could kill a man, but that kind of accident was uncommon. Unless enraged, shades moved away from men who got too close, as if blown by a soft breeze. So long as you were moving slowly—and you *should* be—you would be all right.

She kept the handkerchief around the jar except when she wanted to check specifically the markings nearby. Glowpaste illuminated shades, and shades that glowed too brightly might give warning of her approach.

A groan sounded nearby. Silence froze, heart practically bursting from her chest. Shades made no sound; that had been a man. Tense, silent, she searched until she caught sight of him, well hidden in the hollow of a tree. He moved, massaging his temples. The headaches from William Ann's poison were upon him.

Silence considered, then crept around the back of the tree. She crouched down, then waited a painful five minutes for him to move. He reached up again, rustling the leaves.

Silence snapped forward and looped her garrote around his neck, then pulled tight. Strangling wasn't the best way to kill a man in the Forests. It was so slow.

The guard started to thrash, clawing at his throat. Shades nearby halted.

Silence pulled tighter. The guard, weakened by the poison, tried to push back at her with his legs. She shuffled backward, still holding tightly, watching those shades. They looked around, like animals sniffing the air. A few of them started to dim, their own faint natural luminescence fading, their forms bleeding from white to black.

Not a good sign. Silence felt her heartbeat like thunder inside. *Die, damn you!*

The man finally stopped jerking, motions growing more lethargic. After he trembled a last time and fell still, Silence waited there for a painful eternity, holding her breath. Finally, the shades nearby faded back to white, then drifted off in their meandering directions.

She unwound the garrote, breathing out in relief. After a moment to get her bearings, she left the corpse and crept back to William Ann.

The girl did her proud; she'd hidden herself so well that Silence didn't see her until she whispered, "Mother?"

"Yes," Silence said.

"Thank the God Beyond," William Ann said, crawling out of the hollow where she'd covered herself in leaves. She took Silence by the arm, trembling. "You found them?"

"Killed the man on watch," Silence said with a nod. "The other four should be sleeping. This is where I'll need you."

"I'm ready."

"Follow."

They moved back along the path Silence had taken. They passed the heap of the scout's corpse, and William Ann inspected it, showing no pity. "It's one of them," she whispered. "I recognize him."

"Of course it's one of them."

"I just wanted to be sure. Since we're . . . you know."

Not far beyond the guard post, they found the camp. Four men in bedrolls slept amid the shades as only true Forestborn would ever try. They had set a small jar of glowpaste at the center of the camp, inside a pit so it wouldn't glow too brightly and give them away, but it was enough light to show the horses tethered a few feet away on the other side of the camp. The green light also showed William Ann's face, and Silence was shocked to see not fear, but intense anger in the girl's expression. She had taken quickly to being a protective older sister to Sebruki. She was ready to kill after all.

Silence gestured toward the rightmost man, and William Ann nodded. This was the dangerous part. On only a half-dose, any of these men could still wake to the noise of their partners dying.

Silence took one of the burlap sacks from her pack and handed it to William Ann, then removed her hammer. It wasn't some war weapon, like her grandfather had spoken of. Just a simple tool for pounding nails. Or other things.

Silence stooped over the first man. Seeing his sleeping face sent a shiver through her. A primal piece of her waited, tense, for those eyes to snap open.

She held up three fingers to William Ann, then lowered them one at a time. When the third finger went down, William Ann shoved the sack down over the man's head. As he jerked, Silence pounded him hard on the side of the temple with the hammer. The skull cracked and the head sank in a little. The man thrashed once, then grew limp.

Silence looked up, tense, watching the other men as William Ann pulled the sack tight. The shades nearby paused, but this didn't draw their attention as much as the strangling had. So long as the sack's lining of tar kept the blood from leaking out, they should be safe. Silence hit the man's head twice more, then checked for a pulse. There was none.

They carefully did the next man in the row. It was brutal work, like slaughtering animals. It helped to think of these men as rabid, as she'd told William Ann earlier. It did not help to think of what the men had done to Sebruki. That would make her angry, and she couldn't afford to be angry. She needed to be cold, quiet, and efficient.

The second man took a few more knocks to the head to kill, but he woke more slowly than his friend. Fenweed made men groggy. It was an excellent drug for her purposes. She just needed them sleepy, a little disoriented. And—

The next man sat up in his bedroll. "What . . . ?" he asked in a slurred voice.

Silence leaped for him, grabbing him by the shoulders and slamming him to the ground. Nearby shades spun about as if at a loud noise. Silence pulled her garrote out as the man heaved at her, trying to push her aside, and William Ann gasped in shock.

Silence rolled around, wrapping the man's neck. She pulled tight, straining while the man thrashed, agitating the shades. She almost had him dead when the last man leaped from his bedroll. In his dazed alarm, he chose to dash away.

Shadows! That last one was Chesterton himself. If he drew the shades upon himself . . .

Silence left the third man gasping and threw caution aside, racing after Chesterton. If the shades withered him to dust, she'd have *nothing*. No corpse to turn in meant no bounty.

The Shades around the campsite faded from view as Silence reached Chesterton, catching him at the perimeter of the camp by the horses. She desperately tackled him by the legs, throwing the groggy man to the ground.

"You bitch," he said in a slurred voice, kicking at her. "You're the innkeeper. You poisoned me, you *bitch*!"

In the forest, the shades had gone completely black. Green eyes burst alight as they opened their earthsight. The eyes trailed a misty light.

Silence battered aside Chesterton's hands as he struggled.

"I'll pay you," he said, clawing at her. "I'll pay you—"

Silence slammed her hammer into his arm, causing him to scream. Then she brought it down on his face with a crunch. She ripped off her sweater as he groaned and thrashed, somehow wrapping it around his head and the hammer.

"William Ann!" she screamed. "I need a bag. A bag, girl! Give me—"

William Ann knelt beside her, pulling a sack over Chesterton's head as the blood soaked through the sweater. Silence reached to the side with a frantic hand and grabbed a stone, then smashed it into the sack-covered head. The sweater muffled Chesterton's screams, but also muffled the rock. She had to beat again and again.

He finally fell still. William Ann held the sack against his neck to keep the blood from flowing out, her breath coming in quick gasps. "Oh, God Beyond. Oh, *God . . .* "

Silence dared look up. Dozens of green eyes hung in the forest, glowing like little fires in the blackness. William Ann squeezed her eyes shut and whispered a prayer, tears running down her cheeks.

Silence reached slowly to her side and took out her silver dagger. She remembered another night, another sea of glowing green eyes. Her grandmother's last night. *Run, girl! RUN!*

That night, running had been an option. They'd been close to safety. Even then, Grandmother hadn't made it. She might have, but she hadn't.

That night horrified Silence. What Grandmother had done. What Silence had done . . . Well, tonight, she had one only hope. Running would not save them. Safety was too far away.

Slowly, blessedly, the eyes started to fade away. Silence sat back and let the silver knife slip out of her fingers to the ground.

William Ann opened her eyes. "Oh, God Beyond!" she said as the shades faded back into view. "A miracle!"

"Not a miracle," Silence said. "Just luck. We killed him in time. Another second, and they'd have enraged."

William Ann wrapped her arms around herself. "Oh, shadows. Oh, shadows. I thought we were dead. Oh, shadows."

Suddenly, Silence remembered something. The third man. She hadn't finished strangling him before Chesterton ran. She stumbled to her feet, turning.

He lay there, immobile.

"I finished him off," William Ann said. "Had to strangle him with my hands. My hands . . . "

Silence glanced back at her. "You did well, girl. You probably saved our lives. If you hadn't been here, I'd never have killed Chesterton without enraging the shades."

The girl still stared out into the woods, watching the placid shades. "What would it take?" she asked. "For you to see a miracle instead of a coincidence?"

"It would take a miracle, obviously," Silence said. "Instead of just a coincidence. Come on. Let's put a second sack on these fellows."

William Ann joined her, lethargic as she helped put sacks on the heads of the bandits. Two sacks each, just in case. Blood was the most dangerous. Running drew shades, but slowly. Fire enraged them immediately, but it also blinded and confused them.

Blood, though . . . blood shed in anger, exposed to the open air . . . a single drop could make the shades slaughter you, and then everything else within their sight.

Silence checked each man for a heartbeat, just in case, and found none. They saddled the horses and heaved the corpses, including the scout, into the saddles and tied them in place. They took the bedrolls and other equipment too. Hopefully, the men would have some silver on them. Bounty laws let Silence keep what she found unless there was specific mention of something stolen. In this case, the forts just wanted Chesterton dead. Pretty much everyone did.

Silence pulled a rope tight, then paused.

"Mother!" William Ann said, noticing the same thing. Leaves rustling out in the Forests. They'd uncovered their jar of green glowpaste to join that of the bandits, so the small campsite was well illuminated as a gang of eight men and women on horseback rode in through the Forests.

They were from the forts. The nice clothing, the way they kept looking into the Forests at the shades . . . City people for certain. Silence stepped forward, wishing she had her hammer to look at least a little threatening. That was still tied in the sack around Chesterton's head. It would have blood on it, so she couldn't get it out until that dried or she was in someplace very, *very* safe.

"Now, look at this," said the man at the front of the newcomers. "I couldn't believe what Tobias told me when he came back from scouting, but it appears to be true. All five men in Chesterton's gang, killed by a couple of Forest homesteaders?"

"Who are you?" Silence asked.

"Red Young," the man said with a tip of the hat. "I've been tracking this lot for the last four months. I can't thank you enough for taking care of them for me." He waved to a few of his people, who dismounted.

"Mother!" William Ann hissed.

Silence studied Red's eyes. He was armed with a cudgel, and one of the women behind him had one of those new crossbows, with the blunt tips. They cranked fast and hit hard, but didn't draw blood.

"Step away from the horses, child," Silence said.

"But—"

"Step away." Silence dropped the rope of the horse she was leading. Three fort people gathered up the ropes, one of men leering at William Ann.

"You're a smart one," Red said, leaning down and studying Silence. One of his women walked past, towing Chesterton's horse with the man's corpse slumped over the saddle.

Silence stepped up, resting a hand on Chesterton's saddle. The woman towing it paused, then looked at her boss. Silence slipped her knife from its sheath.

"You'll give us something," Silence said to Red, knife hand hidden. "After what we did. One quarter, and I don't say a word."

"Sure," he said, tipping his hat to her. He had a fake kind of grin, like one in a painting. "One quarter it is."

Silence nodded. She slipped the knife against one of the thin ropes that held Chesterton in the saddle. That gave her a good cut on it as the woman pulled the horse away. Silence stepped back, resting her hand on William Ann's shoulder while covertly moving the knife back into its sheath.

Red tipped his hat to her again. In moments, the bounty hunters had retreated back through the trees toward the roadway.

"One quarter?" William Ann hissed. "You think he'll pay it?"

"Hardly," Silence said, picking up her pack. "We're lucky he didn't just kill us. Come on." She moved out into the Forests. William Ann walked with her, both moving with the careful steps the Forests demanded. "It might be time for you to return to the waystop, William Ann."

"And what are you going to do?"

"Get our bounty back." She was a Forescout, dammit. No prim fort man was going to steal from her.

"You mean to cut them off at the white span, I assume. But what will you do? We can't fight so many, Mother."

"I'll find a way." That corpse meant freedom, *life*, for her daughters. She would not let it slip away, like smoke between the fingers. They entered the darkness, passing shades that had—just a short time before—been almost ready to wither them. Now the spirits drifted away, completely ambivalent toward the flesh that passed them.

Think, Silence. Something is very wrong here. How had those men found the camp? The light? Had they heard her and William Ann talking? They'd claimed to have been chasing Chesterton for months. Shouldn't she have heard of them before now? These men and women looked too crisp, too new, to have been out in the Forests for months trailing killers.

It led to a conclusion she did not want to admit. One man had known she was hunting a bounty today, and had seen how she was planning to track that bounty. One man had cause to see that bounty stolen from her.

Theopolis, I hope I'm wrong, she thought. *Because if you're behind this . . .*

Silence and William Ann trudged through the guts of the Forest, a place where the gluttonous canopy above drank in all of the light, leaving the ground below barren. Shades patrolled these wooden halls like blind sentries. Red and his bounty hunters were of the forts. They would keep to the roadways, and that was her advantage. The Forests were no friend to a Homesteader, no more than a familiar chasm was any less dangerous a drop.

But Silence was a sailor on this abyss. She could ride its winds better than any fort dweller. Perhaps it was time to make a storm.

What homesteaders called the "white span" was a section of roadway lined by mushroom fields. It took about an hour through the Forests to reach the span, and Silence was feeling the price of a night without sleep by the time she arrived. She ignored the fatigue, tromping through the field of mushrooms, holding her jar of green light and giving an ill cast to trees and furrows in the land.

The roadway bent around through the Forests, then came back this way. If the men were heading toward Lastport or any of the other nearby forts, they would come this direction. "You continue on," Silence said to William Ann. "It's only another hour's hike back to the waystop. Check on things there."

"I'm not leaving you, Mother."

"You promised to obey. Would you break your word?"

"And you promised to let me help you. Would you break yours?"

"I don't need you for this," Silence said. "And it will be dangerous."

"What are you going to do?"

Silence stopped beside the roadway, then knelt, fishing in her pack. She came out with the small keg of gunpowder. William Ann went as white as the mushrooms.

"Mother!"

Silence untied her grandmother's firestarter. She didn't know for certain if it still worked. She'd never dared compress the two metal arms, which looked like tongs. Squeezing them together would grind the ends against one another, making sparks, and a spring at the joint would make them come back apart.

Silence looked up at her daughter, then held the firestarter up beside her head. William Ann stepped back, then glanced to the sides, toward nearby shades.

"Are things really that bad?" the girl whispered. "For us, I mean?"

Silence nodded.

"All right, then."

Fool girl. Well, Silence wouldn't send her away. The truth was, she probably *would* need help. She intended to get that corpse. Bodies were heavy, and there wasn't any way she'd be able to cut off just the head. Not out in the Forests, with shades about.

She dug into her pack, pulling out her medical supplies. They were tied between two small boards, intended to be used as splints. It was not difficult to tie the two boards to either side of the firestarter. With her hand trowel, she dug a small hole in the roadway's soft earth, about the size of the powder keg.

She then opened the plug to the keg and set it into the hole. She soaked her handkerchief in the lamp oil, stuck one end in the keg, then positioned the firestarter boards onto the road with the end of the kerchief next to the spark-making heads. After covering the contraption with some leaves, she had a rudimentary trap. If someone stepped on the top board, that would press it down and grind out sparks to light the kerchief. Hopefully.

She couldn't afford to light the fire herself. The shades would come first for the one who made the fire.

"What happens if they don't step on it?" William Ann asked.

"Then we move it to another place on the road and try again," Silence said.

"That could shed blood, you realize."

Silence didn't reply. If the trap was triggered by a footfall, the shades wouldn't see Silence as the one causing it. They'd come first for the one who triggered the trap. But if blood was drawn, they would enrage. Soon after, it wouldn't matter who had caused it. All would be in danger.

"We have hours of darkness left," Silence said. "Cover your glowpaste."

William Ann nodded, hastily putting the cover on her jar. Silence inspected her trap again, then took William Ann by the shoulder and pulled her to the side of the roadway. The underbrush was thicker here, as the road tended to wind through breaks in the canopy. Men sought out places in the Forests where they could see the sky.

The men came along eventually. Silent, illuminated by a jar of glowpaste each. Fortfolk didn't talk at night. They passed the trap, which Silence had placed on the narrowest section of roadway. She held her breath, watching the horses pass, step after step missing the lump that marked the board. William Ann covered her ears, hunkering down.

A hoof hit the trap. Nothing happened. Silence released an annoyed breath. What would she do if the firestarter was broken? Could she find another way to—

The explosion struck her, the wave of force shaking her body. Shades vanished in a blink, green eyes snapping open. Horses reared and whinnied, men yelling.

Silence shook off her stupefaction, grabbing William Ann by the shoulder and pulling her out of hiding. Her trap had worked better than she'd assumed; the burning rag had allowed the horse that had triggered the trap to take a few steps before the blast hit. No blood, just a lot of surprised horses and confused men. The little keg of gunpowder hadn't done as much damage as she'd anticipated—the stories of what gunpowder could do were often as fanciful as stories of the Homeland—but the sound had been incredible.

Silence's ears rang as she fought through the confused men, finding what she'd hoped to see. Chesterton's corpse lay on the ground, dumped from saddleback by a bucking horse and a frayed rope. She grabbed the corpse under the arms and William Ann took the legs. They moved sideways into the Forests.

"Idiots!" Red bellowed from amidst the confusion. "Stop her! It—"

He cut off as shades swarmed the roadway, descending upon the men. Red had managed to keep his horse under control, but now he had to dance it back from the shades. Enraged, they had turned pure black, though the blast of light and fire had obviously left them dazed. They fluttered about, like moths at a flame. Green eyes. A small blessing. If those turned red . . .

One bounty hunter, standing on the road and spinning about, was struck. His back arched, black-veined tendrils crisscrossing his skin. He dropped to his knees, screaming as the flesh of his face shrank around his skull.

Silence turned away. William Ann watched the fallen man with a horrified expression.

"Slowly, child," Silence said in what she hoped was a comforting voice. She hardly felt comforting. "Carefully. We can move away from them. William Ann. Look at me."

The girl turned to look at her.

"Hold my eyes. Move. That's right. Remember, the shades will go to the source of the fire first. They are confused, stunned. They can't smell fire like they do blood, and they'll look from it to the nearest sources of quick motion. Slowly, easily. Let the scrambling city men distract them."

The two of them eased into the Forests with excruciating deliberateness. In the face of so much chaos, so much danger, their pace felt like a crawl. Red organized a resistance. Fire-crazed shades could be fought, destroyed, with silver. More and more would come, but if the men were clever and lucky, they'd be able to destroy those nearby and then move slowly away from the source of the fire. They could hide, survive. Maybe.

Unless one of them accidentally drew blood.

Silence and William Ann stepped through a field of mushrooms that glowed like the skulls of rats and broke silently beneath her feet. Luck was not completely with them, for as the shades shook off their disorientation from the explosion, a pair of them on the outskirts turned and struck out toward the fleeing women.

William Ann gasped. Silence deliberately set down Chesterton's shoulders, then took out her knife. "Keep going," she whispered. "Pull him away. Slowly, girl. *Slowly.*"

"I won't leave you!"

"I will catch up," Silence said. "You aren't ready for this."

She didn't look to see if William Ann obeyed, for the shades—figures of jet black, streaking across the white-knobbed ground—were upon her. Strength was meaningless against shades. They had no real substance. Only two things mattered: moving quickly, and not letting yourself be frightened.

Shades *were* dangerous, but so long as you had silver, you could fight. Many a man died because he ran, drawing even more shades, rather than standing his ground.

Silence swung at the shades as they reached her. *You want my daughter, hellbound?* she thought with a snarl. *You should have tried for the city men instead.*

She swept her knife through the first shade, as Grandmother had taught. *Never creep back and cower before shades. You're Forescout blood. You claim the Forests. You are their creature, as much as any other. As am I . . .*

Her knife passed through the shade with a slight tugging feeling, creating a shower of bright white sparks that sprayed out of the shade. The shade pulled back, its black tendrils writhing about one another.

Silence spun on the other. The pitch sky let her see only the thing's eyes, horrid green, as it reached for her. She lunged.

Its spectral hands were upon her, the icy cold of its fingers gripping her arm below the elbow. She could feel it. Shade fingers had substance; they could grab you, hold you back. Only silver warded them away. Only with silver could you fight.

She rammed her arm in further. Sparks shot out its back, spraying like a bucket of wash water. Silence gasped at the horrid, icy pain. Her knife slipped from fingers she could no longer feel. She lurched forward, falling to her knees as the second shade fell backward, then began spinning about in a mad spiral. The first one flopped on the ground, like a dying fish, trying to rise but its top half falling over.

The cold of her arm was so *bitter*. She stared at the wounded arm, watching the flesh of her hand wither upon itself, pulling in toward the bone.

She heard weeping.

You stand there, Silence. Grandmother's voice. Memories of the first time she'd killed a shade. *You do as I say. No tears! Forescouts don't cry. Forescouts DON'T CRY.*

She had learned to hate her that day. Ten years old, with her little knife, shivering and weeping in the night as her grandmother had enclosed her and a drifting shade in a ring of silver dust.

Grandmother had run around the perimeter, enraging it with motion. While Silence was trapped in there. With death.

The only way to learn is to do, Silence. And you'll learn, one way or another!

"Mother!" William Ann said.

Silence blinked, coming out of the memory as her daughter dumped silver dust on the exposed arm. The withering stopped as William Ann, choking against her thick tears, dumped the entire pouch of emergency silver over the hand. The metal reversed the withering, and the skin turned pink again, the blackness melting away in sparks of white.

Too much, Silence thought. William Ann used all of the silver dust in her haste, far more than one wound needed. It was difficult to summon any anger, for feeling flooded back into her hand and the icy cold retreated.

"Mother?" William Ann asked. "I left you, as you said. But he was so heavy, I didn't get far. I came back for you. I'm sorry. I came back for you!"

"Thank you," Silence said, breathing in. "You did well." She reached up and took her daughter by the shoulder, then used the once-withered hand to search in the grass for Grandmother's knife. When she brought it up, the blade was blackened in several places, but still good.

Back on the road, the city men had made a circle and were holding off the shades with silver-tipped spears. The horses had all fled or had been consumed. Silence fished on the ground, coming up with a small handful of silver dust. The rest had been expended in the healing. Too much.

No use worrying about that now, she thought, stuffing the handful of dust in her pocket. "Come," she said, hauling herself to her feet. "I'm sorry I never taught you to fight them."

"Yes you did," William Ann said, wiping her tears. "You've told me all about it."

Told. Never shown. *Shadows, Grandmother. I know I disappoint you, but I won't do it to her. I can't. But I am a good mother.* I will *protect them.*

The two left the mushrooms, taking up their grisly prize again and tromping through the Forests. They passed more darkened shades floating toward the fight. All of those sparks would draw them. The city men were dead. Too much attention, too much struggle. They'd have a thousand shades upon them before the hour was out.

Silence and William Ann moved slowly. Though the cold had mostly retreated from Silence's hand, there was a lingering . . . something. A deep shiver. A limb touched by the shades wouldn't feel right for months.

That was far better than what could have happened. Without William Ann's quick thinking, Silence could have become a cripple. Once the withering settled in—that took a little time, though it varied—it was irreversible.

Something rustled in the woods. Silence froze, causing William Ann to stop and glance about.

"Mother?" William Ann whispered.

Silence frowned. The night was so black, and they'd been forced to leave their lights. *Something's out there*, she thought, trying to pierce the darkness. *What are you?* God Beyond protect them if the fighting had drawn one of the Deepest Ones.

The sound did not repeat. Reluctantly, Silence continued on. They walked for a good hour, and in the darkness, Silence hadn't realized they'd neared the roadway again until they stepped onto it.

Silence heaved out a breath, setting down their burden and rolling her tired arms in their joints. Some light from the Starbelt filtered down upon them, illuminating something like a large jawbone to their left. The Old Bridge. They were almost home. The shades here weren't even agitated; they moved with their lazy, almost butterfly, gaits.

Her arms felt so sore. That body felt as if it were getting heavier every moment. Men often didn't realize how heavy a corpse was. Silence sat down. They'd rest for a time before continuing on. "William Ann, do you have any water left in your canteen?"

William Ann whimpered.

Silence started, then scrambled to her feet. Her daughter stood beside the bridge, and something dark stood behind her. A green glow suddenly illuminated the night as the figure took out a small vial of glowpaste. By that sickly light, Silence could see that the figure was Red.

He held a dagger to William Ann's neck. The city man had not fared well in the fighting. One eye was now a milky white, half his face blackened, his lips pulled back from his teeth. A shade had gotten him across the face. He was lucky to be alive.

"I figured you'd come back this way," he said, the words slurred by his shriveled lips. Spittle dripped from his chin. "Silver. Give me your silver."

His knife . . . it was common steel.

"Now!" he roared, pulling the knife closer to William Ann's neck. If he so much as nicked her, the shades would be upon them in heartbeats.

"I only have the knife," William Ann lied, taking it out and tossing it to the ground before him. "It's too late for your face, Red. That withering has set in."

"I don't care," he hissed. "Now the body. Step away from it, woman. Away!"

Silence stepped to the side. Could she get to him before he killed William Ann? He'd have to grab that knife. If she sprang just right . . .

"You killed my men," Red growled. "They're dead, all of them. God, if I hadn't rolled into the hollow . . . I had to *listen* to it. Listen to them being slaughtered!"

"You were the only smart one," she said. "You couldn't have saved them, Red."

"Bitch! You killed them."

"They killed themselves," she whispered. "You come to my Forests, take what is mine? It was your men or my children, Red."

"Well, if you want your child to live through this, you'll stay very still. Girl, pick up that knife."

Whimpering, William Ann knelt. Red mimicked her, staying just behind her, watching Silence, holding the knife steady. William Ann picked up the knife in trembling hands.

Red pulled the silver knife from William Ann, then held it in one hand, the common knife at her neck in the other. "Now, the girl is going to carry the corpse, and you're going to wait right there. I don't want you coming near."

"Of course," Silence said, already planning. She couldn't afford to strike right now. He was too careful. She would follow through the Forests, along the road, and wait for a moment of weakness. Then she'd strike.

Red spat to the side.

Then a padded crossbow bolt shot from the night and took him in the shoulder, jolting him. His blade slid across William Ann's neck, and a dribble of blood ran down it. The girl's eyes widened in horror, though it was little more than a nick. The danger to her throat wasn't important.

The blood was.

Red tumbled back, gasping, hand to his shoulder. A few drops of blood glistened on his knife. The shades in the Forests around them went black. Glowing green eyes burst alight, then deepened to crimson.

Red eyes in the night. Blood in the air.

"Oh, hell!" Red screamed. "Oh, *hell*." Red eyes swarmed around him. There was no hesitation here, no confusion. They went straight for the one who had drawn blood.

Silence reached for William Ann as the shades descended. Red grabbed the girl around and shoved her through a shade, trying to stop it. He spun and dashed the other direction.

William Ann passed through the shade, her face withering, skin pulling in at the chin and around the eyes. She stumbled through the shade and into Silence's arms.

Silence felt an immediate, overwhelming panic.

"No! Child, no. No. *No* . . . "

William Ann worked her mouth, making a choking sound, her lips pulling back toward her teeth, her eyes open wide as her skin pulled back and her eyelids shriveled.

Silver. I need silver. I can save her. Silence snapped her head up, clutching William Ann. Red ran down the roadway, slashing the silver dagger all about, spraying light and sparks. Shades surrounded him. Hundreds, like ravens flocking to a roost.

Not that way. The shades would finish with him soon, and would look for flesh, any flesh. William Ann still had blood on her neck. They'd come for her next. Even without that, the girl was withering fast.

The dagger wouldn't be enough to save William Ann. Silence needed dust, silver dust, to force down her daughter's throat. Silence fumbled in her pocket, coming out with the small bit of silver dust there.

Too little. She *knew* that would be too little. Her grandmother's training calmed her mind, and everything became immediately clear.

The waystop was close. She had more silver there.

"M-Mother . . . "

Silence heaved William Ann into her arms. Too light, the flesh drying. Then she turned and ran with everything she had across the bridge.

Her arms stung, weakened from having hauled the corpse so far. The corpse . . . she couldn't lose it!

No. She couldn't think on that. The shades would have it, as warm enough flesh, soon after Red was gone. There would be no bounty. She had to focus on William Ann.

Silence's tears felt cold on her face as she ran, wind blowing her. Her daughter trembled and shook in her arms, spasming as she died. She'd become a shade if she died like this.

"I won't lose you!" Silence said into the night. "Please. I won't lose you . . . "

Behind her, Red screamed a long, wailing screech of agony that cut off at the end as the shades feasted. Near her, other shades stopped, eyes deepening to red.

Blood in the air. Eyes of crimson.

"I hate you," Silence whispered into the air as she ran. Each step was agony. She *was* growing old. "I hate you! What you did to me. What you did to us."

She didn't know if she was speaking to Grandmother or the God Beyond. So often, they were the same in her mind. Had she ever realized that before?

Branches lashed at her as she pushed forward. Was that light ahead? The waystop?

Hundreds upon hundreds of red eyes opened in front of her. She stumbled to the ground, spent, William Ann like a heavy bundle of branches in her arms. The girl trembled, her eyes rolled back in her head.

Silence held out the small bit of silver dust she'd recovered earlier. She longed to pour it on William Ann, save her a little pain, but she knew with clarity that was a waste. She looked down, crying, then took the pinch and made a small circle around the two of them. What else could she do?

William Ann shook with a seizure as she rasped, drawing in breaths and clawing at Silence's arms. The shades came by the dozens, huddling around the two of them, smelling the blood. The flesh.

Silence pulled her daughter close. She should have gone for the knife after all; it wouldn't heal William Ann, but she could have at least fought with it.

Without that, without anything, she failed. Grandmother had been right all along.

"Hush now, my dear one . . . " Silence whispered, squeezing her eyes shut. "Be not afraid."

Shades came at her frail barrier, throwing up sparks, making Silence open her eyes. They backed away, then others came, beating against the silver, their red eyes illuminating writhing black forms.

"Night comes upon us . . . " Silence whispered, choking at the words. " . . . but sunlight will break."

William Ann arched her back, then fell still.

"Sleep now . . . my . . . my dear one . . . let your tears fade. Darkness surrounds us, but someday . . . we'll wake . . . "

So tired. *I shouldn't have let her come.*

If she hadn't, Chesterton would have gotten away from her, and she'd have probably died to the shades then. William Ann and Sebruki would have become slaves to Theopolis, or worse.

No choices. No way out.

"Why did you send us here?" she screamed, looking up, past hundreds of glowing red eyes. "What is the point?"

There was no answer. There was never an answer.

Yes, that *was* light ahead; she could see it through the low tree branches in front of her. She was only a few yards from the waystop. She would die, like Grandmother had, mere paces from her home.

She blinked, cradling William Ann as the tiny silver barrier failed.

That . . . that branch just in front of her. It had such a very odd shape. Long, thin, no leaves. Not like a branch at all. Instead, like . . .

Like a crossbow bolt.

It had lodged into the tree after being fired from the waystop earlier in the day. She remembered facing down that bolt earlier, staring at its reflective end.

Silver.

Silence Montane crashed through the back door of the waystop, hauling a desiccated body behind her. She stumbled into the kitchen, barely able to walk, and dropped the silver-tipped bolt from a withered hand.

Her skin continued to pull tight, her body shriveling. She had not been able to avoid withering, not when fighting so many Shades. The crossbow bolt had merely cleared a path, allowing her to push forward in a last, frantic charge.

She could barely see. Tears streamed from her clouded eyes. Even with the tears, her eyes felt as dry as if she had been standing in the wind for an hour while holding them wide open. Her lids refused to blink, and she couldn't move her lips.

She had . . . powder. Didn't she?

Thought. Mind. What?

She moved without thought. Jar on the windowsill. In case of broken circle. She unscrewed the lid with fingers like sticks. Seeing them horrified a distant part of her mind.

Dying. I'm dying.

She dunked the jar of silver powder in the water cistern and pulled it out, then stumbled to William Ann. She felt to her knees beside the girl, spilling much of the water. The rest she dumped on her daughter's face with a shaking arm.

Please. Please.

Darkness.

"We were sent here to be strong," Grandmother said, standing on the cliff edge overlooking the waters. Her whited hair curled in the wind, writhing, like the wisps of a shade.

She turned back to Silence, and her weathered face was covered in droplets of water from the crashing surf below. "The God Beyond sent us. It's part of the plan."

"It's so easy for you to say that, isn't it?" Silence spat. "You can fit anything into that nebulous *plan*. Even the destruction of the world itself."

"I won't hear blasphemy from you, child." A voice like boots stepping in gravel. She walked toward Silence. "You can rail against the God Beyond, but it will change nothing. William was a fool and an idiot. You are better off. We are *Forescouts*. We *survive*. We will be the ones to defeat the Evil, someday." She passed Silence by.

Silence had never seen a smile from Grandmother, not since her husband's death. Smiling was wasted energy. And love . . . love was for the people back in Homeland. The people who'd died to the Evil.

"I'm with child," Silence said.

Grandmother stopped. "William?"

"Who else?"

Grandmother continued on.

"No condemnations?" Silence asked, turning, folding her arms.

"It's done," Grandmother said. "We are Forescouts. If this is how we must continue, so be it. I'm more worried about the waystop, and meeting our payments to those damn forts."

I have an idea for that, Silence thought, considering the lists of bounties she'd begun collecting. *Something even you wouldn't dare. Something dangerous. Something unthinkable.*

Grandmother reached the woods and looked at Silence, scowled, then pulled on her hat and stepped into the trees.

"I will not have you interfering with my child," Silence called after her. "I will raise my own as I will!"

Grandmother vanished into the shadows.

Please. Please.

"I *will!*"

I won't lose you. I won't . . .

Silence gasped, coming awake and clawing at the floorboards, staring upward.

Alive. She was alive!

Dob the stableman knelt beside her, holding the jar of powdered silver. She coughed, lifting fingers—plump, the flesh restored—to her neck. It was hale, though ragged from the flakes of silver that had been forced down her throat. Her skin was dusted with black bits of ruined silver.

"William Ann!" she said, turning.

The child lay on the floor beside the door. William Ann's left side, where she'd first touched the shade, was blackened. Her face wasn't too bad, but her hand was a withered skeleton. They'd have to cut that off. Her leg looked bad too. Silence couldn't tell how bad without tending the wounds.

"Oh, child . . . " Silence knelt beside her.

But the girl breathed in and out. That was enough, all things considered.

"I tried," Dob said. "But you'd already done what could be done."

"Thank you," Silence said. She turned to the aged man, with his high forehead and dull eyes.

"Did you get him?" Dob asked.

"Who?"

"The bounty."

"I . . . yes, I did. But I had to leave him."

"You'll find another," Dob said in his monotone, climbing to his feet. "The Fox always does."

"How long have you known?"

"I'm an idiot, mam," he said. "Not a fool." He bowed his head to her, then walked away, slump-backed as always.

Silence climbed to her feet, then groaned, picking up William Ann. She lifted her daughter to the rooms above and saw to her.

The leg wasn't as bad as Silence had feared. A few of the toes would be lost, but the foot itself was hale enough. The entire left side of William Ann's body was blackened, as if burned. That would fade, with time, to gray.

Everyone who saw her would know exactly what had happened. Many men would never touch her, fearing her taint. This might just doom her to a life alone.

I know a little about such a life, Silence thought, dipping a cloth into the water bin and washing William Ann's face. The youth would sleep through the day. She had come very close to death, to becoming a shade herself. The body did not recover quickly from that.

Of course, Silence had been close to that too. She, however, had been there before. Another of Grandmother's preparations. Oh, how she hated that woman. Silence owed who she was to how that training toughened her. Could she be thankful for Grandmother and hateful, both at once?

Silence finished washing William Ann, then dressed her in a soft nightgown and left her in her bunk. Sebruki still slept off the draught William Ann had given her.

So she went downstairs to the kitchen to think difficult thoughts. She'd lost the bounty. The shades would have had at that body; the skin would be dust, the skill blackened and ruined. She had no way to prove that she'd taken Chesterton.

She settled against the kitchen table and laced her hands before her. She wanted to have at the whiskey instead, to dull the horror of the night.

She thought for hours. Could she pay Theopolis off some way? Borrow from someone else? Who? Maybe find another bounty. But so few people came through the waystop these days. Theopolis had already given her warning, with his writ. He wouldn't wait more than a day or two for payment before claiming the waystop as his own.

Had she really gone through so much, still to lose?

Sunlight fell on her face and a breeze from the broken window tickled her cheek, waking her from her slumber at the table. Silence blinked, stretching, limbs complaining. Then she sighed, moving to the kitchen counter. She'd left out all of the materials from the preparations last night, her clay bowls thick with glowpaste that still shone faintly. The silver-tipped crossbow bolt still lay by the back door. She'd need to clean up and get breakfast ready for her few guests. Then, think of *some* way to . . .

The back door opened and someone stepped in.

. . . to deal with Theopolis. She exhaled softly, looking at him in his clean clothing and condescending smile. He tracked mud onto her floor as he entered. "Silence Montane. Nice morning, hmmm?"

Shadows, she thought. *I don't have the mental strength to deal with him right now.*

He moved to close the window shutters.

"What are you doing?" she demanded.

"Hmmm? Haven't you warned me before that you loathe that people might see us together? That they might get a hint that you are turning in bounties to me? I'm just trying to protect you. Has something happened? You look awful, hmmm?"

"I know what you did."

"You do? But, see, I do many things. About what do you speak?"

Oh, how she'd like to cut that grin from his lips and cut out his throat, stomp out that annoying Lastport accent. She couldn't. He was just so blasted *good* at acting. She had guesses, probably good ones. But no proof.

Grandmother would have killed him right then. Was she so desperate to prove him wrong that she'd lose everything?

"You were in the Forests," Silence said. "When Red surprised me at the bridge, I assumed that the thing I'd heard—rustling in the darkness—had been him. It wasn't. He implied he'd been waiting for us at the bridge. That thing in the darkness, it was you. *You* shot him with the crossbow to jostle him, make him draw blood. Why, Theopolis?"

"Blood?" Theopolis said. "In the night? And you *survived*? You're quite fortunate, I should say. Remarkable. What else happened?"

She said nothing.

"I have come for payment of debt," Theopolis said. "You have no bounty to turn in then, hmmm? Perhaps we will need my document after all. So kind of me to bring another copy. This really will be wonderful for us both. Do you not agree?"

"Your feet are glowing."

Theopolis hesitated, then looked down. There, the mud he'd tracked in shone very faintly blue in the light of the glowpaste remnants.

"You followed me," she said. "You *were* there last night."

He looked up at her with a slow, unconcerned expression. "And?" He took a step forward.

Silence backed away, her heel hitting the wall behind her. She reached around, taking out the key and unlocking the door behind her. Theopolis grabbed her arm, yanking her away as she pulled open the door.

"Going for one of your hidden weapons?" he asked with a sneer. "The crossbow you keep hidden on the pantry shelf? Yes, I know of that. I'm disappointed, Silence. Can't we be civil?

"I will never sign your document, Theopolis," she said, then spat at his feet.

"I would sooner die, I would sooner be put out of house and home. You can take the waystop by force, but I will *not* serve you. You can be damned, for all I care, you bastard. You—"

He slapped her across the face. A quick, but unemotional gesture. "Oh, do shut up."

She stumbled back.

"Such dramatics, Silence. I can't be the only one to wish you lived up to your name, hmmm?"

She licked her lip, feeling the pain of his slap. She lifted her hand to her face. A single drop of blood colored her fingertip when she pulled it away.

"You expect me to be frightened?" Theopolis asked. "I know we are safe in here."

"City fool," she whispered, then flipped the drop of blood at him. It hit him on the cheek. "Always follow the Simple Rules. Even when you think you don't have to. And I wasn't opening the pantry, as you thought."

Theopolis frowned, then glanced over at the door she had opened. The door into the small, old shrine. Her grandmother's shrine to the God Beyond.

The bottom of the door was rimmed in silver.

Red eyes opened in the air behind Theopolis, a jet-black form coalescing in the shadowed room. Theopolis hesitated, then turned.

He didn't get to scream as the shade took his head in its hands and drew his life away. It was a newer shade, its form still strong, despite the writhing blackness of its clothing. A tall woman, hard of features, with curling hair. Theopolis opened his mouth, then his face withered away, eyes sinking into his head.

"You should have run, Theopolis," Silence said.

His head began to crumble. His body collapsed to the floor.

"Hide from the green eyes, run from the red," Silence said, taking out her silver dagger. "Your rules, Grandmother."

The shade turned to her. Silence shivered, looking into those dead, glassy eyes of a matriarch she loathed and loved.

"I hate you," Silence said. "Thank you for making me hate you." She retrieved the silver-tipped crossbow bolt and held it before her, but the shade did not strike. Silence edged around, forcing the shade back. It floated away from her, back into the shrine lined with silver at the bottom of its three walls, where Silence had trapped it years ago.

Her heart pounding, Silence closed the door, completing the barrier, and locked it again. No matter what happened, that shade left Silence alone.

Almost, she thought it remembered. And almost, Silence felt guilty for trapping that soul inside the small closet for all these years.

Silence found Theopolis's hidden cave after six hours of hunting.

It was about where she'd expected it to be, in the hills not far from the Old Bridge. It included a silver barrier. She could harvest that. Good money there.

Inside the small cavern, she found Chesterton's corpse, which Theopolis had dragged to the cave while the Shades killed Red and then hunted Silence. *I'm so glad, for once, you were a greedy man, Theopolis.*

She would have to find someone else to start turning in bounties for her. That would be difficult, particularly on short notice. She dragged the corpse out and threw it over the back of Theopolis's horse. A short hike took her back to the road, where she paused, then walked up and located Red's fallen corpse, withered down to just bones and clothing.

She fished out her grandmother's dagger, scored and blackened from the fight. It fit back into the sheath at her side. She trudged, exhausted, back to the waystop and hid Chesterton's corpse in the cold cellar out back of the stable, beside where she'd put Theopolis's remains. She hiked back into the kitchen. Beside the shrine's door—where her grandmother's dagger had once hung—she had placed the silver crossbow bolt that Sebruki had unknowingly sent her.

What would the fort authorities say when she explained Theopolis's death to them? Perhaps she could claim to have found him like that . . .

She paused, then smiled.

"Looks like you're lucky, friend," Daggon said, sipping at his beer. "The White Fox won't be looking for you any time soon."

The spindly man, who still insisted his name was Earnest, hunkered down a little farther in his seat.

"How is it you're still here?" Daggon asked. "I traveled all the way to Lastport. I hardly expected to find you here on my path back."

"I hired on at a homestead nearby," said the slender-necked man. "Good work, mind you. Solid work."

"And you pay each night to stay here?"

"I like it. It feels peaceful. The homesteads don't have good silver protection. They just . . . let the shades move about. Even inside." The man shuttered.

Daggon shrugged, lifting his drink as Silence Montane limped by. Yes, she was a healthy-looking woman. He really *should* court her, one of these days. She scowled at his smile and dumped his plate in front of him.

"I think I'm wearing her down," Daggon said, mostly to himself, as she left.

"You will have to work hard," Earnest said. "Seven men have proposed to her during the last month."

"What!"

"The reward!" the spindly man said. "The one for bringing in Chesterton and his men. Lucky woman, Silence Montane, finding the White Fox's lair like that."

Daggon dug into his meal. He didn't much like how things had turned out. Theopolis, that dandy had been the White Fox all along? Poor Silence. How had it been, stumbling upon his cave and finding him inside, all withered away?

"They say that this Theopolis spent his last strength killing Chesterton," Earnest said, "then dragging him into the hole. Theopolis withered before he could get to his silver powder. Very like the White Fox, always determined to get the bounty, no matter what. We won't soon see a hunter like him again."

"I suppose not," Daggon said, though he'd much rather that the man had kept his skin. Now who would Daggon tell his tales about? He didn't fancy paying for his own beer.

Nearby, a greasy-looking fellow rose from his meal and shuffled out of the front door, looking half-drunk already, though it was only noon.

Some people. Daggon shook his head. "To the White Fox." he said, raising his drink.

Earnest clinked his mug to Daggon's. "The White Fox, meanest bastard the Forests have ever known."

"May his soul know peace," Daggon said, "and may the God Beyond be thanked that he never decided we were worth his time."

"Amen," Earnest said.

"Of course," Daggon said, "there is still Bloody Kent. Now *he's* a right nasty fellow. You'd better hope he doesn't get your number, friend. And don't you give me that innocent look. These are the Forests. Everybody here has done something, now and then, that you don't want others to know about . . ."

New York Times #1 bestseller **Brandon Sanderson** made a name for himself in the fantasy genre with his first novel *Elantris* and its sequels as well as the Mistborn series before being chosen to finish Robert Jordan's famous Wheel of Time sequence—left uncompleted on Jordan's death—writing volumes such as *The Gathering Storm*, *Towers of Midnight*, and *A Memory of Light*. His fantasy series for young adults, Alcatraz, consists of *Alcatraz Versus the Evil Librarians*, *Alcatraz Versus the Scrivener's Bones*, *Alcatraz Versus the Knights of Crystallia*, and *Alcatraz Versus the Shattered Lens*. The Stormlight Archive series began with *The Way of Kings* in 2010 and continues with the recently published *Words of Radiance*. He lives in American Fork, Utah, and maintains a website at brandonsanderson.com.

It is funny how a man can see only what he wants to see.
He wants to make her the same as him,
because he thinks he's better . . .

THE PLAGUE

Ken Liu

Lessons on life.

I'm in the river fishing with Mother. The sun is about to set, and the fish are groggy. Easy pickings. The sky is bright crimson and so is Mother, the light shimmering on her shkin like someone smeared blood all over her.

That's when a big man tumbles into the water from a clump of reeds, dropping a long tube with glass on the end. Then I see he's not fat, like I thought at first, but wearing a thick suit with a glass bowl over his head.

Mother watches the man flop in the river like a fish. "Let's go, Marne."

But I don't. After another minute, he's not moving as much. He struggles to reach the tubes on his back.

"He can't breathe," I say.

"You can't help him," Mother says. "The air, the water, everything out here is poisonous to his kind."

I go over, crouch down, and look through the glass covering his face, which is naked. No shkin at all. He's from the Dome.

His hideous features are twisted with fright.

I reach over and untangle the tubes on his back.

I wish I hadn't lost my camera. The way the light from the bonfire dances against their shiny bodies cannot be captured with words. Their deformed limbs, their malnourished frames, their terrible disfigurement—all seem to disappear in a kind of nobility in the flickering shadows that makes my heart ache.

The girl who saved me offers me a bowl of food—fish, I think. Grateful, I accept.

I take out the field purification kit and sprinkle the nanobots over the food. These are designed to break down after they've outlived their purpose, nothing like the horrors that went out of control and made the world unlivable . . .

Fearing to give offense, I explain, "Spices."

Looking at her is like looking into a humanoid mirror. Instead of her face I see a distorted reflection of my own. It's hard to read an expression from the vague indentations and ridges in that smooth surface, but I think she's puzzled.

"*Modja saf-fu ota poiss-you*," she says, hissing and grunting. I don't hold the devolved phonemes and degenerate grammar against her—a diseased people scrabbling out an existence in the wilderness isn't exactly going to be composing poetry or thinking philosophy. She's saying, "Mother says the food here is poisonous to you."

"Spices make safe," I say.

As I squeeze the purified food into the feeding tube on the side of the helmet, her face ripples like a pond, and my reflection breaks into colorful patches.

She's grinning.

The others do not trust the man from the Dome as he skulks around the village enclosed in his suit.

"He says that the Dome dwellers are scared of us because they don't understand us. He wants to change that."

Mother laughs, sounding like water bubbling over rocks. Her shkin changes texture, breaking the reflected light into brittle, jagged rays.

The man is fascinated by the games I play: drawing lines over my belly, my thigh, my breasts with a stick as the shkin ripples and rises to follow. He writes down everything any one of us says.

He asks me if I know who my father is.

I think what a strange place the Dome must be.

"No," I tell him. "At the Quarter Festivals the men and women writhe together and the shkins direct the seed where they will."

He tells me he's sorry.

"What for?"

It's hard for me to really know what he's thinking because his naked face does not talk like shkin would.

"All this." He sweeps his arm around.

• • •

When the plague hit fifty years ago, the berserk nanobots and biohancers ate away people's skins, the soft surface of their gullets, the warm, moist membranes lining every orifice of their bodies.

Then the plague took the place of the lost flesh and covered people, inside and outside, like a lichen made of tiny robots and colonies of bacteria.

Those with money—my ancestors—holed up with weapons and built domes and watched the rest of the refugees die outside.

But some survived. The living parasite changed and even made it possible for its hosts to eat the mutated fruits and drink the poisonous water and breathe the toxic air.

In the Dome, jokes are told about the plagued, and a few of the daring trade with them from time to time. But everyone seems content to see them as no longer human.

Some have claimed that the plagued are happy as they are. That is nothing but bigotry and an attempt to evade responsibility. An accident of birth put me inside the Dome and her outside. It isn't her fault that she picks at her deformed skin instead of pondering philosophy; that she speaks with grunts and hisses instead of rhetoric and enunciation; that she does not understand family love but only an instinctual, animalistic yearning for affection.

We in the Dome must save her.

"You want to take away my shkin?" I ask.

"Yes, to find a cure, for you, your mother, all the plagued."

I know him well enough now to understand that he is sincere. It doesn't matter that the shkin is as much a part of me as my ears. He believes that flaying me, mutilating me, stripping me naked would be an improvement.

"We have a duty to help you."

He sees my happiness as misery, my thoughtfulness as depression, my wishes as delusion. It is funny how a man can see only what he wants to see. He wants to make me the same as him, because he thinks he's better.

Quicker than he can react, I pick up a rock and smash the glass bowl around his head. As he screams, I touch his face and watch the shkin writhe over my hands to cover him.

Mother is right. He has not come to learn, but I must teach him anyway.

⊰⊱

Ken Liu (kenliu.name) is an author and translator of speculative fiction, as well as a lawyer and programmer. His fiction has appeared in *The Magazine of Fantasy & Science Fiction*, *Asimov's*, *Analog*, *Clarkesworld*, *Lightspeed*, and *Strange Horizons*, among other places. He is a winner of the Nebula, Hugo, and World Fantasy awards. Liu's debut novel, *A Tempest of Gold*, the first in a fantasy series, will be published by Simon & Schuster's new genre fiction imprint in 2015, along with a collection of short stories. He lives with his family near Boston, Massachusetts.

"That is outrageous," I said. "And wicked."
"Absolutely, but that does not make it untrue."

THE GRUESOME AFFAIR OF
THE ELECTRIC BLUE LIGHTNING
(FROM THE FILES OF AUGUST DUPIN)

Joe R. Lansdale,
Translated loosely from the French

This story can only be described as fantastic in nature, and with no exaggeration, it deals with nothing less than the destruction of the world, but before I continue, I should make an immediate confession. Some of this is untrue. I do not mean the events themselves, for they are accurate, but I have disguised the names of several individuals, and certain locations have been re-imagined—for lack of a better word—to suit my own conscience. The end of the cosmos and our world as we know it is of considerable concern, of course, but no reason to abandon manners.

These decisions were made primarily due to the possibility of certain actors in this drama being unnecessarily scandalized or embarrassed, even though they are only mentioned in passing and have little to nothing to do with the events themselves. I do not think historians, warehouse owners and the like should have to bear the burden of my story, especially as it will undoubtedly be disbelieved.

There are, however, specific players in my article, story if you prefer, that have their own names to contend with, old as those names may be, and I have not made any effort whatsoever to alter these. This is owed to the fact that these particular personages are well enough recognized by name, and any attempt to disguise them would be a ridiculous and wasted effort.

This begins where many of my true stories begin. I was in the apartment I share with Auguste Dupin, perhaps the wisest and most rational man I have ever known, if a bit of a curmudgeon and a self-centered ass. A touch of background, should you be interested: we share an apartment, having met while looking for the same obscure book in a library, which brought about a discussion of the tome in question, which in turn we decided to share in the reading, along with the price of an apartment, as neither of us could afford the rental of one alone. Dupin is a Chevalier, and had some financial means in the past, but his wealth had somehow been lost—how this occurred, we have by unspoken agreement never discussed, and this suits me, for I would rather not go into great detail about my own circumstances.

In spite of his haughty nature, Dupin is quite obviously of gentlemanly countenance and bearing, if, like myself he is a threadbare gentleman; I should also add, one who in manners is frequently not a gentleman at all. He is also a sometime investigator. This began merely as a hobby, something he did for his own amusement, until I assured him that regular employment might aid in his problems with the rent, and that I could assist him, for a small fee, of course. He agreed.

What I call "The Affair of the Electric Blue Lightning" began quite casually, and certainly by accident. I was telling Dupin how I had read that the intense lightning storm of the night before had been so radical, producing such powerful bolts, it had started fires all along the Rue_____. In fact, the very newspaper that had recorded the article lay before him, and it wasn't until I had finished telling him about the irregular events, that I saw it lying there, and admonished him for not revealing to me he had read the article and knew my comments even before disclosing them for his consideration.

"Yes," Dupin said, leaning back in his chair and clasping his fingers together. "But I appreciate your telling of it. It was far more dramatic and interesting than the newspaper article itself. I was especially interested in, and impressed with, your descriptions of the lightning, for yours was a practical explanation, but not an actual recollection, and therefore perhaps faulty."

"Excuse me," I said.

His eyes brightened and his lean face seemed to stretch even longer as he said, "You described to me lightning that you did not see, and in so doing, you described it as it should appear, not as the newspaper depicted it. Or to be more precise, you only said that the fires had been started by a lightning strike. The newspaper said it was a blue-white fulmination that appeared to climb up to the sky from the rooftops of a portion of the warehouse district rather than come down from the heavens. To be more precise, the newspaper was supposedly quoting a man named F_____, who said he saw the peculiar lightning and the beginnings of the warehouse fire with his own eyes. He swore it rose upward, instead of the other way around. Out of the ordinary, don't you think?"

"A mistake on his part," I said. "I had forgotten all about his saying that. I didn't remember it that way."

"Perhaps," said Dupin, filling his meerschaum pipe and studying the rain outside the apartment window, "because it didn't make sense to you. It goes against common sense. So, you dismissed it."

"I suppose so," I said. "Isn't that what you do in your investigations? Dismiss items that are nonsensical? Use only what you know to be true? You are always admonishing me for filling in what is not there, what could not be, that which faults ratiocination."

Dupin nodded. "That's correct. But, isn't that what you're doing now? You are filling in what is not there. Or deciding quite by your own contemplations that which should not be there."

"You confuse me, Dupin."

"No doubt," he said. "Unlike you, I do not dismiss something as false until I have considered it fully and examined all the evidence. There is also the part of the article where F_____'s statement was validated by a child named P_____."

"But, the word of a child?" I said.

"Sometimes they have the clearest eyes," Dupin said. "They have not had time to think what they *should* see, as you have, but only what they *have* seen. They can be mistaken. Eyewitnesses often are, of course. But it's odd that the child validated the sighting of the other witness, and if what the article says is true, the man and child did not know one another. They were on very distant sides of the event. Due to this—and of course I would question their not knowing one another until I have made a full examination— perhaps more can be made of the child's recollections. I certainly believe we can rule out coincidence of such an observation. The child and the man either colluded on their story, which I find unlikely, because to what purpose would they say such an unbelievable thing? Or, the other possibility is they did in fact see the same event, and their description is accurate, at least as far as they conceive it."

"That lightning rose up from the ground?" I said. "You say that makes more sense than it coming down from the heavens? I would think suggesting Jove threw a bolt of lightning would be just as irrational as to suggest the lightning rose up from the earth!"

"From a warehouse rooftop, not the earth," he said. "And it was blue-white in color?"

"Ridiculous," I said.

"It is peculiar, I admit, but my suggestion is we do not make a judgment on the matter until we know more facts."

"I didn't realize we cared to make a judgment."

"I am considering it."

"This interests you that much? Why would we bother? It's not a true investigation, just the soothing of a curiosity, which I might add, pays absolutely nothing."

"What interest me are the deaths from the warehouse fire," Dupin said. "Though, since, as you noted, we haven't been hired to examine the facts, that pays the same absence of price."

"Horrid business," I said. "But I believe you are making much of nothing. I know that area, and those buildings are rats' nests just waiting for a spark to ignite them. They are also the squatting grounds for vagrants. Lightning struck the building. It caught ablaze rapidly, and sleeping vagrants were burned to death in the fire. It is as simple as that."

"Perhaps," Dupin said. He leaned back and puffed on his pipe, blowing blue clouds of smoke from between his teeth and from the bowl. "But how do you explain that our own acquaintance the Police Prefect, G_____was quoted as saying that they found a singed, but still identifiable arm, and that it appeared to have been sawed off at the elbow, rather than burned?"

I had no answer for that.

"Of course, G_____ is often wrong, so in his case I might suspect an error before suspecting one from the witnessing child. G_____ solves most of his crimes by accident, confession, or by beating his suspect until he will admit to having started the French Revolution over the theft of a ham hock. However, when he has solved his cases, if indeed one can actually consider them solved, it is seldom by any true form of detection. I should also note that there has been a rash of grave robbings of late, all of them involving freshly buried bodies."

Now, as he often did, Dupin had piqued my curiosity. I arose, poured the both of us a bit of wine, sat back down and watched Dupin smoke his pipe, the stench of which was cheap and foul as if burning the twilled ticking of an old sweat-stained mattress.

"For me to have an opinion on this matter, I would suggest we make a trip of it tomorrow, to see where this all occurred. Interview those that were spoken to by the newspaper. I know you have contacts, so I would like you to use them to determine the exact location of these witnesses who observed the lightning and the resulting fire. Does this suit you?"

I nodded. "Very well, then."

That was the end of our discussion about these unique, but to my mind, insignificant events, for the time being. We instead turned our attention to the smoking of pipes and the drinking of wine. Dupin read while he smoked and drank, and I sat there contemplating that which we had discussed, finding the whole matter more and more mysterious with the thinking. Later, I decided I would like to take a stroll before retiring, so that I might clear my head of the drinking and heavy smoke.

I also had in mind the ideas that Dupin had suggested, and wanted to digest them. I have always found a walk to be satisfying not only to the legs and heart, but to the mind as well; many a problem such as this one I had considered while walking, and though, after talking to Dupin, I still turned out to be mistaken in my thinking, I had at least eliminated a large number of my fallacies of thought before speaking to him.

Outside the apartment, I found the rain had ceased; the wind had picked up, however, and was quite cool, almost chilly. I pulled my collar up against the breeze and swinging my cane before me, headed in the direction of the lightning fire in the warehouse district along the Rue_____. I didn't realize I was going there until my legs began to take me. I knew the location well, and no research was required to locate the site of the events, so I thought that for once, having seen the ruins, I might actually have a leg up on Dupin, and what he called his investigative methods of ratiocination.

I will not name the exact place, due to this area having recently been renovated, and keep in mind these events took place some years back, so there is no need to besmirch the name of the new owners. But for then, it was an area not considered a wisely traveled pathway by night. It was well known for unsavory characters and poor lighting. That being the case, I was fully aware it was not the best of ideas to be about my business in this vicinity, but what Dupin had said to me was gnawing at my thoughts like a terrier at a rug. I felt reasonably confident that my cane would defend me, as I am—if I say so myself—like Dupin, quite skilled in the art of the cane, and if I should be set upon by more than one ruffian, it contained a fine sword that could help trim my attacker's numbers.

I came to where the warehouse section lay, and found the burned buildings instantly, not far from a large allotment of land where other warehouses were still maintained. I stood for a moment in front of the burned section, going over it with eyes and mind. What remained were blackened shells and teetering lumber; the rain had stirred the charred shambles and the stench of it filled and itched my nostrils.

I walked along the pathway in front of it, and tried to imagine where the fire had started, determining that the areas where the structure of the buildings was most ruined might be the source. I could imagine that the fire jumped from those ruined remains to the other buildings, which though burned beyond use, were still more structurally sound, suggesting that the fire had raged hottest before it reached them.

I was contemplating all of this, when from the ruins I heard a noise, and saw a shape rise up from the earth clothed in hat and overcoat. It was some distance away from me, and even as it rose, it paused for a moment, looking down in the manner of man who has dropped pocket change.

I can't explain exactly why I thought I should engage, but I immediately set off in that direction, and called out to it. As I neared, the shape looked up, seeing me. I took note of the fact that it carried something, clutched tightly to it, and that this undefined individual was in a kind of panic; it began to run. I wondered then if it might be a thief, looking for some surviving relic that could be swapped or sold, and part of its loot had been dropped when it came up from wherever it had been lurking, and before it could be found, I had startled the prowler.

I took it upon myself to call out again, and when I did, the shape ceased to run, turned and looked at me. I was overcome with fear and awe, for I was certain, even though the being stood back in the shadows, wore an overcoat and had the brim of a hat pulled down tight over its face, that staring back at me was some kind of hairy upright ape clutching a bagged burden to its breast.

Unconsciously, I lifted the shaft of my walking stick and revealed an inch of the hidden sword. The beast—for I can think of it no other way—turned, and once more proceeded to run, its hat blowing off as it went. In a flash, it disappeared behind one of the standing warehouses. I remained where I was for a moment, rooted to the spot, and then, overcome with curiosity, I pursued it, running through the burnt lumber, on out into the clearing that led to the street where I had seen the beast standing. As I turned the corner, I found it waiting for me. It had dropped the bag at its feet, and was lifting up a large garbage container that was dripping refuse. I was granted a glimpse of its teeth and fiery eyes just before it threw the receptacle at me.

I was able to duck, just in time, and as the container clattered along the cobblestones behind me, the thing grabbed up its bag, broke and ran toward a warehouse wall. I knew then I had it trapped, but considering that what it had thrown at me was heavier than anything I could lift, perhaps it would be I who was trapped. These thoughts were there, but my forward motion and determination succeeded in trampling my common sense.

As I came near it again, my previous astonishment was nothing compared to what I witnessed now. The creature divested itself of the overcoat, slung the bag over its shoulder, and with one hand grasped a drain-pipe and using its feet to assist, began to climb effortlessly upwards until it reached the summit of the warehouse. I watched in bewilderment as it moved across the rain-misted night-line, then raced out of sight down the opposite side of the warehouse wall, or so I suspected when it was no longer visible.

I darted down an alley, splashing in puddles as I went, and came to the edge of the warehouse where I was certain the ape-man had descended. Before me was a narrow, wet, street, the R_____, but the ape-man was not in sight.

I leaned against the wall of the warehouse, for at this point in time I needed support, the reality of what I had just witnessed finally sinking into my bones. I momentarily tried to convince myself that I had been suffering the effects of the wine Dupin and I had drunk, but knew this was wishful thinking. I drew the sword from the cane, and strolled down the R_____ in search of the ape, but saw nothing, and frankly, was glad of it, having finally had time to consider how close I may have come to disaster.

Replacing the sword in its housing, I walked back to the ruins of the warehouse. Using my cane to move burnt lumber about, throwing up a light cloud of damp ash, I examined the spot where I had seen the thing pulling something from the rubble; that's when I found the arm, severed at the elbow, lying on top of the ash. It had no doubt been dropped there after the fire, for it appeared un-charred, not even smoke-damaged. I knelt down and struck a Lucifer against the tip of the cane, then held it close. It was a small arm with a delicate hand. I looked about and saw that nearby were a series of steps that dipped beneath ground level. It seemed obvious this was where the creature had originated when it appeared to rise out of the very earth. It also seemed obvious this opening had been covered by the collapse of the warehouse, and that the creature had uncovered it and retrieved something from below and tucked it away in the large bag it was carrying. The obvious thing appeared to be body parts, for if he had dropped one, then perhaps others existed and were tucked away in its bag. I lit another Lucifer, went down the narrow steps into the basement, waved my flickering light so that it threw small shadows about. The area below was larger than I would have expected. It was filled with tables and crates, and what I determined to be laboratory equipment—test tubes, beakers, burners and the like. I had to light several matches to complete my examination—though complete is a loose word, considering I could only see by the small fluttering of a meager flame.

I came upon an open metal container, about the size of a coffin, and was startled as I dipped the match into its shadowy interior. I found two human heads contained within, as well as an assortment of amputated legs, arms, feet and hands, all of them submerged in water.

I jerked back with such revulsion that the match went out. I scrambled about for another, only to discover I had used my entire store. Using what little moonlight was tumbling down the basement stairs as my guide, and almost in a panic, I ran up them and practically leapt into the open. There was more moonlight now than before. The rain had passed and the clouds had sailed; it was a mild relief.

Fearing the ape, or whatever it was, might return, and considering what I had found below, I hurried away from there.

I should have gone straight to the police, but having had dealings with the Police Prefect, G_____, I was less than enthusiastic about the matter. Neither Dupin nor myself were well liked in the halls of the law for the simple reason Dupin had solved a number of cases the police had been unable to, thereby making them look foolish. It was they who came to us in time of need, not us to them. I hastened my steps back to the apartment, only to be confronted by yet another oddity. The moon was turning to blood. Or so it appeared, for a strange crimson cloud, the likes of which I had never before seen, or even heard of, was enveloping the moon, as if it were a vanilla biscuit tucked away in a bloody-red sack. The sight of it caused me deep discomfort.

It was late when I arrived at our lodgings. Dupin was sitting by candlelight, still reading. He had a stack of books next to him on the table, and when I came in he lifted his eyes as I lit the gas lamp by the doorway to further illuminate the apartment. I was nearly breathless, and when I turned to expound on my adventures, Dupin said, "I see you have been to the site of the warehouses, an obvious deduction by the fact that your pants and boots are dusted heavily in ash and soot and are damp from the rain. I see too that you have discovered body parts in the wreckage. I will also conjecture we can ignore having a discussion with the lightning witnesses, for you have made some progress on your own."

My mouth fell open. "How could you know that I discovered body parts?"

"Logic. The newspaper account spoke of such a thing, and you come rushing in the door, obviously excited, even a little frightened. So if a severed arm was found there the other day, it stands to reason that you too discovered something of that nature. That is a bit of speculation, I admit, but it seems a fair analysis."

I sat down in a chair. "It is accurate, but I have seen one thing that you can not begin to decipher, and it is more fantastic than even severed body parts."

"An ape that ran upright?"

"*Impossible!*" I exclaimed. "You could not possibly know."

"But I did." Dupin paused a moment, lit his pipe. He seemed only mildly curious. "Continue."

It took me a moment to collect myself, but finally I began to reveal my adventures.

"It was carrying a package of some kind. I believe it contained body parts because I found an arm lying in the burned wreckage, as you surmised. Something I believe the ape dropped."

"Male or female?" Dupin said.

"What?"

"The arm, male or female?"

I thought for a moment.

"I suppose it was female. I didn't give it considerable evaluation, dark as it was, surprised as I was. But I would venture to guess—and a guess is all I am attempting—that it was female."

"That is interesting," Dupin said. "And the ape?"

"You mean was the ape male or female?"

"Exactly," Dupin said.

"What difference does it make?"

"Perhaps none. Was it clothed?"

"A hat and overcoat. Both of which it abandoned."

"In that case, could you determine its sex?" Dupin asked.

"I suppose since no external male equipment was visible, it was most probably female."

"And it saw you?"

"Yes. It ran from me. I pursued. It climbed to the top of a warehouse with its bag, did so effortlessly, and disappeared on the other side of the building.

Prior to that, it tried to hit me with a trash receptacle. A large and heavy one it lifted as easily as you lift your pipe."

"Obviously it failed in this endeavor," Dupin commented. "How long did it take you to get to the other side of the warehouse, as I am presuming you made careful examination there as well?"

"Hasty would be a better word. By then I had become concerned for my own safety. I suppose it took the creature less than five minutes to go over the roof."

"Did you arrive there quickly? The opposite side of the building, I mean?"

"Yes. You could say that."

"And the ape was no longer visible?"

"Correct."

"That is quite rapid, even for an animal, don't you think?"

"Indeed," I said, having caught the intent of Dupin's question. "Which implies it did not necessarily run away, or even descend to the other side. I merely presumed."

"Now, you see the error of your thinking."

"But you've made presumptions tonight," I said.

"Perhaps, but more reasonable presumptions than yours, I am certain. It is my impression that your simian is still in the vicinity, and did not scale the warehouse merely to climb down the other side and run down the street, when it could just as easily have taken the alley you used. And if the creature did climb down the other side, I believe it concealed itself. You might have walked right by it."

That gave me a shiver. "I admit that is logical, but I also admit that I didn't walk all that far for fear that it might be lurking about."

"That seems fair enough," Dupin said.

"There is something else," I said, and I told him about the basement and the body parts floating in water in the casement. I mentioned the red cloud that lay thick against the moon.

When I finished, he nodded, as if my presentation was the most normal event in the world. Thunder crashed then, lightning ripped across the sky, and rain began to hammer the street; a rain far more vigorous than earlier in the evening. For all his calm, when Dupin spoke, I thought I detected the faintest hint of concern.

"You say the moon was red?"

"A red cloud was over it. I have never seen such a thing before. At first I thought it a trick of the eye."

"It is not," Dupin said. "I should tell you about something I have researched while you were out chasing ape-women and observing the odd redness of the night's full moon, an event that suggests things are far more desperate than I first suspected."

I had seated myself by this time, had taken up my own pipe, and with nervous hand, found matches to light it.

Dupin broke open one of the books near the candle. "I thought I had read of that kind of electric blue lightning before, and the severed limbs also struck a cord of remembrance, as did the ape, which is why I was able to determine what you had seen, and that gives even further credence to my suspicions. Johann Conrad Dipple."

"Who?"

"Dipple. He was born in Germany in the late sixteen hundreds. He was a philosopher and something of a theologian. He was also considered a heretic, as his views on religion were certainly outside the lines of normal society."

"The same might be said of us," I remarked.

Dupin nodded. "True. But Dipple was thought to be an alchemist and a dabbler in the dark arts. He was in actuality a man of science. He was also an expert on all manner of ancient documents. He is known today for the creation of Dipple's oil, which is used in producing a dye we know as Prussian Blue, but he also claimed to have invented an elixir of life. He lived for a time in Germany at a place known as Castle Frankenstein. This is where many of his experiments were performed, including one that led to such a tremendous explosion it destroyed a tower of the castle, and led to a breaking of his lease. It was said by those who witnessed the explosion that a kind of lightning, a blue-white lightning, lifted up from the stones to the sky, followed by a burst of flame and an explosion that tore the turret apart and rained stones down on the countryside."

"So that is why you were so interested in the lightning, the story about it rising up from the warehouse instead of falling out of the sky?"

Dupin nodded, relit his pipe and continued. "It was rumored that he was attempting to transfer the souls of the living into freshly exhumed corpses. Exhumed clandestinely, by the way. He was said to use a funnel by which the souls of the living could be channeled into the bodies of the dead."

"Ridiculous," I said.

"Perhaps," Dupin replied. "It was also said his experiments caused the emergence of a blue-white lightning that he claimed to have pulled from a kind of borderland, and that he was able to open a path to this netherworld by means of certain mathematical formulas gleaned from what he called a renowned, rare, and accursed book. For this he was branded a devil worshiper, an interloper with demonic forces."

"Dupin," I said. "You have always ridiculed the supernatural."

"I did not say it was supernatural. I said he was a scientist that was branded as a demonologist. What intrigues me is his treatise titled *Maladies and Remedies of the Life of the Flesh*, as well as the mention of even rarer books and documents within it. One that was of special interest was called *The Necronomicon*, a book that was thought by many to be mythical."

"You have seen such a book?"

"I discovered it in the Paris library some years ago. It was pointed out to me by the historian M_____. No one at the library was aware of its significance, not even M_____. He knew only of its name and that it held some historical importance. He thought it may have something to do with witchcraft, which it does not. I was surprised to find it there. I considered it to be more than a little intriguing. It led me to further investigations into Dipple as not only the owner of such a book, but as a vivisectionist and a resurrectionist. He claimed to have discovered a formula that would allow him to live for one hundred and thirty-five years, and later amended this to eternal life."

"Drivel," I said. "I am surprised you would concern yourself with such."

"It was his scientific method and deep understanding of mathematics that interested me. My dear friend, much of what has become acceptable science was first ridiculed as heresy. I need not point out to you the long list of scientists opposed by the Catholic Church and labeled heretics. The points of interest concerning Dipple have to do with what I have already told you about the similarity of the blue-white lightning, and the interesting connection with the found body parts, the ape, and the curious event of the blood-stained moon, which I will come back to shortly. Firstly, however was Dipple's mention of the rare book. *The Necronomicon*, written by Abdul Alhazred in 950 AD, partially in math equations and partly in verse. He was sometimes referred to as 'The Mad Arab' by his detractors, though he was also given the moniker of 'Arab Poet of Yemen' by those less vicious. Of course, knowing my penchant for poetry, you might readily surmise that this is what first drew my attention to him. The other aspect of his personality, as mathematician and conjuror, was merely, at that time, of side interest, although I must say that later in life he certainly did go mad. He claimed to have discovered mathematical equations that could be used to open our world into another where powerful forces and beings existed. Not gods or demons, mind you, but different and true life forms that he called *The Old Ones*. It was in this book that Dipple believed he found the key to eternal life."

"What became of Dipple?"

"He died," Dupin said, and smiled.

"So much for eternal life."

"Perhaps."

"Perhaps? You clearly said he died."

"His body died, but his assistant, who was imprisoned for a time, said his soul was passed on to another form. According to what little documentation there is on the matter, Dipple's experiments were concerned with removing a person's soul from a living form and transferring it to a corpse. It was successful, if his assistant, Hans Grimm can be believed. Grimm was a relative of Jacob Grimm, the future creator of *Grimm's Fairy Tales*. But of more immediate interest to us is something he reported, that a young lady Dipple was charmed by, and who he thought would be his companion, took a fall from a horse and was paralyzed. Grimm claimed they successfully transferred her soul from her ruined body into the corpse of a recently dead young lady, who had been procured by what one might call midnight gardening. She was 'animated with life,' as Grimm described her, 'but was always of some strangeness.' That is a direct quote."

"Dupin, surely you don't take this nonsense seriously."

He didn't seem to hear me. "She was disgusted with her new form and was quoted by Grimm as saying 'she felt as if she was inside a house with empty rooms.' She leaped to her death from Castle Frankenstein. Lost to him, Dipple decided to concentrate on a greater love—himself. Being short of human volunteers who wanted to evacuate their soul and allow a visitor to inhabit their living form, he turned to animals for experimentation. The most important experiment was the night he died, or so says Grimm."

"The ancestor of the creator of *Grimm's Fairy Tales* seems an unlikely person to trust on matters of this sort."

"That could be. But during this time Dipple was having exotic animals shipped to him in Germany, and among these was a creature called a Chimpanzee. Knowing himself sickly, and soon to die, he put his experiments to the ultimate test. He had his assistant, Grimm, by use of the formula and his funnel, transfer his soul from his disintegrating shell into the animal, which in turn eliminated the soul of the creature; the ape's body became the house of his soul. I should add that I have some doubts about the existence of a soul, so perhaps essence would be a more appropriate word. That said, soul has a nice sound to it, I think. The experiment, according to Grimm, resulted in an abundance of blue-white lightning that caused the explosion and left Grimm injured. In fact, later Grimm disappeared from the hospital where he was being held under observation, and arrest for alchemy. He was in a room with padded walls and a barred window. The bars were ripped out. It was determined the bars were pulled loose from the outside. Another curious matter was that the room in which he was contained was three floors up, a considerable drop. How did he get down without being injured? No rope or ladder was found. It was as if he had been carried away by something unknown."

"Come, Dupin, you cannot be serious? Are you suggesting this ape pulled out the bars and carried him down the side of the wall?"

"There are certainly more than a few points of similarity between the story of Dipple and the events of tonight, don't you think? Consider your description of how effortlessly the ape climbed the warehouse wall."

"But, if this is Dipple, and he is in Paris, my question is how? And his ape body would be old. Very old."

"If he managed eternal life by soul transference, then perhaps the ape body does not age as quickly as would be normal."

"If this were true, and I'm not saying I believe it, how would he go about his life? An ape certainly could not ride the train or stroll the street without being noticed."

"I am of the opinion that Grimm is still with him."

"But he would be very old as well."

"Considerably," Dupin agreed. "I believe that the body parts you saw are for Grimm. It is my theory that Grimm received a wound that put him near death when Castle Frankenstein blew up. Dipple saved him by transferring his soul to a corpse. Unlike Dipple's lady love, he managed to accept the transfer and survived."

"So why did Dipple go after the body parts himself? Wouldn't he have Grimm procure such things? It would be easier for the one with a human body to move about without drawing so much attention."

"It would. My take is that the human soul when transferred to the soul of a corpse has one considerable drawback. The body rots. The ape body was a living body. It does not; it may age, but not in the way it would otherwise due to this transformation. Grimm's body, on the other hand, has to be repaired from time to time with fresh parts. It may be that he was further damaged by the more recent explosion. Which indicates to me that they have not acquired the healthy ability to learn from their mistakes."

"After all this time, wouldn't Dipple have transferred Grimm's essence, or his own, into a living human being? Why would he maintain the body of an ape? And a female ape at that?"

"My thought on the matter is that Dipple may find the powerful body of an ape to his advantage. And to keep Grimm bent to his will, to maintain him as a servant, he only repairs him when he wears out a part, so to speak. Be it male or female parts, it is a matter of availability. If Grimm's soul were transferred into a living creature, and he could live for eternity, as male or female, then he might be willing to abandon Dipple. This way, with the ape's strength, and Dipple's knowledge of how to repair a corpse, and perhaps the constant promise of eventually giving Grimm a living human body, he keeps him at his side. Grimm knows full well if he leaves Dipple he will eventually rot. I think this is the Sword of Damocles that he holds over Grimm's head."

"That is outrageous," I said. "And wicked."

"Absolutely, but that does not make it untrue."

I felt cold. My pipe had died, as I had forgotten to smoke it. I relit it. "It's just too extraordinary," I said.

"Yet *The Necronomicon* suggests it is possible." With that, Dupin dug into the pile of books and produced a large volume, thrusting it into my hands. Looking at it, I saw that it was covered in leather, and that in the dead center was an eye-slit. I knew immediately what I was looking at was the tanned skin of a human face. Worse, holding the book I felt nauseous. It was as if its very substance was made of bile. I managed to open the book. There was writing in Arabic, as well as a number of mathematical formulas; the words and numbers appeared to crawl. I slammed the book shut again. "Take it back," I said, and practically tossed it at him.

"I see you are bewildered, old friend," Dupin said, "but do keep in mind, as amazing as this sounds, it's science we are talking about, not the supernatural."

"It's a revolting book," I said.

"When I first found it in the library, I could only look at it for short periods of time. I had to become accustomed to it, like becoming acclimated to sailing at sea, and no longer suffering sea sickness. I am ashamed to admit, that after a short time I stole the book. I felt somehow justified in doing this, it being rarely touched by anyone—for good reason, as you have experienced—and in one way I thought I might be doing the world a justice, hiding it away from the wrong eyes and hands. That was several years ago. I have studied Arabic, read the volume repeatedly, and already being reasonably versed in mathematics, rapidly began to understand the intent of it. Though, until reading the newspaper account, I had been skeptical. And then there is Dipple's history, the words of his companion, Grimm. I believe there is logic behind these calculations and ruminations, even if at first they seem to defy human comprehension. The reason for this is simple; it is not the logic of humans, but that of powerful beings who exist in the borderland. I have come to uncomfortably understand some of that logic, as much as is humanly possible to grasp. To carry this even farther, I say that Dipple is no longer himself, in not only body, but in thought. His constant tampering with the powers of the borderland have given the beings on the other side an entry into his mind, and they are learning to control him, to assist him in his desires, until their own plans come to fruition. It has taken time, but soon, he will not only be able to replace body parts, he will be capable of opening the gate to this borderland. We are fortunate he has not managed it already. These monsters are powerful, as powerful as any god man can create, and malicious without measure. When the situation is right, when Dipple's mind completely succumbs to theirs, and he is willing to use the formulas and spells to clear the path for their entry, they will cross over and claim this world. That will be the end of humankind, my friend. And let me tell you the thing I have been holding back. The redness of the moon is an indication that there is a rip in the fabric of that which protects us from these horrid things lying in wait. Having wasted their world to nothing, they lust after ours, and Dipple is opening the gate so they might enter."

"But how would Dipple profit from that? Allowing such things into our world?"

"Perhaps he has been made promises of power, whispers in his head that make him outrageous offers. Perhaps he is little more than a tool by now. All that matters, good friend, is that we can not allow him to continue his work."

"If the red cloud over the moon is a sign, how much time do we have?"

"Let me put it this way: We will not wait until morning, and we will not need to question either the boy or the man who saw the lightning. By that time, I believe it will be too late."

There was a part of me that wondered if Dupin's studies had affected his mind. It wasn't an idea that held, however. I had seen what I had seen, and what Dupin had told me seemed to validate it. We immediately set out on our escapade, Dupin carrying a small bag slung over one shoulder by a strap.

The rain had blown itself out and the streets were washed clean. The air smelled as fresh as the first breath of life. We went along the streets briskly, swinging our canes, pausing only to look up at the moon. The red cloud was no longer visible, but there was still a scarlet tint to the moon that seemed unnatural. Sight of that gave even more spring to my step. When we arrived at our destination, there was no one about, and the ashes had been settled by the rain.

"Keep yourself alert," Dupin said, "in case our simian friend has returned and is in the basement collecting body parts."

We crossed the wet soot, stood at the mouth of the basement, and after a glance around to verify no one was in sight, we descended.

Red-tinged moonlight slipped down the stairs and brightened the basement. Everything was as it was the night before. Dupin looked about, used his cane to tap gently at a few of the empty beakers and tubes. He then made his way to the container where I had seen the amputated limbs and decapitated heads. They were still inside, more than a bit of rainwater having flooded into the casement, and there was a ripe stench of decaying flesh.

"These would no longer be of use to Dipple," Dupin said. "So we need not worry about him coming back for them."

I showed him where I had last seen the ape, then we walked to the other side. Dupin looked up and down the wall of the warehouse. We walked along its length. Nothing was found.

"Perhaps we should find a way to climb to the top," I said.

Dupin was staring at a puff of steam rising from the street. "No, I don't think so," he said.

He hastened to where the steam was thickest. It was rising up from a grate. He used his cane to pry at it, and I used mine to assist him. We lifted it and looked down at the dark, mist-coated water of the sewer rushing below. The stench was, to put it mildly, outstanding.

"This would make sense," Dupin said. "You were correct, he did indeed climb down on this side, but he disappeared quickly because he had an underground path."

"We're going down there?" I asked.

"You do wish to save the world and our cosmos, do you not?"

"When you put it that way, I suppose we must," I said. I was trying to add a joking atmosphere to the events, but it came out as serious as a diagnosis of leprosy.

We descended into the dark, resting our feet upon the brick ledge of the sewer. There was light from above to assist us, but if we were to move forward, we would be walking along the slick, brick runway into utter darkness. Or so I thought.

It was then that Dupin produced twists of paper, heavily oiled and waxed, from the pack he was carrying. As he removed them, I saw *The Necronomicon* was in the bag as well. It lay next to two dueling pistols. I had been frightened before, but somehow, seeing that dreadful book and those weapons, I was almost overwhelmed with terror, a sensation I would experience more than once that night. It was all I could do to take one of the twists and wait for Dupin to light it, for my mind was telling me to climb out of that dank hole and run. But if Dipple succeeded in letting the beings from the borderland through, run to where?

"Here," Dupin said, holding the flaming twist close to the damp brick wall. "It went this way."

I looked. A few coarse hairs were caught in the bricks.

With that as our guide, we proceeded. Even with the lit twists of wax and oil, the light was dim and there was a steam, or mist, rising from the sewer. We had to proceed slowly and carefully. The sewer rumbled along near us, heightened to near flood level by the tremendous rain. It was ever to our right, threatening to wash up over the walk. There were drips from the brick walls and the overhead streets. Each time a cold drop fell down my collar I started, as if icy finger tips had touched my neck.

We had gone a good distance when Dupin said, "Look. Ahead."

There was a pumpkin-colored glow from around a bend in the sewer, and we immediately tossed our twists into the water. Dupin produced the pistols from his bag, and gave me one.

"I presume they are powder charged and loaded," I said.

"Of course," Dupin replied, "did you think I might want to beat an ape to death with the grips?"

Thus armed, we continued onward toward the light.

There was a widening of the sewer, and there was in fact a great space made of brick that I presumed might be for workman, or might even have been a forgotten portion of the sewer that had once been part of the upper streets of Paris. There were several lamps placed here and there, some hung on nails driven into the brick, others placed on the flooring, some on rickety tables and chairs. It was a makeshift laboratory, and had most likely been thrown together from the ruins of the warehouse explosion.

On a tilted board a nude woman . . . or a man, or a little of both, was strapped. Its head was male, but the rest of its body was female, except for the feet, which were absurdly masculine. This body breathed in a labored manner, its head was thrown back, and a funnel was stuck down its throat. A hose rose out of the funnel and stretched to another makeshift platform nearby. There was a thin insect-like antenna attached to the middle of the hose, and it wiggled erratically at the air.

The other platform held a cadaverously thin and nude human with a head that looked shriveled, the hair appearing as if it were a handful of strings fastened there with paste. The arms and legs showed heavy scarring, and it was obvious that much sewing had been done to secure the limbs, much like the hurried repair of an old rag doll. The lifeless head was tilted back, and the opposite end of the hose was shoved into another wooden funnel that was jammed into the corpse's mouth. One arm of the cadaver was short, the other long, while the legs varied in thickness. The lower half of the face was totally incongruous with the upper half. The features were sharp-boned and stood up beneath the flesh like rough furniture under a sheet. They were masculine, while the forehead and hairline, ragged as it was, had obviously been that of a woman, one recently dead and elderly was my conjecture.

The center of the corpse was blocked by the body of the ape, which was sewing hastily with a large needle and dark thread, fastening on an ankle and foot in the way you might lace up a shoe. It was so absurd, so grotesque, it was almost comic, like a grisly play at the *Theatre of the Grand Guignol*. One thing was clear, the corpse being sewn together was soon to house the life force of the other living, but obviously ill body. It had been cobbled together in the past in much the same way that the other was now being prepared.

Dupin pushed me gently into a darkened corner protected by a partial brick wall. We spoke in whispers.

"What are we waiting for?" I said.

"The borderland to be opened."

Of course I knew to what he referred, but it seemed to me that waiting for it to be opened, if indeed that was to happen, seemed like the height of folly. But it was Dupin, and now, arriving here, seeing what I was seeing, it all fit securely with the theory he had expounded; I decided to continue believing he knew of what he spoke. Dupin withdrew *The Necronomicon* from the bag, propped it against the wall.

"When I tell you," he said, "light up a twist and hold it so that I might read."

"From that loathsome book?" I gasped.

"It has the power to do evil, but it also to restrain it."

I nodded, took one of the twists from the bag and a few matches and tucked them into my coat pocket. It was then I heard the chanting, and peeked carefully around the barrier.

The ape, or Dipple I suppose, held a copy of a book that looked to be a twin of the one Dupin held. It was open and propped on a makeshift pedestal of two stacked chairs. Dipple was reading from it by dim lamplight. It was disconcerting to hear those chants coming from the mouth of an ape, sounding human-like, yet touched with the vocalizations of an animal. Though he spoke the words quickly and carefully, it was clear to me that he was more than casually familiar with them.

That was when the air above the quivering antenna opened in a swirl of light and dark floundering shapes. I can think of no other way to describe it. The opening widened. Tentacles whipped in and out of the gap. Blue-white lightning flashed from it and nearly struck the ape, but still he read. The corpse on the platform began to writhe and wiggle and the blue-white lightning leaped from the swirling mass and struck the corpse repeatedly and vibrated the antenna. The dead body glowed and heaved and tugged at its bonds, and then I saw its eyes flash wide. Across the way, the formerly living body had grown limp and gray as ash.

I looked at Dupin, who had come to my shoulder to observe what was happening.

"He is not bringing him back, as in the past," Dupin said. "He is offering Grimm's soul for sacrifice. After all this time, their partnership has ended. It is the beginning; the door has been opened a crack."

My body felt chilled. The hair on my head, as on Dupin's, stood up due to the electrical charge in the air. There was an obnoxious smell, reminiscent of the stink of decaying fish, rotting garbage, and foul disease.

"Yes, we have chosen the right moment," Dupin said, looking at the growing gap that had appeared in mid-air. "Take both pistols, and light the twist."

He handed me his weapon. I stuck both pistols in the waistband of my trousers, and lit the twist. Dupin took it from me, and stuck it in a gap in the bricks. He opened *The Necronomicon* to where he had marked it with a torn piece of paper, and began to read from it. The words poured from his mouth like living beings, taking on the form of dark shadows and lightning-bright color. His voice was loud and sonorous, as we were no longer attempting to conceal ourselves. I stepped out of the shadows and into the open. Dipple, alerted by Dupin's reading, turned and glared at me with his dark, simian eyes.

It was hard for me to concentrate on anything. Hearing the words from *The Necronomicon* made my skin feel as if it were crawling up from my heels, across my legs and back, and slithering underneath my scalp. The swirling gap of blue-white lightning revealed lashing tentacles, a massive squid-like eye, then a beak. It was all I could do not to fall to my knees in dread, or bolt and run like an asylum escapee.

That said, I was given courage when I realized that whatever Dupin was doing was having some effect, for the gash in the air began to shimmer and wrinkle and blink like an eye. The ape howled at this development, for it had glanced back at the rip in the air, then turned again to look at me, twisted its face into what could almost pass as a dark knot. It dropped the book on the chair, and rushed for me. First it charged upright, like a human, then it was on all fours, its knuckles pounding against the bricks. I drew my sword from the cane, held the cane itself in my left hand, the blade in my right, and awaited Dipple's dynamic charge.

It bounded towards me. I thrust at it with my sword. The strike was good, hitting no bone, and went directly through the ape's chest, but the beast's momentum drove me backwards. I lost the cane itself, and used both hands to hold the sword in place. I glanced at Dupin for help. None was forthcoming. He was reading from the book and utterly ignoring my plight.

Blue, white, red and green fire danced around Dipple's head and poured from his mouth. I was able to hold the monster back with the sword, for it was a good thrust, and had brought about a horrible wound, yet its long arms thrashed out and hit my jaw, nearly knocking me senseless. I struggled to maintain consciousness, pushed back the sword with both hands, coiled my legs, and kicked out at the ape. I managed to knock him off me, but only for a moment.

I sat up and drew both pistols. It was loping towards me, pounding its fists against the bricks as it barreled along on all fours, letting forth an indescribable and ear-shattering sound that was neither human nor animal. I let loose an involuntary yell, and fired both pistols. The shots rang out as one. The ape threw up its hands, wheeled about and staggered back toward the stacked chairs, the book. It grabbed at the book for support, pulled that and the chairs down on top of it. Its chest heaved as though pumped with a bellows..

And then the freshly animated thing on the platform spat out the funnel as if it were light as air. Spat it out and yelled. It was a sound that came all the way from the primeval; a savage cry of creation. The body on the platform squirmed and writhed and snapped its bonds. It slid from the board, staggered forward, looked in my direction. Both pistols had been fired; the sword was still in Dipple. I grabbed up the hollow cane that had housed the sword, to use as a weapon.

This thing, this patchwork creation I assumed was Grimm, its private parts wrapped in a kind of swaddling, took one step in my direction, the blue-white fire crackling in its eyes, and then the patchwork creature turned to see the blinking eye staring out of the open door to the borderlands.

Grimm yanked the chairs off Dipple, lifted the ape-body up as easily as if it had been a feather pillow. It spread its legs wide for position, cocked its arms, and flung the ape upwards. The whirlpool from beyond sucked at Dipple, turning the old man in the old ape's body into a streak of dark fur, dragging it upwards. In that moment, Dipple was taken by those from beyond the borderland, pulled into their world like a hungry mouth taking in a tasty treat. Grimm, stumbling about on unfamiliar legs, grabbed *The Necronomicon* and tossed it at the wound in the air.

All this activity had not distracted Dupin from his reading. Still he chanted. There was a weak glow from behind the brick wall. I stumbled over there, putting a hand against the wall to hold myself up. When Dupin read the last passage with an oratory flourish, the air was sucked out of the room and out of my lungs. I gasped for breath, fell to the floor, momentarily unconscious. Within a heartbeat the air came back, and with it, that horrid rotting smell, then as instantly as it arrived, it was gone. The air smelled only of foul sewer, which, considering the stench of what had gone before, was in that moment as pleasant and welcome as a young Parisian lady's perfume.

There was a flare of a match as Dupin rose from the floor where he, like me, had fallen. He lit a twist from the bag and held it up. There was little that we could see. Pulling the sword from his cane, he trudged forward with the light, and I followed. In it's illumination we saw Grimm. Or what was left of him. The creatures of the borderlands had not only taken Dipple and his *Necronomicon*, they had ripped Grimm into a dozen pieces and plastered him across the ceiling and along the wall like an exploded dumpling.

"Dipple failed," Dupin said. "And Grimm finished him off. And *The Old Ones* took him before they were forced to retreat."

"At least one of those terrible books has been destroyed," I said.

"I think we should make it two," Dupin said.

We broke up the chairs and used the greasy twists of paper we still had, along with the bag itself, and started a fire. The chair wood was old and rotten and caught fast, crackling and snapping as it burned. On top of this Dupin, placed the remaining copy of *The Necronomicon*. The book was slow to catch, but when it did the cover blew open and the pages flared. The eye hole in the cover filled with a gold pupil, a long black slit for an iris. It blinked once, then the fire claimed it. The pages flapped like a bird, lifted upward with a howling noise, before collapsing into a burst of black ash.

Standing there, we watched as the ash dissolved into the bricks like black snow on a warm window pane.

I took a deep breath. "No regrets about the book?"

"Not after glimpsing what lay beyond," Dupin said. "I understand Dipple's curiosity, and though mine is considerable, it is not that strong."

"I don't even know what I saw," I said, "but whatever it was, whatever world *The Old Ones* live in, I could sense in that void every kind of evil I have ever known or suspected, and then some. I know you don't believe in fate, Dupin, but it's as if we were placed here to stop Dipple, to be present when Grimm had had enough of Dipple's plans."

"Nonsense," Dupin said. "Coincidence. As I said before. More common than you think. And had I not been acquainted with that horrid book, and Dipple's writings, we would have gone to bed to awake to a world we could not understand, and one in which we would not long survive. I should add that this is one adventure of ours that you might want to call fiction, and confine it to a magazine of melodrama; if you should write of it at all."

We went along the brick pathway then, with one last lit paper twist we had saved for light. It burned out before we made it back, but we were able to find our way by keeping in touch with the wall, finally arriving where moonlight spilled through the grating we had replaced upon entering the sewer. When we were on the street, the world looked strange, as if bathed in a bloody light, and that gave me pause. Looking up, we saw that a scarlet cloud was flowing in front of the sinking moon. The cloud was thick, and for a moment it covered the face of the moon completely. Then the cloud passed and faded and the sky was clear and tinted silver with the common light of stars and moon.

I looked at Dupin.

"It's quite all right," he said. "A last remnant of the borderland. Its calling card has been taken away."

"You're sure?"

"As sure as I can be," he said.

With that, we strolled homeward, the moon and the stars falling down behind the city of Paris. As we went, the sun rose, bloomed red, but a different kind of red to the cloud that had covered the moon; warm and inspiring, a bright badge of normalcy, that from here on out I knew was a lie.

Joe R. Lansdale is the author of over forty novels and numerous short stories. His novella, *Bubba Ho-tep*, was made into an award-winning film of the same name, as was *Incident On and Off a Mountain Road*. His mystery classic *Cold in July* inspired the recent major motion picture of the same name starring Michael C. Hall, Sam Shepard, and Don Johnson. His novel *The Bottoms* will also soon be a film directed by Bill Paxton. His literary works have received numerous recognitions, including the Edgar, eight Bram Stoker Awards, the Grinzane Cavour Prize for Literature, American Mystery Award, the International Horror Award, British Fantasy Award, and many others. His most recent novel for adults, *The Thicket*, was published last fall.

Sometimes all you can do is kneel in the rain and ask
what it is that the universe is trying to tell you.

LET MY SMILE BE YOUR UMBRELLA

Brian Hodge

Forget everything you think you know about yourself. Forget those twenty or twenty-five years of assumptions. However old you are. Instead, try looking at yourself from someone else's perspective for a change. My perspective. Empty out all those pitiful preconceptions and just look at yourself. Look at the effect you're having on the world.

What do you see then? Do you see what's really there? Can you even be that honest with yourself?

If you could, then I think you would agree that there's not much choice of what to do about it, is there? The end result? You've been claiming all along it's what you want.

What I see, it's not a question of saving, not any more. It's too late for that. Now it's come down to quarantine and eradication.

So it'll be the same with you as it's been with the others:

I'll take more pleasure in killing you than you take in being alive.

Who gave you the right to not be happy, anyway? Where did you get the idea that it was okay to throw all that back in the face of a loving, benevolent universe? It's your birthright, for god's sake. It's inscribed right there in the constitution of this great land of opportunity we live in: *life, liberty, and the pursuit of happiness.* So if you squander your liberty by refusing to pursue anything of positive worth, then really, haven't you forfeited your right to life?

And remember: According to you, that's what you've wanted for a long time. Well, just wait, because I'm on my way.

I mean, what kind of attention whore are you, that you would do what you did? Starve yourself to death and blog about the experience so the entire world can share in your sickness—who thinks of a thing like that? If you want to be dead, you just do it, you don't throw a party and invite the world to watch.

And not to belabor the obvious, but if you want to be dead, there are a lot faster ways than starving yourself. Starvation takes a long, long time. As I'm sure you realized. As I'm sure you knew damn well before you ever decided that you'd had your last bite of food and now it was showtime.

Dehydration, now that's a lot quicker. Three or four bad days, then you're done. But obviously that didn't suit your timetable. Obviously you didn't feel inclined to call water and power, and tell them to turn off the taps, nope, won't be needing those anymore.

So I don't know whether or not you're genuinely suicidal. For sure, I believe you're miserable. You don't have to convince me on that account. But more than anything, you're an exhibitionist. You want the attention. You wanted to be found out, and then just *found*, period, before it was too late, because you picked the slowest way possible to kill yourself and gave the world plenty of time to catch up to you. Just sitting there in your apartment there in Portland not eating, oh poor me, poor pitiful me, waiting for the cavalry to ride in and save you, take control of the situation and remove your choice in the matter.

Goddamn sociopath.

Photo updates too. That was a nice touch. One a day, so the world could see your ribs and hipbones standing out a little farther each morning. Like anorexia porn. Just so you could convince the pictures-or-it-didn't-happen skeptics who were calling bullshit on your little experiment. Like, okay, maybe I'm suicidal and masochistic, but don't anyone dare call me a liar.

And they found you. Of course. Well played, applause all around. Hiding your online account behind proxy servers during those first three weeks, so they *couldn't* trace your identity . . . until you weren't. Until you mysteriously "forgot." Because all that hard work of not eating made you loopy and forgetful. Maybe it did, maybe it didn't, but you sure sounded plenty cogent in those last few blog posts.

What a difference three weeks makes, huh? You went from complete anonymity to international celebrity in three weeks. Everybody wondering what was going to happen to HungryGirl234. Everybody loves to watch a good train wreck. You turned viral in the worst sense of the word.

I said three weeks? Less time, actually. Your audience was *huge* before the plug got pulled. Or maybe it was the other way around. The plug got jacked back in. No more worries about life support for *you*. The main thing

I wondered was how the hopes were split. What percentage of people was hoping that someone would get to you in time, and what percentage wanted you to follow this thing to its logical conclusion.

As to which side I came down on? Do you even have to ask?

Wait, wait, don't tell me—you were one of those girls who spent your high school years writing poetry so embarrassingly awful that it would shame a soap opera diva. Yeah, your blog posts had that whiff about them. I bet your favorite color was black and your favorite mood was mope and your classmates voted you Most Likely To Cut Notches Up and Down Her Arms.

Please don't misunderstand. I'm not saying there's anything wrong with being sensitive. Only when you gouge out your eyes to everything on the plus side of the meter, and dramatize and catastrophize everything on the minus side. You live to suffer, and that's all, don't you? You have no interest in dining from life's rich bounty, the good along with the bad, right? All you want to do is revel in eating the shit. Just look up from your dinner table with your helpless sagging shoulders and a shit-eating sob-smile, like you're asking, "Why does this keep happening to me," except you're not the tiniest bit aware of the gigantic ladle waving around in your hand.

You know what it is that I really can't stand about people like you? It's that you're toxic and contagious and you don't even care. You're the runny-nosed moron who wanders up and sneezes on the salad bar. You're the addict who shares the dirty needles even though you know what the test results said.

Can your pathetic little pea-sized soul even begin to comprehend the magnitude of your callous indifference to the effect you're having on the world? It can be hard enough for people to keep their spirits up even when all they have to contend with is the day-to-day mundanity of seeing their dreams end up on the deferred gratification plan. Then they see you, *you*, someone who would seem to have everything to live for, see you squander the most fundamental gifts you've been given and in the process tell them that they might as well not try either. You apparently can't stand the idea of a world going on without you, never even noticing your absence, and now you've made it your mission to drag as many down to your level as you can.

Misery loves company, and you're living proof. You're a professional sufferer and you hung out your shingle years ago: *Abandon hope all ye who encounter me.*

Converts, that's what you want. You want followers. You want to be Queen of the Suicides, only you'll never quite manage to get around to ending the suffering for yourself, will you? No, for you, it would be enough to hear about other people following your lead, only with more commitment. Every casualty you inspire just reinforces your negative worldview that much more.

What a pity. What a waste.

What a tragic perversion of priorities.

I'd ask if you have no shame, but I'm afraid you'd only give me a blank stare and ask what the word means.

I wish you could look up, just once, and see the sun the same way I do, and know its light rather than the shadows. I wish you could take in the first blue of the morning sky and see it as the wrapping paper around the gift of another beautiful day.

And now you're at again, aren't you? HungryGirl234 rides again.

But why use that, when I know your name now. Deborah. You probably hate it, though, don't you? Such a wholesome name. Deborah. It's a cheerleader's name.

Not that you've forced the world to put you back on suicide watch. You've chosen more subtlety this time. You have to know what resorting to the same old hunger strike routine might get you, now that you're a known head-case. You no longer have the luxury of anonymity, the option of teasing the world along, rationing out only as much information as you want it to have about you. You've lost control of that much.

People know who you are now. They know where to find you if they have to.

So you've taken a more measured approach. Every day, another litany of woes. Every day, another dispatch from a world that to your eyes is as colorless and gray as ashes. Every day, further confirmation that life for you really must be a tale told by an idiot, full of sound and fury, signifying nothing.

You're good at it, I'll give you that. You could do this for a living, if there was actually a paying market for it. You're the devil's propagandist, and I don't mean to flatter you when I say that you're dangerous. A person hardly has to get past the titles of your posts to fathom all they need to know about your agenda:

10 Reasons I'm a Cosmic Joke and You May Be Too.

Why Leaving Las Vegas *Was Really a Comedy.*

Why This? Why Me? Why Now?

I Still Resent Eating.

You, Me, and Everybody We Know = God's Chew-Toys.

If your descent into nihilistic spectacle had just been that first time, I would've been willing to overlook it as a cry for help, one that finally ensured that you got what you needed, and once you were discharged, your thinking had been corrected to the point where you could see what a nut-job you really were: *Hoo weee, am I ever glad that's over!*

I would've been willing—deliriously happy, actually—to give you the benefit of the doubt that you were at least going to try. I would've been happy to wish you well, and a life of contentment, from the other side of our shared continent, and we'd each go on our way, and you would never even have to know that I exist.

So remember: You've brought this on yourself.

You have *summoned* me.

What you've been doing all along is a kind of prayer. You've been petitioning the universe, and the universe is kind, so you shouldn't be surprised when it responds via the only avenue you've left open for it. Over time, you have given it all the instructions it needs to see your final wish carried out.

Do you see the beauty of this? Are you even capable of appreciating the wonder of the grand design? You lack the courage to act on your professed convictions, so the universe employs another route to see them carried out. Once again, you're awaiting the arrival of someone who will show up and take control of the situation, and remove your choice in the matter. Only this time, you don't realize it.

It isn't all about you, you know. It's bigger than you, and always has been.

I want to tell you a story, as long as I'm in transit and have nothing better to do than ignore the so-called in-flight entertainment. It's supposed to be a comedy, but I can't say I find it particularly amusing. It's kind of mean-spirited.

But there was this boy, you see, in the neighborhood where I lived before. He was old enough that he probably should've been called a man but, for reasons of his own choosing, that label never seemed to fit. He appeared never to have graduated into manhood, or to have even considered that he should, so I call him a boy.

You remind me very much of him. He was dismal, just like you. He was self- absorbed and sour, just like you.

And every time he stepped outside the house, it was like the day suddenly got cloudy. By his demeanor alone, he could steal the sun from the sky and the moon from the night. You expected flowers to wilt in his wake, grass to die under his footsteps. His projection of negativity was so pronounced it was having an actual visceral effect on me.

He was contagious. Just like you.

I like to think I choose my neighbors carefully. The people you surround yourself with are important. I appreciate the kind of people who look forward to what each day is going to bring. I esteem the company of people who keep it cheerful and positive.

But seeing this dismal, sour boy pollute my environment . . . this disturbed me. It gnawed at me. How could I have been so wrong? How could I have missed this? How could this *weed* have sprouted in my garden? And you know that, before long, there's never just one weed. They spread.

I did try to help, I really did. I asked him why he never smiled. He had black hair that hung down over one eye, and kept flipping it out of the way, but it kept falling right back, and might as well have been stuffed in his mouth for all he managed to communicate.

I really did try to think of something I could do for him. If he would've just made an effort to stand up straight, it might've made a difference. It might've demonstrated a willingness to try and get better. Posture has an enormous effect on mood. But he seemed perfectly resigned to letting his shoulders hang as steep as a couple of ski slopes. And he completely misunderstood my intentions. There's no point in recounting what he called me.

So it became obvious there wasn't anything left to do but pull this noxious weed. They say it takes forty-three muscles to frown, and only four to smile.

Anybody with a good knife can carve a smile into someone's face before they lose their nerve.

It takes real dedication to immortalize the frown.

But I think you'll find that keeping myself motivated is nothing I've ever had a problem with. Especially when I deeply believe in the outcome.

Can you feel my eyes on you, now that I'm finally here? They say people can, sometimes. I've heard that army scouts, observers, snipers—the ones whose success and even lives depend on not giving their position and presence away—I've heard they're trained to avoid letting their gaze linger directly on their enemy for very long. To the side is better. Because some people really can feel eyes on them, following them. The hair on the back of their neck prickles up and they just know.

But I don't think you do. You'd have to be a different kind of person. You'd have to be fully alive.

Here in your neighborhood, there must be a hundred ways to blend in and places to watch you from, and I'd be amazed if you're aware of even a handful of them. It's a busy place, full of life going on all around you, and if you'd just opened up to it and worked to make your disposition a little sunnier and meet the world halfway, we wouldn't have to have this encounter we're about to.

As I watch you, it becomes clear to me that even though I tell myself I'm doing it to learn your habits and timetables, what I'm really doing is giving you one last chance to change my mind. So show me something. Give me a reason not to follow through. Reveal to me some heretofore unsuspected capacity for joy beyond your masochistic perversion of it.

But you're giving me nothing here. *Nothing.* If anything, you're making this too easy. This shouldn't be such a cut-and-dried decision. I should wrestle with this, for god's sake. I should anguish over it.

Instead, I can't help but think it would be a kindness. When you left to go out for another coffee a few minutes ago, I almost expected you to melt under the onslaught of the rain. I've heard it can be like this in Portland. Which doesn't bother me in the least—I love a good rainy day—but even if it did, I still would refuse to let it. But maybe that's just not you. If weather has an influence on mood, and with some people it definitely does, then it may be that this goes some way toward explaining yours. So why have you never thought to just move away?

Although it can't be like this *all* the time. And you, if you're anything at all, are consistent. So let's just dismiss that right now. HungryGirl234 is not a foul-weather creation.

Really, it's unprecedented how much I'm bending over backward for you here. No one else would be giving you the kind of last-minute leeway that I am. It's not very many people who would break cover into the rain, and hurry along the sidewalk on the opposite side of the street to get ahead of you, to beat you to the coffee shop just in time to open the door for you.

And do you offer me a smile for this kindness? No. But then, neither do you act as if you're somehow owed it. You nod, okay, but it's barely perceptible, and looks to be an effort, almost painful.

In you go, just as I decide this has to be your final test. The very last chance to win your future. With the coffee house not two blocks from where you live, you're obviously a regular here. They would know you here. They have to, all of them. So, one laugh with the barista . . . come on, I'm pulling for you. I know you can do it.

Except you don't.

You just stand there encased in your green rain slicker, the hood like a monk's cowl dripping water to the floor, your head down as you count your change, then seem to decide as an aftermath to drop it all in the tip jar.

A nice touch, close, but by itself it's not enough to change anything. The condemned and the terminal often give away their worldly goods, although if you don't realize that's what's actually going on here, that's the least of your problems.

And it's a shame, really, that you don't get to notice the look on the barista's face as you turn from the counter. She knows you, knows you better than you think, maybe even knows who you really are, that you're an Internet celebrity of the sickest kind. She knows what matters, and wishes better for you.

You really should've contributed more to her world, you know.

And look at this! You've at least got one surprise tucked away inside. Your stop with your to-go cup at the spice island? All along I've had you figured you for the no-frills, black coffee all the way type, but you're a cinnamon girl. Who knew?

And it's an extra large for me, because I've got every reason to think it's going to be a long night ahead for both of us, one that I trust we'll both find purifying.

But then you're not even gone two minutes before everything goes wrong. I'm barely out the door and back on the sidewalk myself, so all I can do is watch. Watch, and can't help but think that I've failed you. If I'd been closer, maybe I could've . . .

It's not even your fault. You've got the walk light at the corner. It's yours. Anyone can see that. Even knowing you as I do, there's nothing in me that believes you have any other idea than that you're going to cross from one side of the street to the other, without incident, the same as the hundred thousand times you've done it before.

The thing is, I know what's going to happen even before it does. Look over and see the car, and the hair on the back of my neck prickles up and I just *know*, know that the car's going too fast, that it can't stop in time, and I'm running along the sidewalk, and if I'd been closer I would've pushed you or pulled you, whatever it took to get you clear. Because this isn't the way it's supposed to be.

You were meant for so much more than *this*.

The driver is aware, at least, for all the good that does, the brake lights smearing red and the car fishtailing on the wet pavement. But you don't know any of this. You never even see it coming, and I wonder that if you had, if there was time, even just a moment to react, if looking at the *genuine* prospect of your mortality would've made a difference where nothing else has.

Instead, lost inside that hood, you're blindsided. One devastating impact and there you go, tumbling into the air in the rain and the brown fan of coffee. It's not enough that you're hit the once, is it? No, you have to land on the windshield of the car passing by in the opposite lane, and bounce spinning off that one, too.

Even I have to wince, and shut my eyes for a moment.

And does it verify your worst suspicions about the world and everyone in it, that nobody seems to want to touch you now? They'll crowd around, they'll look, but you're used to that. But I'm used to things they're not, so it doesn't bother me, not in the way it bothers them. I don't mind joining you on the pavement. I don't mind touching you. I don't mind holding you. I don't mind the parts of you that leak onto me.

Or are you even aware of anything at all?

I've never seen anybody breathe that way. This can't be good. A sharp little gulp of breath every few seconds, like a fish drowning in the air. The way your eyes are roving around, they're like a baby's, trying to find something to focus on, and it would surprise me if you have much of any idea what's happened. If you don't, that's okay, and I don't want to tell you.

"Stay with us, Deborah."

Right, that's me saying that. And I *think* it's me you're seeing now. At least your eyes don't leave me, but in a way, that's even worse, because I can see the million questions behind them and I don't know how to begin to answer them. Not here, not now, not this.

I can't even begin to answer my own.

This would've happened whether I was here or not.

I haven't changed anything. I haven't *affected* anything. I've haven't had the chance to make one single point to you.

So I was brought here to what? To witness? That's it? *That's it?*

Sometimes all you can do is kneel in the rain and ask what it is that the universe is trying to tell you. But me, I'm supposed to be way beyond that by now.

You don't mind that I've let myself into your apartment, do you? It's almost like the keys crawled out of your pocket and into my hand.

I thought I'd be seeing the place under such different circumstances. Thought you'd be seeing it anew for yourself, the way it goes when we're with someone seeing something for the first time, and we imagine what it must look like through their eyes.

That's all gone now. The today that never happened.

I have to admit, never in my wildest imaginings did I expect lemon yellow walls. Maybe you *were* trying, in your way.

I'm talking to you like you're still alive, but right now, I don't even know. I just don't know. It didn't look good, down on the street. The state you were in, it didn't look like there was much reason to hope. That's funny, coming from me, isn't it? I always find a reason to hope. I'm the quintessential hope-springs-eternal guy. So if you don't mind, I'll keep the dialogue open for now.

Lemon yellow walls. Bugger me sideways. You really had me fooled. But it's the posters that are the illuminating part.

It takes a while to sink in. At first I wasn't grasping what it is you've really been doing here in the main room, what these posters mean together. I didn't see them as related at first. At the west end of the room, the one of some forest, either early morning or late evening, everything foggy, that one lone figure standing in the middle. And at the east end, the poster looking out on the opening of some enormous cavern, with a tiny boat sailing out into the slanted beams of sunlight coming through. At first glance, who would think these had anything to do with each other?

But it's the one in the middle of the north wall that ties them together, isn't it? That's the link. Except for the crescent moon, it's so dark and indistinct I can't even tell where the person kneeling in the middle is supposed to be. What is that? Is it a prison cell? A dungeon? A storm drain? A log fucking cabin? I'd really like to know.

The title, well, that makes sense. *The Dark Night of the Soul.* If you're going to give the thing a title, that's as good a name as any. And the quote, too, what's that for, just to rub it in? *The mystic heart senses that suffering and sorrow can be the portal to finding the light of what is genuine. Run not from the darkness, for in time it ushers in the light.*

Look. Don't you dare talk to me about the dark night of the soul. Honestly, this is why I'm here? What kind of joke is this?

From what garbage pit did you dredge these deceptions, anyway? Who told you you had to go through these things? They're just illusions. What garden of lies did you pick from to settle for the notion that pain and sadness are anything other than unnatural states of being that it's our duty to repel? What malfunction sent you on this detour, and convinced you that this shadow path you're on was remotely normal?

Me, I was raised better than that. I was promised better than that. I was *promised.*

That is my birthright. *That* is my due. And I *will* have the happiness I deserve. But you? No, you fell for the worst sort of propaganda.

And look at you now.

It didn't have to be that way. It's not *supposed* to be that way. Not for you, not for me, not for anybody, and all of you who think you're going to convince me otherwise, you all find out that the light fights back, don't you? The light doesn't want to go out.

It's so clear now. I was giving you credit for being way more dangerous than you really are, when all you are is another empty puppet. You're a casualty of endless failures of imagination, and your own savage torpor. You just couldn't conceive that you live in a world so generous that everything was yours from the beginning and all you had to do was say yes. You had to make it so much harder than it really is.

If you can't deal with my exceptionalism, fine, but that doesn't mean you get to try to rob me, or drag me down to your level.

You will not rob me.

Not. Not. Not. Not. Do you hear me? *Not.*

You know, I really should leave here, because you've got nothing to teach me and this whole thing's been nothing more than a clerical error, so yes, I should just turn around and leave, but then again, you should take it as a back-handed compliment that it's so hard to turn away.

Because it's not just the posters. No, it's the fine print. My god, what kind of obsessive-compulsive are you? Until this moment I'd been wondering if you'd even seen the comments people left for you during your escapades in starvation, and now it's obvious that you did. And have, every day since.

I'll hand it to you, it's impressive, the patience it must've taken to print out every single hateful thing anyone had to say to you, and tape it to the wall around the forest poster. And then do the same thing with every kind thing someone had to say, and tape those around the cavern picture. Hundreds of them. That's patience.

You know, before, I suspected you hadn't read a word of any of it because I had you pegged for such a narcissist that you wouldn't even bother taking someone else's opinion under advisement.

And I was absolutely right, you *are* a narcissist, just a bigger one than I even dared imagine you could be. Every time your printer spit out some hate mail or a love note, and you tore off a little strip of tape, that's somebody telling you you matter, even the ones who wished you'd just die already, because at least you got a reaction.

Well, you don't. You *don't* matter. Your opinion doesn't matter. Your deluded sense of identity doesn't matter.

Really, I should leave now, but I've just got to read these first, and laugh.

Because I haven't had a laugh this good in a long time. I should be thanking you. And I really should leave. But I need you to know that no matter what you do, now and forever, you can't rob me.

And what's the rush, anyway. I can read these and read these, up and down, across, they're all the same, empty empty empty, and it still feels like I just got here.

And I really should leave. But not until I know how you did it, how you got the walls to start changing color, from lemon yellow to . . . to . . . to whatever the opposite of that is called.

And I really. Should. Leave.

Only your windows are all covered with bars. And the doors are nowhere to be found anymore.

Brian Hodge is the award-winning author of eleven novels spanning horror, crime, and historical fiction. He's also written over one hundred shorter works, and published five full-length collections. His first collection, *The Convulsion Factory*, was ranked by critic Stanley Wiater among the 113 best books of modern horror. Recent or forthcoming titles include *Whom the Gods Would Destroy* and *The Weight of the Dead*, both standalone novellas; *Worlds of Hurt*, an omnibus edition of the first four works in his Misbegotten mythos; a newly revised hardcover edition of *Dark Advent*, his early post-apocalyptic epic; *No Law Left Unbroken*, a collection of crime fiction; and his latest novel, *Leaves of Sherwood*. Hodge lives in Colorado, where a constant supply of mountain air and brewpubs keeps more of everything in the works. Connect through his web site (www.brianhodge.net) or on Facebook (www.facebook.com/brianhodgewriter).

We all feel the melancholy. The taller the trees grow,
the more the melancholy sinks into us.

AIR, WATER, AND THE GROVE

Kaaron Warren

We've got food for seven days. Water for twelve. Because sometimes the Saturnalia doesn't end when it should. It's hard for people to settle, after. Mid slash, mid fuck, mid theft. Do you just stop, then carry on with your suburban life? Leave things half done? Most people prefer to see it through. Take the extra hour or two. Chase away the doldrums for a bit longer.

We've stocked up on hydrogen peroxide and oxalic acid. There are going to be a lot of blood stains and they'll be coming in after with their bundles of clothes, "Oh, I had an accident," is a good one. Or "I was helping an injured person," is another, not one of them wanting to admit what they've been a part of.

Seven days where nobody works. Nothing is open. There are no arrests, although crime occurs, it does, I've had friends murdered. I've lost worldly possessions. But you're not going to be arrested, not during Saturnalia.

We'll be called out to deal with carpets and mattresses. We've stocked up on pepsin powder for those, and we'll charge for travel. It's a good business, stain removal. Especially after Saturnalia. I hate having to go into people's homes, though. Other homes are dirty and they reek and I don't feel safe there. You never know what people will do, what they consider normal, in their own homes. I've had clients stand naked watching me. I've had food offered that I wouldn't feed a dog or a goat. I always need a shower after being in a stranger's home.

Though people are mostly dull these days. They care less than they used to. They're tired and old. I know I feel older.

We've stocked up on sodium percarbonate. That's good for chocolate stains and there will be plenty of those. People think they are original, as if they're the only ones to cover themselves in the stuff. I say, "Seen it before. Seen it plenty."

I'm lining up my stocks, counting the bottles, when my son says, "I'm not staying home this year." He's twenty-one and perhaps I can't keep him safe anymore. "This year, I'm going to be a part of it. I'll help you with the clothes when I get back."

"You should stay at home." I try not to cry. I don't want to make him feel guilty. That is never a good reason to do anything. "We can watch it on TV."

"I want to be the one on TV. Can't I be happy, for a little while?"

"Don't go," I say. "I'll make you a steak dinner tonight. And tomorrow night a chicken dinner. I'll cook you your favorite food every night for a month." He nods, and he eats two steak dinners, but when I check his room at midnight he is gone.

He's slow, though, and loud, so I hear him stumbling to the front door, kicking the umbrella stand as he does every single time, and knocking the Saturn Tree we keep high, under a light, as he does every time as well.

What can I do? Tie him down? Join him to commit our own Saturnalian acts, in our own home?

Maybe it is time to let him free.

He fumbles with the door locks, as he always does, forgetting which turns which way, and how many turns, and whether or not he's already turned one or the other. He looks almost like a shadow in the dark, not a real person at all.

I don't say, "This is why you have to stay home," because it's my fault he's that way.

I'm the one who did it to him.

It's been twenty-three years since the return of the *Tarvos*. Can you call it a return, if the ship never made it back whole? I was only four when it set out amidst a wild fanfare, because they like to make a fuss, don't they? The rocket scientists. As if they are the ones who'll save us all. They're still like it, years on. Discovering new planets. "Earth-like" ones, and you find out it's all bullshit. You know? What they mean is Earth ten million years ago when the only things here were crawly little worms or something.

Speaking of which, there will be dirt to get out. Some of them get buried, up their necks. They showed it on the TV last year. Being used as a toilet, one of them. If those clothes had come in, I would have burnt them and paid the difference.

I was nine by the time the *Tarvos* reached Saturn. Those pictures of the swirling north pole made me dizzy, that's mostly what I remember.

Most people were more interested in watching it suck in samples of the icy particles orbiting the planet.

We've stocked up on bottles of filtered water. The dry cleaners' greatest trick is that air and water are the best cleaners, at the end of the day. We can charge what we like, but our basics costs can be minimal.

I was fourteen when the *Tarvos* returned; I remember that clearly. All the adults so excited by the return of the thing, the rest of us not caring all that much. Happy that they were distracted so they'd leave us alone, and we could party. Skip school without anyone noticing.

But we were all out there, watching the sky for a glimpse, when it blew up.

They calculated wrong, or something. Didn't think the ice would be as heavy as it was. It's all about the micro-millimeters, isn't it? And they get it wrong.

We've stocked up on methylated spirits, and we've got plenty of clean absorbent paper. Candle wax stains are always a problem. People get carried away, and there's spillage. There are fires, too, but that's not up to us. Other people manage that. Or don't.

They love the fireworks, don't they? And the fires, they don't care about safety or property. They'll set things on fire purposely, to see them burn. In the shade of the Saturn Trees, all of it seems to make sense. Is it because of the *Tarvos*? How it burned on entry, exploded in the night sky like fireworks?

Six crew onboard (and the ones with children mattered more, according to the media), all of them now with streets named after them. Suburbs.

It felt like rain but the drops were solid and stayed heavy on your skin if you left it. I wiped all the drops off but some clung to my hair, and my ears, and in my eyebrows.

People dragged their children inside, because there were parts raining down as well. There were deaths, though not in our neighborhood. I heard one girl my age was pierced through the heart by a shard of metal.

Workers in Bangkok offices, Singapore noodle houses, sheep farms. Miners dredging gold and oil and zinc. All of them went out and stood in it. Most of them felt it.

The ice particles, melted. The pieces of ship. The other pieces. Those poor astronauts.

The astrologers told us they predicted it. That this was bound to happen, it was fate. Saturn was in the eighth house and that meant horrible death.

"For who?" people like my dad asked. "What, all of us?"

"Prepare for the grave," the astrologers said.

Wasn't long before many of us wished we'd been one of those early ones. Knocked down flat by debris. Gone in a flash.

We all feel the melancholy. The taller the trees grow, the more the melancholy sinks into us.

We're all whirled up into Saturn's dark heart now.

The ice, the ship, the others. All of this rained upon us.

The ancient alchemists, were partly right; for them, Saturn designated lead. They believed the planet was made of lead. And these water droplets, when they were tested?

Traces of lead. Surprised them all, the so-called smart ones. They hadn't thought that.

Once the particles touched ground, they crystallized. It was beautiful to watch; we all thought so. Especially once they started to grow.

In the forests. In backyards. In bowls set as centerpieces. On roofs and walls, on the heads of statues, in footpath-cracks and sewers.

So many crystal trees. Each of them growing up, up, towards Saturn.

My father worried that the magnetism would shift Earth off its axis, but he didn't finish school. I told him lead isn't magnetic.

It looks like silver, he said. He was one of many who broke pieces off, grew more trees.

Share the wealth, he said. The beautiful crystals shouldn't only be for the rich, he said, and they weren't.

The richest people in the world used to be the ones who owned the land that provided the metal. People like me didn't get a look in. But now we all have own trees; they grow anywhere.

Air quality testing showed that the Saturn Trees were not only beautiful, but healthful; they attracted lead particles, literally sucking lead out of the atmosphere.

Places whose high lead content led to birth defects and early death grew more and more of them. We all did. All you needed was a small piece. Every home soon filled with the air-purifying trees. Every school. Every hospital.

Some trees grew tall as houses.

Some trees grew fat.

The trees were so beautiful you wanted to watch them all the time, and people did.

It seemed the trees absorbed light as well as lead because the world seemed duller, anywhere the trees grew.

They bore no fruit.

Not at first.

Saturn is time. Saturn is the Bringer of Age. Saturn is the bringer of melancholy and dismay. We didn't notice the effect; the tiredness, the melancholy. The graveness.

We didn't notice.

Not at first.

I scoop up the shards my son's clumsiness knocked off and drop them onto the upper branches of our Saturn Tree. If I had the patience I could sit and watch them being absorbed. It's hypnotic. It would distract me from thinking of him, out there amongst it. There are no good people this week. No one who will look after him, bring him home to me.

I wasn't allowed out during the first Saturnalia. I stayed at home, listened to the dogs howl. By the time I was sixteen, though, they were mandatory and I was out amongst it. Blind drunk most of the time. Those crystals! And no regret the next day because who remembered anything?

It's why we don't know who his dad is. Could be one of many. I don't blame any of them. I don't feel used by any of them. It's how it was, it how it still is.

I don't like having methylated spirits in the house. The alcohol smell of it takes me back. I've not touched a drink since the day he was born and we knew. We could see what he was. So many of them like that; damaged by the booze we'd drunk during Saturnalia and beyond. We didn't know. We didn't think. All we knew was that the crystals, dissolved in alcohol, provided an almost instant high and somehow negated the hangovers.

Sparkle, we called it. They still call it. I spent a month in a state of numb euphoria; I didn't care when Saturnalia started or finished.

He came out smelling of booze. I swear it. Not that sweet baby smell they are supposed to have. And his tiny eyes, his flattened cheekbones.

"We're seeing a lot of these," they told me gravely at the time, as if that made it better. Holding that tiny baby, his tiny head, and they say no one was to blame. Because no one wanted the Saturnalias stopped; they still don't.

My son; what worries me most is what happens when I die. But I probably won't die before him. He's clumsy, so accident-prone. His liver is shit and he's impulsive. I can't see him lasting too long. If he survives this Saturnalia, out there with the lunatics (not lunatics though. We're not talking about the moon. The Saturnine) then perhaps he'll be safe for another year.

He should be safe, and return to me and our quiet, clean life. He can help me move some heavy furniture around. It's a good time for change, after Saturnalia. Good time to pretend things are different.

If he comes home in time he can eat with me, but I don't mind eating alone. It's a quick clean up. No spillage.

We are in the Saturnian days, my father used to say. He liked to quote from things he didn't understand. "The days of dullness, when everything is venal," he'd say, nodding as if we should know what he was talking about.

I feel dull. We all feel dull, but they numb that with alcohol. Drugs. Sparkle. With sex and dancing, throwing themselves to the ground in a passion they do not feel. These times are when Saturn is unbound. When we are all so grave on the inside if you cut us we'd bleed tears.

My father always did call me fanciful. I used to talk about Saturn, bound with woolen strips beneath Rome to stop him leaving, unbound only during Saturnalia. I think he is with us now, unbound because we worship him with our dullness, our melancholy.

Satin stains badly and is difficult to clean. I can do it, though, if you give me the time, some cool water and some delicate soap.

I hope my son comes home unbloodied.

I hope he kills no one.

He is back. He leaps and jumps about like a frog in a box; I've never seen him energized before. His clothing is in disarray, stained, his hair is shaved on one side, his face cut, his chin dark, his arms bruised, his legs bleeding. He talks without taking a breather for an hour or more, while I clean his cuts, feed him, and give him tall, cold, sugary drinks. I sponge the stains with cool salted water, then rinse a dozen times with clean water. The rest I remove with hydrogen peroxide.

Dark days follow. After the excitement fades and the ordinary returns, the melancholy seems more intense. As if Saturn is angry that the revels have ended, and is exerting his power, laying his lead-weight against us. Some communities leave up the banners and bright ribbons, but they fade with the sun and became sadder than anything. I could wash them in vinegar but that wouldn't be enough.

I try to help my son. I put him to work, because work distracts, and I need him to keep up. We took in more purple stains than usual; he told me they were passing around a grape drink that tasted like medicine but that numbed the entire body. I tried to find this drink, to give him a taste, cheer him up but there were no supplies in town.

He carries a tiny Saturn's Tree with him everywhere, carefully, as if it was a full cup of tea.

Then a customer tells him about the grove.

"The greatest Saturn Trees you'll ever see!" she says. "And you walk in amongst them and can feel your blood racing, your heart so solid and strong, and you smile, and you should hear the laughter in there. Strangers all together as one. It's beautiful."

I think of our own Saturn Tree, how even standing next to it makes my mouth droop, and my eyelids heavy.

"That doesn't sound right," I say. The customer laughs.

"It's not really for people like you." She actually winks at my son, and he winks back, as if he knows what she is talking about.

He leaves with her. I tell her that he needs help and she laughs at me again, as if I am making things up, have invented all the hours I spent cleaning him up, trying to teach him.

He isn't gone long. He comes back quiet, but he seems happier.

"It's so beautiful there. The sky looks bluer than it does here. But she was wrong, that woman. It is for people like you. It's for everyone. Next time, can you take me?"

"Maybe," I say, the universal, eternally polite parental *No*.

Ninety-seven customers later, he goes out and doesn't return. I know where he's gone; I only wonder how he traveled. I call him. He says, "Come and see, Mum. You'll love it, you really will. I'll meet you at the entrance."

He sounds so bright I wonder if something has changed within him.

I set some clothes to spin and close the shop.

The streets are quiet with the Saturnalia well over. There is a low hum, a low moaning,

I drive to Saturn's Grove. The sign is cracked, tired-looking; the "o" looks like an "a."

From the moment I enter, I am filled with a sense of my own worthlessness. Pointlessness. I am uninteresting. Unlovable. I think the customer was right; this place is not for me.

There are hundreds of metallic trees, growing as tall as redwoods, wide as sequoias. I can barely see the top of them.

I find my son, his arms stretched around the base of one of them.

"Isn't it beautiful?" he says. He's never cared about anything before, beyond food. He reaches his hands up to swing on one shining branch.

He winces, pulls away, and I see that his skin has reddened.

At the base of many of the trees are clothes. Perfectly good, most of them.

"What are these?" I say, smiling. I think *He brought me here, to collect the clothes. It is kind of him, bringing me here.*

"People don't want them any more," my son says. So I start to gather them up, to take home and clean. At least washing clothes gives me a kind of purpose. I feel giddy if I look up, so I look mostly at the clothes on the ground.

"We'll be able to get most of these stains out easily," I say. He was right; I do feel delighted now. Excited.

He doesn't answer. I thought he was behind me but no.

He has stripped naked and is already three meters up a tree. I haven't seen him naked since he was fourteen and insisted that he could wash himself.

"This is the one. This is my tree."

I look up. "It's very high."

With my head tilted back, I can see that many of the trees have do have flowers at the top. Some are bulbous. Some brightly colored.

"I thought they didn't flower?"

"That's the others. That's each one who's climbed. As the tree grows, they reach closer to Saturn."

He drags himself up further.

"Don't go any higher," I say. I fall to my knees. I don't want him up there. "I'll make you any meal you like, just name it. And you don't have to clean the clothes if you don't want to. We'll find you something else. And we'll find you someone nice to be with and don't forget Saturnalia, how much you loved it! Only another ten months and there's another!"

But he climbs up. I watch him and want to follow him, but even the feel of the tree under my palm makes me sick. I sit at the base, waiting for him to come back down again. I can hear him crying.

"Son! Come down! You don't need to feel pain!"

"It's not painful," he calls, but his voice is shaky, withered. "I'll be down soon. Wait there."

I have to trust that he will return. I sort the clothes I've collected by material and color. People watch, asking questions. Distracting me. Until one woman says, "Do you need a hand to get all those things home?"

"I'm waiting for my son. He's climbing up. He'll come down soon."

The woman shakes her head. "Look," she says. She leads me through the trees.

Some have tiny thin trails of blood to the ground, crystallized. "Every last one of them climbed like he did," she says. "Step by step as if there was no other way. This one's my daughter's tree." She stands and puts her hand near a tree that dwarfs many around it. She doesn't touch it.

My son has become one of them.

There are others, lost like me, gazing up and weeping. The woman says to me, "The only certainties in life are air, water and the grave. Saturn's sons: Jupiter, Neptune, and Pluto. The only ones he didn't kill. That's all that's real anymore."

"I'm going to get my son down."

I don't want to go up. The thought of it makes me want to cry and never stop.

But my son is up there and I want to bring him down.

Each step is like climbing on sharpened knives. Blood pouring.

I don't have the strength. I can't do it.

"He won't come down anyway. There's nothing you can do. Once he's climbed all the way up, it's too late," the woman calls. She tugs at my ankles.

As if to demonstrate, one bright green bead of liquid drips down past my face.

Do I love him enough to die trying to get to him? I climb for another hour, making no progress, slipping backwards, dragging the skin from my arms and hands, from my cheek. Then I'm stuck. I can't move up and own. Frozen.

"Stretch your fingers. Spread them. Let go. We'll catch you," they call from below, and I do, and they do.

"It's too late. He's so deep now, you'll never get him out, even if you get him down. They climb up there to die; at least it's a choice. No one has come back down again, not alive." My new friend shakes, rolls her shoulders. "I come back every now and then to take a piece of my daughter's tree," she says. "She's happier now her suffering has ended."

"What about us? What about our suffering?"

She lifts her arms. Smiles. The rest of her is shivering; only her lips are still. She reaches into her bag and offers me a small bottle of vodka. It sparkles. I shake my head at her; not that.

I cry then. I've always known I'll lose him, but I didn't know he'd choose to go. I cry, leaning against his tree, until I realize my tears re being drawn in. Absorbed.

I break a piece of his tree off to bury it. It is stained slightly with his fluids.

I make his grave in a tiny, tiny pot next to my other Saturn's Tree. It will grow if I look after it. Feed it. Water it. It may fruit one day, as do the trees in the grove. We watch them grow, the other grievers and I. I say to them, "Whoever said these trees don't flower? There are our children up there, fruiting." Sometimes one drops and shatters, looking like an arum lily, the corpse kind. Surrounded by crystals worth a lot of money, and I wonder if people will use them, if it will come to that, and what they'd call the drink. A friend brings me some Sparkle, and another does too, and once I remember how good it is, and forget all the rest, things are better.

I re-open my shop when I run out of clothes to clean. My job is so instinctive I can do it Sparkled or not.

Air, water, the grave.

And Sparkle.

Bram Stoker nominee and Shirley Jackson Award-winner **Kaaron Warren** has lived in Melbourne, Sydney, Canberra, and Fiji. She's sold many short stories, three novels (the multi-award-winning *Slights, Walking the Tree,* and *Mistification*) and four short story collections. Her most recent collection, *Through Splintered Walls*, won a Canberra Critic's Circle Award for Fiction, two Ditmar Awards, two Australian Shadows Awards and a Shirley Jackson Award. Her stories have appeared in Australia, the US, the UK and elsewhere in Europe, including *Once Upon a Time: New Fairy Tales*. You can find her at kaaronwarren.wordpress.com and she tweets @KaaronWarren

He did not truly expect some fiend to undo the locks and peer out at him.
Alas, he was living in reality, not a book.

A LITTLE OF THE NIGHT
(EIN BISSCHEN NACHT)

———◆———

Tanith Lee

Preface

Now he was an old man, but you could not entirely think of him in that way. He was lean and tall and hard as steel still, or he looked it. His face was lined, but his eyes had stayed jet black, and he had kept a full head of hair, even if the dark of it had changed to white silver. His teeth were good too—he could crack the shells of walnuts with them, they had seen that only this evening. And in his strong and well-made hands the sabre, when he lifted it, seemed quite as graceful and as dangerous as twenty, thirty years before.

Women had loved his voice, continued to do so. It was a beautiful voice even now, dark in tone, musical. He had persuaded troops into battle with those tones, given them the courage. He was a brave man, and intelligent—as not so many were who were also brave. His name was Corlan Von Antal, and each of the sixteen men here tonight had served under his command. They called him, amongst themselves, Ursus (the Bear), and said it was for his famous cloak of black bearskin. But really it was for his valor and his power, his honor. And for the secret, forest- deep, whatever it was, that they had heard tell of, and that they sensed too about him. Besides, his hound was half wolf, and its pelt, like his, was silver. It would pad courteously from chair to chair when first they were seated, its massive ruffed head level with each man's heart; a colossal beast, but calm as a trained dove. It took a bear to govern a wolf.

The fire shone crystal red and amber, the tasty meal was over and the crimson wine was in the glass goblets, and all around the finely furnished old tower, in which he lived, went up through the eaves of the night, showing its yellow windows to the stars. Would he tell them the story, this year? He was sixty- five if he was a day. Surely he could trust them now, *now*, these officers of his. Surely now he *must* tell them, as they had always hoped he would when they visited him. But they had thought that last time, and the times before. He had been fifty, fifty-five, then sixty. He might live to be ninety, of course. And they— well they might even die, for they were still active soldiers, and though it was hard to recall sometimes, only these three miles from the town of Ruzngrad, the war was going on eighty miles in the other direction.

The young officer Nacek thought this particularly, as he sat watching Von Antal in the firelight. No man, Nacek reflected, old or young, ever knew how long God would give him. Every day ended in a night. The lights in the windows of the highest towers would go out. No one should keep silent forever.

But Ursus did not tell them anything tonight. Just as he never had. As, perhaps, he never would.

One: Night

Forest-deep . . .

The forests—

Corlan ran through them, his coat and shirt sticking to his back in a freeze of sweat, his thick sheaf of hair flattened into black water by icy rain. He was thirty-four. He was afraid.

He had killed a man. For a soldier currently employed in the chess maneuvers of warfare, that would have been a superfluous statement, were it not that the man Corlan had killed belonged to his own regiment, an officer of equal rank. Gerner was a plague-pig, greedy, bloated, crass and vicious. His men suffered from him, which Corlan and his brother Knight-Captains had watched, and said, done, nothing, for Gerner was not the sort to listen. But days ago Gerner had gone into a small village in the forests' outskirts, taken every bit from it that was edible or portable, lined up the men and any male children and had them shot, then made his supper among the females. Some of his battalion had joined him with enthusiasm. Some always would. Others hung back. These village people had had little enough, and were not even counted among the enemy. A day after the "Feast," as Gerner had called it, three of his men deserted. Winter was beginning and the weather was strident; they were easily caught. Gerner had the trio hung up by their ankles from a tree and left in the sleeting rain till their brains should burst. He had also previously made a little supper on them, too.

They were young, not yet sixteen, and—as Gerner remarked—had the "beardless faces of girls."

One evening after that Corlan met Gerner unexpectedly, both of them alone and walking across a half-reaped, spoiled field, under the gray roar of the sky. And Gerner had smiled at Corlan. "You have some difficulty with me, brother Knight?"

"Only one," said Corlan. "You still live."

"Oh," and Gerner laughed, "so I do, so I do."

In that moment Corlan, into whom the discipline of the military had been calcified nearly from birth, felt a cool high hand lift him upwards from his own body, until he stood some seven meters tall. From here, not dazed only a little surprised, he looked down on the ugly face of Captain Gerner. And then, almost gently, Corlan stepped forward and slammed his right fist into Gerner's jaw. Corlan felt nothing much, though he heard the crack of a tooth—or a bone. But when Gerner toppled over, Corlan stamped hard, once, on his guts. After which, as the creature writhed there, bulge-eyed, retching, and wheezing for air like a damaged street-organ, Corlan drew his army sword and decapitated him.

Only when he had wiped off the blade and re-sheathed it, with a certain military precision, did Corlan Von Antal drop back into his own skin. And at once, from a mad retributory angel he became a mad, terrified boy. And the boy turned and sprinted from the field, straight through into the deepest avenues of the trees, nearly mindless, with everything lost and thrown away—Gerner, obviously, but also Corlan's prospects, career, family, friends, ideals—*life*—*heart*—lying in the rotted stalks like pieces of a broken plate.

All told five nights had passed, five days, since the murder in the field.

That fifth night there was a bloody sunset, carmine and implacable. Cut off now from the army, he had found no shelter anywhere, and the few cold-withered roots he managed to grub did him no good. One afternoon he caught a rabbit, a skill from his youth. But then he could not kill it, not even efficiently and cleanly as he knew how to do. He could not kill it because he had, of all things, killed *Gerner*, and the curse of the outlaw was on him. So he let the animal go. Stunned, it kept like a stone long minutes in the frosty grass before bolting out of sight. There were streams where Corlan broke the morning ice and drank the water. He was used to that. By now the little pewter flask in his greatcoat pocket was empty of brandy.

When the blood soaked from the west, he sat on the ground and saw stars appear above, each one like the tip of a polished sabre driven through the uniform of the sky. Or they were shiny bullets.

Then the trees wept. Sleet striped through with a horrible, determined sound.

Well, why not just lie down here, just lie down and let the world that had cursed him finish him off? Or he could fire one of the shiny stars in his revolver through his head.

Eventually he got up, and ran—then only stumbled—on. The stars were washed away.

And darkness fell like a curtain.

Maybe it was the days without food, or the peculiar roots, even the icy *chewiness* of the cold, cold water, that made Corlan think he met his grandfather about an hour later.

Corlan was walking by then, slowly. And the old man simply appeared between two of the pillar-like stems of the black pines. He was made of trees and winter, and his hair of the gray snowy rain. But he had *been* like that.

"Well, Cor, here you are," he said, thoughtfully, the way he had been used to, a couple of decades earlier.

Corlan's father was a bullying sot. The grandfather had often stepped between them. But whereas the father ruled through violence, the grandfather exerted command through his calm iron will. And where, perhaps, this had unhinged his own son, his *grandson* it saved. It was the grandsire, inevitably, who had weaned Corlan towards a military life. He had, too, taught him how to read and value books, to absorb music, to deal well with women, even those he loved. And to kill an animal for food swiftly and without redundant pain. "We are allowed to eat them, my boy," he had said, "which does not mean we should hold them in contempt. We must face the hard nutritional facts, perfect our methods, and cause as little suffering as possible. Respect your food, it was alive only yesterday. Hunting is a necessity, *never* a sport. We have the right to sustain our existence, but not to pretend those other things, upon which we prey, are unworthy of our concern and care."

Yet now, having spoken only his brief greeting, the grandfather merely stood there. And Corlan had the urge to go to him and kneel down and make a confession. The grandfather had nevertheless been dead for fifteen years. Corlan did not forget this. And next minute the old man's image faded in the rain, as the stars had.

And then, through the unfilled gap in the trees, which seemed damaged, Corlan saw the great pile of a building, reared up above the forest. Something in the rain outlined the building on the sky, although no lights showed in the bulk of it. A ruin, perhaps, some long-abandoned architectural hulk from the days of the Rupertian Conclave—centuries out of date.

Corlan stayed where he was, and looking upward at the masonry he felt a profound despair.

It was as if, he later decided, condemned to death, he had witnessed before him the proposed scaffold.

Yet he did not linger very long. He moved free of the dilapidated tree-line and started to climb the steep slope beyond. There was nowhere else to go. Or only one. And he was not ready, despite his previous thoughts, to go *there*.

By the time he reached a sort of fossilized drawbridge, and crossed by it over a type of pit, to a huge, arched, black door, Corlan had seemingly recalled every legend and eerie tale told of these forests. To see a ghostly grandsire was nothing. The vegetal labyrinth contained the strongholds of far worse phantoms, not to mention vampires, were-men, and ghouls.

He had always disdained such stuff. In childhood even he was seldom afraid of anything supposedly supernatural—the *natural* world being adversary enough.

When he struck the door he believed no one and nothing would respond. The door might even simply creak inward, unsecured in the building's abandonment. (It was a castle, towers here and there seemed to rise up from it, and it was far larger than any mansion.) But the door did not give. And all at once a greenish feeble light woke up overhead, in a shoulder of the stone, which was pierced he then saw by the thinnest slits of windows. This light began to crawl down towards him.

Corlan quietly considered taking to his heels. But that was an intellectual joke he was having with himself.

He did not truly expect some fiend to undo the locks and peer out at him. Alas, he was living in reality, not a book.

Something made grinding noises—bolts, keys, hinges, and a quarter of the black door opened.

A fiend looked out at Corlan Von Antal.

For a moment he gaped at it, and then he broke out laughing. "I've died and gone straight to Hell for my crime, yes?"

The poor fiend shook its head, from where narrow gray snakes of hair trickled, shaking in harmony. "Not so, sir. This is the House Veltenlak. What do you seek?" The voice was like rusty nails softly scratching together.

Corlan said, "I've lost my way," smiling still at the awful irony of his words. "I need somewhere to rest. To eat something, drink something not frozen mud, to sleep. Oh," he said unhappily, "if death's just sleep, I'll settle for that."

He was addled, of course, from events and five days without food. He heard himself with censorious dismay.

But the poor fiend, he now realized, eyes adjusting to its waveringly hand-held lantern, was only a skinny, bent-over man, about a hundred years of age, which probably indicated seventy or so. He wore faded dusty eldritch black clothes, perfectly couth though worn out—as was he. His eyes were dull and watery, and his mouth, which now sadly smiled back at the visitor, contained, it seemed, only a third of the teeth God had originally planted there.

"We have not much now. But you are welcome. Come in, sir, come in. A little company will be pleasant for us."

What did Corlan feel as he crossed that threshold? (Where the miniscule bones of a mouse lay like brown needles.) He was never certain, so weary, his head swimming. He always afterward had a vague notion he stumbled, and the old fellow did not reach out to steady him, only moved backward a step, and stood waiting a short way into what seemed to be a vast dark *cave*, whose high walls were of striated rock, and here and there on them something murkily gleamed or glinted, as the lantern-light trembled over it. Then, after Corlan had righted himself, if so he had to, the other man turned and limped off into the darkness.

Corlan looked about him with a sort of oddly uninterested curiosity. He began to see that they moved through and then out of some great hall, a place in the past for banquets and aristocratic councils. Up on the stone walls there were tattered banners fringed with ragged bullion, and antique swords and shields and other warlike implements, that shone and winked from their cobwebbing. A colossal hearth went by on his right, with two savage and enormous stone animals guarding it—he could not make out what they were. There was half an armorial motto, in Latin: *Non Omnis Moriar.* Now what did that mean? The grandfather would have known. *We do not die? We die? All things die . . . ?* No, not that . . .

Here they went round what seemed a very thick pillar, high as the inestimable roof, and possibly having the girth of three or four pines grown together. Now came a passageway, long and curving, like a static worm. The lantern splashed on running wet, puddles, on peculiar stainings and spidery cracks. The enclosure stank of rot and dampness worse than the hall.

Something scrambled across the old man's feet and vanished—as it looked—into the blank wall. A rat, a lizard.

"Where are you taking me?" Corlan asked languidly. He was near to falling down.

"A kitchen below, sir. Teda keeps a fire there."

"Does she? Teda . . . And how do they call you?"

"Tils," the old man said.

"Whose house is this?"

"He is gone, sir." Oddly the old man's voice took on at this a weird harshness. He sounded younger, and more stern.

"*He*," said Corlan. "But what is his name?" The old man did not answer this. He said only, in an inexpressibly unnerving way, "He is dead, sir. Not spoken of. *Never* spoken of."

Corlan thought, Oh, then, one of the bloody story-book ghouls. Dead but still active and in residence. It *is* a story I've walked into. I don't care. Oh God I must lie down.

Just then they turned a corner and before them, along another paved stone walk—this without a roof—another door showed buttery light. Above, the rain—having successfully leaked its way into the house—had given over, and the weaponry stars were back in full force.

They got up a steep and pitted step, and Corlan saw now the roofed kitchen with a few lamps and a fire burning. A pot was slung over it. He smelled soup, and there was a loaf on a table, and coffee had been brewed, and there the white alcohol glittered in its decanter: schnapps or junever. This must be a dream then. He reached a bench and collapsed onto it.

There was also a woman, an old one to match the old man. Teda, presumably. Teda and Tils.

It was the ruined schloss of an undead vampire or werewolf, and these two old bundles of bones were doubtless mad as frogs, and ready to prepare any guest for the monster's delectation. Well, let them. So long as they fed him first.

He pulled some coins from his pocket, all he had—his pay was in arrears. It would save him from being robbed by them later. They were glancing at the money as he offered it, as if they had never seen coins before. Maybe they never had. The ghoul had taken care of them.

We do not altogether die.

That was what the Latin meant, surely?

Of course. How apt.

Corlan fell asleep.

• • •

There is night. And there is the Night—the night-dark void that hides inside the often gilded covers of reality: The Abyss. A little of the latter goes a very long way.

Attributed to the philosopher Anton Woetzsner (1797-1889)

When he came to again Corlan believed he was in the open, out in the dark fracturing of the pine-pillared night. All was pitch-black, but for a row of savage scarlet eyes that seared at him, crouched low down, flickering with lust.

He did not think he would have time to grip the revolver.

One of the eyes blinked, and went out.

It was the kitchen fire. He was in the kitchen of the stone schloss, lying on the bench.

Corlan sat up. He drew out flint and tinder, struck a light. They had left a lamp on the table, which he lit. A bowl of the broth was there too, cold now but no matter, a chunk of the loaf. The coffee was gone, but not the junever-gin.

He ate in the half-light like a starving dog, knew it and cared nothing, his face almost in the dish, growling and grunting. When he was done, for a moment a fierce nausea gushed through him—too much after too little—then faded back, leaving only a dull digestive ache.

He sloshed the gin into a small chipped glass and swallowed two gulps.

Everything would improve now. They, the raddled old couple, had saved his life. Where had they gone to? Oh naturally, to alert, or to hide from, their master, the owner of House Veltenlak.

No, Corlan decided, he would stop that now. He was restored. There were no vampires, none of the other creatures either. This was only a ruinous heap, once grandiose, deserted as several of the ancient castles had been, since an era of war began.

Something hissed and whispered high up. A vaporous serpent came sliding towards him down the wall, and there another—another—

Corlan shook himself. Numbskull. It was only dust or powder escaping the ceiling. The entire habitat was crumbling. All about him, as he concentrated, his ears no longer dinning with fatigue and hunger, he could detect such sighs and grumblings, cracks and masonry groans. Subsiding, these doomed walls due to disintegrate and tumble, leaving only shattered stone blocks and part-standing shafts, through which the winds would blast their cannon-shot.

The fire was dying rapidly now, and the tepid kitchen growing ever colder.

But Corlan drank another glass of junever, and glanced about. He was refreshed. He wanted something to do until the morning came, when he would take himself off.

He wondered idly where Tils slept, and Teda. They had left the sparse column of coins on the table.

Standing up, he took the lamp, and went all round the kitchen, which was not itself very big, and gave on a second kitchen through a broken door. The second kitchen was itself broken, some of its roof down. Beyond, a yard, black with moonless night, and a well, but peering into this it seemed to have gone dry, only rain and muck inside. Three dead rats, coiled tight as rope, lay on the ground.

How long until sunrise? He took a reading from the patterns of the stars, where he could see them. Three, four hours, he thought.

Corlan went back through the kitchen and the corridors.

He reached again the vast hall-cave beyond the pillar with an odd suddenness. As if it had shifted and come to meet him. The unpleasant impression caused him to pull up and rigidly stand there. The flame in the lamp jerked and the stonework jumped with it.

This was when Corlan felt, he thought for the first, (but afterwards he was sure it was not for the first at all) a kind of seeping, leaching yet indescribable dread. Years after he would, to himself, compare all this to an abrupt loss of blood that for an instant made you lightheaded, and then sick, faint, leaden and ashen and barely conscious.

But his senses stayed intact, indeed quite keen.

He wondered had he been poisoned—venom in the food or alcohol. But it was not that. His guts had quieted. Yet—his hands shook, and it took all his will to steady them. He had been, in battle, reasonably cool. What was this? Nothing. Some childish fantasy lingering—

The horror, (for *horror* was in fact precisely what it was) did not let go.

Determined then, Corlan went directly into the enormous hall. He reached the giant fireplace with its sentinel beasts. What were they? Wolves? Dragons? Some mismatch of both? He smashed the lamp straight down on the hearth so it shattered and the flame spilled out. He had immediately seen logs lay on the stone apron, laid ready if evidently for a great while unused. They were damp, too, the huge rainy chimney would have seen to that. But the lamp-oil anointed them, and spluttering, smoking blue and spiking out raw green sparks, they began to burn. Then the smoke went black, but already

Corlan had seen ranks of filthy candles waiting all about, on the mantle, on tall candle-standards either side. The struck flint soon roused them. The smell was vile, animal fat in the wax, the rank unwilling wetness in the wood. Corlan's stomach heaved but he clamped his will upon it. Generally well-trained, his healthy body was used to obeying him.

He stepped back and looked everywhere around him, able to see it all finally, all the splendor of its dying hollowness.

And the horror increased.

It rose up through him as the sickness had done, but worse, much worse. Nor would it permit his steely will to order it down and away. It swelled through his belly and heart and throat and brain. It expanded in his mind and looked out through his fire-burning glaring eyes. It said to him, wordless, voiceless, in a language untranslatable but always known: *Behold, Behold. Behold.*

Corlan rushed across the hall; he did not know what he did, he was in retreat.

So he came to a staircase, the stone treads wide and shallow and rising upward between ranks of stone posts taller than a man, in the tops of some of which were older filthier candles, or only stubs, whose melted greasy lace trailed downward.

Swiftly up the stair he ran. The horror went with him.

It was thick as wax or stone, yet malleable, and it twisted inside him as a snake would.

It's real, he thought, blindly, madly, as he sprang from step to step. (Once, twice, tiny bones crunched under his feet.) *It exists—*

Then he had reached the top and ahead a great opening, like a mouth, toothed with bits of swords and shields hung there, gave on another corridor, very wide. The fluttering light below in the hall penetrated this passage.

Corlan, despite his confusion and fear, slammed to a halt, grabbing at the topmost stair-post.

One of the statuary beasts from the fireplace had got loose. It was here now, poised in the passageway, staring at him, its eyes not like fire at all, but a pearly, nearly opalescent color, between emerald and blue Artic ice.

This fear was nearly welcome. It was so different from the *horror.*

Corlan found he had taken hold of the revolver, but his hand shook again; it was awkward—besides, how could he shoot a beast of stone? In those moments the thing gazed on at him, and all at once furrowing its brow, *frowning,* as a man would, puzzled and affronted by the idiotic antics of a stranger.

It had human eyes, the beast, regardless of their colors and luminosity.

Then he knew what it was. Not a carving come alive but a physical animal, a huge, dark-ruffed wolf. He could kill it, then. Perhaps its splattered gore might appease the evil spirit that now pursued Corlan. But probably not. The wolf would be the monster's own familiar, would it not, beholden to its master. A vampire in legend was inclined to favor the wulven kind. Or again, a werewolf might change into just such an abomination.

I am going insane. Stop this. It's just an animal.

"Hey!" Corlan bawled suddenly at the motionless wolf, and waved his arms.

The wolf lowered its head, then turned from him. It padded off into the passage, not hurrying, neither startled nor enraged.

As it moved, its gait was slow and heavy. If it had been human its shoulders would have sagged. The ruffed head hung down. Halfway off into the dark, just before the darkness swallowed it, Corlan saw it pause. He heard it drinking, sluggishly and not for very long, then it slunk on, dragging its feet now, it seemed to him, as though exhausted.

In the end Corlan snapped off a piece of candle from the last of the posts, lit it, and went after the wolf. A short distance, and there was an old glazed clay bowl on the floor, which held the liquid the wolf had been drinking. Pink in color—milk, Corlan thought, mixed with and curdled by blood.

Closed doors lined the passage. At the end the corridor branched both left and right, but either side was only a wreckage of smashed stone. There was another wide arched doorway in between, this slightly open. The wolf had gone in there; Corlan could smell it. Hesitating outside, he heard it jump up on something, and then settle. He heard it sigh, the same mournful sighing which the House Veltenlak constantly gave. The wolf must have copied it. Corlan did not enter the room.

All this while horror stayed fast inside him. As the wolf had, it seemed to be settling itself, lying down, making itself comfortable within his body, his soul.

He was so weary now. As if he had not eaten, not slept, was ill or wounded, or a slave worn thin with thankless, awful labor, and no hope anywhere, none. No chance at all.

Two: Day in Night

Non Omnis Moriar—
   Behold the voiceless wordless voice proclaimed.

It flung aside the curtains of unknowing and there, before him, lay an infinite vista. But it was a view without a single image in it.

Behold . . .

Non Omnis—the inscription, time-gnawed or hacked away.

BEHOLD—

Corlan woke, sitting bolt upright, like a puppet yanked into position on strings. His head rang and the room cartwheeled. He was back in the bloody kitchen. He could not recall returning here. Perhaps he had never left it, only got up and eaten the food—the bowl stood empty that had held the soup . . . or had it held curdled blood and milk? Crumbs on the table, the decanter of gin one quarter less. So, got up, eaten, drunk, lain down again and slept, dreamed of roaming the stenchful ruins, lighting fires, while some maleficent entity fastened upon him. Utter nonsense.

Deep in his sinews he felt the horror stir. He resisted instinctively, since it did not exist.

The old woman—Teda?—was creeping into the kitchen, sparing him a solitary glance fraught with misgiving, or—could it be compassion?

Corlan rose, nodded to her, and went out into the courtyard behind the other, broken kitchen, to relieve himself, and wash his hands and face in the cleaner pockets of the rain.

These procedures did little for him. He felt like death. He had a fever, he thought. But never mind that, today he must get on. If he could buy a handful more food, some drinkable water, he could continue on his journey to the eastern borders. This was his only method now he had become an outcast. Or, he supposed, he could go back and give himself up to the army, let them strip him of all honor and shoot or hang him amid the trees.

He found Teda had brought him a cracked china cup of coffee, and his eyes filled with sentimental tears. Through them he glimpsed the crooked distortion of her hands. What was it? Old age and rheumatism, no doubt. He thanked her and drank and said, "There's a wolf sleeps in this house."

"Yes," she said, softly. "That is Hris."

"Hris—a wolf. A choice pet."

"Not a pet. Always about. In former days."

He downed the coffee like medicine. "You mean, do you, when your master was—alive." If ever he *was* alive, Corlan added to himself. But deep within his body or his brain, the horror twitched, nearly lazily now, comfortable with him. *Shake it off.* "Who was this *master*?"

"We don't speak of him."

"Why not?"

"It is—" she left a long gap. She said, "There are partings, sir. Severences."

True, he thought. Death severs people. But *The Master* was *not* people—he did not *die*. He *remained*, and drank *his* coffee—blood—or else dined on the flesh and skeletons—of human things.

Corlan got up again and staggered, holding on to the table to keep himself upright. A fever. Damnation—to be ill when it was so urgent to travel far away—

"You've been generous," he said, "but I'll be off in an hour. Is there any food I might buy from you—"

She had gone. He had not seen her go.

Swaying, he allowed himself to sit down again. She had refilled his cup, and he had not seen that, either. He drank it. It did not taste as if poisoned. From somewhere he must wrestle back his strength.

During the day, the castle was no better. Wan light interruptedly yet perpetually splintered through its narrow window-spaces and cracks, littering the stony floors.

Every so often a gushing sigh, or whisper, indicated the stone-dust that poured out of ceilings and walls. In certain spots it ran like water from a tap.

He had meant to leave within the hour, but had felt so weak and sick he had not yet attempted it. An appalling nervousness of going outside again into the forest began to assail him. He had resorted to biting his nails. He had not done this since he was a young boy in his father's cruel presence.

Corlan did return to the hall. It was as he recalled, though more bleak and empty in daylight. Scattered all over lay the shreddings and grains of the bones of rodents, while in all the spider-nets, dead spiders and their unconsumed prey became dabs of sticky tar. The hearth contained burned logs and the blackened glass of the destroyed lamp. He had done that, then. Crazy. God knew what might have happened—the filth-clotted chimney catching alight—he seemed to hear it crash . . . The armorial motto was less evident by day. We do not altogether die.

What about the wolf—Hris? Corlan forced himself up the stair and went along the passage, both of which seemed shorter, in height and length, than during the night. Yet he took an age to walk up and along them.

The bowl was still there. Most of the pink disgusting blood- milk was gone now.

He reached the door under the arch. In the chamber beyond dusty webs hung down like draperies. There was a gaunt bed, with four upright carved posts. The wolf lay there; it was real. As he stared at it, it opened one sluggish eye, which by day was a smoky amber. It watched him, not moving, as he, leaning on the door-frame, did not move either.

"Is *he* real too, Hris?" Corlan asked the wolf. "Your master? The undead lord. Risen like Christ out of some tomb. *Devouring* me. *Eating* me alive. And you, poor bloody animal. Draining you dry, and everything here. So many little corpses, bones—drained, sucked inside out."

The wolf's eye shut. It was clearly too tired to bother with him.

Corlan turned and went away.

Partly down the stair, every step seemed suddenly to spring upward at his face. Almost fainting he clung to the bannister.

Outside, within the dark deep of the forest, silence spread its towering wings like an unseen, unheard, non-existent wind.

In the larder, when he unearthed it, he discovered some pieces of unidentifiable meat, kept cold enough, but unmistakably nibbled by something: just conceivably the band of dead rats lying about. A beggar had no choice. The loaf was the same, somewhat mouthed. And he was stealing too, from the old couple who had, in their way, been helpful. For God's sake, he must shoot something in the forest. Although, in the vicinity of the schloss he had seen nothing animate, nor made out even the call of birds.

He found it difficult to think, let alone plan. Inertia, depletion. But he must get out, now, instantly. He sat down on a stool, and rested his head on the wall.

Corlan was in this position when Teda and Tils came creeping back into the room. They looked at him, he believed, with a kind of bemused contempt.

But the old woman was polishing some glasses, and Tils put a black, webbed bottle on the table. Uncorking this, he exhumed a blood-black wine.

Tils beckoned Corlan to the table, where the old woman now placed the nibbled loaf and a gray slab of curious cheese she unwrapped from a cloth.

Her hands. They appeared as if they had been broken, every bone, then set awry.

"It is pleasant," said Tils, "for us to have a little company." Teda too sat down, though at a slight distance, ready to wait on them. But "Like the days that are gone," she murmured.

"But surely," said Corlan, "those days are still here."

"No, no, done forever," said Tils, drinking deeply.

It was a fine wine, metallic and strong. Corlan was cautious with it, but beginning to feel it made him rather better. His hands steadied, some focus had come back to his vision and brain.

"But this is your joke," he said coldly. "Your nameless master never died."

Tils' head went up. A flash of what—anger? hurt?— for a second ignited in the dullness behind his eyes.

"Not so. He died."

Corlan flung off any restraint with the wine. He too drank deeply. He said, "Perhaps once, long ago. He died *then*, whoever he was, and is, your master of Veltenlak. After which—once again he was—animate, shall I say."

"Ah," said Teda softly. "Ah."

Tils put down his glass and gazed into the wine's thick residue. "The gentleman means that after death, we rise in spirit."

"No, I don't mean that. I mean your master—I'll call him for his house, shall I, since you won't say his name—Herr Veltenlak—is undead. A vampire or some other sort of thing. A ghost even, that preys on humankind without any respect or care, dishonorably, uncleanly, and seldom without unneeded pain. He *likes* to cause pain. He likes to play, like a cat. Hunting is a *sport* to him. And men are his quarry. Which must mean that I am, now, I suppose."

He waited. What would happen? Tils did nothing But Teda rose and brought the wine and refilled both their glasses, and then sat down again at a distance.

Dust rushed from the ceiling. A minute scatter of stones dropped with it, clicketing across the table like thrown dice.

"Veltenlak even devours his own castle," said Corlan. "He's eating it up."

They did not reply.

In God's name, they were not old, but *ancient*. Tils two hundred, she not far short.

Well, finish the glass, *then* get up. Take them, and myself, by surprise. Leave the ruin. God—surely I can?

By day the undead creature should not be able to follow him. Corlan visualized the resumption of his grueling trek into exile. The desolation that there awaited him. A cloud of weakness unfurled. His eyes darkened.

As he surfaced from the lapse, he heard Tils begin to speak again, as if from another room.

"I must tell you, sir, he is gone. I will tell you how and when, and why. You should be told. For some it is no matter. But you—"

"Because I resist—" Corlan inadvertently broke in.

"You must hear me out. It was just over one year back, a few months more. When she lost our child—"

Corlan again interrupted, unable not to. "Who lost a child?"

"I," said Teda, in her soft, dead-leaf voice. "My first. Tils' child, it was. We were only seventeen. It was a terrible thing."

"Wait." Corlan stood. The chair screaked along the stone floor. The wine kept him upright. "*Say to me again the age at which you lost your child—last year.*"

"Why, at seventeen, he and I both. We were very young."

"Christ," said Corlan. "Oh, Christ on his cross. Why are you lying to me? You're lunatics. Or I am."

"She says the truth," said Tils. "Be calm, sir. I'll tell you. There is nothing else to do."

Tils at no point named the Lord of Veltenlak.

At no juncture, even by letting a few words slip, did Tils describe the physical appearance, the age, the manner or personality of his master. Tils did not protest or imply that his master had been noble, or kind, or even wronged.

Tils outlined only what, according to Tils, had gone on one year and two months in the past.

However, he started his narrative with these sentences:

"We were not unhappy. The schloss was mighty, built many centuries. Everything of the best. And the woods full of game. There was a lake with fish, and swans, and wild duck would come. Five wells there were in the yards, each with pure sweet water. And the cellar of the most wonderful. This wine I brought from there. It was laid down in the time of the last true king. It tastes of steel and gold. There are others that taste like rubies and black currants, and white wines like apples and honey and silver."

We belonged to the estate, you will understand. Our parents had worked the fields, or with the livestock or vines . . . "

They were thought fit, Tils and Teda, to serve in the house. And then they were married. He married them, their master, as was usual. It was a nighttime wedding. A great many other servants, of course, worked in the house. There was a lot to do. But the tasks of Tils and Teda were not menial and always there was good food and drink, shelter and luxury.

They felt themselves inexorably secure. The power and might, worldly (and otherwise) of their master, hovered over them always, the pinions of a giant eagle.

And then. Ah, then.

One evening late in autumn there was a strange, thick, greenish sunset, and out of this ominous twilight a column of riders advanced with, walking before them, iron figures in the black robes of priests.

Not many ever came to the castle. The stronghold lay in a wild region, and had, too, a dark reputation that for a great while had safeguarded it. It must seem the master, freely and supernaturally, could range where he wished after prey. (Though Tils did not specify this, it was inherently indicated. For how else did the predatory being nourish himself. Corlan had inferred the servants themselves were never troubled. Probably the vampire assumed some animal shapeshift or semblance. Or grew invisible. Of such talents the undead were capable, in legend. And Corlan himself was now preyed on by an element irresistible and unseen, detectable only by the hideous results despair.)

When the procession of priests and horsemen pressed up from the forest, the castle grew alert and uneasy.

Night was imminent, and although Tils did not stress that his master was most active between sun fall and rise, Corlan had concluded it would be so. And therefore the visitors, whatever their nature or intention, must wish to meet with him.

Were the humans in the house really afraid? Despite their serfdom and inbred loyalty, their faith in their lord's powers, they were.

They had some cause.

In an era of monsters, the arm of the Church that rallied to deter them was militant, obdurate. Sadistic. Fire to fight with fire.

"We are, you see, like infants before them. The aristocracy and the priests, equally," said Tils. "Both hold a sword above our heads. We cannot deny, must not withhold. Yet he—was like our father. And these ones were—" Tils paused.

It was Teda, his ancient young wife, who whispered the single phrase. "Like the Devil," she said. "Like the Devil."

The priestly crusaders thrashed their way into the master's chamber, high up in the König Ragen, a tower which, a month after these events, collapsed and crashed through into the body of the house, just missing the great hall— as if it had tried, yet failed, to crush the heart out of the place.

"Above us we heard them at work. Something was done. Even he could not evade them—"

Corlan thought, How not? He was the bloody Devil, not they. But he did not now interrupt.

It appeared the soldiers and the priests got hold of the Master of Veltenlak. Held down with and by some form of alternate sorcery, in this case named Godfulness, they stripped and flayed him. Undead, yet he was alive enough to feel.

"We heard his cries, terrible shrieking. It was not fear," said Tils in sorrowful pride. "He feared nothing. It was only agony."

At length they smashed the master's jaw, poured boiling mercury into his throat and guts, struck all his bones to shards, and at last, in the hour before dawn, smote off his head with a consecrated sword. After which, there in the upper room, they burned his body.

"There was no smell of flesh," said Tils. He waited, courteously.

Teda spoke; this was her cue? "Only the odor of fire."

Then she got up and tottered out of the kitchen, away into the house.

Tils said, "We lost our baby seven hours later. All the other women in child here lost the fruit of their wombs, through that day, and the next night."

Nevertheless, the priests examined everyone yet living. Every servant must parade before them, and even the part-dead aborted women were carried roughly in. Each was stripped bare, as *he* had been, perused for blighted marks, given a crucifix to kiss. A few had *signs*, abnormal birthmarks or warts, or else were too shocked and frightened to embrace Christ on his cross. All of these were shot, slung together in a heap by the lake, and also burned.

Tils and Teda, along with twenty others judged clean, merely simpletons, were allowed to exist. When at last the invaders went away, the castle was left much as it had been.

As autumn waned to winter, and after the König Ragen fell down, a huge lethargy replaced the terror and confusion. When winter commenced, all the house began, in slight or dramatic, always persistent ways, to disintegrate. Birds died and spun from the sky. The swans perished, and the fish, and the lake turned foul, and in another summer's heat dried up. Just as did all the courtyard wells. Trees nearby began to fail. In the farther forest things died, plants, beasts. The very light grew sickly. Of the castle retainers many determined to leave. None succeeded in getting far. They would sink down, often less than thirty meters from the walls, and never again climb to their feet.

"But I stayed where I was, and she, my Teda, with me. Each day was, and is, to us like a year, so long, so reasonless, so barren, so sad. We have aged, I think? Yes, I think so. In fourteen months she and I, we have aged more than five decades. But we do not go away, you see. Do you see, young gentleman? Nothing does go. Even the wolf that he tamed, the wolf our master called Hris for the pagan god of sunset, even he remains. How strong he must be, the wolf. But he can no longer hunt. We feed him milk and a little blood. But the last cow is dead, since yesterweek. And there is so little in a rat."

Corlan closed his eyes. He saw images of fire and heard a sort of thunder, miles off. An earthquake followed.

Tils was shaking him.

"What?" said Corlan vaguely.

"Did you hear me, sir? Did you hear what I must say?"

Corlan came back. "You're more than fifteen years my junior," said Corlan spitefully, "and a slave. Don't put your damned hands on me. I heard all you said. And now I'll depart this cursed and stinking hole."

"You will never depart," said Tils. "Only through death, perhaps not even then. Some nights," said Tils, "I hear them weeping still, in the walls, the others."

"And what about *him*, your Herren—" snarled Corlan, grabbing the ancient man—seventeen, eighteen?—by his corded throat, "does *he* weep? or does he visit in his doubly undead state, and sink in his teeth?"

"He is done, sir," said Tils, as if the fingers that gripped his windpipe were straws—perhaps they were. "He is over."

Letting go, Corlan said quietly, "He's eating everything up. You, your aged wife, the wolf, the rats, the plaster and the stone. How can such a carnivorous force be *dead*?"

"Oh sir," said Tils. And now tears ran out of his eyes that seemed themselves mostly fashioned of water, "sir—sir—it is not him. He was the strength of this house, its vitality—its soul. No, no, it is—" Tils stared beyond Corlan, beyond the castle, the forest, stared and stared, seeing in horror and anguished acceptance what was not there at all. "It is," Tils concluded, "his absence. All that is left—the emptiness—without him. The hollow. The *nothingness*. The vacant pit. *That* is the vampire. That is the thing which feeds."

Three: The Night

An eagle swept out from the König Ragen, as the masonry cascaded downwards. Its wings filled heaven, darkness, without a spark of light. The captain jumped to his feet. Beyond the door the occluded sky was swarming, not into black but white. Snow, not stonework, fell.

How long now had he slept here, the fool? (The old man was gone. The fire was out.)

Corlan lurched about the kitchen. He felt drunk, as if he had been drinking for days, as once in youth he had, ill with drink yet needing it more. The bottle though was used up. No doubt he had finished it.

He knew he must go up through the House of Veltenlak, and take himself to the small door in the larger one. He must undo it, or beat it down. It was straightforward. One proviso: he must not, at any time, sit, must not even lean on a wall or against any upright thing—post, pillar—

Staggering along the corridors, the snow hitting his head like omissions of life. The passages were longer now. Miles of them. They were catacombs. It was a library shelved and paved with the dead. Bones and tiny corpses stacked everywhere, shriveled remains of beetles, spiders, mice, a slender lizard like a lady's fan, close-folded . . . there had been a dance, the music drifted in his ears, a gorgeous girl in a white lace gown—no, forget the girl, and the music. A dead rat lay on its back—step over. Look, the vast pillar was ahead—Christ help me—wake me up—

Abruptly he was stumbling into the colossal hall.

Absence, not presence.

It is the *Void* that is the vampire. It is the *Void* which feeds—

Corlan cried out, a crazed battle-scream he had heard other men give when hit by blade or shot, crumpling over, ending—

I won't end here.

Nothing is worse than this, whatever it is. I can survive the winter earth, the heartless forest. Or if not, I can die *out there.*

They were seventeen, eighteen, the man, the woman. He believed it, and how they had decayed.

The great tower crashing down. The house giving way when the central support of supernatural life was extracted.

The black eagle of Nothingness filling up the sky. The Night.

Too much of the bloody night—

But the Night was there with him. Finally it showed, unmasked its faceless face.

It must be exactly *here*, just beyond the hall and the passages, just where— somehow—now he found himself. Instead of debris, for a moment he had the impression of the ghosts of walls that had once risen solid as mountains, but they were gone and a crater replaced them, as if the full moon had been thrown down an struck the spot. But what fell was the king Tower. And now, it was Nothingness. Corlan stood on nothing and nothing surrounded him, and all things faded from him. He was blind and deaf and dumb. Even his mind lost its voices and its pictures. All erased. And yet—he *felt*, without sensation, the painless fangs fasten on him, eating him up. The void had hunted him for sport and now the void was feeding, and he was its feast. It had been much simpler with him, obviously, in his human misery, having lost everything. Easy prey—he had believed his life was over already. And here he was in life, in the midst of death, beyond which lay only total annihilation. Let go. Give in. Softly merge with Nothing, and be nothing.

Perhaps no man can strive against a demon, the vampire or the ghoul. But mankind its very self enters the dangerous world already under orders, each a warrior, to resist the Enormous *Nihil* of the abyss. How else would any of us live five minutes?

Years and continents away a crazed voice was bellowing. No denial, for the abyss was *all* Denial. Instead an *assent. Yes!* bellowed the voice. *YES.*

In the center of the hall, while he was flailing and bellowing unintelligibly, Corlan's foot slithered over some mess on the floor—bones, stones—And as he careered and swerved to save himself, he found he had come about to confront the staircase that rose up to the wreckage of floors above.

At the staircase top something stood. It was the ancient ruined wolf.

How heavy was its head. The ruff of fur seemed to weigh it down like a collar of lead. One golden eye, filmed to stagnant treacle, staring. The other stayed shut.

Damn the wolf. It was the monster's familiar. Like the moronic servants, Tils and Teda, stuck here like dying flies in gray jam—No—it was fodder, as they were, of Nothingness—

The wolf put down one paw toward a lower step. Then drew it back, as if afraid of treading in freezing water.

Corlan swayed with fatigue. He flung his arms about his own body in a ludicrous attempt to keep himself upright. *If you fall down you will lie here till Judgment Day.* Longer. You will be *nothing.*

"Hris," he called out to the wolf. Why? But the wolf had remained alive, if only barely, and maybe, just as he did not, it did not want to be consumed, but had not itself been able to fathom a route of escape. It did not grasp what it must fight . . . was Corlan the only one who could? None of the others had wanted to . . . even he—even *he*—

"But I can," Corlan said stubbornly aloud, "I can get free. Hris," he called, his voice strengthening suddenly again, "Hris—come on, my boy—come on."

The wolf dropped its heavy head right down, and turned away. It padded off into the dark above the stair.

A blazing rage filled Corlan Von Antal.

He found he ran forward up the stairs, leaping from shallow stone to stone, all his body, his skeleton, protesting, but never missing a step.

When he reached the very top Hris had vanished.

Corlan stood panting. Then he drew the sabre, and deftly sliced a thin line along his left arm, ignoring vital veins but letting out the blood. Its color astonished him, as if never had he seen a drop till now. Vermilion beads dripping from a thread of air—What in God's name had he done?

"Well, Hris," Corlan said, leaning only his right elbow next on the upright of the door. "Well, wolf. What do you say?"

Outside in the corridor the bowl of blood-milk was dry.

Here the wolf was, fully leaning his side on the four-poster bed, but his head back to look at Corlan through the cobweb draperies. Both the wolf's eyes were open now, if one rather wider than the other.

"Come on."

The long nose of the wolf wrinkled.

Without further preface it shoved itself off from the bed, turned right round, and slunk across the floor. Its claws ticked on the stone. It halted about a meter from him.

"All you've had is blood with this muck in it. And I'm poisoned too, but only yesterday, and I'm still fighting, still *alive*. Let me share the life with you, wolf. *No*, not that way—" for Hris had thrust his head down to the floor to lap up one of the glowing drops. Corlan held out his bleeding arm. (Oh, how the vampire would have exalted. Fresh young blood, offered up. Insanity on insanity. He'll tear my arm off—)

The wolf's tongue slipped along Corlan's wounded skin. It felt like silk. The man reached out and dug his fingers into the coarse rich fur of the ruff. The wolf drank, stopped, politely lifted his head, both eyes wide and gleaming. They were like the eyes of a young man, a comrade. *Human*. Brother.

"Now we go out, Hris." The wolf watched him.

Corlan covered up his arm with the torn coat, and swung out of the room. He felt like a dry husk inside which pain and flame and courage were writhing in a wild knot: the desperate agonies of a living thing.

He did not need to look back. Heard the measured tick of the claws padding after him, and the occasional sponge-like gourmet note as Hris licked his snout.

In the unlight everything had grown ghostly and insubstantial. The stairs, the floor, seemed spinning off in all directions. On the high cliffs of the walls banners and weapons nearly transparent.

Corlan reached the barrier of the outer door. Its bolts—were all undone.

He pushed against it brutally, and the quarter door sighed and tumbled back.

Night was coming in after all behind the snow. The landscape seemed to Corlan like a shattered mosaic, white, black, the whole globe flying to pieces.

A voice without voice or words called behind him, silently, deafening as a trumpet note:

Behold Emptiness. Behold Nothingness. Behold the Abysm of Unremitting Death.

The hot nose of the wolf punched Corlan hard in the side. "Behold," Corlan whispered, grasping the wolf's snow-glittered mane, "behold rebellious life. No surrender." Swaggering, staggering, halting, faltering, they crossed the remains of the drawbridge above the cavity once a lake and white with swans, now patched white with snow. Down the steep hill they went, the man and the wolf. When they reached the first trees, those whose boughs were snapped, Corlan dropped headlong on the ground. He was laughing. Then he forgot to laugh.

He saw a ballroom, lit like topaz. The snow was warm and kind. He was barely aware when Hris came closer and his meat-breath steamed across Corlan's face. *Oh he'll kill and eat me now. God bless him.* "Welcome, my friend," murmured Corlan. And he sank into the depths of what must be the night. But *only* that.

Because of it he did not see, and could only afterwards surmise, how the wolf got hold of him, by coat and boot leather, probably, and hauled him on beneath the first impoverished pines, on and on into the thicker shadow of the forest. Forest-deep Hris dragged Corlan Von Antal, out of the Night of Nothingness and back into the night of the winter world. Behold the rebellion of the living. Pines tall as mountains posted up into the snow- starred ether; later a moon, ivory and aquamarine, rising to pierce and to engulf the dark with the bright.

And Hris lifted his platinum head and howled the lunar love- song of his kind, before the snow closed in again. Then the wolf sat down beside the fallen man. Then the wolf lay down beside him. The snow began to cover them both, as if caringly, with a long pale quilt.

Afterword

Nacek was unable to sleep.

The untold story of Corlan Von Antal kept running through his head.

Of course, for Nacek, it was a compendium of rumor and gossip, which the old Commander—Ursus—had never confirmed or denied.

They said, back then, he had killed a fellow officer, some shameful scum the army was glad to be rid of, the murder therefore blamed on enemy action, and Von Antal exonerated. Yet by then he had gone missing. He was found some two weeks later, in deep snow—and protected by a huge hound at least part wolf, (evidently the progenitor of Von Antal's current companion.) The oddest thing about this tale was not the dog, let alone the murder and its hushing-up, but the fact—according to all versions—that Von Antal, then in his early thirties, appeared to have aged ten years: a man of barely thirty-four had become a man of forty-four. However, if anything he was soon proved stronger than he had been, courageous and cunning in the chess game of conflict. More than a score of secret missions (they said) had been successfully undertaken by him since. While his men loved and admired him, and for the many battles in which he and his troops shone, a whole galaxy of medals and concomitant wealth had been awarded. At last retiring from the field, he had found this remote place among the forests, some antique, ruined castle, and from its stones, its bones, had had rebuilt the colossal keep and lowering tower, a König Ragen more than seven stories high. From miles off, as Nacek had seen, you could make out its crenellated skull looming up above the team of pines, and after dark always with a russet light burning like a beacon, or a vow.

No doubt Ursus was there now, in his rooms, sleeping, or reading—for old men did not sleep the way young ones did. Not that Nacek could sleep.

He swung himself off the narrow cot, pulled on his greatcoat, and went out into the passageway, where a single candle offered light.

Confound the old boy. He must know how they all fretted to hear the truth. Like some coquette, flirtatiously hiding it from them.

Up above the last twist of the stone stair, something shouldered forward. It was the wolf-dog, Hris, caught like a phantom between glim and gloom. It had a ruff like a lion's. Two blue emeralds for eyes.

Nacek braced himself. Hris' Master was not here now, and wolves were wolves—

A voice said mildly from above, "Come up, why don't you?"

In God's name! Had the bloody wolf spoken to him? Then a man's shadow, long and lean, fell sword-like downward from a blur of copper lampshine: Von Antal. Laughing maybe at Nacek, who had thought a dog might talk.

"I couldn't sleep," Nacek said humbly.

"At your age? Well it happens. Come and take a glass of Italian wine. You'll sleep after that. Even I do."

His own rooms were spacious, Nacek presently saw. Some swords, an old flintlock, hung on the walls, and two oil paintings, one a landscape, the other the portrait of a stern and upright old man, not so unlike Ursus himself. "My grandfather," the Bear said, handing Nacek a silver cup of wine.

Afterwards Nacek was aware, given this rare chance with Ursus alone, he had meant to try to persuade from him some of the facts behind the stories. And so, as he sipped the full and fragrant wine, Nacek asked, "Is it true, what they say about your cloak, Sir? The bearskin."

"What *do* they say?" inquired Ursus, almost lazily.

In this lower, older firelight, despite the goblet-silver of his hair, Von Antal gave a definite illusion of youth. He had the effortless physical grace of a young man, while the clearness of his black eyes was remarkable; it always had been.

Nacek told him the consensus was that the dog—that was the first dog (wolf) all those thirty or forty years back—had killed the bear.

Von Antal smiled. He lowered his eyes for a second. Yes, he was a flirt where the truth of this was concerned.

He did not explain to Nacek that the wolf now was the same wolf, Hris, that he had redeemed from Veltenlak, the very wolf too that grappled and pulled him through the forest, and warmed him in the snow. The wolf he had given his blood, as perhaps Hris' original master, the vampire, had given it. As for the bear, they had killed it between them. Hris by leading it to the clearing, Corlan Von Antal by looking into its eyes, then touching it. It had died swiftly, quick and clean, but even in that moment he had learned that he need never kill his prey. As the Herr Veltenlak had done, Corlan required only very little to sustain him, and by a transfer—less will than desire—in return he could give back an incredible enduring energy and vigor to any who served him.

He wore the skin of the bear afterwards not as a boast, but to honor it for the lesson.

Corlan had been hesitant initially, concerned at what he had become. But subsequently, that way, he never harmed another. And soon his doubts were done. When at length he returned to the ruin, as he had surmised, the *Absence* was gone. Hunger had destroyed it. The pines grew close and thick. And so he had the tower rebuilt from its own stones. He did not take on the name of Veltenlak. For it was not the vampire lord of the castle who had remade Corlan Von Antal. It was his own duel with that infinitely more terrible demon, Absence, Nothingness, the *Void*. In such a pass the vampire and its power represented the vitality of Life itself. As Corlan's violent and frantic war with the void had also done. The vessel had been drained—but given that influx of courage and rage, vitality rushed back like a river breaking through a riven dam. This world lives, and, always, Absence must give way to Presence. While the transposition from decay to renewal aged Corlan, thereafter it made him *slow* to age. Just as the same force did with the wolf. They might not now be set to live forever, but they would live longer and more hale than most. The phoenix rises from the ashes because the surrender to the personality of the Abyss must never be. Poor Tils, poor Teda, crumbled away by the hour Corlan reclaimed the Schloss, had not known to fight, had missed the basic principle of survival. But Corlan and Hris knew all along inside their warrior souls.

"Oh," said Ursus, to Nacek, "*that* tale isn't true. I won the cloak in a card game." And next Ursus, looking into the young man's eyes, fixed him in the gentle trance, then touched and took, respectful and with care, leaving him in exchange fitter and more sturdy, handsomer even—as Nacek's fiancée would observe, when again he met her.

But Nacek himself (knowing not a jot of any of that) would always count himself a perfect idiot. He had sat in the Bear's own study, with every possibility to wring from him the whole story. And Nacek had sipped Italian wine and fallen asleep like a child. When he woke in the morning, someone had carried him back to his bed—one of the tower servants, he concluded. And he had slept wonderfully well. They all had, it seemed. And really, if he had not uncovered the truth, none of his fellow officers had either.

As, if it came to it, none of them, ever, would.

Natura Vacuum Abhorret (Nature Abhors a Vacuum)
François Rabelais [1494(?)–1553]
After the Latin of Plutarch

Tanith Lee was born in the UK in 1947. After school she worked at a number of jobs, and at age twenty-five had one year at art college. Then DAW Books published her novel *The Birthgrave*. Since then she has been a professional full-time writer. Publications so far total approximately ninety novels and collections and well over three hundred short stories. She has also written for television and radio. Lee has won several awards; in 2009 she was made a Grand Master of Horror and honored with the World Fantasy Convention Lifetime Achievement Award in 2013. She is married to the writer/artist John Kaiine.

*The house, for reasons I didn't understand,
wasn't acting like a house.*

A COLLAPSE OF HORSES

❦

Brian Evenson

I am certain nobody in my family survived. I am certain they burned, that their faces blackened and bubbled, just as did my own. But in their case they did not recover, but perished. You are not one of them, you cannot be, for if you were you would be dead. Why you choose to pretend to be, and what you hope to gain from it: this is what interests me.

Now it is your turn to listen to me, to listen to my proofs, though I know you will not be convinced. Imagine this: walking through the countryside one day you come across a paddock. Lying there on their sides, in the dust, unnaturally still, are four horses. All four are prone, with no horses standing. They do not breathe and do not, as far as you can see, move. They are, to all appearances, dead. And yet, on the edge of the paddock, not twenty yards distant, a man fills their trough with water. Are the horses alive and appearances deceptive? Has the man simply not yet turned to see that the horses are dead? Or has he been so shaken by what he has seen that he doesn't know what to do but proceed as if nothing has happened?

If you turn and walk hurriedly on, leaving before anything decisive happens, what do the horses become for you? They remain both alive and dead, which makes them not quite alive, nor quite dead.

And what, in turn, carrying that paradoxical knowledge in your head, does that make you?

I do not think of myself as special, as anything but ordinary. I completed a degree at a third-tier university housed in the town where I grew up. I graduated safely ensconced in the middle of my class. I found passable employment in the same town. I met a woman, married her, had children with her—three or perhaps four, there is some disagreement on that score—and then the two of us fell gradually and gently out of love.

Then came an incident at work, an accident, a so-called freak one. It left me with a broken skull and, for a short time, a certain amount of confusion. I awoke in an unfamiliar place to find myself strapped down. It seemed to me—I will admit this too—it seemed for some time, hours at least, perhaps even days, that I was not in a hospital at all, but in a mental facility.

But my wife, faithful and everpresent, slowly soothed me into a different understanding of my circumstances. My limbs, she insisted, were restrained simply because I had been delirious. Now that I no longer was, the straps could be loosened. Not quite yet, but soon. There was nothing to worry about. I just had to calm down. Soon, everything would return to normal.

In some ways, I suppose everything did. Or at least tried to. After the accident, I received some minor compensation from my employer, and was sent out to pasture. Such was the situation. Myself, my wife, my children, at the beginning of a hot and sweltering summer, crammed in the house together with nowhere to go.

I would awaken each day to find the house different from how it had been the day before. A door was in the wrong place, a window had stretched a few inches longer than it had been when I had gone to bed the night before, the light switch, I was certain, had been forced half an inch to the right. Always just a small thing, almost nothing at all, just enough for me to notice.

In the beginning, I tried to point these changes out to my wife. She seemed puzzled at first, and then she became somewhat evasive in her responses. For a time, part of me believed her responsible: perhaps she had developed some deft technique for quickly changing and modifying the house. But another part of me felt certain, or nearly so, that this was impossible. And as time went on, my wife's evasiveness took on a certain wariness, even fear. This convinced me that not only was she not changing the house, but that daily her mind simply adjusted to the changed world and dubbed it the same. She literally could not see the differences I saw.

Just as she could not see that sometimes we had three children and sometimes four. No, she could only ever see three. Or perhaps four. To be honest, I don't remember how many she saw. But the point was, as long as we were in the house there were sometimes three children and sometimes four. But that was due to the idiosyncrasies of the house as well. I would not know how many children there would be until I went from room to room. Sometimes the room at the end of the hall was narrow and had one bed in it, other times it had grown large in the night and had two. I would count the number of beds each morning when I woke up and sometimes there would be three, sometimes four. From there, I could extrapolate how many children I had, and I found this a more reliable method than trying to count the children themselves. I would never know how much of a father I was until I counted beds.

I could not discuss this with my wife. When I tried to lay out my proofs for her, she thought I was joking. Quickly, however, she decided it was an indication of a troubled mental state, and insisted I seek treatment—which under duress I did. To little avail. The only thing the treatment convinced me of was that there were certain things that one shouldn't say even to one's spouse, things that they are just not ready—and may never be ready—to hear.

My children were not ready for it either. The few times I tried to fulfill my duties as a father and sit them down to tell them the sobering truth, that sometimes one of them didn't exist, unless it was that sometimes one of them existed twice, I got nowhere. Or less than nowhere: confusion, tears, panic. And, after they reported back to my wife, more threats of treatment.

What, then, was the truth of the situation? Why was I the only one who could see the house changing? What were my obligations to my family in terms of helping them see and understand? How was I to help them if they did not desire to be helped?

Being a sensible man, a part of me couldn't help but wonder if what I was experiencing had any relation to reality at all. Perhaps there was something wrong with me. Perhaps, I tried to believe, the accident had changed me. I did try my level best, or nearly so, to see things their way. I tried to ignore the lurch reality took each morning, the way the house was not exactly the house it had been the night before, as if someone had moved us to a similar but not quite identical house as we slept. Perhaps they had. I tried to believe that I had three, not four, children. And when that did not work, that I had four, not three, children. And when that didn't work, that there was no correlation between children and beds, to turn a blind eye to that room at the end of the hall and the way it kept expanding out or collapsing in like a lung. But nothing seemed to work. I could not believe.

Perhaps if we moved, things would be different. Perhaps the house was, in some manner or other, alive. Or haunted maybe. Or just wrong. But when I raised the idea of moving with my wife, she coughed out a strange barking laugh before enumerating all the reasons this was a bad idea. There was no money and little prospect of any coming in now that I'd had my accident and lost my job. We'd bought the house recently enough that we would take a substantial loss if we sold it. We simply could not afford to move. And besides, what was wrong with the house? It was a perfectly good house.

How could I argue with this? From her perspective of course she was right, there was no reason to leave. For her there was nothing wrong with the house—how could there be? Houses don't change on their own, she told me indignantly: this was not something that reason could allow.

But for me that was exactly the problem. The house, for reasons I didn't understand, wasn't acting like a house.

I spent days thinking, mulling over what to do. To get away from the house, I wandered alone in the countryside. If I walked long enough, I could return home sufficiently exhausted to sleep rather than spending much of the night on watch, trying to capture the moment when parts of the house changed. For a long time I thought that might be enough. That if I spent as little time in the house as possible and returned only when exhausted, I could bring myself not to think about how unsound the house was. That I would wake up sufficiently hazy to no longer care what was where and how it differed from before.

That might have gone on for a long time—even forever or the equivalent. But then in my walks I stumbled upon, or perhaps was led to, something. It was a paddock. I saw horses lying in the dirt, seemingly dead. They couldn't be dead, could they? I looked to see if I could tell if they were breathing and found I could not. I could not say honestly if they were dead or alive, and I still cannot say. I noticed a man on the far side of the paddock filling their trough with water, facing away from them, and wondered if he had seen the horses behind him, and if not, when he turned, whether he would be as unsettled as I. Would he approach them and determine they were dead, or would his approach startle them to life? Or had he seen them dead already and had his mind been unable to take it in?

For a moment I waited. But at the time, in the moment, there seemed something more terrible to me about the idea of knowing for certain that the horses were dead than there was about *not* knowing whether they were dead or alive. And so I hastily left, not realizing that to escape a moment of potential discomfort I was leaving them forever in my head as not quite dead but, in another sense, nearly alive. That to leave as I had was to assume the place of the man beside the trough, but without ever being able to turn and learn the truth.

In the days that followed, that image haunted me. I turned it over, scrutinized it, peered at every facet of it, trying to see if there was something I had missed, if there was a clue that would sway me toward believing the horses were alive or believing they were dead. If there was a clue to reveal to me that the man beside the trough knew more than I had believed. To no avail. The problem remained insolubly balanced. If I went back, I couldn't help asking myself, would anything have changed? Would the horses still, even now, be lying there? If they were, would they have begun to decay in a way that would prove them dead? Or would they be exactly as I had last seen them, including the man still filling the trough? What a terrifying thought.

Since I'd stumbled upon the paddock, I didn't know exactly where it was. Every walk I went on, even every step I took away from the house, I risked stumbling onto it again. I began walking slower, stopping frequently, scrutinizing my surroundings and shying away from any area that might remotely harbor a paddock. But after a while I deemed even that insufficiently safe, and I found myself hardly able to leave the house.

And yet with the house always changing, I couldn't remain there either. There was, I gradually realized, a simple choice: either I would have to steel myself and return and confront the horses or I would have to confront the house.

Either horse or house, either house or horse—but what sort of choice was that really? The words were hardly different, pronounced more or less the same, with one letter only having accidentally been dialed up too high or too low in the alphabet. No, I came to feel, by going out to avoid the house and finding the horses I had, in a manner of speaking, simply found again the house. It was, it must be, that the prone horses were there for me, to teach a lesson to me, that they were meant to tell me something about their near namesake, the house.

The devastation of that scene, the collapse of the horses, gnawed on me. It was telling me something. Something I wasn't sure I wanted to hear.

At first, part of me resisted the idea. No, I told myself, it was too extreme a step. Lives were at stake. The lives of my wife and of at least three children. The risks were too great.

But what was I to do? In my mind I kept seeing the collapsed horses and I felt my thoughts again churn over their state. Were they alive or were they dead? I kept imagining myself there at the trough, paralyzed, unable to turn and look, and it came to seem to me my perpetual condition. In my worst moments, it seemed the state not only of me but of the whole world, with all of us on the verge of turning around and finding the dead behind us. And from there, I slipped back to the house—which, like the horses, seemed in a sort of suspended state: I knew it was changing, that something strange was happening, I was sure of that at least, but I didn't know how or what the changes meant, and I couldn't make anyone else see them. When it came to the house, I tried to convince myself, I could see what others could not, but the rest of the world was like the man filling the horse trough, unable to see the fallen horses.

Thinking this naturally led me away from the idea of the house and back instead to the horses. What I should have done, I told myself, was to have thrown a rock. I should have stooped and scraped the dirt until my fingers closed around a stone, and then shied it at one of the horses, waiting either for the meaty thud of dead flesh or the shudder and annoyed whicker of a struck living horse. Not knowing is something you can only suspend yourself in for the briefest moment. No, even if what you have to face is horrible, is an inexplicably dead herd of horses, even an explicably dead family, it must be faced.

And so I turned away from the house and went back to look for the paddock, steeling myself for whatever I would find. I was ready, rock in hand. I would find out the truth about the horses, and I would accept it, no matter what it was.

Or at least I would have. But no matter how hard I looked, no matter how long I walked, I could not find the paddock. I walked for miles, days even. I took every road, known and unknown, but it simply wasn't there.

Was something wrong with me? Had the paddock existed at all? I wondered.

Was it simply something my mind had invented to cope with the problem of the house?

House, horse—horse, house: almost the same word. For all intents and purposes, in this case, it was the same word. I would still throw a rock, so to speak, I told myself, but I would throw that so-called rock not at a horse, but at a house.

But still I hesitated, thinking, planning. Night after night I sat imagining coils of smoke writhing around me and then the rising of flames. In my head, I watched myself waiting patiently, calmly, until the flames were at just the right height, and then I began to call out to my family, awakening them, urging them to leave the house. In my head we unfurled sheets through windows and shimmied nimbly to safety. We reached safety every time. I saw our escape so many times in my head, rendered in just the same way, that I realized it would take the smallest effort on my part to jostle it out of the realm of imagination and into the real world. Then the house would be gone and could do me no more damage, and both myself and my family would be safe.

I had had enough unpleasant interaction with those who desired to give me treatment since my accident, however, that I knew to take steps to protect myself. I would have to make the fire look like an accident. For this purpose, I took up smoking.

I planned carefully. I smoked for a few weeks, just long enough to accustom my wife and children to the idea. They didn't care for it, but did not try to stop me. Since my accident, they had been shy of me, and rarely tried to stop me from doing anything.

Seemingly as a concession to my wife, I agreed not to smoke in the bedroom. I promised to smoke only outside the house. With the proviso that, if it was too cold to smoke outside I might do so downstairs, near an open window.

During the third, or perhaps fourth, week after I took up smoking, with my wife and children asleep, it was indeed too cold—or at least I judged that I could argue it to have been such if confronted after the fact. So I cracked open the window near the couch and prepared the images in my mind. I would, I told myself, allow my arm to droop, the tip of my cigarette to nudge against the fabric of the couch. And then I would allow first the couch and then the drapes to begin to smoke and catch fire. I would wait until the moment when, in my fantasies, I was myself standing and calling for my wife and children, and then I would do just that and all would be as I had envisioned. Soon my family and I would be safe, and the house would be destroyed.

Once that was done, I thought, perhaps I would find the paddock again as well, with the horses standing this time and clearly alive.

And yet, the fabric of the couch did not catch fire, instead only smoldering and stinking, and soon I pressed the cigarette in too deeply and it died. I found and lit another, and when the result was the same I gave up on both the couch and the cigarette.

I turned instead to matches and used them to ignite the drapes. As it turned out, these burned much better, going up all at once and lighting my hair and clothing along with them.

By the time I'd flailed about enough to extinguish my body, the whole room was aflame. Still, I continued with my plan. I tried to call to my wife and children but when I took a breath to do so, my lungs filled with smoke and, choking, I collapsed.

I do not know how I lived through the fire. Perhaps my wife dragged me out and then went back for the children and perished only then. When I awoke, I was here, unsure of how I had arrived. My face and body were badly burned, and the pain was excruciating. I asked about my family but the nurse dodged the question, shushed me and only told me I should sleep. This was how I knew my family was dead, that they had been lost in the fire, and that the nurse didn't know how to tell me. My only consolation was that the house, too, the source of all our problems, had burnt to the ground.

For a time I was kept alone, drugged. How long, I cannot say. Perhaps days, perhaps weeks. Long enough in any case for my burns to slough and heal, for the skin grafts that I must surely have needed to take effect, for my hair to grow fully back. The doctors must have worked very hard on me, for I must admit that except to the most meticulous eye I look exactly as I had before the fire.

So, you see, I have the truth straight in my mind and it will not be easy to change. There is little point in you coming to me with these stories, little point in pretending once again that my house remains standing and was never touched by flame. Little point coming here pretending to be my wife, claiming that there was no fire, that you found me lying on the floor in the middle of our living room with my eyes staring fixedly into the air, seemingly unharmed.

No, I have accepted that I am the victim of a tragedy, one of my own design. I know that my family is gone, and though I do not yet understand why you would want to convince me that you are my wife, what you hope to gain, eventually I will. You will let something slip and the game will be over. At worst, you are deliberately trying to deceive me so as to gain something from me. But what? At best, someone has decided this might lessen the blow, that if I can be made to believe my family is not dead, or even just mostly dead and not quite alive, I might be convinced not to surrender to despair.

Trust me, whether you wish me good or ill, I do hope you succeed. I would like to be convinced, I truly would. I would love to open my eyes and suddenly see my family surrounding me, safe and sound. I would even tolerate the fact that the house is still standing, that unfinished business remains between it and myself, that somewhere horses still lie collapsed and waiting to be either alive or dead, that we will all in some senses remain like the man at the trough with our backs turned. I understand what I might have to gain from it, but you, I still do not understand.

But do your worst: disrupt my certainty, try to fool me, make me believe. Get me to believe there is nothing dead behind me. If you can make that happen, I think we both agree, then anything is possible.

Brian Evenson is the author of over a dozen books of fiction, most recently the short story collection *Windeye* (Coffee House Press) and the novel *Immobility* (Tor) which both were finalists for the Shirley Jackson Awards. His collection *The Wavering Knife* (FC2) won the International Horror Guild award, his novel *The Open Curtain* (Coffee House Press) was a finalist for the Edgar Award, and his novel *Last Days* (Underland) won the American Library Association's Award for Best Horror novel of 2009. He has a new collection, *A Collapse of Horses*, forthcoming in 2015. He lives, as weirdly as possible, in Providence, Rhode Island, and works at the college upon which Lovecraft's Miskatonic University is based.

*The ability to keep every active request in his head and accessible at all times,
and to seize on the one particular that might bring the quest
to resolution was what made him who he was.*

PRIDE: A COLLECTOR'S TALE

Glen Hirshberg

Like all their best hunts, this one started as a search for something else, and
ended in failure. They'd been days in the hills above Ruidoso and back and
forth across the Mescalero Reservation in a rented Jeep with canvas sides that
didn't zip, in the middle of winter. They never did find the Kiowa trader the
Collector had heard—somehow, through that impossible, disorganized scatter
of decades-old contacts and private websites and intuition he'd constructed
around himself—was back in the country. They had hoped to fulfill an eight
year-old request from an east coast Numismatic by asking the Kiowa to trade
or sell at least one of the three pre-Mayan axe-head coins he supposedly kept
on his person at all times—for luck, apparently. Luck he actually believed in.

"These people," Nadine told the Collector as they drove through the
blowing snow and gray light, across dead, desert hills that seemed to fade, in
the blizzard, from the dull sepia of old photographs to the dissolving sepia of
ruined old photographs. She had the books she'd tracked down open on her
lap, and her laptop atop those. Doing what she did, what she loved. Filling
the Collector's quests—and life—with meaning, the way he filled hers with
purpose. "This tribe? They had so little use for metal—they were so good
with shells, and wood, and leaves?—that they assigned it the least important
function in their entire cultural system."

"Meaning money," the Collector said, hunching in his seat. Tall and
spindly, he tended to curl forward, which, with his uncombed shock of dark
hair, gave him the look—when he was peaceful and listening—of a windblown
cypress. When he was driving, though, he resembled a bloodhound on point.

He slapped the wheel. "Brilliant." Then he swung his head around so he could look at her some more. As usual, he did that for too long.

"Goddamnit, drive," Nadine said happily, as the Jeep skidded onto the gravel and back off it.

With no real hope left of completing their task, they stopped, in the dead dark of 4:30 in the afternoon, at a reservation bar. Snow roared in clumps across the empty parking lot like a stampeding herd of ghost buffalo. The neon sign over the bar's wooden doors read BAR, and the place radiated all the low, windowless charm of an adult book shop. Inside, instead of the Kiowa, they found Nartana.

Later that night, in the after-storm silence, as they descended from the high desert toward the west Texas waste, Nadine would wonder how the Collector had recognized the man. Or even remembered they were looking for him. But then, that ability—to keep every active request in his head and accessible at all times, and to seize on the one particular that just might, someday, bring the quest to resolution—was what made him who he was. It was also why, despite Smartphones and linked databases and indelible digital footprints, people still sought him out.

In Nartana's case, the Collector had seized on the sandals. Nadine noticed them too, of course, the second her eyes adjusted to the bar's dim, blue light. The thin man wearing them had propped them on the table right by the door. The feet they encased looked hairy, bloody, covered in flaps of dead skin, more like a brace of shot squirrels than feet.

"Nadine," the Collector said, gesturing at the sandaled man. "Go to work."

Surprised—though she shouldn't have been—she glanced at the Collector. He had one index finger in the air and was leaning forward, as though testing for wind. The bartender—a middle-aged Apache woman with salt-and-pepper hair in a neat bun and a dishrag in her hands—watched them without curiosity. On the jukebox, Keith Secola—Nadine recognized the song from an earlier quest—wailed the reservation blues.

Nadine finally got her gaze past the sandaled man's feet, up his long legs and blade-of-grass torso to his face.

"He's sleeping."

"Ask him if he wants a grilled cheese. And a chocolate milk."

"Chocolate milk?"

"Come on. Do your stuff."

"My stuff works better on awake people."

"It works on everyone."

"I *do* want a grilled cheese," said the sandaled man, opening his eyes without lowering his feet from the table. "Yes I do."

Instantly, Nadine felt herself switch on. As though she'd flipped a sign behind her eyes to read OPEN. That's what the Collector always told her it looked like. It wasn't conscious, simply what happened. *And that*, he'd assured her, *is* why *it works*.

"Am I having my sandwich with you?" said the man.

Dropping her bag to the floor and her coat over the back of the nearest wooden chair, Nadine sat. "See to the sandwiches, would you, dear?" she called over her shoulder.

The Collector laughed and moved off.

The sandaled man had removed his feet from the table and sat up, some. His threadbare button-down was too wide but not long enough for him, and hung off his shoulders more like a saddlebag than a shirt. The twiggy thing between his lips, which Nadine had taken first for a cigarette, turned out to be a twig.

"Now then," she said brightly. "Why do you think we're here?"

The Collector returned, pulled up a chair, sat listening a while, then interjected, "You're like the Walking Woman."

And Nartana stopped in mid-tale, blinked, and said, "Who?"

"Like that Mary Austin story. Do you know it? About the woman who wanders from all over the desert, and no one knows where—"

"Back in your box, dear," Nadine said, patting his leg to quiet him. He quieted, smiling, while Nartana bubbled his chocolate milk with his straw. The bubbles rose to the rim of the glass and seemed to rotate there. For a moment, Nadine thought he was going to launch them like smoke rings, do tricks. The bubbles trembled with breath, then sank. When she looked up, she was surprised to find Nartana staring at her.

"You notice," he said. Meaning what he'd done with the bubbles. Which *had* been a trick, after all.

"I do," she told him. And so, before they'd even finished their sandwiches, she worked him around to his flutes.

This time, Nartana's eyes widened comically. "You *know* about those?"

"We've heard about them."

"Are they here?" said the Collector, leaning forward. He'd said nothing the whole rest of the time, just listened, with no trace of impatience. Actually, with the opposite of impatience. That *his* magic. "You have one with you?"

With a shrug, Nartana reached under the table and pulled up a clinking, canvas Trader Joe's bag.

"Perfect," said the Collector. "Oh, God."

For a second, as Nartana struggled to free a recorder-like mouthpiece from whatever it was tangled with, Nadine thought he was about to play the whole bag, that the bag itself was the instrument. Trader Joe bagpipes. Then Nartana got a flute loose and set it on the table.

Together, they gazed at it. A cylindrical reed of something, warping almost apart in several places. The colorless feathers glued to the edges of the finger-holes looked filthy, caked with salt or gypsum sand, as though they'd been dragged behind a snowplow. The mouthpiece was pinched nearly shut, and bent forward just slightly, like a crooked finger.

"Can I hold it?" the Collector asked.

"Knock yourself out, man," said Nartana.

The Collector held it, handed it to Nadine. How, exactly, it felt different than she'd expected, she would never be able to say. Softer? The feathers like fingernails brushing the bottoms of her wrists. Raising goosebumps there.

Nartana seemed pleased by their reaction. But when the Collector asked whether they could trade for or buy the flute—or commission the creation of a new one—the man raised both eyebrows.

"What do you mean?"

"We know a guy," Nadine said. "He . . . well, he collects. Instruments. Handmade breath instruments, from all over the world. In honor of his wife." And then—on impulse, and possibly improvising, because she wasn't completely sure this was right—"She died."

Nartana considered, then shook his head. "How can I give him my flute?" He sounded utterly sincere, and also as though they'd asked for one of his lungs. He put the instrument away. The Collector didn't argue, just removed a card from his pocket and slid it across the table. "In case you change your mind. Ever." He stood.

"Could you play for us?" Nadine said.

And Nartana looked up. And the Collector sat back down.

They still hadn't spoken, fully two hours later, when the Collector turned the Jeep off Route 11 into the parking lot of a Family Pride supermarket that had materialized out of the blowing wisps of snow, lights blazing, like a frontier trading post. "I'm hungry," he said. "Come on."

As she eased into the air, Nadine felt both knees pop. She stretched next to the Jeep, listening to its sides snap in the wind, while snowflakes kissed her outstretched wrists. Disconcerting in their dryness. Even precipitation in this endless, greenless space seemed devoid of liquid, as unlike precipitation in her beloved Ireland as Nartana's fluteplay was to pennywhistling. No less stirring or beautiful. But emptier. Even lonelier.

Theirs was almost the only car in the long, square lot. The new-risen moon poked a pinprick hole in the burl of heavy clouds. Far ahead, at the edge of some low hills, a ribbon of light, or maybe lights, stretched the whole length of the horizon. A town, perhaps. From under the front tire of the Jeep—as though it had been there for hours—a tortoise-shell cat crept out, looked at Nadine with narrowed green eyes, and scurried away. Two more cats she hadn't seen seemed to rise out of the asphalt to join the first, and they glided off together toward the store.

"Hello," chirped a tiny, dark-haired girl in a Family Pride apron, passing in front of the Jeep wheeling a stray shopping cart. Whatever that horizon light was, it flickered in her too-large glasses.

"Uh-uh-uh OH!" sang another girl Nadine hadn't noticed, chugging up behind the Jeep, steering a whole line of shopping carts.

The first girl laughed, spun her cart around so she was pushing from the wrong side, and raced toward the oncoming line. The collision produced a strangely disappointing *ping*, but the girls staggered back as though from a car crash, then leapt into the air and butt-bumped each other. Scream-singing *"Hello!"*

Nadine smiled. Stopped smiling. Watched a snowcloud blow over the girls. Neither one, she realized, was as young as she'd initially thought. The first had to be in her twenties, dark braid thumping down her back, glasses clearly the cheapest she could find, the prescription probably at least a year out of date judging by her squint. The second was taller, pale-cheeked, round and squishy everywhere like an uncooked loaf of bread. Her eyelids not just heavy but set in their heaviness, like a new mom's.

Nadine had known so many of these girls back home in County Clare. Woman-girls who could have gotten away, gone to school, gone to Dublin or London, maybe meant to, but stayed instead to help parents or wait on a boy. And gotten stuck, without realizing. Without even noticing, sometimes. And then spent the rest of their youths wriggling like flies on flypaper.

"Nadine!" called the Collector, standing before the open sliding doors. "They have cactus candy!" He disappeared through another knot of cats into the market.

"It's gross," said the round woman, pushing her carts past Nadine. "Don't do it."

"Tastes like cactus, though," called the woman with the braid. Glasses twinkling.

"And belly lint," said the round woman.

Nadine laughed.

Inside, opening her coat but finding less warmth than she'd hoped, she strolled past closed checkout lanes and a trio of black kittens clustered around a plastic saucer of milk next to the stacked firewood. In the Express Lane, a cashier sat behind the register. Pretty, dusky, Hispanic girl, maybe nineteen, with tired eyes that made her appear almost Asian and a red, glinting mouth, pursed and just a touch lopsided. Kisser's mouth, Nadine thought. Homegrown-tomato mouth.

"*Buenas noches,* welcome to Family Pride," the cashier said, without looking up from the Pauline Kael paperback she had propped against the vegetable scale beside the register.

Smiling without knowing why, Nadine strolled ahead, searching for the Collector. She passed more wandering cats, a few stray shoppers, a drunk guy in a Stetson picking through boxes of sale-priced Cheerios. In the Health and Beauty aisle, she saw another Family Pride employee kneeling to restock tampon boxes along a bottom shelf. This woman actually looked up when Nadine passed. She'd affixed wrapped, taped-together tampons behind each ear, and they bobbed like antennae as she straightened.

"Those," Nadine said, with what she hoped was proper reverence, "are exquisite."

"And you haven't even seen my spatulas," said the woman, and returned to her stocking.

By the time Nadine located the Collector, he'd paid and was on his way out of the store. She caught up as they traversed the lot, and he offered her a candy out of a bag with a painted cactus on it. She took his elbow instead of the candy, and they walked in silence back to the Jeep through the spitting snow. He held her flap open for her, as he occasionally thought to, took too long making his way to his own side, then stood with his own flap unzipped. Any heat left in the cabin streamed out, and the chill poured in. A long, gray tabby hopped in, too, sat in the driver's seat as though preparing to take the wheel, then hopped down again.

"Like Scott himself, he looked," Nadine finally intoned, in her best BBC documentary voice. "Frozen to the side of his Jeep. His beautiful, brilliant companion frozen inside. One turn of the key from safety, warmth, civilization..."

The Collector dropped into his seat, keyed the ignition, and turned on the car. Then he turned it off again, while wind battered the canvas and the chill chased down their bones.

"What?" Nadine said, following his gaze but seeing only the woman with the braid, hunched over, burrowing to the far corner of the lot to collect a cart that had wandered all the way to the barrier.

"Nothing," said the Collector. Not starting the car. He wiped the windshield free of breath.

Nadine waited. Sure it would be worth it, though she had no idea what *it* was. As usual.

Eventually, he turned, his face unreadable. His posture even more stiff than usual. As though he really had frozen. "It's just that I know a collection when I see one," he said.

Then he slid through the flap and set out across the lot.

She was too surprised to follow, and too cold. So she just watched as he went, popping another cactus candy in his mouth. His clothes whipped around his stick-figure frame. He stopped a few feet from the girl, not helping with the cart. The girl spoke to him. When the conversation showed no signs of abating, Nadine clambered out and made her way to them. Airborne snow danced along her scalp and neck like little fingers, tickling and teasing. And freezing.

The girl was laughing as she removed her glasses and wiped them on the edge of the sweater sticking out under her coat. The Collector just stood, his smile for show, not his real smile. Nowhere near.

"So. What time do you get off?" Nadine heard him say, and stopped. The question startled her, despite the fact that she knew better.

The girl's answer got swallowed by the wind, but the Collector said, "Uh-huh. And what time did you come on?"

The girl started to answer that, too, laughing some more. Then she stopped laughing. Put her glasses on, but not before Nadine got a good look. And saw.

The person in there. The woman-girl. Panicking. Without making a sound.

Almost casually, never disengaging his gaze from the girl's, the Collector lifted his foot and kicked the cart toward the edge of the lot. It bumped against the curb.

"Stop," the girl said.

"Hey," said Nadine. "You're freaking her out."

The Collector moved to the cart. Popping it up on two wheels, he shoved it over the curb onto the gravel shoulder of the road on the other side. Then he went over the curb himself and pushed the cart just a little farther away. Right to the edge of the asphalt.

When Nadine looked at the girl, she was stunned to see tears streaming down her cheeks. "I'm from Juarez," she said abruptly.

"Honey, it's all right," said Nadine, moving to her side. "He's . . . I don't know what he's doing. But he won't hurt you. He's never hurt anyone."

"That isn't true," said the Collector.

Nadine whirled on him. "What's wrong with you? Stop torturing this poor—"

"Come on," said the Collector to the crying girl, gesturing at the cart. "Go get it."

Wind whistled past, dry as dust, heavy as breath. The girl from Juarez just stood and wept.

"Okay," he said. "I guess I better talk to the manager."

"Oh, God, you can't do that," the girl breathed.

"For fuck's sake," said Nadine, "what's *wrong* with you? I'll get it." Letting go of the crying girl's arm, she moved for the cart. The sensation didn't seize her until she'd reached the curb, had her foot off the ground and halfway over. And when it hit—like the yank of a leash, but *inside*, around her esophagus and also her hips, not painful, not strangling, but *permanent*, impermeable, as inescapable as her own skin—Nadine gasped in surprise. And glanced up at the Collector. Who looked even more surprised. Only then did she get scared.

"What is this?" she said.

He didn't answer. Her fear intensified. She tried starting over the curb again, realized she'd never make it, stumbled back.

"It's not so bad," said the girl with the braid, stepping forward. Taking Nadine's hand. Tears freezing on her wind-whipped cheeks like the tracks of something that had just raced past. Footprints in desert sand. "Really, it isn't."

The Collector looked at them both. Abruptly, he grabbed Nadine around the waist, as though he were going to sling her over his shoulder and break for the Jeep.

But the girl clamped tiny fingers around both of their arms. Squeezed hard. "Don't," she whispered. She glanced toward the market, then down at her feet, where the gray tabby who'd jumped into the Jeep twined about her ankles.

Nadine felt the Collector let go. He caught her eyes, but not for long enough so she could see what he was thinking.

"Right," he said. "Be right back."

"What?" Nadine snapped.

But he'd moved away, returning to the Jeep without turning around. And the girl with the braid was pulling Nadine gently across the lot toward the market, where the register woman had just emerged through the sliding doors. She had her book in one hand, a freshly lit cigarette in the other.

Perching against the frost-caked front window, she settled into a cloud of her own breath, staring past Nadine and the braid-girl at the empty road. The pinprick moon.

Nadine felt herself start to panic. Or—no, *not* panic—which frightened her even more, because it made even less sense. "You can't be serious," she called to the Collector. And then, "You're *leaving* me here?"

Stroking her arm, the braid-girl left her by the open sliding doors. The warmth from inside and the cold out here met on her skin, shooting shivers through her. In disbelief, she watched the Collector close himself into the Jeep, start the motor, and drive off into the night.

Later, and forever afterward, when she thought of those days—only six, the Collector assured her, and the longest of his life, though sometimes she suspected he was lying, that it had taken him much longer—Nadine would try to remember if she'd ever actually seen the Doña. Certainly, she remembered the cats. Dozens of them, their claws clattering over the linoleum as they chased each other down the aisles. Their head-bumps and purrs whenever any of the women who worked at the market knelt or sat to stock or just sit. Their very occasional, quiet meowing at the front windows, almost always just at dawn. Sometimes, even now, Nadine believed she could perfectly recall— could sketch from memory—every single one of their faces. Their whisker-twitches. Their eyes that glowed, radiated, overflowed.

Of course she remembered the women, too. Their faces, though she couldn't recall a single one of their names. Had she ever learned their names? Had she told them hers? Had she known hers?

She wasn't sure. But the braided girl had proven right. The days themselves weren't bad. In fact—and this was the worst, the scariest thing of all—they'd rung with laughter. With broom hockey games played with margarine stick-pucks, and tiniest-bubble-blowing contests using Free-Affix, the worst-tasting gum on Earth. With murmured, sleepaway-camp conversations while they all sat with their backs against the dairy cooler, the chill like the shock of diving into a snowdrift moments after fleeing an overheated house. Purifying, somehow. The conversations about nothing: proper ingredients for fry-bread, and how accordions sound over distant gunfire; the first times they'd tasted Yoo-hoo, and the stupidity of Stetsons; their far-away moms.

Did they eat? Sleep? Where had they slept? Nadine didn't know, didn't want to. What she did remember, could not get away from, was that feeling. That sense that every single moment had been suffused with a sensation she'd forgotten she'd ever felt, and so hadn't been able to identify at the time. A specific sort of effortlessness. A restlessness so old and familiar and permanent, it felt like peace.

As though she'd been sucked all the way across the Atlantic and landed on her backside in the middle of the Burren, then hiked from there to the sea, where she'd made her way along the cliffs to Doolin. All of this in the company of her sisters. If she'd had sisters.

As though she'd wandered up the mud-riven road between the hills to the cabin of her childhood and found her mother still living, just standing there waiting for her.

He came back on a Sunday morning, was waiting on the mat when they unlocked the doors. Newspaper in one hand and a steaming Styrofoam cup in the other. When he saw Nadine, who'd been stacking Duraflame logs beside the woman with the tampon-antennae, he grinned. His grin did nothing, she thought, to hide his relief. Then thought itself erupted through her, and she dropped the logs she'd been cradling and swayed in place. Tingling. Stinging. As though every inch of her had been asleep.

"Hi," he said. "So, okay. Cactus candy? No." He raised the cup. "But pinon nut coffee? *Yes*." He took a steaming sip.

Glancing sideways, almost all the way awake, now, Nadine noted that her companion had frozen, too. Tampon-antennae quivering, as though she were trying to make sense of something. Or admit what she'd already sensed.

"He's here to help," Nadine said—forcefully, to convince herself, really, or maybe just remind herself, because he *really had left her here*—and slid an arm around the woman's waist. "He's with me."

"With you . . . " the woman murmured.

"I'd like to see the Doña, please," said the Collector.

Nadine felt her companion stiffen. Unless that was her own arm tightening. As far as she knew, she'd never heard that word spoken here. And yet she knew exactly whom he meant.

"You can't," the woman beside her said.

"Don't," said Nadine. And then, "You left me here."

"She's not back there," said her companion. "She's—"

"Back there?" said the Collector, gesturing down the soup aisle toward the stockroom. "Right." And he looked at Nadine. And winked. Stupidly. And right then, Nadine saw it all. What leaving her had cost him. How scared he'd been of what he'd find when he came back.

How scared he still was.

Down the aisle he went. Nadine followed. Her first impulse was to stop him, pull him back, but she couldn't make herself run, and so couldn't quite catch him. Cats foamed and fled before him like a wake. He was still several feet from the metal stockroom doors, had just pulled the snub-nosed revolver from his pocket, when the doors swung open and the Doña appeared.

He didn't stop moving. Nadine would always remember that. She saw the impact hit him, his knees half-buckling and his back twitching while cats scattered and Nadine herself flinched as she fought her feet to a standstill. Stayed where she was.

The Doña stood in a halo of her own light. Or maybe that was her hair, a shale-and-white cascade that tumbled all the way to her waist. Her tawny skin seemed to glow, too. Lion's skin, under lion's mane.

The Collector stopped, lowered gun in one hand, pinon nut coffee in the other.

"Don't," she heard herself whisper, edging closer. "Oh, please."

To her surprise, the Doña spoke first. It took a long time. Mostly, the Collector just stood, or took nervous sips of his coffee. He never once turned around.

"Safe's in the back," the Doña told him, eyes black, shoulders high. Smile blinding-bright.

"You have something of mine," said the Collector, and for a second, as he bent, Nadine thought he was going to kneel. Kiss the Doña's hand. She thought that might be a good idea. Instead, he placed the coffee cup at his feet and straightened. "Someone."

Now, the Doña laughed outright. Somehow, she seemed to coil and straighten at the same time, so that she loomed over the Collector like a bobcat in a tree. "If she's here, she's not yours. Otherwise, it wouldn't work."

For the second time, the Collector's shoulders twitched. But again, he held his ground. Lifted the gun, though not to point it. "This either, I suppose."

"Oh, that will work. On me. It won't do what *you* want, though."

"Thought not," the Collector muttered. He laid the gun atop a stack of Cream of Mushroom cans.

For a time—though Nadine would never know how long, time being lost to her, then—the two of them just eyed each other. The Doña, the Collector. Like cats. The Doña's smile, when it came, wasn't completely without pity.

"You men. You grasping, stupid, lonely men." She turned back toward the stockroom.

"Tell me how it works," the Collector said.

Pleaded? Was he pleading?

The Doña turned back, no longer smiling. "Sure," she said.

And told him. Not about herself, but her girls: the braided one, whose sister, cousin, *and* mother had had their lives ended for them in the alleyways of Ciudad Juarez, the cousin and mother on the same night, in different alleys; the checkout-stand woman, who'd left the University of New Mexico to nurse the sick uncle who'd molested her as a child into his grave, and then stopped here for a string cheese on her way back to Albuquerque; the tampon girl, who'd literally walked off the reservation, because no one would drive her, with no destination in mind except elsewhere; the junkie hooker from El Paso who'd somehow cold-turkeyed herself one summer night—though not in time to save her hearing or one of her kidneys—and spent her off-shift hours humming to herself in the bakery aisle.

Others. So many others.

"But it's not *all* women," the Collector said, when the Doña finally stopped. "It doesn't work on all women."

"No, indeed," said the Doña. "On very few women, actually. They have to be worth saving. They have to *deserve* the home I've given them."

"And be far from their old one."

"That's right," said the Doña. Clearly surprised.

The Collector's voice came out sadder than Nadine had ever heard it. "With no way back."

"Right again. Oh, you are a rare one."

"And whole worlds inside them."

The Doña positively swelled, throwing her arms wide and gazing around at where her employees had gathered by the dairy cases, in the produce aisle. All of them watching. Cats crouched under nearby shelving or hunched, submissive, at her feet. "That, most of all."

The Collector started to say something else, but she cut him off. Couldn't help herself now.

"That's why I am here. That's why I came."

"To trap. To imprison."

In mid-gesture, the Doña froze. Swayed. Her smile dissolved. "And here, I thought you understood."

"I'm hoping you do," said the Collector. "I'm here to help."

Now, finally, the Doña laughed. "Help. You. Scarecrow man. You already know better, I think. What help can you give, in comparison to mine?"

"I can help you let them go."

"But . . . that's the beauty of it. Don't you see? That's what makes it so powerful. So unbreakable. You *do* see, don't you? It's not me. It's nothing I've done. I simply . . . created the opportunity. That's the real secret. These women. All these beautiful, marvelous women. They *want to stay*." And with that, she raised her arms again, like a faith healer. Like an angel. Transcendent. Triumphant. Shining. "They *want* to."

"Unbreakable, you said?"

The Doña looked too ecstatic to answer.

"It can never be broken, you said."

"Not by me. Certainly not by you."

"That's what I thought."

And there it was again, Nadine realized with a shudder. That undertone of regret. He glanced at her, half-smiled, turned back to the Doña. "That's why I decided to call your brothers."

Silence flooded the market, and the world outside, too. As though whatever was coming had already happened. Its impact pre-determined, just not yet felt. The seconds between lightning and thunder.

"You did what?" the Doña finally answered. Arms still outstretched.

"I'm so sorry," said the Collector. "I know you meant well. They're on their way."

"But . . . how could you . . . how did you even learn who . . . "

"You should go now. You really don't have long."

The Doña lowered her arms. While from every side, the cats—*all* of them, dozens—crawled from their hiding places, edging nearer. Bumping each other. *Meowing* their confusion. If that's what it was.

Raising trembling fingers to her lips, the Doña stared at the Collector. While everything in Nadine screamed, *Run*.

But all the Doña said was, "Why? Why would you do that?" Then she dropped into a crouch, snapping her fingers at the cats, waving her employees close. "Come. All of you. We have to hide you. Keep you safe."

And that, of all things, triggered the worst. The moment when the Collector turned sidelong, and Nadine got a clear look at his face. And knew that whatever he'd planned wasn't working.

Brows knitted, long fingers curled uselessly around the coffee cup, the Collector shook his head. Then, abruptly, he turned again to the Doña and said, "Wait."

"We cannot wait, thanks to you." She was gathering cats, pushing them through the swinging door into the stockroom, waving her employees closer, her whole frame a whirl of motion.

"If they want to stay . . . why the spell?"

Once more, the Doña stopped. Turned. Looked up, from her knees. Nadine felt herself leaning forward.

"If you're right," the Collector said, "and the women want to stay . . . what do you need the magic for?"

For a long moment, the Doña just crouched, as though considering. Or preparing to spring. Then she shrugged. "I didn't invent it," she said. In the blackness of her pupils, like fireflies in a cave, was a wildness Nadine had never seen in another living thing. But the voice was a controlled, low purr. "All I did was set it loose. To save them from the world. From themselves. From what they've been taught they want. And so your calling my brothers won't work, either. See? There is *not one thing* you can do. Except perhaps get us all killed."

The Collector's shoulders sagged, and he glanced at Nadine again. The words were out of her mouth before she even realized what she was saying.

"That's why *I* called them."

For the first time—lightning-fast, like a nictitating lid flicking shut and open—the Doña blinked. Then she stood. "What?"

"That was our plan all along. Tell her, Hon."

But the Collector had gone blank. Looked as baffled as the Doña. Nadine plunged ahead anyway.

"My getting in here. Pretending to be trapped in the market, so we could make sure it was really you behind it all. Right?"

Now, the Collector nodded, repeatedly, while the Doña stared. "Exactly right. Yep. Worked like a charm, too. We had to make sure you were who we thought. Make sure we were earning the Cartel's money, because one wants to be sure to *earn* the Cartel's money, after all."

"*Callar*," the Doña whispered, wild eyes locking on Nadine's, which set her shaking. "*Puta.* What have you done?"

Somehow, Nadine held still. "Just one mama lion ridding herself of another."

"*Callar*," the Doña shrieked. "Shut your whoring mouth. *Puta perra. Esclavo. Diablo.*" She had her arms out again, and stepped forward while cats squealed under her feet.

How soon did the Doña realize what she'd done? Nadine knew only what had happened—to all of them—the moment she started shouting. Got angry. It really did feel like a leash snapping loose. A hand at her neck, letting go. Her throat falling open. The outside world—the vast, empty, ordinary world—rushing in.

The Doña had whirled for the stockroom, spitting and screaming in her rage. "Them, first," she was shouting toward her girls. "We'll deal with these two first. Come on, *niñas*." She vanished through the doors, and the Collector turned, brow sweating, eyes blinking furiously, as though trying to twitch away sunspots.

"You're quite brilliant," he said. Then he was talking to all the women around him. "Don't be scared. Don't think. Don't worry about the boundary. It's gone. Just run."

There should have been hesitation. They knew, even if the Collector didn't, about the cats. Had known all along, Nadine realized now, but had somehow set the knowledge aside during their time with the Doña. Or been lured away from it, back into the dreaming present.

But every woman there had experienced exactly what Nadine had, moments ago. Felt their old lives engulf them. And now every single one of them dropped whatever they had in their hands and ran.

Nadine would remember only fragments of those next, hurtling moments. The doors sliding open. The blast of frigid air against her face, seemingly shoving her back. Her screaming for the braided girl, the only one near her in the lot, to come with her, to jump in the Jeep. That single moment, crossing the threshold onto the freeway, when she grabbed the dashboard with both hands and closed her eyes and held tight. Until they were out of the lot, their wheels grinding on the open road.

And that last moment. The sound, or collection of sounds, behind her. Audible, utterly clear somehow over the wheels and the engine and the whistling in the wind.

The cats. Reaching the curb at the edge of the lot. Leaping into the air to cross it. Screaming as they froze, started to crack . . .

"See, it was mostly protective," the Collector told her, days later, in the Las Cruces hotel room where they'd holed up since leaving the braided girl at the pedestrian checkpoint over the Rio Grande and fleeing west out of El Paso.

He poured her yet another cup of pinon nut coffee. Had already told her he was going to keep making her drink it until she agreed that it was good.

"Protective." She was still hunched in blankets she could not seem to leave, She'd long since decided she *did* like the coffee, but she wasn't going to tell him that, yet. "But . . . how did you even know she was there? *We* didn't see her until that night. At least, I don't remember . . . "

"I didn't know," the Collector said, hunching forward.

He made like he might touch her, and she shrank back. Apparently, she was still angry about his leaving her, though she knew she shouldn't be. Probably shouldn't be.

"Nadine, all I knew was what I saw in those girls. And then in you. And I knew that whatever had hold of you, it was powerful. Not something I could break by just carrying you out of there. It had to be powerful, to stop you. To stop *those* women."

"But . . . " Nadine stared over the rim of her cup. A new round of shivering rippled up her spine, and yet, somehow, she held the cup straight, the coffee un-spilt. "How did you get onto her?"

The Collector shrugged. "That wasn't hard. Everyone in the area knew she was there. Given who she turned out to be—who her family was—that's hardly surprising, is it? The hard part was coming to the realization that she really did believe exactly what she told us. She really was out to save you all, from everything and everyone. From families like hers. That's what was so hard to grasp. That particular magic . . . it only works when cast in kindness. Her kind of kindness. That was the piece I needed. That's why it broke. When you broke it."

"There was nothing kind about what she did to the cats."

"Ah, but see," and the Collector hunched forward more, his enthusiasm for discovery manifesting itself even now, "she didn't actually *do* that. At least, *she* wouldn't say so. All she did was create the boundary. A safe haven, in a world almost utterly devoid of them. If any of her guests—*daughters,* really— were fool enough to try and leave the place she'd created for them . . . leave Heaven . . . " He shrugged.

"So why didn't they . . . " Nadine shook her head, put the coffee down on the night table as her wrists, then her arms started shaking once more. "Why couldn't they just turn back into whoever they'd been? Why did that have to happen to them? Once the boundary was broken?"

The Collector watched until she settled. "I don't know. I didn't know that would happen. I didn't even know what the cats were, or *who* they were, until you told me. Maybe, when they tried to escape before you and I arrived, and got transformed . . . maybe, at that moment, they really became *hers.* Maybe they could never go back, after that."

"Creatures of Heaven," Nadine said, tears forming yet again. "Members of the Pride."

But the Collector gazed at her so long, so quietly, that the tears never came. "Maybe. Yeah. Creatures of Heaven."

Nadine leaned forward, was about to grab him and kiss him, when he said, "Unless."

She sat back. "Unless?"

"Unless the transformation spell—the cat spell—was different magic entirely. Something the Doña created to protect *herself,* from what *she* feared most."

"*Cats?*"

"The women those cats had been. Women who'd tasted all she had to offer—home, Heaven, call it what you will—and decided to leave anyway."

Nadine thought of Ireland, then. Of the little houses they'd passed on the reservation, their leaning walls and flaking roofs. The junked cars in the snow. There really was a difference, she thought, between accretion and collecting. The one simply an accumulation of detritus from the life you'd lived. The other a collage of bits scavenged from other lives and hung on your wall like a mirror. One accidental, the other willed. The home you were born into, and the one you made. Which was the truer?

Then she thought of the Doña's home. The one *she'd* been born into. The family she'd escaped.

"Tell me one thing," she whispered. "You didn't really call them, did you? You didn't really get in touch with the Cartel. With her brothers. You wouldn't."

And the Collector let go of her hands. Looked down at the bed, over her shoulder at the window. "You keep being wrong about that, Nadine," he said.

Nadine stared. "Can you go away for a while, now?"

"Okay," he said. And stayed right where he was. And took her hand again, and held onto it, until she held him back.

Glen Hirshberg's novels include *The Snowman's Children* (2002), *The Book of Bunk,* 2010), and *Motherless Child* (2012), which has just been republished in a new, revised edition by Tor. He is also the author of three story collections: *The Two Sams* (a *Publishers' Weekly* Best Book of 2003), *American Morons* (2006), and *The Janus Tree* (2011). In 2008, he won the Shirley Jackson Award for novelette, "The Janus Tree." He is also a three-time winner of the International Horror Guild Award, and a five-time World Fantasy Award finalist. With Peter Atkins and Dennis Etchison, he cofounded the Rolling Darkness Revue, an annual reading/live music/performance event that tours the west coast every fall and has also made international appearances. He lives in the Los Angeles area with his wife, son, daughter, and cats.

Inside, illuminated by candles, crowded a multitude of statues:
Our Lady of Ruins, repeated over and over . . .

OUR LADY OF RUINS

Sarah Singleton

A winter forest: dark stripes of trees against the snow, and the girl's red coat. He followed her, away from the glistening road and inert car. She moved through the black and white, folding herself into the trees.

He was two hours' drive from the city. The car had died in the narrow corridor of road. No phone signal, no passing traffic. He lifted the bonnet and stared, perplexed, at the engine, its incomprehensible hieroglyphs of steel.

To north and south, he saw twin vanishing points, neatly ruled: road, snow, trees, sky.

Then he saw her, impossible, mythological—a running girl.

"Hey!" he called out. "Hey! I need help!"

The forest swallowed his words. The girl didn't hear him, didn't stop. He looked again at the car and stepped away from the road.

He found her footprints in the snow. The road disappeared behind him. Silence—except for the crunch beneath his boots. Prepared for the cold he wore a hat and black sheepskin mittens. His mobile lay in his zipped up pocket, a protective charm proved useless.

The trail wound to left and right, sometimes circled a tree, backtracked and looped, as though to tease. He'd lost sight of the girl, wondered about wolves and bears, and when the snow grew deeper, sweated. The light would fade in another hour. What then?

He heard a clink, observed a stab of color.

He stopped and looked up, shading his eyes to see. A dense net of twig and branch, ink-black, drawn against the sky and a blot, a knot of color—scarlet, blue—turning on the air.

He stretched out his hand and grabbed. The branch bent and rebound, like a bow, spraying him with snow. He shook his head, wiped his face and stared at the object in his hand.

A round, white face: bead eyes, stitched mouth and nose. A dress of rags, cunning strips of cloth, a tiny bell hanging from wooden feet. He rolled it from side to side, observing sequins, fragments of glass, silver embroidery, a stuffed pouch made for a body. As his fingers probed, the doll lay like a dead bird in his hand, lolling and gaudy.

He'd broken the string from which the doll depended so he propped it in a cleft of the same tree and walked on. The footprints veered east. He followed.

Another doll, then a few paces, three more on one tree. He felt them watch, bead eyes turning in his direction. Then dark pines gave way to silver birches with peeled-paper trunks. He saw the girl again, vivid, only yards away. The birches melted on the air to make a clearing in the forest, a lake of sunlight— and a church with a high turret.

The church floated above the snow.

He blinked, struggling to make sense of it: a wooden church with a steep shingled roof, narrow stained-glass windows, the tilted cone of a spire jostling with statues and gargoyles. A church with six huge wooden wheels to carry it through the forest.

"What's your name?" The girl in red was standing in front of him, a hood pulled over her head. She was about fourteen, with dark hair, tawny skin, and a slight squint.

"Rider," he said. "Dan Rider."

"What are you doing here, Rider?"

"My car broke down."

"You followed me."

"Yes. I need help—a phone. Someone who can fix cars. Or give me a lift." He gestured vaguely at the forest, the way he'd come.

The girl didn't respond. She narrowed her eyes.

"The church," Rider said. "Does it actually move?"

"Of course." Her voice was deadpan. "You want to go inside?" She didn't wait for an answer but turned away holding out an arm to guide him.

As they drew closer, he saw an encampment of caravans beyond the church, horses tethered and browsing on hay, the twining smoke of a dozen small fires where several anonymous figures huddled.

They climbed a flight of wooden steps at the front of the church to an arched door. Above it, in a tall niche, stood a statue of the Virgin Mary made of dark, polished wood. Her gaze was raised, her hands pressed together in prayer.

"Come in," the girl urged.

Rider glanced back, aware of time passing, the imminent approach of night.

"I need to—I have to . . . "

"Come on." The girl was impatient, imperious. Rider's words died. He followed.

They entered a wooden box with an uneven floor. Light leaked through stained glass windows—three narrow slots on each side and one elaborate circle above the altar. The walls were not quite true, creating a sense of vertiginous hallucination. The church seemed to totter. Rider's brain struggled to make sense of it, the out-of-true walls, the shadows punctuated by candles burning in lanterns. He grabbed the back of a pew.

The girl seemed immune. She walked up the aisle, pushing her hood back, and stood before another statue, beside the altar.

"The church is dedicated to the Virgin," she announced, the tour guide. "Our Lady of Ruins."

Rider, grasping each pew ended as he proceeded, stared up at the statue. Of painted wood, taller than he was, Our Lady of Ruins wore silver armor and a sky-blue cloak. Her right arm, stretched out to her side, held a sword, and on her left a shield painted with white lilies. A snake languished beneath bare feet. Her face was pure and insane.

"So pray," the girl said. "Kneel—here."

Rider dropped to his knees, lost and perplexed. He'd never prayed in his life, didn't know how to. He stared at the Virgin, opened and closed his mouth, his mind a perfect void. Outside the sun sank behind the trees. Darkness swilled through the forest and filled the church.

Rider crouched by the fire. An ancient man, sunken-faced with feathery white hair, nodded and smiled at him beyond the flames. Rider's questions about his car and need for help made no impression. He could hear them talking, but apart from the girl in red, struggled to make out what they said. The conversations were opaque. Were they speaking another language?

The old man nodded again. They'd given him a bowl of oily rabbit stew and a slab of black bread. Something in the stew, herbs perhaps, left an acrid taste in his mouth. Red (the girl wouldn't tell him her name) had unstrung one of her many necklaces as they left the trundle church and slipped it over his head. The pendant, a carved, painted effigy of the Lady of Ruins, dangled from his chest as he hunched over his bowl.

"We make them for pilgrims," she said.

"I'm not a pilgrim," Rider answered.

Sitting at the front of the caravan, an elderly woman sewed the face of another doll.

"They represent the saints," Red said. The dolls were hung in trees as prayers and petitions to God in the forest. Saint Michael, Saint Catherine, Saint Perpetua, Saint Sara the Black, Saint Maxentia, Saint Caesaria. Rider saw the old woman stab her needle in the cloth face as she stared at him across the fire.

When he'd eaten, the travelers gathered. Some carried lanterns, others crucifixes and statues. Myrrh smoked in a silver censer. Rider stood up. Around him the travelers murmured. Above the miasma of hot breath, wood smoke and incense, he looked up to clear cold air, a circle of treetops and a bowl of stars. From far away he heard the low, wandering chorus of wolves.

"It's time." Red held out her hand.

"For what?"

She smiled, encouraging: "The church, Rider. The church."

They walked in procession and oddly Rider's unease deserted him. He accepted the situation, the strange faces, the low, untuneful hymn rising from the procession and wondered briefly if the stew had been drugged because his gums were numb, his tongue stinging.

The church door was open, the interior lit with a host of candles. The travelers watched as he climbed the steps and went inside. He looked back at the uncanny faces, the calm, well-meaning smiles, and he stepped inside. They closed the door behind him.

He stood on the threshold. A single figure stood before the altar. The statue, Our Lady of Ruins, presided over the empty space. Yellow light played over the multitude of figures painted on the walls, monsters and angels, winged and fanged.

"Thus saith the Lord: Behold, waters rise up out of the north, and shall be an overflowing flood, and shall overflow the land, and all that is therein; the city, and them that dwell therein: then the men shall cry, and all the inhabitants of the land shall howl." The man at the altar had his back to Rider but his words filled the church.

Rider took a step forward. On the walls the painted figures swam, a mass of limbs and faces, gesturing, reaching out, rolling their eyes.

"Lift up thy feet unto the perpetual ruins; *even* all *that* the enemy hath done wickedly in the sanctuary," the voice said.

"And they shall build the old wastes, they shall raise up the ruin, and they shall repair the waste cities, the desolations of many generations."

The man turned. He watched Rider approach and gestured for him to kneel.

"How long have you searched for this place?"

Rider raised his face. The priest had long white hair and aged, riven skin. The Lady of Ruins gazed over the priest's head. Her sword shone.

A ribbon of thought ran through Rider's mind: his home, the city with its glass towers, offices and housing estates, his distant wife, meaningless business, journey, the dead car by the roadside. His memories seemed thin and false. The ribbon dissolved into nothing.

"I don't know," he said, bowing his head. He hadn't been searching. This place, the church on wheels, a dream he'd fallen into—and from which he might yet wake up to resume in that other faraway place, his life.

A swelling sound filled the church—a multitude of voices, a storm wind, the choir of wolves—or perhaps just the roar of blood in his eardrums. The priest pressed Rider's forehead with his thumb and made the sign of the cross above his head. He took a silver cup from the altar and held it to Rider's lips. Rider sipped, tasting honey on his tongue, feeling dust and ash in his throat. He coughed, choking, unable to breathe, losing balance.

He tottered, his body a helpless column of flesh and bone, without its bearings. Slowly, slowly he fell to the wooden floor and then he was looking up at the dark shape of the priest. Beyond him, the hectic paintings on the walls, the snarling demons, the dancing angels, each merged into the other. Then the priest was gone. Rider lay on his back, helpless, in the giant cradle of the church. The light in the church intensified, blinding, bleaching out the paintings, burning his brain.

He opened his eyes. Daylight colored the windows. The spot on his forehead burned. Rider sat up.

A woman was standing in front of the altar, tall and lean, with a face so exact it was almost androgynous. Rider struggled to his feet.

"I've been waiting for you," she said. "For a long, long time. I was afraid you'd never come back."

Rider stared. "I don't know who you are."

"Yes, you do. You know. Everyone knows. You were looking for me, but you lost sight. You forgot you were looking." She had pale-almond skin; black, crow-feather hair. They stared at one another. Then she smiled.

"Time to go," she said.

Outside the church, the forest had disappeared. Tracks wended from the giant wooden wheels, a twisting parallel line in the dry dirt that disappeared into the distance, illustrating its journey. Now the church stood at the heart of a ruined village, on a wide, paved square blown with dust from the desert.

They walked, Rider and the woman, seeing walls like broken teeth, trees rooted in cracked stone, yellow grass spouting from a clay bowl lying on the ground. In a tiny courtyard they found an orange tree, still covered in leaves and fruit. Rider picked an orange, split it open with his fingers, and found inside a ring made of buttery gold which he slipped over his thumb.

In a small, dark house a book lay open on a table. The words had run from the pages, covering the top of the table, the legs, the floor, and had begun to climb the wall. Rider tried to read them, but couldn't.

In a square, between half a dozen white houses, stood a well with a wooden lid, which the woman pushed back. Rider leaned over, seeing far below the glim of water. He heard voices, cries, whispered conversations in the column of air. When he stood up, the darkness inside the well seemed to have tipped out, filling the sky. A huge round moon loomed over the village. The trundle church had gone, moved on. Tracks indicated the way it had come, and the direction of its leaving.

"Where are we?" Rider asked.

"In the ruins," the woman said.

They walked from the village across the desert, finding old paved roads. Once a ghost funeral passed, and at one of the several carved stone waymarks, a multitude of rusty keys hanging on a fig tree.

At the end of the desert, they passed into ancient woodland. One evening, by a pond, a nightingale began to sing and Rider saw, over the tops of blossoming hawthorns, the tiled roof of a circular tower. He climbed the spiral staircase winding around the tower to a single door at the top. Inside, illuminated by candles, crowded a multitude of statues: Our Lady of Ruins, repeated over and over, the largest towering over him, the smallest, perched in a niche, thumb-sized.

The woodland passed from spring to smoke- and mud-scented autumn. They found a suit of armor by a smoldering fire and later, an orchard of wild apple trees beneath which lay the skeleton of a horse, caparisoned in silver.

At the wood's end, on a grassy plain, Rider saw the banners of two opposing armies, heard the cries of soldiers, blood leaking into a river. All melted on the air, but as they walked, Rider felt innumerable phantoms passing through his body.

That night, in a roofless marble temple, Rider and the woman undressed and lay, shivering, in each other's arms. For a measureless time they kissed and caressed. The shadow land melted: they contained it, marked its boundaries. Rider held her gaze when she came. His body burned.

"I do know who you are," he said. "How did I forget?"

"Because you always forget," she said.

He was cold when he woke, clothes soaked and filthy. Leaves moved above as he lay alone, body aching.

A car passed on the long straight road through the forest. Seeing it, Rider's mind seemed to collapse on itself. Memories fell over each other, shaken up, a kaleidoscope of images.

Deftly his mind knitted back to the time (how long ago?) when his car died by the roadside. The vast in-between, the trundle church, the woman, the landscape of dreams, seemed to shunt sideways into a parallel realm of dubious memory.

Rider struggled to his feet. He was still wearing the clothes of that day in the snow, and zipped into his pocket, a mobile phone, battery dead. Considerable time had passed—his hair was long, face bearded, clothes soiled. One boot had vanished.

He lurched to the road, guessing, from the weather and vegetation, it was April. Had he been gone five months? He'd have to hitchhike, though he wasn't a good prospect, a wild man covered in filth. Eventually a truck stopped, offering a lift to the city. They talked, Rider and the driver. Rider asked the date. He'd been gone not five months, but seventeen.

His wife cried and shouted when she saw him. She'd believed him dead, had grieved, moved on, and now seemed put out he was inserting himself back into her life. She asked what had happened, where he'd been. He had no plausible explanation. She followed him into the bathroom as he undressed, asked about the gold ring on his thumb, the pendant, the odd red scar in the middle of his forehead, the picture inked across the skin of his back, a woman in a blue cloak, dressed in armor and carrying a sword. When he couldn't answer, she shouted and cried again, pummeling his chest with her fists. His disappearance was unfathomable. He'd taken no money from their account, he had returned in the clothes he'd left in. The car had been recovered not long after he'd disappeared, on the forest road.

Rider shaved but didn't cut his hair. He'd aged: lines etched his face, strands of white grew in the mass of dark hair but he was thinner, stronger, lacking the soft paunch of two years before. The first night back, his wife dragged him into bed, evidently intrigued by the stranger who'd returned, the lean, muscular, tattooed man, the mystery of him. Before they slept, she pressed her hand to the side of his face and asked him again:

"Where did you go?"

"I don't know, Marion. I can't remember. The car broke down, I followed a girl in the wood to get help. And then? I don't know. My mind's blank."

"You're different," she said.

"Am I? In what way?"

"I don't know. Before you went you seemed—well, absent." She gave a short laugh. "I thought—I was afraid, when you disappeared. Depression maybe."

"You thought I'd killed myself."

"Yes. We did—the police. You didn't leave a trail—no money gone, nothing."

While she slept, Rider lay awake wondering who he was. It wasn't true, that his memory was empty. He remembered a sequence of images and emotions—the saint doll lying in his hand, the trundle church in the forest, the woman, the orange tree in a courtyard. He turned the ring on his thumb as his wife slumbered, her hand resting on his chest. Most of all he felt loss and exile.

Marion didn't have to go to work the next day, allowed leave for the unsettling reappearance of her dead husband. He heard her speak quietly to a man on the phone, in tender, familiar terms and realized she had indeed moved on. After breakfast, they drove into the city and over a coffee she explained she'd started seeing someone, but that was over now. She apologized and cried again. Rider reassured.

Beyond the café window, traffic passed on the city road before a backdrop of shops and offices—so many smooth surfaces, cut-outs pressed against a sky of cloud and rain showers. Marion was still talking. He studied her face, the short blond bob she pushed back over her ear from time to time, saw the wedding ring back on her finger.

"You're not listening to me," she said. "You've not heard a thing I've said."

"What? I'm sorry." He shrugged. "It's hard," gesturing to the window, the city scene. "Nothing seems real."

He saw hurt in her face. "I didn't mean—not you, I didn't mean you."

"Yes, you did," she said. "Yes, you bloody did. Do you know what it was like for me all that time? Not knowing where you were, what had happened, all I had to deal with?" More tears, angry this time. "I lost a year of my life too. Everything stopped. And you can't even tell me where you were!"

She tried to stand up and get away but Rider grabbed her hand. The couple sitting at the next table stared.

"Don't go," he said, voice low. "You're the only real thing. I need you, Marion. I'll be lost if you go."

She stood where she was for a moment, hand pinned to the table. She blinked.

"Okay," she said, dropping back to her seat. "Okay, I'll stay. But you've got to help me too. You've got to *be* here."

Rider resumed his life, after a fashion. He found a new, if less important job. He worked hard, managed his occasional wayward thoughts and plunging moods. Marion seemed resigned, treated him kindly. Sometimes he wondered if she still met, or merely longed for, the other man, the one who'd briefly taken Rider's place.

One feeling never left him—that his true life had stopped the moment he woke up at the side of the road, unwashed, wild-haired. Every day since he made an effort to accept and to appreciate the life he had but it was an effort, a falsehood. Marion wanted a child, and he agreed, but no pregnancy ensued. He sensed this was his failure, that he was dried up and infertile. Some nights, lying awake, he heard Marion crying in the bed beside him, in the dark. She seemed to age quickly over the following years, as though infected by his ruin. He was destroying her chance of a life. When Rider refused the tests and medical interventions, Marion left him, swiftly remarried and conceived. Rider felt only relief. He wished her well.

He lived alone, through a succession of thin gray days. He bought a motorbike and at the weekends, rode around the country, to the mountains and the coast, the long forest roads. Sometimes, sleeping outside, he'd dream of the wooden church on wheels, Our Lady of Ruins, and wake, as though drunk, desperate to hold onto the image, the tumult of emotion. Each time the memory faded within minutes, leaving him emptier, drained out, lacking substance.

Seven years. When the snow fell he rode along the forest road to find the place, as he'd done every winter since. Hard to be sure of the exact location: the road was featureless. He relied on intuition, an unreliable tool, waiting for a particular quiver of feeling, a sign in the landscape. He listened to the familiar note of the engine, longing for a breakdown. The road reeled past, the forest stripes of black and white. An image rose in his mind—Marion playing with a child in a bright warm house, a man in the background, familial comforts he'd declined.

The cold made Rider's hands and feet ache. Wind stung his face. Ruts of gray ice glistened at the edges of the road. His speed crept to ninety.

Then he saw it—a splash of blood-red.

He braked so hard the bike slewed under him, pitching on a skim of ice.

The bike skidded, on and on, Rider's leg caught underneath, helmet dragging against the rough asphalt.

At last, it came to rest in the middle of the road. For several stunned moments Rider lay there, staring up at the strip of cloud between the treetops. The engine died. He smelt petrol, and a vague metallic burning. His leg began to throb.

"You have to move," he said. His body didn't respond but the pain rose a notch.

"You have to move," he repeated. Rider pulled himself free. He stood for a moment, stupefied by shock and pain. The winter trees seemed to tilt. He squeezed his eyes shut, gathering strength, and hobbled to the side of the road.

Rider tugged off the helmet and dropped it in the snow. Blood leaked from his knee through torn leathers but, ignoring the pain, he scanned the tree-line. Where? How far back? He lurched along the road, like a monster, like Caliban, desperate for another glimpse.

Nothing. He almost wept with frustration.

"Where are you?" he yelled. The snowy forest soaked up his voice. He shouted again, choice words. Trees absorbed the sound. Nothing moved. Rider limped away from the road. A trail of blood, chthonic, marked the virgin snow—a perilous choice, to leave the road in the dead of winter, with an injury. He ignored his mind's sensible advice and proceeded. What did he have to lose?

His lame leg dragged a rut through the snow. He sweated, though his hands were numb. His thoughts, like thin ice, seemed to break up and drift away. The forest filled him, the black and white of it, the spaces of sky between trees. Then he saw them: splashes of color, saint dolls suspended from branches. He cried out and sank to his knees, oblivious to pain. Above his head the dolls turned on strings embroidered to their heads.

Saint Michael, Saint Catherine, Saint Perpetua, Saint Sara the Black, Saint Maxentia, Saint Caesaria.

Rider recited their names from memory, repeated them like a rosary. Sunlight flashed into his eyes. He felt himself falling, finally losing grip. The ground seemed to rise up, banging against his back, his head.

When he opened his eyes the light had changed and he was moving. Nothing made sense at first: he was still on his back, in the snow, and sliding through the trees. He tried to shift his position, but could not. He was tied and someone was pulling him on a low sled. Late, golden sunshine flooded through the trees.

"Hey, hello." He tried to speak but his voice was hoarse. He tasted stale blood. He raised his head as far as he could to see a red cloak, the back of a figure pulling him through the forest. His heart soared; he felt a surge of emotion so powerful he couldn't breathe. His head dropped back. His body shook.

Time blurred. When they stopped, night had blacked in the gaps between the trees. A small wooden house stood close by, a lantern burning on the porch. A statue perched on a lintel by the door. The yolky light painted the angles of its female face, robe and outstretched arms. The red-cloaked figure dropped the rope and turned to Rider. Beneath the hood he saw an old woman's face, shadowed, deeply lined, with hooded eyes. She loosened the straps binding him to the sled and helped him to his feet. Her age belied her strength.

As they crossed the threshold into the cabin, Rider glanced at the statue.

"Our Lady of Ruins," he said. The old woman raised her head. She didn't smile, precisely: some other more inscrutable expression.

She tended his leg, and he slept. She fed him some kind of spiced, meaty gruel. Day and night passed through the tiny window above the bed. He smelled wood smoke, the blood and meat of animals, herbs, burnt apples.

The cabin had one room, a large fireplace along one side, a table with two wooden chairs where the old woman sat sewing dolls, amid shreds of fabric and glittering scraps. Icons covered the walls—too many to count—pieces of wood painted with the depictions of saints, angels and demons, the face of the Virgin. On shelves he saw fragments of statues—marble, granite, painted wood -hands and broken feet, half heads, pieces of wings. Amid these ruins he saw parts of plastic dolls, some sanctified by halos of wire, wings made of birds' feathers.

The old woman didn't speak but in the long winter evenings, sewing or painting, she hummed to herself. At night, dreams like long golden ribbons unraveled in Rider's mind. He tried to catch hold of them, to follow, but failed.

After three days Rider sat up in bed. Cloth bandages wrapped his frost-bitten fingers. The old woman was out, the fire low.

He struggled to his feet and stood up, weak and swaying. He crept, hunched like an ancient, across the room to the door and looked out at the forest. Above the treetops he saw the peaks of mountains.

When the old woman returned, he had revived the fire and was sitting beside it on one of the two chairs. She nodded and smiled to see him up and began preparing a meal—a broth of meat and roots. After they'd eaten the old woman said: "I've been waiting for you," she said. "For a long time. I was afraid you'd never come back."

"I searched for seven years," he said. "The church on wheels, the other people."

The old woman picked up one of her dolls. She squeezed its cloth body. "They're stuffed with ashes, did you know that?" She gave a tiny smile. "Little pouches of ash."

"Can I go back?" Rider said. "To the church, to the other place?"

The old woman shook her head. "I don't know."

"So what are you doing here?"

"Waiting."

"You left it all behind?"

"All?" she said. "The *other*, other place? The world? The nothing."

"Ruins," Rider said.

"Yes. Ruins."

They lapsed into silence. The fire crackled. Beyond the window, snow fell, blown flakes swirling in lantern light.

"So you wait," Rider said. "Maybe you'll wait in vain."

"Maybe," she said. "So what? There's nothing else—only waiting. I pass the time, walking in the forest—making dolls, the pictures."

Rider's thoughts flew briefly to the road, the motorbike, to Marion. Might he have waited with her, after all? Would time with Marion have offered more pleasing distractions? The idea lasted only a moment. The other world had gone. Here, at least, he would wait on the threshold of his dream, with someone who knew what he'd seen.

When the fire had burned down they went to bed, lying side by side. The old woman gently took his bandaged hand in hers and touched the gold ring on his thumb.

"Tell me what you remember," she said. "What did you see?"

"Hundreds of keys hanging on a fig tree," he said.

She squeezed his hand, not hard enough to hurt, but tears filled his eyes and one leaked, burning, on his face.

"I remember," she said.

The scene rose up in Rider's mind, a memory so bright and charged his heart seemed to swell and shine beyond the narrow confines of his body. He shook with pleasure. The tears ran over his cheeks.

"I could paint it," he said, like a boy. "A picture."

Rider felt her tremble, the brush of her long, old-woman's hair on his shoulder. He touched her forehead, where he'd seen the old red scar.

The wind moaned in the cabin's crevices. He stared into the glittering dark.

Sarah Singleton is an award-winning writer of fiction for adults and teenagers. Her first novel, *The Crow Maiden,* was a finalist for the IAFA William L. Crawford Fantasy Award and her eight novels for young adults, published by Simon & Schuster, include *Century,* which won the Booktrust Teen Award 2005, the premier award for YA fiction in the UK. Her short stories have been published in magazines and anthologies including *Interzone, Black Static, Time Pieces, and Spectrum* SF. She was a journalist for many years and now works as a teacher of English literature and language at a secondary school in Wiltshire, England—county of ancient forests, chalk downlands, standing stones, long barrows and white horses.

They inhabit all the absences, the voids unfilled . . .

THE MARGINALS

Steve Duffy

They picked up Howard from the bus stop in town, early in the morning of his first day.

"Bit of a change for you, then, off to work with the rest of 'em?" said the driver, a thickset shaven-headed man in his fifties. His voice was incongruously mild and affable; it took Howard a while to process the statement and decide that it wasn't any sort of dig.

"I've been doing bits and bobs," he said, with the air of injured defensiveness that had become more or less habitual since he'd left college and signed on the dole.

"Not like this you haven't," said the man in the back seat.

Howard caught a glimpse of him in the rear-view mirror, and decided to address himself to the driver.

"I suppose you've done this for a while, then," he said.

"Ooh, a good while now," agreed the driver. "I'm Dave. That's Barry in the back, he's leaving us, aren't you, Barry?"

"Too right," Barry said flatly. "Is that a Wetherspoons? You can drop me here."

Dave seemed surprised. "You off, then? Aren't you going to give me-laddo the talk or anything?"

"Talk?" Barry was halfway out of the back door before the car had come to a full halt. He had to stoop to Howard's wound-down window to reply. "What 'talk' is that, then? You mean tell him about the job, what he's signed up for? Tell him what goes on, like? Where's the point in that? You tell him now, he'd laugh in your face. Even when he's done it, he won't understand it. Look at me. I've done it the best part of six months and I still don't understand fuck all, I don't. I can tell him that if you'd like." He thrust his head into the passenger window, causing Howard to recoil slightly. "Get that, did you, mate? Fuck, all. There you go, consider yourself up to speed."

"Righto," Dave said to the sound of Barry's door slamming shut behind him. "Phew. Well, so much for Barry. He's moving on, like I say." He considered a while, while around him the high street traffic honked and swerved. "I think the best thing to do's just to take you there and show you the ropes meself, so to speak. There's some of them little Scotch eggs in the glove compartment, help yourself."

They drove on in silence, more or less, till the business parks and industrial estates gave way to the wide flat fields of the Cheshire plain. The day was sunny, mild for March, and with Dave's window rolled down the car was filled with the sweet loamy smell of fertilized farmland. After a while, Howard caught the first whiff of what lay up ahead.

"You getting that, are you?" Dave must have seen his nose wrinkle. "It's alright, you get used to it after a while. I don't hardly notice it at all, now, me." Chuckling, he rolled the window up.

At the junction with the motorway, Dave took an unmarked turn off the roundabout that led to a five-bar gate, beyond which lay a farm lane that ran parallel with the motorway.

"Do us a favor," Dave said, unhooking a big bunch of keys from his belt. "It's that one there, look, the Chubb with the bit of blue tape on it."

Howard undid the padlock and opened the gate. Closing it behind him he felt an odd little shiver run up the back of his neck.

On their right was the raised bank of the motorway; away to their left ran an evil-looking stream, a tidewater branch of the Dee estuary, and beyond it the refinery. The track, fringed with wasted hedgerow, led them through scrubby uncultivated fields that had all but reverted to marshland. The stink of the refinery was getting stronger and stronger.

A couple of miles down the track, Howard was beginning to appreciate the weird isolation of the place. The cars and lorries up on the motorway were, to all intents and purposes, as far removed from them as the airplanes scratching contrails across the bright spring sky. Across the mudflats and the stream, the refinery, an abstract of metal piping and brick chimney, looked so unfamiliar as to be almost alien, the space-age architecture of a moon base. Howard had heard the place was largely automated; more than anything it looked abandoned, a relic of the industrial age left behind to perplex some band of post-apocalyptic refugees. Not for the first time, he wondered whether he'd done the right thing in answering the advertisement in the newsagent's window.

"This is us, then," Dave said, indicating ahead.

With a sinking feeling, Howard saw what lay at the end of the dirt track. "What, the caravan?"

"Home away from home." Dave braked to a halt on a wide waste patch in front of the static caravan. When he turned the engine off, the silence took Howard almost by surprise. For a few seconds, the two men sat in the front seats and said nothing. Then Dave nudged Howard and said, "Okey-doke, let's get you started."

The keychain came into play once more. "It's a Chubb again, see, but the black tape this time," Dave explained, popping the padlock that secured the caravan door. "Upsy-daisy, there we go. Door shuts like so—" and he shot home the bolt on the inside. "Now, let's have the fire on, shall we? Gets a bit damp in here otherwise, bit parky."

While Dave lit the propane heater, Howard took stock of his new workplace. There was a sort of counter or low shelf made of plywood, running around two sides of the caravan; there was a fold-out bunk bed; there were a couple of office chairs, one from the typing pool, one from middle management, both having seen better days. There was a gray metal filing cabinet, and on top of it a large industrial clamp lamp with a reel of extension cable.

"I left the generator running," Dave was saying, "you can turn that off if the noise gets on your nerves, but you want to make sure it's on again well before it gets dark, 'cos that's your only electricity, see?" He reached up, tapped the twin fluorescent tubes above his head. "Gonna need your light there, later on."

"You'll be back before it gets dark, though, won't you?"

"Oh, I should think so," Dave said, not wholly reassuringly. "Right, well, let me see. Talk you through it. Blimey. Okay, well, here goes, then—"

Watching Dave's aging Volvo out of sight across the flats, Howard found himself prey to a mixture of emotions. There was tedium, or more accurately the anticipation of tedium, which to be fair had been predictable from the get-go. There was the nagging conviction that here was a waste of a third-rate degree in media studies, and by extension the life it had been expected to transform. Over and above these things, though, he hadn't expected to feel quite so lonely; nor, all things considered, quite so apprehensive. Not knowing why he felt these things didn't really help—quite the opposite, in fact.

The Volvo's receding engine merged into the ambient din of the distant motorway, and Howard suddenly felt absurdly isolated, standing in front of the caravan. He looked to the north, towards the refinery where thick white smoke belched incessantly from the chimneys. Howard guessed—wrongly, it turned out—that he would, as Dave had suggested, get used to the smell. Away to the east, the polder stretched flat and unlovely for five miles or so, till the land rose to the big power plant at Rocksavage. To the south lay the motorway, of course, and beyond it the hills of Helsby and Frodsham. Feeling at once hemmed-in and exposed, Howard cast a wistful glance west towards the trees, in which direction Dave's Volvo had disappeared.

Within these boundaries of his space lay little enough to capture Howard's attention. Over by the raised carriageway of the M56 there was a large articulated trailer, detached from its cab, parked at an angle to the eastbound traffic. Howard knew from frequent journeys on the motorway that on the far side of the trailer was painted the slogan CAR BOOT SALES EVERY SUN A.M. JUNCT 12. On the side now visible to him, the side hidden from the traffic, he could see nothing . . . except, as he squinted into the low March sunlight, a couple of men in business suits standing in its shade. Howard guessed they were shaking hands on some new advertising for the side of the trailer: PAY DAY LOANS, perhaps, or WE BUY BROKEN GOLD. He'd been looking at them for a few minutes, drawn to this only sign of activity in all that dead space, before he remembered Dave's instructions. Dutifully he climbed the steps into the caravan, settled himself in the better-upholstered of the two office chairs, and pulled down the big loose-leaf ledger from its shelf.

"09.23," he wrote in the first ruled column, just as Dave had shown him, and in the next: "2 men." In the wider space to the right he wrote: "Standing by trailer near motorway—" He paused before adding a period. Really, what else could he say?

His entry lay at the top of a new page. Before leaving, Dave had extracted the preceding few sheets, stuffed them in a manila folder and taken them away with him. On a whim, he leafed back to a tabbed divider with DECEMBER written in underlined capitals. The first entry was "2 / nr. tralor" followed by "3 / same", then "2 again" over a time period ranging from half-past seven in the morning to just gone nine.

Howard swiveled in his chair and peered through the back window. There they were, the same two men, barely visible in the shadow. Regular visitors, clearly. But why?

On the shelf above where the big ledger was kept was a smaller ring-binder. "Have a look in there later on, if you like," Dave had told him. "Might come in handy to show you the lie of the land, like."

Howard, feeling disorientated less than ten minutes into his new job, pulled it down and opened it.

The contents seemed to be in no particular order. Some entries were handwritten, some word-processed; each page seemed to be an entry separate in itself. The first began didactically, in spaced caps:

LEARN TO RECOGNIZE THEM

You WILL have come across them, even if you didn't realize it at the time.

In the motorway services, for example, at off-peak hours of the daytime, or through the lonely stretches of the night. In the cafeterias, the Happy Chefs and Costa Coffees. They're drawn inescapably to places like these: the margins, the places in between. They can pass for businessmen, commercial travelers, middle management, representatives. Cups of tea grow cold on the table in front of them as they sit, hands folded, apart from everyone. Other customers come and go while they remain—if you stayed long enough, you would notice it, you'd have to.

You will never see them arriving, nor will you see them leave. Their eyes will never meet your own.

Another example:

Next time you buy a daily paper from one of those city newsstands, take special notice of the vendor. Try to fix his face, so that you can describe it later—you won't be able to, but make the effort anyway. Pay attention, too, to the paper he sells you— read it carefully when you get a chance, compare it to another copy of the same edition. Somewhere in its pages there will usually be a clue.

They seem at home in cities, as much as they seem at home anywhere. Check out the pavement crowd beneath the would-be jumper on his high ledge. Not all of them are the conventionally anxious or the drearily morbid.

Once you learn to recognize them, try this exercise: look very closely at the people around you in the Underground carriage or the bus. The law of averages is adamant on this point.

• • •

Howard looked up from the ring-binder, feeling more confused than ever. Over by the trailer there were now four men in suits.

On the shelves inside the caravan was a pair of not very good binoculars. Howard spent most of the rest of that morning peering through them, trying to get a better look at the men standing by the trailer. In their ones and twos they came and went, though never while Howard was looking, it seemed. He'd developed a kind of anxiety compulsion about checking both windows, front and rear: there was something going on, he felt sure, along the course of the stream, but the banks were just too high for him to be able to make it out. Perhaps it was nothing more than a black post, uncovered by the tide. A black post, that's all. But every time he turned away, satisfied or otherwise, from the tidewater creek, it seemed that through the other window there were one or two more of the men, or one or two fewer, over by the trailer.

Where they came from, why they gathered there, what they were doing . . . Howard could work none of it out. The notion they were coming out of (or going back into) the trailer had occurred to him as the most likely explanation for the first part of it, and he spent several hours trying to catch them in the act. By lunchtime he was only half convinced this might really be the explanation. But even if so, what did it actually explain?

He set it all down in the ledger, as best he could. As the day wore on into its slow dragging afternoon, and the shadows began to lengthen across the waste land, he pulled down the small ring-binder once more, flipped through it in a search for answers he half-knew would never really come to anything:

A PARADOX

They inhabit all the absences, the voids unfilled. You would not necessarily expect to see them in churches, but this may be subject to change. Hospitals have always been a favorite place; waiting rooms and reception areas, at all hours. And of course the ocean: the oldest jumping-off point of them all.

Visit any out-of-season seaside town and stand on the promenade. Look out across the tidal flats, the people who go walking there, mid-mornings, mid-afternoons. Disregard the dog-walkers, the fishermen digging for lugworm, the retired couples with their happy little camper vans. Concentrate on the others—the ones who don't fit in. Ask yourself this:

If you were to walk out across the damply rippled sand to the dishwater ebb of the surf—out into the liminal zone—and then look back towards the land, would you see more or less what they see? The shift in perspective, the sudden remoteness that colors all things; imagine it. This is all they know now, anywhere. Imagine how it feels, day in, day out, to patrol these hopeless frontiers; think of the isolation, unyielding, all-encompassing.

Of course, this will be easier for you to understand, the longer you stay on the job.

"Yeah, thanks for that," said Howard aloud. His voice sounded odd in the cramped space inside the caravan; somehow not like his own. For the first time, he wondered how he himself, a small man in a caravan, might appear to a traveler on the motorway glancing out of the car window. That traveler would probably not see anybody over by the trailer—its bulk, its shadow, the angle of its parking; all would serve to render its occupants invisible from the road. All they would see was a man at the window of the caravan, binoculars clamped to his face, the loneliest figure in that lonely landscape.

Without Howard noticing, the propane heater had run out of fuel. Obviously, he told himself, that was why he was shivering. The replacement cylinders, according to Dave, were in the exterior storage locker. He'd have to go outside to fetch one.

Standing in the open doorway, he peered towards the trailer; for the time being, there was nothing to be seen. After a minute's hesitation, Howard stepped down, moved quickly around to the front, fumbled the locker open, and hauled out the spare cylinder. As he started back towards the door, something—a dark shape, a blur on the periphery—moved quickly out of sight around the further corner of the caravan. Sheer fright made Howard drop the cylinder; it caught his toe painfully, and by the time he'd limped back inside the caravan sweat was standing out on his forehead.

Over by the edge of the stream, what he'd originally taken for a wooden post sank gradually from his view till it was hidden by the bank.

After about half-an-hour had passed, thirty minutes of confused and unilluminating internal dispute, Howard felt recovered enough to be able to resume his duties (such as he understood them), checking fore and aft and making the relevant notes. By now the trailer men had reappeared, and he logged their comings and goings, their incomprehensible loiterings, with a fair pretense of detachment. He wondered how easy he'd find it to be blasé about the whole affair once the sun went down.

With a glance every few minutes or so towards the windows, front and rear (it was pretty much force of habit by now), he returned to the ring-binder, in the forlorn hope that it might all suddenly fall into place, everything he'd seen, everything he'd read, all he'd experienced in the course of this weirdest of days.

DEFINITIONS

Remember, these are not the dead and buried, the loved ones taken to the graveyard in rented limousines and wept over for a season while their flowers rot on the bare turned earth. These are different. Nobody grieves for them. The majority are not even missed.

Nor yet should you think of them as zombies—but then, it has always been easier to say what they aren't, than what they really are. To see them clearly, to see them for what they are, we need to look beyond those categories we understand.

What these unfortunates have in common, it seems safest to say, is the experience of lessening. The drip-drip-drip of psychic diminution. The attenuation of the psyche. Call it what you will. They are drained, one and all, at the most profound and fundamental level. Months, maybe years of unremitting reduction . . . till the day, long after they'd become oblivious to the whole process, on which they reached the tipping-point and passed over, unnoticed, unmourned. A day on which they did not go home.

And in this way they were given over to the margins, to the space around the edge of things. In this way, they became the sort of creatures for whom these places—these inhospitable thresholds they're forever on the verge of crossing—might have been invented.

Though there was no author's name, no way of telling who'd written these strange pages, Howard felt fairly sure it hadn't been Barry. Nor yet Dave, he suspected: in fact, he wondered whether Dave had spent much time at all in the caravan when not dropping people off or picking them up. He didn't seem the type, thought Howard; and then wondered whether this meant that he himself might be that very type. He didn't really want to think about it at this stage; what it would say about the terminal poverty of his choices, were he to be the type of person who could actually be said to belong here, in this shabby gas-stinking caravan, with night falling over the Cheshire plain, the shadow of the trailer deepening, helping to conceal whatever might be hiding within it.

With an involuntary body-length shudder, he turned a page of the ring-binder and read on:

DARKNESS

Some, the newly translated perhaps, are drawn to certain houses in the night. While the occupants are asleep they move in close, position themselves outside the unlit curtained windows and press their faces to the panes, as if—though it's pointless to ascribe to them any motives we would recognize—some memory of refuge, of belonging might move in them still. Why these houses? Why these feelings? Who can say? We could assume the houses evoke in them something like nostalgia; probably we'd be wrong. All we really know is that there they are, leaning in against the glass, resigned, unwearied, still and noiseless in their vigils.

Occasionally, it has been observed, tears will leak from their wide unblinking eyes, and sometimes in the morning the low-angled sunlight will catch the impressions of their faces on the pane. Hundreds of times you've seen these marks. Now you know what causes them.

Howard closed the ring-binder sharply. Already it was too dark to see outside: the fluorescent tubes above his head served only to cast his own white-faced reflection back at himself. There was an hour to go still before Dave might come to pick him up. Would it be better with the lights switched on, or off?

For the life of him he couldn't decide.

Steve Duffy has written/coauthored five collections of weird short stories. *Tragic Life Stories*, *The Five Quarters*, *The Night Comes On* (all From Ash-Tree Press), and his most recent, *The Moment of Panic* (PS Publishing). His work also appears in a number of anthologies published in the UK and the US. He won the International Horror Guild Award for Best Short Story, was shortlisted for a World Fantasy Award in 2009, and again in 2012.

"My final act," the magician said. "Into the heart of the matter. To the core of it. We have worlds to create."

DARK GARDENS

⟜⟝

Greg Kurzawa

Sam bought the foreclosure on Enfield at auction, sight unseen. He assumed its history would be questionable, but as the plan was to gut, remodel, and resell—history was irrelevant. Not until the day he took possession did Sam learn the previous owner had been a semi-professional magician, stage name of Kurricke. The magician had vanished after living in the two-bedroom ranch for seventeen years, leaving spoiled milk in the refrigerator, dishes in the sink, and all the tools of his trade in unlocked trunks.

Sam wanted none of it: not the costumes and stage props in the second bedroom, nor the closets full of dresses, shoes, and wigs. The winch and stand in the basement might have been saleable, but the wicker trunk of journals and 8mm tapes was utterly worthless. He had no use for the mannequins in the attic—some upright on stands, some dismembered and crated. Stage paraphernalia had no place in his investment strategy. Sam made drastic inroads that first weekend, hauling the magician's junk down from the attic and out through the garage. Without ceremony, he resigned everything to the rented dumpster occupying the driveway.

His plans didn't change until Monday afternoon, when he rolled up an oil-stained carpet in the basement and uncovered the hatch.

Ascending from the basement Monday evening, Sam went to the garage looking for the wicker chest he'd wrestled out earlier that morning. This, he dragged back into the house and parked in front of the dark green couch, which he'd already decided would be the last thing to go—immediately after the 32-inch Magnavox. Settling on the couch, he unfastened the latches and lifted the lid.

Composition notebooks and 8mm tapes. Tucked to one side was a Sony hand-held camera wrapped it its own cables, and on top of everything, a 4x6 photograph in a thin pewter frame. Sam lifted the picture out to study it more closely.

Professionally done, the photograph captured a mismatched couple. She: young and pretty, seated on a chair with hands in her lap, her expression somewhat bewildered. He: presumably the magician Kurricke, standing behind her, his hand on the bare skin between shoulder and neck. He was perhaps fifty. His hair, going to gray, looked unaccustomed to the comb. Here was a man who couldn't iron a shirt, who'd forgotten how to knot a tie. He grinned at the camera with an excited, boyish charm, thrilled at his own good fortune.

The woman was too young to be the magician's wife or lover, Sam decided. A daughter, maybe. But his fingers on her throat were too possessive—too intimate for that relationship. Her skin was perfect, smooth and cream-colored, her hair a flossy brown silk utterly at odds with her skin type. To Sam, her beauty seemed inviolate, although there was something unusual in her posture. It didn't look, Sam thought, as though she'd applied her own makeup.

Sam set the frame aside.

A cursory inventory of trunk's remaining contents revealed that the notebooks were neither numbered, nor dated. Similarly, the tapes were loose and unlabeled. Feeling certain that something left behind by the magician would explain the hatch, Sam chose a notebook off the disordered pile. Opening it to the middle, he read:

How God must detest us. How revolting to Him our helplessness and stupidity.

Hitler exterminated the crippled and the weak for no better reason than that they were crippled and weak. Even though he too was human—a bag of flesh no different than those he gassed. How much greater the divide between us and God? How much more profound His hatred of us?

Why should the suffering of the weak evoke hatred?

I heard a story about a boy who crushed the head of a wounded dog because it hadn't the decency to die. I understand now that it wasn't the piteous animal's misery he sought to end, but his own. How miserable then is God, watching us flail about, blind and bleating, in His dark garden? We are ignorant of our own ignorance, rolling and stamping over all His creation.

How are any of us still alive?

Sam closed the book and once more took up the photograph. This time, he slid it from its frame and turned it over.

To E.—Love J.

"J. Kurrick," Sam said. "What happened here?"

He lifted out the hand-held Sony camera and its bundle of cables. It was time to watch a tape.

Kurricke the magician, in white shirt and glittering black vest, takes the stage of what appears to be a high school gymnasium. The camera records from behind a sparse audience; the quality of the tape is poor. The magician brandishes scarves, hoops, and giant playing cards for an audience that hardly acknowledges him. The constant murmur of peripheral conversations obscure his sad jokes. Occasionally, an adolescent face leans in from the side to leer into the camera.

Twelve uncomfortable minutes into his show, Kurricke ducks into the wings. Returning a moment later, he is pushing in front of him a mannequin on a wheeled chair. She sits woodenly in a gray skirt and white blouse, hands composed in her lap, bare head glossy under the stage lights.

Wheeling the chair to center stage, Kurricke asks a question of the crowd in a voice that is audible, but incomprehensible. Someone throws a crumpled wad of paper. It makes a high, slow arc before falling short.

Unconcerned by this reaction, Kurricke throws his arms wide with a shout, as though introducing an act superior to his own.

Nothing happens.

Kurricke has forgotten the mannequin's wig, which hangs on a hook behind the chair. The hair is brown and luxurious. Embarrassed, Kurricke shows it quickly to the now-silent audience, then slips it over the mannequin's head. Hair in place, he leaps back and throws up the same grand gesture. This time his shout is clear.

"Evelyn!"

The mannequin's eyes open. The magician—arms still raised—beams proudly at his audience, who fail to share his triumph. Behind him, Evelyn has but little control over herself. Her head jerks as though palsied. Her legs kick out then back again, heels scraping the stage floor.

Kurricke grins as though at a beloved daughter.

"Evelyn," the old magician croons. "Evelyn, will you dance?" Holding both her hands, Kurricke draws her out of the chair, and encourages a lurching step forward.

Pause. Rewind.

Sam left the couch to put his face closer to the television's quivering image.

Play.

Her eyes open. Her head turns. She grabs for Kurricke's offered hands and rises. A step. A stumble. He catches her, and his lips are near her ear. Is he whispering to her? His hands hold her slight waist. She clings to him, but her eyes are on the audience.

Pause.

Was that fear in her eyes?

Rewind. Play.

Evelyn falls into Kurricke, throwing her arms around his neck. He holds her, lips to her ear. His knees are bent to support her weight. Over his shoulder, her eyes are wide. Yes, she is afraid. More than afraid.

They dance—or rather, Kurricke drags her across the stage. Evelyn is shockingly graceless. A spin—she stumbles. A dip—she clutches him, terrified. The spectacle goes on too long. The audience grows restless.

When Kurricke at last returns her to the chair, her wig has come askew. Kurricke straightens it for her, and arranges her hands in her lap. Wheeling her around to face the audience, he stands behind her, hands on her shoulders.

"Evelyn, you were splendid this evening," he declares to the audience. "Will you wave goodnight to the kind people?"

Evelyn begins to look back at him, but the magician faces her forward with one hand on either cheek. He will not stop grinning at his audience. He waves, as though to demonstrate what is expected. Evelyn rotates a rigid hand in a shy parade wave.

While her arm is still in the air, Kurricke wrenches her head to the side, so she is looking suddenly over her own shoulder. Her body jerks, and Kurricke lifts her head away. Evelyn's arm drops—*clack*—to her side. Her leg kicks out from under her skirt.

There is some scattered applause, but mostly he has provoked an uneasy silence.

Kurricke bows, and bows again, though the applause has died. He leans back to look into the wings because the curtains are not closing. He raises a hand to catch the attention of someone only he can see. He is still smiling—still waving—when the curtains, like walls of black water, sweep in to engulf him.

Sam's ad in the Austin classifieds read: *Need services of one SCUBA diver. Caving experience and camera required. Will pay for time.*

• • •

Sam stepped outside when the black Jeep backed boldly into the narrow slice of driveway beside the dumpster. The driver had the door pushed open before the engine quieted. Bald and unsmiling, the man who stepped down was older than Sam had expected.

"David?" Sam asked as he crossed the dead grass.

"And you must be Sam."

Sam offered his hand, which David squeezed harder than necessary. Sam waved an arm back at the house. "It's inside," he said.

"Well, then," said the diver, lifting a backpack from the rear bed. "Let's have a look."

Sam had arranged two portable worklights around the hatch in the basement. He switched them on, and shadows burned away under the brilliant stare of twin 500-watt halogen bulbs.

"Looks like a sub's escape hatch," David said. Twenty-four inches in diameter, the hatch was bolted to the concrete floor with twelve thumb-sized rivets. The diver glanced up. "What's this for?"

Suspended over the hatch, a pulley system had been bolted to the underside of a supporting beam.

"It was all here when I moved in," Sam said. He saw David about to ask so added, "Five days ago."

Before there were more questions, Sam took a knee and turned the handwheel counterclockwise. From below came the solid *thunk* of internal mechanisms retracting. Getting his feet under him, Sam pulled up on the hatch, which opened smoothly on its hinge and locked into a leaning position twenty degrees past the apex.

He rose and stepped back. Side by side, the two men stared into a pool of dark water.

Blandly, David said, "Wow."

Sam agreed.

"Bomb shelter?" David asked.

Having already considered and dismissed that idea, Sam gave a skeptical shrug. "I don't think so. There's no ladder."

David's brow furrowed. He knelt next to the hatch, and with his face near the water, breathed deep. "It's not septic." He dipped his fingers and tasted. "Not salt, either."

Without warning, he plunged his arm in the water, reaching not down, but along the underside of the floor. Sam watched him feel around the entire perimeter, then again, this time lying on his stomach, shoulder-deep in water. When he got back on his knees, he looked concerned. Sam imagined it was exactly how he himself had looked after completing the same exercise. Predicting where David's mind was leading him, Sam offered him a broom handle.

"I couldn't find the sides," Sam said. "I already tried, but you've got a longer reach than me."

Holding the broom by its end, David slipped it into the water and probed for anything that would hint at the dimensions of the chamber below them. Finding nothing, he sat up and laid the broom handle aside, mystified.

"Broom handle's sixty inches," Sam said. "My arm's another twenty-four." He went to stand at the chalk mark he'd made on the concrete exactly eighty-four inches from the lip of the hatch. He pointed out the chalk marks he'd drawn around the basement, outlining the minimum circumference of the chamber. It wasn't the entire basement, but it didn't leave much room.

David pulled his backpack next to him and unzipped it. Out came a black mask and an underwater light. Pressing the mask to his face, he switched on the light and plunged his head into the water. He was back in a moment to report, "Nothing. I can't see the sides or the bottom. Have you tested for depth?"

Sam showed David the five hundred foot spool of utility rope and the twelve-pound river anchor he'd tied to the end of it. "I looped it over the pulleys," he said. "Then just dropped it in."

David waited.

"A hundred and eighty-eight feet," Sam said.

David blinked at the hatch. "Odd," he said.

Sam credited the man's composure. His own reaction, upon realizing that his mid-town home was supported over an abyss by a slab of concrete six inches thick, hadn't been nearly so indifferent.

"At this point, I just want to know what's down there."

"Right," David said, all business. "Let's get the gear."

Five minutes later they had David's equipment piled beside the hatch. After looping the yellow line through the pulley, they cast the anchor and let it sink. While the pulley rattled and the rope played out, David stripped off his T-shirt and cargo shorts. He proceeded to stuff himself into a neoprene wetsuit.

When the anchor hit bottom, David looped the line around the handwheel and pulled out the slack. After knotting it, he looked at Sam. "That's a good knot," he said. "Don't touch that knot."

From one of his bags, David produced a spool of braided nylon rope and a handheld underwater light. "I'll clip onto the anchor line up here and follow it all the way down. On the bottom, I'll tie off with this—" He shook the spool of rope. "—and go exploring. I've only got about twenty-five minutes of bottom time, so I can't go far."

David shrugged into his vest—burdened with gauges, dials and hoses—and zipped up. He had a spare everything. Sitting at the ledge with his legs in the water, he forced his bare feet into a pair of stiff, black flippers.

"Aim those big lights into the water after I'm down," David said. "If all mine go black and I lose the anchor line, I'll need them to get back."

With a little heave, David slipped legs first into the water. "Tanks," he said.

One at a time, Sam passed the tanks into the water, and David attached them to fittings under his arms, where they dangled like a pair of strange wings. He jerked a thumb at his bag. "There's a little book in there with a few names and numbers. I'd appreciate you letting them know what happened if I don't make it back.

"Relax," he said when Sam balked. "Me dying won't come as a shock to anyone." He held up his camera, safe in its clear little box. "I'm going to swim around, have a nice time, take some pictures. You won't even miss me."

With that, he fitted his mask and stuck a regulator in his mouth. Then he disappeared into the black water. His descending lights were obscured by darkness much sooner than Sam would have thought.

Forty-five minutes later, the hiss of breaking bubbles preceded David's return. On surfacing, he peeled away mask and regulator.

"What did you find?" Sam asked.

David hefted a tank out of the water, which Sam took and stood to the side. The next came immediately after.

Twisted into sitting position, David hauled himself out of the hatch. He nodded to his bag while reaching back down to pull off his fins. "Pass me a water, will you?"

Sam handed him a plastic bottle, then watched the diver twist it open and drink deeply.

"What's down there?" he asked again.

David ran a hand over his bare scalp, then lifted the camera. "Easier to just show you."

David sat squarely in the center of the couch, Sam's laptop on the coffee table in front of him. Sam sat beside him.

"This is a hundred and sixty feet," David said.

Mostly dark, the picture featured a circle of illumination on what appeared to be a muddy slope.

"The anchor hit here," David said, touching the screen at the start of a long gouge in the mud. "Then slid off this way." He traced the groove across the otherwise smooth surface to the lip of a sudden abyss. Barely visible, the yellow anchor line faded into the darkness.

"This is about ten feet above the structure," David said.

Sam hadn't finished processing the word 'structure' before David tapped the keyboard.

Next picture: clear, black water and darkness crowding in from all sides; the anchor resting in three inches of black mud, yellow rope angling towards the surface.

"I tied off at the anchor and dropped a flare, just in case."

Next picture: a doorless frame in a featureless wall. Beside it, a glassless double window opening into a black room, the edge of a mantle barely visible at the limit of the light's reach.

"What's that?" Sam touched a vague blur inside the room, barely within range of the flash.

David answered with the next picture: a much closer view. A figure sat in a plain wooden chair in an otherwise empty room. Hands arranged in its lap, it faced an open doorframe on the opposite wall. It wore no clothes, and had no hair. They could not see its face.

Sam sat back. "You went *inside?*"

"I put the camera through the window."

Leaning forward again, Sam said, "It's a mannequin."

"All those pictures were from the first house," David said. "The one right below us."

Sam stared at him. "The *first?*"

Staring at the screen, Sam became aware of David watching him closely. Realizing he had his hand over his mouth, he took it away and nodded at the laptop. "Keep going."

David clicked through a series of images, leaving each one up for just a few seconds. There were bare rooms and bloated furniture, stairways leading into darkness. And mannequins. Some of them were seated, some lying down. One of them stood at a window, another slumped in a dark corner of a drowned room, legs splayed.

"I didn't like it," David said. "I was uncomfortable."

Before Sam could reply, David cleared his throat. "I was running low on mix at that point, so I headed back. At that first house, the one right below us, I thought I'd take a few more pictures before coming up. Maybe go inside."

David tapped a key. The chair was empty.

Sam leaned back, but it wasn't enough distance. Pushing himself out of the couch, he walked a few feet before realizing he had nowhere to go.

"At first I thought I had the wrong house," David continued. "But I could see the glow from my flare, and I never left my guideline. So I went around."

Sam watched from behind the couch, arms folded.

The flare, a brilliant shard of harsh light, illuminated a wide expanse of flat mud in the next picture. Half-buried beside the flare was the anchor. Rising from it to the surface, the yellow line. And there, the silhouette of a figure standing beside the anchor.

"It wasn't moving," David said. "It was like it had been *moved*. Like someone had come while I was gone and just . . . moved it there."

The next picture was closer, but no more detailed.

"That's as close as I wanted to get," David said. "I'd seen enough, and I was out of gas, so I got out of there. I dropped the rope and swam for the anchor line about fifteen feet up."

David's final picture had been taken from maybe twenty feet up the anchor line, looking back down. Below, the light of the flare seemed crushed by the weight of the darkness around it. Even at that distance, in that darkness, Sam could see how the human-shaped blur had taken hold of the anchor line and lifted its gaze to follow David's ascent.

Sam dragged the trunk in front of David and squatted next to it. "I found this in the attic," he said. Lifting the lid of the trunk revealed the notebooks and tapes. "The previous owner was a stage magician. This was all his."

Seeing that it meant nothing to David, Sam picked up the top notebook. Opening it to one of the pages he'd marked, he read aloud:

There is no food there. They chose the weakest among them to devour. Does that make their world an imitation of ours? Or is it we who imitate them? Who is the higher being: a creature who is exactly as it seems, or we who cower behind civilized performances? Do layers of artifice make us more human, or less so?

Imagine I mold a primitive man from a lump of mud. I might teach him to dance and whistle. I might teach him to speak. Because I am proud, I will dress him like myself. His buttons will always be polished, and his cuffs clean. He will learn to smile, and to laugh. But to whatever majestic heights he aspires, I will

*always know his secret—even if he forgets it himself. It is the same as mine: under
our masks, we are only so much mud.*

*If we, who think ourselves so fine, were stripped down to our bare essence,
would we be any different? I think not. Mud and spit are all that is real. The rest
is masks and lies heaped layer upon layer.*

"He knew something," Sam said with confidence. "I haven't read all of
them, or watched everything yet. But there's got to be something in there that
explains *that.*" He stabbed a finger at his laptop.

Sam could see that David remained unconvinced, so he turned on the
television and put the first tape into the camera.

After the closing of the curtains, Sam felt a grim satisfaction at the stunned
look on David's face.

"That mannequin . . . " David said.

"There were more in the attic."

David shifted in discomfort. "Where are they now?"

"The dumpster. In pieces."

"But did they . . . I mean, do you think he got them from down there?"

"They had to come from somewhere."

Sam watched David thinking. After a moment, the older man's eyes shifted
to the open trunk. Pushing aside the layers of notebooks, he uncovered the
8mm tapes beneath. "What's on the rest of these?"

"More of the same."

David handed one to Sam. "Show me."

They spent all afternoon watching the tapes. Both agreed that Kurricke was
a mediocre magician, at best. They took to fast-forwarded his act to get to
Evelyn's appearances.

In the earlier tapes, Evelyn couldn't so much as rise from her chair. Her
hands fluttered in her lap, her head jerked helplessly—an epileptic parody.
During one show she spasmed off the chair. Back arching, heels drumming
the stage. In later shows, she remained in her chair and responded to simple
commands. At the end of those shows, a proudly grinning Kurricke would
lift her arm to help her wave. Once, after helping her stand, Kurricke stepped
back to applaud her when a seizure shook her legs from under her. One of her
arms broke off when she hit the floor, but she continued waving. The crowd
was appalled.

As the timeline progressed, Evelyn became less awkward. Like a child learning to walk, she stumbled stiff-legged across the stage, groping for the encouraging magician. In one show, she danced an awkward solo number under the spotlights, during which she seemed a horrid, life-sized puppet jerked about on unseen strings. She performed a clumsy curtsy when finished, and blew a kiss to the audience. Out came Kurricke from the wings: grinning, waving, smiling—the proud showman. Evelyn sat obediently in her chair, soundless as he twisted off her head and held it aloft for all to see.

Sam peeled a cold slice of pizza from the box on the counter, then couldn't decide if he wanted it reheated or cold. It was 11:37 p.m. by the clock on the stove.

"Listen to this," David called from the living room.

Sam dropped his cold pizza on a dirty plate and carried it to the living room. David had one of Kurricke's notebooks open on his lap. They'd been searching the journals while watching the tapes, reading to one another the most intriguing excerpts.

David waited for Sam to sit, then read:

"Eat not of the blood," said Yahweh to His people. "For the blood is the life."

It is forbidden fruit, this eating of flesh and blood. Yet Christ gave His to the disciples, and they drank of it. He gave them His flesh, and they ate that, too.

We know what happened to those wretches in the Garden of Eden when they ate what they ought not have. And we know what happened to the disciples when they feasted on their Christ. But what if He had eaten of their flesh? What if He had tasted their blood?

I have read that true evil is the forceful attempt to ascend to a higher plane. Was this not Lucifer's sin, and all those angels deceived by him? It was, God's throne being as high above the angels as the angels are above Man. He stormed Heaven to take what was not his, and his punishment was terrible. For him, and for us. The same can be said of those in Babel and their offensive tower.

The message is clear: to ascend is forbidden.

But what of ascension as a gift? Is it not what Christ promises His believers? A place in a higher world? A position for which we are not suited as we are, but for which we must be groomed. The fruit that must be had is the same as it ever was. The blood is the life. Eat of the flesh. Become more like Me.

If true evil is striving for ascension where it is not permitted—what, then, is true goodness? It must be the reverse: a willing descent. This also is in keeping with the Christian mythology. Did not the Christ descend to us from a higher world? And was it not deemed good? He did, and it was.

This is my blood: drink of it.

This is my body: eat of it.

These symbols are more than metaphor. They are the reality. And the rules must be the same regardless of the direction one travels. The fruit is the blood is the life.

And so her elevation is good. It is my gift to her.

As for my descent—she has no blood, but she has flesh, or something like it. Will it suffice?

We shall see.

Stripped of appetite, Sam dropped his plate of untouched pizza on the coffee table. "I can't do this anymore tonight."

David glanced at his watch. "I want to go down again," he announced. "Tomorrow."

"You're not serious."

"We should take more pictures. Collect evidence. I'll bring up some samples."

"Samples? Of what? Evidence of what?"

"You want people to think you're crazy?"

"No."

"So we take pictures. We document."

Sam rubbed his face.

David pulled a thick wallet from his back pocket. Sliding out the folded check Sam had given him earlier, he tore it in half and put the pieces on the coffee table. He tapped them with two fingers.

"We shouldn't stop now," he said. Then he pushed up from the couch, one of the magician's notebooks in hand. "You mind if I take a couple of these with me? I probably won't sleep anyway."

Sam waved his permission.

At the door, David looked back. "Listen, I'm not trying to tell you what to do, okay? But I don't think you should stay here tonight. It doesn't seem safe."

It only took a moment for Sam to tick off every friend he had in the area, none of whom he wanted to call at midnight to admit he was frightened to spend the night alone.

"Sleep at my place," David offered. "My couch is big."

Sam hesitated.

"I have beer," David added.

Sam laughed despite himself. "I'll be fine. Go on, I'll see you tomorrow."

"Early, okay?" David said.

"Early," Sam agreed.

Sam ventured down the long hall to the master bedroom only to retrieve a blanket and pillow, which he dragged back to the couch. He felt safer there, and thought it must be the proximity to the refrigerator that made it seem so.

At 2:15 a.m. his phone buzzed.

"I thought you might still be awake," David said.

"I wasn't."

"Listen to this: he used the winch."

Sam put his feet on the floor and his forehead in his palm.

"The winch in the garage," David continued. "And the pulleys. He lowered—get this—a grappling hook on the end of a chain. He left it down there for days at a time. He was trolling."

Sam heard pages rustling over the line.

"Then he caught Evelyn," David said. "She got tangled up in the chain. She wasn't Evelyn at first though—she was just a bunch of hard clay shaped like a person. He only named her Evelyn later. Are you hearing this?"

"Have you been up all night?"

"I don't sleep much."

"What else?"

"That's all. I thought you'd want to know."

"I do. But maybe stop reading until tomorrow."

"Right," David said. Then hung up.

Knowing he wouldn't sleep again, Sam inserted a tape, then went to the kitchen for a glass of milk and whatever pizza remained. He was eating hard crusts when Kurricke's familiar voice spoke from the living room.

"This one stops it," the magician said. "I've showed you this before. You know how this works."

Sam spit a mouthful of crust into the trash and went to the doorway. The television showed a steady shot of the basement and the open hatch.

Kurricke shuffled into view, only it wasn't the magician Sam had come to recognize. This man's hair had fallen out in patches. His skin was waxen, and he moved stiffly, every step an effort.

Positioning himself beside the hatch, he turned toward the camera. It became immediately apparent that something was wrong with his face. His muscles were rigid, the skin nearly perfect in its smoothness. Holding up his hands, he displayed fingers sealed together.

There he stood a long moment, his intent forgotten. Then he pawed at the buttons of his shirt with useless hands.

"Help me," he said, looking up at the camera.

Giving up on the buttons, the magician advanced until he moved out of the shot. For a long while there was only the sound of rustling clothing, labored breathing, and urgent whispers.

When Kurricke hobbled back into view he was naked. His skin everywhere was glossy and hairless. He had lost his sex. He—or someone—had fixed a weighted belt around his hips.

"My final act," the magician informed the camera as he knelt beside the hatch with difficulty. "Into the heart of the matter, yes? To the core of it. I will—if I am able—return. We have worlds to create."

Tipping forward, Kurricke disappeared with a muted splash.

Barely breathing in the resulting silence, Sam watched the onscreen hatch. Something bumped the camera, and Sam jumped, having forgotten that someone else watched with him. He sat forward, waiting to see if she would show herself. The camera shifted again, lifted off its support. The basement leaned and whirled, then blackness.

Sam paused the tape and sat in the quiet half-light of the living room. A board creaked in a back room. A window rattled. Sam got up to make sure the door to the basement was shut securely, then retreated back to the couch. He wanted to be gone from the house, but the distances seemed too great, the empty spaces between himself and everywhere else too threatening. He started the tape rewinding, and pulled the blanket up to his chin. He told himself he would wait for dawn, then leave and never come back, but he was asleep before the tape reached the beginning. He woke briefly when it started again. The glow from the television, coupled with the gentle click and whir of the camera, offered comfort, so he muted the volume and let it play.

Somewhere in a half-dream, a door opened.

She was standing near the television when Sam woke, transfixed by Kurricke's old familiar act playing out in silence. Her wig was crooked, her dress backward and inside-out. Sam's first thought was that someone had reclaimed limbs from the dumpster and assembled the parts in his living room as a horrid joke. Then she moved.

Sam threw off his blanket and scrambled over the back of the couch. He quelled his panic as she turned her whole body to face him.

Her time away from the magician had been unkind to her. Peels of thick skin had dried, cracked, and were curling from her face and arms. Her eyes were something out of a taxidermist's kit. With rusted effort, she bent an arm to waist-level, and aimed it toward the television by rotating her upper body. Her head tilted to one side in a mechanical gesture of inquiry.

"He's gone," Sam said.

Her eyes remained on the set, following Kurricke as he capered about throwing colored scarves into the air. Reluctant to draw her attention again, Sam watched her watching the magician. She was not quite still; her arms moved in tiny increments, as though desiring to mime Kurricke's abundant gestures.

"You're Evelyn," Sam said.

Her head twisted toward him. Her mouth, which Sam had thought hardened shut, parted to emit a throaty choking. She lifted both arms in a gesture of supplication. Her fingers were fixed together, her wrists immobile. Arms thus raised, she lurched forward.

It was 6:00 a.m. when David's Jeep swung onto the quiet street and threw itself into the driveway. Sam rose from where he had been sitting on the curb across the street and went to meet him.

"What happened?" David asked as he stepped down from the Jeep,

They found Evelyn's body at the bottom of the basement stairs. One of her arms had broken off, and her left leg was folded back at the knee. Using her one arm, she had dragged herself a few feet toward the closed hatch. Now, her hand scrabbled feebly at the floor, and her legs moved with the futile motions of a crushed animal. At the sound of footsteps on the stairs, Evelyn lifted her head to emit strangled, tongueless glottals. If they were efforts to communicate, her capacity to speak was more primitive than her body.

Standing over her, Sam felt himself beginning to loathe her for being so wounded, for clinging to life in a place she'd never belonged, for this suffering that made him feel he had done her some terrible wrong. He hated her for needing so much, and for being so far beyond help. He looked up to see David still on the top stair.

"I'm going to need your help," Sam warned him. He went to plug in the standing halogens, and garish light crushed back the shadows. When he pulled up the hatch, Evelyn began to make different sounds, a high keening broken by abrupt consonants and sharp barks. He went back to stand over her with David, where he saw that she was trying to touch the diver's sandaled feet.

They could see into her torso from where her arm had broken off at the shoulder. She was full on an airy, sponge-like webbing. She would be light. Sam didn't really need help at all. He just didn't want to do it alone.

He took Evelyn under the shoulders, and waited for David to lift her legs. She was still twisting weakly when they fed her through the hatch. She listed, her dress fanning out to tangle her remaining limbs. In slow, dreamlike turns she he moved. An arm rose from the water, trailing the sopping fabric of her dress like weeds. Sam couldn't tell, but she seemed to be grasping for the ledge.

He fetched a shovel to hold her under.

Long after she had sank into blackness, Sam remained, unsure of what to expect next. After a while, he closed the hatch and spun the handwheel until it locked. He wiped his face on his sleeve. When he turned to thank David— to tell him that he should leave now, and not come back—he found himself already alone.

In the days that followed, Sam read each of Kurricke's notebooks. He ordered them chronologically as best he could, then read them again. He studied them. In time, he began to understand what Kurricke had done right, and where he had gone wrong. He learned from the magician's mistakes, and resolved not to repeat them.

One day he read:

The hatch was never necessary. Egress can be found anywhere. There have always been so many other ways: paintings and music and books. Books, most of all. There are doors to be found everywhere, and where they do not already exist, we create them. We engender worlds so blithely, then abandon them to their own misery. We care so little because it is not we who suffer for our recklessness.

I have heard it argued that God became human so that none could accuse Him of being unsympathetic to His own creation. He walked a mile, as they say. What must we become, then, to understand Him? Where does our mile begin, and where end? God descended, and still loved. Is the same required of us?

We accuse God of neglect, but are we kinder to our own creations? Or to any living thing unfortunate enough to find itself subject to our dominion? We hypocrites shake our fists at Heaven. But if we had a world to create, and a people to rule, could we do better?

Sam closed the journal and looked at its frayed cover. He had been using the picture of the magician and Evelyn to keep his place, but removed it now. "I can do better than you, J. Kurricke," Sam said. He ripped the photograph in half, keeping only Evelyn.

• • •

David returned to the house on Enfield three weeks later. The rented dumpster was gone, and the lawn unkempt. No one answered his knocking. The garage door complained at being opened, but the door to the house had been left unlocked.

"Sam!" he called.

Getting no answer, David stepped inside, and his shoe squelched on waterlogged carpet. He noticed then the sagging ceiling and the water-blistered walls. The air was dense with moisture. On the magician's trunk, David found a composition notebook bloated with water damage. Two-thirds of the pages were filled with script ruined by water. Only the final page remained legible.

The Outsider had been gone many years when the children of the village began telling stories of a tall stranger living beside the river. He had eyes full of light, and charmed them with gifts of honeycomb and pearls. The men and women of the village—search as they might—could find no trace of him, and soon understood that they would not until he willed it.

Every night of that vibrant summer, Evelyn went alone to the riverbank to wait for him, until one evening she arrived to find him emerging from the shallows. His shoulders were like the bull's, and his eyes like the stars. His smile was kind.

"You are Evelyn," he said to her.

"And by what name do I call you, Master?"

"Here, you will know me as Samael."

Evelyn knelt before him.

Samael took her fragile chin in his hand and turned her face upwards. "You were but a girl when I left."

"But I am a woman now, Samael."

And so Samael became her king, and she his queen. In time, he shared with her all the wonders of that world, which were his to command.

Greg Kurzawa studied theology before stumbling into an information technology career. His work has appeared in *Interzone*, *Clarkesworld*, *Beneath Ceaseless Skies*, and *Orson Scott Card's Intergalactic Medicine Show*. He has a passable impression of Gage Kurricke, with whom he coauthored the bleak fantasy novel, "Gideon's Wall." He can be found online at gregkurzawa.com.

Do whatever you need to survive.
Do whatever you need to be free.

RAG AND BONE

Priya Sharma

I leave Gabriel in the yard and go into town, taking my bag with the vials of skin and bone, flesh and blood, my regular delivery to Makin. The Peels are looking for body parts.

I love the grandeur of The Strand. High towers of ornate stone. The road's packed with wagons and carts. Boats choke the river. The Mersey is the city's blood and it runs rich. Liverpool lives again.

I can hear the stevedores' calls, those kings of distribution and balance, whose job it is to oversee the dockers loading the barges. The boats must be perfectly weighted for their journey up the Manchester Ship Canal. Guards check them to ensure no unlicensed man steals aboard. Farther along, at Albert Dock, there's a flock of white sails. The Hardman fleet's arrived, tall ships bringing cotton from America.

The Liver birds keep lookout. Never-never stone creatures that perch atop the Liver Building where all the families have agents. I keep my eyes fixed on the marble floor so that I don't have to look at the line of people desperate for an audience. Peels' man has the ground floor. The Peels' fortune came from real estate, small forays such as tenements at first, but money begets money. They took a punt when they redeveloped Liverpool's waterfront, a good investment that made them kings of the new world.

The other families have managers on other floors, all in close proximity as nothing's exclusive, business and bloodlines being interbred. The Hardmans are textile merchants, the Rathbones' wealth was made on soap, of all things, while the Moores are ship builders.

The outer offices contain rows of clerks at desks, shuffling columns of figures in ledgers. A boy, looking choked in his high-necked shirt, runs between them carrying messages. No one pays me any mind.

Makin's secretary keeps me waiting a full minute before he looks up, savoring this petty exercise of power. "He'll see you now."

Makin's at his desk. Ledgers are piled on shelves, the charts and maps on the walls are stuck with pins marking trade routes and Peel territories.

"Have a seat." He's always civil. "How did you fare today?"

"A few agreed."

I hand him the bag.

"They're reluctant?"

"Afraid."

There are already rumors. That the Peels, Hardmans, Rathbones, and Moores, these wealthy people we never see, are monstrosities that live to a hundred years by feasting on Scousers' flesh and wearing our skins like suits when their own get worn out. Their hands drip with diamonds and the blood of the slaving classes. They lick their fingers clean with slavering tongues.

Makin taps the desk.

"Should we be paying more?"

"Then you'll have a line that stretches twice around the Mersey Wall consisting of drunken, syphilitic beggars."

"Do we have to order obligatory sampling of the healthy?"

"That's unwise."

His fingers stop drumming.

"Since when are rag and bone men the font of wisdom?"

I'm not scared of Makin but I need the money so I'm respectful. Besides, I like him.

"At least wait 'til it's cooler before you announce something like that or you'll have a riot."

That brings him up short.

"I'm feeling fractious today." He rubs the top of his head like a man full of unhappy thoughts. "Don't be offended."

"I'm not."

"You're a good sort. You work hard and don't harbor grudges. You speak your mind instead of the infernal yeses I always get. Come and work for me."

"Thank you but I hope you won't hold it against me if I say no."

"No, but think on it. The offer stands." Something else is bubbling up. "You and I aren't so different. I had to scramble too. I'm a Dingle man. My daughters are spoilt and innocent. My sons no better." His rueful smile reveals the pain of parenthood. "It's their mother's fault. They're not fit for the real world, so I must keep on scrambling."

I envy his children, wanting for nothing, this brutal life kept at arm's length. Makin must see something in my face because he puts the distance back between us with, "Have you heard any talk I should know about?"

He's still chewing on my unpalatable comment about riots.

"All I meant was that it's unseasonably hot and a while since the last high day or holiday. Steam builds up in these conditions."

I hear craziness in the ale houses all the time that I'm not going to share with him. Talk of seizing boats and sailing out of Liverpool Bay, north to Blundell Sands and Crosby to breathe rarefied air and storm the families' palaces. Toppling the merchant princes. A revolution of beheading, raping, and redistribution of riches.

Tough talk. Despairing men with beer dreams of taking on armed guards.

"They can riot all they like. Justice will fall hard. Liverpool's peaceful. There'll be no unions here. We'll reward anyone who helps keep it that way."

I want to say, *The Peels aren't the law*, but then I remember that they are.

I cross Upper Parliament Street into Toxteth. My cart's loaded with a bag of threadbare colored sheets that I'll sell for second-grade paper. I've a pile of bones that'll go for glue.

"Ra bon! Ra bon!" I shout.

Calls bring the kids who run alongside me. One reaches out to pat Gabriel, my hound, who curls his lip and growls.

"Not a pet, son. Steer clear."

When I stop, the children squat on the curb to watch. They're still too little for factory work.

"Tommy, can I have a sweet?"

"No, not unless you've something to trade and it's Tom, you cheeky blighter. Shouldn't you be in school?"

There are elementary classes in the big cathedral. I convinced Dad to let me attend until he decided it was too dangerous and taught me himself instead. Hundreds of us learnt our letters and numbers by rote, young voices raised in unison like fevered prayers that reached the cavernous vaults. The sad-eyed ministers promised God and Jerusalem right here in Liverpool and even then I could see they were as hungry as we were, for bread and something better.

"Are you the scrap man?" It's a darling girl with a face ravaged by pox. "My ma asked for you to come in."

"Don't touch my barrow," I tell the others. "After the dog's had you, I'll clobber you myself."

I wave my spike-tipped stick at them. It's not a serious threat. They respond with grins of broken teeth and scurvy sores. They're not so bad at this age. It's the older ones you have to watch for.

I follow the child inside. The terraces seethe and swelter in the summer. Five stories from basement to attic, a family in every room. All bodies fodder to the belching factories and docks; bargemen, spinners, dockers, weavers, and foundry workers. Dad reckoned Liverpool got shipping and industry when the boundaries were marked out and other places got chemicals, medicines, food production, and suchlike. He said the walls and watchtowers around each county were the means by which the martial government quelled civil unrest over recession, then biting depression. It was just an excuse to divide the nation into biddable portions and keep those that had in control of those that didn't.

Dad also said his grandfather had a farm and it was a hard but cleaner living. No cotton fibers in the lungs, fewer machines to mangle limbs. Less disease and no production lines along which contagion can spread.

The girl darts into a room at the back. I stand at the door. The two women within are a pair of gems. One says, "Lolly," and the child runs to her. She looks like an angel, clutching the child to her that way.

"We've stuff to sell," says the other one with the diamond-hard stare. "I'm Sally and this is Kate."

Sally's dazzling. I take off my cap and pat down my hair.

They share the same profile, long hair fastened up. Sisters. Sally's still talking while Angel Kate puts a basket on the table. I catch her glance. This pitiful collection's worth won't meet their needs.

"Let's see." I clear my throat. "These gloves might fetch something. The forks too." The tines are so twisted that they're only worth scrap value. There's a jar of buttons and some horseshoe nails that look foraged from between cobbles. "I'll give you extra for the basket."

Kate looks at the money in my outstretched hand with hungry eyes but Sally's got the money in her pocket before I can change my mind.

"Are you both out of work?"

"Laid off." Sally makes a sour face.

"I'm sorry. Laid off from where?"

"Vicar's Buttons."

A good, safe place for nimble-fingered women.

"I'll let you know if anyone's hiring."

"Lolly, play outside." Lolly jumps to Kate's order, dispelling any doubt about which woman is Lolly's mother.

"We need more money." Mother Kate is fierce. "I've heard that you're looking to collect things for one of the families . . . "

"Which one?" Sally butts in.

"The Peels," I answer.

"The Peels have taken enough from us already."

I want to ask Sally what she means but I don't get a chance.

"*We need more money, Sally.* Peels, Vicars, Hardmans. What's the difference?"

"There is."

"No, there isn't, Sal." Kate sounds flat. "Lolly needs food and a roof. She comes above pride or principles."

Nothing could make me admire Kate more. I'm gawping at her.

"We'll get work."

"Not soon enough." Kate turns to me. "Tell me more."

"It's just in case one of the Peels get ill." I feel foolish trotting out this patter. "Should they need a little blood or skin, or bit of bone."

"Are they too proud to ask one another?" Sally's sharp. "I've heard that they take the bits they want and toss the rest of you to their lapdogs. And what if they want an eye or kidney?"

"They wouldn't want anything vital and the compensation would be in keeping, of course."

"Compensation?" Sally presses me. She's the sparring sort.

"That's up for discussion. Someone got granted leave to live outside Liverpool for their help."

Outside. Myth and mystery. That shuts her up.

"Yes, but what will you give me now?" Kate has more pressing concerns.

Both women are bright-eyed. They don't look like they buy backdoor poteen or have the sluggish, undernourished look of opium fiends. They've worked in a button factory, not a mill, so they've young unblemished lungs, engine hearts, and flawless flesh, except for their worn hands. Just the sort I've been told to look for. I feel like a rat, gnawing on a dying man's toes.

Do whatever you need to survive, Dad would say. *Do whatever you need to be free.*

I put a silver coin on the table.

"I'll do it," Kate says.

"Don't." Sally's like a terrier. I don't know whether to kiss or kick her.

"We've queued for weeks with no luck."

The indignity of hiring pens and agency lines. At the respectable ones they just check hands and teeth. At others, they take women and boys around back for closer inspection.

"What if they want something from you? What then?" Sally sounds panicked.

"All they ask is a chance to speak to you. No one's forcing anyone." It's what I've been told to say, but the rich always have their way.

"Do it." Kate's firm.

I take off the bag strung across my chest and sit down at the table.

"What's your name?"

"Kate Harper."

Kate's hands are calloused from factory work but her forearms are soft.

"It'll hurt." I remove the sampler's cap.

I put it over her arm and press down. I feel the tip bite flesh and hear the click as it chips off bone. It leaves a deep, oozing hole. Kate gasps but doesn't move. It's only ever men that shout and thrash about.

"I'll give you some ointment to help it heal. What about Lolly's father?" I try and make it sound like easy banter as I write her details in the log book and on the tube.

"He was a sailor on *The Triumph*."

"You're Richard Harper's wife?" A name said with hushed reverence.

"Yes, and before you blather on about heroism, he didn't give us a second thought. Everything we'd saved went on his sailor's bond."

The Triumph was a Peel ship that landed in the Indies. You can't send men across the ocean on a boat and not expect them to want to get off on the other side and walk around. It's a foul practice to stop sailors absconding, resulting in cabin fever, brawling and sodomy. The crew of *The Triumph* mutinied.

The leader, Richard Harper, was a martyr for his part. The authorities tied him to the anchor before they dropped it. His sailor's bond, held with the port master, was forfeit.

"You were widowed young."

Kate's nod is a stiff movement from the neck. She tries to soften it with, "It's just us now."

"I understand. It used to be me and my dad until he died. He was a rag and bone man too." I'm overcome with the need to tell her everything, but I can't. "He wanted a horse instead of pulling the barrow himself. One day I'll get one, if I can save enough."

I'm trying to impress them. Sally sighs as if I'm tiresome but Kate pats my hand like an absentminded mother. Her unguarded kindness makes me want to cry. I want to put my head on Kate's knee and for her to stroke my hair.

Sally watches us.

"I won't do it. I don't trust them."

I realize that I want to touch Sally too, but in a different way. I have a fierce urge to press my mouth to the flesh on the inside of her wrist where the veins show through.

Sally stares me down and I want to say, *I'm not the enemy. I'm not a flesh-eating Peel up in an ivory tower*, but then I realize that I might as well be.

I sit in my room at The Baltic Fleet. Mother Kate's essence shouldn't be contained in a vial. I don't want anyone else to possess her. Not some sailor, bound and drowned, and definitely not a Peel. She should be free.

Times are hard. I've filled in a whole page of Makin's log book.

I go walking to clear my head, Gabriel at heel. Mrs. Tsang, the publican, is stocking the bar with brown bottles of pale ale. She's good to me, just like she was good to Dad. She lets me the room and I keep my barrow in the yard under a tarp.

"Okay, poppet?" she asks as I pass.

On impulse I lean down and kiss her cheek. She swats me away, hiding her smile. Mrs. Tsang's tiny but I've seen her bottle a man in the face for threatening her. The jagged glass tore his lips and nose.

The factories are out and everyone's heading home. Workers pile into the terraces. Some sun themselves on doorsteps. A tethered parrot squawks at me from its perch outside a door, talking of flights in warmer climes. Kids play football on the street.

I head to Otterspool Prom where I stand and consider, looking out at the river. Herring gulls scream at me for my foolishness. Gabriel lies down and covers his face with his paws.

I drop Kate's vial and stand on it. Then I kick every single fragment into the water and don't leave until the Mersey's taken it all away.

I pause outside Makin's office.

"I'd advise caution with his sort, sir." A stranger's voice.

"What's *his sort* then?" That's Makin.

"Loners, in my experience, are freaks or agitators."

"Tom's neither."

Behind me, someone clears his throat. I turn to find myself on the sharp end of a pointed look from Makin's secretary. No doubt he'll tell later.

"I told you to knock and go in." He opens the door.

"Ah, Tom, this is Mr. Jessop."

Jessop's the most handsome man I've ever seen, with good teeth and all his hair. He's no gentleman. He has the swagger of the law, not a regular policeman but a special.

"Tom, we were just talking about you." He sounds like a Scouser now, a rough edge to his voice that was missing before. He must talk it up or down, depending on the company. "Can I see the log book that Mr. Makin gave you?"

I look at Makin who nods. Mr. Jessop flicks through it, checking against the ledger where a clerk copies the details.

"Is this address correct?"

It's Kate's.

"Yes." I shrug. "I filled it in at the time."

"Anyone else live there?"

"Her sister and daughter."

"And you broke one of the samplers that day?"

"Yes. An empty one. I'm a clumsy oaf." I try and sound like I'm still berating myself. "I dropped it and stepped on it. I reported it straight away, didn't I, Mr. Makin? I offered to pay for it."

"No one's accusing you of anything, Tom."

"Do you know where Kate Harper is now?" Jessop doesn't let up.

"Isn't she there?"

I know she isn't. I knocked at her door and an old man answered. *Bugger off. I've no idea where they went.*

"No, but you know that already because you went back." Jessop smiles, the triumphant conniver. "You do know that she's Richard Harper's widow, don't you?"

"Yes, but what's that got to do with me?"

Jessop's hands are spotless. He must scrub them nightly to get out suspects' blood. Specials with manicured hands don't come in search of factory girls without reason.

Makin sits back, waiting. Of course. They're terrified of Harper. That his wife will be a rallying cry.

"I didn't know who she was until she gave the sample."

"And why would she do that?"

"She needed money."

"So she's not being looked after by her Trotsky pals?" Jessop won't let it go.

"I don't think so." I try and catch Makin's eye.

"Why did you go back?"

Makin's holding his breath, waiting.

"The thing is"—I shift about, embarrassed by the truth—"they were pretty and I wanted to see them again."

"There's no shame in that." Makin seems relieved. Thank God that good men like him can rise in this world that favors politicians who use smiles, wiles and outright lies.

I feel bad about lying to him.

"We need to speak to her," Jessop says.

"But I don't know where she is."

"But you'll tell us if you do find her?" His smile makes me want to bolt for the door. "You've never had a job, have you?"

"I work."

My dad would say, *We're free. Never subject to the tyranny of the clock. The dull terrors of the production line. No one will use us as they please.*

"Bone grubbing. Piss-poor way to make a living."

"Enough." Makin tuts.

"So sorry." Jessop's oily and insincere. "If you do find her, be a good lad and run up here and tell Mr. Makin."

I want to say, *Shove your apology*, but keep my gob shut.

The bastards follow me about all day. Jessop and his pals, got up like dockers. I pretend I've not seen them but they stand out. They're too clean to look real.

I look for Kate and Sally in the hiring lines, strolling past with my barrow as if on my way elsewhere. I wouldn't give her away. I just want to see her face. I ask the washerwomen at the water pumps and the old men standing around the fires at night.

Kate, Sally, Lolly. There's not a whiff of them.

I go up to the destitute courts of the Dingle, each court comprised of six houses set up around a central yard. The noxious stench from the shared privy is of liquid filth. I look through open doors: blooming damp patches on the plaster, crumbled in places to bare brick. I see faces made hard by deprivation. Infants squalling from drawers because they're hungry. It was a miracle that Makin clawed his way out of here.

"You."

A priest accosts me. He's on his rounds, demanding pennies from the poor to give to the even poorer.

"Come here."

Closer and he's unshaven and smells. He's ale addled. I feel for him, driven to despair and drink by the gargantuan task of saving so many lost souls. He follows me out of the court, onto the street.

"I've heard about you, Thomas Coster."

I tie Gabriel to the cart in case he goes for the man and wait for the rage of the righteous. I don't feel so well-disposed towards him now.

"You're in league with evil." He shoves his face into mine. Gabriel goes crazy. We're drawing quite an audience. "The Peels keep people in tanks like fish, cutting off the bits they want."

I'm panting from pushing the cart uphill and trying to outpace him. Jessop's up ahead, leaning against a wall.

"A man should be buried whole in consecrated ground."

The priest's enraged when the crowd laughs. Burial's expensive. The poor are cremated on pyres.

"You'll be damned. You'll suffer all hell's torments. You'll be flayed. The devil will sup on your gizzards and crack the marrow from your bones."

Jessop laughs under his breath as I pass.

It's a rare day that a Peel comes to town.

The Peel factories have closed an hour early to mark the day. Men loiter on Hope Street, outside the Philharmonic pub. Rowdy clerks from the insurance offices and banks are out, seeking white-collar mayhem. One turns quickly and shoulder barges me as I pass. He's keen to prove he can push more than a pen. His friends laugh.

His mates all line up across the pavement to block my path. I step into the gutter. One of them steps down to join me. He's wearing ridiculous checked trousers and his hands are in his pockets. I wonder what's in there.

"You walked into my friend. You should apologize."

I open my mouth but someone's standing at my shoulder. It's Jessop.

"I think you're mistaken," Jessop says as he opens his jacket. Whatever's glinting within is enough to put this bunch off.

I glance around. Jessop's traveling in numbers, all of them in black suits.

"I'm sorry, sir."

Oh, to wield so much power that you don't have to exert it.

Jessop picks up his pace, looking back to give me a final grin. I follow in their wake, pushing through to the barrier. There's a big crowd. Lord Peel's here to give a special address to his foremen. They must be in need of bucking up if he's got to come down here to talk to them himself.

The doors of the assembly rooms open and a pair of specials come out, eyes scanning the crowd. The foremen follow, dressed in their Sunday best. They look uncertain as they emerge, blinking in the afternoon sunlight. Makin and his secretary follow. Makin looks stiff and starched. I'm used to seeing him with his shirtsleeves rolled up, fingers inky from his calculations.

Then Lord Peel steps out, the brim of his hat angled to shade his face. I realize there's silence. Not even the sound of shuffling feet.

Some lackey shoves a child forward and she holds up a bunch of pink roses. Peel turns his face as he takes them. He's a shocker close up. His nose and eyes are leonine. Thin lipped. Skin stretched to a sickening smoothness that rivals the silk of his cravat. His blue eyes are faded by age.

Then it begins. A low baritone from deep within the crowd.

> The sea takes me from my love . . .

Another voice joins in, then another, then more so there's a choir.

> The sea takes me from my love
> It drops me on the ocean floor
> The sea tempts me from my true love's arms
> And I'll go home no more.

Peel smiles, thinking this impromptu serenade's for him. He doesn't know that each ship has its own shanties and ballads and this one's famed as *The Triumph*'s.

Makin leans over and whispers in Peel's ear and his smile fades. There's another chorus and it sounds like the whole of Liverpool is singing.

> The sea takes me from my love
> It drops me on the ocean floor
> The sea tempts me from my mother's knee
> And I'll go home no more.

There are no jeers or shouts. Just the people's indignity dignified in song. The police don't know how to respond. They form a ring around Peel and his retinue. The foremen are outside this protective circle. Someone motions for Peel's carriage.

The air's filled with fluttering white sheets. They're being thrown down onto the street from the roof of the infirmary. Hands reach for them. Makin plucks at a sheet, reads it and crumples it in his fist. Peel's caught one too. He's angry. He turns to Makin and jabs at his chest with a gloved forefinger as if he's personally responsible.

I pick up one. It's *The Echo*, a dissident rag, printed on cheap, low-grade paper, the ink already smudging. It advocates minimum wages, safety measures and free health care. This edition's different. It bears the words *Lord Peel's Triumph*, with a drawing of Richard Harper floating on his anchor. It's the anniversary of his death. A bad day for Peel to show his face.

Once Peel's departed the police will demonstrate their displeasure for this display. Jessop's already giving orders. It's time to leave.

Peel's in the carriage as the singing continues. Makin turns as he climbs in and his gaze fixes on me, *The Echo* still clutched in my hand.

It's an official match day, when the factories close for the machines to be serviced.

Football's a violent and anarchic game where passions are vented, on and off the pitch. The crowd wears the colors, red or blue. They're no longer just a dark mass of serge and twill that pour into the black factories.

Jessop and his sidekick are behind me. I try and lose them in the crush. The hoards of Everton, Toxteth, Kensington, and Dingle come together for this sliver of pleasure.

The constabulary are mounted, their horses stamping and pawing the cobbles. They'll tolerate fisticuffs amid the crowd to vent rising tensions. A good-natured kicking or black eye, as long as everyone's fit for work the following day no harm's done.

The coppers know if they weigh in the crowd will turn on them, but I can see in their eyes how they'd love to beat about with batons and hand out indiscriminate thrashings in the guise of peacekeeping.

I see my chance. A chanting group comes up the street towards Anfield's football pitch, waving Evertonian flags. Red banners are at my back. The two groups meet, posturing and jostling. I dart down an alley, ducking to avoid the lines of washing. Jessop's lost.

There's one place I've not looked for them. The dirty terraces where parlors of women wait for the game to end. It makes me shudder.

I peer into windows and am shocked by what's on show. It's just another factory, churning up girls, making fodder of their flesh. I go around the back. Women line the wall, waiting to be hired. My heart stops when I see her. I push past the other girls who try to lure me in with promises that make me blush.

"Where's Kate?"

"You." Sally looks tired and bored. "Are you paying?"

Hard and heartless. I rifle in my pocket, glancing up and down the street. "Here."

"It's double that." She scowls.

I give her more. We have to get indoors.

She leads me to a house. A room's free at the top of the stairs. It's painted an oppressive red that would look fashionable somewhere grand. The window's dirty. There's a bed with a sheet and pillow on it. A pitcher and bowl on the dresser. A headboard rattles on the other side of the wall.

"What are you doing, Sally?"

"Earning a living."

"Here?"

"I can't get work."

"And Kate?"

"Dead."

The mattress sinks even farther as I sit beside her. She moves away.

"When?" Then, "How?"

"A week ago. We moved in with a family in Croxteth. The woman was sick that day so Kate went to work in her place. She got her sleeve caught in a roller. It took her arm. They were too slow tying the stump off. She bled to death."

Sally's matter-of-fact. Her lip doesn't quiver. Her eyes are dry.

"I'm sorry." Words clog my throat. "Where's Lolly?"

"At home, where else?" She's glad of an excuse to be angry. "What sort do you think I am, to bring a child here?"

"The best sort." I try and soothe her.

Kate's dead. I wish I'd gone back to their terrace sooner but posthumous offers of help mean nothing to the dead.

"I'm the best sort, am I? Is that why you think you can buy me with a few coins? You men are all loathsome."

I'm angry too. I want to shut her up. I grip her head and cover her mouth with mine. She pulls away.

"Don't kiss me with your eyes shut and pretend I'm Kate. Fuck me for my own sake."

I don't relent. I'm too busy kissing Sally to correct her. The tension in her is like a wire.

We lie down. She's thin, a skeleton wrapped in skin. I'm not much better, but I take the weight of my large frame on my knees and elbows.

"This doesn't mean anything. Understand?"

She's wrong. It means everything.

"You're crying," she says.

"So are you."

She undoes my trousers and puts her hand between my legs. No one's ever touched me there before.

"Oh," she says. Then louder, "Oh."

I feel the wire snap, and her whole body relaxes. She kisses me, finally yielding. My whole life's been leading to this moment of sex and solace.

I want to say, *Thank you, thank you, thank you*, but I'm too breathless to speak.

Sally's head is on my chest. Sleep slows her breathing. My trousers are around my thighs, my shirt's undone. Her petticoat's rucked up around her waist. I don't move for fear of disturbing this lovely girl. The sudden roar from Anfield carries over the rooftops and into the room. It masks the quiet click of the door opening and closing.

Jessop stands at the end of the bed, chuckling. I leap up, struggling with my trousers.

"So Tom," he says, sarcastic. "Who's your pretty friend?"

I do up my fly. Sally retrieves her blouse from the floor and pulls it over her head. Jessop's sly look scares me. He takes off his jacket.

"We've all afternoon. Why don't you both lie down again?"

I go at him like a cornered dog. Dad used to say, *Fight if you're cornered.* I stick him in the throat with my pocketknife. Bubbles of blood mark the wound. I put my hand over his mouth to stop him crying out. He grips my wrist and twists. Sally's fishing about under the bed and I wonder what the hell she's doing, then I see the docker's hook. It's the weapon of choice in Liverpool. The handle sits snug in the palm, the hook protruding between the first and second fingers. She comes around behind him and plants it in his skull.

Jessop pitches into my arms. I lower him to the floor.

"Hold his legs."

I grab them to stop his boot heels from hammering on the floor. Sally helps. How he clings to life. It seems like forever before he's still.

"Are you okay, Sal?" A woman's voice.

"Fine."

"Sure?"

Sally gets up. I wipe the blood spray from her face. She goes to the door and opens it a crack. She whispers something and the woman laughs. Then Sally locks the door.

"Who was he?"

"A special."

"Jesus. We'll both swing."

She's right. We'll go straight from the law courts to the noose in Victoria Square. But before that there'll be long days and nights in a cell with Jessop's friends queued outside.

I'd rather die.

"What did he want with you?"

"He was looking for Kate. They think she can lead them to trade unionists."

"That's crazy."

"Sally, we've not got much time. I'll deal with this. You need to go."

"No. We stay together."

"Get Lolly. Wait at The Baltic Fleet. Don't speak to anyone but Mrs. Tsang. Tell her I sent you. You can trust her." It kills me to say this. I want to be a coward and say, *Yes, stay. Never leave my side.*

She kisses me. Why did I ever think her hard?

"I'm sorry that I got you involved with this." I usher her out. "Go on now, quickly." Once she's gone, I splash cold water on my face and button up my jacket to hide my bloodied shirt.

All the while I'm thinking of Sally. Of how my parting words were *I'm sorry that I got you involved with this,* when what I meant was *I'm sorry that you think I love Kate more.*

I roll Jessop under the bed and pull the rug over the stained floorboards. I'm thankful for the room's violent color as it hides the blood sprayed across the walls.

The specials must be going house to house. I'm on the stairs when I hear outraged shouts from the room below. A pair of them come up the narrow stairs. I grapple with the first one and he knocks me down. The other tries to hold my thrashing legs. Like Jessop, I struggle against the inevitable.

A third clambers over us, pretty tangle that we are, and checks the rooms. There's a pause, then a hoarse shout. Jessop's been found.

"Take the bastard outside."

They've cleared the street. Faces peer from the window. Someone kicks my legs from under me. I land on my knees.

"Mike, remember what Makin said." The man holding my arm is young and nervous.

Mike, who's looking down on me, pauses, but then he decides I'm worth it. He kicks me in the chest. I feel the wind go out of me.

"Bugger Makin. He killed Jessop."

I curl up on the floor, hands over my head. My view's of the boots as they pile in. It doesn't matter. I've had a kicking before.

I'm in Makin's office. The clock sounds muffled and voices are distant. The hearing in my left ear's gone. The vision in my right eye's reduced to a slit. Breathing hurts.

Makin's furious.

"Get out."

"Sir, the man's a murderer," Mike whines.

"I gave specific orders. Tom wasn't to be harmed under any circumstances. You were to bring him straight to me if anything happened."

"Sir, Jessop . . ."

"Are you still here? Go before I have you posted to Seaforth."

Mike flees at the ~~~~~~ Merseyside's hinterlands. Makin fetches a pair of glasses and ~~~~~~ urs out the port. It looks like molten rubies.

"D~ ~~~~~~ ve called for a doctor."

I dra~ ~~~~~~ contents. His sits, untouched.

"You'r~ ~~~~~~ want to help you." The chair's legs scrape the floor as ~~~~~~ own. "Did you kill him?"

I nod. Th~ ~~~~~~

"It happen~ ~~~~~~ ~rst in. I was with a girl." I'm babbling. A stream of snot, tears, a~ ~~~pair. "I'm not a trade unionist."

"Who was the girl?"

"Not Kate Harper, if that's what you're thinking. Jessop didn't do his job very well. She's dead. He should've checked the register."

"He did. The body didn't match the sample you gave me for her." Makin tips his head. "You have to trust me. Is Kate really dead or were you with her?"

"No. All I know is that she's dead."

"Who did the sample belong to? Was it the woman you were with?"

"Does it matter?"

He looks down at his hands. Ink stains his fingers. "More than you think."

He tops up my glass.

"Let's suppose Lord Peel's keen to find this woman, whoever it is. Let's say Lady Peel needs medical attention that requires a little blood or perhaps a bit of skin. It would be a wealth for this woman and a reward to whoever helps me find her." He lets this sink in. "Suppose Jessop got himself into a spot of bother with some girl. He played rough from what I've heard. There's no proof. The girl's long gone. An unsolved case."

My nose starts to bleed. Makin hands me his handkerchief. Blood stains the fine linen.

"You could do that?"

"I'll do what's necessary." Makin, not afraid to scramble.

"I want somewhere away from Liverpool. Out in the country. A farm with cows and chickens where nobody can bother me," I blurt out. "And I want to take a woman and child with me."

"That's a lot, just for information."

"It's more than that. Peel will be pleased. It'll make up for that day when he made his speech. But promise me first, that we have a deal."

Makin looks at me with narrowed eyes.

"A deal then, as long as you deliver her."

We shake hands.

"The sample's mine."

"That's not funny."

"I'm not joking."

He stares at me.

"Test me again and you'll see." I'm an odd-looking woman, but I make a passable man. I'm too big, too ungainly, too flat chested and broad shouldered. My hips narrow and features coarse. "I'm not trying to make a fool of you. I live this way."

"Why?"

"Sarah, my mother, got me when she was cornered on the factory floor by men who resented a woman who could work a metal press better than them. She swore she'd never go back. She became Saul after I was born."

Rag and bone men. We're free, Tom. Never subject to the tyranny of the clock. The dull terrors of the production lines. No man will use us as he pleases.

"What's your real name?"

"Tom." It's the only name I've ever had. "Do we still have a deal?"

"Yes. The girl you were with when you killed Jessop. Is she the one you want to take with you?"

His face is smooth now, hiding disgust or disappointment.

"Yes."

"I'll need to know who she is and where to find her if I'm going to get her out of Liverpool."

I tell him. When I say Sally's name he takes a deep breath but doesn't ask anything else.

I want to ask, *What do the Peels want from me?* But then I decide it's better not to know.

I've never been on a boat. I've never seen Liverpool from the sea. My stinking, teeming city's beautiful. I've never loved her more than I do now. I love the monumental Liver birds, even though they're indifferent to the suffering below. The colonnades and warehouses. Cathedrals and crack houses. The pubs and street lamps glowing in the fog. Workers, washerwomen, beggars, priests, and princes. Rag and bone men. Liverpool is multitudes.

The boat's pitch and roll makes me sick. A guard follows me to the rail. He's not concerned about my health. He's scared I'll jump. I get a whiff of the Irish Sea proper. Land's a strip in the distance.

We don't moor at Southport but somewhere nearby. I'm marched down the rattling gangplank and onto a narrow jetty. Miles of dunes roll out before us. It's clean and empty. I've never known such quiet. There's only wind and shifting sands. I wonder if it's hell or paradise.

The dunes become long grass and then packed brown earth. I've never seen so many trees. Their fallen leaves are needles underfoot, faded from rich green to brown.

There's a hatch buried in the ground. One of my guards opens it and clambers down, waiting at the bottom.

"You next."

The corridor leads downwards. Our boots shed sand and needles on the tiles. There's the acrid smell of antiseptic.

"In here." One of them touches my arm.

The other's busy talking to someone I can't see because of the angle of an adjoining door. I catch the words, "Makin sent her this way. She'll need time to heal."

"Take your clothes off and put them in the bin. Turn this and water will come out here. Get clean under it." My guard's talking to me like I'm a child. "Soap's here. Towel's there. Put on this gown after."

I'm mortified, thinking they're going to watch, but they're keen to be away.

I drop my clothes into the bin. I can still smell Sally on me but she doesn't stand a chance against the stream of hot water and rich suds.

A woman's leaning against the far wall, watching. I pull the towel about me and try to get dry. She looks like a china doll, with high, round cheeks and blue eyes. Her long yellow hair swings as she walks.

"Sit there."

She tuts as she touches my cheek where the skin's split. Then she checks my eyes and teeth. A needle punctures my vein. Blood works its way along a tube into a bottle. She takes scrapings from the inside of my mouth.

"Disrobe."

I stand up and let the towel drop to a puddle at my feet. I stare ahead of me. She walks around me like a carter considering a new horse. Her hand floats across the plane of my back, around the garland of yellow and purple bruises that run from back to front. She touches my breasts, my stomach, my thighs. From the steadfast way she avoids my gaze, I know there's more chance that the Liver birds will fly than of me leaving here.

I try and stay calm. I was dead from the moment Jessop opened the door of the red room. From the moment I put the sampler to my arm. It's either this or a jig at the end of a rope. There's no point in me going cold into the warm ground to rot when I can help Sally and Lolly. I hope they'll remember to take Gabriel with them.

Ink-fingered Makin, the artful scrambler, making his calculations. The possibility I've got him wrong is a cold, greasy knife in my belly. If I have, I've served up Sally, Lolly, and Mrs. Tsang into the constabulary's hands.

The woman seems satisfied. I want to say, *Look at me. Look me in the eye. I'm a person, not a piece of meat*, but then I realize I just might as well be. A piece of meat. Rag and bone.

"Rag and Bone" is based in Liverpool, UK, the beautiful city where **Priya Sharma** was a medical student. She is now a doctor but writes whenever she can. Her short stories can be found in various publications including *Interzone*, *Black Static*, *Alt Hist*, *Tor.com*, and more will be available in 2014. She has been anthologized in several "Year's Bests." More information is available at www.priyasharmafiction.wordpress.com.

I swear to you, that day the Angel of Death wore a face
and that face was the face of the slipway gray.

THE SLIPWAY GRAY

Helen Marshall

Sit by me, my bokkie, my darling girl. Closer, yes, there.

I am an old man now, and this is a thing that happened to me when I was very young. This is not like the story of your uncle Mika, and how he tricked me in the Breede River and I almost drowned. It is also not like the story of my good friend Jurie Gouws whom you called Goose when he was alive, which was a good name for him. He used to hitchhike all across Rhodesia until he blew off his right thumb at that accident at the Selebi mine, which I will say something about. Afterward the trucks would stop anyway, even when he wasn't trying to hitch a ride, because of the ghost thumb, he used to say, which still ached with arthritis when it rained.

These are what your father would call fables or fancies or tall tales, and perhaps he is right that they have grown an inch or two in the telling, but the story I will tell you is a different sort of story, my bokkie, because it is my story and it is a true story. It has not grown in the telling because I have never told anyone about what happened except for your Ouma, God rest her soul, to whom I told all the secrets of my heart and let her judge them as she would. Still, even she did not know what it meant, and neither of us could ever come to much agreement on this.

I am getting older, and I can feel the ache Jurie complained of in his thumb. It lives in every part of me, but my lungs most of all, which the doctor tells me are all moth-eaten by the mining work, even though that was many years passed. Perhaps you will say that moths are not made for lungs. They are made for closets and for fine things such as the silk your Ouma wore on our wedding day—white silk, the finest Tsakani government silk, so fine it felt like water in my hands, but then after she died and I went to see to her things, there it was, so thick with moths in the crawlspace where she had hid it, so thick it was as if she had made the dress of these little white-winged creatures with their dark nesting eyes, and maybe she had, maybe there had been nothing but moths on her as she walked down the aisle to marry me. But the way that dress looked when the moths had scattered—all coming to pieces in my hands, this beautiful thing, this beautiful thing I had loved so much when I had seen it that day, the doctors say that is what my lungs are like now, from the mine dust.

When a man gets older a man starts to think about all the things in the world—like you, my bokkie, the things that he loves and the things that he will leave behind—but then he also thinks about the place that he might be going to and the people he might see there, like Jurie and the others and especially like your Ouma who has had to wait far too long for me to catch up with her.

The story goes like this, and I know you have not heard it before, but even so, if you have heard parts before or heard something like it then keep still, my bokkie, keep still and listen, for a thing that starts the same does not always end the same.

I first met Jurie at Howard College when I was studying. He was an Afrikaner like I was and he was also studying engineering. From that first look, I judged Jurie to be something of a NAAFI, which is to say, No Ambition and Fuck-All Interest, if you don't mind me saying so and please don't repeat it to your father, but that is the kind of man he was. Skinny as a bushwillow, with a mess of bright red hair. He had the look of a traveling man, and that is an untrustworthy sort of look. As it happened, though, I spent much of my time studying and Jurie spent little enough time at the same endeavor, still when our grades were posted he consistently beat me. I knew he was not a more diligent student than I, and I guessed he was not a smarter one. I confess this rankled somewhat, particularly because I was only there because your Uncle Mika had paid my way to University instead of going himself, and even then he had just been drafted into the National Service, though it was as a cook, thank God, and not a proper service man because he had flat feet. So it was that near the end of term, after I had had a somewhat ill-informed dalliance with a particular lady who was not your Ouma, because this was before your Ouma and before I found out what love was, that my grades started to slip. You see, my bokkie, the thing about women is that they have a power about them that is not unlike that story Jurie told you about his thumb. Women are like that, they've got the power to stop you in your tracks. You will be the same, my bokkie, just you wait.

But I won't go further into that matter here, for the sake of your Ouma who, if she was listening, wouldn't like to hear it much repeated. The important thing is that I found myself in a somewhat precarious position in terms of my schooling. I had watched Jurie, who, as I say, seemed no smarter than I was, rise higher and higher in the postings while my own place suffered. As the end of term stepped closer and closer, I found myself in what you might call desperate straits, so it was then I approached Jurie and inquired in what might have been rather ruder terms than I shall repeat as to the nature of his successes. Jurie did not answer in the manner I expected. He was, you see, used to that sort of line of questioning, and had developed a limp and the occasional black eye from answering badly. That smile of his, well, I'll tell you that it didn't hang quite so straight on his face back then. Remember, I wasn't an old man and so all this skin you see hanging off my bones and my lungs raggle-taggled, well, it wasn't much like that. It had been remarked more than once that I could have been a champion boxer if I had applied my mind to that instead of engineering. I confess I might have asked Jurie in such a way that he considered it wisest to answer quickly. So he tells it, anyway.

He told me that he had learned a special trick to train his mind. Now I know, my bokkie, that this might sound something like those other tales I started off with, but I swear to you that isn't the way of it. What Jurie could do I had seen with my own eyes, and this is it: he would sit in a certain chair suited to relaxation, and then he would take a certain word, which I shall not tell, and he would repeat it over and over and over again. He described the sensation to me as standing at the top of a stairwell partially submerged in water, and as he would say the word, he would take a step farther and farther downward until such time as he had drifted into the water, until it reached his knees and then his belly and then his shoulders and then his chin.

When he was deep into the water, so deep he was floating and he could feel nothing but the warmth of the water and all weight had left him, then he would imagine three boxes adrift in the water. As he continued to say the word, he would swim one stroke closer until at last he had reached the boxes. Then he would open each box and he would place inside each box some part of the day's lessons. Once the whole process was complete, he would begin to stir again, and his eyelids would flutter wild and delicate, then the rest of him would stretch and yawn, but the knowledge would be lodged firmly in his memory.

I thought this sounded a fine thing. When I saw it at work it seemed no harm so I asked him to show me how it was done.

Jurie was reluctant. He said that it took time to master the skill properly, but after some time and some insistence eventually he relented. It is difficult to tell you exactly what the experience of that meditation was like, as I have never felt its likeness at all except for, perhaps, the look in your Ouma's eyes after we had come to the decision together about what should happen, which was a thing both frightening but somehow also calming in the end.

That is what the experience was like.

I stepped into the water, lower and lower, but he had not told me how lifelike it would be. For Jurie's eyes had a furious calm to them, as if he was stepping into a bath, but for me the water was strange and dark. Instinctively, I did not want to go into it.

To understand this properly, I must tell you something about your Uncle Mika and the Breede River. I know, my bokkie, that he has told you this story before, but as I said earlier, a thing that starts the same does not always end the same.

There was a time when we were much younger and we lived along the Breede River. As boys, he and I would go diving in the waters because unlike most of the waters in those parts it was free of crocodiles and mosquitoes and hippopotamuses. Because we were boys, and because I was bigger than Uncle Mika even though he was older, he would often make challenges to me. He would say, "I expect you cannot swim as fast to the other side of the river as I can," or, "I expect you cannot take that man's prized rod and tackle," and so forth. That day, he said to me that he reckoned he could stay under the water longer, and I, of course, reckoned otherwise, and so it was set that we would swim out a ways and then we would both go under together. Your Uncle Mika was a damn sight smarter than me in those days, and he took with him a straw he had fashioned for the purpose of breathing under water. The Breede, you see, was so murky in that part that though I could see him, I couldn't see anything like the straw he had fashioned.

So down we went, the two of us boys, and out came your Uncle Mika's straw, and he blew and he blew until it was cleared of water and he could breathe as if he were upon dry land. Down I went, and I sank right to the bottom because I was heavier than he was, and I kept my cheeks puffed out and I stared at your Uncle Mika, so close to the surface and I confess I might have laughed to myself, I confess I might have thought him something of a moegoe or a coward as you would say it, so close to the surface where he could just pop his head up when he was tired. Even then I knew it is not good to have the thing you want too close to you, not if you want to resist it. No, I knew I would do better in the depths where I would forget what sunlight looked like and forget the taste of the Sunday morning air.

Of course, as you would have guessed it your Uncle Mika could hold out for far longer than me, what with his straw, and though I sat at the bottom, heavy as a stone, smart as a crocodile and laughing in my head at him, I began to feel a burning in my lungs. A little thing at first, but need is need and the need for the Sunday morning air was not likely to diminish. Your Uncle Mika sucked away at it, but me, down there in the darkness with the weeds, I had to live off only what I had taken down with me. So my lungs got to burning, and my lungs got to burning, and all I got see was your Uncle Mika happy near the surface and looking like he might go on forever.

There is only so much a man can take, my bokkie, and I had long past reached it. So finally when I tried to push to the surface, my lungs feeling like they'd take in the water as happily as the air and my vision all gone strangled and dim, well, wouldn't you know it but down there in the muck I had managed to hook myself well and good on the trunk of an old yellowwood, it being, as I have said, a sight murky at the bottom.

It wouldn't have been a difficult thing to get free of. I was a strong boy and a good swimmer, but I was weak from holding in my breathing, and the first thing to set upon me was a panic so strong and so terrible that I flailed like a mad thing.

Your Uncle Mika, he was just about getting tired of playing that old game anyway, and he looks down and he sees me flailing about, and all he can think is the tales the old fishermen used to tell him about the things that lived in the water, the things that none of us quite believed would ever come so far inland. So your Uncle Mika, he hightails it out of there, thinking I'm already dead, thinking that the thing, whatever it is, has already got me. I can't fault him for it, even if he were my own brother, but still to this day I think that is why he sent me off to University even though I was never quite as clever as he was. He always felt the shame of tricking me with that little straw and then leaving me to drown.

So there I am at the bottom of the Breede River, caught up in a tangle with an old yellowwood and not long for the world, I reckon, and soon sure enough the water on the other side of my lips is looking sweeter and sweeter if only so that it'll stop that damn fire in my lungs. That's when I see it: to this day your Uncle Mika doesn't believe me even though he's seen the old lady himself, but I swear that I saw something dark moving through the water, and to be sure, it was exactly the same thing that your Uncle Mika had been afraid of—an old Zambezi bull shark, the grand dame of river sharks, I reckon, her body like a torpedo with a slit-open mouth across the front, head wavering back and forth as she slid oh so delicately through the waters.

They say those sharks are killers, man-eaters, they call them, the slipway grays. Sure as Hell if I had thought drowning would be bad, it had nothing on being taken apart bit by bit by those teeth of hers.

But this one, she just glided past me, a solemn thing, beautiful even though I can't tell you how, until the darkness and the murk closed around her once more.

Who can say if I really saw it? I certainly believed it. It was only a moment later that your Uncle Mika was in the water again, and he was hauling me out by the shoulder, by the hair, by any bit of me he could grab hold of. You see, he'd realized there was no blood, and if there had been a shark, there would've been blood. So after a minute up on the banks, gasping like a son of a bitch, he was in the water again and he was after me and I'm sure that I owe him my life for it.

But that shark, that slipway gray . . . I swear to you, my bokkie, there was nothing more frightening in the world, not even the fear of drowning, than seeing that old thing gliding past. My father, he was a religious man and he spoke to us boys about angels and signs and such, and I swear to you, that day the Angel of Death wore a face and that face was the face of the slipway gray.

I have told you all this for a reason, though, and that is to say that deep water has always had such an effect on me. It is enough to shiver my blood and tighten my balls, if you don't mind me saying. I still cannot shake the feeling that deep water, it was not made for the likes of you and I. It was made for the angels and the demons of this world.

So when Jurie set me to walking down those steps into the cold blackness of those waters, saying that word over and over again, a kind of creeping terror stole over me. All I could imagine was the feel of something against my legs as I crawled through darkness towards the three boxes he told me about, but I did as he told me, and I opened them one by one, and into them I placed the day's lessons. When I woke, cold-soaked and sweating, there it was in my head, and to this day I still know the things I learned. I only have to travel in my mind to the boxes.

As you know, Jurie and I became close friends, and I suspect I owe much of my career to him and his tricks. Indeed, it was the very next semester that

I met your Ouma, God rest her soul, and if I thought the first woman had a kind of pull about her, well, there has never been another woman like your Ouma.

The next part of the story happened some time later once Jurie and I had both taken jobs at the Selebi mine in Botswana. I know you have not been to the mines and so you do not know what it was like there. The job of an engineer is to make a place unfit for man livable, and that is what I did. I was the winding engineer, it was my job to inspect the shafts and make sure there were no obstructions for the man winder, that little elevator the workers used to ride, ninety, a hundred-fifty, up to three-hundred-sixty meters down to the bottom where they loaded the copper and tin into bins.

On this particular day, Jurie and I were riding on the top of the cage of the man winder in order to perform an inspection upon its gears. This was the part that I disliked most about the job, that great fall into the black, just watching that cable unwind slowly as the winding engine driver lowered us down. Jurie, of course, was Jurie and it never bothered him in the slightest, he was the sort of man who could raise a smile on the Devil's lips if he had to. In those days we could not get a radio signal in the mines so we used a system of bells to communicate with the surface: one chime to stop, two chimes to raise slowly, and three chimes to lower. So this time it was three chimes to lower, and down we went, one, two, just like that and the winding engine driver sent the cage a hundred meters, two hundred meters into darkness.

It was at about the two hundred-fifty meter mark where Jurie was fooling around as he did sometimes, knowing that I was a nervous man about such things. Sometimes he would joke about the other men, and sometimes he would sing that old mining song. "Shosholoza," he would sing, "shosholoza, you are running away on these mountains. Eh, boss? Sing it with me." And the sound would echo back up through the mines like Jurie was the tongue kicking around at the bottom of some enormous throat. "Shosholoza, shosholoza," he was singing like a mad man, and me chiming three times for the winding engine driver to take us the rest of the way down. And Jurie's just been singing along—"shosholoza, shosholoza," he's singing like a drunk, "go forward, go forward," he's singing—and suddenly he's hollering up a storm. Underneath us the cage starts to shudder and shake—snick, snick, snick— making a noise. Oh, my bokkie, I don't have to tell you that it is every mine worker's nightmare. That sound. The feeling of the world shifting under your feet and a straight plunge into darkness waiting for you. It sends shivers through me even now, just remembering.

But there it was, the man winder tilting sideways until there's a shower of sparks as it scrapes along the side of the shaft, but not budging too much because now it's jammed solid in the shaft. Then I can see something flashing like a snake in the bright cone of my mining light, something winding through the air, fast now, hooking back and forth. I'm looking around and then I see what it is, one of the stabilizing guy wires snapped free.

It's snapping mad like a hyena put off her dinner for too long, and Jurie's still shrieking, and I can see he's over by the cage's metal guide, and now he's waving his hand around and the air has gone heavy and sour with the smell of blood.

You've seen Jurie smile that goose smile of his, yes, I know it, but you've never seen the way a man smiles, you've never seen the way a man's lips might become something else, might change the very shape of his face when he's staring at the stump of his thumb down there in the mine's darkness, two hundred meters from a sunlight you don't know you'll ever see again.

That snapped guy wire, you see, that wasn't enough to drop us solid— thank God for that—but it was enough to jam us down there. Jurie with just that stub of his thumb bleeding out on the cage. Me with nothing but that bell to tell them what had happened. "Eh, boss," says Jurie, and I don't even know if he can tell what he's saying, but he's whispering, "go forward, go forward" still as if the song's just kept running through his head, teeth flashing white and glowing in that thin beam of mining light.

I chime the bell once, and the cage, it stops grinding away. At least it's steady for a moment.

I look at Jurie, and Jurie looks at me. He's licking his lips now, I don't know if he can feel the pain, but he's licking his lips just like he's going to settle down to a chicken dinner, like he's so hungry and that scares me all the worse.

"We'll get you, Goose," I say to him, "they'll be coming down here for us, you know that." I'm tearing off something of my shirt, and you can hear that noise, that long rip echoing back up the throat of the mine. Then I'm wrapping it around him, wrapping it around that hand, and I can feel the blood pooling sticky onto my hand, and I can hear him breathing heavy now in my ear. "Eh, boss," he's saying, as he holds his other hand over mine till I can feel them almost tacking together with the blood. "Eh, boss. You gotta climb, you gotta climb now."

I know he's right. I know that bell isn't enough, and if we wait, well, Jurie's bones wouldn't be the first to feed the darkness, his blood wouldn't be the first dripping down into the great dark black. But, dammit, if there isn't a worse thing I can imagine at that moment than climbing. But there is need, and I know it, and I know that if I do not climb then Jurie will be dead.

There are vertical ladders—five, six meters each—running up the side of the shaft, so before I think about it, before my brain slams on the brakes, there I am, twenty meters up, Jurie's mine light winking away below me, him slumped over away from the broken guy wire. And then I was climbing. I was climbing and the shaft wall was wet with groundwater leakage, and it was running down the metalwork too, down those ladders I was clinging too. And my hands, my hands were wet with Jurie's blood, but I pull myself up, I pull myself up until after a while I can hear Jurie singing, "go forward, go forward" in that crazy, pain-mad voice of his, or maybe I'm just dreaming it by then.

Because it is just like being underwater. It is just like that, the darkness close around me, and my muscles burning, burning. But I know that if I slack for a moment now, then I will plummet all that way and the dark will take me too.

So I start saying a word.

I started saying that word that Jurie taught me years before, and with every hoist upward I am saying that word now, I am breathing that word out and I am breathing that word in again and I am getting higher and higher and higher away from the blood and the cage and the pool of light beneath me.

And as I climb higher, it is like I am swimming up from deep water now, swimming from the ocean floor up and up and upto sunlight and the Sunday morning air.

But I know I will not make it. I know my strength is failing me.

I am a hundred meters up now. I am a hundred and twenty meters up. If I fall, I will die.

And there is something in the darkness with me. Something in those dark waters of my mind, something that I sensed was always there with me, has always been with me since I was a child, since the day I was born. And she is sleek, gorgeous and deadly. This thing with me. This thing I know is my own death.

The killer. The man-eater. The slipway gray.

She is coming for me now, drifting along the currents, slick and terminal. Cold and quiet as the lights turning off one by one by one. Her mouth open and tasting. The wide, dark, liquid space of her eyes. The shadow of her, the shape of her. My death come for me at last.

I said, my bokkie, that I have never told this to another person, and that is true. But it was real. It was real to me. I swear it to you and I swore it to your Ouma and, for everything, I know she believed me.

I could feel my hands going slack on the ladder. My back humping out into the open shaft of the mine.

She was beautiful. I wanted her to come for me.

But then. But then, my bokkie, there was something else. Three boxes. I could see them as well as I can see you here, all dressed up fine for Sunday church and maybe a bit impatient no?—with your Oupa's stories. Three boxes.

So my hands are slipping and in my mind I am opening those three boxes. And do you know what I find? In the first is your Uncle Mika who had taken on the National Service for me. In the second is Jurie, lying in the darkness below me, singing that damn stupid song of his. And in the third is your Ouma who was everything to me. My piece of sunlight. My Sunday morning air. In those three boxes were all the things worth living for.

So I set myself to climbing again and oh, even though it hurt, even though it hurt more than anything, it was still easier than dying. So up I am coming, and I can see that shape of darkness so near me I could touch her. I can see those teeth of hers.

But for the second time she passes me by. For the second time she lets me go, and up I came out of the mine. Up I came into the light, and there was the winding engine driver and all the others, waiting for me.

They got Jurie out, not fast, of course, not fast enough to save his thumb but fast enough that even though he was pale and shaking he was still alive. Still singing that damn song of his. "Go forward, go forward," he was singing, "you are running away on those mountains, the train from Zimbabwe."

Now, as I said to you, your Ouma and I, we could never much agree on what it all meant, what it was that I had seen there drifting in the darkness. But let me tell you this one thing, my bokkie, this one thing that I have not told another soul. At the end, after your Ouma and I had come to that decision together and I could see that the lights were going out, one by one, she drew me close to her. Her skin was as pale as old silk, and her touch was as light as a moth's wing, but she pulled me close to her and she whispered into my ear, "I see it. Oh, love, I see it, and I am scared, and I see it, and she is come for me."

Now I know you do not want to listen longer to an old man's ramblings, but as I said, this is a true story. Not a fable. Not a fancy. And I swear to you that it has not grown in the telling. But even now. Even now as I am drawing in breath through these raggle-taggled lungs of mine, these lungs that the doctors tell me will not last much longer, these lungs that feel as if they are breathing in water instead of Sunday air. Even now I know she is coming for me. The grand dame of the river. The slipway gray.

There are three boxes.

Jurie has gone into one, your Ouma has gone into another, and I fear, my bokkie, the last box is mine. But this is how it should be. A man should not live forever.

Because that is what death is. That beast in the darkness where no beast should be. Death is the thing that hooks you and will not let you go. Death is the slow undoing of beautiful things.

You should know this, my bokkie, while you are young. Your father will not teach you this.

But here is another secret. The slipway gray has her own kind of beauty, and when you meet her you will know that. There is more to her than the teeth. This is how it is, my bokkie. I want you to know that. When she comes for me the third time, I shall be ready for her. I shall welcome her as an old friend. And when she comes to you, and pray God let that be many years from now, I know that you will do the same.

Helen Marshall is an award-winning Canadian author, editor, and doctor of medieval studies. Her debut collection of short stories *Hair Side, Flesh Side* (ChiZine Publications, 2012) was named one of the top ten books of 2012 by *January Magazine* and won the 2013 British Fantasy Award for Best Newcomer. Her second collection, *Gifts for the One Who Comes After*, will be released from ChiZine in September 2014. She lives in Oxford, England— that is, medieval Disneyland.

Knowing of his family's curse, Kyle Murchison Booth
was determined never to marry . . .

TO DIE FOR MOONLIGHT

Sarah Monette

I cut off her head before I buried her.

I had no tools suitable to the task—only my pocketknife and the shovel—
and it was a long, grisly, abhorrent job, but I had to do it, and I did.

I could not leave the chance that she might return.

I had been weeping when I started; by the time it was done, the last tattered
string of flesh severed, I had no tears left in me, and my mouth and eyes and
sinuses were raw with bile and salt.

I stuffed her mouth with wolfsbane, wrapped a silver chain around her
poor hands, placed silver dollars over her staring eyes.

Then, at that most truly God-forsaken crossroads, under a full and leering
moon, I began to dig Annette Robillard's grave.

How, exactly, the Robillards were connected to Blanche Parrington Crowe, I
never discovered. Cousins in some degree of her long-dead husband, but whether
it was a Crowe daughter who married into the Robillards, or a Robillard daughter
who married into the Crowes, the link was many generations in the past—surely
not enough to count as kinship except in the genealogical sense. Nevertheless,
I was informed, Mrs. Crowe considered the Robillards to fall under the
umbrella of her family obligations; thus, when Marcus Justus Robillard asked
for a cataloguer to come make sense of his family's long-neglected library, Mrs.
Crowe felt it incumbent upon her to send one.

By which, I was further informed, she meant me.

I tried to argue that one of the junior archivists—all of whom certainly
needed the practice more than I did—would be both eminently suited to

the task and far less disruptive to the Parrington in his absence, but Dr. Starkweather glared me into silence, and then said, "Mrs. Crowe was very specific, Mr. Booth. It appears that she trusts you."

The grim incredulity in his tone told me that if Mrs. Crowe could have been talked out of the idea of sending me to Belle Lune, the Robillard estate, he would have done it. He had been heard on more than one occasion to say, publicly and loudly, that I could not be trusted to come in out of the rain.

"Then I suppose I, er, have no choice," I said. "Does Mrs. Crowe anticipate . . . er, that is, is it supposed to be a *long* job?"

"No," Dr. Starkweather said, even more grimly. "I have been instructed to release you from your duties for a week. That will be sufficient, Mr. Booth. I trust I make myself clear?"

"Yes, sir," I said, and was occupied for the rest of the day in the unsatisfying tedium of preparing my office for a week's absence.

It would be unwise to specify the location of Belle Lune. I will say only that it was in the mid-Atlantic states, close enough to the coast that the wind, when in the right quarter, would bring the smell of salt. Robillards had lived there since sometime in the seventeenth century, and the house had been expanded and remodeled so many times that nothing of its original character remained. It was more brick than wood, with the columns beloved of the Neoclassical Revival added to the front as a dowager pins a diamond brooch to her bosom, and it stood on the edge of a tarn. I call it a tarn, although there are no mountains in the vicinity of Belle Lune, because I do not know of a word that better conveys the secretive aspect—dark and uninviting—of its waters. The Robillards called it the Mirror, although I never saw it to reflect anything at all.

I was met at the train station on Monday by a young man and a horse-drawn trap. He had apologized as he introduced himself: "Justin Robillard—I'm sorry about the antiquated transport, but my grandfather has an abhorrence of engines and won't have them at Belle Lune."

"Kyle Murchison Booth." His gloved grip was strong, but not punishing; I was glad to be released from it all the same. "And I, er, I have no objection to horses."

His smile revealed strong white teeth and made his brown eyes glint almost yellow. "That's good. I appreciate it, Mr. Booth. Is it 'mister'? Or ought I to say 'doctor'?"

He swung my suitcase into the back of the trap, and swung himself up just as easily.

"I don't have a doctorate," I said, climbing up beside him.

"Good. Don't want to be rude." He smiled at me again, and the impression of teeth was so strong that it took an effort to keep from edging away from him. I upbraided myself for being nervy and ridiculous, but I was nevertheless glad when his attention shifted from me.

He clucked the horse into motion and said as we rattled out of the yard, "We'll have to make one stop. My sister Annette insisted on coming with me. She wanted to go shopping without my mother or any of my aunts."

He seemed to be waiting for a response, although I could not imagine what he thought I might say. I could hardly insist that he abandon his sister. I mumbled awkward compliance, and that was the end of the conversation until the trap drew up in front of a building with the words FOLKOW BROS. emblazoned in gaudy red and gold script across its windows.

"She promised she'd be waiting," said Justin Robillard, but he did not sound surprised that she was not. He consulted his watch. "I'll give her five minutes, then I'll have to go in after her. We want to get home before dark."

Again, he seemed to want a response from me. " . . . Yes," I said, and was either rewarded or punished with another tooth-baring smile.

At the four-minute mark, Annette Robillard appeared, a young man at her side. She was much younger than Justin; I guessed him to be twenty-five or twenty-six, and she was no more than eighteen. She was slight-boned, brunette, and very pretty, with large dark eyes of the sort referred to in novels as "speaking." The man with her was close to her own age, little more than a boy, blond where she was dark, and obviously, hopelessly smitten. It was notable that neither of them was carrying any packages.

Justin Robillard jumped down from the trap. "So *this* is why you wanted to come to town," he said unpleasantly, and to the younger man, "Clear off, Folkow."

"Justin!" protested Annette. "Don't be horrid. Roy was bringing his father a message, and we just happened to bump into each other as I was coming in."

"Grandfather's already spoken to you, Annette. There's no excuse for this."

"Love doesn't need an excuse," Roy Folkow said, and perhaps if he had been even slightly older, it would not have sounded quite so pompous.

Justin laughed, and the sound made me shiver. "Is that the kind of bilge he's been filling your head with, Annette?"

"It isn't bilge!" But her voice wavered.

"Get in the trap," Justin said, his voice a snarl almost like a dog's, and he turned his head sharply to glare at Roy Folkow. "Come near my sister again, and I'll tear you to pieces."

It should have been as much a cliché as Folkow's platitude, but it was not. Justin sounded not merely as if he meant what he said, but as if it would be no difficulty to him to carry out the threat.

Folkow backed away, one step, two, and then he stopped, his gaze fixed pleadingly on Annette's face.

"Go on, Roy," Annette said, and she was trying to make it sound as if her decision had nothing to do with her brother's threat. She added with clear defiance, "I'll talk to you later."

"All right," said Folkow. "G-good bye, Annette." He gave Justin a nervous sideways glance and went back into the store like a rabbit into a hole.

Justin watched him go.

Annette turned toward the trap and—visibly—noticed me for the first time. "Oh! I beg your pardon! Are you the man from the museum?"

"This is Mr. Booth," said Justin, "and I'm sure he found your little melodrama most edifying."

"*I* wasn't the one being melodramatic," she said. "I don't know what you have against Roy Folkow, but honestly, Justin—"

"Let's go home, Annie," Justin said, and instead of menacing, now he sounded merely tired.

She gave him a quick sidelong look, then hopped up nimbly into the trap, taking the seat back-to-back with her brother and immediately twisting around to keep talking. "I'm sorry you were kept waiting, Mr. Booth," she said. "I told Justin I'd walk home, but—"

"And I've told you, and Grandfather's told you, and Aunt Olive's told you, not if you can't make it home before dark." The trap lurched into motion like a physical echo of Justin's hard-edged words.

"Is the area so dangerous?" I said, surprised.

"Oh, there have been stories of wolves for years and years," Annette said, with a coquette's toss of her head, "but it's all nonsense. I think Grandfather's afraid I'll elope."

That made Justin laugh, and again the sound made me cold. "I'd like to see Roy Folkow try. But don't go out after dark, Mr. Booth. Whether there are wolves or not, the local geography is very treacherous, and frankly, I wouldn't advise wandering alone even in daylight. People fall into sinkholes every year, and sometimes their bodies can be retrieved and sometimes they can't."

"What a horrid way to welcome the poor man!" Annette said, laughing. Her laugh was nothing like her brother's. "I'm sure we all hope you'll be very comfortable at Belle Lune, Mr. Booth, and not want to go wandering about *regardless*. I think Grandfather said you'd be staying a week?"

"I, er . . . those are my instructions, yes." I had become rather anxious on the train about what I was supposed to do if, at the end of the week, Belle Lune's library was still not completely catalogued, and here was a chance to get a little more information. "Is the library, er, very large?"

"Oh, no," said Annette. "None of the Robillards have ever been great readers."

"Properly," said Justin, "it's Great-Grandmama Josephine's library. She brought most of the books with her when she married Samuel Justus Robillard in 1846."

"There'd be more books," Annette said with a sigh, "but Great-Grandmama Josephine died young."

"Grandfather kept the books in her memory," Justin said, "and then that lawyer said they might be valuable."

I doubted it, but at least, from their description, the task I faced was a manageable one, and might even prove interesting. I was relieved.

I should—I thought drearily Friday night, five purgatorial days later—*have known better*. The library was, in fact, much as Annette and Justin's comments had led me to surmise, but what they had not mentioned was that Belle Lune's library was also the sitting room, and as such, was never free of one or another of Marcus Justus Robillard's daughters.

Of the four of them, Olive, Sophia, Christina, and Sarah, three spinsters and one widow, I minded Sarah the least. She had been struck deaf by a fever when she was a small child, and she lived a strange silent existence among her family. They never spoke to her, and rarely *of* her, but her eyes, large and dark, very much like her niece's, were bright and intelligent. She was the only one of the family who read Josephine Robillard's books, and she had watched my preliminary examination with great interest, going so far as to fetch for me a handful of books which (I gathered) she felt were particularly worthy of note: Lydia Maria Child's first novel, *Hobomok*; all four volumes of *The Dial*, sadly foxed; and the *American Bestiary* of Matthias Claybourne Cullen—not the rare 1839 edition, but the cheap octavo of 1845. It was still an interesting find, with its entries on Seal-Maidens, Thunder-Birds, and Were-Wolves; I thanked Sarah Robillard with a nod, and she smiled as if it were far more than she had expected.

The other three sisters, as if to compensate for Sarah's silence, never stopped talking, and they had hard, harsh voices that kept jangling in my head for some time after I had escaped their company. They were horribly inquisitive, as well, asking questions about the museum, about the city, about my life (did I have family? was I married? was there a lady I was courting?), even about the books—their own books, which had been in their house their entire lives—and I found that even more offensive than the rest put together.

Marcus Justus Robillard, a stocky white-haired paterfamilias, seemed merely ironically resigned to his daughters' behavior—and indeed, he did not seem to think me worth rescuing from them. Or perhaps he knew the enterprise was doomed before it began: both Justin and Annette made efforts to distract their aunts, but it was hopeless. Annette might successfully lure Olive and Christina away, but that would be the signal for Sophia to come in. And if Justin, with an apologetic and embarrassed glance at me, contrived a reason to get Sophia out of the room, by then Olive would have returned. The only respite I had, before I pleaded fatigue each night and fled ignominiously to my room, was at dinner. Even that was a precarious haven, for if conversation lagged, one or another of the sisters was sure to turn her attention to me. The only night I was able to eat undisturbed was Wednesday, and that was because Justin and Annette's widowed mother made what was evidently a very rare appearance.

Patrick Robillard had died when Annette was scarcely old enough to toddle, and Marian Robillard had instantly embarked on an epic career as an invalid. Having been exposed to her sisters-in-law, I could not blame her. She had the look of a woman addicted to opiates, thin and hollow-eyed and languid, as if she moved through water no one else could feel. Her presence at the dinner table meant that the conversation revolved around illnesses rather than me, and I was grateful to her for it, even though it took no exceptional intelligence or sensitivity to see that I was entirely irrelevant to her. Justin must have told her about Roy Folkow, for around and between Olive, Sophia, and Christina's inexhaustible fund of embarrassing questions and grisly anecdotes, Marian Robillard was exerting herself to try to question her daughter.

She did not have a great deal of success, since she seemed reluctant to ask outright—perhaps, from her glances toward the head of the table, fearing her father-in-law's reaction—and Annette was adroit at dodging. When Marian rose from the table, kissed her father-in-law's temple, and murmured that she was returning to her room, I saw guilty triumph on Annette's face. She had known that all she had to do was outlast her mother's limited stamina. It was an unpleasant insight, and it did not make the Robillard ménage easier to bear.

At least the best guest bedroom was worthy of its name. It was a large airy room, much less oppressive than the main rooms of Belle Lune, decorated in blue and white and featuring a lovely cherrywood secretary that looked to me like a museum-quality antique, although American decorative arts were not my specialty. The bed was large, the mattress firm, and I only wished I had had any particular success in using it for its intended purpose.

I had, however, on Friday night as on the four nights before, no expectation of sleep—at least not for a good many hours. I went through the motions of preparing for bed; it was much better to make use of the bathroom before the family came upstairs, and I locked the bedroom door on my return with a feeling almost of safety. I turned the covers back and changed into my pajamas, for I had learned long ago that making myself uncomfortable was a useless punishment as far as my insomnia was concerned. I had brought Sascha Fleury-Dubois's *Letters from the Guillotine* to keep me company through the long, cold nights, and it had proved worth its iron weight in my suitcase.

I was just buttoning the top button of my pajamas when someone knocked on the door.

I must have looked abjectly ridiculous, had there been anyone to see, trying both to turn around and dive for my dressing gown at the same time, but I am sure I looked even more ridiculous when I opened the door, for it was Marcus Justus Robillard standing in the hallway.

He had paid almost no attention to me all week long, and indeed, I had been glad of it, for if he had asked me, I would have had to tell him that bringing me out here had been a waste of my time and his best guest bedroom. The books Sarah Robillard had showed me on Monday were the only ones worth a second look; the rest, aside from their poor condition, were merely foot soldiers in the army of paper that had marched across mid-nineteenth-century America. There was nothing of interest to a museum, nor even anything valuable, and I had had suspicions all week, which I had tried to quash, that Marcus Justus Robillard knew it.

And now he was standing outside my bedroom, giving me an ironic look that made his eyes glint as yellow as his grandson's. "May I speak to you a moment, Mr. Booth?"

"Er . . . ah, that is, certainly, if you wish." I could see no option; I stood aside and let him in.

He sat on the chair by the secretary, leaving me the choice of floundering in the middle of the room or sitting on the bed, either of which would combine well with my dressing gown and pajamas to set me at a disadvantage. I sat on the bed.

Marcus Justus did not waste time. He said, "Your cousin sends his regards."

The words made no sense at first, and even when I understood them, they continued to make no sense. " . . . My . . . er, my *what?*"

"Your cousin," said Marcus Justus distinctly, his eyes glinting at me. "L. M. Ogilvy."

"You . . . you know my cousin?" It was not a recommendation if he did. I had met my cousin, Luther Murchison Ogilvy, once, and I never wished to meet him again.

"We have corresponded for many years," said Marcus Justus. "I suppose you could say we have interests in common."

"What interests?"

He bared his teeth, but it was not a smile. "Family curses."

" . . . Oh." I had learned about the Murchison curse from my cousin Ogilvy. I bore the mark of the curse in my prematurely white hair, and if I ever married, the curse would kill my wife just as it had killed my father. My mother had committed suicide; I was determined never to marry, never to allow myself to become close enough to anyone that the curse might recognize them as a target.

"My family suffers under a curse just as yours does, Mr. Booth, a curse that there seems to be no hope of breaking. But your cousin had a suggestion. He told me of the success the Murchisons had had in marrying each other, that the curse didn't come into effect when both parties carried it. And while that option is not available to me, as the Robillards have never bred far from Belle Lune, your cousin asked if it was possible that the Murchison curse and the Robillard curse might . . . " He brought his hands together sharply. "Might cancel each other out."

"I don't understand what you're talking about," I said; it was hard to get the words out, for my face felt stiff and numb.

"Oh, I think you do," Marcus Justus said. "Now, it would be unreasonable to ask you to marry one of my daughters—old maids the lot of them, and I could see you didn't take to them."

"I like Sarah," I said inanely, defiantly.

He waved that aside. "But my granddaughter's a pretty girl. Well brought up. And we've money, of course." His sneer said he had noticed the threadbare elbows of my dressing gown, the frayed hems of my pajamas.

"You want me to marry Annette," I said slowly, struggling to keep my voice level.

"It's a gamble," said Marcus Justus, "but it seems worth it. It won't keep the curse from afflicting her, of course, but it should keep you safe. And it may lessen the effects on your children."

"Or they may be doubly cursed," I said.

"Ogilvy and I considered that. We don't think it likely."

I had no faith in their opinions, and every faith in the Murchison curse's power to kill Annette if she became my . . . I had to force myself to finish the thought: my bride.

Something I could never have.

I knew that arguing with Marcus Justus would be useless, or worse than useless, and I very badly wanted him out of my room, but there was one other question first.

That lawyer said they might be valuable, Justin had said. I had assumed that he meant the Robillard family lawyer, but my cousin Ogilvy was a lawyer, and I knew from experience that he was good at fabricating pretexts. "That's why you contrived to have me sent here. It was never about the books at all."

"Oh, the books," Marcus Justus said with a shrug that showed how heavily muscled he was; I guessed he was seventy or more, but he was still formidable. "They can be your wedding present, if you're interested in them. Ogilvy told me it was the only way to get you here."

"Yes, of course," I said. There was no comfort in being right. The numbness seemed to be spreading, and I was beginning to feel light-headed.

Marcus Justus smirked. "He doesn't think much of you, you know."

"He can hardly think less of me than I do of him." I was not even listening to myself, occupied with trying to find some way to get Marcus Justus out of the room before I passed out—or succumbed to hysteria—so that I startled violently when he laughed.

"You may not be such a milksop as you seem," he said, and to my amazement and relief, got to his feet. "I know I've given you a lot to think about, and I don't expect an answer tonight. Sleep well." And he let himself out, closing the door tidily behind him.

I scrambled up, locking the door as if it might actually be any protection. But even illusory safety was better than the helplessly exposed feeling with which Marcus Justus had left me.

I took a deep breath, then another. He could not *force* me to marry Annette; I had only to avoid giving an answer until Sunday, and then I could return to . . .

What if Marcus Justus would not let me leave?

The thought was nonsense, surely, but the more I thought about the situation—the isolation of Belle Lune; the way that generations of Robillards had been in essence lords of their own bleak fiefdom; the truth I had seen all week, that Marcus Justus's word was law to his family—the less nonsensical it seemed. He could ban automobiles; why should anyone cavil at imprisoning an archivist? And I could not pretend that there was anyone who would care particularly if I vanished into this desolation. My colleagues would be inconvenienced and Dr. Starkweather would be irritated, but no one would pursue the matter beyond the most perfunctory inquiries.

No one would rescue me.

On Saturday morning, Marcus Justus announced that he thought Annette should take me to see the Robillard burying ground. The speed with which the rest of the family agreed was alarming; it indicated that they were both aware and approving of the plan to marry me to Annette. I could find no excuse not to go, especially after Marcus Justus said outright, "Oh, don't worry about the books." Annette herself seemed perfectly happy to have her day disposed of so high-handedly, but it was obvious from her lack of self-consciousness that she did not know her grandfather was trying to dispose of more than an afternoon.

She did not know about the curse.

We took a picnic lunch, provided by Sarah and Christina, both beaming like idiots, and walked the quarter-mile from Belle Lune proper to the burying ground. It was an entirely private cemetery, Annette told me; no one but Robillards had the right to be buried there, and it was exempt from state and county laws about the disposition of the dead. It seemed an all too apt metaphor for Belle Lune itself.

And it seemed even more so when we arrived. The landscape stretched out in cold brown desolation as far as I could see. On three sides, the cemetery was fenced with forbidding iron spikes; on the fourth, it crumbled into one of the sinkholes Justin Robillard had mentioned. Annette told me that some graves had been lost when the cave-in occurred almost forty years ago, but they thought the rest of it was stable. I was not reassured.

The gravestones ranged from well-tended modern plaques (Annette's father; Olive's husband; Marcus Justus' elder son, Philip Justus, who had died when he was Annette's age), to ornate nineteenth century obelisks, to crumbled illegible slabs laid full-length in the ground as if they were the covers of sarcophagi. Annette said no one knew any longer which Robillard ancestor lay beneath which slab, although she pointed out the one said by family legend to memorialize Marie-Marthe de Givère, who had run away from a French convent to join her Robillard lover in the New World.

Annette was a conscientious tour guide. She showed me the Civil War graves—the Robillards had lost a son to each side, Henry Justus to the North and Clarence to the South—and Josephine Robillard's grave (the most ornate of the ornate obelisks). Over lunch, she told me the stories of as many of the graves as she knew; I noticed that the majority of them were women in their twenties or very early thirties, all of them bearing Robillard as their married name and all of them presented to posterity as "Wife and Mother." It was indirect proof of Marcus Justus's claims for a family curse, and I knew I should use it as a way to broach the subject with Annette, but I could not do it.

All the way to the burying ground, I had tried to think of a way to tell her about the curse, but every gambit I imagined foundered on my lack of information. Marcus Justus had been—I realized belatedly—very careful not to provide any details, anything *useful*. Simply announcing, *Your grandfather says your family is cursed,* would achieve nothing.

And without that to build on, how could I tell her that her grandfather wanted her to marry me? Every time I opened my mouth to try, I looked at her, lovely and young and vibrant in a flowered dress and a wide-brimmed straw hat, and I thought of the incredulous laughter with which she would surely respond. I did not at all blame her—what other reaction could any rational young woman have?—but the prospect killed my voice in my throat.

All that afternoon, I did not speak.

When we returned, Annette was called into her grandfather's private study. Someone had told him about Roy Folkow. Over dinner, Annette's aunts scolded her in relays: "A *shopkeeper's* son," Olive said, her entire face pursing around the words as if they tasted of vulgarity. Or sour milk. "*Really,* Annette." Annette broke and fled the table in tears before the coffee was brought out. The atmosphere did not improve; I claimed a migraine rather than face any after-dinner conversation.

No mention was made of Sunday trains.

I lay down on my bed with *Letters from the Guillotine,* and must have dozed off, for I woke suddenly to the sound of someone tapping on the window. I jolted upright, and for a moment as she stood framed against the night, the light caught Annette Robillard's eyes and made them glow gold.

I opened the window, and she said at once, "Mr. Booth, please, you have to help me."

"Er," I said. She was still red-eyed, and I did not like the grim set of her mouth. "With what?"

"I told Roy I would meet him tonight at the Ussher crossroads, and I can't, not with everyone *snooping*. But *you* could go for a walk."

"Your brother told me not to," I said stupidly.

"*Please,*" she said.

I wondered with a chill if Marcus Justus had confided his plans to her. "What's wrong?"

She glanced over her shoulder, at the banked violet clouds and fierce pinprick stars of the night sky. The moon was not yet up. "It's true," she said. "The full moon is a chancy time in this part of the world. And I know Roy. He'll *wait*."

"*Are* you going to elope with him?"

"No," she said. She looked down, pleating the delicate flowered fabric of her dress between her fingers. Then, "Maybe. I don't know! I don't want to be stuck *here* for the rest of my life."

"Your grandfather," I started, still not sure what I was going to say, and she interrupted me.

"My grandfather is going hunting tonight."

"Your grandfather hunts at *night*?"

"At the full moon. It's a family tradition." She burst out suddenly, savagely, "I hate it! My father was killed on a night-hunt, and Grandfather takes Justin out sometimes, and Aunt Olive and Aunt Christina, and sometimes I feel like I'm just waiting for one of them to die, too! And I'm afraid for Roy."

"You think your grandfather would shoot him?" I said. I only wished I found it unlikely.

"It would be an excuse," she said, her eyes wide and dark and dreading. "Hunting accidents happen all the time."

"And what's to prevent one from happening to *me*?"

"Grandfather doesn't make mistakes," she said, so flatly that I could not doubt the truth of it.

And I knew that Marcus Justus had every reason to view Folkow as, not merely a nuisance, but an impediment. And perhaps . . . perhaps I could tell Folkow that Marcus Justus proposed a marriage between me and Annette. Remembering his earnestness, the worship of Annette so naked in his face, I thought he would be quicker to believe than Annette would herself. And I could not make myself say it to her face: *Your grandfather wants you to marry me. Because of a curse.*

"Let me . . . er, that is, I need to get dressed," I said.

Annette smiled at me brilliantly, although not quite brilliantly enough to erase the darkness from her eyes, and said, "I'll get you a flashlight."

Annette returned with the promised flashlight mere moments after I had knotted my tie–a futile and ludicrous gesture of respectability, but it made me feel better. She showed me down the back stairs and out through the kitchen, where Sarah Robillard was washing the dishes. She did not notice us.

"Does your family not keep servants?" I asked Annette, once she had closed the door of the mudroom behind us. I had been wondering all week.

"No one stays out here who doesn't have to," she said and changed the subject briskly. "Now, what you want to do is go around the house and back to the main road. Turn left, and it's about three miles to the crossroads. There's a sign there, and it says Ussher, so you'll know you're in the right place. And anyway, you'll see Roy." She turned the flashlight on and handed it to me.

I opened my mouth to protest, but realized I had no idea of what to say, nor even quite what I wanted to protest–except the general damnable unfairness of the whole situation, and that was not Annette's fault.

She must have seen something of what I felt in my face, for she said suddenly, "Thank you—thank you so much, Mr. Booth. And here. For your buttonhole." She caught my lapel before I could evade her and tucked something in my buttonhole, although I could not see it clearly.

"Wolfsbane," she said; her laugh was uneasy—not the bright ripple of the daylight hours. "Local people grow it to keep away those wolves I mentioned."

"It's, er, quite poisonous," I said dubiously.

"So don't eat it," she said. Her laugh sounded better that time. She might have kissed my cheek then, but I turned away before I was sure that was her intention and did not let myself look at her again.

She could never be my bride.

I reached the road without difficulty—and without running into any other Robillards, which was what I had chiefly feared. I turned left, as Annette had directed me, and started walking.

The moon rose shortly thereafter, a vast bright disk. It was, I thought, the Hunter's Moon, as the autumn equinox was a month gone. I remembered that the Hunter's Moon was also called the Sanguine Moon, and I walked a little faster.

But I could not walk very fast, even trying to hurry. The road was not in good repair—as I had noticed Monday afternoon, jouncing in Justin Robillard's trap—and I did not have the aid of familiarity. Even with the flashlight, I fell twice; the second time, I knocked the air out of my lungs, and it was some little while before I was able to continue. I told myself it was ridiculous to be anxious—as the wide white moon rose higher in the sky— but I could not rid myself of a feeling of urgency, a feeling that Annette was right, that Roy Folkow was doomed unless I could get to him in time.

Ridiculous, I said again, more firmly, and tried to walk faster all the same.

Even walking as fast as I could, it took me nearly an hour, but finally, I crested a slight rise and saw a crossroads. I did not see anyone waiting there, but Folkow might have decided to sit down—or he might sensibly have chosen to wait in concealment. I picked my way down the hill as quickly as I could.

The flashlight and moonlight together let me read the sign, which did indeed say *USSHER.* "Folkow?" I called, not loudly.

There was no response.

Annette had been so certain that Folkow would wait for her—I wondered if perhaps I had somehow reached the crossroads ahead of him. I turned in a circle, slowly, to see if there were any signs of movement on the other branches of the road. There was nothing. I stepped cautiously toward the side of the road, in hopes of finding somewhere to sit; regardless of whether Folkow had not waited or had not yet arrived, I wanted at least to rest for a few moments before I started back to Belle Lune—or perhaps, in defiance of Justin Robillard, struck out for the nearest town or human habitation. But I had not reached the verge when the smell struck me: blood and excrement, both nauseously fresh.

I wished, desperately and pointlessly, to be anywhere other than where I was. Then I took another step, the flashlight leading the way, and I found Roy Folkow.

He was dead, and he had not been shot.

He had been . . . I leaned closer and then had to turn away and fight not to vomit. He had been disemboweled, and I thought he had been partially eaten, as well. And it had happened very recently.

Annette had laughed at the stories of wolves, but what else could have done this?

The howl came as if in answer, a long rising ululation that sounded like grief. It did not seem close, which was barely any comfort at all. I could not stay out here with Roy Folkow's corpse and a wandering predator, and there was nothing closer than Belle Lune. I had to go back.

I looked at the Hunter's Moon, the Blood Moon; I looked at the flashlight Annette had given me. I wondered if I would break my neck trying to run.

• • •

I did run, at least part of the way, but I was still a good half-mile from Belle Lune when the horizon began to show blood-red and I smelled smoke.

"No," I said, barely more than a whisper. "Oh, no."

But denial made no more difference to the truth than it ever does. Belle Lune was burning.

I ran faster, recklessly, and that I did not break my neck is astonishing. I was limping by the time I came down Belle Lune's driveway, blisters scraping raw on both feet and my left ankle throbbing from yet another fall.

The house blazed, flames seeming to lean out of every window. There was no possibility of a heroic dash inside, even if I had been capable of it; there was no "inside" left, and the idea of survivors seemed entirely impossible. Either they had already gotten out or they were already dead. And those valueless books were nothing but ashes.

I stood by the dark water of the Mirror, feeling, if I am honest, more bewildered than anything else. There were no neighbors that I knew of, and it was ten miles or more into town. I did not know where the horse was, nor the trap, and even if I had known, I had not the first idea of how one went about putting the two together. I supposed, finally, dimly, that I ought to circle the house and see if any of the Robillards was there—perhaps in the back garden? Perhaps the back of the house had not burned as quickly as the front? But I was still standing stone-like when I heard the howl again.

I knew it was the same creature, although I do not know how I knew. And it sounded much closer than it had at the crossroads. I told myself that wild creatures avoided fire, and that Belle Lune was surely a fire that even the most ferocious and bloodthirsty beast would fear, but I did not find myself convincing. If it *was* closer, and if it was coming this way, I needed either shelter or a weapon. I remembered there was a gardener's shed in back of the house; if it did not provide one, it might provide the other, and in any event, I had to look for survivors, even if I believed it utterly futile.

I skirted the burning house carefully, trampling through the flowerbeds rather than get too close.

There was no one behind Belle Lune. Unless Marcus Justus had indeed gone out hunting, the entire Robillard family was almost certainly destroyed. I wondered, as I fought the warped door of the shed, how they could all have been trapped. No one had been asleep when I had left; they had all still been on the ground floor. How could it have sprung up so quickly that not one of them made it out? Sarah Robillard had been fewer than twenty feet from the back door, and although she was deaf, she could smell smoke as easily as any hearing person.

The shed provided: a pair of rusty secateurs which I decided dubiously would be even less use as a weapon than my pocket knife; a ladder which did me no good at all; a rake missing half its tines; and a shovel. The shovel at least had a broad iron blade and was sturdily constructed. I felt a fool carrying it as I completed my circle around the house, but I comforted myself with the thought that at least, as a weapon, it was one I could use as well as anyone else.

I had been hoping, mostly without articulating the idea, that by the time I made it to the front of the house, someone would have shown up: a Robillard, or a neighbor, or a police officer. Someone who would know what to do, someone who could take responsibility for this burning house and the dead bodies presumably inside it, not to mention the dead body at the Ussher crossroads. There was no one standing in front of the house—rationally there was no reason to expect otherwise—and I was conscious of a strong desire simply to sit down and weep with exhaustion and fear and uselessness.

But before I either gave into that desire or chose a more constructive course of action, the howl rose for the third time, and it had not died away when something came bounding down the driveway and stopped barely ten feet from me, where it crouched and panted, great heaving breaths like sobs.

It was not, quite, a wolf. It was *like* a wolf, but it was much too large, and its legs did not bend in the correct directions. Its front feet, where it had braced itself against the gravel, were lumpish and misshapen, but I could not mistake the fingers—the torn fingernails, the bloody knuckles. When it raised its head to howl again, I saw the blood staining its muzzle and throat and chest. I also saw that the muzzle was too short for a wolf, the teeth too flat. And when it lowered its head and looked at me, I saw that its eyes were not a wolf's eyes.

It opened its mouth, tongue lolling, and said, "Kill me."

The voice was harsh and unpleasantly thick, as if the creature were on the verge of choking, but the words were unmistakable.

I fell back a step; I could hear my own breathing, too fast and sharp.

"*Kill me,*" the creature repeated, and I watched as it lurched upright. It seemed almost unable to balance, the grotesque hands flailing against the air.

I realized that it was wearing the remains of Annette Robillard's flowered dress, and my legs folded under me. My knees hit the ground with a jolt that clacked my teeth together painfully, but I could only stare at the monster in Annette's dress, the monster that had killed Roy Folkow—the monster that wanted to die.

"Kill me," it begged again, taking a lurching, staggering step toward me. I scrambled up again, because I was too terrified to stay on the ground. If I did not kill it, it seemed all too likely that it would kill me—I did not think it was approaching me in order to lay its head in my lap like the unicorn of legend. But how I could possibly kill it with only a shovel?

I thought that it tried to say, "Kill me," again, but the words garbled into a roar even as its legs bunched under it, and it sprang.

I swung the shovel. It was purely instinctual, and I think my eyes were closed, but the shovel-blade connected with some part of the creature's body, for the blow jarred in my shoulders, and I heard the creature yelp. Moreover, it did not rip my throat out; although I felt the heat and force of its body passing near mine, it did not touch me.

My eyes came open, and I spun to face it. It had its back to the fire now, which I suspected was a bad thing for me, and it had its head lowered, its eyes glinting yellow up at me, the way Justin Robillard's eyes had glinted. It looked more like a wolf now, and I did not think it would ask me to kill it again.

I wondered—if I could keep my eyes open the next time it leapt, could I land a solid enough blow on its head to knock it unconscious? It seemed my only, though vanishingly unlikely, hope. I tightened my grip on the shovel and tried to watch for the creature to spring.

A voice cried behind me, "Down!"

I am afraid it is not due to any good sense that I obeyed. I was so startled that in trying to turn to see who was behind me, I lost my balance and fell, very nearly ending up in the Mirror.

The shotgun blast sounded utterly like the end of the world.

It was some moments before, ears ringing, winded, I managed to pick myself up. When I did, I saw Marian Robillard, in a nightgown dyed lurid red by the flames, kneeling beside the creature's body. I edged a little closer and saw that the body, rent and broken and dead, was Annette.

Marian did not turn, although I saw by the way she stiffened that she knew I was there. After a moment, she said, "It was a family curse."

"Lycanthropy?" No wonder Marcus Justus had been so carefully reticent.

"Yes. As far back as they could trace their genealogy, Robillards have been werewolves. Sometimes only one in a generation, sometimes all of them. It skipped Sophia in my husband's generation, and I prayed—dear God how I prayed—that it would skip Annette."

"Sarah was a werewolf?" I said stupidly.

"They were beasts, but they were not *loveless*," Marian said. "There is no other reason I can think of that Marcus Justus would not have sent her to a proper school for the deaf. But he could not take the chance—the curse could hit them at any age from nine to twenty-nine—and, of course, it turned out he was right. She started changing when she was barely twelve."

Marcus Justus' "night-hunts" took on a dreadful new dimension. "What happened to your husband?" I asked.

"A better question is, what didn't happen to me?" she said. She stood and turned to face me, and I saw that it was not the fire dyeing her nightgown red. She was covered in blood. "Sooner or later, every werewolf turns against the person he loves. Or she loves." She glanced down at her daughter's body. "Marcus Justus' mother was killed by his father when he was a tiny boy. Marcus Justus killed his wife—none of her children would ever talk about her, do you know that? And Patrick tried to kill me."

"He failed," I said; it was half a question.

"He was a strange man," Marian said. "He armed me—gave me a Bowie knife as a wedding present and told me always to have it by my bed at the full moon. And I did. When the monster broke down my door, I fought it, and I won. And I killed my husband."

The corners of her mouth lifted in a tiny, distant smile. "Marcus Justus was furious. I begged him to let me take the children away—I have always thought, since I learned of the curse, that it must be something in the situation of Belle Lune that brings it, some poison in the water or the soil. He refused utterly, warned me that if I tried, I would be hunted down—and Marcus Justus and his daughters were a formidable hunting pack, make no mistake, Mr. Booth. I begged him again, when Justin turned, to let me try to save Annette, but he told me it was too risky. He told me he thought Annette might not be a werewolf anyway."

I remembered Marcus Justus saying calmly, *It won't keep the curse from afflicting her, of course,* and I knew he had lied to his daughter-in-law. He had known full well that Annette was a werewolf. It seemed the only one who had not known was Annette herself.

"I told him," Marian Robillard said grimly, drearily, "that if she were, I would know who to blame. He just smiled. I don't think he understood what I meant. Until tonight."

"You killed them," I said, realizing. "And set the house on fire."

"There are only two ways to be sure a werewolf is dead, Mr. Booth," she said. "Burn it to ashes, or cut its head off. Or both. I did both."

"All of them?" My voice was no stronger than a whisper, but either she heard me or she knew what I was asking.

"All of them. Marcus Justus, Olive, Christina, Sarah, Sophia. Justin. And, in the end, Annette."

"I thought you said Sophia wasn't a werewolf," I said stupidly.

"She was raised among werewolves," Marian said, with chilly, logical insanity. "And she was still young enough to bear children."

She had killed her entire family. Even knowing why she had done it, even knowing that she had been right to do so by any standard one cared to name, I found myself shrinking away from her, as if she instead of the dead girl at her feet were the monster.

"I don't want my daughter to burn," Marian said. "Will you bury her, Mr. Booth?"

"Yes," I said in witless reflex. "But wait. Why can't you—"

"Bury her at the crossroads," she said. She reached up and unclasped a chain from around her throat. "This is silver. I think you know what to do."

"Mrs. Robillard," I said, "I don't—"

"Don't bury her with *them*," she said and turned away. At the steady drifting pace that was all I had ever seen from her, she walked into the conflagration of Belle Lune. I could not reach her in time to stop her, and in truth, I do not know that I would have if I could.

I listened—I could not keep myself from listening—but Marian Robillard did not make a sound.

If I had known that Annette Robillard was cursed with lycanthropy, I would have told her. Even knowing that she would not have believed me, that she would have thought me insane or gullible or merely cruel, I have to believe that I would have spoken, that I would not have let my cowardice rule me.

I am a weak man, and not a good one, and maybe I am lying to myself to think I am not a monster. But I have to believe that I kept silent only because I did not know.

And then I remember that if I had spoken, and Annette had not died, then her mother would not have murdered the werewolves of Belle Lune. I remember what Annette told me about her grandfather's night-hunts. I remember what Justin said about bodies unrecovered.

If I *had* known, *should* I have spoken? Would saving her life have been a worse sin than letting her die?

I do not know. I have no answers, only grief. Grief for her and for that travesty that is as close as either of us will ever come to a wedding night, when I cut her head off and buried her beneath the gloating Hunter's Moon.

Sarah Monette grew up in Oak Ridge, Tennessee, one of the three secret cities of the Manhattan Project, and now lives in a 108-year-old house in the Upper Midwest with a great many books, two cats, one grand piano, and one husband. Her PhD diploma (English Literature, 2004) hangs in the kitchen. She has published more than fifty short stories and has two short story collections out: *The Bone Key* (Prime Books, 2007—with a new second edition in 2011) and *Somewhere Beneath Those Waves* (Prime Books, 2011). She has written two novels (*A Companion to Wolves*, Tor, 2007, and *The Tempering of Men*, Tor, 2011) and four short stories with Elizabeth Bear, and hopes to write more. Her first four novels (*Melusine*, *The Virtu*, *The Mirador*, *Corambis*) were published by Ace. Her latest novel, *The Goblin Emperor*, published under the pen name Katherine Addison, came out from Tor in April 2014. Visit her online at www.sarahmonette.com or www.katherineaddison.com.

Evil used to be more obvious.
Nowadays everyone is tainted to some degree.

CUCKOO

Angela Slatter

The child was dead by the time I found her, but she suited my purposes perfectly. Tiny delicate skin suit, meat sack, air thief. The flesh was still warm, which is best—too hard to shrug on something in full rigor—and I crammed my bulk into the small body much as one might climb into a box or trunk to hide. A fold here, a dislocation there, a twinge of discomfort and curses when something tore, stretched just too far. The rent was in the webbing of the right hand. Only a little rip, no matter. The sinister *manus* was my favored choice of weapon anyway. I sat up, rolled my new shoulders—gently, carefully—then stood, rocking back slightly on legs too tender, too young to support my leviathan weight. I took a step, felt the world tilt, caught my balance before I fell and risked another tear; looked down at the single pink shoe, with its bows and glitter detail; took in the strange white cat face that ran around the hem of the pink and white dress; rubbed my miniature fingers against the dried brown stains that blotched the insides of my thighs. The child had died hard.

The sliver of me that retained empathy ached, just a bit. But I could smell the scent of the one who'd done this and I would follow that scent. The hunt was on, my blood was up. Time was of the essence—my presence will speed decay. I pitched my head up so my nostrils caught the evening breeze and breathed deeply, filling my borrowed lungs, so the memory would remain. Again, I took a step, more, all steady. Determined. Forward.

Here's the thing: evil used to be different.

It used to be black and white. It used to be more *obvious*. Nowadays?

Everyone on this planet is tainted to some degree. Once upon a time, there were villains of a memorable—perhaps even admirable—scale. But now?

Without contrast it's hard to see the differences.

I miss that—the delineation of great evil from banal nastiness.

I'd walked for two hours and the girl's legs were sore. I sighed and stepped into his front garden with its fastidiously dug flowerbeds planted with purple, red, and saffron blossoms. The house was neat and tidy, a thin building running the length of the block, rather than across—I didn't need eyes to tell me that, just the child's memories. I dug around in her fading box of remembrances and found the floor plan of the house, vague as if seen in a rush. Hallway, all the doors to the left: a living room, then two more rooms, then a kitchen at the very back where he'd taken her for a glass of water. A staircase near the front door leading up: two bedrooms at the front and a bathroom at the back. The second bedroom she remembered most.

The walls had a shimmer to them and dancing fairies were stenciled around the baseboards and just beneath the architraves. The bed was covered in a Barbie-branded duvet and so many frilly purple cushions they seemed like an eruption of fabric mumps. Shelves ran across two of the walls, burdened with My Little Ponies in every hue and style, too high for a child to reach.

And the cupboard, painted pink so it appeared as a mouth in a white face. And inside the cupboard, all those shoes, all those single left shoes, tossed in like so much refuse, as if the fetish could never be tidy. As if the inner workings would always be *messy*. Somewhere in that pile, maybe balancing precariously on the top, maybe toppled down the back, was the shoe he'd taken as she sat on the bed, before he did *anything*.

The mind began to shut down, the memories becoming the blurred white-blue of blind eyes. I clenched a hand, heard the joints crack. Time was running short.

I didn't need long.

A knock on the door, harder than intended, hurt my knuckles. I heard him moving around inside. I coiled inside the body, bracing myself against the slow wash of congealing blood and decaying organs, against the sea of human soup the child was becoming, and prepared to spring the moment I saw what I needed.

He opened the door.

Mr. Timmons gave me nothing. Nothing but a slow steady blink. His eyes shifted from the dark marks around the delicate throat, down past the bruised thighs, and lit on the bare foot.

No fear. No guilt. No remorse.

I felt sawn off at the knees. Robbed. At a loss.

He twitched a sort of smile in my direction and slowly closed the door once more.

And I didn't do a thing.

I, who once commanded legions, who fell through fire and rose again, who felt the earth shudder beneath my feet, who took into me the souls of the greatest of the worst, I . . . did nothing.

The woman was in the wrong place at the wrong time.

But then, aren't they all?

I'd lain quiet for ages in the alley, just the bare foot sticking out to get attention. About four in the morning, she staggered along in her high heels, saw the pale flash of flesh and stumbled over to kneel beside me. The woman leaned in and I grabbed her. I wrapped my arms around her neck and covered her mouth with one hand, pinching her nostrils shut with the fingers of the other. I held her that way until the life drained out and she released her last breath, emptying herself in a final humiliating gesture of humanity. It's easier when they're dead, they no longer have the will to fight; if you have to expend energy battling for a body, you're not in best shape for the contest to come. I stood over her and let the child's form go, unpicked myself from the rapidly putrefying corpse, then watched as it hit the asphalt heavily. It made a wet noise as the side of the face gave way on impact and the belly burst like an over-ripe melon.

I stayed outside for a few moments, stretching, feeling the night on what passes for my skin, just for a few moments, then did my contortionist's act and plunged into the woman. Roomier, to be sure, broad across the hips, fleshy thighs, the strange weight of breasts hanging at the chest—I cupped them, jiggled them about, found nothing to justify the fascination with them. Then I felt the fizz and buzz of alcohol in the veins, the unsteadiness of the legs, the jelly of the knees and that ache in the lower back from being pushed at the wrong angle by the height of the shoes.

I'm sorry, I said to no one in particular. I don't even know if I was. It'd been a long time since I'd expressed sentiment to anyone; anything beyond disgust and a sort of righteous boredom. I said it again, just to hear my voice, *I'm sorry. I need . . .*

But I didn't continue. Didn't finish. Had neither necessity nor desire to offer explanations to the dead.

• • •

I sat next to him on the park bench.

He was feeding the birds, watching all the little girls on the jungle gym, nodding, friendly, to their mothers and nannies. He didn't notice me. At least, not until his nose began to twitch. An unwashed body will garner attention sooner rather than later. His head swiveled and his eyes took me in; not that I would have been of any interest to him. He smiled and pointed towards the children as they played.

"Which one's yours?" he asked, although he must have known, couldn't have thought for a moment that my shell, still in its nightclub finery with smudged make-up and bird's-nest hair, had care of any child. He grinned slyly, as if we were in cahoots.

I turned towards him, shifted my torso, the body beginning to lose its flexibility; my clumsiness made it look as though I was showing him the woman's breasts, *presenting* them.

Disdain. Contempt. Amusement. All of *these* were in his face.

I raised my stolen hand and clicked its fingers. Sparks flew but didn't take. I did it again and there were flames; at first just at the tips, then they crept to engulf the hand, scorching the arm, catching quickly on the synthetic fabrics of the woman's outfit. It sped across the shoulders, split its forces and half-leapt downward, while the other continued upwards to set the bleached blond coif ablaze. I smiled at him from lips that curled and blackened and shriveled back against teeth furred from no brushing.

I watched him long and hard, waiting, poised for that look, that hint, that signal.

For the light in his eyes that said he was afraid—because they're all afraid, in the end, and that's why I can take them—for the whimpering as he begged for his life.

His eyes remained dead, but for a lazy curiosity.

He stood and walked away as my body burned to a symphony of children's screams.

I followed him all the next day, incorporeal.

Vengeance has been my path for so many years. Centuries. Eons. It's all I've known; or all I remember. I have taken what was just, from men great and ordinary, their only commonality being they had stolen lives that did not belong to them. One life or thousands unjustly snuffed out will bring my kind like a hunting hound. I have seen them all learn fear, all tremble when faced with their crimes and beg for forgiveness, more time, another chance. But this man . . .

There was *nothing* great about this man. There was nothing special but his refusal to *fear*.

I ventured into his house, picked through his things while he went about his daily chores. Sat on the sad mountain of shoes in the closet and wracked my brain. I heard the phone ring and he let the answering machine get it. An official voice, tired, disinterested, left him a message, obviously used to no response, but duty-bound to follow through. I listened, then watched intently as he quite deliberately erased the recording, not bothering to take down the number or name the caller had left.

I thought I had my answer.

The smell of antiseptic was sharp enough to sting.

Soft-soled shoes squeaking on waxed floors, clangs of metal trays and bedpans, trolleys banging through swinging doors, alarmed squeals from heart rate monitors as people died, the constant "blip" of the lesser machines, the swoosh of uniforms as staff hurried by.

And finally, a private room, a quiet space, oddly enough in shades of pink, a room meant for two patients but in which only one was in evidence. The bed was a striking piece of machinery, up-down-sideways buttons, the not-quite-white linen from too many washings, a curtain around it all, ostensibly for privacy, but really so no one is forced to watch someone dying.

The woman was younger than she appeared, but still older than I imagined. She looked, no matter her real age, like a crone. She was shriveled, cannulas in both hands, tied to a battery of technology; a slit marred her throat with a tube poking through it, and a machine breathed for her. Her hair was wiry iron gray, her face etched with lines, her eyelashes absent. Her mouth, which I imagine to have been often pursed with disapproval in life, hung slack. Saliva gathered in the deep furrows at the corner, some dried and flaking beneath the new layers of damp spittle.

I doubted she had much spirit left, no will to fight.

I touched fingers to her thin, thin chest and looked for a way in. Through the skin, through the very pores and I felt . . . I felt almost as if I was being pulled down as much as I was entering in. She didn't fight me as her life limped away, rather she swum around like the dregs swirled in a coffee cup and I sensed myself . . . contaminated.

But still, I sat the wizened carcass up, and carefully turned the machines off before I tore out probes and the sticky pads of plastic that connected us. No use causing a stir, sending a signal. It was going to be hard enough to walk the old bat out of the hospital.

I swung my blue-veined legs off the edge of the bed and gauged the distance to the door. One chunk at a time would suffice: bed to door; door to fire stairs; fire stairs to parking lot; parking lot to the end of the first block; first block to the second block; then his house, halfway down that very street, not so far away.

The linoleum was cold beneath my feet.

The house was dark, but not as dark as inside the woman's head. Insistent thoughts of her son papered the walls of her memory. He was small, so small in there. So tender, so sweet, so *vulnerable*.

Ill. I felt ill.

I stood at the door to the main bedroom, watching the moonlight sheer through the curtains. I traced its trajectory to the bed. It was empty, the coverlet undisturbed. I backed away. The brittle bones in the feet seemed friable, liable to snap at any moment. The steps down the hallway, the thin tightly woven carpet, gave no comfort. The door to the princess room was ajar. I pushed it open. It did not creak as I slipped inside.

He lay flat, head thrown back, mouth open. Snores issued forth. The mountain of cushions had suffered an avalanche and I couldn't help but trip against them as I approached. Light streamed in, hitting the sequins and glitter on the scattered squares of over-stuffed fabric, throwing beams around the walls.

I drew in my own weight until the body was as light as a bird's bones and I crawled onto the bed. My movements caused no ripple. I knelt on his chest and began to gradually let the weight loose.

His breathing became irregular; he started to struggle and soon enough he opened his eyes. Blinked to try and make out the face that hovered above his in the moonlit dark. His lids peeled back, widened in astonishment. I leaned forward, hungering for that look, that hint . . .

His right hand wrapped around the old woman's ankle. I glanced down as his fingers caressed the cool, corrugated flesh, tracing the ridges of ancient veins, moving upwards.

I fled. I shot out of every aperture I could find and pressed myself against the ceiling as the barely-alive body slumped onto Mr. Timmons.

His hand did not stop moving.

I did not cling there long. I flew through the window and fell, tumbling, to the garden beds, pressed the dirt rough against my skin, breathed deeply the fertilizer's acrid perfume. All of this felt clean compared to the contagion that seemed to still coat to me.

I stood, shaking, and slid into the clean black of night.

Specializing in dark fantasy and horror, **Angela Slatter** is the author of the Aurealis Award-winning *The Girl with No Hands and Other Tales*, the World Fantasy Award finalist *Sourdough and Other Stories*, and the Aurealis finalist *Midnight and Moonshine* (with Lisa L. Hannett). She is the first Australian to win a British Fantasy Award (for "The Coffin-Maker's Daughter" in *A Book of Horrors*, Stephen Jones, ed.). In 2013 she was awarded one of the inaugural Queensland Writers Fellowships. She has an MA and a PhD in Creative Writing, and is a graduate of Clarion South 2009 and the Tin House Summer Writers Workshop 2006. She blogs at www.angelaslatter.com about shiny things that catch her eye.

He promised them bounty, all the treasure they'd wished for
for so many years, all they'd prayed for and never received

FISHWIFE

Carrie Vaughn

The men went out in boats to fish the cold waters of the bay because their fathers had, because men in this village always had. The women waited to gather in the catch, gut and clean and carry the fish to market because they always had, mothers and grandmothers and so on, back and back.

Every day for years she waited, she and the other wives, for their husbands to return from the iron-gray sea. When they did, dragging their worn wooden boats onto the beach, hauling out nets, she and the other wives tried not show their disappointment when the nets were empty. A few limp, dull fish might be tangled in the fibers. Hardly worth cleaning and trying to sell. None of them were surprised, ever. None of them could remember a time when piles of fish fell out of the nets in cascades of silver. She could imagine it: a horde of fish pouring onto the sand, scales glittering like precious metals. She could run her hands across them, as if they were coins, as if she were rich. Her hands were chapped, calloused from mending nets and washing threadbare clothing. Rougher than the scale that encrusted the hulls of the boats.

Her husband had been young once, as had she. Some days she woke up, and in the moment before she opened her eyes, she believed they were still young. His arms were still strong, and she would guide them around herself, until he was holding her tightly against him. A fire burned in her gut, and she felt as she had the night after their wedding, both sated and still hungry, arrogantly proud that he belonged to her forever. She always knew which boat was his, of the dozen silhouetted against the horizon on the far end of the bay.

Then she opened her eyes, saw the creases of worry in his face, the streaks of gray in her own once-dark hair, and remembered that years had passed, and nothing had gotten better. She clung to the pride she once felt. She remembered what it had been like, and on those days she wanted so badly to seduce him. But he was too tired to be seduced, and she was too tired to keep trying. The best she could do was take a small geranium from her flowerbox to stick in his buttonhole or behind his ear. Sometimes when she did, he smiled.

Every day, the fishermen returned empty-handed, and they bowed their heads, ashamed, as if they really had thought today, this day of all days, their fortunes might change. Once a week they went to the village's small church, where the ancient priest assured them, in the same words he'd used every week for decades, that their faith would be rewarded. Someday.

Basket in hand, she would pick a path through the sand to his boat. He would greet her silently, frowning. The shame, apology, in his eyes had faded over time. Now, there was only defeat, and habit. He goes out in the boat because he always has, because he has nothing else to do, because she is always standing on the beach with her basket, waiting for him and a catch that never quite materializes.

She was always too tired to touch his face, to offer a smile of comfort. Dutifully, silently, she gathered up the day's catch from where it flopped on the wet sand. A few dull creatures, sickly whitefish no bigger than her hand. Not enough to cover the bottom of her basket, but she would scale them, gut them, clean them, and take them to the square to sell.

Their village did not have a market of its own. Instead, a buyer in a rickety truck, its sides built up with wooden slats, came to buy what they offered. The only reason the man came at all was because he could pay less here than anywhere else. They should ask for more money, she always told herself, they deserved more money. But when she stepped forward, shoulders set and chin raised to stand up for herself, the other women held her back. They couldn't afford to drive him away. Sometimes, though, she recalled the pride she once felt and made her demand.

He simply turned his back, threatening to get in the truck and drive away. She had to beg him to stay, and when he offered less than he ever had before, she had to accept. He fed on their desperation with a smug smile. They did not have a choice; no one else would ever come to make an offer.

Now, she was the one to feel shame peeling back her face. She'd take the few coins in exchange for the scant catch, and think of the impossibility of even wishing for something better. She kept on, for no other reason than her husband made the effort to take out the boat at dawn. Going through the motions was the least she could do. So the circle played out, and would play out for all the days to come. To do anything else would upend the order of the universe. At least they didn't have children, as if the village's population had thinned as thoroughly as the bay's.

The last thing she did each day, after their dinner of soup and hard bread, as the sun went down, was water the box of flowers in the single window of their one room clapboard home. The red geraniums usually flowered and granted some color to her tired, washed-out world. They even smelled a little, a faint perfume cutting through the stink of fish. As long as she had fresh water for the flowers, as long as the flowers sparked green and red against the salt-scoured drabness of her house, she could continue to wake each morning and imagine that she was young, imagine that today was the day her husband would return to shore with a boatful of fish, and their fortune.

One day she woke up, opened her eyes, got herself and her husband out of bed. Fed him and sent him off to the boats, but he returned a short hour later, and asked her to come with him to the beach. They'd found something.

On the sand, the fishermen and their wives gathered, standing in a semicircle around a figure: a man, shoeless, in torn and weathered clothing, lying face up at the tideline, unconscious. The waves lapped at his feet, and there were grooves in the sand that hinted that he must have clawed up from the surf. A castaway perhaps, but no other debris littered the beach, no broken spars or ripped sails, no other bodies or survivors. No storm raged last night, to account for a body washed up on their shore.

Disbelief at the oddness, the disruption in the eternal routine, kept anyone from moving closer. So she was the one who went to the man, brushed his tangled black hair from his pale face and touched his neck, feeling for his pulse. When he opened his eyes, she flinched. Not a drowned body, but a man, alive. His eyes were the gray of slate.

He smiled at her.

Seeming hale and strong now, he sat up and smiled at them all, not at all like a man who'd been found on the beach, baking under the morning sun after freezing in the night air. She stared at her hand; he'd been cold, where she touched him.

When he spoke, his voice wasn't at all parched like it should have been, washed up from the sea as he was. Instead, it was clear, deep, beautiful, and he made them an offer. He promised them bounty, all the treasure they'd wished for for so many years, all that they'd prayed for and never received. To prove he could make good on his vast assertions, he asked to borrow one of the fishermen's nets. Her husband gave him his. Taking the net, the stranger waded into the water, until the waves met his knees, and he cast. The net settled, sank, and, skillfully, as if he'd fished all his life, as if he'd come from a place where men had fished for hundreds of years, perhaps even a small poor village like this one, he held on to the net, dragged it, gathered it in, hauled it to shore. He leaned against the weight of it, because the net was full.

A hundred fish thrashed against the net's fibers. But more than fish, there was gold: he reached in among the flopping bodies and drew out a cup, a plate, and a circlet—a band of twisted gold that might fit around a woman's arm. The bend of it spiraled one way and another, resembling the infinite curl of a seashell. The shape drew the gaze, which fell into it, spiraling down until you believed you might fall in truth, and then you looked up into the sky, and realized the sky too went on forever. She stopped thinking at all, lest she become ill.

The castaway reached out, offering her the band of gold. She took it; it was cold, burned her hand with its chill, but she held it tightly, drawn close to her breast. This was all the riches she had ever dreamed of.

The god of the village's old priest had never given such glittering proof of his good faith.

The price they had to pay was blood. It didn't even have to be their own. Just blood, shed in sacrifice, which, when she thought of it, made a certain kind of sense, as much sense as the wealth the castaway drew forth with his net—a concrete wealth that she could feel and taste, not a wish and hope for something that might never come. What else did they have to trade but blood? Never mind all the blood she and her husband had already shed, stabs from fishhooks, burns from rough nets, bruises, broken bones, blisters, a slip of a knife, chapped hands from so much washing, washing, washing, until the water she rinsed in ran red.

Accidental blood didn't count. The bargain needed fresh blood, clean and intentional.

She knew exactly where to find the blood they needed.

While the others glanced between them, uncertain, she rounded her shoulders and caught her husband's gaze. Convinced him she knew what to do, took his hand, and marched to the village square.

Everyone followed her, except for the old priest in his faded gray robes. The cloth might have been white once, before she was born. The old man was afraid and begged her, all of them, to stop. He could barely look at the castaway and made the sign against evil at him. For his part, the castaway laughed, and that was all it took to drive the priest into his church. She saw the priest one more time trying to light a candle in the window, but his matches were damp, and the wick was moldy. He stood there, striking over and over, his motions sharp and desperate, his face pursed in concentration. She looked away, didn't look again. He'd never helped them, in all her years of praying for fish, for health, for salvation. How wonderful now, to be doing something more than praying.

At the same time she always did, she went to the square, her basket in hand, waiting for the man in the rickety truck. She looked like she did any other morning, waiting for what their buyer thought of as charity, what the wives knew was shame. The air seemed very quiet, not even the gulls crying over the water.

The buyer arrived in a puff of stinking exhaust, climbed from the rusted cab of his truck like he always did, his smile broad as if he had just finished laughing at a joke. Faced her, arms spread, as if to say good morning and what fine weather. She didn't give him time to look surprised as she dropped her basket and slashed his throat with the hooked gutting knife she'd kept hidden at her side.

It was a cut she'd made a thousand times, designed to part flesh instantly and spill the guts cleanly. His throat opened, shining red like the inside of a fish's gills. His eyes bulged, round and unblinking. The man fell soundlessly, and his blood spilled. A much darker red than her geraniums.

How nice, to see some color in their faded world.

She showed them all how easy it was to make a strike for a better future.

The next day, every boat was filled with fish and gold.

The new god provided. She spent hours studying the gold band around her arm, tracing her fingers along its arcs and spirals, sighing at its color, an inspiring glow, what she imagined the sun must look like in a fairy-tale kingdom, so perfect and warm. Along a certain curve, she could imagine that the metal caressed her back.

The second sacrifice was even easier.

The village had one inn, a decayed plankboard house, two stories, with a cupola that looked over the bay. It might have been elegant, once, and was still the most stately building in the village, with its overgrown yard and peeling façade. In summer months, a handful of tourists might decide the village was quaint and choose to spend a night here. They never stayed more than one.

But this was winter, and no one had passed through for months—until today, which must have been a sign. She spied on the man, a sickly young thing with an ill-fitting suit and scuffed hand-me-down briefcase. The innkeeper said he was a scholar studying the region's history, and had asked many outlandish questions about economic depression and whether it might be brought on by curses. Depended on how you defined curses, she thought.

Approaching midnight, a whole crowd of them went to the inn to do the deed. Again, she held the weapon and made the cut. The rest stayed behind to ensure the sacrifice could not flee.

He didn't escape. He hardly made a sound when she struck. She stood over his bed as he gaped, and he didn't even seem surprised as he bled out.

Her husband brings her trinkets of gold that he draws up in his nets, along with fish, though she cares less and less about the fish. Now, when she pulls herself to him and guides his hands to her hips, he digs in his fingers greedily, clutching her to him so that her breasts are flattened by his chest. His eyes are bright enough to match the flashing of jewels in sunlight as he kisses her, and she is warm as fire, no matter how clammy the winter air outside grows.

The flowers have died. Their scent has long ago faded, and for a time, she continues to water the dried out, blackened stems, the broken petals lying shattered on the cracked soil of the planter box. It's out of habit rather than hope. One day she forgets, distracted by the twisted gold band around her wrist. Its light draws her like a sun, if she could remember what the sun looks like. She follows the pattern of its spirals, the depth of its whorls, and she can almost hear the chanting of the beings who made it. They must be beautiful.

The fisher folk gather in the square in front of the old priest's church. The old priest hasn't been seen in some time. She hardly wonders what has happened to him, and can't remember what he looked like or what he preached. She forgets the old life, because what of it is worth remembering? Though she notices the splash of red across the church door. It reminds her of her geraniums, and she always liked flowers.

These days, her husband comes home smiling and rushes at her, arms outstretched to grab her up, to feel every inch of her, carry her to their cot and pin her there. She burns, answering him. It's no longer work to seduce each other, and they rut like eels, writhing around one another. After wearing each other out, they fall asleep smiling, wake smiling, and they kiss deeply, wetly, before she sends him off to the boats. The ocean has become a joy instead of the torment it was. She can smell nothing now but salt and slime.

She bathes sometimes in the old tub that has stood behind their shack for years, gathering debris. She cleaned it out, scrubbed it, filled it with water from the sea, and now soaks in it for hours. Her graying hair coils and snakes around her like the limbs of some leviathan. When she pulls at the strands, they come out, and she stares, studying them. Wraps them around her fingers and wrists, twining them with the twisted gold she wears. She'll fall asleep like this, floating, suspended, dreaming of deep places and distant voices; then wake submerged, staring up through the distorted lens at a wavering world, gray and dimly lit, and hardly notice that she has not drowned.

Once, she looks up through the warped glass of the water and sees the castaway above her, looking back, seeming to study her, taking in every inch of her naked body, curled up in the tub. She recalls that she should be embarrassed at the very least, mortified and blushing. She should hide herself. Ought to be angry and cry out for her husband. But she doesn't. Though her skin is cool, her mouth clammy, her gratitude for him burns, and she would take his hand and draw him down with her, to show him how deep her faith runs. But he touches her face, strokes back what's left of her hair, smiles like a father showing affection for a favorite daughter.

And she thinks, he does love me, he loves us all.

They perform the rituals, make the sacrifices. They watch the little-used roads for signs of travelers, whom the innkeeper invites into his decrepit building with a hungry gaze and grasping hands. So eager, most guests are suspicious. Some listen to their instincts and leave, in which case they'll be taken on the road leading out of the village. Some stay, though soon the keeper won't have a room to offer that isn't stained with blood.

Her husband loses his thick brown hair, leaving a scalp like a whale's hide. She still loves to rub her scaled hands over it, stroking him to a frenzy as he lays his now-toothless mouth against her neck for sucking kisses. His boneless arms fit so tightly around her, and her legs cling to him with a sinuous determination, like an octopus gripping its rocky mount. They lie in the salty bathtub together, and it feels like home.

Their new priest preaches of a time when they will go to the sea. This is their reward, eternal life in the holy depths. No longer slaves to the sea, but masters of it. So he says. They gather, chanting, and the rituals make her feel like that first glimpse of gold did: overwhelmed, soaring over an abyss, the infinite spirals, so much greater and terrific than anything she had ever seen before. She has kept that gold band around her wrist, where it remains locked, her peeling gray flesh swelling in folds around it.

There comes a time when they are gathered, chanting and writhing, performing their sacred rites of blood, when she isn't sure anymore which of the gray-skinned, eel-headed men is her husband. If she calls out his name, none of them will answer, but she doesn't call, because she doesn't remember. They seem like such small things, names and husbands. Now, she only dreams of the time which must come soon—always, must come soon—when they will go to their reward, to dwell in the eternal kingdom in the darkest places under the ocean.

She remembers one thing. Tiny, so small and inconsequential she has forgotten to forget. A day, a moment in a day, in her young and newly married life, before the future stretched unbreaking. She found a wooden box which she filled with dirt and mulch. She planted flowers, watered them, kept them alive for years, until she didn't. Reds and greens and yellows, a memory of color that stings her mind like the cut of a knife. She flinches at the sting, hardly knows why. Instead, she turns again to the sound of chanting, which by now has become the sound of resolve.

When she slips under the waves and lives forever more in a world of gray, she wonders if her resolve will break. Because even then, she'll remember the warmth of the sun on her face, and the scent of the flowers.

<hr />

Carrie Vaughn is the bestselling author of the Kitty Norville series. The twelfth novel, *Kitty in the Underworld*, is due out in July 2013. She has also written young adult novels, *Voices of Dragons* and *Steel*, and the fantasy novels, *Discord's Apple* and *After the Golden Age*. Her short fiction has appeared many times in *Lightspeed* and *Realms of Fantasy*, and in a number of anthologies, such as *Fast Ships, Black Sails,* and *Warriors*. She lives in Colorado with a fluffy attack dog. Learn more at carrievaughn.com.

"Have you committed a crime? In your dreams?"

THE DREAM DETECTIVE

———✦———

Lisa Tuttle

In the beginning, I was not attracted to her at all. Quite the opposite.

I don't know if it was intentional on her part, and honestly, I'm not the sort of dick who always judges women on how hot they are, but if there's *any* situation in which a person's attractiveness matters, I think everybody would agree it's a blind date.

Hannes and Mardi, my so-called friends, so worried about my single state, had once more stepped into the breach and invited me to dinner to meet someone "very special." They had introduced me to several very nice, lovely, smart, sexy women in the past, and all had been good company even though there'd never been the necessary, mutual spark that would ignite a love affair—but not this time.

My first sight of Mardi's old house-mate Grace was of a lumpy little figure in drab, ill-fitting clothes. Her hair probably hadn't been brushed since she'd rolled out of bed, her eyebrows looked like hairy caterpillars, and apart from a slash of bright red lipstick, she hadn't bothered with makeup. "Couldn't be bothered" was a good description of her in general, and from her sullen look, she was equally unimpressed by me.

As it was only the four of us for dinner, I couldn't ignore her without being rude. But my first few attempts to engage her attention fell flat.

Hannes kept the ball rolling with some stories I hadn't heard before—he's very funny, especially considering English isn't his first language—until Mardi shrieked for his help in the kitchen, and we were left alone together.

"So what do you do?" I asked.

I could have kicked myself as soon as the words were out. I didn't want to talk about my own tedious job, so why put her on the spot?

She stared at me for a long moment while I tried to figure out a way of withdrawing the question that wouldn't make things worse, and finally she said, "I'm a dream detective."

I thought I'd heard wrong. "Dream?"

She nodded. "Detective," she added, helpfully.

If it was a joke I didn't get it. "You mean you solve dreams?"

"What does that mean?"

"I don't know. You said it."

"I didn't say I solved *dreams*. I solve *crimes*, and other mysteries, in dreams."

"What's your success rate?"

"Quite good, actually." She made a modest face. "Although, I shouldn't brag; I have to admit I haven't done much of anything lately . . . "

She was playing it straight, so I had to do the same. "But you've solved a few, over the years?"

"Oh, yes."

"How long have you been helping the police with their enquiries?"

She looked as if she was about to laugh, but stopped herself, and simply shook her head. "The police aren't interested in dreams."

"But—I mean, if you are solving crimes—"

"Dream crimes."

"What's a dream crime?"

She sighed, as if I were deliberately obtuse. "A crime committed in a dream."

"In a dream."

"That's what I said."

This fey game of hers was really getting up my nose. It wasn't funny, and it wasn't clever—if it *was* a game. Just checking, I said, "But not in the real world."

I was reminded of one of my least favorite teachers by the snooty look she gave me and her retort: "In your opinion, dreams aren't part of the real world?"

"I don't know. *You're* the one who—"

"You don't dream?"

"Everybody dreams."

"You'd be surprised how many people say they don't. Or that they can't remember. It's not for me to say they're lying, but forgetfulness can be a cover for things people find too painful to think about."

"I dream a lot." Since childhood, I'd enjoyed my dreams and enjoyed thinking about them; if I rarely told them to anyone, it was out of the fear that my descriptions would be inadequate, and they'd sound boring or nonsensical, instead of the fascinating adventures they were to me.

She leaned across the table, fixing me with eyes that were larger, darker and more eloquent than I'd realized. "Have you committed a crime? In your dreams?"

I felt a sudden surge of adrenaline, as if she'd come too close to a deeply guarded secret. My heart was racing, and I felt a powerful urge to run, the need to hide—and what an admission that would be!

I faced her down, smiling, although maybe it looked more like a snarl. "Is that how you solve your mysteries? You ask everyone you meet to confess to an imaginary crime? No wonder if your success rate is high! Who would dare to say no?"

"I'll take that as a yes," she said, staring at me so hard her twin caterpillars became one. Her eyes no longer held the slightest allure; they were like laser-beams, science fictional weapons able to bore right through the bones of my skull, into my brain, where her unnatural vision would find the image of something I had done that was so shameful, so deeply buried, that even *I* couldn't remember it.

Hannes came through the door then, thank God, carrying a platter, announcing dinner was served, followed by his wife carrying a covered bowl.

Over the meal, conversation was general, on the subjects of food, travel, movies, and then food again when Mardi brought out cheesecake and fruit salad for dessert. It was not the most scintillating conversation; in fact, it was one of the most restrained and boring I could remember ever having around that table, as if we were four random strangers forced to share in a crowded restaurant.

When Hannes left the room to make coffee there was a silence until Mardi turned to speak to Grace as if I wasn't there: "How's the job-hunting? Any luck?"

Grace shook her head.

"Still at the charity shop?"

"Two days. They'd have me for more hours, which would be great if I was getting paid, but, you know, I need to make some money."

"So your dream detecting doesn't pay?" I don't know what possessed me to jump in with that.

Mardi stared hard at the other woman. "You *told* him?"

The chair creaked as Grace leaned back and crossed her arms. Her face was flushed. She spoke flatly. "I had a feeling he might need my help."

"What?" Mardi's voice rose almost to a wail. "You're still doing that? You never told me!"

Hannes poked his head through the door. "Stop it; no fair having fun without me."

Mardi's hair was messy, her lipstick eaten away, her face as red as Grace's—but on her it looked good. "Oh, honey, you won't believe it, but Gracie—she's still—you know, remember that dream thing she did?" She groped with her hand in the air above her head.

Grace looked at me and said earnestly, "I don't do it for money. I would never—it would be wrong; it's a *gift*. It would be wrong for me to try to exploit it."

"Exactly! " Mardi exclaimed. "Like me and the tarot. I'll read the cards if someone asks, but I'd never, ever charge money."

"I'm astonished," said Hannes, deadpan. "I thought they only talked about these things in private, when all three witches got together."

"We're not witches."

"Who's the third?" I asked.

"Remember little Holly?"

"From your wedding? Ah, yes." I recalled the tiny yet perfectly formed maid of honor everyone had wanted to dance with.

He nodded. "The three weird sisters. Or former flat-sharers—but that doesn't sound so good, does it?"

I wondered if Grace had been at the wedding, too, and sneaked a look at her. I saw a frumpy, shapeless lump who didn't know how to make herself interesting. I wondered if the idea of the dream-investigation had been her own, or borrowed from one of her smarter roommates. She did not notice me looking, just went on staring at nothing, seemingly undisturbed by the queasy excitement roiling around the room even when Mardi shouted:

"We're not *witches*."

"Sorry, darling, how silly of me. You predict the future, and Holly heals people by stroking their auras, and Grace goes into people's minds to affect their dreams, and all that is completely ordinary and normal and not at all witch-like or weird."

"You're horrible."

"Horribly irresistible." She scowled at him, then giggled; he invited me to help him get the coffee, and I jumped up, happy for any excuse to leave.

In the kitchen, I asked: "Fortune-telling?"

"I'm surprised she's never dealt the cards for you. She still has them in a velvet bag. True, she doesn't often get them out these days, hardly ever since we were married, but back then, when she was living with Holly and Grace . . . they scared me sometimes, I don't mind telling you, those three women in the same room together, looking like they could read your mind and tell your future from the way you sipped your coffee." He shuddered melodramatically. "But each girl on her own . . . a different proposition."

"I wouldn't want to proposition Grace," I said sourly. "Is that what you thought? She's *really* my type. "

He gave me a sheepish smile and pressed the plunger down on the cafetiere. "Sorry, man. It wasn't supposed to be like this. We had invited two other people, and at the last minute they couldn't make it."

"Two? A couple?"

"Sister and brother. Both single. One for each of you. I swear."

"Well, better luck next time," I sighed, and lifting the tray of mugs, followed him out of the room.

After I went home that night I did not give Grace a second thought. But she wasn't done with me.

I was a turkey-farmer, somewhere in the country, rounding up my herd and then driving them, on foot, down a dirt road until I reached London, which was like the set for a low-budget TV version of Dickens' *A Christmas Carol*. I sold the big birds to an East Ender in a patched coat and shabby top hat ("Aow! God bless you, Guvnor!") and took my little velvet bag of gold coins to buy myself a drink, but at this point wintry London morphed into Paris in the spring, so I walked into a sidewalk café and ordered *un cafe, s'il vous plait*. It was as I was sitting there, waiting for my coffee, that I realized, from the nervous clenching in my gut, that I'd been followed.

She was sitting at another table, pretending to read a newspaper, and although she looked nothing like the woman I'd met over dinner—she looked like Edith Piaf, or, rather, like Marion Cotillard playing Piaf in *La Vie en Rose*—I knew her. I knew she was on to me. But she couldn't follow me into the men's toilet, so I was able to get away from her quite easily, although there was still some running and dodging down narrow alleys and in and out of shops before I woke up, heart pounding, feeling I'd had a narrow escape, but with no idea why. Was she police, or a foreign agent? Was I the good-guy spy, or an innocent who knew too much? Dreams feel like stories, but they leave out a lot of the information we'd need to make sense of a movie or a book.

• • •

Another night, another dream: I was in a theatre, up in the gods, where the rows of seats kept morphing into chutes and ladders, and every time I tried to get out, I ran into a little blonde girl in a blue dress, blocking the exit. She looked like Disney's Alice, but when she trained her eyes on me like a twin-bore shotgun, I knew who she really was, and knew I was in trouble.

Another time, in the midst of a ripping yarn featuring neo-Nazi conspirators and a fabled treasure hidden at the heart of an Egyptian pyramid, I became aware of her again. I never saw her, but felt the disturbing presence of an outsider; someone female who did not belong, an uninvited visitor who was spying on me. Only afterwards, awake, thinking it over as I showered and dressed for work, I became convinced that it was Grace; and I began to wonder what she was after, and how to get rid of her.

On my way home that night—I'd been working late, required to be on hand for a conference call with partners in other time zones—I stopped to buy a few things. It wasn't the store where I usually shopped, but I'd just remembered there was almost nothing in my fridge when I spotted a sign for Morrison's, and nipped in.

I found Grace in the wine aisle, inspecting the bottles. At the sight of her I felt disoriented, almost dizzy; that may have been the first time in my life when I genuinely wondered if I was really awake or only dreaming.

But maybe it wasn't her. The woman shopping for wine was dressed up and looked quite sexy. Had I become obsessed, was I starting to see the detective of dreams everywhere I went?

She turned her head and the recognition on her face told me I wasn't fantasizing. "Oh, hi! How are you? Do you live around here?"

"Sort of, not too far—but I don't usually shop here; how about you?"

She shook her head. "I'm on my way to . . . a party. Thought I'd better bring a bottle."

She wore a snug, scoop-necked top and short skirt, clothes that revealed that she wasn't fat at all, perhaps a little thick-waisted, but she did have a pair of enormous breasts. Maybe she hadn't wanted to show them off to me, but, clearly, she didn't feel obliged to keep them hidden all the time; I wondered what made the party she was on her way to now so very different from the dinner at Mardi and Hannes'. She was still far from beautiful, but just then she had a glow about her that made up for any small deficiencies in her appearance.

I saw her look in my basket, recognize the pathetic shopping of the single man (frozen chips, pizza, bacon, eggs, and a loaf of bread) and felt suddenly defensive, almost angry are her presumption in judging me, spying on me.

Without pausing to think, I asked her, "How do you do it?"

She looked honestly bewildered.

"The dreams . . . " Before I got it out, I'd realized how utterly idiotic my question was. She hadn't done anything. This meeting was coincidence; my dreams were my own. I stalled and fumbled and finally managed: "I was just wondering . . . You said you were a dream detective . . . I guess you were joking?"

"Oh. No, it wasn't a joke." She looked apprehensive. "It was true, but . . . I really don't know why I said it. I don't usually tell people. Mardi knows, because I used to do it when we lived together. But not anymore."

I know that's not true. I kept my accusation to myself, though, and only said, "Yeah? It's odd. I'd never heard of a dream detective before."

She cleared her throat and glanced around at the ranks of wine bottles. "No . . . that's not surprising. Neither had I. I guess I made it up. I was sharing a house with two friends, one read cards and the other read auras; they did it to help people and it was kind of cool and I wanted something I could do, so . . . " She shrugged and moved away from me to read a price-label.

"But how did it work? Did people invite you into their dreams, or did you just kind of dream your way inside their heads, or—"

"What?" Now she was staring at me.

"How—how did you do it? The dream-detecting?"

"People told me about their dreams and I interpreted them. What did you think?" Her eyes had widened, and I could see that she knew perfectly well what I had thought, and I realized how crazy it was. Why had I imagined for a moment that this less-than-ordinary woman could see inside my brain, even enter my dreams to spy on me?

To distract her from my idiocy, I asked another question. "And it worked?"

She shrugged. "People seemed to think so. They liked it, anyway. It was something I could do, it seemed vaguely useful, I had a lot of free time and no money—"

"So why did you stop? I mean, you must still have a lot of free time and no money, and since you're looking for a job—why not create your own employment? You'd have it to yourself, you'd be the expert, the only dream detective in England—"

"Oh, shut up. What did I ever do to you?"

I was surprised to realize she was angry. I hadn't meant to offend her, but she wouldn't let me explain.

"You don't know anything about it! You think it's a joke, but it's *not*."

"No, I don't think that—I really do take you seriously, that's why—"

"I *told* you, I couldn't charge money for using this gift—it would be wrong. It's not a job, it's a calling. Have you ever seen a rich and famous so-called psychic? What they're like? Do you think I'd ever be one of those media-whores?"

"Sorry," I said, holding up my hands as if her shiny eyes were loaded guns. "Sorry, I didn't understand; I didn't mean anything . . . "

She grabbed a bottle off the shelf without looking. "Forget it."

My dream that night began like a road trip, a pleasurable sort of dream I've enjoyed for years. As usual, it was set in the American West, a place I've never seen except in movies, out on a flat, open highway, Route 66, maybe. I was in one of those big old-fashioned sedan cars from the 1950s, white and shiny, with fins. Inside, the front seat was like a big leather couch, and the gearshift stuck out the side of the steering wheel. No seatbelts, no airbags, just a cigarette lighter and an AM radio tuned to a station belting out songs by Buddy Holly, the Everly Brothers, Elvis Presley.

I myself had more than a touch of Elvis about me, my hair in a quiff with long sideburns, wearing tight jeans, cowboy boots, and a black shirt with pearl-covered snaps, a packet of Camels squashed into the breast pocket. Sitting behind the wheel of that automotive behemoth, singing along to "Jailhouse Rock," driving through the desert towards somewhere unknown, I was free, and as purely happy as I've ever been. Everything was fine, better than fine, it was *perfect* until, glancing in the rear view mirror, I spotted a little black dot in the distance. Just in case, I checked my speed.

I was right; it was a cop. As the motorcycle drew closer, I told myself not to worry. I was going just under the speed limit, my tax disc was valid, the exhaust and tires were good, there was absolutely no reason for him to pull me over . . . but he did.

Even as I was slowing to obey his peremptory command I was no more than annoyed. It was only when I was stopped, watching the cop dismount, that I remembered there was a dead body in the trunk of the car.

I knew I must not panic, that I had to stay calm and convince the cop I was a good, law-abiding citizen he could have no interest in detaining. He came over to my window, asked to see my driver's license, told me to get out of the car and step away, keeping my hands where he could see them. I obeyed, but perhaps not quickly enough, or maybe there was something in my attitude he didn't like, because he became more aggressively authoritarian with every passing second. He sneered at my hairstyle, asked where I went to church, and about my political affiliations, and when I reminded him that this was America, the land of the free, he said I sounded like a limey bastard, and demanded my passport.

The tedious, threatening argument went on and on, and I was relieved to wake up before my guilty secret was revealed.

I found that dream unusually disturbing. I had no idea whose body was in the boot, or how it had come to be there. I didn't even know if I was a killer. In the dream there had been no guilt or shame attached to the knowledge that I was driving around with a dead body, only anxiety about the consequences if it was found. Did that mean I wasn't a murderer? Or did it indicate the opposite, that my dream persona was a cold-blooded psychopath?

Over the next few weeks, the dream continued to haunt me. I'd had recurring dreams before, anxiety dreams in which I was forever doomed to miss my flight, getting lost on my way to take an exam, or finding I had to give a speech wearing nothing but a skimpy bathrobe. Now, my pleasurable dream of driving across America had been spoiled, turned into another variant of angst.

After the first time, as soon as it began I was obsessed with the problem of how to dispose of the body. My every attempt to find a hiding place was foiled: There were fishermen on the lake, a family having a picnic in the woodland glade, kids playing in the old quarry, people with their prying eyes everywhere I went.

Gradually I came to understand that the body was that of my former girlfriend, but what had actually happened, and why I was burdened with her corpse remained unclear. I knew that my past connection with her would make me the prime suspect if her body was discovered, but I didn't actually know how she had died, and I didn't feel guilty.

In my waking hours I thought more and more about this dream, although I wished I could forget it. I wondered if talking to someone might help, and I thought of Grace.

Another coincidental meeting would have been perfect, but of course that wasn't going to happen. If I knew where she lived, though, I could make it happen, so in the end I phoned Mardi.

"Her *address?*" She made my simple request sound outrageous.

"I thought I might send her a card."

"Oh, really." Her skepticism was palpable.

"All right, then, phone number."

"I don't think so."

"Why not? You try to match us up, and then—"

"I did *not*. Anyway, that was a month ago, and you clearly didn't get on. In fact—"

"That's not fair. She was quite interesting, actually. Not my type, but—I'd like to talk to her again. I've been thinking about her."

"Well, don't."

I wished we were speaking face to face instead of on the phone. "Why do you say that? Did she say something about me?"

"Of course not."

But there had been a pause before she answered. "Did she tell you we ran into each other about a week after dinner at yours?"

She made a noise and I winced, remembering how Grace had suddenly taken flight. What had she said about me to Mardi? How bad was it?

"I want to apologize. Please, Mardi."

"I'll tell her." When I said nothing more, she sighed. "I promise. I'll call her tonight and give her your number, and then, if she wants, she can call you."

Grace did not phone me, but about a week later, she returned to me in a dream.

I was on the road again, and had pulled into a service station to fill the tank. When I came back from paying, there she was, in the front seat. She was a prettier, idealized version of Grace in a tight-fitting cashmere sweater beneath a trench coat. Her hairstyle was long, old-fashioned, hanging down in waves, one dipping across an eye like Veronica Lake's in an old black and white movie. I think the dream was in black and white, too.

"Drive," she said.

It was night now, and raining, but there was enough traffic on the road for the passing headlights to reveal her to me in occasional, strobe-like glimpses.

"I hear you've got a case for me," she said.

An enormous wave of relief washed over me, and between the pulsing beats of the windshield wipers I told her my story: brief, laconic, just the facts, ma'am. When I had finished, she continued to gaze straight ahead for a while before saying, her voice low, "Pull over."

"Where?"

"Doesn't matter. Wherever you can."

There was an exit just ahead, sign-posting a roadside picnic area, so I pulled off the highway and drove even deeper into darkness, away from the lights and the traffic, to a secluded spot, utterly deserted on this dark and rainy night.

When I had parked, I turned to face the detective. Light from an unknown source gently illuminated her features. She looked wise and gentle and I was suddenly certain she was the one person who could save me from this nightmare.

"Do you know who killed her?" I asked.

"Of course."

"Will you help me?"

"Yes." She touched my hand. "I'll take you in."

"What?"

"To the police. You have to turn yourself in."

"No."

"It's the only way."

"I can't. I won't. They'll think I'm the killer."

"You *are* the killer."

I looked into her eyes (one half-obscured by a silky fall of hair) and knew she told the truth.

"Give me the keys," she said. "I'll drive. They may not go so hard on you if you confess, if you can explain . . . "

But how could I explain something I could not remember?

As in a montage of scenes from an old black and white movie I saw my future: the grim faces of the jury, the old judge banging his gavel, the bleak and lonely cell, the walk—shuffling in ankle chains—to the electric chair, the hood coming down over my face, the soft voice of the priest exhorting me to confess and repent before I died . . .

It wasn't fair! I wanted to live!

Driven by desperate need, I reached for Grace. My hands closed around her slender neck and squeezed. My reaction took her by surprise, and my thumbs must have been in just the right spot to inflict maximum damage, for she scarcely even struggled; when she could not draw another breath she went limp. I continued to squeeze, making sure, venting my terror and rage on her frail and vulnerable neck, and by the time I let go, she was dead.

There was no one around to see, but I did not want to take the risk that some tired motorist might decide to drive in next to me, and considered simply pushing the detective's body out of the car and driving away. Then I had an idea: why not get rid of both bodies at once? I discovered a shovel in the trunk, and with it I dug a single grave, deep enough to hold them both. I drove away feeling satisfied, certain the evidence of both my crimes was now hidden so well they would never be found. Even if in future years someone found the bones, there would be nothing to link them to me.

I woke filled with regret and sorrow and a sense of terrible loss, but also with the cooler, steadying awareness that I'd done what I had to do, and it was over. I never had that dream again. Case closed. I would have liked to see Grace's reaction if I told her about it—but not enough to make any effort to find her. More than a year went by, actually closer to two, before I found out what had happened to her.

Hannes had asked me to meet him in Waterstone's at around six—I thought we were going for a drink, and had no idea why he'd suggested the bookshop rather than the pub across the street, not even when I saw him standing, grinning, beside the sign announcing a book-signing. He pointed at the author's photograph, and still I didn't twig, didn't recognize her until the title of the book—*Dream Detective*—gave me a clue.

"Grace Kearney—that's your Grace?"

"Not mine, mate!"

The woman in the photo looked ordinary: was blandly pretty, smiling, heavily made-up, the eyebrows plucked into anorexia. "Really? That's her? Mardi's old friend? She wrote a book?"

"And sold it for a bundle, and that's the least of it. Have you never seen her on TV? First it was guest appearances, but now I've heard she's going to have her own show."

I looked at the picture again, trying to summon up a mental image of the woman I'd met to compare it to, and failing. All I could think of was Veronica Lake struggling feebly in my murderous grasp.

"Are we meeting Mardi?" I hadn't seen her in months; although I tried to keep in touch, the two of them no longer entertained the way they'd used to, and rarely went out, since their baby had been born.

"No way! She doesn't approve."

"Of what, the book?"

"The book, the TV show, the celebrity clients, the publicity, glitz, bling, dosh . . ."

I recalled how badly Mardi had responded to Grace's telling me what she did. "Grace charges people money to investigate their dreams?"

"You sound like Mardi! Yeah, well, everybody's got to make a living. But my dear, idealistic wife does not approve. She thinks her old friend has gone over to the dark side. They don't speak anymore."

The long-ago dinner party conversation came back to me. "Grace said she didn't believe in taking money for her gift."

"That was the *old* Grace. She changed. Even before all this—" he gestured at the sign and the bookstore beyond. "Something happened. I have no idea what it was, but it changed her, like, overnight."

I felt a chill, an unwanted memory intruding, and repressed it.

"Does Mardi know what happened?"

He shook his head. "I told you, they don't talk. 'She's dead to me,' says my lovely wife. Or was it 'She's dead inside'—maybe both those things." He shrugged it off. "Want to go for a drink?"

"Maybe I'll just get a book signed, first. Since we're here." I felt no nervousness about seeing her again, and I was curious. That mousey little girl, a celebrity! Recalling her vehemence about how wrong it would be to take money for using her gift, I realized I had met her at a moment of crisis, sounding out other people and arguing with herself over the decision she had to make. What I found harder to understand was how her imaginary profession could be taken seriously by so many. A TV show!

Picking up a book, taking it to the counter to pay, I reflected that people were eager to believe in all sorts of nonsense. And there was the "entertainment" argument—that justified the regular publication of horoscopes in newspapers, and psychics making their predictions on television. Just a bit of slightly spooky fun. Grace had simply tapped into that. Why not? It might upset someone like Mardi, who believed she could see the future in her special deck of cards, but a realist like me ought to applaud her initiative.

There was a small, orderly queue near the back of the shop. I joined the end of it by myself—Hannes said he'd meet me in the pub across the road—and while I waited my turn I wondered if Grace would recognize me, and decided she would not.

But I was wrong. When I reached the front of the queue and put the book down, open, before her, she raised her eyes to mine, and at once, although there was no change in her mild, professionally pleasant smile, greeted me by name.

I looked into her eyes and saw nothing there. The emptiness was unsettling.

"I'm surprised—I didn't think you'd remember me," I said, stammering a little.

"How could I forget? After what you did . . . If not for you, I wouldn't be here now. In a way, I owe my whole career to you."

A woman standing near the wall behind her took notice and stepped forward. "Really? That's *very* interesting! I don't recall this from your book . . . Will you introduce us, Grace?"

Grace went on smiling mildly at me and staring at me with her dead eyes; without turning she said, "Not now"—and although there was nothing threatening or even unpleasant in her tone, it was enough to make the other woman fall back.

"I don't know what you mean," I said.

"I think you do."

If I said Grace was dead, that the woman signing books was only a simulacrum, or some kind of zombie, who would believe me? Yet I knew, and so did she, that it was true. Mardi had sensed it as well. She was physically still alive, but dead inside—and it was my fault.

"Thank you for coming," she said. While I had stood there speechless, she had finished writing in my book and now she handed it back to me. "Thank you. Next!"

At her command, I stumbled away. I'd forgotten everything else in the horror of my discovery, forgot I was supposed to meet Hannes, and made my way home, alone, across the city. There was no one I could talk to about it, and I could think of nothing else. What had I done to that poor girl?

Poor? I could just imagine what Hannes might have said: "Are you kidding? She used to be poor, and now she's not. She's a success! I can't see how it's anything to do with you, but she thanked you, right? She's changed, sure, and maybe her old friends don't like it, but that's life."

Mardi alone might have understood—but if I told her what I'd done to the dream-Grace, she would have hated me, and however much I deserved it, I couldn't bear the thought.

When I got home, I took a cursory look at *Dream Detective,* reading a few pages, wondering if it would give me any answers, but there was something smug and flat and false about the paragraphs I skimmed that killed that hope. I turned back to the title page where I found what I later learned to be the author's standard inscription: My name, and *Dream well! Sincerely yours, Grace Kearney.*

Her signature was a florid scribble, which I imagined she had worked up as an impressively individual, if nearly illegible, autograph. Yet there seemed to be something wrong with it. A closer look revealed that something had been written in the same space *before* she signed; two words in tiny letters, hand-printed, almost obliterated by the signature. I knew they had not been there when I bought the book, were not on the page when I opened it before her, and they were written with the same pen—Grace herself was the only possible author. Had she started to write a more personal message, then changed her mind?

Under the brightest light I had, with the aid of a magnifying glass, I examined the page until the half-hidden words became clear:

save me

Those words have changed my life. I've been asked to do something, and although I don't know how, I will find a way.

Some things, once broken, can never be mended. Murder, no matter how deeply the killer repents, can't be undone—except, of course, in dreams.

Lisa Tuttle began writing while still at school, sold her first stories at university, and won the John W. Campbell Award for Best New Science Fiction Writer of the year in 1974. Her first novel, *Windhaven,* was a collaboration with George R. R. Martin published in 1981; her most recent is the contemporary fantasy *The Silver Bough,* and she has written at least a hundred short stories— science fiction, fantasy and horror—as well as essays, reviews, non-fiction, and books for children. Born and raised in Texas, educated in New York, later a resident of London, she now makes her home in a remote, rural part of Scotland.

*I don't know why he started feeding the house,
but I think about how hard it is to look away from it,
how hard it is to keep from going there . . . it calls us.*

EVENT HORIZON

—◆—

Sunny Moraine

On Tuesdays and Thursdays we go to feed the house.

Zhan takes me. We walk down the cracked sidewalk, hopping the places where the cracks are almost chasms. At points we have to push through high weeds. We go in the middle of the day when the sun is a hammer beating on your head and it's too hot for the flies to buzz. There's hardly anyone outside then and never anyone down this end of Pine Street, which is probably the only reason we can come and feed the house at all.

Because if the rest of them had their way they'd just let it starve.

Can you starve a house? I asked Zhan once, and he just spat tobacco at me and smirked. It was a stupid question and I know that now. Of course you can starve a house. You can starve anything that's alive.

Zhan flips his shaggy black hair back from his face, huffs out a laugh at nothing in particular. Zhan is three years older than me and all angles and he doesn't know I'm in love with him.

In my mind, all three of those things are of equal importance. In my mind, none of them can exist independently of the others.

Zhan has two squirrels in a steel box trap under his arm. They scurry back and forth and rattle the wire mesh on the ends. I can feel their panic. Once it would have bothered me but I'm over that now. I'm focused ahead, trying not to trip over anything but also because I want to see the house the second that seeing it is possible. I don't want it sneaking up on me. It keeps up the appearance of dormancy but we know that it's like any predator; it only seems passive when it has to.

"Step it up, Tom." Zhan glances back over his shoulder and speeds up a little. We're not supposed to be here. If we're seen by an adult nosy enough we'll get busted for truancy and they'd probably want to know what we were going to do with the squirrels. I move faster, grass whispering around my ankles.

Then I see it.

It's two stories. There's a porch running around its front and a little way onto the sides. Its blue paint has faded and peeled until it's almost gray. Its front yard is dead and brown. The four front windows—two on each floor— are broken. They're black holes. We've never seen what's inside. We've never gotten close enough to do so. A rusty PRIVATE PROPERTY KEEP OUT sign hangs crooked on the wire mesh fence but that's not why we hang back.

Zhan and I stand there for a few minutes. The squirrels are still and silent, and I know without looking that it isn't because they're afraid. They're beyond fear.

Finally Zhan drops into a crouch and sets down the trap, points the front at the gap where the gate used to be before it rusted off its hinges. He opens the trap. I lose the fight against the shiver that wants to roll through me; there's sweat trickling down between my shoulder blades, but that's not where the shiver is coming from.

The house is staring at me. At both of us.

The squirrels walk out of the trap. They aren't moving in that funny little hop that squirrels do. They're *walking*, one foot in front of the other, stiff. They're little squirrel zombies. They walk through the gate without hesitation, up the broken pavement of the front path and right up to the door.

Here's the thing about the door: It's there. And it's not.

They walk right up to it and through it. It never opens.

No sound. No movement.

"Every fuckin' time," Zhan murmurs. I nod.

Zhan picks up the trap. We back away. Twenty yards clear and we turn and walk back the way we came. Neither of us says a word.

The house has always been there. Or it was there when we moved here, which was before I can remember anything, so as far as I'm concerned that's *always*.

Zhan and I have been friends since I was old enough to have friends and he's been my hero since I was old enough to have heroes. A lot of this is because he accepted me from the first when a lot of other kids laughed and called names and threw rocks and never gave me a moment's peace at school—

most particularly the ever-present trio of Kyle Patterson, who has hated me for reasons of his own since the third grade, Jake McDonnell, who's his best friend, and Drew Carter, who usually just tags along because he has nothing better to do—because of my hair and the clothes I insisted on wearing and how I bristled every time anyone called me *her*. I could never have explained to them why I wanted these things; they just felt right in a world that was nothing but wrong. But Zhan, if he didn't understand, at least accepted without question or complaint. For Zhan, I just was. I am.

Like the house.

I was ten when Zhan first took me to the house. He had caught a neighbor's cat, a mangy thing that always came after us with claws fully extended. It hissed and yowled in the trap but then it walked through the front gate and we never saw it again.

Zhan swore me to secrecy. I swore.

That was three years ago. In those three years Zhan has never answered any of my questions, not where it came from, what it really is, how he found out about it, or whether or not we could kill it. I think if there were answers, Zhan would give them to me.

Later in the woods, after we've fed the house, he sticks a hot dog into fire we made in a ring of stones and holds it out to me when it's split down the middle and steaming. The light is touching his face with soft, shifting fingers. I look at him and I hope—oh, God, I *hope*—that he can't see what I'm thinking.

I knew I was in love with Zhan a year after he showed me the house. I think the house is why it happened. He shared a secret with me. It made me want to share all of mine.

It's getting tough to do the twice-a-week-sneaking-out thing.

Back in summer it was easier. We could get away for entire days, spend the morning tossing a baseball back and forth in the dusty lot two blocks from our street, check the traps, feed the house, and devote the rest of the afternoon to shooting crows with an air rifle from the bushes that surround the parking lot of the Los Vientos industrial park. In the summer it's pretty empty so no one runs us off. But I think Zhan always enjoys that part more than I do.

Regardless, it's not summer anymore. School's back in session, never mind how hot it is and will be for at least two more months, and it's not all that hard to go truant from lunch with all of us crowded into the blacktop yard—*blasting* heat at us—but we're running a little bit of a risk every time.

Thank Christ no one really cares. *That fucking dyke and her faggot friend.* Neither of us is especially popular, so okay, we have each other.

We have each other. I love how that sounds.

Here we are again. This time it's three chipmunks, walking in stately procession up the path. Zhan and I are standing close enough to touch. I glance at him—it always feels hard to look away from the house, dangerous even, but I can manage it for him—and for the first time I wonder *How much longer are we going to do this?*

What would happen if we stopped?

I don't know why Zhan started feeding the house. But in bed that night I start thinking about the steady plod all the animals do up to that not-there door. And I think about how hard it is to look away from the house, how hard it is to even keep from going there, the way we'll get around almost any obstacle to do it.

It calls us.

I fall asleep thinking about it there in the dark, alive, hungry, waiting for the next time we bring it meat.

I dream about it. It's not a good dream.

I'm standing where Zhan and I always stand, looking at the house. But it's not like it usually is. We never go to the house after dark but it's dark now, starless and moonless. And I'm alone.

Except I'm not. Because the house is there. And while I know that every time we stare at it, it's staring back . . . I've never felt it like this before. It's this dark hulk sitting there, and while it's not moving I feel like it is. Creeping closer to me. Reaching out.

The front yard is full of bones.

We've never seen it like that. The house leaves nothing. It takes everything in. Flesh, bone, blood. Light. Air. I want to turn around and walk away. Run away, maybe. But I can't. My muscles are locked. And instead I find myself walking forward in that walk that hundreds of animals have been forced into before me. Bones crunch under my feet. The air is weirdly hot.

What are you? Where did you come from?

I reach out and put my hand through the door, and I feel it disappear into the nothing beyond.

"I wonder if it was from some kind of experiment."

Zhan grunts and passes over the cigarette we're sharing. It's an off day for us—at least as far as the house is concerned—and we're sitting on the concrete wall outside the abandoned Sunoco, drinking flat soda, smoking. Watching the sunset. My hand brushes his when I take the cigarette, and he isn't looking at me.

I can't decide which is harder to stop thinking about, Zhan or the goddamn house—and maybe they can't be separated. Maybe neither can exist without the other.

But it's been a while and I should really figure it out.

"I mean," I persist, "like maybe it's like a black hole or something? Like a scientist was doing shit and it went wrong."

Another grunt.

"Or maybe it's haunted," I say. "I read about something like that. Haunted houses. People go into them, never get seen again."

Zhan takes the cigarette back and taps ash onto the asphalt. "Whatever, man."

No, not whatever. But I'm not irritated with him. I'm irritated with the house. I get the sense, subtle but increasingly hard to ignore, that we don't talk about it because it doesn't want us to.

"You know it's not haunted," Zhan says after about ten minutes of silence. I jump, and then I stretch my arm back to scratch at a fake itch on my shoulder blade so he won't think I was startled, but it probably doesn't work.

"You know it's not, Tom. That shit is *alive*."

It never really feels like autumn, but the days get shorter. I don't ask Zhan about the house, not for a while. If it really is trying to silence me, I give up and let myself be silenced. I'm thinking about other things. I'm getting to the point where every week I can feel myself changing, getting older. Two weeks ago I looked at myself in the mirror and I'm getting tits, *shit*, still small but I can feel them coming. Mom took me out to get a couple of sports bras. I got them one size too small and so far it's working okay. I'm still flat. And Mom doesn't seem like she cares what I do. She watched me come out of the changing room and look at myself and all she did was ask me if the bras were okay.

Not asking questions is a kind of support, isn't it?

Whatever. *Zhan*. And the Winter Formal is coming up and last year I wouldn't have ever thought about going because I'm *that fucking dyke* but now I'm fantasizing about it, me in a tux and Zhan in a tux, matching pair except he's taller with longer hair, and we'd dance in the dots of mirrorball light and everyone would leave us alone.

I don't even know why I want this. I wish I could stop. I wish the house would make me quiet about this like it does about itself.

Maybe the animals don't die. Maybe they go somewhere better. Maybe that's why none of them ever come back.

"We're moving."

It takes me a minute to get it. We're walking to school, taking our circuitous route that sends us through the blacktop yard, and I get lost in the rhythm of my own steps.

He's moving. Well, aren't we both? Together?

Then, "The fuck you mean?"

"End of the month." He kicks a rock into the scrubby grass. "Dad's got a new job. He told me this morning."

"You can't," I say. It comes out without me thinking. It's a statement of fact, like what he just said. He can't. Of course he can't. We're a matched pair, like when I think about dancing with him; we go together. We don't make any sense apart.

He huffs a laugh. "Yeah, well."

We're at the fence. We're through the fence, where some of our classmates are heading inside and the others are screaming all around us in those play screams that escalate out of control; one person starts being loud and then everyone gets louder and louder until no one can hear anything anymore but no one shuts up. I stop and I stare at him. He stops and stares back. His hair is falling in his face. I can only see one black eye. He has crow's eyes. Like the crows he shoots.

"I don't want you to." I take a breath, and I latch onto the only argument I can think of that isn't about what I want, because I don't think what I want ever carries a lot of weight. "What about the house?"

He shrugs. "That'll be on you, I guess."

"I can't. I don't have the traps."

"I'll give them to you."

"I *can't*." I'm so close to crying. I've never cried in front of him. I hate it so much. "I can't, I can't, I don't *want* you to." Jesus Christ, I sound like a two-year-old, and he's just looking at me and he's like the goddamn *house*, I have no idea what the hell he's thinking.

I was working up to asking him to the Formal. Like a joke. *Be my date.* And he'd take it as a joke and we'd spend the whole night smirking at everyone like we're too cool for them instead of the other way round, and we probably wouldn't even dance but you know? I think I would have been okay with that. But it's not like it even matters now.

"I have to." And for those three words he sounds so gentle that suddenly I'm sobbing and pushing myself forward, my arms going around his skinny frame, those tits that I don't like and don't want pressing against his chest.

I don't mean to kiss him but I do. I don't really mean to do anything. Like ever. Shit just happens. He's happening. He tastes like cigarettes and toothpaste.

Oh, God, he's kissing me back.

We just stand there. If I could hold onto this it wouldn't even matter. Now I'm the house and I'm pulling him into me. *Stay here. Stay in me. I'll never let you go. Not a single part of you, not even your bones.*

All around me the screams are rising into a surprised, mocking crescendo.

We get a day of peace, like a gift. Then they come for me.

I'm walking home. Isn't that always when shit like this happens? People get mugged. Raped. Dragged into vans and never seen again. None of that is what happens to me, but one moment the sidewalk ahead of me is clear and the next it's crowded with guys. Looking at me. Clenching their fists.

Kyle, Jake, and Drew. They're big enough to count as a *crowd*.

I stop. On some level I suppose I expected this. I took a risk; more often than not risks have costs. And I was getting too lucky with not getting beaten up much anymore. But I look at them there in the twilight and I have this awful feeling that today I'm in for more than an average beating.

I can't run. Their legs are longer. But I take a step back anyway. I'm still blocks from home. If I screamed I'm not sure anyone would come to the door.

"Hi, *Tessa*."

That gets me bristling. I think of that cat, his fur all bushed out and his lips drawn back from his teeth; he always looked like a snake. Maybe I can be like that.

Jake tips his chin toward me. It would be easier if he was sneering or something; instead he just looks cold. "So you were making out with your girlfriend the other day. That was real fucking sweet, Tessa."

"I'm not Tessa." They use my name like a punch. Names shouldn't get used like that. No one should be *able* to use them like that. I feel guilty for letting them. "The fuck you guys want?"

"We want your girlfriend," Kyle says, and he sounds like he's doing me a favor, telling me. "You know where *she* is. We wanna see you make out again. It was real hot, Tess."

I shake my head, but Drew steps forward and grabs me by the arm and squeezes so hard I feel my bones grind and I choke back a cry. I'm getting a sense of it, what's looming in front of me out of the dark. Behind them. It's more than them. Bigger. Nastier. Driving them. Do they know? Would they care if they did? There's something like that behind everything like this that anyone does anywhere in the world. I don't think people can do things like this on their own. Not that people are *fundamentally* good or any shit like that but just because I honestly don't think people are strong enough for this kind of bad.

I'm trying to figure a way past this, and I'm not smart enough to wriggle free no matter how much I wish I was—but I think I might be strong enough for a different kind of bad.

I have no idea if this will work. Probably it won't. They aren't like Zhan and me. They haven't been called.

But I incline my head down the street, breathing hard. I hurt. It's hard to think over the hurt; I'm sort of impressed that I can do it at all. "Okay. I was . . . I was gonna meet him. I'll take you. Just don't hurt us, okay?"

It sounds lame. They laugh. I don't expect anything but more hurt. We all know, there's this kind of understanding between all four of us, even if none of us acknowledge it. I think gazelles have this kind of understanding with lions.

I start walking. Drew doesn't let go of my arm. I swallow down the pain. All I'm thinking about is black empty spaces, open to the night. And the day. And always.

Kyle frowns. Drew gives my arm a hard wrench and this time I do cry out. They're not happy. I knew they wouldn't be happy.

"The fuck is this?"

We're standing a few yards away from the gate. It's full dark now and the streetlights make everything look orange and too hard and just plain weird. Nothing is the right shape.

But the house looks exactly the same as it does in the daylight.

"I was meeting him here," I gasp. "He's here. I swear."

We're not close enough. That has to be it. Please, let that be it.

"So where is he? *She*," Jake corrects with a glance back at Kyle. A little nervous. I get it; this is a conceit he came up with and they're following his lead like when dogs want to make someone happy. But at this point it's sort of ridiculous and I have to bite my lip to keep from laughing. They'd hate that. They'd hurt me even worse and they wouldn't wait for Zhan to do it.

Zhan is at home.

No one is coming for me.

So I point toward the house with my free hand. "He's in there. We go in there to drink sometimes."

Jake and Drew look like they at least sort of buy it, but Kyle is staring at me with narrow eyes. Shit, he doesn't. *Shit*. Not that I really thought this would work, but *shit*.

Kyle nods toward Jake. "Get in there and check it out."

And then I know I'm screwed. There are two ways this can go and neither of them help me.

Jake will go in there and whatever gets the animals won't work on him because he's not that bright but he's still *human* and it doesn't work on humans the same way. And inside he'll find nothing. Just an abandoned house with broken furniture and peeling wallpaper and whatnot.

Or Jake will go in there and not come out. And then Drew and Kyle will be pissed at me beyond what I can imagine now. Pissed and maybe *scared*. And we're really close to the woods, and the woods go back a long way from the road. They get deep.

For the first time it occurs to me that I might not make it home tonight.

Jake starts walking. I can't breathe. He's three yards from the gate. Then two. *It won't work on him*. He's not walking the way the animals do. He's still got that *I can fuck you up* swagger. One.

He steps through.

And nothing changes.

I want to yell. Scream for help, for all the good it'll do me. These are the last few minutes before something black and awful hits me in the face. I can't avoid it, I can't duck. I can just stare and wait for it.

My gaze hits the windows. Those black, empty holes in space. And I swear one of them flickers out of existence for a split second and then back in again.

It's winking at me. The fucking house is *winking at me*.

Jake is pulling out his phone, calling up the flashlight app, and it's just going on and beaming out across the remaining path and toward the door when he stops. Drops the phone. I watch it fall in slow motion—I thought that shit only happened in movies, but no. It hits the concrete and it shatters. It glitters in its own light before the light goes out.

Jake steps forward. Stiff. Plodding. Staring straight ahead.

The rest of it happens so fast. He gets to the door and then he steps *through* the door and he's gone. Drew and Kyle are yelling his name, demanding that he come back; they're not total idiots, they *know* that something's wrong here even if they don't know what it is, and when Jake doesn't appear again after a minute their cries start getting angry.

Drew's hand is loosening on my arm. I could twist free, I know it. I could turn and run back down the street. They might not catch me? But I know that's bullshit. They'd catch me. They'll be pissed, and they will be scared, and I'll have run and they'll be pumped up and bursting with adrenaline and I know what happens to a lot of kids like me in hick towns like this and I know it's bad and I know sometimes you walk through that door and you never come out again.

Everywhere in front of me are doors. There are no good endings behind any of them. There's no good choices here.

But there is this one.

Fuck it.

I break free. Drew is yelling the second I do, lunging forward, but that second I have on him is what I need and I'm tearing ass toward the gate and through it and up the path. Toward the door. All those processions of animals, all those zombie creatures, walking without ever turning back. In all the months and years we've been feeding the house none of them have ever turned back. I'm a living conglomeration of rhythm, my heart and my lungs and my pumping arms and the pounding of my feet. I don't even know if they're chasing me. They probably aren't. But even if they don't follow—

It's like everything in my brain folds in on itself.

I stop. One by one all of my muscles are locking up. I can't get them to respond to anything I do. I don't even think my lungs are working like they were because suddenly I can't get my breath. I'm looking at the house and it occurs to me that I shouldn't fight this. The house is my friend, because it helped me and it's still helping me now. The house doesn't care who I am; the house will let me be whatever I want to be. I should go to it. I should go in there.

It can't turn it off, I think distantly. *Not even for me. It can't.*

My legs are carrying me forward. I think I'm smiling.

I'm kissing Zhan on the blacktop. We're sitting shoulder to shoulder and I'm imagining that I can taste his mouth on the cigarette we pass back and forth. We're in the woods, doing fuck-all the way we do. We're lying in Riverside Park and my head is on his stomach and I can hear his heartbeat and that soft little gurgle that stomachs make even when you're not hungry. There are birds taking off, landing, all around us. We're standing in front of the house and watching animals go where we won't go. Where he wouldn't let me go. The first time he took me there. He told me to stand clear.

I try to stop before I even get why I'm trying. My legs don't really stop moving but my body stops, and that makes them walk right out from under me and I drop onto my ass. The pain drowns out everything else and something in me snaps, a tether coming loose, and I roll onto my stomach, clawing at the dry ground. Trying to crawl. That pleasant hum in my head that was drowning out everything jerks into a *screech*, angry and loud, and I scream, clapping my hands over my ears but I can't block it out.

It wants me. It wants me and it's going to have me and there's nothing I can do about it.

Something heavy and hard comes down on my ankle and twists it sideways. If I cry out I don't hear myself. Turning over is like rolling a log down a hill; it's tough to get going but once you're there it's tough to stop. My vision is blurring, bursting with light at the edges, but I can see enough.

Drew and Kyle. Standing there, locked in place. They came for me. The stupid fuckers actually *came* for me.

And they're moving forward toward the door.

With them there, it feels like the focus is swinging away from me and onto them. I can pull myself up to my hands and knees, one hand still against the side of my head. The screech has faded. The house is getting what it wants. And so much of it, too. Three big, meaty courses. Drew and Jake step onto the porch and together, without hesitation, they walk through the door.

My arm hurts. I don't feel sorry for them. I don't feel sorry when I think, at the edge of the hum in my brain, I can hear them start to scream.

I'm floating around the periphery. The house can't or won't pull me in now, so it's locked me into a stable orbit. Around and around. I think it might be waiting.

Things have happened. Things are still happening. I can't go back, even if I get free. I'm a singularity. Everything has changed and is always changing forever.

I open my eyes once in the dawn light and I'm surrounded by bones. I'm looking into the empty eye sockets of a skull. Totally clean. Polished. Sunlight gleams off it at a low angle and looks red. I don't know whose it is.

They weren't as digestible as squirrels. As cats. I guess.

I slide my fingers into the sockets like a bowling ball. I float back down like that. There's something comforting about it. I'm not alone. Or I won't be. If I just wait long enough, I have a feeling he'll come. He always has.

"Tom."

I'm locked into an orbit, but my name pulls me back. Barely. I lift my head off the hard-packed dirt and Zhan is there, at the gate, and dawn light is washing all the remaining color out of the world, and I know my time itself was sucked into the house and I'll never get it back, and I'm not sure I care. Zhan's eyes are taking up his whole face. God, he's so beautiful.

"Jesus Christ, Tom, what did you *do*?"

But I don't need to answer him. In this place, he should understand. We're compressed into each other. No real space between him and me.

Just like I always wanted.

I had to do it. You weren't here.

When he showed me the house three years ago he had to have known we were doing more than just feeding it. He must have felt that. You don't feed something like this and get nothing in return.

Come here, Zhan. Be with me.

My gaze meets his. I can't move any more than I have but I think if he were closer to me, folded into me, I could move a lot more. We could circle together. We could dance.

"Please." I don't know who says that.

For a moment I think he's going to step through the gate and I'm so happy I can't breathe. For a moment I'm *sure* he is. One foot in front of the other, Zhan, just like that. You've seen how easy it is, over and over and over.

And he turns around and walks away.

He doesn't run. We never ran.

My head drops down again. *Just let me fall, then.*

Without him, my orbit decays.

I never know, afterward, if it's just that the house demanded both of us and I was unacceptable alone, if I was bait for him and I failed, or if I was stronger than I knew. But at some point I get up. I walk past the bones. I'm plodding, slow and steady, pulled back every second of the way. I go home and I sleep and I don't dream, and part of me feels like it's just gone. Like I left it behind. Or like I'm carrying around something new. Or both things at once.

I never hear anything about any bones. No one ever asks me about Drew or Kyle or Jake. That's good. I don't know anything.

• • •

At the end of the month Zhan moves away.

I never saw him again. But I also see him every day, in the part of me carved out by the house to contain itself.

He can't stop himself returning. Neither of us could.

Once it had us, it had us. We always thought we were better than the animals, better than the boys I tossed through that door to save myself, better because we didn't let ourselves get pulled in. Better because the house knew us. Better because we had an understanding.

But we always went back there. We were always called. We never said no. In the end he and the house are pretty much the same, devouring me before I can even begin to fight. If I even wanted to.

So half of me moves on with life, high school and college and whatever the hell comes after that, becoming freer, becoming more *myself* . . . and part of me is still there. Unchanged by time but shaping everything around it. I don't exist apart from it. I don't make any sense beyond the arc I carve around it, spiraling inward and out. Small and scared and trying so hard. Waiting for him to come to me.

Live here. I have enough room for you.

There's never any escaping that orbit. There's never any going back.

Sunny Moraine is a humanoid creature of average height, luminosity, and inertial mass. They're also a doctoral candidate in sociology and a writer-like object whose work has appeared or is forthcoming in *Lightspeed, Shimmer, Clarkesworld,* and *Long Hidden: Speculative Fiction from the Margins of History,* as well as multiple Year's Best anthologies, all of which has provided lovely reasons to avoid a dissertation. Their first novel *Line and Orbit,* co-written with Lisa Soem, is available from Samhain Publishing. Their solo-authored novel *Crowflight* is available from Masque Books. Its sequel, *Ravenfall,* will be released this summer.

Bravery is perseverance through fear.

MOONSTRUCK

Karin Tidbeck

They lived on the top floor in a building on the city's outskirts. If the stars were out, visitors would come, usually an adult with a child in tow. Alia would open the door and drop a curtsy to the visitors, who bade her good evening and asked for Doctor Kazakoff. Alia would run halfway up the stairs to the attic and call for the Doctor. At the same time, Father would emerge from the kitchen in a gentle blast of tea-scented air. Sometimes he had his apron on, and brought a whiff of baking bread. He would extend a knobby hand to pat the child's head, and then shake hands with the adult, whom he'd invite into the kitchen. While the parent (or grandparent, or guardian) hung their coat on a peg and sat down by the kitchen table, Father poured tea and wound up the gramophone. Then Mother, Doctor Kazakoff, would arrive, descending the spiral staircase in her blue frock and dark hair in a messy bun. She'd smile vaguely at the visiting child without making eye contact, and wave him or her over. They'd ascend the stairs to the darkened attic and out onto the little balcony, where the telescope stood. A stool sat below it, at just the right height for a child to climb up and look into the eyepiece.

Alia would crawl into an armchair in the shadows of the attic and watch the silhouettes of Mother and the visiting child, outlined against the faint starlight. Mother aimed the telescope toward some planet or constellation she found interesting, and stood aside so that the child could look. If it was a planet, Mother would rattle off facts. Alia preferred when she talked about constellations. She would pronounce each star's name slowly, as if tasting them: *Betelgeuse. Rigel. Bellatrix. Mintaka. Alnilam.*

Alnitak. Alia saw them in her mind's eye, burning spheres rolling through the darkness with an inaudible thunder that resonated in her chest.

After a while, Mother would abruptly shoo the child away and take his or her place at the telescope. It was Alia's task to take the child by the hand and explain that Doctor Kazakoff meant no harm, but that telescope time was over now. Sometimes the child said goodbye to Mother's back. Sometimes they got a hum in reply. More often not. Mother was busy recalibrating the telescope.

When the moon was full, Mother wouldn't receive visitors. She would sit alone at the ocular and mumble to herself: the names of the seas, the highlands, the craters.

Those nights (or days) she stayed up until the moon set.

On the day it happened, Alia was twelve years old and home from school with a cold. That morning she found a brown stain in her underwear. It took a moment to realize what had really happened. She rifled through the cabinet under the sink for Mother's box of napkins, and found a pad that she awkwardly fastened to her panties. It rustled as she pulled them back up. She went back into the living room. The grandfather clock next to the display case showed a quarter past eleven.

"Today, at a quarter past eleven," she told the display case, "I became a woman."

Alia looked at her image in the glass. The person standing there, with pigtails and round cheeks and dressed in a pair of striped pajamas, didn't look much like a woman. She sighed and crawled into the sofa with a blanket, rehearsing what to tell Mother when she came home.

When the front door slammed a little later, Alia walked into the hallway. Mother stood there in a puff of cold air. She was home much too early.

"Mother," Alia began.

"Hello," said Mother. Her face was rigid, her eyes large and feverish. Without giving Alia so much as a glance, she took her coat off, dropped it on the floor and stalked up the attic stairs. Alia went after her out onto the balcony. Mother said nothing, merely stared upward. She wore a broad grin that looked misplaced in her stern face.

Alia followed her gaze.

The moon hung in the zenith of the washed-out autumn sky, white and full in the afternoon light. It was much too large, and in the wrong place. Alia held out a hand at arm's length; the moon's edges circled her palm. She remained on the balcony, dumbfounded, until Father's thin voice called up to them from the hallway.

· · ·

Mother had once said that when Alia had her first period, they would celebrate and she would get to pick out her first ladies' dress. When Alia caught her attention long enough to tell her what happened, Mother just nodded. She showed Alia where the napkins were and told her to put stained clothes and sheets in cold water. Then she returned to the attic. Father walked around the flat, cleaning and fiddling in quick movements. He baked bread, loaf after loaf. Every now and then he came into the living room where Alia sat curled up in the sofa, and gave her a wordless hug.

The radio blared all night. All the transmissions were about what had happened that morning at quarter past eleven. The president spoke to the nation: *We urge everyone to live their lives as usual. Go to work, go to school, but don't stay outside for longer than necessary. We don't yet know exactly what has happened, but our experts are investigating the issue. For your peace of mind, avoid looking up.*

Out in the street, people were looking up. The balconies were full of people looking up. When Alia went to bed, Mother was still outside with her eye to the ocular. Father came to tuck Alia in. She pressed her face into his aproned chest, drawing in the smell of yeasty dough and after-shave.

"What if it's my fault?" she whispered.

Father patted her back. "How could it possibly be your fault?"

Alia sighed. "Forget it."

"Go on, tell me."

"I got my period at a quarter past eleven," she finally said. "Just when the moon came."

"Oh, darling," said Father. "Things like that don't happen just because you had your period."

"Are you sure?"

Father let out a short laugh. "Of course." He sighed, his breath stirring Alia's hair. "I have no idea what's going on up there, but of this I'm sure."

"I wish I was brave," said Alia. "I wish I wasn't so afraid all the time."

"Bravery isn't not being afraid, love. Bravery is perseverance through fear."

"What?"

"Fancy words," said Father. "It means doing something even though you're afraid. That's what brave is. And you are."

He kissed her forehead and turned out the light. Falling asleep took a long time.

• • •

Master Bobek stood behind the lectern, his face gray.

"We must remain calm," he said. "You mustn't worry too much. Try to go about your lives as usual. And you are absolutely not allowed to miss school. You have no excuse to stay at home. Everyone will feel better if they carry on as usual. Itti?" He nodded to the boy in the chair next to Alia.

Itti stood, not much taller than when he had been sitting down. "Master Bobek, do you know what really happened?"

The teacher cleared his throat. "We must remain calm," he repeated.

He turned around and pulled down one of the maps from above the blackboard. "Now for today's lesson: bodies of water."

Itti sat down and leaned over. "Your mum," he whispered. "Does she know anything?"

Alia shrugged. "Don't know."

"Can you ask? My parents are moving all our things to the cellar."

She nodded. Itti gave her a quick smile. If Master Bobek had seen the exchange, he said nothing of it, which was unusual for him. Master Bobek concentrated very hard on talking about bodies of water. The children all looked out the windows until Master Bobek swore and drew the curtains.

When Alia came home from school, she found the door unlocked. Mother's coat hung on its peg in the hallway.

"Home!" Alia shouted, and took off jacket and shoes and climbed the stairs to the attic.

Mother sat on the balcony, hunched over the telescope's ocular. She was still in her dressing gown, her hair tousled on one side and flat on the other.

Alia forced herself not to look up, but the impossible moon's cold glow spilled into the upper edge of her vision. "Mother?"

"The level of detail is incredible," Mother mumbled.

Her neck looked dusty, as if she'd been shaking out carpets or going through things in the attic. Alia blew at it and sneezed.

"Have you been out here all day?" Alia wiped her nose on her shirt sleeve.

Mother lifted her gaze from the telescope and turned it to somewhere beyond Alia's shoulder, the same look that Doctor Kazakoff gave visiting children. Gray dust veiled her face; the rings under her eyes were the color of graphite. Her cheekbones glimmered faintly.

"I suppose I have," she said. "Now off with you, dear. I'm working."

• • •

The kitchen still smelled of freshly baked bread. On the counter lay a loaf of bread rolled up in a tea towel, next to a bread knife and a jar of honey. Alia unfolded the towel, cut a heel off the loaf and stuffed it in her mouth. It did nothing to ease the burning in her stomach. She turned the loaf over and cut the other heel off. The crust was crunchy and chewy at the same time.

She had eaten her way through most of the loaf when Father spoke behind her. He said her name and put a hand on her shoulder. The other hand gently pried the bread knife from her grip. Then her cheek was pressed against his shirt. Over the slow beat of his heart, Alia could hear the air rushing in and out of his lungs, the faint whistle of breath through his nose. The fire in her belly flickered and died.

"Something's wrong with Mother," she whispered into the shirt.

Father's voice vibrated against her cheek as he spoke.

"She's resting now."

Alia and her father went about their lives as the President had told them to: going to work, going to school. The classroom emptied as the days went by. Alia's remaining classmates brought rumors of families moving to cellars and caves under the city. The streets were almost deserted. Those who ventured outside did so at a jog, heads bowed between their shoulders. There were no displays of panic or violence. Someone would occasionally burst into tears in the market or on the bus, quickly comforted by bystanders who drew together in a huddle around him.

The radio broadcasts were mostly about nothing, because there was nothing to report. All the scientists and knowledgeable people had established was that the moon didn't seem to affect the earth more than before. It no longer went through phases, staying full and fixed in its position above the city. A respected scientist claimed it was a mirage, and had the city's defense shoot a rocket at it. The rocket hit the moon right where it seemed to be positioned. Burning debris rained back down through the atmosphere for half a day.

As the moon drew closer, it blotted out the midday sun and drowned the city in a ghostly white light, day and night. At sunrise and sundown, the light from the two spheres mixed in a blinding and sickly glare.

Mother stayed on the balcony in her dressing gown, eye to the ocular. Alia heard Father argue with her at night, Father's voice rising and Mother's voice replying in monotone.

Once, a woman in an official-looking suit came to ask Doctor Kazakoff for help. Mother answered the door herself before Father could intercept her. The official-looking woman departed and didn't return.

Alia was still bleeding. She knew you were only supposed to bleed for a few days, but it had been two weeks now. What had started as brownish spotting was now a steady, bright red runnel. It was as if it grew heavier the closer the moon came.

Late one night, she heard shouts and the sound of furniture scraping across the floor. Then footsteps came down the stairs; something metallic clattered. Peeking out from her room, Alia saw Father in the hallway with the telescope under one arm.

"This goes out!" he yelled up the stairs. "It's driven you insane!"

Mother came rushing down the stairs, naked feet slapping on the steps. "Pavel Kazakoff, you swine, give it to me." She lunged for the telescope.

Father was heavy and strong, but Mother was furious. She tore the telescope from him so violently that he abruptly let go, and when the telescope crashed into the wall she lost her grip. The floor shook with the telescope's impact. In the silence that followed, Father slowly raised a hand. The front of Mother's dressing gown had opened. He drew it aside.

Vera." His voice was almost a whisper. "What happened to you?"

In the light from the hallway sconce, Mother's skin was patterned in shades of gray. Uneven rings overlapped each other over her shoulders and arms. The lighter areas glowed with reflected light.

Mother glanced at Father, and then at Alia where she stood gripping the frame of her bedroom door.

"It's regolith," Mother said in a matter-of-fact voice.

She returned upstairs. She left the telescope where it lay.

A doctor arrived the morning after. Father gave Alia the choice of staying in her room or going over to Itti's. She chose the latter, hurrying over the courtyard and up the stairs to where Itti lived with his parents.

Itti let her into a flat that was almost completely empty. They passed the kitchen, where Mrs. Botkin was canning vegetables, and shut themselves in Itti's room. He only had a bed and his box of comics. They sat down on the bed with the box between them.

"Mother's been making preserves for days now," said Itti.

Alia leafed through the topmost magazine without really looking at the pictures. "What about your father?"

Itti shrugged. "He's digging. He says the cellar doesn't go deep enough."

"Deep enough for what?"

"For, you know." Itti's voice became small. "For when it hits."

Alia shuddered and put the magazine down. She walked over to the window. The Botkin's apartment was on the top floor, and Alia could see right into her own kitchen window across the yard. Her parents were at the dinner table, across from a stranger who must be the doctor. They were discussing something. The doctor leaned forward over the table, making slow gestures with his hands. Mother sat back in her chair, chin thrust out in her Doctor Kazakoff stance. After a while, the physician rose from his chair and left. He emerged from the door to the yard moments later; Alia could see the large bald patch on his head. The physician tilted his head backward and gave the sky a look that seemed almost annoyed. He turned around and hurried out the front gate.

Father was still in the kitchen when Alia came home. He blew his nose in a tea towel when he noticed Alia in the doorway.

"Vera is ill," he said. "But we have to take care of her here at home. There's no room at the hospital."

Alia scratched at an uneven spot in the doorjamb. "Is she crazy?"

Father sighed. "The doctor says it's a nervous breakdown, and that it's brought on some sort of skin condition." He cleared his throat and crumpled the tea towel in his hands. "We need to make sure she eats and drinks properly. And that she gets some rest."

Alia looked at her hand, which was gripping the doorjamb so hard the nails were white and red. A sudden warmth spread between her legs as a new trickle of blood emerged.

Father turned the radio on. The announcer was incoherent, but managed to convey that the moon was approaching with increased speed.

Mother's dressing gown lay in a heap on the chair next to the balcony door. Mother herself lay naked on the balcony, staring into the sky, a faint smile playing across her face. Alia could see the great wide sea across her chest, and the craters making rings around it. All of the moon's scarred face was sculpted in relief over Mother's body. The crater rims had begun to rise up above the surface.

Alia couldn't make herself step out onto the balcony. Instead, she went down to the courtyard and looked up into the sky. The moon covered the whole square of sky visible between the houses, like a shining ceiling. It had taken on a light of its own, a jaundiced shade of silver. More blood trickled down between Alia's legs.

With the burning rekindling in her stomach, Alia saw how obvious it was.

It was all her fault, no matter what Father said. Something had happened when she started bleeding, some power had emerged in her that she wasn't aware of, that drew the moon to her like a magnet. And Mother, so sensitive to the skies and the planets, had been driven mad by its presence. There was only one thing to do. She had to save everyone. The thought filled her with a strange mix of terror and anticipation.

Father was on the couch in the living room, leafing through an old photo album. He said nothing when Alia came in and wrapped her arms around him, just leaned his head on her arm and laid his long hand over hers. She detached herself and walked up the stairs to the attic.

Mother was as Alia had left her, spread out like a starfish.

Alia crouched beside her still form. "I know why

You're ill."

Mother's bright eyes rolled to the side and met Alia's gaze.

"I'll make you well again," Alia continued. "But you won't see me again." Moisture dripped from her eyes into the crater on Mother's left shoulder, and pooled there.

Mother's eyes narrowed.

"Goodbye." Alia bent down and kissed her cheek. It tasted of dust and sour ashes.

The plain spread out beyond the city, dotted here and there by clumps of trees. The autumn wind coming in from the countryside was laden with the smell of windfallen fruit and bit at Alia's face. The moonlight leached out the color from the grass. The birds, if any birds remained here, were quiet. There was only the whisper of grass on Alia's trouser legs, and an underlying noise like thunder. And the moon was really approaching fast, just like the radio man had said: a glowing plain above pressed down like a stony cloud cover. The sight made Alia's face hot with a shock that spread to her ears and down her chest and back, pushing the air out of her lungs. She had a sudden urge to crouch down and dig herself into the ground. The memory of her mother on the balcony flashed by; her body immobile under the regolith, her despairing eyes. Bravery was perseverance through fear. Alia took another step, and her legs, though shaking, held. She could still breathe somehow.

When Alia could no longer see the city behind her, a lone hill rose from the plain. It was the perfect place. She climbed the hill step by slow step. The inside of her trousers had soaked through with blood that had begun to cool against her skin, the fabric rasping wetly as she walked. At the top of the hill, she lay down and made herself stare straight up. Why did they always describe fear as cold? Fear was searing hot, burning a hole through her stomach, eating through her lungs.

She forced out a whisper. "Here I am," she told the moon. "I did this. Take me now, do what you're supposed to."

Alia closed her eyes and fought to breathe. The muscles in her thighs tingled and twitched. The vibration in her chest rose in volume, and she understood what it was: the sound of the moon moving through space, the music of the spheres.

She had no sensation of time passing. Maybe she'd fainted from fear or bleeding; the sound of footsteps up a hillside woke her. She opened her eyes. Mother stood over her, the terrain across her body in sharp relief against the glowing surface above. The whites of her eyes glistened in twin craters. She held the broken telescope in one hand.

"Go home." Mother's voice was dull and raspy.

Alia shook her head. "It's my fault. I have to make everything okay again."

Mother cocked her head. "Go home, child. This isn't about you. It was never about you. It's my moon."

She grabbed Alia's arm so hard it hurt, and dragged her to her feet. "It was always my moon. Go home."

Mother didn't stink anymore. She smelled like dust and rocks. Her collarbones had become miniature mountain ranges.

Alia pulled her arm out of her mother's grasp. "No."

Mother swung the telescope at her head.

The second round of waking was to a world that somehow tilted. Alia opened her eyes to a mess of bright light. Vomit rose up through her throat. She rolled over on her side and retched. When her stomach finally stopped cramping, she slowly sat up. Her brain seemed to slide around a little in her skull.

She was sitting at the foot of the hill. Over her, just a few meters it seemed, an incandescent desert covered the sky.

The moon had finally arrived.

Afterward, when Father found her, and the moon had returned to its orbit, and the hill was empty, and everyone pretended that the city had been in the grip of some kind of temporary collective madness, Alia refused to talk about what happened, where Mother had gone. About Mother on the top of the hill, where she stood naked and laughing with her hands outstretched toward the moon's surface. About how she was still laughing as it lowered itself toward the ground, as it pushed her to her knees, as she finally lay flat under its monstrous weight. How she quieted only when the moon landed, and the earth rang like a bell.

Karin Tidbeck lives and works in Malmö, Sweden. She's published prose and poetry in Swedish since 2002, with publications in journals like *Jules Verne-magasinet* and *Lyrikvännen*. Her English publication history includes *Weird Tales, Tor.com, Lightspeed,* and the anthologies *Steampunk Revolution* and *The Time Travelers Almanac*. Tidbeck's stories have appeared in *The Year's Best Dark Fantasy and Horror: 2013, The Best Science Fiction and Fantasy of the Year: Volume Eight, The Year's Best Science Fiction and Fantasy: 2014,* and *The Year's Best Weird Fiction, Volume One*. Tidbeck's 2012 short story collection *Jagannath* won the Crawford Memorial Award in 2013 and was shortlisted for the Tiptree Award and World Fantasy Award. One of the stories, "Augusta Prima," won the SF & Fantasy Translation Award.

Among the shadows between the pillars, a man wielding a narrow,
curved sword fought silently—desperately—valiantly—for his life . . .

THE GHOST MAKERS

Elizabeth Bear

The faceless man walked out of the desert at sunset, when the gates of the City of Jackals wound ponderously closed on silent machinery. He was the last admitted. His kind were made by Wizards, and went about on Wizards' business. No one interrogated him.

His hooded robe and bronze hide smoked with sun-heat when the priest of Iashti threw water from the sacred rivers over him. Whether it washed away any clinging devils of the deep desert, as it was intended, who could have said? But it did rinse the dust from the featureless oval of his visage so all who stood near could see themselves reflected. Distorted.

He paused within and he lowered the hood of his homespun robes to lie upon his shoulders. The gates made the first sound of their closing, a heavy snap as their steel-shod edges overlapped and latched. Their juncture reflected as a curved line up the mirror of the faceless man's skull. Within the gates, bars as thick as a man glided home. Messaline was sealed, and the date plantations and goats and pomegranates and laborers of the farms and villages beyond her walls were left to their own devices until the lion-sun tinted the horizon again.

Trailing tendrils of steam faded from the faceless man's robe, leaving the air heavy with petrichor—the smell of water in aridity—and the cloth over his armored hide as dry as before. His eyeless mask trained unwaveringly straight ahead, he raised his voice.

"Priest of Iashti." Though he had no mouth, his voice tolled clear and sonorous.

The priest left his aspergillum and came around to face the faceless man, though there was no need. He said, "You already have my blessing, O Gage . . . of . . . ?"

"I'd rather information than blessings, Child of the Morning," said the Gage. The priest's implied question—to whom he owed his service—the faceless man left unacknowledged. His motionlessness—as if he were a bronze statue someone had draped in a robe and left inexplicably in the center of the market road—was more distressing than if he'd stalked the priest like a cat.

He continued, "Word is that a poet was murdered under the Blue Stone a sennight since."

"Gage?"

The Gage waited.

The priest collected himself. He tugged the tangerine-and gold dawn-colored robed smooth beneath his pectoral. "It is true. Eight days ago, though—no, now gone nine."

"Which way?"

Wordlessly, the priest pointed to a twisting, smoky arch towering behind dusty tiers of pastel houses. The sunset sprawled across the sky rendered the monument in translucent silhouette, like an enormous, elaborate braid of chalcedony.

The faceless man paused, and finally made a little motion of his featureless head that somehow still gave the impression of ruefully pursed lips and acknowledgement.

"Alms." He tossed gold to the priest.

The priest, no fool, caught it before it could bloody his nose. He waited to bite it until the Gage was gone.

The Gage made his way through the Temple District, where great prayer-houses consecrated to the four major Messaline deities dominated handfuls of lesser places of worship: those of less successful sects, or of alien gods. Only the temple to the Uthman Scholar-God, fluted pillars twined about with sacred verses rendered in lapis lazuli and pyrite, competed with those four chief temples for splendor.

Even at dusk, these streets teemed. Foot traffic, litter bearers, and the occasional rider and mount—mostly horses, a few camels, a mule, one terror-bird—bustled through the lanes between the torchbearers. There were soldiers and merchants, priests and scholars, a nobleman or woman in a curtained sedan chair with guards crying out *"Make way!"* The temples were arranged around a series of squares, and the squares were occupied by row upon row of market stalls from which rose the aromas of turmeric, coriander, roses, sandalwood, dates, meat sizzling, bread baking, and musty old attics—among other things. The sweet scent of stitched leather and wood-pulp-and-rag paper identified a bookseller as surely as did the banner that drifted above his pavilion.

The faceless man passed them all—and more than half of the people he passed either turned to stare or hurried quickly along their way, eyes fixed on the ground by their shoes. The Gage knew better than to assign any quality of guilt or innocence to these reactions.

He did not stay in the temple district long. A left-hand street bent around the temple of Kaalha, the goddess of death and mercy—who also wore a mirrored mask, though hers was silver and divided down the centerline. The temple had multiple doorways, and seemed formed in the shape of a star. Over the nearest one was inscribed: *In my house there is an end to pain.*

Some distance behind the temple, the stone arch loomed.

At first he walked by stucco houses built cheek to cheek, stained in every shade of orange, red, vermilion. The arches between their entryways spanned the road. But soon the street grew crooked and dark; there were no torchbearers here. A rat or two was in evidence, scurrying over stones—but rodents went quickly and fearfully here. Once, longer legs and ears flickered like scissors as a slender shadow detached itself from one darkness and glided across the open space to the next: one of the jackals from which Messaline took its epithet. From the darkness where it finished, a crunch and a squeak told of one scurrying at least that ended badly for the scurrier.

In these gutters, garbage reeked, though not too much of it; things that were still useful would be put to use. The people passing along these streets were patch-clothed, dirty-cheeked, lank of unwashed hair. Many wore long knives; a few bore flintlocks. The only unescorted women were those plying a trade, and a few men who loitered dark doorways or alleys drew back into their lairs as the Gage passed, each footstep ringing dully off the cobbles. He was reminded of tunnel-spiders, and kept walking.

As he drew closer to one base of the Blue Stone, though, he noticed an increase in people walking quickly in the direction opposite his. Though the night sweltered, stored heat radiating back from the stones, they hunched as if cold: heads down and shoulders raised protectively.

Still no one troubled the faceless man. Messaline knew about Wizards.

Others were not so lucky, or so unmolested.

The Gage came out into the small square that surrounded one foot of the Blue Stone. It rose above him in an interlaced, fractal series of helixes a hundred times the height of a tall man, vanishing into the darkness that drank its color and translucency. The Gage had been walking for long enough that stars now showed through the gaps in the arch's sinuous strands.

The base of the monument separated into a half-dozen pillars where it plunged to earth. Rather than resting upon a plinth or footing, though, it seemed as if each pillar had thrust up through the street like a tree seeking the light—or possibly as if the cobbles of the road had just been paved around them.

Among the shadows between those pillars, a man wearing a skirted coat and wielding a narrow, curved sword fought silently—desperately—valiantly—for his life.

The combat had every appearance of an ambush—five on one, though that one was the superior swordsman and tactician. These were advantages that did not always affect the eventual result when surrounded and outnumbered, but the man in the skirted coat was making the most of them. His narrow torso twisted like a charmed snake as he dodged blows too numerous to deflect. He might have been an answer to any three of his opponents. But as it was, he was left whirling and weaving, leaping and ducking, parrying for his life. The harsh music of steel rang from the tight walls of surrounding rowhouses. His breathing was a rasp audible from across the square. He used the footings of the monument to good advantage, dodging between them, keeping them at his back, forcing his enemies to coordinate their movements over uneven cobblestones.

The Gage paused to assess.

The lone man's skirts whirled wide as he caught a narrower, looping strand of the Blue Stone in his off hand and used it as a handle to swing around, parrying one opponent with his sword hand while landing a kick in the chest of another. The kicked man staggered back, arms pinwheeling. One of his allies stepped under his blade and came on, hoping to catch the lone man off-balance.

The footpad—if that's what he was—huffed in pain as he ran into the Gage's outstretched arm. His eyes widened; he jerked back and reflexively brought his scimitar down. It glanced off the Gage's shoulder, parting his much-patched garment and leaving a bright line.

The Gage picked him up by the jaw, one-handed, and bashed his brains out against the Blue Stone.

The man in the skirted coat ran another through between the ribs. The remaining three hesitated, exchanging glances. One snapped a command;

they vanished into the night like rain into a fallow field, leaving only the sound of their footsteps. The man in the skirted coat seemed as if he might give chase, but his sword was wedged. He stood on the chest of the man he had killed and twisted his long, slightly curved blade to free it. It had wedged in his victim's spine. A hiss of air escaping a punctured lung followed as he slid it free.

Warily, he turned to the Gage. The Gage did not face him. The man in the skirted coat did not bother to walk around to face the Gage.

"Thank . . . "

Above them, the Blue Stone began to glow, with a gray light that faded up from nothingness and illuminated the scene: glints off the Gage's bronze body, the saturated blood-red of the lone man's coat, the frayed threads of its embroidery worn almost flat on the lapels.

"What the—?"

"Blood," the Gage said, prodding the brained body with his toe. "The Blue Stone accepts our sacrifice." He gestured to the lone man's prick-your-finger coat. "You're a Dead Man."

Dead Men were the sworn, sacred guards of the Caliphs who ruled north and east of Messaline, across the breadth of the sea.

"Not anymore," the Dead Man said. Fastidiously, he crouched and scrubbed his sword on a corpse's hem. "Not professionally. And not literally, thanks to you. By which I mean, 'Thank you.' "

The faceless man shrugged. "It didn't look like a fair fight."

"In this world, O my brother, is there such a thing as a fair fight? When one man is bestowed by the gods with superior talent, by station with superior training, by luck with superior experience?"

"I'd call that the opposite of luck," said the faceless man.

The Dead Man shrugged. "Pardon my forwardness; a true discourtesy, when directed at one who has done me a very great favor solely out of the goodness of his heart—"

"I have no heart."

"—but you are what they call a Faceless Man?"

"We prefer the term Gage. And while we're being rude, I had heard your kind don't leave the Caliph's service."

"The Caliph's service left me. A new Caliph's posterior warms the dais in Asitaneh. I've heard *your* kind die with the Wizard that made you."

The Gage shrugged. "I've something to do before I lie down and let the scavengers have me."

"Well, you have come to the City of Jackals now."

"You talk a lot for a dead man."

The Dead Man laughed. He sheathed his sword and thrust the scabbard through his sash. More worn embroidery showed that to be its place of custom.

"Why were they trying to kill you?"

The Dead Man had aquiline features and eagle-eyes to go with it, a trim goatee and a sandalwood-skinned face framed by shoulder-length ringlets, expensively oiled. Slowly, he drew a crimson veil across his nose and mouth. "I expected an ambush."

Neither one of them made any pretense that that was, exactly, an answer.

The Gage reached out curiously and touched the glowing stone. "Then I'm pleased to see that your expectation was rewarded."

"You discern much." The Dead Man snorted and stood. "May I know the name of the one who aided me?"

"My kind have no names."

"Do you propose then that there is no difference between you? You all have the same skills? The same thoughts?"

The Gage turned to him, and the Dead Man saw his own expression reflected, distorted in that curved bronze mirror. It never even shivered when he spoke. "So we are told."

The Dead Man shrugged. "So also are we. Were we. When I was a part of something bigger. But now I am alone, and my name is Serhan."

The Gage said, "You can call me Gage."

He turned away, though he did not need to. He tilted his featureless head back to look up.

"What's this thing?" The Gage's gesture followed the whole curve of the Blue Stone, revealed now as the light their murders had engendered rose along it like tendrils of crawling foxfire.

"It is old; it is anyone's guess what good it once was. There used to be a road under it, before they built the houses. A triumphal arch, maybe?"

"Hell of a place for a war monument."

The Dead Man's veil puffed out as he smothered a laugh. "The neighborhood was better once."

"Surprised they didn't pull it down for building material."

"Many have tried," the Dead Man said. "It does not pull down."

"Huh," said the Gage. He prodded the brained man again. "Any idea why they attacked you?"

"Opportunity? Or perhaps to do with the crime I have been investigating. That seems more likely."

"Crime?"

Reluctantly, the Dead Man answered, "Murder."

"Oh," said the Gage. "The poet?"

"I wonder if it might have been related to this." The Dead Man's hand described the arc of light across the sky. The glow washed the stars away. "Maybe he was a sacrifice to whatever old power inhabits . . . this."

"I doubt it," said the Gage. "I know something about the killer."

"You seek justice in this matter too?"

The Gage shrugged. "After a fashion."

The Dead Man stared. The Gage did not move. "Well," said the Dead Man at last. "Let us then obtain wine."

They chose a tavern on the other side of the block that faced on the Blue Stone, where its unnerving light did not wash in through the high narrow windows. The floor was gritty with sand spread to sop up spilled wine, and the air was thick with its vinegar sourness. The Dead Man tested the first step carefully, until he determined that what lay under the sand was flagstone. As they settled themselves—the Dead Man with his back to the wall, the Gage with his back to the room—the Gage said, "Did it do that when the poet died?"

"His name was Anah."

"Did it do that when Anah died?"

The Dead Man raised one hand in summons to the serving girl. "It seems to like blood."

"And yet we don't know what they built it for."

"Or who built it," the Dead Man said. "But you believe those things do not matter."

The girl who brought them wine was young, her blue-black hair in a wrist-thick braid of seven strands. The plait hung down her back in a spiral, twisted like the Blue Stone. She took the Dead Man's copper and withdrew.

The Dead Man said, "I always wondered how your sort sustained yourselves."

In answer, the Gage cupped his bronze fingers loosely around the stem of the cup and let them lie on the table.

"I was hired by the poet's . . . by Anah's lover." The Dead Man lifted his cup and swirled it. Fumes rose from the warmed wine. He lifted his veil and touched his mouth to the rim. The wine was raw, rough stuff, more fruit than alcohol.

The Gage said, "We seek the same villain."

"I am afraid I cannot relinquish my interest in the case. I . . . need the money." The Dead Man lifted his veil to drink again. The edge lapped wine and grew stained.

The Gage might have been regarding him. He might have been staring at the wall behind his head. Slowly, he passed a brazen hand over the table. It left behind a scaled track of silver. "I will pay you as well as your other client. And I will help you bring her the Wizard's head."

"*Wizard!*"

The Gage shrugged.

"You think you know who it is that I hunt."

"Oh yes," the Gage said. Scratched silver glittered dully on the table. "I can tell you that."

The Dead Man regarded his cup, and the Gage regarded . . . whatever it was.

Finally, the Gage broke the impasse to say, "Would you rather go after a Wizard alone, or in company?"

Under his veil, the Dead Man nibbled a thumbnail. "Which Wizard?"

"Attar the Enchanter. Do you know where to find him?"

"Everyone in Messaline knows where to find a Wizard. Or, belike, how to avoid him." The Dead Man tapped the nearest coin. "Why would he kill a *poet*? Gut him? In a public square?"

"He's a ghost-maker," the Gage said. "He kills for the pleasure it affords him. He kills artists, in particular. He likes to own them. To possess their creativity."

"Huh," said the Dead Man. "Anah was not the first, then."

"Ghost-makers . . . some people say they're soulless themselves. That they're empty, and so they drink the souls of the dead. And they're always hungry for another."

"People say a lot of shit," the Dead Man said.

"When I heard the manner of the poet's death, and that Attar was in Messaline . . . " The Gage shrugged. "I came at once. To catch up with him before he moves on again."

"You have not come about Anah in particular."

"I'm here *for* Anah. And the other Anahs. Future and past."

"I see," said the Dead Man.

His hand passed across the table. When it vanished, no silver remained. "Is it true that darkness cannot cloud your vision?"

"I can see," said the faceless man. "In dark or day, whether I turn my head aside or no. What has no eyes cannot be blinded."

"That must be awful," the Dead Man said.

The lamplight flickered against the side of the Gage's mask.

"So," said the Gage, motionless. "When the Caliph's service left you, you chose a mercenary life?"

"Not mercenary," the Dead Man said. "I have had sufficient of soldiering. I'm a hired investigator."

"An . . . investigator."

The corners of the Dead Man's eyes folded into eagle-tracks. "We have a legacy of detective stories in the Caliphate. Tales of clever men, and of one who is cleverer. They are mostly told by women."

"Aren't *most* of your storytellers women?"

The Dead Man moved to drink and found his cup empty. "They *are* the living embodiment of the Scholar-God."

"And you keep them in cages."

"We keep God in temples. Is that so different?"

After a while, the Dead Man said, "You have some plan for fighting a Wizard? A Wizard who . . . killed your maker?"

"My maker was Cog the Deviser. That's not how she died. But I thought perhaps a priest of Kaalha would know what to do about a ghost-maker."

"Ask the Death God. You are a clever automaton."

The Gage shrugged.

"If you won't drink that, I will."

"Drink it?" the Gage asked. He drew his hands back from where they had embraced the foot of his cup.

The Dead Man reached across the table, eyebrows questioning, and waited until the Gage gestured him in to tilt the cup and peer inside.

If there had been wine within, it was gone.

When the lion-sun of Messaline rose, haloed in its mane, the Gage and the Dead Man were waiting below the lintel inscribed, *In my house there is an end to pain.* The door stood open, admitting the transient chill of a desert morning. No one barred the way. But no one had come to admit them, either.

"We should go in?" the Dead Man said.

"After you," said the Gage.

The Dead Man huffed, but stepped forward, the Gage following with silent precision. His joints made no more sound than the massive gears of the gates of Messaline. Wizards, when they chose to wreak, wrought well.

Beyond the doorway lay a white marble hall, shadowed and cool. Within the hall, a masked figure enveloped in undyed linen robes stood, hands folded into sleeves. The mask was silver, featureless, divided by a line—a join—down the center. The robe was long enough to puddle on the floor.

Behind the mask, one side of the priest's face would be pitted, furrowed: acid-burned. And one side would be untouched, in homage—in sacrifice—to the masked goddess they served, whose face was the heavy, half-scarred moon of Messaline. The Gage and the Dead Man drew up, two concealed faces regarding one.

Unless the figure was a statue.

But then the head lifted. Hands emerged from the sleeves—long and dark, elegant, with nails sliced short for labor. The voice that spoke was fluting, feminine.

"Welcome to the House of Mercy," the priestess said. "All must come to Kaalha of the Ruins in the end. Why do you seek her prematurely?"

They hesitated for a moment, but then the Dead Man stepped forward. "We seek her blessing. And perhaps her aid, Child of the Night."

By her voice, perhaps her mirrors hid a smile. "A pair of excommunicates. Wolf's-heads, are you not? Masterless ones?"

The supplicants held their silence, or perhaps neither one of them knew how to answer.

When the priestess turned to the Gage, their visages reflected one another— reflected distorted reflections—endlessly. "What have you to live for?"

"Duty, art, and love."

"You? A faceless man?"

The Gage shrugged. "We prefer the term Gage."

"So," she said. She turned to the Dead Man. "What have *you* to live for?"

"Me? I am dead already."

"Then you are the Goddess's already, and need no further blessing of her."

The Dead Man bit his lip and hid the hand that would have made the Sign of the Pen. "Nevertheless . . . my friend believes we need her help. Perhaps we can explain to the Eidolon?"

"Walk with me," said the priestess.

Further along the corridor, the walls were mirrored. The priestess strode beside them, the front of her robe gathered in her hands. The mirrors were faintly distorted, whether by design or flaw, and they reflected the priestess, the Gage, and the Dead Man as warped caricatures—rippled, attenuated, bulged into near-spheres. Especially in conjunction with the mirrored masks, the reflections within reflections were dizzying.

When they left the corridor of mirrors and entered the large open atrium into which it emptied, the priestess was gone. The Dead Man whirled, his hand on the hilt of his sword, his battered red coat swinging wide to display all the stains and shiny patches the folds of its skirts hid.

"Ysmat Her Word," he swore. "I hate these heathen magics. Did you see her go? You see everything."

The Gage walked straight ahead and did not stop until he reached the middle of the short side of the atrium. "I did not see that."

"A heathen magic you seek, Dead Man." A masked priestess spoke from atop the dais at the other end of the long room.

It was unclear whether this priestess was the same one. Her voice was identical, or nearly so. But she seemed taller and she walked with a limp. Of course, it would be easy to twist an ankle in that trailing raiment, and the click of wooden pattens as she descended the stair said the truth of her height was a subject for conjecture.

She came to them through shafts of sunlight angled from high windows, stray gleams catching on her featureless visage.

"Forgive me." The Dead Man inclined his head and dropped one knee before her. "I spoke in haste. I meant no disrespect, Child of the Moon."

"Rise," said the priestess. "If Kaalha of the Ruins wants you humbled, she will lay you low. The Merciful One has no need of playacted obeisance."

She offered a hand. It was gloved, silk pulled unevenly over long fingers. She lifted the Dead Man to his feet. She was strong. She squeezed his fingers briefly, like a mother reassuring a child, and let her grip fall. She withdrew a few steps. "Explain to me your problem, masterless ones."

"Are you the Eidolon?" the Gage asked.

"She will hear what you speak to me."

The Gage nodded—a movement as calculated and intentional as if he had spoken aloud. He said, "We seek justice for the poet Anah, mutilated and murdered nine—now ten—days past at the Blue Stone. We seek justice also for the wood-sculptor Abbas, similarly mutilated and murdered in his village of Bajishe, and for uncounted other victims of this same murderer."

The priestess stood motionless, her hands hanging beside her and spread slightly as if to receive a gift. "For vengeance, you wish the blessing of Rakasha," she said. "For justice, seek Vajhir the warrior. Not the Queen of Cold Moon."

"I do not seek vengeance," said the Gage.

"Really?"

"No." It was an open question which of them was more immovable. More unmoving. "I seek mercy for all those this murderer, this ghost maker, may yet torture and kill. I seek Kaalha's benediction on those who will come to her eventually, one way or another, if their ghosts are freed. As you say: the Goddess of Death does not need to hurry."

The priestess's oval mask tilted. On her pattens, she was taller than both supplicants.

The Gage inclined his head.

"A ghost maker, you say."

"A soulless killer. A Wizard. One who murders for the joy of it. Young men, men in their prime. Men with great gifts and great . . . beauty."

Surely that could not have been a catch of breath, a concealed sob. What has no eyes cannot cry.

The Gage continued, "We cannot face a Wizard without help. Your help. Please tell us, Child of the Moon: what do you do against a killer with no soul?"

Her laughter broke the stillness that followed—but it was sweet laughter, glass bells, not sardonic cruelty. She stepped down from her pattens and now both men topped her by a head. She left them lying on the flagstones, one tipped on its side, and came close. She still limped, though.

"Let me tell you a secret, one mask to another." She leaned close and whispered. Their mirrored visages reflected one another into infinity, bronze and silver echoing. When she drew back, the Gage's head swiveled in place and tilted to acknowledge her.

She extended a hand to the Dead Man, something folded in her fist. He offered his palm. She laid an amethyst globe, cloudy with flaws and fracture, in the hollow. "Do you know what that is?"

"I've seen it done," said the Gage. "My mistress used one to create me."

The priestess nodded. "Go with Kaalha's blessing. Yours is a mission of mercy, masterless ones."

She turned to go. Her slippered feet padded on stone. She left the pattens lying. She was nearly to the dais again when the Dead Man called out after her—

"Wait!"

She paused and turned.

"Why would you help us?" the Dead Man asked.

"Masterless ones?" She touched her mask with both hands, fingertips flat to mirrored cheeks. The Dead Man shuddered at the prospect of her face revealed, but she lifted them empty again. She touched two fingers to her mask and brushed away as if blowing a kiss, then let her arms fall. Her sleeves covered her gloved hands.

The priestess said, "She is also the Goddess of Orphans. Masterless Man."

The Dead Man started to slip the amethyst sphere into his sash opposite the sword as he and the Gage threaded through the crowd back to the street of Temples. Before he had quite secured it, though, he paused and drew it forth again, holding it up to catch the sunlight along its smoky, icy flaws and planes.

"You know what this is for?"

"Give it here."

Reluctantly, the Dead Man did so. The Gage made it vanish into his robe.

"If you know how to use that, and it's important, it might be for the best if you demonstrated for me."

"You have a point," the Gage said, and—shielded in the rush of the crowd—he did so. When he had demonstrated to both their satisfaction, he made it vanish again and said, "Well. Lead me to the lair of Attar."

"This way."

They walked. The Gage dropped his cowl, improving the speed of their passage. The Dead Man lowered his voice. "Tell me what you know about Messaline Wizards. I am more experienced with the Uthman sort. Who are rather different."

"Cog used to say that a Wizard was a manifestation of the true desires, the true obsessions of an age. That they were the essence of a time refined, like opium drawn from poppy juice."

"That's pretty. Does it mean anything?"

The Gage shrugged. "I took service with Cog because she was Attar's enemy."

"Gages have lives before their service. Of course they do."

"It's just that you never think of it."

The Dead Man shrugged.

"And Dead Men don't have prior lives."

"None worth speaking of." Dead Men were raised to their service, orphans who would otherwise beg, whore, starve, and steal. The Caliph gave them everything—home, family, wives. Educated their children. They were said to be the most loyal guards the world knew. "We have no purpose but to guard our Caliph."

"Huh," said the Gage. "I guess you'd better find one."

The Dead Man directed them down a side street in a neighborhood that lined the left bank of the river Dijlè. A narrow paved path separated the facades of houses from the stone-lined canal. In this dry season, the water ran far down in the channel.

The Gage said, "I told you I chose service with Cog because she was Attar's enemy. Attar took something that was important to me."

"Something? Or someone?"

The Gage was silent.

The Dead Man said, "You said Attar kills artists. Young men."

The Gage was silent.

"Your beloved? This Abbas, have I guessed correctly?"

"Are you shocked?"

The Dead Man shrugged. "You would burn for it in Asmaracanda."

"You can burn for crossing the street incorrectly in Asmaracanda."

"This is truth." The Dead Man drew his sword, inspected the faintly nicked, razor-stropped edge. "Were you an artist too?"

"I was."

"Well," the Dead Man said. "That's different, then."

Before the house of Attar the Enchanter, the Dead Man paused and tested the door; it was locked and barred so soundly it didn't rattle. "This is his den."

"He owns this?" the Gage said.

"Rents it," the Dead Man answered. He reached up with his off hand and lowered his veil. His sword slid from its scabbard almost noiselessly. "How much magic are you expecting?"

"He's a ghost maker," the Gage said. "He travels from murder to murder. He might not have a full workshop here. He'll have mechanicals."

"Mechanicals?"

"Things like me."

"*Won*derful." He glanced up at the windows of the second and third stories. "Are we climbing in?"

"I don't climb." The Gage took hold of the doorknob and effortlessly tore it off the door. "Follow me."

The Gage's footsteps were silent, but that couldn't stop the boards of the joisted floor from creaking under his armored weight. "I hate houses with cellars," he said. "Always afraid I'm going to fall through."

"That will only improve once we achieve the second story," the Dead Man answered. His head turned ceaselessly, scanning every dark corner of what appeared to be a perfectly ordinary, perfectly pleasant reception room—unlighted brass lamps, inlaid cupboards, embroidered cushions, tapestry chairs, and thick rugs stacked several high over the indigo-patterned interlocking star-and-cross tiles of that creaking floor. Being on the ground floor, it was windowless.

"We're alone down here," said the Gage.

The staircase ascended at the back of the room, made of palm wood darkened with perfumed oils and dressed with a scarlet runner. The Gage moved toward it like a stalking tiger, weight and fluidity in perfect tension. The Dead Man paced him.

They ascended side by side. Light from the windows above reflected down. It shone on the sweat on the Dead Man's bared face, on the length of his bared blade, on the bronze of the Gage's head and the scratched metal that gleamed through the unpatched rent at his shoulder.

The Gage was taller than the dead man. His head cleared the landing first. Immediately, he snapped— "Close your eyes!"

The Dead Man obeyed. He cast his off hand across them as well, for extra protection. Still the light that flared was blinding.

The Gage might walk like a cat, but when he ran, the whole house shook. The creak of the floorboards was replaced by thuds and cracks, rising to a crescendo of jangling metal and shattering glass. The light died; a male voice called out an incantation. The Dead Man opened his eyes.

Trying to focus through swimming, rough-bordered blind spots, the Dead Man saw the Gage surrounded by twisted metal and what might be the remains of a series of lenses. Beyond the faceless man and the wreckage, a second man—broad-shouldered, shirtless above the waist of his pantaloons, of middle years by the salt in his beard but still fit—raised a flared tube in his hands and directed it at the Gage.

Wood splintered as the Gage reared back, struggling to move. The wreckage constrained him, though feebly, and his foot had broken through the floor. He was trapped.

With his off hand, the Dead Man snatched up the nearest object—a shelf laden with bric-a-brac—and hurled it at the Wizard's head. The tube—some sort of blunderbuss—exploded with a roar that added flash-deafness to the flash-blindness that already afflicted the Dead Man. Gouts of smoke and sparks erupted from the flare—

—the wall beside the Gage exploded outward.

"Well," he said. "That won't endear us to the neighbors."

The Dead Man heard nothing but the ringing in his ears. He leaped onto the seat of a Song-style ox-yoke chair, felt the edge of the back beneath his toe and rode it down. His sword descended with the force of his controlled fall, a blow that should have split the Wizard's collarbone.

His arm stopped in mid-move, as if he had slammed it into the top of a stone wall. He jerked it back, but the pincers of the steam-bubbling crab-creature that grabbed it only tightened, and it was all he could do to hold onto his sword as his fingers numbed.

Wood shattered and metal rent as the Gage freed his foot and shredded the remains of the contraption that had nearly blinded the Dead Man. He swung a massive fist at the Wizard but the Wizard rolled aside and parried with the blunderbuss. Sparks shimmered. Metal crunched.

The Wizard barked something incomprehensible, and a shadow moved from the corner of the room. The Gage spun to engage it.

The Dead Man planted his feet, caught the elbow of his sword hand in his off hand, and lifted hard against the pain. The crab-thing scrabbled at the rug, hooked feet snagging and lifting, but he'd stolen its leverage. Grunting, he twisted from the hips and swung.

Carpet and all, the crab-thing smashed against the Wizard just as he was regaining his feet. There was a whistle of steam escaping and the Wizard shouted, jerking away. The crab-thing's pincer ripped free of the Dead Man's arm, taking cloth and a measure of flesh along with it.

The thing from the corner was obviously half-completed. Bits of bear and cow-hide had been stitched together patchwork fashion over its armature. Claws as long as the Dead Man's sword protruded from the shaggy paw on its right side; on the left they gleamed on bare armature. Its head turned, tracking. A hairy foot shuffled forward.

The Gage went to meet it, and there was a sound like mountains taking a sharp dislike to one another. Dust rattled from the walls. More bric-a-brac tumbled from the shelf-lined walls. In the street or in a neighboring house, someone screamed.

The Dead Man stepped over the hissing, clicking remains of the crab-thing and leveled his sword at the throat of the Wizard Attar.

"Stop that thing."

The Wizard, his face boiled red along one cheek, one eye closed and weeping, laughed out loud. "Because I fear your sword?"

He grabbed the blade right-handed, across the top, and pushed it down as he lunged onto the blade, ramming the sword through his chest. Blood and air bubbled around the blade. The Wizard did not stop laughing, though his laughter took on a . . . simmering quality.

Recoiling, the Dead Man let go of his sword.

Meanwhile, the wheezing armature lifted the Gage into the air and slammed him against the ceiling. Plaster and stucco-dust reinforced the smoky air.

"You call yourself a Dead Man!" Attar ripped the sword from his breast and hurled it aside. "This is what a dead man looks like." He thumped his chest, then reached behind himself to an undestroyed rack and lifted another metal object, long and thin.

The Dead Man swung an arc before him, probing carefully for footing amid the rubble on the floor. Attar sidled and sidestepped, giving no advantage. And Attar had his back to the wall.

The Gage and the half-made thing slammed to the floor, rolling in a bear hug. Joists cracked again and the floor settled, canting crazily. Neither the Gage nor the half-made thing made any sound but the thud of metal on metal, like smith's hammerblows, and the creak of straining gears and springs.

"I have no soul," said Attar. "I am a ghost maker. Can your blade hurt me? All the lives I have taken, all the art I have claimed—all reside in me!"

Already, the burns on his face were smoothing. The bubbles of blood no longer rose from the cut in his smooth chest. The Dead Man let his knees bend, his weight ground. Attar's groping left hand found and raised a mallet. His right hand aimed the slender rod.

"ENOUGH!" boomed the Gage. A fist thudded into his face; he caught the half-made thing's arm and used its own momentum to slam it to the ground.

The rod detonated; the Dead Man twisted to one side. Razors whisked his face and shaved a nick into his ear. Blood welled hotly as the spear embedded itself in the wall.

With an almighty crunch, the Gage rose from the remains of the half-made thing, its skull dangling from his hand. He was dented and disheveled, his robe torn away so the round machined joints of knees and elbows, the smooth segmented body, were plainly visible.

He tossed the wreckage of the half-made thing's head at Attar, who laughed and knocked it aside with the hammer. He swung it in lazy loops, one-handed, tossed it to the other. "Come on, faceless man. What one Wizard makes, another can take apart."

The Gage stopped where he stood. He planted his feet on the sagging floor. He turned his head and looked directly at the Dead Man.

The Dead Man caught the amethyst sphere when the Gage tossed it to him.

"A soul catcher? Did you not hear me say I am soulless? That priest's bauble can do me no harm."

"Well," said the Gage. "Then you won't object to us trying."

He stepped forward, walking up the slope of the broken floor. He swung his fist; Attar parried with the hammer as if the blow had no force behind it at all. The Gage shook his fist and blew across it. There was a dent across his knuckles now.

"Try harder," the Wizard said.

He kept his back to the corner, his hammer dancing between his hands. The Gage reached in, was deflected. Reached again. "It's not lack of a soul that makes you a monster. That, beast, is your humanity."

The Wizard laughed. "Poor thing. Have you been chasing me for Cog's sake all these months?"

"Not for Cog's sake." The Gage almost sounded as if he smiled. "And I have been hunting you for years. I was a potter; my lover was a sculptor. Do you even remember him? Or are the lives you take, the worlds of brilliance you destroy, so quickly forgotten."

The Wizard's eyes narrowed, his head tipping as if in concentration. "I might recall."

Again the Gage struck. Again, the Wizard parried. His lips pursed as if to whistle and a shimmer crossed his face. A different visage appeared in its wake: curly-haired, darker-complected. Young and handsome, in an unexceptional sort of way. "This one? What *was* the name? Does it make you glad to see his face one last time, before I take you too? Though your art was not much, as I recall—but what can you expect of—"

The Gage lunged forward, a sharp blow of the Wizard's hammer snapping his arm into his head. The force knocked his upper body aside. But he took the blow, and the one that followed, and kept coming. He closed the gap.

He caught Attar's hammer hand and bent it back until the bones of his arm parted with a wet, wrenching sound.

"His name was Anah!"

The Wizard gasped and went to his knees. With a hard sidearm swing, the Dead Man stepped in and smashed the amethyst sphere against his head, and pressed it there.

It burst in his opening hand, a shower of violet glitter. Particles swirled in the air, ran in the Wizard's open mouth, his nostrils and ears, swarmed his eyes until they stared blank and lavender.

When the Dead Man closed his hand again, with a vortex of shimmer the sphere re-coalesced.

Blank-faced, Attar slumped onto his left side, dangling from his shattered arm. The Gage opened his hand and let the body fall. "He's not dead. Just really soulless now."

"As soon as I find my sword I'll repair that oversight," the Dead Man said. He held out the amethyst. Blood streaked down his cheek, dripped hot from his ear.

"Keep it." The Gage looked down at his naked armature. "I seem to have left my pockets on the floor."

While the Dead Man found his blade, the Gage picked his way around the borders of the broken floor. He moved from shelf to shelf, lifting up sculptures, books of poetry, pottery vases—and reverentially, one at a time, crushing them with his dented hands.

Wiping blood from his sword, the Dead Man watched him work. "You want some help with that?"

The Gage shook his head.

"That's how you knew he didn't live downstairs."

"Hmm?"

"No art."

The Gage shrugged.

"You looking for something in particular?"

"Yes." The Gage's big hand enfolded a small object. He held it for a moment, cradled to his breast, and bowed his scratched mirror over it. Then he pressed his hands together and twisted, and when he pulled them apart, a scatter of wood shreds sprinkled the floor. "Go free, love."

When he looked up again, the Dead Man was still staring out the window. "Help me break the rest of these? So the artists can rest?"

"Also so our friend here doesn't grow his head back? Soul or no soul?"

"Yeah," the Gage answered. "That too."

Outside, the Dead Man fixed his veil and pushed his dangling sleeve up his arm, examining the strained threads and tears.

"Come on," the Gage said. "I'll buy you a new coat."

"But I like this one."

"Then let's go to a bar."

This one had better wine and cleaner clientele. As a result, they and the servers both gave the Dead Man and the Gage a wider berth, and the Dead Man kept having to go up to the bar.

"Well," said the Dead Man. "Another mystery solved. By a clever man among clever men."

"And you are no doubt the cleverest."

The Dead Man shrugged. "I had help. I don't suppose you'd consider a partnership?"

The Gage interlaced his hands around the foot of his cup. After a while, he said, "Serhan."

"Yes, Gage?"

"My name was Khatijah."

Over his veil, the Dead Man's eyes did not widen. Instead he nodded with satisfaction, as if he had won some bet with himself. "You're a woman."

"I was," said the Gage. "Now I'm a Gage."

"It's supposed to be a selling point, isn't it? Become a faceless man and never be uncertain, abandoned, forsaken again."

"You sound like you've given it some thought."

The Dead Man regarded the Gage. The Gage tilted his featureless head down, giving the impression that he regarded the stem of his cup and the tops of his metal hands.

"And yet here you are," the Dead Man said.

"And yet here I am." The Gage shrugged.

"Stop that constant shrugging," the Dead Man said.

"When you do," said the Gage.

Elizabeth Bear was born on the same day as Frodo and Bilbo Baggins, but in a different year. When coupled with a childhood tendency to read the dictionary for fun, this led her inevitably to penury, intransigence, and the writing of speculative fiction. She is the Hugo, Sturgeon, Locus, and Campbell Award winning author of twenty-five novels (The most recent is *Steles of the Sky*, from Tor) and almost a hundred short stories. Her Promethean Age novel, *One-Eyed Jack*, will be published by Prime Books in August 2014. Her dog lives in Massachusetts; her partner, writer Scott Lynch, lives in Wisconsin. She spends a lot of time on planes.

The ministry had recruited Iseul because she was able to write Yeged-dai and speak it with any of three native accents. She also had a reasonable facility with the language of magic, a skill that never ceased to be useful.

ISEUL'S LEXICON

Yoon Ha Lee

kandagghamel, *noun*: One of two names the Genial Ones used for their own language. The other, *menjitthemel*, was rarely written. Derived from *kandak*, the dawn flower of their mythology and a common heraldic device; *agha*, or "law"; and *mel*, "word" or "speech." Note that *mel* is one of a small class of lexical elements that consistently violates vowel harmony in compounds. The Genial Ones ascribe considerable metaphysical importance to this irregularity.

She went by the name Jienem these days, a proper, demure Yegedin name that meant something between "young bud" and "undespoiled." It was not her real name. She had been born Iseul of Chindalla, a peninsula whose southern half was now occupied by the Yegedin, and although she was only the bastard daughter of a nobleman and an entertainer, she never forgot the name her mother had given her.

The Empire of Yeged had occupied South Chindalla for the past thirteen years, and renamed it Territory 4. Yeged and free Chindalla had a truce, but no one believed it would last for long, and in the meantime Chindalla had no compunctions about sending agents into South Chindalla. People still spoke the Chindallan language here, but the Empire forbade them to write it, or to use Chindallan names, which was why Iseul used a Yegedin name while operating as a spy in the south for the Chindallan throne. Curiously, for people so bent on suppressing the Chindallan language, Yeged's censors had a great interest in Chindallan books. Their fascination was enormous and indiscriminate: cookbooks rounded out with gossip, military manuals, catalogues of hairstyles, yearly rainfall tabulations, tales of doomed love affairs, court annals, ghost stories, adventures half written in cipher, everything you could imagine.

Iseul worked for Chindalla's Ministry of Ornithology, which, despite its name, had had nothing to do with birds or auguries for generations. It ran the throne's spies. The ministry had told her to figure out why the books were so important to the Yegedin. Iseul had a gift for languages, and in her former life she had been a poet, although she didn't have much time for satiric verses these days. The ministry had recruited her because she was able to write Yeged-dai and speak it with any of three native accents. She also had a reasonable facility with the language of magic, a skill that never ceased to be useful.

In the town the Yegedin had renamed Mijege-in, the censor was a magician. Iseul was to start with him, especially since tonight he was obliged to attend a formal dinner welcoming an official visiting from Yeged proper. It would have been more entertaining to spy on the dinner—she would have had a chance of snacking on some of the delicacies—but someone else was doing that. Her handler, Shen Minsu, had assigned her to search the magician's home because she had the best chance of being able to deal with magical defenses.

Getting into the house hadn't been too difficult. The gates to the courtyard and all the doors were hung with folded-paper wards inscribed with barrier-words of apathy and dejection to discourage people like Iseul. She had come prepared with a charm of passage, however, and a belt hung with tiny locks worn around her waist under her sash. The charm of passage caused all the wards to unfold, and reciprocally, most of the locks had snapped closed. One time, early in her career as a spy, she had run out of locks while infiltrating a fort, and the thwarted charm had begun throwing up random obstacles as she attempted to flee: a burst pipe, crates almost falling on her, a furious cat. Now she erred on the side of more locks.

It was a small house, all things considered, but magicians were a quirky lot and maybe he didn't want to deal with the servants necessary to keep a larger house clean. The courtyard was disproportionately large, and featured a tangle of roses that hadn't been pruned aggressively enough and equally disheveled trees swaying in the evening wind. Some landscaper had attempted to introduce a Yegedin-style rock garden in the middle. The result wasn't particularly harmonious.

She circled the house, but heard nothing and saw no people moving against the rice-paper doors. Then she went in the front door. She had two daggers in case she came across someone. After watching the house for a few days, she had concluded that the magician lived alone, but you never knew if someone had a secret lover stashed away. Or a very loud pet. That time with the peacock, for instance. Noisy birds, peacocks. Anyway, with luck, she wouldn't have to kill anyone this time; she was just here for information.

Her first dagger was ordinary steel, the suicide-blade that honorable Yegedin women carried. It would be difficult to explain her possession of the blade if she was searched, but that wasn't the one that would get her in trouble.

Her second dagger was the one that she couldn't afford to be caught carrying. It looked more like a very long needle, wrapped around and around by tiny words in the Genial Ones' language. It was the fifth one Iseul had constructed, although the Ministry of Ornithology had supplied the unmarked dagger for her to modify.

The dagger was inscribed with the word for human or animal blood, *umul*. The Genial Ones had had two more words for their own blood, one for what spilled out of them in ordinary circumstances, and another used in reference to ritual bloodletting. The dagger destroyed the person you stabbed it with if you drew blood, and distorted itself into a miniature, rusting figure of the victim: ghastly, but easy to dispose of. Useful for causing people to disappear.

The house's passages had creaky wooden floors, but nobody called out or rushed out to attack her. Calligraphy scrolls decorated the walls. Yeged had a calligraphy tradition almost as old as Chindalla's, and the scrolls displayed Yegedin proverbs and poetry in a variety of commendably rhythmic hands. She could name the styles they were scribed in, most of them well-regarded, if a little old-fashioned: River Rocks Tumbling, Butterfly's Kiss, Anaiago's Comb . . .

Iseul looked away from the scrolls. She shouldn't get distracted, even though the scrolls might be a clue of some kind. There was always the chance that the magician would find some excuse to leave the dinner early and come home.

She found part of what she was looking for in the magician's study, which was dismally untidy, with scraps of paper on every conceivable surface. There was still some light from outside, although she had a lantern charm just in case.

The magician had brought home two boxes of Chindallan books. One of them mostly contained supernatural stories involving nine-tailed foxes, a genre whose appeal had always eluded her, but which was enduringly popular. She had to concede the charm of some of the illustrations: fox eyes peering brightly from behind masks, fox tails curving slyly from beneath layers of elaborate robes, fox paws slipping out of long gloves.

Stuffed into the same box was a volume of poetry, which Iseul pulled out in a spirit of professional interest. With a sigh, she began flipping through the book, letting her eye alight on the occasional well-turned phrase. She kept track of syllable counts by reflex. Nothing special. She was tempted to smuggle it out on principle, but this collection had been popular sixteen years ago and there were still a lot of copies to be had in the north. Besides, the magician would surely notice if one of his spoils went missing.

The next book was different. It had a tasteful cover in dark red, but that wasn't what caught her attention. She had seen books with covers in every conceivable color, some of them ill-advised; hadn't everyone? No. It was the fact that the book shouldn't have been in the box with the others. She went through a dozen pages just to be sure, but she had been right. Each page was printed in Yeged-dai, not Chindallan.

However, Iseul could see why whoever had packed the box had gotten confused. She recognized the names of most of the poets. More specifically, she recognized the Yegedin names that Chindallan poets had taken.

Iseul knew from experience that a poet's existence was a precarious one if you didn't come from a wealthy family or have a generous patron. Fashions in poetry came and went almost as quickly as fashions in hairstyles. Before the Ministry of Ornithology recruited her, she had written sarcastic verses for nobles to pass around at social functions, and the occasional parody. Slightly risky, but her father's prominence as a court official had afforded her a certain degree of protection from offended writers.

The poets who survived in occupied Chindalla could no longer rely on their old patrons, or write as they had been accustomed to writing. But some of them had a knack for foreign languages, as Iseul did, or had perhaps learned Yeged-dai even before the invasion. Those poets had been able to adapt. She had known about such people before this. But it still hurt her to see their poems before her, printed in the curving Yeged-dai script, using Yegedin forms and the images so beloved of the Yegedin: the single pebble, the grasshopper at twilight, the song of a heartbroken lark sitting in a bent tree.

Iseul put the book back in its place, wishing for something to staunch the ache within her. It would have been easy to hate the southern poets for abandoning their own language, but she knew that resistance carried a considerable risk. Even in Mijege-in, which had fallen early and easily, and which the Yegedin considered well-tamed, the governor occasionally burned rebels alive. She had passed by the latest corpses on the walls when she entered the city. Mainly she remembered them as shadows attracting shadows, charred sticks held together by a conglomeration of ravens.

There were also those who had died in the initial doomed defense of the south. Sometimes she thought she would never forgive her father, whose martial skills were best not mentioned, for dying with the garrison at Hwagan Fort in an attempt to slow the Yegedin advance. There were poems about that battle, all red-stained banners and broken spears and unquiet pyres, all glory and honor, except there had been nothing glorious about the loss. She hated herself for reading the poems over and over whenever she encountered them.

Iseul went through the second box. More Chindallan books, the usual eclectic variety, and no clue as to what the Yegedin wanted with them. Maybe it was simple acquisitiveness. One of the Yegedin governors, knowing the beauty and value of Chindallan celadon, had taken the simple expedient of rounding up all the Chindallan potters in three provinces and sending them to his homeland as slaves along with their clay, as well as buying up everything from vases to good forgeries of antique jewelry boxes.

The rest of the box didn't take her long to get through. It included a single treatise on magic. Those were getting harder and harder to find in the south, as the Yegedin quite reasonably didn't trust magic in Chindallan hands. The treatise in question concerned locator charms. Like all magic, locators were based on the writings of the Genial Ones, who had once ruled over the human nations the way Yeged desired to rule over the known world. Humans had united under General Anangan to destroy the Genial Ones, but not long after that, a chieftain assassinated the general and the alliance dissolved.

People discovered that, over time, magic started to fail because its masters were no more. Locators had stopped being reliable about a century ago or Iseul would have had some uses for them herself. On the occasions that you could get one to activate at all, it tended to chew a map into your entrails. Some people would still have used them anyway, but the maps were also inevitably false.

The treatise's author had included a number of gruesome illustrations to support her contention that the failed magic was affected by the position of the user's spleen. The theory was preposterous, but all the same, Iseul wished she could liberate the treatise. She didn't dare risk it, though. The magician would be even more sure to notice a missing book on magic.

Iseul froze. Had she just heard footsteps? How could the magician be back so early? Or had she spent more time looking through those damnable poems than she had realized? She ducked behind a coat rack. Under better circumstances, she would have critiqued the coats, although a quick glance suggested that they were in fact of high quality. That cuff, for instance; hard to find embroiderers these days who were willing to put up with the hassle of couching gold thread that had to be done in such short segments. Iseul's mother had always impressed upon her the importance of appearances, something that Iseul had used against a great many people as a spy.

The footsteps were getting closer and their owner was walking briskly. A bad sign. Contrary to popular belief, magicians couldn't detect each other; being a magician was merely a matter of study, applied linguistics, and a smattering of geometry. Magicians could, however, check the status of their charms by looking, just like anyone else with a working pair of eyes. Or by touch, if it came to that. The problem with the passage charm that Iseul used was that it made no attempt to hide its effects. The older version that disguised its own workings had stopped working about 350 years ago.

It might be time to flee. Iseul was willing to bet that she was more athletic than a magician who worked in an office all day. Her glimpses of him hadn't suggested that he was particularly fit. The study's window was covered in oiled paper, and was barely large enough for her to squeeze through.

More footsteps. Iseul headed for the window, but her sleeve snagged on a coat, and it rustled to the floor. Just her luck: the magician had left a coin purse in it, and the coins jangled as they landed. She cursed her clumsiness. Now he probably knew her location. Indeed, halfway on her way to the window, flowers with shadow-mouths and toothy leaves started growing in hectic tangles from the window, barring her passage.

Iseul knew better than to believe the illusion, no matter how much the heavy, heady scent of the blossoms threatened to clog her sinuses; no matter how much her hands wanted to twitch away from the jagged leaves and the glistening intimation of poison on the stems. She had seen these flowers in her dreams as a child, when she was afraid that she would fall asleep in the garden during hide-and-seek and be swallowed up by the spirits of thorn and malice. They were only as real as she allowed them to be.

Her father had once, uncharacteristically, given her a piece of military advice, probably quoted from some manual. They had been playing baduk, a board game involving capturing territory with stones. As usual, he refused to give her any handicap despite the disparity in age. She had been complaining about the fact that she was sure to lose. In her defense, she had only been ten. *It doesn't matter how good your position is,* he had told her, *if you're already defeated in your head.*

If the magician thought that a childhood nightmare was going to get her to give up so easily, he was sorely mistaken. She could have punched through the window, which was only covered with paper, and gone on her way. But he already knew someone with knowledge of magic had broken into his home. She might as well have it out with him right now, even if she ordinarily preferred to avoid confrontations. Minsu was going to lecture her about taking risks, but the dreadful timing couldn't be helped.

Iseul's pulse raced as she drew her second dagger and angled herself back behind the coat rack. For a moment she didn't realize the magician had entered the room.

Then a figure assembled itself out of shadows and dust motes and scraps of paper, right there in the room. Iseul was tall for a Chindallan woman, but the figure was taller, and its arms were disproportionately long. She thought it might be a man beneath the strange layers of robes, which weren't in any fashion she'd seen before. She could see its eyes, dark in a pale, smudgy face, and that it was holding up a charm of a variety she didn't recognize.

Iseul had killed people before. She lunged with her dagger before the magician had a chance to finish activating the charm. He brought up his arm to protect his ribs. The dagger snagged on his layers of sleeves. She gave it a good hard yank and it came free, along with strands that unraveled in the air.

She made one more attempt to stab him, but he twisted away, fiendishly fast, and she missed again. She bit back a curse. It was only with great effort that she kept herself from losing her balance.

Iseul ran past the figure since momentum was taking her there anyway and out of the study. The dagger was needle-keen in her hand, with blood showing hectic red at its point. It should have shrank into a misshapen figure amid shivers of smoke and fractured light the moment she marked her target. She flung it aside in a fit of revulsion and heard it clattering against the wall. It made a bright, terrible sound, like glass bells and shattering hells and hounds unloosed, and she had never heard anything like it before.

If the dagger hadn't changed, then that meant the magician was still alive. She had to go back and finish the job. She swung around. The dagger was visible where she had cast it. The blood on the blade seemed even redder.

Words writhed in the sheen of the metal's surface. Probably no good to her if it hadn't worked the first time. She plunged past it and into the study without hesitating at the threshold.

The magician was waiting for her. The mixture of amusement, contempt, and rage in his eyes chilled Iseul more than anything else that had happened so far. He threw his charm at her as she cleared the doorway.

The charm didn't grow thorns or teeth or tendrils. Instead, it unfolded in a twisting ballet of planes and vertices. For a single clear second, Iseul could see words in the Genial Ones' language pinned to the paper's surface by the weight of the ink, by the will of the scribe. Then, with a thready whispering, the words flocked free of the paper and spread themselves in the air toward her, like a net.

Iseul knew better than to be caught by that net. She twisted around it, thanking her mother for a childhood full of dance lessons, although some of the words brushed her sleeve before they dispersed. Her entire left forearm grew numb. No time to think about that. The magician was reaching for something in a pouch. She ignored that and went instead for his throat. People never expected a woman to have strong hands.

The magician croaked out half a word. Iseul pressed harder with her thumbs, seeking his windpipe, and felt the magician struggle to breathe. His hands, oddly chilly, clawed at her hands.

How could someone as skinny as the magician have such good lung capacity? Iseul hung on. The magician's skin grew colder and colder, as though he had veins of ice creeping closer to his skin the longer she choked him. Her hands ached with the chill.

Worse, she felt the scrabbling of her lantern charm in response to the magician's proximity. Belatedly, she realized he was trying to scratch words into her skin with his fingernails. Her teeth closed on a yelp.

Like all her charms, the lantern charm was made of paper lacquered to a certain degree of stiffness. It scratched her skin as though it were struggling to unfold itself just as the magician's original charm had done. For the first time, she cared about the quality of the charm's lacquer, hoping it would hold fast against another word-cloud.

Iseul could barely feel her left hand. She kept pressing against the magician's throat and staring at the ugly purple marks that mottled his skin. "Die," she said hoarsely. The numb feeling was spreading up her forearm to her elbow, and at this rate, she was going to lose use of the arm, who knew for how long.

The lantern charm was starting to unfurl. Iseul resisted the urge to close her eyes and give up. But the magician was done struggling. The cold hands dropped away, and he slumped.

Iseul was trembling. But she held on for another count of hundred just to be certain. Then she let the figure drop to the ground and staggered sideways.

The magician's eyes slitted open. Careless of her. She should have realized his physiology might be different. She scrabbled for her ordinary dagger with her good hand and cut his throat. The blood was rich and red, and there was a lot of it.

The magician wheezed something, a few words in a language she didn't recognize. Her first instinct was to recoil, remembering the cloud of words. Her second and better instinct, which was to stab his torso repeatedly, won out. But nothing more emerged from those pale lips except a last cool thread of breath.

She sat back and forced herself to breathe slowly, evenly, until her heart wasn't knocking at the walls of her ribs anymore. Then she went back out into the hallway. The magical dagger showed no sign of shrinking. She brought it back with her into the study and its mangled corpse.

Iseul wanted to drop both daggers and huddle under the coats for the rest of the night. Instead, she wiped off both daggers on the magician's clothes and tucked them back into their sheaths. She took off her jacket. There was a small basin of water, and she washed her hands and face. It wasn't much, but it made her feel better and right now she would take what she could get. She hunted through the magician's collection of coats for something that wouldn't fit her too poorly and put it on.

Since she had killed the magician, she might as well complete her search of the house. She wouldn't get another opportunity once they found out about the murder.

Yes. Think about logistical details. Don't think about the corpse.

Except she had to think about the corpse. It would be remiss of her not to search it to see if the magician had been carrying any other surprises.

She couldn't think about the fact that the dagger would have disintegrated a human. It might simply be that the charm no longer worked, the way any number of charms had stopped working. There was an easy way to test that, but she wasn't about to kill some random victim just to test whether her dagger really had lost its virtue.

Iseul thought about the fact that its blade repeated, over and over in a winding trail, the word for human blood. *Umul.*

About the fact that she might have killed a Genial One, and the Genial Ones were supposed to be over a thousand years extinct.

Someone would find the corpse. But first, the search. See what the corpse wanted to say to her in the language of violence and clandestine corners.

Iseul went through the magician's robes, all of them, layers upon layers that clung clammily to her fingers. Next time she did this she was going to bring gloves. All the while she puzzled over the magician's last words. She had believed that she was fluent in the language of magic. The longer she thought about it, the more she became convinced that the magician had said, *You can kill one of us, but not all of us. We won't accept this*—and then there was one more word that she couldn't get to slot into place no matter how much she shifted the vowels or roughened the fricatives.

The most unhelpful thing she found in the magician's pockets was the candy. It smelled like ordinary barley candy, but she wasn't about to put it in her mouth to check.

The one useful thing was a charm. Iseul recognized it because it was folded very similarly to her own charm of passage, except it had a map-word inscribed on some of its corners, which meant that it was meant to interact with a specific lock rather than being intended for general use. The magician had worn it on a bracelet. Iseul cut it away, then set about stuffing the magician's corpse into a closet and wiping down the room. It wouldn't pass a good inspection, but she would be long gone by the time anyone came searching.

It was hard not to flinch every time a branch knocked against the walls of the house as the wind outside grew stronger, but eventually she found the secret passage by paying attention to the way the charm quivered in her hand. The door was in the basement, which had a collection of geometrically sorted blocks of bean curd, bags of rice, and other humble staples. Curious thought: had the magician cooked his own food? She wasn't sure she liked the thought of a Genial One enjoying Chindallan food.

The secret room was situated so it was under a good portion of the oversized garden. Brandishing the magician's charm opened the door. Lantern charms filled the space with a pale blue light. It was hard not to imagine that she walked underwater.

Iseul checked the shadows for signs of movement, but if an ambush awaited her, she would have to deal with it when it came. She stepped sideways into the room.

A book lay open on a cluttered escritoire. Next to it was a desk set containing a half-used, sumptuously carved and gilded block of ink. The carving had probably once been a dragon, judging by the lower half: conventional, but well-executed. A charm that had been folded to resemble a quill rested against the book. The folds had been made very precisely.

Iseul's gaze went to a small stack of paper next to the book. The top sheet was covered with writing. Her hackles rose as she realized that that wasn't precisely true. It sounded like someone was writing on the paper, and the stack made a rustling sound as of furtive animals, but there was no brush or graphite stick, and the ink looked obdurately dry.

Against her better judgment, she approached the desk. She looked first at the charm, which was covered with words of transference and staining, then at the papers. Black wisps were curling free from the book, leaving the page barren, and traveling through the air to the paper, where they formed new words. She flipped back in the book. The first thirty or so pages were blank, as faceless as a mask turned inside-out. Iseul flipped forward. As before, the words on the next page, which were in somewhat archaic Chindallan, continued sizzling away in ashy curls and wisps.

Iseul reminded herself to breathe, then picked up the top of the pile and began paging through. All of the words were in the Genial Ones' language. It appeared to be some sort of diatribe about the writer's hosts and their taste in after-dinner entertainment. She squinted at the pages: only three of them so far. She pulled out the page currently being written on.

More words formed on the new sheet. Iseul had expected a precise insectine march, but that wasn't the case. There seemed to be someone on the other end; it wasn't just a transfer of marks. Sometimes the unseen writer hesitated over a word choice, or crossed something out. At one point a doodle formed in the margin, either a very fat cow or a very large hog, hard to tell. The writer, a middling artist at best, had more unflattering comments about the people they were staying with.

Would she alert the person on the other end if she made off with the letter, which was becoming increasingly and entertainingly vituperative? She didn't know how close by they were. How much time did she have? Her left arm felt less numb than before, which was reassuring, but that didn't mean she should let down her guard. Time to read the letter and see if there was anything she should commit to memory. Sadly, the writer was cagey about revealing their location, although she learned some creative insults.

It was tempting to linger and find out if the writer was going to regale the dead magician with more misshapen farm animals, maybe a rooster or a goose, but Iseul made herself turn away from the escritoire and examine the rest of the hideout. There were more books with the writing worn away, and a number of what she recognized as ragged volumes of a torrid adventure series involving an alchemist and her two animal-headed assistants, popular about five years back. Since she preferred not to believe that one of the Genial Ones had such execrable taste in popular fiction, it seemed likely that the books were convenient fodder for this unusual method of exchanging letters.

Still, it paid to be thorough. Iseul didn't like turning her back on the escritoire, but she still needed to search the rest of the secret room, which was well-supplied with books.

She was starting to think that most of the books would fall into the two previous categories—blank and about to be blank—when she found what the magician had been so keen on hiding. These books, unlike the others, were only labeled by number. Each was impressively thick. An amateur, albeit a moderately accomplished one, had stitched the binding. The binder— probably the magician—had a fondness for dark blue linen thread.

Iseul picked up the first book and flipped rapidly through the pages. Thin paper, but high quality, with just a hint of tooth. The left-hand pages were in a writing system unfamiliar to her. Unlike Chindallan, the letterforms consisted of a profusion of curves and loops. She wondered if it, like the language of the realm of Moi-quan to the south, had originally been incised into large leaves that would split if you used straight strokes.

The right-hand pages were in the Genial Ones' writing, in script so small that it hurt her eyes, and it was immediately obvious that they were compiling a lexicon. Definitions, from denotations to connotations; usage notes, including one on a substitute word to be used only in the presence of a certain satrap; dialectal variations; folk etymologies, some amusingly similar to stories in Chindalla, like the one about a fish whose name changed twice in one year thanks to a princess discovering that something that tasted delicious when you were starving in exile didn't necessarily remain so after you had returned to eating courtly delicacies. And look, there was a doodle of a sadly generic-looking fish in the margin, although it was in a different style than the earlier pig-cow. (Like many Chindallans, Iseul knew her fish very well.) How long had it taken the magician to put this together?

The unfamiliar writing system was summarized in five volumes. Iseul went on to the next language. Four volumes, but the notes in the Genial Ones' language were much more terse and had probably been compiled by a different researcher or group of researchers. She estimated the number of books, then considered the number of languages. Impressive, although she had no way of knowing how many languages there were in the world, and what fraction of them this collection of lexicons represented.

She sampled a few more languages at random. One of the sets was, interestingly, for Yeged-dai. Judging by its position in the pile, it had been completed a while ago. She was tempted to quibble with some of the preferred spellings, but she had to concede that the language as used in occupied territories probably diverged from the purer forms spoken in Yeged proper.

Then she came to the last set. Only one volume. The left-hand pages were written in Chindallan.

It turned out that the second volume hadn't yet been bound, and was scattered in untidy piles in drawers of the study. The words were sorted into broad groups more or less by Chindallan alphabetical order, although it looked like they were added as they were collected. For instance:

Cheon-ma, the cloud-horses that carry the moon over the sea. Thankfully, the magician hadn't attempted to sketch one. It probably would have ended up looking like an ox. The *cheon-ma* were favorite subjects of Chindalla's court artists. There was a famous carving of one on a memorial from the previous dynasty, which Iseul had had the privilege of viewing once.

Chindal-kot, the royal azalea, emblem of the queen's house. This included a long and surprisingly accurate digression on the evolution of the house colors over the lifetime of the current dynasty as new dyes were discovered. Iseul bristled at the magician's condescending tone, although she didn't know why she expected any better from a Genial One.

Chaebi, the swallow, said to be a bearer of good luck. Beneath its entry was a notation on the Festival of the Swallows' Return in the spring. And, inevitably, a sketch of a swallow, although she would have mistaken it for a goose if not for the characteristic forked tail.

Iseul put the papers back. Her throat felt raw. The magician couldn't be up to anything good with this, but what did it mean?

Especially puzzling: what did it mean that all the lexicons were copied out by hand? The rough texture of ink on paper had been unmistakable. She had already witnessed a magician sending a letter by manipulating the substance of text from a book already in existence. Surely magicians could use this process to halve the work? Or did it only work on the language of magic itself?

She had spent too long here already. It was time to get out and report this to her handler, who might have some better idea of what was going on.

Iseul hesitated, then gathered up the Chindallan lexicon and the four volumes of the Yeged-dai lexicon. For all she knew there were duplicates elsewhere, but she would take what she could get. If she had more time to inspect the lexicons once she was far from here, there might be valuable clues. She was going to look odd hauling books around at this hour, but perhaps she could pretend to be running an errand for some Yegedin official.

Cold inside, she headed back up the stairs, and out of the house with its secrets wrapped in words.

The Genial Ones believed in the sovereignty of conservation laws. This may be illustrated by a tale that begins in the usual way by naming the Genial Ones as the terrible first children of the world's dawning. In due course (so the story goes), the sun grew red and dim and large, threatening to swallow the world. Determined to preserve their spiraling towers and their symphonies and their many-bannered armies, the Genial Ones unlanterned a younger star in order to rejuvenate their own.

It is likely that they did this more than once.

Many of Chindalla's astronomers believe that, since this sun indisputably supports learned civilizations, other stars must do the same. Some astronomers have produced lengthy essays, complete with computations, to support this position.

Reckoning whether any such civilization would survive the extinction of its sun, on the other hand, requires no arduous calculation.

Iseul's handler, Shen Minsu, was a tall, plain woman with a strong right arm. Before the invasion, she had been known for her skill at archery. Iseul had seen her split one arrow with another at 130 meters during a private display. "Useless skill," Minsu had said afterwards, "people dead of arrows to the heart find it hard to confess what they're up to. Much better to make use of the living."

They met now in the upper storage room of a pharmacy in a small town. The Shen family had risen to prominence by running pharmacies. One of the earlier Shens had been elevated to a noble after one of his concoctions cured a beloved king-consort's fever. Even in the south, the Shen family maintained good ties with medicine-sellers and herb-gatherers. Yegedin medicine was not terribly different in principle from Chindallan medicine, and the Yegedin prized Chindalla's mountain ginseng, which was said to bestow longevity. Iseul had grown up drinking the bitter tea at her mother's insistence, but from observation of her mother's patrons, it didn't do anything more for you than any other form of modest living.

Minsu didn't care for ginseng tea, ironically, but she always insisted that they drink tea of some sort whenever they met. Iseul took a sip now. She was wearing clothes cut more conservatively, and she had switched her hairstyle to the drab sort of thing a widow might favor. Shen Minsu was wearing subdued brown and beige linen, which suited her surprisingly well, instead of the sumptuous embroidered robes she would have worn in northern Chindalla.

Minsu was going methodically through the incomplete Chindallan lexicon. She had already glanced through the Yeged-dai lexicon. "You're certain," Minsu said for the third time this meeting, which showed how unsettled she was.

"I killed a Yegedin guard on the way out, to be sure," Iseul said bleakly. She had agonized over the decision, but it wouldn't be the first time she had killed a Yegedin on Chindalla's behalf. The dagger had performed flawlessly, which meant the issue wasn't that the charm had stopped working; the issue was that the charm only triggered on human blood. "And the last thing the Genial One said—"

You can kill one of us, but not all of us. We won't accept this—and then the unfamiliar term.

"My guess is that the Yegedin are as much in the dark as we are," Minsu said. "I find it hard to believe that even they would knowingly ally with the Genial Ones."

"I wish I believed that Yeged conquered Chindalla so handily by allying itself with monsters," Iseul said bitterly.

Both of them knew that Yeged's soldiers hadn't needed supernatural help. In the previous century, Chindalla had turned inwards, its court factions squabbling over ministry appointments and obscure philosophical arguments. The Yegedin had also been a people divided, but that division that taken the form of vicious civil wars. As a result, when a warlord united Yeged and declared himself Emperor, he was sitting on a brutally effective army that had grown accustomed to the spoils of war. It had only been natural for the Emperor's successor to send his soldiers overseas in search of more riches to keep them loyal.

"I feel as though we've walked into a children's story," Minsu said. "When I was a child, the servants would scare us out of trouble by telling us tales— you know the ones. Don't pull the horses' tails, or the Genial Ones' falcons will come out of the shadows and eat your eyes. If you pinch snacks from the kitchens at night, the Genial Ones will turn your fingers into twigs and use them for kindling. Or if you tear your jacket climbing trees, the Genial Ones will sew you up with your little brother and use you as a ceremonial robe. That sort of thing."

"Except they were real," Iseul said. "All the histories in all the known nations agree on the basics. It's difficult not to believe them."

Minsu sighed. "The Yegedin haven't mentioned anything in their official dispatches so far as we know, but one of my contacts in Mijege-in has remarked on how the censor has been terribly quiet. A very long-running hangover after entertaining the guest from Yeged. No doubt the Yegedin authorities are looking for the murderer as we speak." She looked sideways at Iseul; her eyes were dark and very grave. "And that means the Genial Ones are looking for the murderer, too.

"We don't know how many of them there are," Minsu went on, "although if they're researching the world's languages it's certain that they're widely dispersed. You're lucky to have survived, and you're also lucky that he tried to take care of you himself instead of raising the alarm."

"He probably didn't want to risk anyone else finding out about his collection of lexicons," Iseul said, "if he ran afoul of some Yegedin magician."

"This is a complication that I didn't need," Minsu said, "but it can't be helped. We're going to have to pull out."

"It's hardly unexpected," Iseul said. People were talking about it in the markets, not least because the prices for ordinary necessities had gone up again.

The Yegedin were preparing to break the thirteen-year truce and move on free Chindalla to the north. Reinforcements had been filtering into the territory, some crossing the ocean from Yeged itself.

"I assume you have dedicated assassins," Iseul said, "but we need to find out if there are any Genial Ones associated with the Yegedin army. One of them might have been mediocre at hand-to-hand combat, but we don't know how closely connected they are with Yeged's plans. If they intervene as magicians, or trained the Yegedin magicians, the border defenses could be in a lot of trouble. At least we know that they can be killed."

Humans had battled the Genial Ones as a matter of necessity, even if they hadn't done as thorough a job of obliterating them as everyone had thought.

"Well," Minsu said, "it's clear you can't rely on the charms anymore since they'll be suspicious of anyone using magic. You're in a lot of danger."

Iseul looked at her bleakly. Like everyone in Chindalla, she had grown up with stories of the Genial Ones' terrible horses, whose hooves opened cracks in the earth with bleak black eyes staring out until they boiled poisonously away; the Genial Ones' banquets, served in the skulls of children; the Genial Ones' adulthood ceremonies, where music of drum and horn caused towers of glistening cartilage to grow out of mounds of corpses. Even in the days of their dominion, the histories said, there had been humans who objected not to the Genial Ones' methods, but to the fact that they didn't have mastery of those terrible arts for themselves. After the Genial Ones' downfall, they had lost no time in learning. The wars in the wake of General Anangan's assassination had been wide-reaching and bloody.

"Everything has been dangerous," Iseul said. "We just didn't realize it until now. And who knows—maybe if I can lure them out, we can get them to reveal more about whatever it is they're up to."

They discussed possible options for a while. "Your tea's getting cold," Minsu said eventually. "Drink up. You never know when you'll next taste Three Pale Blossoms tea harvested before the Yegedin took over the plantation." Her smile was bitter. "I keep track, you know. Not many people care, especially when the stuff is a luxury to begin with, but it matters."

"I know," Iseul said. "You don't have to remind me." She drank the rest of the cup with slow sips. She didn't like the tea, but that wasn't the point.

> **himmadaebi,** *noun*: More literally, "great white horse rains." A Chindallan term used of the worst storms. Originally reserved for the storms that the Genial Ones used to call down on cities that defied them. Usage shifted after the Genial Ones' defeat by General Anangan, although attempts to date the change have been hampered by the fact that literacy rates in Chindalla at the time were much lower than they are now, and only a few reliable sources are extant.

Not long after Iseul's run-in with the magician, the second Yegedin invasion began with a storm, and with horses.

The horses were the color of foam-rush and freezing ice. They had wide, mad eyes and hooves that struck the earth as though it were a breaking drum. Their shadows broke off behind them every fourth stride and unfurled into tatters that sliced off tree branches and left boulders in crumbled ruins.

Iseul had been traveling with the soldiers ever since they decamped from the city that the Yegedin had renamed Mijege-in, heading north toward the border of free Chindalla. The infantry soldiers had wan, anxious expressions, and the highborn cavalrymen didn't look much better. Their horses were blinkered, and the blinkers were made of paper covered with cryptic words: charms. She had checked one night. Too bad she couldn't cause a little confusion by making off with all the blinkers, but it wasn't feasible and she had a more important task.

She had been tempted to report to Minsu for further instructions the moment she saw the horses. The storm-spell had been defunct for over two centuries. There were accounts of it in the old histories. One of the northwestern Chindallan forts had been thundered down by such a storm generations past. To this day the grasses and trees grew sickly and stunted where the stones had once stood. It wasn't surprising that the Yegedin had more magicians in their employ, but the fact that an old charm had been resuscitated suggested that at least one of the magicians was a Genial One, or had been trained by one. Perhaps a Genial One could pass the charm off as a brilliant research discovery, even though the problem of magic that didn't work anymore had vexed the human nations ever since the phenomenon was noted.

But Iseul needed better information. It had taken an alliance of all the human nations to defeat the Genial Ones the last time, and some of them had survived anyway. There were probably much fewer of them now, but she was under no illusions that the human nations of the present time were likely to unite even for this, especially if they had a chance of claiming the Genial Ones' magics for themselves.

She had spent cold hours thinking about the fact that at least one of the old spells worked again, which meant others might, too. And which meant that human magicians and their masters would seek those spells for their own ends, no matter how horrible the cost.

Tonight Iseul was dripping wet and huddled in a coat that wasn't doing nearly enough to keep out the chill. She had killed a scout early on and was wearing his clothes. Her hair was piled up underneath his cap and she had bound her chest tight. It wouldn't pass a close inspection, but no one was looking closely at anyone in such miserable weather.

Iseul was helped by the Yegedin themselves. Not that the Chindallans were known for tight military discipline either, but the Yegedin force was doing unusually poorly in this regard. Part of the problem was that no one felt comfortable near the storm-horses. The other part was that orders from Yeged had apparently assigned the initial attack to not one but two rival generals. No doubt the theory was that the two would spur each other on to ever greater feats in battle, but in practice this meant the two generals' soldiers squabbled over everything from watch assignments to access to the best forage. Iseul had situated herself at the hazy boundary between the two armies so she could claim to be on either side as necessary.

Tonight she had decided that she would try approaching the magicians' tent again. The Yegedin were sheltering in hills perhaps two days' march from the nearest Chindallan border-fort. The Chindallan sentries would have seen the storm, although the knowledge wouldn't save them. They almost certainly wouldn't realize what it signified.

She was tempted to assassinate the Yegedin magicians. But she would undoubtedly die in the attempt. Besides, as terrible as it would be to lose the fort, it was more important to determine how the Genial Ones meant to threaten all of Chindalla.

Iseul eased her way toward the magicians' tent a little at a time. She had learned that there were two of them and that they kept to themselves, although not much else. Even the officers didn't like speaking of them too loudly. When they did mention the magicians, it was with careful distaste. Iseul was only a little reassured to find out that Yegedin attitudes toward magicians weren't far different from Chindallan attitudes, considering that she knew how to use charms herself.

Most of the soldiers who weren't on watch were, sensibly, sleeping. But a few exchanged ribald jokes about shapeshifting badgers, or spoke of how much they missed proper plum pickles from home, or mentioned pilgrimages they had made to Yeged's holy mountains in the past. Some of them looked quite young.

One of the younger ones mentioned a pretty Chindallan woman who was waiting for him in a southern town. Iseul kept her face blank at the coarse remarks that followed. She had long practice controlling her expression, and it wasn't news that a number of the Yegedin had taken lovers among the Chindallans. South Chindalla had been occupied for thirteen years, after all. There were Chindallans who had grown up thinking of the Yegedin as their natural rulers, and whose only memories of freedom were a child's memories of stubbed toes and overripe persimmons and picking cosmos flowers in the fall.

Iseul clutched the satchel of the unfortunate scout and continued to the magicians' tent, which stood by itself with two reluctant sentries at the tent flap. A pale, unsettling light burned from the tent. She wound her way to the back. The sentries were exchanging riddles. She wished she could stay and listen; the Yegedin, for all their faults, knew the value of a good riddle.

She was going to have a hard time getting past the sentries into the tent, and from the sounds of it the magicians were having a discussion. The fact that there were always sentries was bad enough. She might have dealt with them, but usually at this hour the magicians were speaking to one or the other of the generals in the command tent. Rotten luck.

Of course, all the rotten luck in the world didn't make a difference when the magicians' defensive charms were certain still to be in place. She had glimpsed some the first time she approached the tent nights ago. While some of them were unfamiliar, she recognized the ones that would have detected the use of concealment magic. Another was a boundary-warden, which would have caught her if she had attempted to cut her way into the tent.

This was no doubt just punishment for developing a dependence on the Genial Ones' tools all these years, but Iseul couldn't help but grit her teeth. She wondered if a passage charm would work, but the Genial Ones might have a countermeasure for that, too. Keeping her expression placid, she strolled on by.

The magicians' voices carried remarkably well in the chilly damp. They spoke the language of magic with an accent similar to that of the Genial One Iseul had killed. She had difficulty understanding their pronunciation, as before, but her mother had taught her how to sing in foreign languages by concentrating first on the sounds without worrying about the meaning. As she traced a meandering path, she committed the conversation, which had the rhythms of an argument, to memory.

Iseul slouched her way to a less conspicuous location, avoiding contact with Yegedin soldiers as much as possible. She had only two days to figure out a better approach. If she had Minsu's astonishing skill with a bow—but going around with a Chindallan weapon, especially one so difficult to conceal as a bow, would be a sure way of getting herself killed for no gain.

The storms grew worse in the next two days. Iseul drifted to the rear with other laggards. The generals had people whipped for it, but nothing could change people's opinion of the storm-horses.

She tried again the next night. The guards were clearly bored. One of them kept peeling back the tent flap to look in and make snide comments about the magicians' furnishings. Time to risk a more direct approach if it would get her a glimpse of the tent's contents. She made sure to spill some of the scout's rice wine on her coat and take a long sip before she strolled on by just as one of the guards was finishing up a joke about an abbot and an albino bear.

"Hey, you'd better move on," the other guard said, noticing Iseul. "The only things that go on in there are related to spiders." He shuddered.

The guard was probably referring to the moving shadows. Iseul staggered a little as she approached him. Inside, there was a charm on the small table right next to a telltale sheaf of papers, but it was hard to see—ah, there it was. Two quills, curving in opposite directions. She guessed that they complemented each other, one to send letters and one to receive.

"If he's drunk, maybe he's drinking something better than we are," the first guard said. "Want to share what you have, friend?"

"It's no good if they catch us drinking on duty," the second guard said.

"Like they pay attention to people like us."

"Ah, what's the harm," Iseul said in her gruffest voice, which wasn't very, and handed over her flask. It was terrible wine, but maybe terrible wine was better than no wine. She didn't hang around to find out what the guards decided to do with the flask.

The information about the quills was all she had gotten out of the miserable journey, but it might allow her to figure out a charm to spy on the Genial Ones' future communications. She worked her way to the rear again, and left six hours before dawn the day the siege began. Without an army's impedimenta to trouble her, she could make better time. Not that the storm wasn't obvious, but it wasn't clear to her the Chindallan watchers would realize just what it signified.

She shed the Yegedin clothing while hiding behind some shrubs, exchanging it for the plain brown dress—now quite rumpled—she had been carrying with her, although she resented even the moments that this took. Then she ran for the border-fort, pacing herself. It was hard to make herself concentrate on the dubious paths, but she would be no use if she sprained an ankle on the loose rocks. She had not eaten well while she traveled with the Yegedin army, and it took its toll now. Her breath came hard, and she could feel the storm-winds drawing ever closer behind her.

She had kept the Yegedin boots on because she hadn't brought spare shoes—they would have been a nuisance to carry around—but she discovered that the boots were even worse than she knew from days of marching around in them. Every step jolted the soles of her feet, and the toes were starting to pinch. The scout she had killed hadn't had notably small feet, so she was guessing the boots had caused him even more discomfort than they were causing her. Ill-fitting shoes were apparently a military universal: she knew Chindallan soldiers complained about it, too.

The sky to the north was yet clear, but every time she glanced over her shoulder she saw the stormclouds.

The gate guards to the border-fort must have been bemused to see a small, disheveled woman huffing as she came up the road. Iseul was gratified to see the wall sentries training their bows on her: at least they were prepared for the enemy. "I work for the Ministry of Ornithology," she called out. Iseul trusted that the purity of her Chindallan accent, high court from the north, would convince them that she was no Yegedin. "That's an army a few hours south, as you've guessed, but it has magicians."

The guards conferred, and after a few moments escorted her in to see the guard captain. "You must have made a narrow escape, sister," he said. He was a stocky man, much scarred, with kind eyes, and he spoke Chindallan with the unhurried rhythms of the hill people. Iseul had never been so grateful to hear her people's language. "The outriders had thought as much. Follow me. We can at least give you something to eat."

The guards let Iseul in, and a young soldier led her to the kitchens, where the cook gave her some rice and chicken broth. Iseul was glad of the opportunity to sit and rest her aching feet.

The captain came in with her and asked her questions about the disposition of the enemy. Iseul reported everything she had observed about the rival generals and their temperaments, the disarray of their army as it marched, and the estimated numbers of cavalry and infantry. "But it's the magicians you must worry about, Captain," she said, determined to impress this point upon him.

"It doesn't matter," the captain said quietly. "We're the first thing that stands in their way, and stand we must, however terrible the thunder that comes for us."

He didn't have to mention the fact that two of the three first land battles in the original Yegedin invasion had involved Chindallan commanders abandoning their forts, destroying all the supplies, and fleeing north. It was a shame that no Chindallan would soon forget.

"You won't stand for long unless you have magical defenses of your own," Iseul said.

The captain was already shaking his head. "The Yegedin will next have to pass Fort Kamang on the River Hwan," he said. "They have two magicians there. That will have to do." He eyed Iseul's soup bowl, already empty, with affectionate amusement. "We've sent word north, but it won't hurt to give them more recent intelligence. You undoubtedly have business of your own in that direction. Could I trouble you to—?"

"Of course, Captain," Iseul said.

The captain insisted on making her eat more soup, and she was given rice and barley hardtack and clear, sweet water for the journey. They let her rest for half an hour. The captain asked if she could ride, and she replied that she could, as her mother had taught her. They mounted her on a steady mare, a plain bay without markings, but one who responded calmly and quickly to each of Iseul's aids.

She set out on the bay mare. She had pulled her coat tightly about her in response to the air, which tasted increasingly of ice even though winter was months away. Then, looking back only once, she rode north, knowing as the distance unribboned behind her that she had failed her people.

The terrible thing about the Genial Ones was not that they held nations as their slaves, or that they destroyed cities with firefall and stormlash, or that they concocted their poisons from corpses. After all, human empires have done similar things.

It was not even that they were fond of sculpture. The Genial Ones regarded it as one of the highest arts. A favorite variant was to attune a slab of marble or a mossy boulder to a particular individual. As the days passed, the victim's skin would crack and turn gray, and their movements would slow. When the process was complete, only a dying, formless lump would remain of the victim, and the statue would be complete.

As much as people dreaded this art, however, the Genial Ones could only kill one person at a time with it.

Two hours before the siege of the border-fort, six arrows flew.

The senior general wore a back banner in livid red and a great helmet that resembled the head of a beetle. Only a small part of his face was exposed.

The first arrow took him through the side of the face, beneath the left eye, and even so he didn't die of it.

At the time he was consulting with the two magicians. In the gray light and the fine haze of rain, it was difficult to discern their otherwise distinctive blue robes. Three arrows took one of the magicians in the chest. She wore no armor and the arrowheads' barbs caught in her heart.

Two more arrows killed one of the general's servants, who happened to wear clothing that you might mistake for a magician's robes from a great distance on a day where the visibility was terrible to begin with.

This left the Yegedin army in disarray: someone notified the junior general, who wished to take command, while the senior general was shouting orders even as his servants tried to call for a physician. Both generals were keen on capturing the assassin, but by the time the two of them had organized search parties—since both groups of soldiers were confused as to whose orders should take precedence—the assassin had gotten away.

All that the Yegedin searchers found, at a distance sufficiently far from the command tent that everyone agreed the archer had taken the shots from some other, closer location, were goose feathers dyed red, damp from the rain, stuck into a hill at the base of a tree in the shape of an azalea.

> **Hwado**, *noun*. The way of fire. At one point the Chindallan bow and arrow were believed to be sacred to the spirits of sun and moon. A number of religious ceremonies involve shooting fire-arrows. Such arrows are often fletched with feathers dyed red. There is a saying in Chindalla that "even the wind bleeds," and most archers propitiate the spirits of the air after they practice their art.

Minsu was late for the rendezvous. Iseul had taken advantage of one of the safehouses in the town of Suwen, which was some distance to the north and out of the likely path of the Yegedin advance. She took advantage of the lull to experiment with making her own charms, even though she knew Minsu would have preferred her not to risk working with magic. Still, Iseul had a notion that she might be able work out something to spy on the Genial Ones' communications if she could only exploit certain of the charms' geometries.

After her latest failure, which resulted in words of lenses and distance charring off the attempted charm, Iseul sought comfort in an old pleasure: poetry. She could barely remember what it was like when her greatest problem had been coming up with a sufficiently witty pun with which to puncture some pretentious noblewoman's taste in hairpins. After a couple hours failing to write anything entertainingly caustic, she ventured to one of the town's bookstores to buy a couple volumes of recent poetry so she could pick them apart instead.

Iseul had once wondered what the Yegedin were getting out of piles of Chindallan books when the majority of them were simply not very good. Especially when the Yegedin were famed for their exquisite sense of aesthetics. It was almost difficult, at times, to hate people who understood beauty so thoroughly, and who even recognized beauty when it was to be had in a conquered people's arts.

She returned to the safehouse with her spoils. One of the books was an anthology by highborn poets. All of the poems were written in the high script, which Iseul had learned as a child at her mother's insistence. She had hated it then. The high script was based on the language of the great Qieng Empire to the north and east, but the Qieng language had little resemblance to Chindallan, necessitating a whole system of contrivances to make their writing work for Chindallan at all. Complicating the matter was the fact that the high script had come into use in Chindalla's earlier days, when Chindallan itself had been different, so you had to compensate both for the Qieng language and for the language shifts within Chindallan.

The other volume was a collection by an entertainer who had made a specialty of patriotic poems. He wrote in the petal script, which had been invented by a female entertainer, Jebi the Clever, to fit Chindallan itself. The shapes of the letters even corresponded to the positions of the tongue as it made Chindallan's speech sounds. Sadly, while the collection was beautifully illustrated—the artist had a real eye for the dramatic use of silhouettes— the poetry itself was trite and overwritten. How many times could you use the phrase "hearts of stout fire" in the space of twenty pages without being embarrassed for yourself, anyway?

Minsu met her at the safehouse two days later. She was wearing modestly splendid robes of silk embroidered with cavorting quails. "I am tired of hearing about battles with no survivors," she said. She was referring to the border-fort.

"I heard about the supernatural archer who came back from the dead to defend the fort," Iseul said, raising her eyebrows. "A rain of arrows to blacken the sky, people falling over pierced through the eye, that sort of thing. I didn't even know you had that many arrows."

"You should know better than to listen to hearsay," Minsu said. "Besides, I'm sure I got one magician, but I missed the other. Damnable light, couldn't tell who was who and couldn't risk getting closer, either. And it made no difference in the end."

Iseul nodded somberly. People in the town spoke of nothing else. The storm clouds, the white hands of lightning, the tumbling stones. Skeletons charred to ash, marrow set alight from within. The kindly guard captain at the border-fort was almost certainly dead.

Despite the city magistrate's attempts to keep order, the townsfolk had been gathering their belongings to flee northward. One of them had insisted on explaining to Iseul the best things to take during an evacuation. "Don't take rice," the old woman had said. "Only fools weigh themselves down with rice." She had shown Iseul her tidy bundles of medicines, small and light and pungent. "Someone always gets sick, stomach trouble or foot pains, or some woman has a hard childbirth, if you're unlucky enough to bring a child into the world in these times. You trade the medicine for the food someone else has had to carry, and you fill your belly without having to break your back." Bemused, Iseul had thanked the old woman for her advice.

"I couldn't get into the magicians' tent," Iseul said, "and I still haven't figured out if there's a way to spy on their letters. The trip was for nothing."

"Overhear anything useful?" Minsu said, looking at her with such an expression of calm trust that Iseul felt even more wretched.

Iseul thought over the magicians' exchange while she waited for Minsu. "They were arguing about how destructive to make the storm, I think. That was all. But there was something—" She frowned. Something about their words had just reminded her of the poetry, but what could Chindallan poetry possibly have to do with the Genial Ones?

"Have some tea," Minsu said, her solution to everything, "and maybe it will come to you."

Iseul gave a tiny sigh. The safehouse's tea might as well have been mud steeped in rainwater, but Minsu gave no sign that she noticed its inferior quality. Iseul recounted the rest of her meeting with the border-fort's captain, although there wasn't much to tell.

"I don't think the magicians at Fort Kamang will do us much good," Iseul said. "How are mere human magicians going to stand up to the Genial Ones themselves? Magic clearly prefers to serve its original masters if the Genial Ones can so casually invoke spells we all thought had decayed to uselessness."

"I'd send you to kidnap one of the Genial Ones," Minsu said, "but I don't think we have a safe way of holding one for questioning."

Over and over Iseul heard the two magicians arguing in her head. "Their accent," she said slowly. The threads were in her hands. She only had to figure out how to weave them together. "Their accents, and the accent of the one I killed. The fact that I didn't recognize the language at first."

Minsu eyed her but knew better than to interrupt. Instead, she poured more tea.

"Minsu," Iseul said, going pale. "I was wrong just now. We've all been wrong. Magic didn't die because the Genial Ones were wiped out. Because we know now that they were never wiped out. Magic stopped working for the humans piece by piece because it's their language, and *their language changed over time* just as Chindallan has changed, which everyone who has studied the high script knows. Their language became different. We've been trying to use the wrong words for magic."

"You could make more powerful charms, then," Minsu said. "Using the proper words now that you know them."

"Now that I know some of them, you mean. It would take trial and error to figure out all the necessary changes, and magical experimentation can get messy if you do it wrong."

"So much for that," Minsu said. "What about the lexicons? What do they signify?"

"I still don't know what they're doing, but I will find out," Iseul said.

"We have some time," Minsu said, "but that doesn't mean we can afford to relax. The fact that Yegedin have learned from their mistakes in the first invasion may, in some sense, work in our favor." Originally the Yegedin armies had raced north, far ahead of their supply lines, and eventually had to retreat to the current border. "This time they're making sure they can hold what they take: conquest is always easier than subjugation. Still, tell me what you need and I will make sure you are well-supplied."

"More paper, for a start," Iseul said. "A lot of paper. I will have to hope that the Genial Ones don't track me down here."

"Indeed." Minsu's eyes were unexpectedly grim. "I would get you the assistance of a Chindallan magician, but you do realize that there's every possibility that the Genial Ones have been hiding among our people, too."

"It had occurred to me, yes." Iseul was starting to get a headache, although in all fairness, she should have had one ages ago. "I don't suppose you have any of that headache medicine?"

"I have a little left from my last detour to a pharmacy," Minsu said, and handed it over. "I'll get you more. I have other business to attend to, but I will check back with you from time to time. The safehouse's keeper will have instructions to assist you in any way she can."

"Thank you," Iseul said. She didn't look up as Minsu slipped out.

The first Chindallan dynasty after the fall of the Genial Ones only lasted four abbreviated generations. Its queens and kings were buried in tombs of cold stone beneath mounded earth. Certain Chindallan scholars, coming to the tombs long after they had been plundered, noted that many of the tombs, when viewed from above, seemed to form words in the high script: *wall*, for instance, or *eye*, or *vigilant*. The scholars believed that this practice, like that of burying terracotta soldiers with the dead monarchs and their households, arose from a desire to protect the tombs from grave robbers. Like the terracotta soldiers, the tombs' construction was singularly inadequate for this purpose.

Iseul slept little in the days that followed. She was making progress on the scrying charm, though, which was something. It required suspending the charm along with two of the quill-charms in a mobile. Sometimes, when her exhaustion overcame her, she found herself staring at the charms bobbing back and forth in the air.

She also developed a headache so ferocious that Minsu's medicine, normally reliable, did her no good. Finally she ventured out in search of a pharmacist. It turned out that the pharmacist had fled town, to her vexation, but an old man told her that one of the physicians, a somewhat disreputable man who had evaded registration with the proper ministry for his entire life, was still around. Since she didn't have much option, she went in search of him.

The physician lived in a small hut at the edge of town. He was sitting outside, and he had finished ministering to a pair of grubby children. One of the children was eating a candy with no sign that her splinted wrist bothered her. The other, an even younger girl, was picking wildflowers.

The physician himself was a tall man who would have been taller if not for his hunched shoulders, and he had a wry, gentle face. His clothes were very plain. No one would have looked at him twice in the market square. He stood at Iseul's approach.

"This will be quick, I promise," Iseul said. "I've been having headaches and I need medicine for it."

The physician looked her up and down. "I should think that a few good nights' sleep would serve you better than any medicine," he said dryly.

"I don't have time for a few good nights' sleep," Iseul said. "Please, don't you have anything to take the edge off the pain? If it's a matter of money—"

He named a sum that explained to Iseul what he was doing in such plain clothes. Any respectable licensed physician could have charged three times as much even for something this simple.

"I can pay that," Iseul said.

The girl with the splint tugged at the physician's sleeve, completely unconcerned with the transaction going on. "Do you have more candy?"

"For pity's sake, you haven't finished what's in your mouth," he said.

"But it tastes better when you have two flavors at once."

He rolled his eyes, but he was smiling. "Maybe later."

"You should be all right so long as you don't fall out of any more trees." But the melancholy in his eyes told Iseul that he knew what happened to children in wartime.

The younger girl handed him the wildflowers. She didn't speak in complete sentences yet, but both Iseul and the physician were given to understand that she had picked him the prettiest and best wildflowers as payment. The physician smiled and told her to go back to her parents with her sister.

"You can come in while I get the medicine, if you like," the magician said.

Iseul looked at him with worry as he began to walk. Something about the way he carried himself even over such a short distance intimated a great and growing pain. "Are you well?" she asked.

"It's an old injury," the physician said with a shrug, "and of little importance."

The hut had two rooms, and the outer room was sparsely furnished. There were no books in it, which disappointed Iseul obscurely. On a worn table was a small jar with a crack at the lip and a handful of wilting cosmos flowers in it. He added the newly plucked wildflowers to the jar.

Iseul couldn't help looking around for weapons, traps, stray charms. Nothing presented itself to her eye as unusually dangerous, but the habit was hard to lose.

"Here it is," the physician said after a moment's rooting around in a chest. "Take it once a day when the pain sets in. Ideally you want to catch it before it gets bad. And try not to rely on it more than you have to. People who take this stuff every day over long periods of time sometimes get sick in other ways."

"That shouldn't be an issue," Iseul said, *one way or another.* She hesitated, then said, "You could do a lot of good to the military, you know. They're sure to be looking for physicians, and they'd probably give you a temporary license."

The physician held out the packet of medicine. "I am a healer of small hurts," he said, "nothing more. Everything I accomplish is with a few herbal remedies and common sense. A surprising number of maladies respond to time and rest and basic hygiene, things that soldiers don't see a lot of when they go to war. And besides, the people here need someone too."

Iseul thought of the little girl picking flowers for him. "Then I will simply wish you well," she said. "Thank you." She counted out the payment. He refused her attempts to pay him what he ought to be charging her.

She took a dose of the medicine, then headed back to the safehouse. She passed more people heading out of the town. Mothers with small, squalling children on their backs. Old men leaning on canes carved in the shape of animal heads, a specialty of the region. The occasional nervous couple, quarreling about things to bring with them and things to leave behind. One woman was crying over a large lacquered box with abalone inlay. The battered box was probably the closest thing to a treasure she owned. Her husband tried to tell her that something of its size wasn't worth hauling north and that nobody would give them much money for it anyway, which led to her shouting at him that it wasn't for money that she wanted to bring it.

Merchants were selling food, clothes, and other necessaries for extortionate sums. People were buying anyway: not much choice. Iseul paused to glance over a display of protection charms that one woman was selling, flimsy folded-paper pendants painted with symbols and strung on knotted cords.

The seller bowed deeply to Iseul. "They say the storms are coming north," she said. "Why not protect yourself from the rains and the sharp-toothed horses?"

"Thank you, but no," Iseul said, having satisfied herself that the charms' symbols were beautifully rendered, but empty of virtue. "I wish you the best, though."

The seller eyed her, but decided not to waste time trying to sway her. Shrugging, she turned away and called out to a passing man who was wearing a finer jacket than most of the people on the street.

There was a noodle shop on the way back to the safehouse. The noodles were just as extortionately priced, but Iseul was tired of the safehouse's food. She paid for cold noodles flavored with vinegar, hoping that the flavor would drive out the foul taste of the medicine. The sliced cucumbers were sadly limp, so she added extra vinegar in the hopes of salvaging the dish, without much luck. At least her headache seemed to have receded.

Iseul sat down with her papers and began her work again. She had been keeping notes on all her experiments, some of which were barely legible. She hadn't realized how much her handwriting deteriorated when she was in pain. This time she adjusted the mobile to include a paper sphere (well, an approximate sphere) to represent the world, written over with words of water and earth and cloudshadow.

When the scrying charm did begin to work, hours later, Iseul almost didn't realize it. She was staring off into space, resigned to yet another failure. It was a bad sign that the tea was starting to taste good, although that might possibly be related to the desperation measure of adulterating it with increasing quantities of honey. Not very good honey, at that.

The safehouse's keeper had come in with another pot of tea and was staring at the mobile. "My lady," she said, "is it supposed to be doing that?"

Iseul stifled a yawn. She didn't bother correcting the keeper, although a mere spy didn't rate "lady." "Supposed to be doing—oh."

The sphere was spinning at a steady rate, and black words were boiling from its surface in angry-looking tendrils. Iseul stood and squinted at them. Experimentally, she touched one of the tendrils. Her fingertip felt slightly numb, so she snatched it back. The safehouse's keeper excused herself and left hastily, but Iseul didn't notice.

Iseul had a supply of sheets of paper and books of execrable poetry. She opened one of the poetry books, then positioned one of the sheets beneath the sphere's shadow. Sure enough, words began to condense from the shadow onto the paper, and lines of poetry began to fade from the books. The lines were distorted, probably because they were traveling from a curved surface to a flat one, but the writing was readable enough, and it was in the Genial Ones' language, as she had expected it would be.

Not far into this endeavor, Iseul realized she was going to need a better strategy. There was only one of her, and only one of the scrying charms. Based on the sphere locations, there looked to be at least a hundred Genial Ones communicating with each other. She could make more scrying charms, but she couldn't recruit more people to read and analyze the letters.

Minsu stopped by the next day and was tactfully silent on Iseul's harried appearance, although she looked like she wanted to reach out and tidy Iseul's hair for her. "That looks like some kind of progress," she remarked, looking around at the sorted stacks of paper, "but clearly I didn't provide you with enough paper. Or assistants."

"I'm not sure assistants would help," Iseul said. "The Genial Ones seem to communicate with each other on a regular basis. And there are a few hundred of them just based on the ones who are writing, let alone the ones who are lying low. How many people would you trust with this information?"

She had worse news for Minsu, but it was hard to make herself say it.

"Not a lot," Minsu said. "There's that old saying: only ashes keep secrets, and even they have been known to talk to the stones. What is it that the Genial Ones are so interested in talking about? I can't imagine that they're consulting each other on what shoes to wear to their next gathering."

"Shoes are important," Iseul said, remembering how much her feet had hurt after running to the border-fort in the Yegedin soldier's completely inadequate boots. "But yes. They're talking about language. I've been puzzling through it.

There are so many languages, and they work in such different ways. Did you know that there are whole families of languages with something called noun classes, where you inflect nouns differently based on the category they fall into? Except the categories don't usually make any sense. There's this language where nouns for female humans and animals and workers share a class, except tables, cities, and ships are also included." She was aware as she spoke that she was going off on a tangent. She had to nerve herself up to tell Minsu what the Genial Ones were up to.

"I'm sure Chindallan looks just as strange to foreigners," Minsu said. Her voice was bemused, but her somber eyes told Iseul she knew something was wrong. "I once spoke to a Jaioi merchant who couldn't get used to the fact that our third person pronouns don't distinguish between males and females, which is apparently very important in his language. On the other hand, he couldn't handle the formality inflections on our verbs at all. He'd hired an interpreter so he wouldn't inadvertently offend people."

The "interpreter" would have been a spy; that went without saying. Iseul had worked such straightforward assignments herself, once upon a time.

"You haven't said how bad things are down south," Iseul said. She couldn't put this off forever, and yet.

"Well, I'm tempted to have you relocate further north," Minsu said, "but there's only so far north to go. The Yegedin have taken the coastal fort of Suwen. We suspect they're hoping to open up more logistical options from their homeland. I don't, frustratingly, have a whole lot of information on what our navy is up to. They're probably having trouble getting the Yegedin to engage them." During the original invasion, only the rapacious successes of Chindalla's navy—always stronger than its army—had forced the Yegedin to halt their advance.

"I have to work faster," Iseul said, squeezing her eyes shut. Time to stop delaying. Minsu was silent, and Iseul opened them again. "Of course, every time the safehouse keeper comes in, she looks at me like I'm crazed." She eyed the mobiles. There was only room for eleven of them, but the way they spun and cavorted, like orreries about to come apart, was probably a good argument that their creator wasn't in her right mind. "What I don't understand . . . " She ran her hand over one of the stacks of paper.

When Iseul didn't continue the thought, Minsu said, "Understand what?"

"I've tested the letter-scrying spell," Iseul said, "with languages that aren't the Genial Ones'. I'm only fluent in five languages besides Chindallan, but I tried them all. And the spell won't work on anything but the language of magic. The charms spin around but they can't so much as get a fix on a letter that I'm writing in the same room."

"Did you try modifying the charm?" Minsu asked.

"I thought of that, but magic doesn't work that way. I mean, the death-touch daggers, for instance. If you had to craft them to a specific individual target, they'd be less useful. Well, in most circumstances." They could both think of situations where a dagger that would only kill a certain person might be useful. "But I think that's why the Genial Ones have been so quiet, and why they've been busy compiling the lexicons by hand for each human language. Because there's no other way to do it. They know more magic than I do, that goes without saying. If there were some charm to do the job for them, they'd be using it."

"I have the feeling you're going to lead up to something that requires the best of teas to face," Minsu said, and stole a sip from Iseul's cup before Iseul had the chance to warn her off. She was too well-bred to make remarks about people who put honey in even abysmal tea, but her eyebrows quirked a little.

Iseul looked away. "I think I know why the Genial Ones are compiling lexicons," she said, "and it isn't because they really like writing miniature treatises on morphophonemics."

"How disappointing," Minsu said, "you may have destroyed my affection for them forever." But her bantering tone had worry beneath it.

Iseul went to a particular stack of papers, which she had weighted down with a letter opener decorated with a twining flower motif. "They've been discussing an old charm," she said. "They want to create a variation of the sculpture charm."

"That was one of the first to become defunct after their defeat," Minsu observed. "Apparent defeat, I should say."

"That brings me to the other thing," Iseul said. "I think I've figured out that word that the first Genial One said, the one that was unfamiliar. Because it keeps showing up in their conversations. I think it's a word that didn't exist before."

"I remember that time that satirist coined a new word for hairpins that look like they ought to be good for assassinations but are completely inadequate for the job," Minsu said. "Of course, based on Chindalla's plays and novels, I have to concede that we needed the word."

Minsu's attempts to get her to relax weren't helping, but Iseul appreciated the effort. *You can kill one of us, but not all of us. We won't accept this—* "'Defeat,'" Iseul said softly. "The word means 'defeat.'"

"Surely they can't have gone all this time without—" Minsu's mouth pressed into a flat line.

"Yes," Iseul said. "These are people who had separate words for their blood and our blood. Because we weren't their equals. Until General Anangan overcame them, they had no word for *their own defeat*. Not at the hands of humans, anyway, as opposed to the intrigues and backstabbing that apparently went on among their clans."

"All right," Minsu said, "but that can't be what's shadowing your eyes."

"They want to defeat us the way we almost defeated them," Iseul said. "They're obsessed with it. They've figured out how to scale the sculpture charm up. Except they're not going to steal our shapes. They're going to steal our words and add them to their own language. And Chindalla's language is the last to be compiled for the purpose."

In the old days, the forgotten days, the human nations feared the Genial Ones' sculptors and their surgeons and their soldiers. They knew, however, that the greatest threat was none of these, but the Genial Ones' lexicographers, whose thoroughness was legendary. The languages that they collected for their own pleasure vanished, and the civilizations that spoke those languages invariably followed soon afterwards.

Iseul was in the middle of explaining her plan to thwart the Genial Ones to Minsu, which involved charms to destroy the language of magic itself, when the courier arrived. The safehouse's keeper interrupted them. Iseul thought it was to bring them tea, but she was accompanied by a young man, much disheveled and breathing hard. He was obviously trying not to stare at the room's profusion of charms, or at Iseul herself. She couldn't remember the last time she had given her hair a good thorough combing, and she probably looked like a ghost. (For some reason ghosts never combed their hair.) Her mother would have despaired of her.

"I trust you have a good reason for this," Minsu said wearily.

"You need to hear this, my lady," the keeper said.

The young man presented his papers to Minsu. They declared him to be a government courier, although the official seal, stamped in red ink that Iseul happened to know never washed out of fabric no matter what you tried, was smeared at the lower right corner. Minsu looked over the papers, frowning, then nodded. "Speak," Minsu said.

"A Yegedin detachment of two thousand has been spotted heading this way," the courier said. "It's probably best if you evacuate."

Iseul closed her eyes and drew a shuddering breath in spite of herself.

"All this work," Minsu said, gesturing at the mobiles.

"It's not worth defending this town," Iseul said bleakly, "am I right?"

"The throne wishes its generals to focus on protecting more important cities," the courier said. "I'm sorry, my lady."

"It'll be all right," Iseul said to Minsu. "I can work as easily from another safehouse."

"You'll have to set up the charms all over again," Minsu said.

"It can't be helped. Besides, if we stay here, even if the Yegedin don't get us, the looters will."

The courier's expression said that he was realizing that Iseul might have more common sense than her current appearance suggested. Still, he addressed Minsu. "The detachment will probably be here within the next five days, my lady. Best to leave before the news becomes general knowledge."

"Not as if there are a whole lot of people left here anyway," Minsu said. "All right. Thank you for the warning."

Iseul was used to being able to pick up and leave at a moment's notice, but she hadn't reckoned on dealing with the charms and the quantities of text that they had generated. There wasn't time to burn everything, which made her twitch. They settled for shuffling the rest into boxes and abandoning them with the heaps of garbage that could be found around the town. Her hands acquired blisters, but she didn't even notice how much they hurt.

Iseul and Minsu joined the long, winding trail of refugees heading north. The safehouse keeper insisted on parting ways from them because she had family in the area. Minsu's efforts to talk her out of this met with failure. She pressed a purse of coins into the keeper's hands; that was all the farewell they could manage.

Minsu bought horses from a trader at the first opportunity, the best he had, which wasn't saying much. The price was less extravagant than Iseul might have guessed. Horses were very unpopular at the moment because everyone had the Yegedin storm-horses on their mind, and people had taken to stealing and killing them for the stewpot instead. Minsu insisted on giving Iseul the calmer gelding and taking the cantankerous mare for herself. "No offense," she said, "but I have more experience wrangling very annoying horses than you do."

"I wasn't complaining," Iseul said. She was credible enough on horseback, but it really didn't matter.

Most of the refugees headed for the road to the capital, where they felt the most safety was to be had. Once the two of them were mounted, however, Minsu led them northeast, toward the coast.

In the evenings Iseul would rather have dropped asleep immediately, but constructing her counterstroke against the Genial Ones was an urgent problem, and it required all her attention. Not only did she have to construct a charm to capture the Genial Ones' words, she had to find a way to destroy those words so they could never be used again. Sometimes she caught herself nodding off, and she pinched her palm to prick herself awake again. They weren't just threatened by armies; they were threatened by the people who had once ruled all the known nations.

"We're almost there," Minsu said as they came to the coast. "Just another day's ride." The sun was low in the sky, but she had decided they should stop in the shelter of a hill rather than pressing on tonight. She had been quiet for most of the journey, preferring not to interrupt Iseul's studies unless Iseul had a question for her.

Iseul had been drowsing as she rode, a trick she had mastered out of necessity. She didn't hear Minsu at first, lost in muddled dreams of a book. The book had pages of tawny paper, precisely the color of skin. It was urgent that she write a poem about rice-balls into the book. Everyone knew rice was the foundation of civilization and it deserved more satiric verses than it usually received, but every time she set her brush to the paper, the ink ran down the bristles and formed into cavorting figures that leapt off the pages. She became convinced that she was watching a great and terrible dance, and that the question was then whether she would run out of ink before the dance came to its fruition.

"Iseul." It was Minsu. She had tied her horse to a small tree and had caught Iseul's reins. "I know you're tired, but you look like you're ready to fall off."

Iseul came alert all at once, the way she had trained herself to do on countless earlier missions. "I have to review my notes. I think I might have it this time."

"There's hardly any light to read by."

"I'll shield a candle."

"I'll see to your horse, then," Minsu said.

Minsu set up camp while Iseul hunched over her notes. Properly it should have been the other way around, but Minsu never stood on formalities for their own sake. She was always happy to pour tea for others, for instance.

"If they think to do scrying of their own once I get started," Iseul said while Minsu was bringing her barley hardtack mashed into a crude cold porridge, "our lifespans are going to be measured in minutes."

"We don't seem to have a choice if we want to survive," Minsu said.

"The ironic thing is that we'll also be saving the Yegedin."

"We can fight the Yegedin the way we'd fight anyone else," Minsu said. "The Genial Ones are another matter."

"If only we knew how General Anangan managed it the first time around," Iseul said. But all that remained were contradictory legends. She wondered, now, if the Genial Ones themselves had obfuscated the facts.

"If only." Minsu sighed.

Iseul ate the porridge without tasting it, which was just as well.

A little while later, Minsu said quietly, "You haven't even thought to be tempted, have you?"

"Tempted how?" But as she spoke, Iseul knew what Minsu meant. "It would only be a temporary reprieve."

She knew exactly how the lexicon charm worked. She had the Yeged-dai lexicon with her, and she could use it to destroy the Yegedin language. The thirteen-year occupation would evaporate. Poets could write in their native language without fear of attracting reprisals. Southern Chindallans could use their own names again. No more rebels would have to burn to death. All compelling arguments. She could annihilate Yeged before she turned on the Genial Ones. People would consider it an act of patriotism.

But as Minsu had said, the Yegedin could be fought by ordinary means, without resorting to the awful tools of humanity's old masters.

Iseul also knew that turning the lexicon charm against the Genial Ones' own language would mean destroying magic forever. No more passage charms or lantern charms; no more convenient daggers that made people vanish.

No more storm-horses, either, or towers built of people's bones erupting from pyramids of corpses, as in the old stories. It wouldn't be all bad. And what kind of spy would she be if she couldn't improvise solutions?

Besides, if she didn't do something about the Genial Ones now, they would strike against all the human nations with the lexicons they had already compiled. Here, at least, the choice was clear and narrow.

"I don't want to be more like the Genial Ones than I have to," Iseul said with a guilty twitch of regret. "But we do have to go through with this."

"Do you have ward spells prepared?" Minsu said.

"Yes," Iseul said. "A lot of them. Because once we're discovered—and we have to assume we'll be—they're going to devote their attention to seeking out and destroying us. And we don't know what they're capable of."

"Oh, that's not true," Minsu said. "We know exactly what they're capable of. We've known for generations, even in the folktales."

"I should start tonight," Iseul said. "I'm only going to be more tired tomorrow."

Minsu looked as though she wanted to argue, but instead she nodded.

Iseul sat in the lee of the hill and began the painstaking work of copying out all the necessary charms, from the wards—every form of ward she knew of, including some cribbed from the Genial Ones' own discussions—to the one that would compile the lexicon of the language of magic for her by transcribing those same discussions. That final charm was bound to fail at some point when its world of words was confined to the sheets of blank paper she had prepared for it, but—if she had done this correctly—she had constructed it so that it would target its own structural words last.

The winds were strong tonight, and they raked Iseul with cold. The horses were unsettled, whinnying to each other and pulling at their ropes. Iseul glanced up from time to time to look at the sky, bleak and smothered over with clouds. The hills might as well have been the dented helmets of giant warriors, abandoned after an unwinnable fight.

"All right," Iseul said at last, hating how gray her voice sounded. She felt the first twinge of a headache and remembered to take the medicine the physician had given her. "Come into the circle of protection, Minsu. There's no reason to delay getting started."

Obligingly, Minsu joined her, and Iseul activated each warding charm one by one. It was hard not to feel as though she was playing with a child's toys, flimsy folded shapes, except she knew exactly what each of those charms was intended to do.

At the center of the circle of protection were four books as empty as mirrors in the darkness, which Iseul had bound during her time in the safehouse. She hoped four books would be enough to cripple the Genial Ones, even if they couldn't contain the entirety of their language. Iseul began folding pages of the empty books, dog-earing corners and folding them into skewed geometries. When she wasn't watching closely, she had the impression that the corners were unfolding and stretching out tendrils of nascent words, nonsense syllables, to spy on her. She didn't mention this to Minsu, but the other woman's face was strained. There was a stinging tension in the air; her skin prickled.

Lightning flickered in the distance as she worked. It cut from one side of the sky to the other in a way that natural lightning never did, like the sweep of a sword.

"Hurry if you can," Minsu said, head raised to watch the approach of the storm.

"I'm hurrying," Iseul said.

The winds were whipping fiercely around them now. One of Minsu's braids had come unpinned and was flapping like a lonely pennant.

The candle flickered out. Minsu brought out a lantern charm.

"I'm all for ordinary fire if you can get it to work for you," Minsu said at Iseul's dubious look, "but you need light and this will give you light for a time."

Iseul continued with the lexicon charm, double-checking every fold, every black and twining word, every diagram of spindled lines. The sense of tension sharpened. If she dared to look away from the books' pages and at the suffocating sky, she imagined that she would see words forming amid the clouds, sky-words and wind-words and water-words, words of torrential despair and words of drowning terror, words that had existed in some form since the first people learned to speak.

She slammed each book shut counterclockwise, shuddering, suddenly hoping the whole affair was an extension of the dream she had had and that she would wake to sunlight and flowers and a warm spot by some fire, but no. With a dry creaking voice—with a chorus of voices that rose and rose to a roar—the books wrenched themselves open in unison.

For a second the pages fluttered wildly, like birds newly freed. Then they darkened as words inundated them. Slowly at first, then in a steady pouring of black writhing shapes. Postpositions. Conjunctions. Nouns that violated vowel harmony and nouns that didn't. Verbs in different conjugations, tenses, aspects. A stray aorist. Scraps of syntax and subclause generators. Interjections snatched from between clenched teeth. Sacred names rarely spoken and never before written.

One of the horses was thrashing about, but Iseul was only peripherally aware of it, or of Minsu swearing under her breath. A dark shape plunged up before Iseul, but she was intent upon the books, the books, the terrible books. Who knew there were so many crawling words in a language? Years ago, when reviewing a cryptology text, she had seen an estimate of the number of words a literate Chindallan needed to be able to read. She had thought the number large then. Now she knew the estimate must be low. It wasn't possible for more words to flood the four books' pages, but here they came, again and again and again, growing smaller and smaller as they crushed each other in the confines on the pages.

The dark shape was one of the horses, which had pulled free of the rope in its panic. Minsu had her riding crop out and struck the horse. Iseul had a vague idea of how desperate she must be. The other woman had always been softhearted about the animals. But the horse wheeled and ran toward the hills, neighing wildly.

Iseul's attention was abruptly drawn to the horse when, having passed the circle of protection, lightning scythed through the horse. Except it wasn't lightning, precisely: pale light with eyes in it, and black waving feelers sprouting from each pupil, and the feelers ate holes into the unfortunate animal's spine. The horse screamed for a long time.

More lightning zigzagged down from the sky, crackling around the circle. Rain was pelting down all around them, and muddy water sluiced down the hillside. Voices whispered out of the darkness, murmuring liplessly of entrails and needlepoints and vengeance. The light from the lantern charm glittered in the raindrops and the sheets of water like an unwanted promise. The lantern, although flimsy in construction, seemed to be in no danger of being toppled by the rising winds.

One of the protective wards began to unfold itself.

Minsu said a word that Iseul hadn't even realized she knew.

"We can't let them win this," Iseul said breathlessly. Stupid to just stand here watching, as if the Genial Ones would simply submit to the destruction of their magic. She began constructing an additional ward to reinforce the one that was disintegrating.

Chasms of fire opened in the air, then closed, like terrible fierce smiles. The rain hissed where it met the fire, and Iseul flinched when tendrils of steam were repelled by the circle of protection. Leaves spun free of the hillside wildflowers and the nearby copses of trees, formed into great screaming birds, battered themselves fruitlessly against the wards before dissipating into shreds and slivers of green and yellow.

Iseul spared a glance for the books. Was it possible for them to hold any more words? She set the current ward in place, then flipped through the pages of the fourth book in spite of herself, in spite of the conviction that the paper would hold her hands fast and drag her in. And then the teeth began.

The teeth grew from the corners of the pages. They distended into predatory curves, yellow-white and gleaming. Iseul flinched violently.

The teeth took no notice of her, but the books fanned themselves out like a hundred hundred mouths. Then, with a papery crumpling sound, they began to eat the words.

Minsu was holding Iseul's shoulder. "This is not," she said thinly, "at all what I thought it would be."

The storm crackled and roared above them. The two women clung to each other as rain and lightning crashed inland. If the winds grew any stronger, Iseul felt she would fall over sideways and not stop falling until she had gone through the world and out the other side. But she didn't dare rest, and she didn't dare contemplate leaving the circle of protection

More of the wards were unfolding. Despite her shaking hands, Iseul bent to the task of making more charms, except now the charms were fighting her. *Of course,* she thought, cursing herself for her carelessness. She had thought to specify that the lexicon charm would spare itself as long as possible, but she had done no such thing for the wards. She would have to try synonyms, circumlocutions, alternate geometries; she would have to hope that the Genial Ones were having as much difficulty sustaining their attacks as she was her defenses.

The lantern charm abruptly guttered out. Iseul couldn't see, through the water in her eyes, whether the words upon it had been devoured, or whether the Genial Ones had discovered them and snuffed it themselves.

Faces of fire scattered downward and struck a hilltop perhaps thirty meters from them. All the faces were howling, and their eyes were hollow sooty pits. For a moment everything was crowned in sanguinary light, from the silhouetted grasses swept nearly flat to the hunched rocks.

"We're done for," Iseul whispered. Was it her imagination, or did she hear horses in the distance, sharp-toothed horses with hooves that struck savage rhythms into the earth's bones?

More charms uncurled, crumpled, made the kinds of sounds you might imagine of lost love letters and discarded prayers.

"Hold fast," Minsu said, although she had to repeat herself over the drumming storm so that Iseul could hear her. Her expression was obscure in the darkness.

Iseul was holding down the covers of one of the books, small futile gesture. The whole thing should have been drenched. Ordinarily she would have been appalled at herself for leaving a book out in the rain, but the teeth seemed just as happy to devour water as words.

A swirl of flame made it past the circle of protection. Minsu's hair caught on fire. She beat at the flames with her hands. For a bad moment, Iseul thought that the fires had spread to her eyes, her ears, the marrow of her hands. But after one horrifying white-red flare, the fire shook itself apart in an incoherent dazzle of sparks, then sizzled into silence.

"I'm fine," Minsu shouted, although her voice shook. She went to retrieve the lantern charm. "No words," she said, squinting at it during the next lightning-flash. The charm had unfolded completely. There were only faint rust-colored marks where the words had been, like splotches of blood.

Hurry, Iseul bid the books with their gnashing teeth. *Hurry.*

There was no way to guide the books' hunger now, no way to tell them to eat words of storm and fire above all others. They were indiscriminate in their voracity. More and more of the pages were spotted rust-red, like the former lantern charm.

Then the storm broke. There was no other word for it. It came apart into smaller storms, and the smaller storms into eddies of wind, the rain into a fine wandering mist. In the distance they heard the tolling of dark bells and the screams of sharp-toothed horses.

The teeth receded. The books' pages twitched upward, yearning, then subsided. A sullen light rippled from their covers. Every single one of their pages was covered with splattered blood, a slaughterhouse of words. Fighting her revulsion, Iseul closed each one and put them away. The light sloughed away.

Iseul and Minsu were drenched through. "We'll catch our death of chill out here," Iseul said. Her throat felt raw although she had hardly spoken. After what had just happened, a great lassitude threatened to drag her under, but she couldn't afford to sleep, not yet.

"We have to see what became of the coastal fort," Minsu said. "If we walk through the night we might make it. Assuming the place hasn't been overrun by the Yegedin navy."

The books felt like chains all the way through the night. They found a trail through the hills, difficult to see in the darkness and dangerously slippery at that, but Minsu had experience of this region and was able to lead them in the right direction. She insisted that Iseul ride the remaining horse while she led it. By that point, Iseul didn't care where they were going or how they got there so long as she was allowed to collapse and sleep at the end of it. Any flat surface would do.

"Oh no," Minsu said at last.

Iseul almost fell off the horse. She had slipped into a half-doze, except she kept seeing black spidering shapes behind her eyelids.

They had stopped on the crest of a hill: risky to be silhouetted if there were enemies in the area, especially archers, but an excellent vantage point otherwise.

The sea crashed against broken white-gray cliffs. The bones of ships could be seen floating in the newly formed harbor along with uprooted trees. "They destroyed the coast," Minsu said, bringing out a spyglass and looking north and south. "Fort Jenal used to be out there—" She gestured toward the horizon, toward the frothing waves. "Now it's all water and wreckage."

"Do you suppose there are any survivors?" Iseul said. But she knew the answer.

Minsu shook her head.

"If only I had figured it out sooner," Iseul said, head bowed. If only she had been able to make the lexicon charm work faster.

"We'll have to notify the nearest garrison," Minsu said, "so they can search for survivors, Chindallan or Yegedin. But for now, we must rest."

She said something else, but Iseul's knees buckled and she didn't hear any of it.

The Genial Ones originally had no word for *medicine* that did not also mean *poison*. They ended up borrowing one from a human language spoken by people that they slaughtered the hard way for variety's sake, person by person dragged from their villages and redoubts and killed, cautery by sword and spear.

Minsu said very little to the garrisons they visited about the real reason the storm had broken, which was just as well. Iseul wasn't sure what she would have said if asked about it. She did, at Minsu's urging, write a ciphered account of the lexicon charm and the devouring books to send to the Ministry of Ornithology with a trusted courier.

They were sitting in a rented room at the time, and Minsu had scared up a tea that even Iseul liked.

"I only wrote the account," Iseul said, very clearly, "because none of the charms work anymore." With the Genial Ones' language extinguished, the magic it empowered was gone for good. She had attempted to create working charms, just to be sure, but all of them remained inert. "Imagine if Yeged's Emperor had figured out how to use this on Chindallan or the language of any other nation he desired to conquer."

"The way we could have?" Minsu said sardonically. "It's done now. Finish your report, and we can get out of this town."

There were still refugees on the road north. They might have deprived the Yegedin of magical assaults, but then, they had also deprived the Chindallans of magical defenses. Given that both sides had spent the uneasy peace preparing to go to war, it was anyone's guess as to who would prevail.

At one point they ended up at a wretched camp for those who were too sick to continue fleeing, and the few people who were staying with them, mostly their families and a few monks who were acting as caretakers. Iseul remained prone to headaches and was running low on medicine. Minsu had insisted that they seek out a physician, even though Iseul tried to point out that the people at the camp probably needed the medicine more than she did.

As it turned out, they forgot all about the question of who deserved the medicine when Iseul saw a familiar little girl. She was picking flowers, weeds really, but in her hands they became jewels.

Iseul approached the girl and asked her if she knew where the physician was. The girl seemed confused by the question, but after a little while her older sister appeared from one of the tents and recognized Iseul. "I'll take you to him," the girl said, "but he's very sick."

"I'm sorry to hear that," Iseul said. Despite the monks' best efforts to enforce basic sanitary practices, the camp reeked of filth and sickness and curdled hopes, and she couldn't help but imagine that the physician had taken sick while helping others.

She and Minsu followed the older girl to a tent at the edge of the camp. Flowers had been weighted down with a rock at the tent's opening: the younger girl's handiwork, surely. They could smell the bitter incense that was used to bring easeful dreams to the dying.

The tent was small, and there were more flowers next to the brazier. Their petals had fallen off and were scattered next to the pallet. The incense was almost all burned away. The physician slept on the pallet. Even at rest his lined face suggested a certain weary kindness. Someone had drawn a heavy quilted blanket over him, stained red-brown on one corner.

"What happened?" Minsu said. "Will he recover? I'm sure he could be a great help here."

"He fell sick," the girl said. "One of the monks said he had a stroke. He doesn't talk anymore and he doesn't seem to understand when people talk to him. They said he might like us to visit him, though, and our mother works with the monks to help the sick people, so we come by and bring flowers."

He doesn't talk anymore. Iseul went cold. He had spoken Chindallan; shouldn't that have saved him? But she didn't know how language worked in the brain.

Without asking, she lifted the corner of the blanket. The physician had

longer arms than she remembered, like the Genial One she had killed at
his house a lifetime ago. Who was to say they couldn't change their shapes?
Especially if they were living among humans? Tears pricking her eyes, she
replaced the blanket.

"I'm very sorry," Iseul said to the girl. "It's probably not long before he
dies."

She couldn't help but wonder how many Genial Ones had lingered into
this age, taking no part in the conspiracy for vengeance, leading quiet lives as
healers of small hurts to atone for their kindred who summoned storm-horses
and faces of fire. There was no way to tell.

The Yegedin had tried to destroy Chindalla's literature and names, but
Iseul had destroyed the Genial Ones themselves. It hadn't seemed real until
now.

"Thank you," she said to the dying Genial One, even though his mind was
gone. She and Minsu sat by his side for a time, listening to him breathe. There
was a war coming, and a storm entirely human, but in this small space they
could mourn what they had done.

For a long time afterwards, Iseul tried to come up with a poem about the
Genial Ones, encapsulating what they had meant to the world and why they
had had to die and why she regretted the physician's passing, but no words
ever came to her.

—. A noun, probably, pertaining to regret or cinders or something
of that nature, but this word can no longer be found in any lexicon,
human or otherwise.

Yoon Ha Lee's Crawford Memorial Award-nominated short fiction collection
Conservation of Shadows was published in 2013 by Prime Books. She lives in
Louisiana with her family, used to design constructed languages as a hobby,
and has not yet been eaten by gators.

ACKNOWLEDGEMENTS

"Postcards from Abroad" © 2013 Peter Atkins. First publication: *Rolling Darkness Revue 2013* (Earthling Publications).

"The Creature Recants" © 2013 Dale Bailey. First publication: *Clarkesworld*, Issue 85, October 2013.

"The Good Husband" © 2013 Nathan Ballingrud. First publication: *North American Lake Monsters* (Small Beer Press).

"Termination Dust" © 2013 Laird Barron. First publication: *Tales of Jack the Ripper*, ed. Ross Lockhart (Word Horde).

"The Ghost Makers" © 2013 Elizabeth Bear. First publication: *Fearsome Journeys*, ed. Jonathan Strahan (Solaris).

"The Marginals" © 2013 Steve Duffy. First publication: *The Moment of Panic*, (PS Publishing).

"A Collapse of Horses" © 2013 Brian Evenson. First publication: *The American Reader*, February/March 2013.

"A Lunar Labyrinth" © 2013 Neil Gaiman. First publication: *Shadows of the New Sun: Stories in Honor of Gene Wolfe*, eds. J. E. Mooney & Bill Fawcett (Tor).

"Pride" © 2013 Glen Hirshberg. First publication: *Rolling Darkness Revue 2013,* (Earthling Publications).

"Let My Smile Be Your Umbrella" © 2013 Brian Hodge. First publication: *Psycho-Mania!*, ed. Stephen Jones (Robinson).

"The Soul in the Bell Jar" © 2013 KJ Kabza. First publication: *The Magazine of Fantasy & Science Fiction*, November/December 2013.

"The Prayer of Ninety Cats" © 2013 Caitlín R. Kiernan. First publication: *Subterranean Online*, Spring 2013.

ABOUT THE EDITOR

Paula Guran serves as senior editor for Prime Books. She edited the Juno fantasy imprint from its small press inception through its incarnation as an imprint of Pocket Books. In addition to the annual Year's Best Dark Fantasy and Horror series, she edits a growing number of other anthologies as well as novels and single-author collections. In an earlier life she produced weekly email newsletter *DarkEcho* (winning two Stokers, an IHG Award, and a World Fantasy Award nomination); edited *Horror Garage* (earning another IHG and a second World Fantasy nomination) and other periodicals; and has contributed reviews, interviews, and articles to numerous professional publications. The mother of four, mother-in-law of two, and grandmother of one, she lives in Akron, Ohio with two cats and—depending on the day or week—a variable number of adult children and/or two of their dogs. Her website is paulaguran.com. Find her on facebook (www.facebook.com/paulaguran) or on Twitter: @paulaguran.